Turin, 19 March 1888

The girl sits alone in what seems to be little more than a deep pit and wonders what she has done to deserve her incarceration. She cannot tell how long she has been there because she cannot see when the night ends and the day begins, but it feels like weeks at least. Too long anyway to be in what she has come to think of as her cell. There is not much in the way of comfort, just a thin mattress, a bucket for relieving herself, and a few cotton strips, presumably for her monthly visitor, which is due quite soon.

Sometimes she hears movement and voices. Maybe she is not alone in her experience, but it is impossible to know for sure.

Occasionally food and water is lowered down to her, but she cannot see by whom. Other than that she is left quite alone with only her own increasingly desperate thoughts for company. Reaching into her pocket, she pulls out a rosary and begins to pray. Perhaps if she does this for long enough, the Virgin Mary will come to her assistance. But the hours pass, as the days have already, and no one arrives to release her. She begins to think they never will.

Yet she is not alone. Through a peephole roughly carved into the wooden cover that is her ceiling, she is being closely watched. Though she does not know it, her release is imminent – but when it finally comes, she will wish that it had not.

Diana Bretherick is a former criminal barrister and now a senior lecturer in criminology and criminal justice at the University of Portsmouth. She won the *Good Housekeeping* new novel competition in 2012.

Find out more at Diana's website www.dianabretherick.co.uk and follow her on Twitter at @DianaBretherick

Also by Diana Bretherick

City of Devils

THE DEVIL'S DAUGHTERS

DIANA BRETHERICK

An Orion paperback

First published in Great Britain in 2015
by Orion Books
This paperback edition published in 2016
by Orion Books,
an imprint of The Orion Publishing Group Ltd,
Carmelite House, 50 Victoria Embankment
London EC4Y 0DZ

An Hachette UK Company

1 3 5 7 9 10 8 6 4 2

A CIP catalogue record for this book
is available from the British Library.

ISBN 978 1 4091 5031 2

Typeset at The Spartan Press Ltd,
Lymington, Hants

Printed in Great Britain by
Clays Ltd, St Ives plc

FSC
www.fsc.org
MIX
Paper from
responsible sources
FSC® C104740

www.orionbooks.co.uk

To David, who is everything.

Turin, 1 March 1888

The dark changes everything.

She moves quickly through the early winter morning and wishes fervently for the sun to rise. In the daylight this would be an unremarkable journey. But now, in the darkness, the mundane slips seamlessly into the sinister, and threat surrounds her. Every corner is a hiding place for a monster, and every sound, no matter how slight, is from someone or something that wishes to do her harm.

As she makes her way to work through the familiar streets, now shrouded in shadows, she pulls her thin shawl around her in an attempt to fend off the icy cold and damp. It reaches through her clothing right to her skin, caressing her like the clammy hands of an unwanted suitor.

The freezing wind whistles round her ankles as she goes on her way, blowing dust, dead leaves and bits of old newspaper into her path. She blinks, and her eyes water in the cold air. The gas lamps are still lit, but she can take no comfort from them. The flickering yellow flames merely add to the phantoms that surround her. She tries her best to look straight ahead, but every now and again she thinks she hears something, a sharp sound – an unidentified footstep or a door creaking open to reveal . . . who knows what.

She has reached the Via Garibaldi in the oldest part of the

city when her imagined sound becomes real. It is distinct – a cracking sound; an opening perhaps. She is reminded that the gates to Hell are never far away in this city. There is the sound again, sharp and resonating, almost like someone breaking a cane in two. A little way down the street she sees a light, a lantern perhaps, swaying as if someone is looking for something. It seems to be coming towards her. She backs away from it but still it approaches. Instinctively she begins to run. She does not know why. It is only a light after all. Eventually she stops and tells herself to be calm. But then she sees that the light has followed her, so she runs again and tries to lose it, ducking into another street only to find it blocked by a carriage halfway up. The door opens. She hesitates, holding her breath. A gloved hand beckons to her. The gloves are lace. The hand is long and slim.

'Come, child, come!' says the figure in the carriage.

She sees the light again. It seems to be getting closer. She walks to the carriage door and peers inside. There is one occupant – a woman in a large-brimmed hat swathed in a veil.

'Get in, child,' says the woman.

She hesitates. The voice is strange, with a sing-song quality to it. It captivates her. A hand comes over her mouth from behind. It holds a handkerchief and smells odd – like the cleaning fluid the housekeeper gives her to use on the polished wooden floors. She struggles, but it is useless. She is becoming weaker as she is bundled into the carriage.

As they drive away, she slips gently into oblivion. The fears that haunted her have finally come true.

The bearer of the light stops and leans against the wall, trying to relieve himself whilst still holding his lantern. He's getting too old for this. He slumps to the ground and sits with his eyes closed. Everything is spinning. He shouldn't have had that last grappa. But it was a celebration, although of what exactly he cannot quite remember. And it seemed rude to refuse a drink or two, particularly as it was free. 'Come on, Pietro,' they said. 'It isn't a real party without you!' Well who was he to disagree?

Now, though, sitting in a puddle of his own piss in the darkness, he is full of regret. And as if that wasn't enough, he is seeing things – some girl being dragged into a carriage again and spirited away. He takes off his tatty old straw hat and shakes his head at his own folly, but it hurts, so he stops. He pulls himself to his feet and starts his journey home to his bed, to sleep it off and forget. The city is quiet again, as if, having been awoken for a few brief moments, it is settling back to sleep. Everything appears to have returned to its former equilibrium. But this is merely an illusion.

1

The morally insane repay hatred with hatred. Even when the cause is slight, they react with anger, envy and vengeance. Incapable of family life, they flee the paternal home, sleeping under bridges and devoting themselves to refined cruelties. Lombroso, 1884, p. 215

Edinburgh, 18 March 1888

'I know what you are.'

The voice cut through the silence, the edge jagged with hatred.

The mourners stared, first at the man who had made this statement and then at his subject.

The funeral had been difficult enough even before this intervention. James Murray had stood and watched the coffin being lowered into the grave and wondered if his empty heart would ever be full again. He wanted more than anything to regret his father's passing, but instead he felt only relief.

There was Arthur's Seat, rising imposingly behind the church – a green mass giving a hint of colour in an otherwise grey landscape. He and his father had often walked there together, deep in conversation about their shared fascination with the workings of the human brain. He had been the student, his father the teacher. But those were happier times. Now everything was different.

Another memory had lurched into his mind, this time unwanted – his father strapped to a bed in the asylum where he had ended his days, screaming and raving. James had tried to shake the vision away, but he knew that it would haunt him until his own death. He should have done something earlier to prevent this tragedy. Instead, like a coward, he had run away to a foreign city, leaving everything and everyone behind.

Sobbing came from beside him. His sister Lucy was weeping steadily. Wispy tendrils of strawberry-blonde hair surrounded her pretty heart-shaped face. He longed to tuck them gently behind her ears as he had seen his father do. Instinctively he reached out to her, but she shrugged away from him, giving him a reproachful glare. Unlike him, Lucy was truly in mourning, but then she did not know the truth about what kind of man was being buried – a lunatic and a criminal, guilty of the theft of a man's soul.

As the final words were intoned by the suitably gloomy minister, the church clock chimed as if it too was sounding an end to his father's life. James had been about to escort Lucy away when he heard a commotion. A man pushed his way through the mourners and stood for a moment peering down at the coffin. He was smartly dressed in the black frock coat customary for these occasions. His cravat, however, was of a vivid scarlet, and so great was the contrast with everything else that it seemed to glow. James stared at him. Who was he? The man was familiar but he could not place him. Gaunt and pale, he resembled Death himself, but it was his eyes that were his most striking feature. They were steel grey, and when the man lifted his head to focus them on James, it felt as if they were boring holes into his skull.

'I know what you are.'

The words ripped into James, through his skin and through his bones until he felt their icy touch around his heart.

The man walked away. At first there was silence, then what felt like a collective intake of breath among the few that were present. They began to stare at James and mutter to each other. He tried to look straight ahead, knowing that if he acknowledged the man's words it might give them credence, but he sensed the disapproval. He had begun the occasion as the chief mourner, but now he was a source of gossip. That was nothing. He deserved it after all. But Lucy didn't.

Eventually the mourners began to make their way to their carriages. There was to be no wake. At least they had that to be thankful for. It had seemed wrong somehow, given the circumstances.

Lucy turned away, her eyes full of hurt and confusion. James watched her for a few seconds and realised how alone he felt. His parents were both gone, and now even his sister seemed lost to him. But then she stopped, as if she was waiting for him. James walked towards her. Could there be some hope for them after all? The question was still there, an invisible barrier between them as they began their journey home. They sat in silence, together but still far apart, as the carriage with its black-plumed horses, upon which Lucy had insisted, made its way slowly through the narrow, winding streets of the old town to the broad, straight ones of the new.

For a moment James was transported back to Turin, from where he had not so long ago returned. He had gone there to study the nature of the criminal and to find out if his father's evil might have infected him, just as the man at the funeral had suggested. He had learnt not just about crime but also about what it was to love and lose someone. He had put his duty first. He did not regret it, but neither could he quite forget what he had left behind. Still, that was another world and another time. He had returned home to face his fears, but he had been too late.

He glanced out of the window and for a split second he thought he saw her, standing on a corner dressed in a long hooded cloak, a basket in her arms. Everything around him came to a halt, as if he was in a photograph. Even his ability to breathe seemed to desert him. Logic told him that it could not be her, but still the anticipation made every one of his senses sharpen. Then she turned towards him and he saw that she was a stranger. The woman he longed for was in Italy, and he and his duty still belonged in Edinburgh.

'Who was that man, James?' Lucy asked. It was clear from the strain in her voice that she was struggling to keep her emotions under control.

'I'm not sure.'

'What did he mean about knowing what you are?'

James shrugged. He had been badly shaken by the accusatory tone of the man at the graveside but did not want to admit it.

'I just don't know, Lucy.' What else could he say? If he started to tell her of his suspicions, he would not be able to stop. He could not put her through that. It just wouldn't be fair.

The carriage lurched and James and Lucy were thrown together. She leant quickly away from him, as if he was some kind of threat. He put out his hand to hers, but she pulled it away. James understood why she was behaving like this. She had lost her father, and she blamed him. He had abandoned her, and by the time he had returned home, their father was dead. Lucy knew nothing of his sacrifice, and he would not tell her. He deserved her anger, but he would fight for her forgiveness. After all, they had only each other now, and that was all that mattered.

They were not quite alone. They arrived home to find their Aunt Agnes seated primly reading the Bible in the drawing room, grim-faced, like a parasite sucking away at their grief. An ostentatiously devout woman, she had been shocked by their father's decline and the scandal it had threatened to bring upon the family, virtually disowning him since his incarceration. She had even refused to attend his funeral, claiming that it was not decent behaviour for a woman. Lucy, of course, had insisted on being there, notwithstanding – or perhaps because of – her aunt's objections, saying that this was an old-fashioned view and that it was perfectly acceptable these days. James was not certain that she was right, but he did not have the heart to forbid it. Aunt Agnes had merely pursed her lips and stood her ground, her expression making it clear that she blamed James for his father's fate.

Now she sat there in her crêpe mourning gown, having insisted on all the usual customs that accompanied death despite her views on the deceased himself. Agnes Kennedy was small and joyless, embittered by her husband's infidelity. Her mouth was permanently downturned and her thin dark hair was tinged with grey and worn in what seemed to be a mercilessly tight bun secured firmly at the back of her head – an outmoded coiffure that reflected her outlook exactly. He decided not to tell her about the man at the funeral, knowing that it would merely confirm her opinion.

'I'm going up to my room to lie down,' Lucy declared.

Aunt Agnes nodded. 'Very well, child.' She turned to James once his sister had left. 'There is a letter for you,' she said in a faintly disapproving tone, holding out a small cream envelope.

He examined it curiously. It did not have the black borders of a letter of condolence. Who could it be from? Then, as he saw the Turin postmark and recognised the handwriting, his heartbeat quickened with anticipation.

'Who is writing from Italy, James?' asked his aunt, her eyes narrowing suspiciously.

'A friend,' he replied tersely. 'If you'll excuse me, Aunt, I will also rest for a while. It has been a difficult afternoon.'

She gave a curt nod. No doubt, James thought, she was annoyed to be denied further information about the letter. He didn't care. This was for his eyes alone, and was more precious to him than anything in the world.

Up in his room, he stared at the page before him. He lifted it to his face and breathed in its aroma – a faint suggestion of lemons and spice. As he sat there with his eyes shut, he imagined her arms around him, and for a moment he was returned to her. But when he opened them again, he realised that he did not know quite how to feel. Ever since he had left Italy, he had dreamt of hearing from Sofia, and yet he had dreaded it too. He had loved her and left her. They could not be together because their pasts and their futures were so different. All the same, he had hoped that somehow he would see her again. He had continued to write to her, but no reply had come. He had almost reconciled himself to staying in Scotland and making a life for himself there. But now she had finally written to him and thrust him into a state of confusion.

Per favore, aiutami, the letter said in characteristically cryptic terms. Please, help me.

Turin, 19 March 1888

The girl sits alone in what seems to be little more than a deep pit and wonders what she has done to deserve her incarceration. She cannot tell how long she has been there because she cannot see when the night ends and the day begins, but it feels like weeks at least. Too long anyway to be in what she has come to think of as her cell. There is not much in the way of comfort, just a thin mattress, a bucket for relieving herself, and a few cotton strips, presumably for her monthly visitor, which is due quite soon.

Sometimes she hears movement and voices. Maybe she is not alone in her experience, but it is impossible to know for sure.

Occasionally food and water is lowered down to her, but she cannot see by whom. Other than that she is left quite alone with only her own increasingly desperate thoughts for company. Reaching into her pocket, she pulls out a rosary and begins to pray. Perhaps if she does this for long enough, the Virgin Mary will come to her assistance. But the hours pass, as the days have already, and no one arrives to release her. She begins to think they never will.

Yet she is not alone. Through a peephole roughly carved into the wooden cover that is her ceiling, she is being closely watched. Though she does not know it, her release is imminent – but when it finally comes, she will wish that it had not.

2

One need only to look at pictures of women of genius of our day to realise that they seem to be men in disguise.

Lombroso, 1893, p. 83

Edinburgh, 20 March 1888

James stood outside the door of the lecture hall and listened carefully. A man's voice, soft but authoritative, was holding forth about the importance of observation. 'How does your patient move? Does he drag a foot, suggesting evidence of some former injury? Does he leap around, thereby showing himself to be fit and healthy, if something of a show-off? Does he have any marks upon him – a tattoo, perhaps – gained in some foreign clime, indicating that he has travelled and wishes us all to know it? It is these small things that make up the larger and more significant whole.'

James smiled to himself, remembering when Professor Joseph Bell had given him the same lecture during his own medical training, what seemed like a century ago. He opened the door gently and attempted to sidle in unseen, the better to hear what remained of the lecture. This turned out to be a mistake.

'Ah! I do believe we have a subject, gentlemen!'

James stood and grinned as a ripple of laughter went through the students.

'Come into the centre, sir, and make yourself visible. Now, who can make some observations about our subject? Remember, it is small things we are looking for.'

A couple of hands went up. Professor Bell peered out at them before pointing at a nervous young man sitting at the front. 'Mr Davies, what can you tell us?'

'He looks a bit shifty . . . up to no good.'

'I see. In what way?'

'It's his eyes. They move about.'

James frowned.

'I see . . . Anything else?'

'His shoes are scruffy. Looks like he's done a fair bit of walking recently,' someone called out.

'And what might that indicate about his occupation?'

'Is he a policeman?'

'Interesting . . . Are you a man of the law, sir?' Bell asked James, with a twinkle in his eye.

'I like to think so, but not in the way you mean,' James replied.

'He's a Scot!' a student shouted.

'Aye, he can't be all bad!' said another.

'Let us confine ourselves to the physical for now, gentlemen,' Bell said. 'We've time for one more observation.'

'The subject has a slight stoop,' someone called from the back.

Instinctively James straightened up. 'Not any longer, it seems!' Bell said. 'What does that tell you?'

'He is unsure of himself . . . or about something.'

'Perhaps he is not confident. He prefers not to stand out in a crowd?' someone said tentatively.

'Well the good doctor has failed in that enterprise today, to be sure!' Bell said to general laughter. 'Yes, Dr Murray is a medical man, and not so long ago sat where you are now, listening to me, poor fellow. Thank you, gentlemen. We shall continue this tomorrow.'

As the students filed obediently out, Professor Bell seized James's hand. 'I hope you didn't mind me using you as a subject.'

'Not at all, Professor. It was, as always, very instructive.'

'Good. That is, after all, what we aim for. Now, how about a drink of something?'

Minutes later they were sitting in the professor's cavernous office sipping at a decidedly acceptable malt whisky. The shelves were crammed with books, untidy piles of papers and one or two jars holding pickled body parts. James felt another twinge of regret for what he had left behind in Turin. His employer in Italy had been similar in many ways to Professor Bell – and yet in others they were almost diametrically opposed to each other. Professor Bell was precise and careful in both his investigations and the expression of his findings. Criminal anthropologist Cesare Lombroso, on the other hand, preferred, as he often said, to let the facts speak for themselves. In practice this often meant that the facts were altered in order to fit the theory, and occasionally vice versa, which made working with him sometimes difficult but never, ever dull.

Professor Bell peered at James curiously over the rim of his glass. 'So tell me, Murray, were any of the students correct in their observations?'

James paused. 'To an extent, perhaps . . . There is a matter that I am unsure of, as one of them mentioned.'

'Is it connected to what happened at your father's funeral?'

'You have heard about that?'

Bell nodded. 'I am afraid it is the subject of speculation in some quarters.'

'I still do not know the man's identity, though I am sure I have seen him before.'

'Perhaps it is best left. It will be yesterday's news soon enough. It is your future that should be occupying your mind now, Murray.'

'You are right. In fact that is why I am here. I wish to ask your advice about something.'

'I see.' Professor Bell paused for a moment. 'I deduce that something is a woman.'

James smiled. 'I suppose I must ask how you reached that conclusion. Was it my demeanour that gave me away, the way I was standing . . . or something I said perhaps?'

The professor laughed and shook his head. 'No, no, my dear boy, none of that . . .'

'So how did you know?'

'When I see a young man wearing a troubled expression, believe me, the cause is almost always a woman.'

'I'm not sure that is quite fair, although you are right on this occasion, Professor.'

'Your tone suggests that she is not the only matter that concerns you.'

'Again you are right. There is more to it.' James hesitated, struggling to find the right words.

'Go on.'

'I want to return to Turin . . . indeed, I feel that I must.'

'May I ask why?'

'The woman I speak of . . . she has asked for my help.'

'And you feel duty bound to answer her call?'

'It is not so much a matter of duty.'

'Ah, I see – a matter of the heart, then. And what else?'

Bell paused. 'You travelled to Italy to study with Professor Lombroso, but you found more, did you not?'

'There was something that had been troubling me and, to an extent, the professor reassured me. I felt that I was just beginning to make sense of his theories when I had to leave. I did not want to go.' As James spoke, the feeling of regret he had experienced became sharper, almost painful.

Professor Bell nodded thoughtfully. 'I have read one or two articles by him. He has some original ideas. I am not sure that I agree with all his methods, but still they are fascinating. I am not surprised that he has inspired you.'

'He is unusual in his approach, but some of his ideas have definite possibilities for the solution of crimes. I would relish the opportunity to work with him again.'

'So what is stopping you?' Bell asked.

'As you know, Professor, I have a sister, Lucy. If I abandon her again, I don't think she would forgive me.'

'Ah, I see,' Bell said. 'So you have come to me because you think I will tell you that your work must take precedence. In other words, you want me to give you permission to leave your sister here in Edinburgh.'

James stared down at his glass and swirled its amber contents round, watching the viscous liquid cling to the sides. 'I suppose you're right, Professor.'

'You must know that I cannot do that,' Bell said gently. 'It is a personal matter that only you can decide upon.'

James nodded miserably. He felt like a fool. How could he ever have thought that asking Professor Bell for advice was the right thing to do?

'Your work is important to you. I understand that. But is a choice really necessary?' Bell asked.

'What do you mean, Professor?'

'Sometimes you're a little slow on the uptake, Murray. There are only two possible solutions. All you have to do is choose one.'

James shook his head in confusion.

Professor Bell smiled at him. 'Give it some thought, young man, and I'm sure the answer will come to you before too long. Remember what I used to say to you at the beginning of each case.'

'Never ignore the obvious. It is often an investigator's only friend.'

'Indeed! I am most gratified that you have not forgotten. Now all you have to do is go away and apply it.'

'Return to Turin! I have never heard such a preposterous idea!' Aunt Agnes declared. 'You cannot possibly be thinking of shirking your responsibilities again! What of your sister?'

'Yes, James, what about me?' Lucy repeated, her eyes flashing with anger. 'Am I to be abandoned yet again?' A look of despair crossed her face.

'No, Lucy, you are not,' he heard himself saying. 'You will travel with me. It would do us both good.'

Lucy looked at him in surprise. 'You want me to come with you to Turin?'

'Yes, I do. '

'You most certainly will do no such thing!' Aunt Agnes got to her feet and strode towards him. For a brief moment he thought she was going to attack him. Instead she stood inches away and wagged her finger in his face. 'Lucy was too young to travel with you before. You admitted it yourself. Nothing has changed.'

'I am older now! I am almost eighteen,' Lucy protested.

'That is still far too young to go gallivanting across Europe, young lady!'

'Things are different now, Aunt,' James said.

She glared at him. 'How, exactly?'

'For one thing I have been there and I know Lucy will be safe.'

'Safe! There were two killers on the loose! That does not sound safe to me.'

'They have been . . . dealt with.'

'One has been dealt with. The other is still at large.'

'My employer, Professor Lombroso, is a good man, a family man, with two daughters of an age similar to Lucy.'

'So you have said before, but he is not . . .' she paused and took a deep, almost theatrical breath, 'suitable as a guardian for your sister.'

James wondered how else he could persuade his aunt of Lombroso's good character. 'The professor is an eminent scientist, extremely well respected in his field.'

'I do not doubt it, but Lucy is a young lady at an impressionable age. She requires moral guidance, particularly in the light of her parental background.'

There was a pause as James struggled to ignore this slight. 'And she shall have moral guidance, Aunt Agnes. I will make sure of that.'

'I am almost eighteen,' Lucy repeated. 'I require no guidance, moral or otherwise.'

'Your words demonstrate the exact opposite, young lady,' Aunt Agnes said, an expression of deep satisfaction on her face. 'However, I have a solution . . .'

Lucy sat in her room with her pencil poised, but inspiration would not come to her tonight. How could it? She was far too excited. Her life was about to change beyond recognition. She was to have a new home, a new city, a new country... and all without the presence of Aunt Agnes. Thank heavens James had put his foot down when she had offered to accompany them! That would have been a disaster. As it was, Lucy would have to put up with some stuffy companion hand-picked by her aunt. Still, that in itself provided a challenge, which was something she always enjoyed. She pictured herself climbing through a window to escape as her companion dozed in an armchair. Yes, she would enjoy pitting her wits against Aunt Agnes's spy, whoever she turned out to be.

Lucy was in the middle of writing one of her stories. Her heroine, the intrepid lady detective Lydia Loveday, was trapped in an underground cavern in the search for some stolen diamonds. The trouble was, having got Lydia into this predicament, she couldn't think of a way of getting her out. She studied the illustration she had sketched last night. Lydia stood with her hands on her hips looking reproachfully out at her. Reluctantly Lucy closed her notebook, carefully tying the ribbons as her father had taught her. 'If you do it like that,' he'd said, 'you'll always know if someone has been poking their nose where they shouldn't.'

The memory of her father made her catch her breath. It still caused her so much pain just to think of him. She cast her mind back to the funeral, and that strange man who had said such a peculiar thing. Who was he, and what on earth had he meant about James? She thought of the expressions on the faces of the few mourners present – an uneasy combination of pity and prurience. Now that they were leaving them all behind, they could think what they liked. It would be a fresh start.

Having no parents made her feel adrift. Perhaps both she

and James needed to put down some new roots. But wasn't that a kind of betrayal – leaving the city where they had lived as a family? Yet the thought of staying here with Aunt Agnes depressed her. It would be like being buried alive, albeit in a silk-lined coffin.

No. She had to go. It seemed strange and somehow wrong that she knew so little of the country where her mother had been born. Lucy's father Robert had been on a walking tour of the Piedmont countryside when they had met. Elena was helping her aunt, her only surviving relative, to run a small hotel in the town of Alba. He was a guest. Her mother would always smile as she told them how he had complained about something and she had argued with him. Apparently he hadn't expected it, and his face was such a picture of shock that she'd laughed. 'Yes,' Robert would say. 'And she has never stopped arguing with me from that day to this!'

Despite the protestations of Elena's aunt, they were married a few months later and returned to Edinburgh. Lucy could only imagine how hard it must have been for her mother to adjust to such a different way of life. Perhaps that was why she had insisted that both Lucy and James spoke Italian. It kept her country alive in her heart. They had often conversed in the language at home and their mother was full of stories about the place, but they had never visited. Perhaps Robert feared that once she was back in Italy, she would not want to return to Scotland. Lucy herself had always dreamt of travelling there with her mother when she was old enough, but it had not been possible, and then it was too late. Her mother had died and her father was never really the same man again.

This then could be a sort of pilgrimage. No – more of a tribute to her mother. She would at last make proper contact with the half of her that was Italian. The prospect seemed inviting. Lucy didn't know whether she was prepared to turn her back on her father and on Scotland completely. Only time and distance would tell.

3

A special type of criminality among females, particularly in the higher animals, is hatred for individuals of their own sex. Envious of her companions, the dove will hide food that she herself does not need under her wing. Among the anthropomorphic monkeys, particularly orang-utans, females treat one another with an instinctive animosity, beating and sometimes even killing one another.

Lombroso and Ferrero, 1893, p. 92

3 April 1888

The train jolted James awake and, for a moment, he wondered where he was. Out of the window he saw the snow-covered peaks of the Alps rising in the distance, and it all came back to him in one glorious rush. It had been only two weeks since he had received Sofia's letter, and now he was on his way back to her. Across from him Lucy was dozing gently, her head lolling onto the shoulder of the woman next to her. Fortunately they were quite well acquainted by now, as she was Lucy's new companion, Miss Euphemia Trott.

'It will not be long before we arrive, I imagine,' she said.

'Perhaps another hour or so, if memory serves,' he replied.

Miss Trott seemed unremarkable in almost every way. She

was in her late forties, short and roundish, with pleasant features and faded-blonde hair that was pinned up rather untidily. She had an air of competence about her, as if little would shake her; this, James presumed, was why Aunt Agnes had decided to engage her. He knew little else about her other than her name, that she attended the same church as his aunt and was fluent in Italian. She seemed nice enough, though a little dull. But then perhaps that was what Lucy needed – someone to keep her grounded in her new life.

Miss Trott sat with her hands folded in her lap, the forefinger of one tapping on the other as if keeping time with an imaginary orchestra. As James watched, he realised that it was the rhythm of the train that she was marking. Her small round glasses began to slide slowly but surely down her nose, but she did not touch them. How long would she resist the temptation? he wondered.

She turned her head briefly to peer out of the window, and when she looked back, the glasses had mysteriously returned to where they had started, apparently without her intervention.

James stared at her. How on earth did she do that? She raised her eyebrows, as if challenging him to ask. He turned away, embarrassed. It was probably best left. There were other, more pressing, matters on his mind.

He looked out at the Alps again and thought, with an unfamiliar contentment, of what was to come. He was to take up his old position as assistant to Professor Lombroso, and they were to stay with the professor while they found their feet. And that of course meant that he would be in close proximity to the only person other than his sister who really mattered to him – Sofia, the woman he loved. Whatever it was she needed him for, it was surely an excuse, a ruse to get him to return. Why else would she be so oblique? For him their time apart had merely served to emphasise the strength of his feelings, which surely meant that it must have been the same for her.

At last everything seemed to be righting itself to its proper order. He and Lucy had left behind their old life in Edinburgh, with all its difficulties and strains. Finally they could start afresh and everything would be as it should be. He would help Sofia, and somehow, despite her past, they would be together. For once, after the dark days he had suffered, all James saw ahead of him was hope. Because now he had a plan. It had come to him following his conversation with Bell. Its simplicity had surprised him. It was clear that he could not be with Sofia in Scotland. It would be almost as difficult for them in Turin, where everyone knew her background. The answer then was, as Bell had said, quite obvious. They would have to go somewhere else entirely.

'What are your first impressions, Lucy?' James asked as they stood side by side on the platform of Turin's Porto Nuevo station.

'It isn't very . . . different.'

James laughed. 'What did you expect? People with two heads? Blue rain?'

'Not that kind of difference. Just a feeling that we're not in Scotland.' Lucy had expected some kind of foreignness at least, but all she had seen was . . . well, sameness. The architecture of the station was almost exactly like that of Waverley. The people rushed about just as they did in Scotland, and she felt as much of a stranger here as she did in her own city. It was even raining, as it had been in Edinburgh when they began their journey.

It was true that there had been plenty of contrast during

their travels, and Lucy had experienced a sense of invigoration with each new experience. The trip by boat had been, in her imagination, a voyage to the new world with a pirate ship on the horizon and the possibility of being shipwrecked on a desert island arriving with even the suggestion of a cloud. The train rattling through the French and Italian countryside towards Turin was the setting for an encounter between her detective and a network of spies. When she tired of that scenario, Lucy had started to peer out of the window at every station and examine the people milling about in almost forensic detail. Once she had jotted down a few observations in her notebook, she would set about giving each person a story that she would then relate to James and Miss Trott. The large woman in the dress with the too-tight arms at a small station near the border was wearing an anxious expression because she was fleeing from justice. She had either poisoned her lover or was a retired baby farmer, or possibly both. James had entered into the spirit of it and had suggested that she might be wearing a disguise, because 'no one would wear that dress voluntarily'. Miss Trott had merely kept her nose in her book. Lucy had hoped it would at least be a novel that was holding her attention, but it turned out to be a collection of accounts of the lives of various saints, or what Aunt Agnes would call 'an improving text'. What normal person would read such a dull narrative? she wondered.

Lucy had done her best to give her new companion an interesting backstory, but it was an uphill struggle. In the end she had settled for either a tragic love affair that had come to a premature end when her lover had been killed in a faraway conflict, or some kind of scandal. She liked the idea of an affair much more than the scandal, but had to abandon it due to implausibility. Love and Miss Trott just didn't go together. If propositioned, she would be more likely to raise her eyebrows, give a small shake of her head and walk away rather than do or say anything that might involve passion of any kind. This was based on what Lucy had observed so far, which was Miss Trott variously reading, nodding off or making comments about the weather, with which she seemed to be obsessed. James appeared happy enough with her, although no doubt his criteria were different to Lucy's own.

A sense of disappointment began to overwhelm her. Why wasn't there more evidence of Italian-ness? She could hear the difference in the language, and that was something. But everything smelt of damp and seemed grey when it should have been a new aroma and a different kind of light that had greeted them. Perhaps it was just a matter of the rain.

She watched James, in his element organising their luggage, moving from one trunk to another, checking them off in a notebook. He liked order. Having his equilibrium disturbed in any way depressed him, which was one of the reasons why their father's downfall had hit him so hard. He grinned, and Lucy gave him a small smile. She had not yet forgiven him for his attitude towards their father. He was dead and should be properly mourned, whatever he had done, yet all James had been able to demonstrate, it had seemed to her, was relief.

'I cannot pretend to feel what I do not,' he had said when she had challenged him. 'There are things you do not know.'

'Then tell me!' she had cried. 'He was my father too!'

But it was no good. James would not be drawn on the matter, leaving her trapped in a kind of lonely limbo wherein she could not forgive either her brother or her father, and wondering what the words 'I know what you are' actually meant. She had thought she knew what James was – kind, sometimes funny, protective, impulsive about some things, cautious about others; at any rate nothing bad – at least until her father had been taken away. Then he had changed, becoming secretive and strained, until one day he too had disappeared. She remembered it only too well, for it had marked the beginning of her own incarceration with Aunt Agnes. At least that was over, for the time being anyway.

'Are you ready, dear?' Miss Trott enquired. 'I think we are all set to go. I am told it isn't far.'

She was right. It seemed that they had hardly sat down in the waiting carriage before they arrived at the professor's house. The touch of James's hand was cool and reassuring as he helped Lucy to alight. She looked up at the building with its tall windows and occasional architectural flourishes in the form of scrolls and flowers. Here and there were faces carved into the stone, squinting down at her malevolently as if warning her not to enter. Defiantly she pulled her cloak around her and waited for the door to be opened.

There was only one thing on James's mind from the moment they had arrived in Turin, and that was Sofia. Why had she called him back to her? There had been no communication other than her letter, which had been so brief it had told him almost nothing. Sofia was not one for idle chatter, but still he would have liked at least a suggestion of what help she required. It was as if she knew that her request alone was all it would take. And, of course, she had been absolutely right.

As they stood outside Lombroso's imposing front door, he yearned to see her. He looked at his sister to see if she had noticed anything, but fortunately she seemed oblivious to how he felt. The time would come to tell Lucy about Sofia, but it had not yet arrived. He had no idea how to broach the subject – and that was before he mentioned his plans for all of their futures. For now, though, all that mattered to him was Sofia. He had rehearsed the moment of their reunion many times since receiving her letter, and all he wanted was to see her. But to his dismay and surprise, when the door opened, she was not there.

Instead they were ushered in by a capable housemaid, who showed them into the drawing room. James was instantly transported back to his last meeting with the professor and Ottolenghi, his fellow assistant. They had sat around the fire and reflected on the tragic events that had taken place. Lombroso had seemed humbled by all that had happened, even questioning his own actions. He had been so certain that criminal anthropology could be used to catch a killer, but he had been proved wrong in a very public way. Instead all they had learnt was that science could not always explain criminal behaviour. James wondered what developments in Lombroso's theory of the born criminal this might have led to. It made him realise how much he was looking forward to getting back to work.

The door was thrown open and the professor bounded in, a small, bearded bundle of energy fizzing like a newly opened bottle of champagne.

'Murray, my dear fellow. How good it is to see you! How are you?'

He seized James's hand and pumped it up and down. A grey-haired woman stood in the doorway, watching them and smiling patiently.

'Now, there is much to discuss. I have started a new investigation. We will be revolutionising the study of crime. What do you think of that?' He went on before James could answer, his heavy eyebrows moving up and down, marking time with his words. 'I think – no, I am certain that we will shake the very foundations of criminal anthropology! And there is more . . . so much more to talk about!'

The woman in the doorway cleared her throat.

'What is it, my dear?' he asked.

She came into the room and indicated Lucy and Miss Trott. 'We do have other guests, Cesare.'

He gave a short bow. 'Ah, Miss Lucy Murray, I gather, and this lady is . . . ?'

'This is Miss Trott, Professor,' James said. 'My sister's companion.'

Miss Trott gave Lombroso a nod of acknowledgement. The professor peered at her and frowned. Steadfastly she returned his gaze. There was an awkward silence, which was eventually broken by the woman with the grey hair.

'Why don't you take Signor Murray to your study, Cesare, whilst I look after the ladies?' She paused. 'I am Nina Lombroso, as my husband neglected to inform you.' She tutted at him, and James was amused to see a sheepish look pass over his face just for an instant before he moved towards the door.

'Yes, my dear . . . an excellent notion. Come, Murray, we have much to discuss.' With that he swept out of the room without so much as a backward glance.

'I do apologise for my husband,' Signora Lombroso said. 'He is rather prone to getting carried away. He's been so excited about your return, Mr Murray.'

'Should I . . . ?' James said, looking towards the door.

'Yes, do. I think you know the way, do you not?' she said, her eyes twinkling. 'Now, ladies, let me show you to your rooms. Then, later, you must allow me to introduce you to my daughters. They are very much looking forward to meeting you, Miss Murray.'

James took his leave and began to make his way to Lombroso's study. It was almost as if he had never left . . . except for the one thing that was missing. Where on earth was Sofia?

4

... the female born criminal surpasses her male counterpart in the refined, diabolical cruelty with which she commits her crimes. Merely killing her enemy does not satisfy her; she needs to watch him suffer and experience the full taste of death.

(Lombroso and Ferrero, 1893, p. 182)

Lucy had been left to rest in her room. She was finding it difficult to settle. Surely the sudden pang she was experiencing could not be homesickness, could it? She had been so eager to leave, after all. Still, it was a strange feeling not having your own home. Professor Lombroso was a funny little man, not at all the grave and serious scientist she had been expecting. James had always seemed to be in awe of him. Lucy could not think why. He was so friendly... almost like a favourite uncle.

There was a light tap on the door. It opened to reveal two girls, one of a similar age to herself and the other slightly younger, perhaps about fifteen – the Lombroso sisters, she imagined. The elder was taller than the younger and had more pronounced features. She wore a slight frown, making her look serious and bookish. Her sister was a little dumpy, with a rounder face and a flatter nose. Neither could be called pretty. They both had dull brown hair, and both were dressed in drab school outfits that did nothing to flatter their shape. But there was something engaging about them nonetheless, and Lucy felt instantly comfortable in their company.

'I am Paola Lombroso,' said the older girl, stepping forward and extending her hand. Lucy shook it solemnly.

Her sister grinned. 'And I am Gina. Really, Paola, there is no need to be so formal!'

'I was just being polite. Remember what Mama told us about how to greet a stranger.'

'I hope we shall not be strangers for long,' Lucy said.

Paola frowned slightly. 'We have met, so we can't be strangers now.'

Gina groaned. 'Always analysing!' Paola opened her mouth as if to protest, but her sister interrupted her. 'I know, I know . . . Papa would say that was a good thing, but you can go too far.'

Paola shook her head impatiently. 'How are you finding Italy, Miss Murray?'

'Call me Lucy, please, or should I say Lucia, now that I am here. That is my given name after all.'

'Oh yes,' Gina said, flopping down on to Lucy's bed. 'I like that. Miss Lucia Murray – it is much more serious-sounding. That is what we shall call you – a new name for a new city.'

Lucy nodded. 'Perhaps, though I don't know what my brother will say.'

'Ah yes, Signor James. We watched as you arrived. He's quite handsome, isn't he?' Paola said, perching sedately on a chair.

Lucy considered this view of her brother. 'Really? I've

never thought of him in that way, but I suppose he might be considered so by some.'

Gina laughed. 'Let us analyse, as Papa would. Not tall – more stocky, I'd say – with thick dark hair, pale skin, generous lips, nice smile, grey eyes, I think?'

Lucy nodded, enjoying the game.

'An infectious laugh,' Paola added, 'oh, and a flat head at the back. That might be significant, don't you think?'

'Only if you're Papa,' Gina said. 'I doubt Signor Murray is a criminal!'

Lucy began to laugh, but it turned into a yawn, which she tried desperately to stifle, not wishing to seem rude.

'Perhaps we should leave you to rest a little,' Paola suggested. 'We will have plenty of time to get acquainted.'

'Yes, yes . . . a good idea,' Gina said. 'We shall see you at dinner. Papa has invited Anna, you know.'

'Anna?' Lucy asked.

'You'll like her,' Gina said. 'She is wonderful.'

'Madame Anna Tarnovsky. She has come all the way from Prague to work with Papa on a new project,' Paola said. 'If we are lucky, they will tell us about it.'

Lucy nodded. 'I think the professor mentioned it earlier. It all sounded rather strange.'

Gina smiled. 'You'll get used to it. Before long, that is all your brother will be able to talk about.'

'Anyway, we will see you at dinner,' Paola said. 'The first of many, no doubt.'

Lucy watched them as they left. Then it struck her. *Plenty of time*, Paola had said, and she was right. They would be here for a few months at least, and who knew what would happen after that. The recent past had not been kind to them, but it was the future that was important now – an unknown and mysterious landscape unpunctuated by the familiar landmarks of her childhood. This was the beginning of a new part of her life.

James was on his way up to Lombroso's study when he saw her – framed in a doorway, the light surrounding her as if she was some kind of vision. He felt a surge of joy travel through him. With her dark hair, almond-shaped eyes and enigmatic half-smile, Sofia was every bit as beautiful as he had remembered. He had fallen for her almost as soon as they had met, but her past had always come between them. She had been working as a prostitute when Lombroso had found her and brought her to Turin. It meant that she and James could never allow their relationship to be anything but a secret either in Turin or in Scotland. When his father's illness had taken him away from her, James had promised that he would find a way for them to be together. Now he thought he had, and he couldn't wait to tell her his plans.

'*Buongiorno*, James.'

He walked towards her, but before either of them could speak, Lombroso called from his study on the floor above. 'Murray, where the devil are you?'

Sofia whispered in his ear. 'I will meet you after dinner. Wait for me on the corner.'

He breathed in her scent – a heady aroma of spices and citrus – and then in an instant she was gone, as ever leaving him wanting more.

'Murray, are you ever going to join me?' Lombroso called out. An indignant face peered over the banisters at him.

'On my way, Professor . . .' Had Lombroso seen him with Sofia? If so, how would he react?

He ran up the stairs, but when he got to Lombroso's study,

the professor was standing at one of the bookcases that lined it, peering intently at a set of leather-bound volumes, as though he hadn't been calling impatiently for him at all.

'Sit, sit. I'll be with you in a moment,' he said distractedly.

James did as he was told, seating himself on a small, faded velvet sofa to one side and gazing round the room in an effort to reacquaint himself with the world of criminal anthropology. Sitting on Lombroso's desk was a skull belonging to a brigand. According to the professor, it was the artefact that had given him the idea that lay at the heart of all his theories – that some criminals were throwbacks to primitive man and had been born that way. Privately James had thought this a little too simplistic, though it was certainly interesting. He was even less convinced by Lombroso's certainty that one could identify these born criminals by their physical characteristics. Could one really be certain, as the professor maintained, that habitual murderers had a cold, glassy stare and bloodshot eyes, or that thieves had thick eyebrows, thin beards and sloping foreheads? Still he did not know enough to challenge these theories. Hopefully, now he was back, he would be able to learn more so he could reach his own conclusions.

On the shelves were a selection of water pitchers decorated with writing and drawings done by criminals from Le Nuove prison in Turin. There were many more of these in Lombroso's personal crime museum at the university, which was where he kept most of the items he had collected over the years. His aim was to examine such artefacts and by doing so identify signs of criminality. To Lombroso, the items were criminal objects – signs and indicators of the criminal nature of their creators.

James remembered his reaction when he was first shown round the museum. Everything had seemed so strange and alien – as if he was entering a different world. One minute he was in a perfectly ordinary hallway; the next he had stepped into a strange and exotic hinterland filled with death masks, rows of skulls and shrunken heads, a selection of fearsome weapons and even a large facsimile of a carnivorous plant. It seemed like a lifetime ago, though less than a year had passed.

Lombroso finally put down the book he had been studying and sat behind his desk. 'I do apologise, Murray. There was something that occurred to me and I wanted to look it up before I forgot it.'

'May I ask what it was?'

'Oh, just a proverb.'

'Really?' James was intrigued.

'Yes, now how did it go . . . something to do with deception . . . "Women always tell the truth, but they don't tell all of it."'

'What made you think of it, Professor?'

'Nothing you need to worry yourself about, Murray. Really, you are so easily distracted. We need to focus on work.'

James decided not to react. 'Is Ottolenghi at the museum?'

'Ah yes, your fellow student . . . No, he is not.' Lombroso sniffed briskly. 'Signor Ottolenghi has seen fit to take a short sabbatical in order to study with someone else.'

'Really, who?'

'Oskar Reiner in Vienna. They are conducting a study on criminal vampirism, of all things.'

James remembered that his friend Ottolenghi, with whom he had shared his adventures during his last visit to Turin, had been fascinated by Reiner's work. He was not in the least surprised that the young man had decided to take a break from

Lombroso, who, though undoubtedly brilliant in his field, could be difficult to work with. And vampirism did sound interesting.

Lombroso leant back in his chair and peered at James. 'He'll be back with us soon enough, but still it means that we shall have our work cut out. Are you ready for the challenge?'

'Yes, Professor, I believe I am.'

'And what of... other distractions?'

Obviously Lombroso was referring to Sofia; perhaps after all he had seen them together just now. It was difficult to know what to say. He was not yet sure exactly where he stood. A few months ago he had left with promises about their future, but he could tell by her response that Sofia had been doubtful about his sincerity, and indeed his capability of conquering the social difficulties that might impede them. And for all he knew, she was right. For now he would have to bluff his way through and hope it would suffice.

'I will deal with these should they arise, Professor, you can be assured of that.'

'Splendid. I am glad to hear it. I would not want your attention to be diverted from the matters at hand. They are too important for that. Our project must take absolute precedence. I am relying on you.'

'Can you tell me more about what it entails?' James asked.

'All in good time, young man, all in good time. Suffice to say that we shall be conducting some very interesting experiments indeed. Madame Tarnovsky will be assisting us too, bringing some data from Prague.'

'And this is a new kind of criminal anthropology, you say?'

Lombroso looked smug. 'Yes, Murray, in a way. We are certainly going to do something different, something that has never been attempted before.' He stood up and walked over to the window, beckoning to James to follow him. 'What do you see out there on the street?'

'People . . . just people walking . . . and some trams and carriages.'

'Exactly! You have performed what we would call a blind observation of facts, albeit a rudimentary one. You have looked out of this window and given an account of what you have seen from an objective point of view – a scientist's view.'

'So?'

'So, that is how we differ from our contemporaries. They do not approach things objectively, but deduce from universal principles. We, on the other hand, view things empirically.'

'And the new aspect? '

'We will turn our attention to women as criminals and study them in the same way that I have been doing with the male criminal.'

James nodded. 'And no one has attempted this before?'

'Not like this.' Lombroso put his hand on James's shoulder and beamed at him. 'I don't think it is an overstatement to say that we are going to make history in the study of crime.'

James wanted more than anything to embrace the professor's enthusiasm, but something made him pause. Though the subject matter might make them pioneers in the new science of criminal anthropology, he rather suspected that the end result might not have the effect Lombroso yearned for.

The smile disappeared. Had the professor realised what he was thinking? He had often displayed an uncanny ability for such mind-reading. James braced himself, waiting for an admonishment, but none was forthcoming. Instead Lombroso spoke in an uncharacteristically hesitant manner.

'There is another matter that I hope will engage your interest.'

'What is that?'

Lombroso cleared his throat. 'Before we go any further, I need your honest answer to what might seem like an odd question.'

'Go on, Professor.'

'Do you believe in the Devil, Murray?'

5

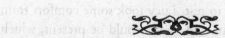

Everyone agrees that the few violent women far exceed men in their ferocity and cruelty. The brigand women of southern Italy and the female revolutionaries of Paris invented unspeakable tortures. It was women who sold the flesh of policemen; who forced a man to eat his own roasted penis; and who threaded human bodies on a pike.

Lombroso, 1876, p. 67

Lucy had mixed feelings about the dinner that evening. She was excited at the prospect, but she was also nervous. She was loath to admit it, even to herself, but the nerves were there nonetheless, jabbing at her like an impish child armed with a pin. Her life in Edinburgh had been mostly quiet and uneventful. Before her father's downfall, she had socialised with friends from school. Afterwards, just as she was becoming old enough for such things as small gatherings, dinners, concerts and visits to the theatre, invitations had seemed to dwindle until they became non-existent. Then her mother had died and she had gone into mourning. This meant that social occasions were confined to Aunt Agnes's church-related activities, and she was forced to watch as her peers enjoyed all the things that she was missing. Lucy had, therefore, never been invited to a formal dinner that included academics, scientists and thinkers as guests. In Aunt Agnes's social circle, ideas were rarely exchanged, perhaps because everyone held the same opinions about everything. And they were always dull, dull, dull.

Miss Trott had abandoned her, claiming that she had a bad headache and needed to rest. Lucy took some comfort from the fact that both Gina and Paola would be present, which would give her an example to follow.

The door opened after a sharp knock. James strode in. He seemed surprised. 'You look different.'

'How different?'

He shrugged. 'I don't know. Just different, grown up.'

'I'm almost—'

'Eighteen, yes, I know. I suppose I shall have to get used to it.'

'To what?'

'To you being . . . well . . . you know . . .' He cleared his throat and avoided her glance.

'What, James? What am I?'

'I think you know without me telling you. The word is beautiful. Now come on, Lucy. We need to go down. It is not polite to keep our hosts waiting.'

She took a last look at herself in the full-length mirror, turning this way and that to get the full effect. She hardly recognised herself. Instead of the slightly untidy figure she was used to seeing, a young woman stood in front of her – taller, more elegant and more poised than before, red-gold hair piled elegantly on top of her head to reveal a long, swan-like neck. Yes, she liked that expression. Lydia Loveday should definitely have a swan-like neck.

Lucy had always thought it most unfair that it was James who resembled their mother, with his shock of dark hair and fine features, whereas she took after their father's side of the family. Now, however, she was beginning to think that it might not be such a bad thing after all. Still, despite the evidence in front of her, James's words had startled her. Beauty was not something she had thought about very much, but as she stared at her reflection, she wondered if perhaps, just perhaps, he might be right.

Dinner, it appeared, would be less formal than James had expected. It began with a small gathering of guests in the drawing room. He watched Lucy take in her surroundings and smiled to himself at her reaction to the various strange artefacts dotted about the place, mingling with the more normal ornaments and knick-knacks. Even here Lombroso had made his mark.

James had told Lucy all about Lombroso, the museum at the university and its contents, so she was, to an extent, forewarned. Still, he could see that experiencing the professor and his curios in the real world might be something of a shock to the uninitiated, particularly as, on close inspection, even the most innocuous of items sometimes turned out to be anything but.

All were examples of prisoners' art collected by the professor during his career. There were ceramic vases and pots that looked quite ordinary at a distance but were decorated with lurid depictions of various crimes. A small piece of sculpture taking pride of place on the mantelpiece re-created a trial complete with judge and jury. There was even an extremely lifelike object made, according to Lombroso, out of bread and showing an insane thief being strapped to his bed.

Lucy seemed to be taking all of this in her stride, perhaps because of Lombroso's daughters, who were now guiding her through the collection. It was the first time he had set eyes on them, and he could certainly see their father in both of them. The elder girl, Paola, watched studiously as her younger sister talked animatedly to Lucy, waving her arms about exactly as Lombroso did when addressing an audience. Every now and again Paola would interject, her eyes lighting up in her evident passion for her subject. In her expression James could see her father, transported to another world by his ideas and wanting his listener to accompany him there.

James wandered over to take a closer look at one of the professor's latest acquisitions – a small clay sculpture of two men apparently fighting. It was a primitive representation, roughly hewn and resembling a carving on a totem pole or similar, like something from the British Museum. When examined more closely, it was clear that the two men were melded together, almost as if they were Siamese twins. The other thing of note was that one was clearly choking the other, the victim's tongue protruding quite horribly. The perpetrator's expression was determined, ruthless, cold – evil. It reminded James of someone he would far rather forget, a multiple murderer he had encountered in Turin on his last visit. He could see him in his mind's eye – a sharp-featured American carrying a silver-topped cane and wearing a coat with a distinctive astrakhan collar. He was ruthless and calculating, with a quick tongue and a penchant for ripping people to shreds. He had managed to slip away whilst they had been preoccupied with another set of crimes, and now his absence had made him even more of a threat. James and Lombroso had revealed his identity, and he was not a man who was likely to forgive or forget. He was out there somewhere, almost certainly plotting his revenge. The thought made James feel cold, though Lombroso's drawing room was nothing of the kind.

'I wonder who you're thinking of,' Lombroso said, joining him.

'I think you know the answer to that, Professor,' James replied.

'Indeed I do. A finer example of the morally insane criminal I have yet to meet.'

'Where could he have gone?'

'Who knows. No doubt he is perpetrating ever more monstrous deeds in some unfortunate place. He had killed before we encountered him and I see no reason to suppose he will stop of his own volition.'

'I take it there is no chance he has remained in Turin?'

'I doubt it. The city was thoroughly searched. Even Machinetti managed that, though I imagine our friend Inspector Tullio had a hand in it. Still, you can ask him yourself. He will be joining us this evening.'

'You have invited Machinetti?' James said in surprise. Machinetti, Lombroso's nemesis, was a carabinieri marshal whose methods of investigation were almost as primitive as one of the professor's criminal throwbacks.

'Why not? I like to keep an eye on him. Don't worry. I have invited Tullio too.'

James was relieved. Tullio, an officer in the public security police who had also been involved in the case, was a very different prospect from the bombastic Machinetti. He disliked Machinetti almost as much as Lombroso did, and was forever complaining about him.

'Ah, and here they are, together with our remaining guests! Inspector Tullio, Machinetti, I am delighted you could spare the time from your criminal exertions. And Father Vincenzo . . . and Professor Gemelli, welcome!'

James grinned at Tullio, who responded in kind. It was

good to see a friendly and familiar face. Something about the inspector seemed to have changed, though. It wasn't so much his appearance – slight in build, neatly clipped beard, well-polished shoes; a picture of understatement and efficiency just as James remembered – as his demeanour. When they'd first met, James had considered him to be a little unsure of himself, which at the time had seemed comforting. Now, however, Tullio had a new air of confidence, and it suited him.

Looking at Tullio's fellow guests, James wondered if Lombroso was operating under the epithet 'Keep your friends close but your enemies closer.' Father Vincenzo, an extremely influential priest who sat on various university boards, disapproved wholeheartedly of the professor's work, seeing his ideas as a direct attack on the Catholic Church. A born criminal could not be held responsible for his actions, which in turn meant that he was not a sinner and therefore did not require forgiveness or salvation. That, as Lombroso had pointed out more than once in Father Vincenzo's company, made the Church somewhat redundant.

Professor Gemelli, dean of the university faculty within which Lombroso worked, was almost as hostile. This was partly due to academic jealousy, James thought, but he too did not support Lombroso's ideas, preferring to criticise his admittedly somewhat erratic methods rather than his findings. Both men had been heavily involved in impeding last year's investigation, although neither would ever admit it.

'I was just saying to Murray here that I think we can be sure, thanks to Inspector Tullio, that our killer is long gone,' Lombroso said.

Machinetti bristled with indignation at being left out. He was wearing his dress uniform, an ostentatious combination of shining brass buttons and gold brocade. His stomach strained at the seams of his jacket and a small bead of sweat glistened as it made its way down one of his temples.

Tullio was about to reply when he was interrupted.

'I hope you are right, Lombroso. It would not reflect well on either you or the faculty if he returned to Turin,' Professor Gemelli said. He was a small, rotund man who had a habit of standing with his chin elevated, as if he were perpetually peering over the edge of something. His hair was plastered to his shining skull in an apparent effort to hide the fact that there was so little of it.

Lombroso smiled patiently at him as if he were a child. 'No need to be concerned, Gemelli. If the killer was still with us, he simply would not be able to resist for long. He would feel a compulsion to commit new crimes and to lay each atrocity out for us in an effort to share them with the widest audience possible. Even Machinetti here could catch him!'

'Now look here, Lombroso . . .' Machinetti's large moustache quivered with indignation.

'I seem to recall that your own efforts in that regard were not particularly fruitful, Lombroso,' Gemelli said. It was the professor's turn to bristle.

'So you are certain that he has left the city?' Father Vincenzo asked, arching his eyebrows. He was an entirely different kind of man to Gemelli. Everything about him exuded understated power, from his bearing – which was upright, almost regal – to his sharp features, including a prominent aquiline nose. He looked a little like a Roman emperor, albeit one dressed as a priest.

Lombroso acknowledged him with a brief respectful nod. 'Indeed I am, Father. It is my considered view that he has gone to a place he knows, a place where it is easy to hide.'

'I hope you're right, Professor,' James said.

Lombroso patted him on the back. 'I am always right, you know that!'

James caught Tullio's eye. The events of the previous year had surely proved that the professor was as fallible as anyone else, given that he had failed to spot the identity of a killer who was right under his nose. Still, he seemed to have recovered from any self-doubt that might have plagued him. In fact he sounded just as he had before it had all happened. And now it seemed there might be a venture into psychical research. Lombroso had been coy about the details. After James had answered his question about believing in the Devil with a puzzled 'not really', Lombroso had declined to comment further. James wondered, just for a moment, whether he had done the right thing in returning to Turin to continue his studies, even if it was only to be a temporary arrangement.

Then the door opened and in an instant all his doubts were gone. There stood Sofia, as captivating as ever, smoothing down her drab grey dress. Anna Tarnovsky passed her in a vivid blue gown with lace around the neck and sleeves and tiny sparkling crystals on the bodice. Her attire was a good deal more elaborate than Sofia's, but she might as well have been standing in a dark shadow for all the impact she made on James. He tried unsuccessfully to prevent himself from grinning stupidly as Sofia walked over to Signora Lombroso and whispered in her ear. Then, without warning, she left the room as abruptly as she had entered it.

James had watched her as she carefully ignored him. She had not exactly been welcoming when they met earlier, but one could never tell with Sofia. She was almost always inscrutable. It was one of the things he had found most enticing about her. Still, at least it would not be long before they met properly. It could not come quickly enough for James.

'Murray!' Lombroso said sharply. 'Madame Tarnovsky is here!'

He flushed at this admonishment, though he deserved it. There was no excuse for ignoring someone so eminent in her field.

Anna Tarnovsky smiled. 'Ah, Mr Murray – how nice to see you back with us in Turin. I see that we have that in common. Neither of us could stay away.'

He stared at her. Was she being pointed? It was unlike her.

'Murray!' Lombroso said again, more impatiently.

James recovered himself and bowed. 'Do forgive me, Madame Tarnovsky. It has been a very long day.'

'Not at all, Mr Murray, though perhaps as we are to work together, we could dispense with the formalities. Do call me Anna.'

'Then please, call me James.'

'I'm "Professor" to you, Murray, before we get carried away,' Lombroso said. 'Now, shall we go in to dinner? I believe I have quite an appetite!'

James escorted Lucy into the dining room. She seemed excited, coltish – skittish even. He supposed it was natural given that prior to this her usual company had been their Aunt Agnes, but still there was something odd about her demeanour. He smiled ruefully to himself. The closer to adulthood Lucy got, the more of a mystery the workings of her mind became to him.

The conversation at dinner was lively, and Lucy was relieved that the atmosphere was a good deal more relaxed than she had anticipated. She was pleased to note that her Italian was sufficient to keep up with most of what was being said, although there were one or two words and phrases that eluded her. Soon, she hoped, she would be as fluent as a native. Other than her brother, the only scientists present were Professor Lombroso and Anna Tarnovsky, and a small man with hardly any hair and what Lucy thought was a mean-spirited expression. They and the rather intimidating priest sitting with them were engaged in their own discussion for much of the meal. This meant that she could watch and listen. She had already learnt something of great interest by doing exactly that, and hoped that further close observation would reveal more. When Anna Tarnovsky had arrived, the change in James had been palpable. His usually pale skin had become flushed as if he was lighting up from the inside, and he had smiled quite stupidly. It was perfectly clear to Lucy what was happening here. She had known that her brother was hiding something from her about his previous trip to Turin, and here it was, plain for all to see if they bothered to look. He was in love with Anna Tarnovsky.

Lucy could understand why. It was true that she was a little older than James, and not exactly beautiful – well, not classically so, anyway. But her face was interesting, some might say striking, with its slightly prominent nose and high cheekbones. She had hazel eyes and a smile that put you immediately at ease. Her hair was a deep chestnut colour – the same hue that Lucy herself had always hoped for instead of her strawberry-blonde locks. But it was Anna Tarnovsky's obvious intelligence and wit that made her stand out. What Lucy admired most was her ability to stand up to the professor, whose opinions were put forward in such a way as to make it absolutely clear that he did not expect them to be challenged.

But had she not been referred to as Madame Anna Tarnovsky? Had James fallen in love with a married woman? Surely not! That would be scandalous. Lucy allowed her imagination to run riot. It must be an unhappy match. She did not even wear a wedding ring. That must be significant. James was no doubt trying to rescue her from her cruel and abusive spouse. He liked to rescue people. It was why he had become a doctor, he had told her once.

Now who might the husband be? Of course! She would obviously be married to a Russian count or similar, who refused to release her from her vows. She had probably met him when she was a student and fallen for his charms. Gradually he had restricted her freedom until she had no option but to escape to Turin. There she had met James and they had fallen in love. No wonder he had been so desperate to return! Poor James and Anna, forced to meet in secret until… well, until what? Oh, if only she had thought to bring her notebook down with her. She must observe the interaction between the guests with extra care to ensure that she remembered every last detail.

'It is quite clear that our hypothesis should be that criminal women are inferior to their male counterparts,' Lombroso was stating firmly.

'Now, Cesare, I am not so sure that I agree,' Anna said. Lucy noticed the way she addressed the professor, with an easy kind of informality that made it clear that she viewed them as equals, even if the professor did not. No doubt she was enjoying her freedom from the cruel count.

'Why ever not?' he asked.

'Because it makes no sense to begin there when the figures are so contradictory.'

'In what way?'

'There are so few women criminals . . . that is why. It muddies the ground.'

Lombroso frowned. His face was reddening. Clearly he did not enjoy being contradicted. Whether this was because it was done by a woman, or just in general, Lucy could not tell. The little bald man, who she'd discovered was called Gemelli, was sitting back in his seat, a contented smile on his face. Perhaps he was enjoying the food and wine, which were, Lucy had to admit, rather good. Signora Lombroso had told her that she disapproved of the fashion for serving French dishes and much preferred local cuisine. Having said that, they had dined on chicken Marengo, which according to Paola had been created by Napoleon Bonaparte's chef during his Italian campaign. The aroma of Madeira, garlic and lemon that had wafted across the table was so appetising that Lucy found it agonising to wait for everyone to be served before she could tuck in.

She looked again at Gemelli. No, it was not the food that had made him smile. There was a glint of satisfaction in his eyes that told her it was Professor Lombroso's evident discomfort that he was really relishing.

'A very interesting point, Madame Tarnovsky. What do you say to that, Lombroso?' Gemelli said, smirking.

'It is a question of atavism. These women are throwbacks to their primitive ancestors, as are their male counterparts,' the professor replied.

'I am not sure that atavism is the right way to describe it,' said Anna. 'If they are throwbacks, then why are there not more female criminals? That is what we need to be wary of. What do you think, James?'

James paused. His thick dark hair fell forward over his eyes and he pushed it back impatiently. It must be difficult for him, Lucy thought. He would not want to offend anyone, and yet he would still have an opinion. Would he be sufficiently confident to share, it and whose side would he take? She urged him on in her head. Come on, James, be bold.

'It is a conundrum, that is certain,' he said finally. 'Perhaps before continuing with the experiments, it might be useful to consider our subject pool.'

'Then we are bowing to the critique of the French before we have even got started!' Lombroso said with a note of exasperation.

'Now, Cesare, let us have no more discussion of work,' admonished Signora Lombroso. 'Dr Murray will be tired after his long journey. There will be time enough for that in the days and weeks to come.'

Lombroso acceded to his wife's wishes with a smile, but Lucy could see that he was reluctant to change the subject.

'So, Miss Murray, what will you do whilst James is busy with his work?' Anna Tarnovsky asked.

Lucy frowned. The truth was, she wasn't certain what James had planned for her. Would she have a governess, or would Miss Trott take that position?

'I expect you will do a little sightseeing first of all, won't you, Lucy?' James said. 'Get acclimatised to your surroundings?'

'Could we take Miss Murray to see your museum, Father?' Gina asked.

'I don't see why not,' Lombroso replied. 'I'm all for women in the sciences, am I not, Madame Tarnovsky?'

Lucy noticed Anna Tarnovsky raise her eyebrows ever so slightly.

'Any objection, Murray?' Lombroso asked.

James shrugged. 'If you would like to, Lucy, then I don't mind.'

'I thought she was changing her name to Lucia,' Gina whispered loudly to her sister.

'Ah, a change of identity . . .' Lombroso said. 'That reminds me of a young female swindler I once encountered. She had the most extraordinarily large—'

'Cesare!' interrupted his wife. 'This is not the time or the place!'

Lucy noticed James hiding a smile. What would Aunt Agnes think if she was here – or Miss Trott, for that matter? The professor really was the most extraordinary person. One simply didn't know what he would say next.

Before long the dinner drew to a conclusion and the ladies withdrew, leaving James and Lombroso in deep conversation about something or other. As she got up to leave, Lucy saw Anna Tarnovsky linger for just a few seconds, but it was enough. She was clearly reluctant to go. How difficult it must be for her. She was excluded from the discussion just because she happened to be a woman, even though she was their equal in every other way. It was so very unfair.

The ladies having left, James sat with Tullio whilst Gemelli and Father Vincenzo talked about this and that, mostly university business from what he could hear. Machinetti sat with them, leaning towards them slightly as if he was hoping to catch them out in some indiscretion.

'How's the family, Tullio?' James asked.

'They are well as far as I know. I hardly get to see them these days.'

'Busy fighting crime, then?'

'It seems never-ending sometimes,' Tullio said. 'We have a devil of a case on at the moment.'

'Go on.' James was not surprised by Tullio's comment. This was a city of devils, after all. The events of the previous year had more than proved that.

'A few days ago a woman's body was discovered in a shallow grave outside the city. We have no leads, and the cause of death is difficult to establish with any certainty.'

'Really? How come?'

'Without going into unsavoury detail, the body is in an unusual state. In fact I would go so far as to say that I have never seen anything like it before. Whoever did this . . .' Tullio shook his head.

James was quiet for a moment, his mind travelling swiftly to the scene depicted by the inspector. He could only imagine what Tullio had meant, but it was enough to shock him, as evidence of the level of depravity to which a man could sink always did.

'So the state of the body indicates murder?'

'It appears so.' Tullio seemed reticent. James was tempted to probe further, but something about the policeman's demeanour made him pause.

'Have you identified the victim?'

'No, not yet,' Tullio replied. 'But the area is full of seasonal workers, particularly in the rice farms and vineyards, so it could be difficult.'

'Sounds intriguing. Have you asked the professor about it?'

'Not yet. I wondered if you could mention it. I have already asked him for one favour recently, and I don't want to push my luck.'

'What favour was that?'

Tullio furrowed his brows slightly, as if wondering how

much to say. 'I think I'd better let the professor fill you in when he's ready, but if you could mention the other matter . . .'

James nodded. 'I'll do my best.'

'That would be useful. If you both have time, I'd like you to come down to the mortuary and take a look.'

'I'm sure the professor would be only too happy to lend a hand. You know how he likes a mystery.'

'True enough.'

'What's Machinetti's view?'

Tullio lowered his voice. 'Oh, the usual . . . pull in all known offenders, whatever their crime, and wait until someone points the finger at someone else. It's time-consuming and won't get us anywhere but, strictly speaking, it is his case, as it happened in the countryside, not the city.'

'How come you're involved?' James asked.

'Intervention from the mayor, who is taking a personal interest in the case for some reason. The marshal doesn't know about my involvement yet, and when he finds out . . . Let's just say I'd prefer to be out of range, as it were.'

Machinetti's beady little eyes were gleaming as he sipped his brandy and puffed on a cigar. He was a bully, and a stupid one at that. He resented Tullio, who, being educated and intelligent, represented all that the marshal and his ilk despised.

James could see the strain etched on his friend's face. His earlier confidence seemed to be waning. 'Don't worry, Tullio,' he said. 'I'm sure you'll get there in the end . . . and if we can help, then all the better.'

Tullio gave a wan smile. 'Thanks, I appreciate it, but we will have to be discreet. We don't want the newspapers getting hold of the story until we know more.'

'I'll do my best,' James said, 'but I make no promises. You know that discretion is not exactly the professor's forte.'

'I tell you, Gemelli, we will break new ground here. It can only be good for the university,' Lombroso was booming.

Gemelli looked doubtful. 'I have heard this before, Lombroso. In my experience, you breaking new ground usually means two things.'

'And what are they?' Father Vincenzo asked with an amused smile.

'Large sums of money being wasted on all kinds of . . .' Gemelli seemed to be searching for the word, 'equipment,' he said with disdain.

Lombroso nodded enthusiastically. 'I'm glad you mentioned that. We will need some new measurement pieces and, of course, components for my lie-detecting machine.'

'And what is the second thing?' Father Vincenzo asked.

'The university being discredited, that's what.' Gemelli was warming to his theme, his face reddening with each word.

Lombroso shook his head. 'On the contrary, we . . . you will be applauded for your foresight in supporting such pioneering work.'

Gemelli paused, apparently considering this possibility. 'You know as well as I do that all research involving prisoners has been forbidden.'

'I am sure there are ways to circumvent such unreasonable constraints,' Lombroso said.

'No, there are not, and after last year's business you would be well advised to take care with any plans you might have.' Gemelli's voice went up an octave.

'What is this I hear about psychical research, Professor?' Father Vincenzo asked. It seemed like a perfectly innocent question, but James saw from the priest's expression that it had been asked for precise and, perhaps even uncharitable, reasons.

'What's this?' Gemelli said. 'Didn't I tell you to refrain from such activities, Lombroso?'

'Ah, yes . . . well, perhaps unsurprising after what happened last time,' Father Vincenzo said, shaking his head. Machinetti watched in satisfaction as Lombroso blushed.

'That was unavoidable, and anyway, no one was hurt. The shopkeeper was reassured and I paid for the damage . . . most of it, anyway.'

'So you are considering another investigation?' Gemelli asked.

'I am, though it is in the early stages at present,' Lombroso replied. 'I have a venue in mind, although it has yet to be confirmed. As soon as the preliminaries have been completed, I plan to launch a psychical enquiry as soon as possible.'

'What kind of enquiry?' Gemelli asked.

'We are going to be searching for the Devil . . . or possibly demons.'

Father Vincenzo seemed pleased at this, which James thought odd. Surely a priest should be reluctant to endorse any encounter with Satan or those who served him.

'Well think again, Lombroso. I expressly forbid it,' Gemelli said.

'Oh dear,' James murmured to Tullio, 'that's done it.'

Lombroso frowned for a moment, then his brow cleared as if a cloud had moved away from the sun. 'I promise you that I will not embark on any form of psychical research that involves the university.'

Gemelli's expression was one of surprise. He clearly had not expected such a complete climbdown. 'Well, good, just as long as we are clear.'

'Oh, you've been very clear, Gemelli,' Lombroso said, for some reason winking at Tullio, whose mouth twitched slightly. 'Very clear indeed.'

In the drawing room, Lucy sipped at her strong, aromatic coffee and watched as Gina and Paola played at cards, with their mother watching over them fondly. Anna came across and sat with her. 'Your brother tells me that you write literature, Miss Murray.'

'I would hardly call it that,' Lucy said, 'but yes, I do write stories.'

'Then I wonder if you would like to accompany me tomorrow. I am visiting the Marchesa Vittoria Carignano for tea, and I'm sure she would enjoy meeting you.'

'I should like that very much.'

'Good. I think you will find it interesting. The lady is very influential in the city. She seems to know almost everyone, and she is the patron of many intellectual pursuits, including literature and poetry as well more scientific subjects.'

'She sounds fascinating.'

'Oh she is, she is, as is the company she keeps.'

Lucy could hardly wait. She had only just arrived, and already her life in Italy seemed full of possibilities. It would be an ideal opportunity to get to know Anna better and perhaps find out more about her past. She might even be able to ask her about James. Glowing with the anticipation of what tomorrow might bring, she took her leave and went up to bed.

The house was smaller than it looked from the outside. As Lucy climbed the central staircase, she saw that the floors were covered with rugs that had once been vibrantly patterned but were now faded and worn. There were display cabinets holding what she assumed were yet more examples of prisoners' art, as if the professor could not bear to be parted from his work even for a second. She heard a noise coming from downstairs and peered over the banisters.

That was odd, she thought. It was late, almost midnight, time for any sensible person to be going to bed. But not, it would seem, her brother. There was James slipping out of the front door, shutting it quietly behind him as if he did not want to be seen. Where on earth was he going at this time of night? Perhaps he was waiting for Anna Tarnovsky to join him for a romantic assignation. It seemed rather risky behaviour, though typically impulsive. Lucy was tempted to peep out of the front door to see where he was going, but just as she was about to creep down the stairs, Anna emerged from the drawing room and said good night to Signora Lombroso before leaving herself.

Lucy smiled. So she was right. They had to be secretive, given the nature of their liaison. And since they all had to work together, the professor might well disapprove of such a match, so poor Anna and James had to meet in secret. This appealed to Lucy's sense of the romantic. Could she perhaps work it into a story?

A door opened on the landing and Miss Trott came out. She was wearing her outdoor coat and carrying a large canvas bag. 'What are you doing standing about, Lucy? Time for bed!'

Lucy paused for a second and then nodded and did as she was told. There would be plenty of time to find out more tomorrow.

6

Female love is, essentially, nothing more than a secondary aspect of maternity. All those feelings of affection that bind woman to man are born not of the sexual impulse, but from instincts of subjection and devotion acquired through adaptation. Lombroso and Ferrero, 1893, p. 76

James made his way with some trepidation to the corner of the Via Legnano. He had been longing for this moment, but now that it was here, he was apprehensive. A carriage went past and instinctively he stepped into the shadows so that he was not seen. Then there she was, walking towards him with her distinctive gait. His breath quickened with desire at the sight of her. She beckoned to him and he followed.

'Let us walk for a while, *caro*.'

He took heart at the familiar term of endearment. They strolled through the deserted streets side by side, the tension between them forming a barrier that he longed to break through. He remembered their final embrace all those months ago, when they had said their last goodbye. He could bear it no longer. He stopped and gently touched her arm. The feel of her sent a jolt of longing through him.

'Sofia, please . . . we must talk.'

She pointed to a small piazza nearby. A fountain played

at its heart and there were some wooden benches around it. They went over and sat on one of them. The silence was filled only with the gentle playing of the water and a slight breeze rustling through the trees.

'I have come back,' James said quietly. 'You asked for help and I am here.'

Sofia avoided his eye. 'Back, yes, but not alone.'

James was puzzled for a moment at the bitterness in her voice and then realised who she meant. 'Lucy...'

'You are not free.'

'I had no choice. I could not leave her again. It would not have been right.'

'I understand. You have a duty to her. She is your family.'

Sofia's voice was stilted. He could sense her hostility, but he had to try.

'We can still be together. It would have to be our secret for a while, as it was before, until I tell Lucy about us... but we could meet.'

'No.' Her refusal rang out across the piazza.

'But you asked me to come back.'

'That was for another reason.'

'What reason?'

'As I said in my letter, I need your help.'

'Sofia, I will do anything for you, you know that. I love you.'

There was a pause. It told him everything.

She did not look at him. 'We are from different worlds. It is not possible. *We* are not possible. It is as I said when we parted last time.'

'And I told you that I would find a way. Everything has changed since the death of my father. I am independent now.

We could leave Turin and start a new life somewhere else... America perhaps.'

'America! That is so like you, James. You do not think things through. I cannot go away. I have a life here. But you did not think of that, did you?'

'Then why ask me to come back?'

'I had no choice.'

'What do you mean?'

'I need your help. My cousin Chiara. She has been staying with me. Now she has gone missing. I have to find her.'

'When did she go missing? Do you remember?'

'Of course I remember! How could I forget? It was the first day of March, her thirteenth birthday. She was on her way to work as a maid at the Marchesa di Carignano's palazzo. '

There was a pause as James took in this information. Sofia's cousin was younger than he had thought. 'So why not tell the carabinieri? You don't need me for that.'

'I tried, but they would not listen. They told me that she had probably run away, but she is so young – still a child, though she looks older. She would never have left without a word like that.'

'There are others you could turn to, surely – the professor, Tullio, Ottolenghi.'

'None of them would help. The professor is too busy with his experiments. You know how preoccupied he gets. Inspector Tullio was sympathetic, but he is dealing with other crimes and does not have the time, and the *dottore* is away. I was desperate. That is why I did not tell you in the letter.'

'What do you mean?'

'Everyone else seemed to think that she had run away. Why should you be any different?'

'I thought you wanted us to—'

Sofia stood up and faced him, her eyes flashing with anger. 'To what? To carry on as before? For me to be your secret mistress, there when you want me and invisible when you don't... your whore!' She spat the word out as if she could not bear to have it on her lips.

'All right, I'm sorry. I can see how it looks, but that wasn't... isn't what is in my heart. I had planned it all – our escape.'

'*Your* escape, you mean!'

'I thought you wanted to be with me.'

She sat down next to him again. 'It cannot be, James. I will not carry on as before. I cannot live like that – meeting in secret, deceiving the professor. You must understand. No matter what I feel for you, that part of my life is over.'

'But if we went somewhere we could be together...'

'And what of your sister? Have you told her of your plans... about me?

James looked away just for a moment, but it was long enough.

Sofia threw her hands in the air in exasperation. 'You have not told her anything, have you?'

James shook his head. 'I am waiting for the right time.'

'Oh well, if that is all we are waiting for,' Sofia said, her voice heavy with sarcasm. 'What made you think that she would accept me?'

'She will love you, Sofia. As I do.'

'I doubt that – an ex-prostitute and a servant who steals her brother away and leaves her alone in a strange city?'

'She could come with us.'

'Even better! Two new countries in the space of a year. I am sure she will be delighted.'

'Sofia, we could make it work. We love each other.'

There was silence. Sofia's hands were clenched by her sides as if she was readying herself to fight. Her eyes were dull.

'I do not love you.'

Of all the words he had thought she might utter, these were the ones he had least expected. 'How can you say that, after everything? I said that I would come back, and here I am. Are you really telling me that you do not want me?'

'*Sì*. You ask me to sacrifice everything, but I do not love you . . . enough.'

'Enough?'

Sofia nodded.

'So you just asked me here for my help and nothing else?'

'I am sorry. I have misled you. I can see that. I made you come back to Turin with hope in your heart when really . . .'

'There is none?' Each breath seemed like a labour. How could she be so cruel?

She was still unable to meet his eye. He grabbed her arm and swung her to him, furious now. 'So you have used me. Knowing how I felt about you, you have lured me back here to help you.'

'I had no other option. I was desperate!'

'You are not the woman I thought you were, Sofia,' he said.

'What do you mean? I have not changed.'

'Perhaps it is because of your background . . . your criminal background,' he spat. 'Lies and deceit seem to come easily to you.'

Sofia gasped. 'I see you are becoming like the professor.'

'Why? Because I see you now for what you are?'

Her eyes flashed with anger. 'And what is that?'

The words slipped from his mouth all too freely in his hurt and fury. 'You're a born criminal, Sofia. You cannot help yourself.'

She shook her head. 'It is not I who have changed. You are not the man I thought you were. Goodbye, James.'

He watched her walk away and almost went after her, but he could not bring himself to be near her. He was just too angry – both with her for misleading him and with himself for saying those hateful things to her.

It was only once she had gone that his mind cleared enough for a terrible possibility to enter it. A missing girl, a body in the woods – could they be one and the same?

She hears the stone cover being pushed away. It makes her jump. She can feel someone's eyes upon her.

'Why won't you let me go?' she asks.

There is no answer.

'What are you keeping me here for?'

Again no answer. Unable to contain her misery any longer, she starts to sob.

She hears her captor sigh, as if her weeping is a mere inconvenience. Or could it be that they have realised they have made a mistake?

'Let me go, please.'

'Atone.' The voice comes from above. It is light, almost musical. Is it male or female?

She looks up. 'What did you say?'

'Atone,' the voice repeats, and the covering is slid back into place. Is she being left to consider this advice?

She hears the sound of retreating footsteps.

'No, come back. I don't know what you mean!' she cries out in desperation. 'Atone for what?'

But it is to no avail. She is alone yet again. She does not know when her captor will return, or even if they will return at all. Hours pass, empty of everything – even hope. Despite herself, she dozes off for a little while. She is awoken by a noise. She rubs the sleep from her eyes and sits up eagerly. What is it? She hears it again, a high, keening sound, almost like an animal, but not quite. She recognises the humanness of it because it is a sound she has made herself. Someone is weeping. She is not alone.

'Hello?' she shouts. 'Can you hear me?'

The weeping stops.

'Hello,' she calls again. 'Who are you? Where are you?'

There is no reply. She sits, waits and reasons. Perhaps whoever it is needs time to think... to trust. Whoever made that sound must be frightened. When one is removed from everything one knows and placed in the darkness with no explanation, then of course it is difficult to know who or what to believe in.

She tries again. 'Please, we are the same. Tell me who you are.'

There is no more noise at first. Only silence. And then the screaming begins.

7

Women have something close to what might be called an instinct for lying... Unconsciously all are a little false.

Lombroso and Ferrero, 1893, p. 77

James was walking through the city streets, his mind restlessly turning over his encounter with Sofia. How could she have been so cruel? To bring him back to her, knowing how he felt, just so that he could help her find her wretched cousin, who had probably just run away... well, that demonstrated how little she cared about him. He had never been good at affairs of the heart. Falling for the wrong woman was becoming something of a habit. Why could he not find some uncomplicated, acceptable and suitably adoring young woman to settle down with? Perhaps love was too much to ask for. It was not as if he deserved such happiness.

He turned in to yet another dark street. He probably shouldn't be doing this. Turin was full of criminals, as Lombroso was always commenting, and he was just the sort of target a thief might be looking for.

A sign was swinging gently in the breeze. As he listened to it creaking, he realised that he had seen it before. Something had brought him back to the tavern where he had first been taken by Sofia. It was only a few months ago, but it seemed as if years had passed. He paused outside and peered up at the sign: La Capra – the goat, Satan's symbol. The animal stared back at him defiantly as if daring him to enter. He heard laughter. The place was still open despite the lateness of the hour. It seemed like fate. He decided to go in for a drink.

The tavern didn't seem to have changed much since his last visit. The smell was the same – tobacco, stale beer and sweat – the barman, Gambro, was still there, and one of the regulars was sitting in his usual spot, muttering to himself. As James walked in, there was a palpable hush. He was still dressed for a formal dinner in his black tail coat and white waistcoat, so it was hardly surprising.

Gambro sneered as he approached. 'Well if it isn't the Inglese. Back to cause more trouble, are you? I'm not sure I should serve you.'

'Firstly, I'm a Scot, and secondly, I can easily take my custom elsewhere.'

Gambro laughed. 'No, no, I'll take your money. What'll it be?'

'Grappa . . . large.'

'It's like that, is it? Better take a carafe.'

James slammed his money down on the counter and picked up his drink. Despite the hour, the tavern was packed. The clientele hadn't improved. It was still comprised of wastrels and vagabonds, none of whom would have looked out of place in one of the illustrations to Lombroso's *Criminal Man*. There were a few women too, mostly prostitutes, he assumed, judging from their appearance. He remembered from his previous visit that there was a state-registered brothel not far from La Capra, so it wasn't surprising that some of its employees ended up there.

There was nowhere to sit except for a space opposite the

resident drunk, who glared at him as he approached and snatched up his tatty straw hat, hugging it to himself as if it might be worth stealing. James was not in the mood for an argument, so he scowled back and sat down anyway. He planned to stay until oblivion descended in an attempt to blot out his conversation with Sofia.

He drank quickly and steadily, welcoming the warmth of the clear liquid as it burned its way down his throat. Lombroso had once told him that drunkenness caused crime as well as insanity, something James knew about only too well thanks to his father. But tonight he didn't care. He drained his glass and poured himself another. The man opposite shoved out his own glass. James shrugged and filled it for him. He knocked it back in one gulp and held it out again. James poured another glass.

'That's all you get, old man.'

His companion shrugged. 'Woman trouble, is it?' he asked, wiping his nose on his dirty cuff.

'How did you guess?'

'Easy. It's always a woman that makes a man turn to drink. What did she do? Go with someone else?'

James shook his head. 'She lied.'

The old man nodded. 'They all do that.'

'I wouldn't care,' James said as he emptied his glass, 'but she knew I loved her. She used me.'

'I hope you told her.'

'Oh I told her all right. I said some terrible things to her. I wanted to hurt her, you see.'

'Should have given her the back of your hand. It's the only thing they understand.'

James stared at him in distaste. 'I need more grappa.'

'Good idea,' the old man said, burping gently into his

glass and slumping forward until his forehead met the table in front of him.

James went back to the bar and put the empty carafe down. Gambro grinned. 'Are you sure, Inglese? It's stronger than it looks.'

'I'm sure.'

'I'll get this,' came a voice from behind him. 'How are you, Signor Murray?'

James turned and saw a man with a pointed nose and thin lips wearing a bowler hat pushed jauntily to the back of his head. 'Just when I thought the night couldn't get any worse... Baldovino, what are you doing here? Following me again?' They had last met during his previous visit to the city, when Baldovino, a reporter on the local paper, *The People's Voice*, had been shadowing him in the hope of a story.

The journalist smirked. 'That's all in the past, my friend. Let me buy you a drink to make up for that... unpleasantness.'

James waved his hand and made his way to a recently vacated table, well away from the old drunk, who now appeared to be unconscious. Baldovino soon joined him, clutching another carafe of grappa. The sight of his rat-like face reminded James of the terrible events of the previous year. He had arrived in Turin to work with Lombroso just as the first of a series of macabre murders was being committed. Each of the victims was left with a note implicating Lombroso.

'So how are things in the world of crime reporting?' he asked. 'Written any more letters to yourself?' Baldovino had sent letters to his own newspaper purporting to be from the killer. It had led them up a blind alley, delayed the investigation and caused Sofia to be hurt.

'It sold a few papers. What's wrong with that?'

'You know perfectly well what the consequences were.'

'I thought your professor was an expert. It's hardly my fault if he couldn't tell they were fakes, now is it?'

James shook his head. 'I see you haven't changed.'

'Thanks,' Baldovino said. 'I can't say the same for you.'

'I'm having a bad day.'

'I thought you'd gone home to England.'

'Scotland . . . I did, but now I'm back.'

'Unfinished business?'

'Well I thought so, but now I'm not so sure.'

'How come?'

James ran his hands through his thick dark hair and peered blearily at Baldovino. 'I came back for a woman. She asked me for help. Stupidly, I thought she wanted me too.'

Baldovino nodded sympathetically and poured him some grappa. 'And she didn't?'

'No, she just wanted me to find her cousin, who's probably run away. That's what the carabinieri seem to think, anyway.'

Baldovino raised his eyebrows and sat forward on his chair. 'What is this cousin's name?'

'Chiara.'

'Chiara Esposito?'

James nodded. 'Yes. How did you know?'

Baldovino did not answer him. 'How old is she?'

'Young, still a child really. She was . . . is thirteen, though apparently she looks older.'

'When did she go missing?'

'A few weeks ago, on her way to work. Why?'

'What was the date?'

'March the first.'

'Drink up, my friend. You're going to need it.'

James peered at him through the fog of his drunkenness. 'What is it? Tell me!'

Baldovino paused, as if wondering whether it was a good idea to say anything more.

'The thing is, I don't think this girl you're talking about is a runaway.'

'How do you know?'

The journalist picked up a copy of *The People's Voice* and pointed at the headline: MISSING GIRLS MYSTERY – HAUNTED ABBEY LINK? BALDOVINO INVESTIGATES.

James took it from him and began to read.

> Could history be repeating itself? A century ago, girls started to go missing from the city and its outskirts. Shortly afterwards, the nearby Abbey San Callisto was closed and its monks dispersed to other monasteries. There were reports that the monks and the girls had become INSTRUMENTS OF THE DEVIL. The monks were banished and most of the girls were never seen again . . . except for one. Found wandering in a state of confusion near the abbey, covered in cuts and bruises, the traumatised girl could utter only one word: DIAVOLO.
>
> Now there have been a number of similar disappearances in MYSTERIOUS circumstances. Is there a link? If there is, you can be certain that Baldovino will find it.

Baldovino sat back smugly. 'One of my contacts gave me some information and . . . well, as you can see, your girl is not the only one to disappear.'

'And they are all still missing?'

Baldovino nodded.

'How many?'

'Six that I know of, but there may be more.'

James wondered if the journalist knew about the body in the woods. Presumably not, or he would have mentioned it in his article. 'Is there anything else to connect the girls other than the fact that they're missing?'

'They are all aged between thirteen and eighteen and disappeared in the early morning on their way to work.' Baldovino handed him a scrap of paper. It was a list of names, including Chiara's.

'And the abbey. You mention a link?' James asked.

'My sources told me that there have been reports of strange lights and noises coming from the building, which is odd considering it is practically derelict. I asked around the town nearby, and the people I spoke to all confirmed it. There is definitely something going on up there.'

'Sources?'

Baldovino tapped his nose and smiled. 'You know I can't say.'

'So from what these sources said, you put two and two together . . .'

'I have to make a living. Besides, the missing girls all have links to the town near the abbey. That can't be a coincidence, surely?'

'Perhaps, though I assume you're not claiming that the monks are back.'

Baldovino grinned and waved at the barman for more grappa. 'Hardly, but they're not the only ones in this city to dabble with the Devil, now are they?'

James had to agree. When he was in Turin before, he had been told of the city's status as a centre for satanic ritual, apparently owing to its location on a pole of both black and white magic. If people believed that nonsense, then it was at least a possibility that someone could be reaching back to the past and drawing inspiration from a century-old scandal. And now that a body had been found, it looked as if it was more than abduction. A killer was at large.

8

The passion that most often leads women into crime is love. Lombroso and Ferrero, 1893, p. 202

As Lucy awoke for the first time in her Torinese bed, she heard the rain pattering lightly on the window pane. Hopefully it was just a shower. There seemed to be as many here as there were in Edinburgh. She was planning a walk around the city to orientate herself and was looking forward to it so much that even the weather would not deter her. Of course Miss Trott would be there to act as chaperone, but at least it would give Lucy the opportunity to find out a little more about her companion. The older woman had said little of note since they had met in Edinburgh, and up until the previous evening had given the overwhelming impression that she was dull. Now, though, her nocturnal wandering had given her an air of mystery that Lucy was rather enjoying. And there was also the question of James's affair with Anna Tarnovsky to investigate. Things were definitely getting interesting.

Step one in any investigation was to accumulate information about one's suspects. Lucy knew this to be so because it was how Mrs Paschal, the heroine of her favourite novel, *Revelations of a Lady Detective*, would approach such a problem. Lucy was an avid reader of both sensation and detective fiction whenever she could get her hands on it, which wasn't often, given Aunt Agnes's disapproval of such material. This particular volume had been a secret gift from James, and reading it had inspired Lucy to create her own stories.

There was a knock at her door and Miss Trott poked her head round it. 'Are you up yet, Lucy?'

'Almost.'

'Well hurry, dear. We don't want to inconvenience anyone. And you don't want to waste valuable time lingering up here when we could be exploring the city, now do you?'

Lucy observed Miss Trott with a little more care than she had done in the past. Her hair was still the same, fading blonde in colour, pinned up a little untidily, and she was wearing her usual uniform of a plain dress with no evidence of any embellishment. In fact she looked every inch what she was – a lady's companion, hand-picked by Aunt Agnes. But there was something different about her today. She sounded rather tetchy, for one thing, which was unusual, and there was a change in her demeanour. She seemed more guarded in the way she carried herself. It was clear to Lucy that her subject required close study if any secrets were to be uncovered.

'Did you go out last night, Miss Trott?'

'What do you mean, dear?'

'I saw you in your coat when we said good night, and I wondered . . .'

Miss Trott hesitated. Was that a slight flush in her cheeks? 'I just wanted a little fresh air before bed – my headache, you know – so I took a short stroll.'

'I hope it was successful.'

'Sorry?'

'Your headache . . . the walk dispelled it?'

'Yes, yes it did, thank you, dear. Now hurry along. We do not want to waste the day.'

'I'll be down directly,' Lucy said.

Miss Trott paused as if she was about to speak, but evidently thought better of it and merely nodded and departed, leaving Lucy only partly satisfied by the explanation offered. If one was taking a short stroll, why would a large canvas bag be required?

James could not at first work out where he was. He was lying on a shabby settee in lodgings that could only be described as basic. The walls were punctuated with damp patches and the carpet was so threadbare that it did not deserve the name. The place stank of stale sweat with a hint of urine, not unlike La Capra. James groaned as the events of the previous night came back to him and he remembered Sofia walking angrily away.

He tried to move his head but it felt as if someone was burrowing through his brain from the inside. Every time he opened his eyes he found that the room was moving. Slumped in a chair opposite him was Baldovino. His mouth was hanging open and a thin line of dribble was coursing its way slowly down the side of his chin. He shifted slightly in his sleep but did not wake.

It was light outside. James had to speak to Sofia before she went to work. It would be risky. He would have to be discreet. It was important for the sake of propriety that he was not seen anywhere near her lodgings. He would also have to find a way of getting into the professor's house undetected and just hope that he could reach his room before his absence was noticed. He would have to claim a lack of appetite if anyone asked about him missing breakfast. It would not be easy, but he had to try.

Having heard what Baldovino had told him the previous night, James had realised his mistake and knew that he had to put it right, whatever the consequences. He had been dismissive of Sofia's concern for her cousin, and now it was clear that she was not the only girl to have disappeared. Would Sofia have read the newspaper? She hadn't mentioned it. For a moment he considered telling her about the body in the woods but quickly decided that it would be better to wait until he and the professor had examined it. There was no sense in upsetting her unless it became necessary. Besides, first of all he had to persuade her to speak to him, and after last night that might not be an easy thing to accomplish.

Not twenty minutes later, he was standing outside Sofia's rooms. It was raining, and he was ill equipped for the weather. Water dripped down his face onto the end of his nose. He wiped it with his hand and thought what a sight he must represent: haggard from the combined effects of lack of sleep and far too much grappa, and now damp through and through. He looked around him. Fortunately the early hour and the rain had kept most people indoors, and those who were about were too busy getting to their destination to be interested in him.

He had rehearsed what he wanted to say as he walked through the quiet streets of the early morning. But when he saw her in the doorway, his careful words went from his head and he was left struggling to express himself. Sofia did not help him, and who could blame her after the way they had parted the previous evening? Everything about her manner was hostile. Her usual enigmatic smile was gone and her lips formed a thin line of disapproval. He must, he supposed, come across as dishevelled and seedy; not, in fact, unlike Baldovino.

Having made sure that no one was watching, Sofia beckoned him inside. They stood for a moment in the shelter of a small lintel.

'Sofia, I'm sorry.'

'You are sorry… I see. And I am supposed to forgive you just like that? You may have forgotten all you said last night.' She looked at him with disdain. 'Drink will do that.' There was a pause, as if she was trying to retain some control over her emotions. 'As no doubt your father will have told you.' James was shocked by the cruelty of her tone, though he knew he could hardly blame her.

'Sofia, please…'

'I have not forgotten a single word you said to me, and will never do so. You are wasting your time.'

'Wait, please! I know I do not deserve your forgiveness and I respect your decision, but…'

'But what?'

'I have learnt something – some information that you should hear.'

'About?'

'About your cousin.'

Sofia swore under her breath. 'If you are using this, James, so help me…'

'No, no!' he protested. 'I would never do such a thing. You must know me better than that.'

'I thought I did, but after last night…'

'I was angry. It made me say things. I wanted to hurt you because you hurt me.'

She hesitated for a moment. 'You'd better come up.'

James followed her up the rickety stairs to her rooms. He was not stupid enough to think that her invitation changed anything between them, but at least it was a start.

As soon as they reached her small sitting room, he remembered the last time he had been here with her; how they had sat on her threadbare settee and held each other, trying desperately to shut out the impossibility of their situation – two people who loved each other but could never be seen together in public. They had eaten meals at her table, laughing as it wobbled to and fro when James forgot its flimsiness and leant on it. He saw the curtain that separated this room from where she slept and where they had made love. For a moment he was almost overwhelmed by the memories until the smell of coffee wrapped itself around him, reviving him just in time to feel the sting of regret.

Sofia faced him. Her stance was defiant. 'So tell me, what is it about Chiara that I should hear?'

There was no point in prevaricating. 'She is not the only one to have gone missing. Other girls of her age and . . .' He paused.

'Background?' Sofia said.

James nodded and showed her the list that Baldovino had given him the previous night.

'I do not recognise any other names.'

'There is this as well.' He unfolded a copy of the newspaper with Baldovino's article in it. Sofia took it from him and read, a frown spreading across her face. She looked tired. 'It does not say much.'

'I know, but at least it's something.'

Sofia blinked. 'What is all this about the abbey?'

'Baldovino had a tip-off. His source hinted that there might be a connection.'

'I see, and he thought this nonsense would make a good article.'

'That's it. There have been sightings of mysterious figures, and people claim to have heard noises and seen strange lights.'

Sofia shook her head and tossed the newspaper onto the table. 'There have been rumours about that place for years. It means nothing.'

'I know that, but it at least brings the question of the missing girls into the public eye.'

'So six girls have disappeared in the last few months.'

'At least, although Baldovino says that more cannot be ruled out.'

'How much does he know?'

'Only what his source told him, I think. He asked around the town near the abbey, too. Apparently all the girls are linked to the place. '

'*Sì*. Chiara lived there before she came to stay with me. But he has not mentioned the town in his article.'

'I suppose the Devil is more newsworthy.'

Sofia gave a snort of derision. '*Madonna mia!* Young girls go missing and he does nothing except write a story about the Devil and a haunted abbey.'

'The paper wouldn't print it until he got the lead on the abbey, and even then they told him to keep it vague.'

'Of course they wouldn't. Girls like Chiara are not important. They have no money, no status, so they do not matter to anyone. It takes some stupid story about the Devil and a haunted abbey to get it into the paper. Who gave him the tip-off? I suppose he has told the carabinieri?'

'He won't reveal his source. The carabinieri made some initial enquiries, but when they couldn't find anything, they gave up, claiming that the girls were runaways.'

'That is what they said to me . . . but six of them?'

'Perhaps they will reopen the case now it is in the newspaper.'

Sofia sank onto a nearby chair as if all her energy had been drained away. James went over to her and knelt down by her side. 'Please allow me to help you, Sofia.' He placed his hand on hers, but she shook it away and gave him a scornful glare.

'What help can you offer a born criminal like me? Chiara and I are related. She's probably a criminal too, is she not? No doubt she has fallen into bad company. That's what women like us do, isn't it?'

'Sofia, I am so sorry for saying those things.'

'Maybe, but it changes nothing. Chiara is still gone, and so are those other girls, if Baldovino is right.'

'Sofia, I want to help. Please let me do what I can.'

'What do you think you can do?'

'I can investigate.'

'Like you did with the pilgrim last year? He had to come to you before you found him!'

'I would have found him given a little more time, I'm sure of it.'

There was a long pause. Her face was devoid of all expression. A barrier had come down between them.

Finally she spoke. 'Very well. What have I to lose? No one else will listen. But, James . . .'

'Yes?'

'It changes nothing between us.'

'I understand.' He heard himself say the words but he knew there was hope in his heart. 'I will need your help. You know Chiara; I do not.'

Sofia nodded. 'What do you need to know?'

He took out his leather notebook and a pencil. 'Tell me about her. Tell me everything.'

The showery rain of the early morning had not dispersed, so Lucy and Miss Trott had decided to visit the Galleria Sabauda.

It was a fine old building containing a collection of paintings that had once been owned by the dukes and kings of the Savoy dynasty, whose power had dominated Italy and particularly Turin for many years. There were also examples of the Italian masters and the Piedmont school, as well as a number of Dutch and Flemish paintings. Lucy had readily agreed when Miss Trott suggested it as a destination. It seemed somehow to be a way of reaching out to her mother. A love of art was something they had shared. In fact, so keen had her mother been on encouraging this interest that she had engaged an art master for her, or to be more accurate, two.

The first, Monsieur Rabbe, a tall, skinny young man with a patchy and untidy beard, had escorted Lucy to several London galleries. Unfortunately, he was rather too taken with his charge and was much given to staring adoringly at her rather than teaching her. He was quickly replaced by a much older man, Signor Giovanni: short, stout and in possession of an overly inflated idea of his own importance. Unhappily, he was also enamoured, this time of the bottle. He was asked to leave after an unfortunate incident with a decanter of port and a pair of brocade curtains – he drank the first and pulled down the second, much to the amusement of James and Lucy, but not their mother, who dismissed him on the spot.

It was Miss Trott who had suggested that they visit a gallery, but once they got there, she declared herself to be suffering a moral dilemma. Although, she said, she was herself a champion of self-improvement, and encouraged such opportunities to learn, she also felt that the sight of so much naked flesh might not be suitable for a young lady's eyes.

'Whatever would your aunt say?' she asked anxiously, before doing her best to guide Lucy away from paintings she felt were unsavoury in any way, much to her charge's irritation. Finally they reached a compromise. Miss Trott would go ahead and select those paintings that she felt were appropriate. This, though a somewhat annoying prospect, at least meant that Lucy would have an opportunity to take in some of what she had come to see without her companion's unwelcome and tiresome interventions.

The problem was that the paintings she most wanted to study seemed to be the very same ones that Miss Trott found unsuitable. Lucy wanted to look at works that had some kind of story attached to them, or at least a narrative that she herself could embroider with detail. For example, she had been drawn to a painting of *The Beheading of St John the Baptist* by Volterra, which had a headless body at its heart, with a figure leaning over it picking up the severed head. This work pulled her in not because of its gruesome centrepiece, but because in the background, seen through a window, was a woman looking in at the scene and holding an empty platter. She presumed that this was Salome, who had danced so well for King Herod that he had granted her wish for the head of John the Baptist. Miss Trott, however, steered her away from the painting, calling it 'quite horrid', and instead planted her in front of a tedious picture of *St Peter and a Worshipper* by Ferrari.

'He looks bored, don't you think, Miss Trott?'

'Who does, dear?'

'St Peter. I think he is wishing that his fat little worshipper with the irritating, pious expression would leave him alone.'

Miss Trott frowned at her, though just for an instant Lucy thought she had noticed the beginnings of a smile.

'Come and look at this Rembrandt, Lucy,' she said. 'Isn't the detail startling?'

Dutifully Lucy obeyed. The picture was of an elderly man dozing on a chair. 'I suppose so, but the subject's so tedious.'

'Art doesn't have to be exciting,' Miss Trott replied. 'That is not the point.'

'Is that a severed hand at his feet?' Lucy asked, spotting something in a shadowy part of the painting. 'That would make it interesting.'

Miss Trott peered closely. 'No. It is a pair of tongs, dear.'

Lucy sighed. 'Yes, I think you're right. How dull.'

They continued on their artistic journey, with Lucy being guided away from anything she considered potentially interesting in favour of more wholesome examples, as Miss Trott put it. As they went on, however, this insistence became not just tiresome but suspicious, until it began to occur to Lucy that her companion's piety was not genuine. It was as though that was how she thought she should be, rather than how she was. Lucy was unsure what to do with this idea. Was she creating a mystery where there was none, just to make Miss Trott more interesting?

Lucy was admiring a particularly beautiful depiction of the Madonna and Child by Spanzotti, a prominent member of the Piedmont school, according to Miss Trott, when a light, almost musical, voice interrupted her reverie.

'The form is well constructed enough, but the end result is a little trite, don't you think?'

A tall, slim figure approached her. He raised his hat politely and she saw that he had a mass of dark, wavy hair beneath. She wanted to lean forward and smooth it into some kind of order. Instead she nodded her acknowledgement. 'I don't agree. The word trite suggests that it is ordinary, and in my opinion it is anything but that.'

'Perhaps it is not ordinary, but it lacks a certain spark of life, I feel. It is dull and flat, without originality or realism.'

Lucy had to stop herself from giving a sharp intake of breath as she observed the man more closely. He was younger than she had thought, surely no more than twenty-five, and was like no one she had ever encountered before. His features were delicate, almost feminine, and his eyes were green and piercing. It was the kind of face that, once seen, was never forgotten, and such was its beauty that she did not want to take her gaze from it.

Miss Trott, it seemed, was not quite so smitten, or at least not at first. She had noticed their conversation from a distance and had rushed over to ensure that no further impropriety took place. The man bowed. Miss Trott seemed to start a little but quickly recovered.

'Lucy, I do not think your brother, or indeed your aunt, would approve of you conversing with a stranger.'

The man smiled his extraordinary smile. Lucy felt a pang of regret that it had not been reserved exclusively for her.

'I'm quite all right, Miss Trott.'

'That's all very well, but let it not be said that Euphemia Trott neglects her duties.'

'Euphemia – what an unusual name, and how it suits you, madam, if I may say so,' said the young man. 'I believe it means well-spoken, and so you are.'

Lucy was amused at the compliment. Miss Trott smiled for an instant, a victim of unfamiliar charm. This, however, was only momentary, and she soon recovered her wits.

'It is unseemly for a gentleman, if you could be called such, sir, to address a young lady in such a familiar manner!'

The young man bowed and adopted a sorrowful expression that Lucy suspected was not entirely sincere.

'If I have offended, I am distraught. We were merely conversing as one student of art to another. But perhaps my opinion was unwelcome. Good day, ladies.'

With that he withdrew as quickly and mysteriously as he had arrived, leaving both Lucy and Miss Trott to gaze after his retreating form. The rest of the visit continued without incident, but neither of them was able to banish the thought of the young man entirely from her mind.

She is not completely alone . . . or at least she was not. She does not know whether to be pleased or upset. There was definitely someone nearby, and from the little she heard, they were in the same terrifying situation as her. But when the crying turned to screaming, then . . . she could not forget that sound. A great roar of pain, as if the girl's very soul was being tortured. Dare she call out again? She yearns for human contact until it almost overwhelms her, but does she really want to antagonise whoever it was that caused those screams? Eventually, as she stares into the void that is her existence, she decides to risk it. Even pain is better than this emptiness.

'Are you there?' she cries.

There is nothing for a while, and she thinks she is still alone. Then she hears weeping, and a barely audible 'hello' between the sobs. 'Help me . . . please. It hurts so . . .'

'I cannot. I wish I could,' she calls, tugging at the manacle around her ankle. 'But at least we are not alone.'

There is more silence. She cannot bear it. 'What . . . what has he done to you?' she asks.

She waits, unsure that she wants her question answered. Then she hears the unmistakable sound of a stone being slid slowly back. She has a visitor. It seems that it is her turn.

She sits and stares ahead of her into the darkness. She can

hear her captor breathing. Is it a man or a woman? She cannot tell. All she can see is a shadowy outline. Whoever it is wears a cloak with a hood, like some kind of habit. They have not hurt her, at least not yet, and she supposes she should be grateful for that. But she cannot help but want to know more, even if it might provoke her captor.

'Who was that girl?' she asks. 'What did you do to her?'

Silence.

'How many of us are there?'

Silence.

'What do you want?'

The darkness and the silence press down on her like the stone that her captor slides across when they leave her.

'Clean yourself. Then put this on.' Her visitor finally speaks. It is a whisper – loud, though: a stage whisper. Something is thrown down to her – something soft. A lantern is lit and hung on the wall, and she cranes her neck to see who is there. Then a pail of water is lowered, and a bar of soap follows it wrapped in a towel. The stone is slid back into place and she is alone again. She breathes a sigh of relief. Whatever her captor did to the other girl, he did not want to repeat it . . . or not yet, anyway. She has survived, and now she has light.

The soft cloth that has been thrown to her is pale, and simple in design. She examines it for a second or two, then catches her breath as she realises what it resembles – a shroud.

9

Criminals and the mad frequently lack affection entirely, showing neither pity nor benevolence nor remorse. They are capable of eating and dancing near the cadaver of their victim, all the while boasting of their crime. In addition they manifest little affection for their companions.

Lombroso, 1876, p. 82

The mortuary was situated in the basement of Turin's main hospital, a building that although not old in years still gave an impression of shabbiness, as if whoever had built it was afraid that to do otherwise might be considered frivolous. When James had returned from seeing Sofia, he had passed on to Lombroso Tullio's request about examining the remains. As he had predicted, the professor had been only too pleased to accept once he was told that some kind of mystery surrounded them.

The two of them sat in the waiting room and waited for Tullio to arrive. Lombroso was bright-eyed and eager to begin. James, though intrigued, had other things on his mind. The thought that the body they were about to examine might be that of Chiara was overwhelming him, making it difficult to think of anything else.

'I cannot think why Tullio did not mention this at dinner,' Lombroso said.

'I seem to remember that he had already asked you for something,' James said. The after-effects of the previous night's grappa were catching up with him. 'Perhaps he didn't want to seem too demanding.'

'Ah yes. That is correct. He did make a request a day or two ago . . . something rather curious, in fact.'

'What was it?' James asked.

'Later, Murray, later. Be patient.'

James knew that it was useless trying to get Lombroso to tell him anything. Besides that, he had a headache and felt queasy. The prospect of examining a dead body in his current condition was not a pleasant one, notwithstanding any secrets that it might be concealing. He was not in the best of physical states to be grappling with body fluids oozing out of every orifice. Already he could smell the familiar underlying odour of decomposition, and they were only in the waiting room. It took all his concentration to stop himself from being sick, knowing that if he was he would never be allowed to hear the last of it.

Luckily Tullio soon arrived and they followed him down some worn stone steps into the largest part of the mortuary, where the body was laid out. Standing to attention next to it was the mortuary assistant, a large man with a face full of dimples, strange unruly blonde hair and an incongruously beaming smile. His name, he informed them, was Boris, and he was happy to help. James noticed that Lombroso viewed him with suspicion, paying particular attention to his ears, which stuck out almost at right angles from his oversized head. No doubt it was the sign of some criminal type or other. If he wasn't careful, Boris would end up having his head measured and appearing in one of the professor's academic papers, or worse, perhaps even being forever preserved after death as an exhibit in the museum.

With a flourish Boris pulled back the sheet covering the body. It was immediately clear that it could not be Chiara. The victim had not died recently. James was relieved. At least he would not have to break such terrible news to Sofia... not yet, anyway.

He peered down at the body. It had reached an advanced state of decomposition, being devoid of the telltale swelling produced by the gases of putrefaction. He tried to remember the book that he had been referred to by Professor Bell. What was it called? Ah yes: *Legal Medicine*, by Charles Meymott Tidy – two very handy volumes indeed, particularly for propping open the door to his rooms in the summer months. Professor Bell was especially dismissive of the section on hair and nails growing after death. He was of the view that they didn't, whereas Tidy was certain that they did.

Whatever the truth, they had long since stopped doing so here. James leant over to take a closer look. The body was clearly that of a woman. It resembled a shrunken leather-skinned corpse, bent almost double like a foetus. Next to it were placed what looked to be internal organs, dark brown, almost black, and shrivelled in consistency. On closer inspection the body seemed to be covered in some kind of crystalline substance, not unlike salt. Some hair was still present, but it was sparse – no more than thin brown strands. The jaw gaped open in a macabre smile. A scarlet ribbon was still tied around the head. A picture of the girl when she was alive flashed into James's mind, with glossy hair shining in sunlight and long, slender fingers playing coquettishly with its scarlet adornment.

The flesh, if you could still call it that, was strange – tough and brown. An attempt had been made to open up the body, revealing that it had been stuffed full of vegetation, dried now: herbs, flowers and grasses. The clothes had been removed and lay on an adjacent table. They were mostly intact, though ripped in places – a plain dress of faded blue cotton with an apron tied around the middle. Another picture arrived unbidden in James's head. This time the girl with the long brown hair was standing with an enigmatic smile on her face, her hands on her hips. Her face was Sofia's.

The remains were certainly unusual. 'As you can see, the body is not recent,' Tullio said.

Lombroso peered at it. 'I'd say she has been dead for at least six months . . . perhaps even longer. Where was she found?'

'In woods outside the city, near a small town called San Callisto.'

'Still no clues on identity?' James asked.

'Nothing solid, as I told you last night. We have made some enquiries in the town and surrounding area, but nobody has noticed anyone missing for that length of time. Mind you, it is a rural community and there are quite a few itinerant workers, so it is hard to be sure. '

'Will you be giving details to the newspapers? Someone might come forward.'

'I wanted to, but the mayor has asked me to keep it quiet for the time being. He doesn't want people to panic.'

'Are they likely to?' In James's experience, the Torinese were not easily shocked.

'I would not think so,' Tullio replied.

'The mayor is hoping for another term of office, is he not?' Lombroso said pointedly.

Tullio nodded and gave a shrug.

'Did you know that the reporter Baldovino has a list of girls who have disappeared?' James asked.

'I am aware that other girls have gone missing, yes,' Tullio replied. 'Marshal Machinetti thinks that they are most likely to be runaways.'

'Even now, with this body?' James said.

Tullio shook his head. 'They have all gone in the last few months, and as the professor has confirmed, these remains are far older.'

'But they are all connected to the town.'

'Do not complicate things, Murray,' Lombroso said. 'Girls like that run off all the time, wherever they are from. It is the way they are made. Indeed, poor women generally are increasingly likely to travel around the country looking for employment as maids, casual labourers or even prostitutes. It is becoming a real social problem. But then what do we expect from women? They are inherently inferior and cannot help the way they are made.'

James could see that he was fighting a losing battle, but he knew he had to persevere. If there was one body now and girls were missing, then there could be more.

'How was the body left?' he asked.

'In a shallow grave,' Tullio said. 'At least it was shallow enough to be dug up by a truffle hog.'

'That's interesting. Any insect activity?' Lombroso asked.

'Some but not much,' Tullio replied. 'Why do you ask?'

'Haven't the French been doing some work on using insect activity to indicate time of death?' James asked.

'Indeed, Murray, though the Chinese started it as far back as the thirteenth century.' Lombroso indicated the pile of internal organs. 'I take it these were removed by the pathologist?'

'No,' Tullio replied. 'They were in a small sealed container next to the body, exactly as you see there.'

'May I look at it?' Lombroso asked.

Tullio nodded, and Boris held up a stone pot with a lid. Lombroso took it and examined it. The handle was fashioned in the likeness of a snake.

'There are no distinguishing marks, though I am sure I have seen something like it before. I can't for the life of me remember where,' he said.

'It is interesting that there is no sign of activity from foxes and the like,' James said.

'Yes, well spotted, Murray. That indicates a recent burial, and yet the state the body is in shows that it is older.'

Tullio nodded. 'That would tally with what the truffle hunter said. He goes there regularly apparently, and claims he would have found the body earlier.'

'Or the pig would,' James said. 'At any rate, it looks like this woman died elsewhere.'

'Cause of death?' Tullio asked.

'It is difficult to say with any certainty, given the state of the body,' Lombroso replied. 'Various things have been done to it, but I cannot tell if that is ante, peri or post-mortem.'

'What kind of things?' Tullio asked.

'It appears that attempts have been made to preserve the body. In order to achieve that, certain procedures must have been conducted.'

James looked again at the leathery bundle beside the body. 'That would explain the organ removal. What other procedures?'

'Eviscerate, bleed and dry, Murray. Just as the Egyptians did. The brain is removed through the nasal passage. Take a look and tell me what you see.'

James peered at the girl's face. 'Yes, there is disturbance to the nasal cavity. I think you might be right.'

'Naturally. There might well have been draining of fluids, but that is mere speculation. I would have to ask a specialist to be sure.' Lombroso looked at the body again. 'Yes, see here, Murray, just to the left of the abdomen – an incision. Interesting that the heart has been removed. As I recall, it was usually left *in situ*, along with the kidneys.'

'What is this salty residue?' James asked.

'Natron, I would think. After evisceration, the body was covered with it. It is a kind of preserving salt.'

'Is there any possibility that the woman was subjected to these techniques whilst still alive?' Tullio asked.

Lombroso nodded grimly. 'I cannot rule it out. However, there is damage to the hyoid bone, which indicates strangling or perhaps garrotting.'

'A murder, then,' Tullio said.

'It would certainly seem so,' Lombroso said. 'But it may not have been sufficient to kill her, so it is at least possible that the embalming took place whilst she was living.'

'My God! What kind of animal would do something like that?' James said.

'Someone exhibiting signs of moral insanity . . . possibly an epileptic,' Lombroso said.

'Really?' Tullio said. 'So that is who I should be looking for here?'

'These are conclusions I have been drawing recently, based on past work,' Lombroso said breezily. 'I have found certain overlaps between epileptics, the insane and born criminals that indicate to me the likelihood of a link. This killer will certainly lack any moral sense and be intrinsically unstable; he will probably be agile, and of course may have a propensity for drinking blood – common in epileptics.'

Tullio and James exchanged glances. It was difficult to work out exactly how Lombroso had reached these conclusions.

Tullio cleared his throat. 'I see. Thank you . . . very useful, I'm sure.'

Undeterred, Lombroso continued, clearly warming to his theme. 'Physically, you are seeking a fairly common criminal type – a voluminous jaw, jutting cheekbones and a propensity towards sexual perversion. I once heard of a very intelligent example who ate excrement as he fitted and also orally masturbated his own penis. Extraordinary!'

Tullio frowned, momentarily lost for words. 'Well that's something to go on, anyhow.'

Lombroso beamed at him. 'Quite so. I do like to think that my work has a practical application.'

'How about the burial site?' James asked, hoping to bring the professor back to something less speculative.

'Yes,' Tullio said with a grateful glance. 'Was the grave shallow because he wanted the body to be found, do you think?'

'I would say that is possible,' Lombroso replied.

'But isn't it equally possible that he thought the location was sufficiently remote to make it unlikely that it would be found?' James said. 'Or perhaps he didn't care either way.'

'Oh he cared all right,' Tullio said.

'How can you be so sure?' James asked.

'Firstly because the body was buried right at the centre of a clearing. The measurement is exact to the last inch.'

'Interesting,' James said.

'And secondly there is the container full of organs.'

'That is unusual,' Lombroso agreed. 'It is almost as if he wanted us to think of them as an exhibit in a museum.'

James frowned. 'No,' he said. 'It's more ritualistic than that.'

'What do you mean?' Tullio asked.

'Think about the care that has been taken here. He made sure that the body was placed right in the middle. The burial indicates to me that he's not putting her on show,' James said. 'He's laying her to rest. And where she was found isn't a museum. It's a graveyard.'

10

Prostitutes have bigger calves than honest women.

Lombroso, 1893, p. 126

'We know, do we not,' Lombroso said as he sat back in his chair, his fingers pressed together in front of him like the steeple of a church, 'that women are arrested and convicted far less frequently than men.'

The professor, James and Anna Tarnovsky were sitting in Lombroso's study at the museum discussing their project about criminal women. James felt his eyes becoming heavy. He had experienced something of a second wind at the mortuary when faced with the mystery of the strange leathery corpse, but that was fast disappearing as he sat and listened to Lombroso. All he could see when he let his eyelids droop even for a moment was a vision of brown wrinkled skin and a red ribbon tied gaily round what was left of a head.

'Murray, try to concentrate! This is important!' Lombroso said.

'Of course, Professor.' Surreptitiously he pinched himself on the wrist – an old trick he had occasionally used during some of his more tedious lectures at medical school.

'And that is the problem, as I outlined last night, Cesare,'

Anna said. 'If you keep to your previous claims about female inferiority, then you may well find that there is a contradiction.'

The professor was nodding sagely and stroking his beard. He did not seem to have noticed the irony of being told that his findings were flawed by a woman who was anything but inferior. It was as if he did not recognise her sex at all.

'I see the problem . . . but what is the solution?'

'James, you mentioned last night about reconsidering our research pool,' Anna said. 'What did you mean exactly?'

'If we look at normal as well as criminal women, then we could do a comparison.'

'That is a capital idea!' Lombroso beamed at him. 'Of course I had been considering doing something of that nature, but I wanted to see if either of you would think of it.'

James caught Anna's eye. Was she angry or amused by Lombroso's claim? It was hard to tell. She was fond of the professor, he knew, but still there was a limit.

'It might be quite difficult to compile that kind of information. After all, how can we be certain what is normal and what is abnormal?' she said.

Lombroso frowned. 'Yes, that might be a problem. Perhaps you could do a little research into existing data, Murray?'

James agreed enthusiastically, eager to start work. It should not be too difficult to fit it around his investigation.

'There is another possibility,' Anna said.

'Which is?' Lombroso asked.

'Prostitutes,' she replied. 'Surely they should be included in the research.'

Lombroso looked thoughtful. 'Perhaps they should. After all, criminal women in primitive times were all prostitutes of one kind or another. Why should today's be any different?'

James exchanged perplexed glances with Anna. He somehow doubted that this view of primitive women was true. He hoped their research would demonstrate some rather more credible conclusions. Still, the role of the prostitute might well be relevant.

'I have some data that might assist,' Anna said. 'I did some work on local prostitutes in Prague this spring and have a number of interesting photographs. I also used a control group for a short while.'

'*Eccellente!*' Lombroso declared. 'I think we are on our way. But I would also like to try to collate my own data. I have some already from a local brothel, so this would be a good opportunity to build on that.'

'Of course, Cesare. Mine was only a small study,' Anna said.

'And we shall use it, I am sure. But as I say, I have been to this particular establishment before, and I think we shall get some interesting material from visiting it again.'

'What establishment is it?' Anna asked.

'Madame Giulia's,' Lombroso replied. 'I've taken some preliminary cranial measurements, but I'd like us to measure other characteristics as well as conducting interviews. They're delightful ladies on the whole, despite their criminality. I hope to arrange it for tomorrow afternoon.'

'It all sounds very interesting,' Anna said. 'I'll look forward to it.'

Lombroso shifted in his seat and avoided her glance. 'I'm afraid it will just be Murray on this occasion. It's not a suitable place for a lady, even when she is as eminent in her field as Madame Anna Tarnovsky.'

'But I did my own research in Prague and no one seemed to mind.'

'That may be so, but I do not want the girls to feel uncomfortable or to upset the owner. I'm sorry, but it cannot be helped. One must always ensure that one's subjects are comfortable with one's methods.'

James thought it most unfair for Anna to be excluded. It seemed that Lombroso remembered that she was a woman only when it suited him. Since they had all begun to work together, he had detected a definite change in the professor's attitude to her. During the symposium last year, Lombroso had been charming, almost deferential. Now he seemed to be undermining her at every opportunity. He also noticed that the professor had not mentioned the body they had just examined. Of course that could be an attempt at discretion, as requested by Tullio, but such things did not usually trouble Lombroso.

'Now,' the professor said in a hearty tone, 'I think we have earned ourselves a decent luncheon. Shall we continue our discussions at Caffé San Carlo over a bite to eat?'

The food was more than decent, James thought as he tucked into a bowl of fragrant wild mushroom risotto and a few glasses of a white wine called Gavi di Gavi that tasted of pears and peaches. The flavours almost seemed to explode on the tongue and revived him after the overindulgence of the night before. But even that could not dull his sense of outrage at his mentor's views on the nature of women.

'They are no more than big children!' Lombroso declared.

'And does this apply to all of my sex,' Anna enquired, her cheeks becoming ever more flushed, either from the effects of the wine or, more likely, the direction of the conversation.

'Or is it just criminals and prostitutes who have never grown up?'

Lombroso nodded enthusiastically. 'They are like men in so many ways, but men who have been somehow arrested in their intellectual and physical development.'

'Cesare . . .' Anna began.

'Yes, my dear Madame Tarnovsky?' Lombroso said, smiling at her in that way he had – a sort of dreamy confidence, as if he took his own rightness for granted to such an extent that he didn't regard it as needing his complete attention.

'What shall we be asking the girls at Madame Giulia's?' James said, in an effort to divert Anna from a course that he suspected might be unwise.

'I think we should regard Madame Tarnovsky's work in Prague together with mine as an experimental preliminary study.'

'Are you sure my work is sufficiently mature?' Anna asked pointedly.

'Yes, of course, my dear. What a question to ask!' Lombroso shook his head and tutted. 'You really must have more confidence in your abilities.'

'And our questions?' James asked.

'They will be designed to ascertain a propensity or otherwise to dishonesty,' Lombroso said. 'Women lie. It is a well-known fact. Countless proverbs tell us that. The question is, do criminal women lie more?'

'How will we measure that?' James asked.

Lombroso smiled the smile of a man who had a trick up his sleeve. 'We shall use my lie-detecting machine.'

'Really?' Anna said, frowning. 'I would like to see that. I did help you develop it after all, Cesare.'

'Yes, that is true, of course . . . Ah!' Lombroso beamed at

them both. 'We shall conduct the interviews at the university. Then Madame Tarnovsky will be able to join us!'

Anna smiled in satisfaction. 'Thank you, Cesare. It is much appreciated.'

'Are you sure that is wise, Professor?' James asked. 'Won't inviting prostitutes to the university be somewhat controversial?'

Lombroso grinned. 'I do hope so, Murray. I like people to know what we're up to, and Gemelli will no doubt make sure that everyone hears about it.'

'You must take care, Cesare,' Anna said. 'You know that regulations do not allow for the girls to move around the city outside of their curfew.'

'We shall time our inquiry accordingly,' Lombroso said. He beamed at them. 'I think this will be very interesting indeed.'

At this point Anna took her leave to meet Lucy and Miss Trott. James was delighted that she had taken his sister under her wing. She was just the sort of person that Lucy would admire – independent-minded, intelligent, but with a sense of humour. She would be an excellent role model for Lucy and something of an antidote to the dry Miss Trott. The two women would complement each other and together provide all the guidance that a young girl like Lucy might require, leaving James free to concentrate on finding Chiara and winning back Sofia. That afternoon he intended to visit the place where Chiara worked and speak to her fellow servants. Sofia had already done so but had not learnt much of use. It would be good to do something practical.

'You look pleased with yourself, Murray,' Lombroso said. 'I am glad you are in a good mood. I have something to tell you.'

What now? James wondered. Before Lombroso could say more, a familiar gangling figure came into view and waved at them, almost knocking over some glasses on a tray carried by a short and rather haughty waiter.

'It's Ottolenghi!' James exclaimed.

'Now we are complete,' Lombroso said with satisfaction.

The young man made his way over to them and they shook hands and exchanged greetings. James felt himself relax at the sight of his friend and ally. They had shared so much during James's last visit, and Ottolenghi alone knew how he felt about Sofia. But something about his friend had changed. He was paler, and there were new lines on his forehead. His clothes were rumpled and he had dark circles under his eyes. Whatever it was that he had experienced with Oskar Reiner in Vienna, it did not look as if it was pleasant.

'I was sorry to hear about your father, James,' Ottolenghi said. 'It must have been hard for you.'

'Thank you, Salvatore. It was difficult, but perhaps it is time to look to the future.'

'And it will be a full one, you can be sure of that, Murray,' Lombroso said.

'Have you told our friend about tonight yet, Professor?' Ottolenghi asked, pushing his wire-rimmed glasses up the bridge of his nose.

'Told me what?' James was apprehensive. Expeditions led by Lombroso always seemed to end in trouble, and he suspected that this one would be no different.

Ottolenghi grinned. 'The professor sent me a telegraph in Vienna a few days ago asking me to return. I could not resist!'

'I hope that you have nothing planned for this evening, Murray,' Lombroso said cryptically.

'I haven't, as it happens,' James said. 'So what are we doing?'

Ottolenghi handed him a copy of Baldovino's article. 'We're looking for the Devil, my friend. What else?'

11

Very often in women the criminal type is disguised by youth; the lack of wrinkles and plumpness of youth mask the size of the jaw and the cheekbones, softening the virile and savage aspects of the features. When the hair is abundant and black and the eyes are bright, these criminals can even present a pleasant appearance. Moreover, sex appeal may affect our judgement, encouraging us to think erotically and making the offender seem more beautiful and free of degenerative traits than she really is.

Lombroso and Ferrero, 1893, p. 140

Lucy and Miss Trott had arranged to meet Anna Tarnovsky at the marchesa's palazzo, on the hill that rose up from the city and its river. True to her word, she was waiting for them in a carriage outside. The palazzo itself seemed to Lucy to be too small a residence for a woman of such influence and standing. She had been expecting something magnificent and imposing, like some of the buildings that James had told her he had visited when he was last in the city. This, by comparison, seemed quite modest.

Inside, however, the palazzo still bore some of the hallmarks of ostentation that James had described. It was as if whoever had furnished it could not resist the temptation to leave the odd touch of splendour behind – a splash of gilt here and there; a solitary alabaster cherub peeping out from the ceiling as if it had been abandoned when all the others had flown off to somewhere more opulent. They were shown into a large room filled with comfortable chairs. On the walls between the many bookshelves were oriental silk hangings in vivid colours, and every available surface was covered with assorted ornaments and knick-knacks.

The marchesa rose to greet them. She was tall, angular and elegant, with silver hair, and as she talked, she gesticulated gracefully to emphasise her words. The effect was almost balletic. Standing next to her was a girl of about Lucy's age, dark-haired, dark-eyed but with a sulky expression that quite spoiled her otherwise pretty face. Her lips seemed to fold automatically into a pout and her nose wrinkled as if she could smell something sour.

'This is Fabia Carignano, my niece. She is staying with me at the moment.'

Fabia nodded curtly, as if she could only just be bothered to acknowledge them.

The marchesa smiled at Lucy. 'I think I remember your brother from the symposium last year – a handsome young man, dark-haired, rather pale?'

'That sounds like him,' Lucy replied, quite forgetting her host's aristocratic background, so informal did the occasion seem.

'And how does our city compare to Edinburgh?'

Lucy hesitated. 'I have only seen a little so far, but in many ways they don't seem too different, certainly with regard to the weather.'

The marchesa laughed. 'Ah yes, I'm afraid you have arrived during one of our dampest seasons, but soon the sun will shine, I am sure of it.' She sat down gracefully, indicating for Lucy to join her on a large sofa strewn with velvet cushions. 'Now tell me, my dear, what are your plans whilst you are with us?'

'Miss Murray writes stories,' Anna said.

'Ah . . . I thought you might be creative,' the marchesa said. 'Something about your eyes, a glint of . . . well now, what could it be? Yes, devilment, I believe.'

Lucy blushed. She did not know what to say to that. Was it a compliment or a criticism? Before she could respond, a voice came from the doorway. 'I cannot believe that there is anything remotely devilish about this young lady!'

'Francesco! I'm so glad you could join us,' the marchesa said, beaming. 'And Bianca too. How lovely.'

Lucy examined the new arrivals with interest and was surprised to see that the first was the young man that she and Miss Trott had encountered in the Galleria Sabauda that morning. Standing next to him was a dark-haired woman of about thirty, who despite this seniority seemed almost to shrink into his shadow. She was dressed in browns of various hues, which gave her a birdlike quality, enhanced by bright, intelligent eyes and a slightly aquiline nose. She could hardly be described as a beauty. Her features were uneven and her jawline was a little too heavy. This plainness was highlighted by her companion's striking looks. Lucy speculated on their relationship and found herself hoping they were brother and sister. She also noticed that Fabia's expression had brightened considerably at Francesco's arrival.

Francesco strode into the room and kissed the marchesa's hand. 'How could I resist an invitation from the Lady Vittoria? It would be unconscionable.' He caught sight of Miss Trott, who was sitting in a corner apparently trying to be unobtrusive. 'And what a wonderful coincidence! How enchanting to meet you again, Miss Euphemia Trott, and Miss Lucy, the art critic, too. I am spoilt!'

Lucy could not help but smile, though she thought him a little precocious and rude. He had completely ignored both Anna Tarnovsky and Fabia. She could not imagine James behaving so badly. And could their earlier meeting really have been a coincidence as he claimed? As she studied him, she noticed that he had managed to dominate the room to the extent that the woman with him seemed almost invisible.

'I should introduce you formally, even though it seems that some of you are already acquainted,' the marchesa said, with an amused expression. 'Miss Lucy Murray, Miss Trott, Madame Tarnovsky, may I present Francesco Rambaudi and his sister Bianca. You know Fabia, of course.'

Still Francesco ignored the marchesa's niece. Was there a history to his hostility, or was it that his interest in Lucy was feigned in order to make Fabia jealous? Whatever the reason, Lucy was becoming more and more intrigued by him.

Soon after the introductions, refreshments were brought and the conversation began to flow. 'Tell me more of your writing, Miss Murray,' the marchesa said.

'Let me guess,' Francesco said. 'Are you a poetess as well as an art critic, Miss Lucy?'

Lucy blushed again, this time at his familiarity. 'No, I write stories.'

'You are a novelist. How clever of you. Are you published?' Fabia asked, as if she knew the answer already.

'No. They are just short stories. I write them for my own amusement really.'

'That is surely the best of motives for creation,' Francesco declared.

'Have you been in Turin long, Miss Carignano?' Anna asked Fabia.

'I arrived yesterday,' Fabia replied in a tone that suggested it was none of her business.

'I will be throwing a ball next week in Fabia's honour,' the marchesa said. 'To celebrate her eighteenth birthday. Needless to say, you are all invited.'

'How delightful,' Francesco declared. 'And no doubt your niece will be the belle of the ball!'

Fabia blushed and smiled, transforming her face in an instant.

Lucy studied the assembled company as the conversation went on. Ever the writer, she was less interested in the details of the ball than the opportunity it would give her to observe the people around her. She watched Francesco as he entertained the marchesa and Fabia, noting that his easy manner did not seem quite authentic. Beneath the surface was something deeper and more serious. His eyes did not reflect the lightness of his conversation. What lay behind this facade?

At first Bianca Rambaudi, in contrast to her brother, did not utter a word, apparently preferring to allow Francesco to take centre stage. She gazed at him intently, as if everything he said was of the utmost importance. The siblings could not have been more different. Francesco fitted into the marchesa's circle quite naturally, whereas Bianca seemed decidedly ill at ease, fiddling with the tea things in front of her, lining them up in neat little rows as if creating a barrier between her and the rest of the company. It was only when the marchesa asked her about the Rambaudi estate that she appeared to come to life. Lucy gleaned from what was said that the family's wealth stemmed from their rice fields just outside the city, and that since the recent death of their father, Bianca had been running the business almost single-handedly.

'You are to be congratulated, Miss Rambaudi,' Anna said. 'Not many women could do as you have, and with such success too.'

Bianca's face reddened. 'Thank you, Madame Tarnovsky. You are most kind.' Her voice did not match her mannish features. It was light, almost musical, not unlike her brother's.

'Bianca always had an interest in such things,' Francesco said airily. 'Even when she was a child she would follow my father and me around the fields. He was intent on teaching me the business, the old fool, and ignored her. But she was always the one with the brains, just like our mother.'

'You have studied at the university, Francesco,' the marchesa said. 'That hardly makes you a dunce. I remember one of your teachers telling me that you could have been a professor, had you wanted to travel that path.'

'I have dabbled in many areas,' Francesco admitted. 'But without Bianca the Rambaudis would be in a sorry state.'

'What have you studied?' Lucy asked.

'European literature, Philosophy, Art, Egyptology . . .'

'Egyptology! How fascinating!' Miss Trott said.

'Our Museo Egizio holds one of the most prestigious collections of Egyptian artefacts in the world,' the marchesa said.

'How wonderful!' Miss Trott said. 'We must pay it a visit, don't you think, Lucy?'

'And I shall escort you,' Francesco said, much to Fabia's annoyance, judging from the expression on her face.

The conversation rumbled on for a while until it was time

to leave. As they were about to do so, Francesco took Lucy's hand and shook it solemnly. 'I look forward to our Egyptian expedition, Miss Murray.'

'So do I, Signor Rambaudi.'

He bowed and escorted his sister to their carriage, waving at Miss Trott, who managed to nod her acknowledgement and yet simultaneously make her disapproval clear.

'Should you not seek agreement from your brother, Lucy?' she asked.

Lucy watched as Anna left. 'I think you'll find he has other things on his mind, Miss Trott. I doubt he will even care.'

'I'm sure that is not so. In any event, you must ask his permission. And assuming he agrees, I of course must be present.'

As their cab began to trundle towards the Via Legnano, Lucy wondered what it would be like to be free of this endless supervision. It must be wonderful to be male and able to go where you wanted whenever you felt like it. Why should the fact that she was a girl mean that she had to be chaperoned constantly?

Before long they arrived at their destination and Lucy alighted. Miss Trott, though, stayed in her seat.

'Are you not coming in, Miss Trott?'

There was a pause. 'I have somewhere to go,' she said firmly. And with that she leant forward, slammed the door shut and banged on the roof with her umbrella. '*Avanti!*'

Lucy watched as the carriage drove swiftly away. She envied her companion, who, it appeared, thought nothing of exploring the city alone. If only she had thought to stay with her. Perhaps then the evening would hold a better prospect than a quiet dinner and some sitting about until it was time to go to bed. Still, at least she had a visit to the Museo Egizio with Francesco Rambaudi to look forward to, and that promised to be very interesting indeed.

She hears her captor coming with a mixture of relief and trepidation. It is always unnerving, because she does not know what their arrival might bring. Up to now she has been left untouched. Instead that sing-song voice has merely murmured things to her through the bars that form her roof to the world. None of it makes any sense to her. She is urged to atone but is not told what she might be atoning for. She is not a bad person, although some might say she has done bad things. But then what choice did she have? Surely those who employed her have committed greater sins. Why should it be her rather than they who must atone? But she has no influence on anything either here or in the establishment where she worked.

Reluctantly she has changed into her new white gown. Her clothes were beginning to smell and felt scratchy. Her new outfit is soft and scented. It could almost be a wedding dress. She has washed as instructed and waits now for whatever her fate might be. As the hours pass, she has become more and more afraid.

Gradually her apprehension is buried beneath more physical needs. She is hungry. She has not been fed now for at least three days. It might have been more, but she has not been able to keep count accurately in the darkness of her captivity. All she knows is that the rumbling in her stomach has been replaced by an emptiness more acute than she has ever experienced before. Times were occasionally hard during her childhood, but there was always at least something to eat. Her mother made sure of it. A picture comes into her mind – her family sitting round the dinner table; her father cracking jokes and teasing her mother, her brothers and sisters squabbling. A solitary tear runs down her cheek as she remembers how keen she was to leave all that behind in order to work in the city. And now this.

She realises that her captor is watching her. She can sense the presence in the shadows. The grid is removed and a basket is lowered down to her. The lack of food means that she is not thinking clearly, and she wonders for a moment about grabbing hold of the basket and pulling her tormentor in, but in any event her hunger gets the better of her. As the basket reaches her, she can smell meat and gravy, a rich savoury aroma that makes her feel faint with anticipation. She lifts out a bowl of bollito misto – a stew of fried meats that is a local speciality. Mindful of what her captor said before, she gives a slight smile. 'Thank you.'

She puts her hands piously together and says grace. Once she has finished, she hesitates. Should she eat or wait until she is alone again? Which would be preferred? Throughout her captivity, compliance has become increasingly important. It seems that it might be the only way she is ever going to get out of here.

'Please, eat,' the voice says.

She picks up the spoon that has been thoughtfully provided and does as she is told. She is too hungry to appreciate the flavour or quality of what she is eating, and bolts it down giving no thought at all to her meal. As she eats, though, something does enter her mind. Might she use the spoon to dig her way out? It is only small, so it would take forever – but then perhaps forever is exactly what she has. It isn't as if there is anything else to do. She decides to try to keep hold of it, just in case.

When she has finished, she puts the bowl back into the

basket and watches as it is pulled back up and the grid above is replaced.

'You have atoned,' says her captor. 'Now we can begin.'

A key is thrown down to her and she uses it to undo her shackles.

'What do you mean, I have atoned?' she asks as she rubs her ankle. But she is already alone.

She sits and puzzles over what has just happened. Perhaps the intention is to release her, or to keep her as some kind of slave. At least now that she is no longer shackled, she might be able to escape. If she could win some trust, there might just be a chance. She needs to wait for the guard to slip and then she can get away. And if that doesn't work, there is always her back-up plan. She pulls the spoon from beneath her skirts. Perhaps things are not quite so desperate after all.

She sits back. For a moment or two her eyelids begin to droop and she allows herself to start drifting into sleep. But before she can escape into unconsciousness, she feels herself being lifted from the pit by some kind of hoist. At last she is being liberated. But she is drowsy and her limbs are heavy and useless, so she cannot make a bid for freedom however much she tries in her mind. She is carried over someone's shoulder. She can smell his body – earth and sweat mingling with leather. They reach a garden of some kind. As she is lowered into a chair, she sees candles, food and wine. But there is something else, something so terrifying and strange that at first she cannot make sense of it. When she eventually does, she screams and cannot stop until she is punched so hard that she can no longer open her mouth. She passes out.

Later – she does not know how much time has passed – she wakes, but only just. Her dress is being removed gently by soft, sensual hands. Soon she is naked. She has never felt so defenceless in her life. She wants so much to struggle, but her body refuses to obey her. Now she is being lifted again . . . up and up, higher and higher . . . Someone is touching her softly where no one should without permission as she is held there, suspended in mid-air as if she is floating, helpless. The arms that were holding her let go and she is left to swing. The shock jolts her awake. She is strung up like a carcass – and now the pain, oh such pain, begins.

12

Haunted houses furnish an important factor in the solution of the problem as to the post-mortem activity of the spirits of the departed... Popular legend, and frequently history also, attributes the noises heard and the appearance of spectral forms, often blood stained and fierce, to scenes of violence that happened on the spot many years or many centuries previous.

Lombroso, 1909, pp. 269–81

According to Lombroso, it was not worth beginning any psychical investigation of a place such as the Abbey San Callisto before nightfall.

'The manifestations will not begin until at least midnight,' he stated with confidence as he, James and Ottolenghi sat in a cab making its way to their dining destination. The abbey was situated in the hills above the city, and Lombroso had declared that this was an ideal opportunity for James to taste more of the local cuisine; there was a little place he knew that served some of the best on offer in the region. The little place turned out to be a trattoria run by a cousin of Paolo, a friend of Lombroso's who had a similar establishment in the city. It was indeed small, with plain wooden tables and chairs and murals of rural scenes on the walls. Outside, though, there was a vast covered terrace with a magnificent view of Turin and the Alps beyond.

It was only early April, but the evening was fine and clear, though there were a few clouds gathering in the distance. The air was filled with the smell of woodsmoke and enticing aromas coming from the kitchens. The hills and the rooftops of the city were glowing gently in the light of the setting sun. James felt that he had finally come home. But for all that, he was more than prepared to leave it all behind if only Sofia would go with him. He had spent the afternoon questioning Chiara's workmates, but discovered that Sofia had been right about them having little to say. Chiara had only been there for a few weeks before she went missing, so they scarcely knew her. Apparently she had seemed diligent and rather quiet – mousy had been one description. Other than that, there was nothing of note. No one was surprised at her sudden absence. He was told that it was quite common for servants to move on without giving notice, particularly in the first few weeks of employment.

'What do you know of the history of the abbey, Murray?' Lombroso asked.

'Not a great deal, except what I read in Baldovino's article. It was secularised a century ago, wasn't it?' He felt uncomfortable lying, but he did not want Lombroso to know that he had been out drinking in La Capra in the company of a reporter, particularly Baldovino, whom the professor despised.

'That much is common knowledge, locally at any rate,' Ottolenghi said. 'The question is why.'

'And that is what no one knows,' Lombroso said. 'It happened a long time ago, after all. There have been rumours ever since.'

'What kind of rumours?' James asked.

'Mostly to do with young girls from the town,' Lombroso replied. 'It is said that they were lured to the abbey with promises of employment and then forced to take part in satanic rituals.'

'Really? What kind of rituals?'

'That is where the mystery lies,' Lombroso said. 'Nobody knows the truth except those involved. The Church was not keen to discuss the matter, as you might imagine.'

'So what happened to the monks?' James asked.

'Once the abbey was closed down, they were dispersed to other places throughout the country,' Lombroso replied.

'Or at least that is what the Church would have us believe,' Ottolenghi added.

James reached for his glass and took a gulp of wine. 'And what of the missing girls that Baldovino speaks of in the article, and the body we examined this morning?'

Lombroso pursed his lips. 'I don't see an obvious connection, given the age of the corpse. Besides, Baldovino is hardly a reliable source of information. Look at how he tried to link the missing girls to events that happened a century ago. His only interest is in selling newspapers.'

'But as you know, several girls have disappeared over the last few months. Do you still not think it suspicious?'

Lombroso shrugged. 'And as I said to you, girls of that type run or move away all the time. It is in their nature. I doubt there is anything to be concerned about.'

'That is not what Sofia thinks!' James knew immediately that he had said too much. Ottolenghi seemed surprised, and Lombroso was frowning.

'What has this to do with Sofia?' he said. 'You led me to believe that the attachment between you was severed. If it is not…'

'It was . . . it is,' James said. 'But she told me about her cousin.'

'Yes, yes, I am aware of it, but that young girl is an example of the type I was speaking of – flighty, incapable of loyalty or any form of commitment. All women have characteristics that bring them closer to the level of savages, as you will see when we continue our investigations.'

'But why should she run away? Sofia said that she had a good position with the marchesa.'

'Oh come now, Murray, it is hardly surprising. They run off at the slightest provocation, wherever they are employed. She has most likely gone in pursuit of some man or other. Girls like that have an inferior moral sense.'

'And is that what you told Sofia when she asked for your help?'

There was a long silence. James realised that he had overstepped the mark, though he could not bring himself to regret it. But still he forced himself to adopt a more conciliatory tone. 'Surely you must at least accept the possibility that the body found in the woods might be linked to the girls who have gone missing recently.'

'Perhaps . . . perhaps not. Really, Murray, I wish you would leave these things to the authorities and concentrate on the matters at hand.'

James glared at him. One minute he was part of something, and the next he had been demoted to the role of assistant. Lombroso's inconsistency was absolutely infuriating, not to mention his stubbornness. Fortunately at that point their host arrived with dinner and the tension was broken.

They began with vitello tonnè – sliced veal served cold in a delicious thick sauce with capers, anchovies and cinnamon. This was accompanied by a white wine made from a grape called Arneis. It had a scented, almost flowery perfume, and the flavour of apricots and melons was so wonderful that James almost did not want to swallow. 'This wine is excellent,' he said.

'Of course. One always gets the best in places like these,' Lombroso said, an expression of satisfaction on his face. He held up his glass. 'Let us drink a toast to our investigation, this evening and beyond. To the Devil and the Abbey San Callisto!'

They raised their glasses. James noticed that there was consternation among their fellow diners, who were muttering to each other and staring.

'What's the fuss about?' Lombroso asked the waiter who had come to collect their plates.

The waiter pulled a copy of *The People's Voice* from his pocket. The professor frowned as he read it, then held it up. James squinted at the headline in the fading light: HAUNTED ABBEY MYSTERY: LOMBROSO INVESTIGATES.

'How did Baldovino find out?' Ottolenghi asked.

Lombroso tutted. 'I told him it was for tomorrow's edition!'

James was incredulous. 'You sold the story to Baldovino? I thought you disliked him.'

Lombroso shrugged. 'He has his uses. Besides, people have a right to know what I am doing.'

'You sound just like him,' James said.

'I don't know why people are so upset about our expedition,' Ottolenghi said. 'The abbey's reputation goes back years.'

'*Sì, Dottore*, but we do not like to speak of it in these parts, particularly now,' the waiter said. 'It is because of *le figlie del Diavolo* . . . the Devil's daughters.'

'Interesting,' Lombroso said, stroking his beard. 'Who are they?'

The waiter looked around, as if worried who might hear him. He bent closer and whispered. 'As you know, it is said that a century ago the Devil walked freely among the monks at the abbey, assisted by his handmaidens, girls from San Callisto he had persuaded to serve him. They disappeared when he did.'

'*Le figlie del Diavolo?*' Ottolenghi asked. The waiter nodded.

Lombroso sipped at his wine. 'I remember the stories, certainly. But surely they belong to the past, as the *dottore* said.'

'If only, Professor, if only. But now it is thought that Satan has returned. Apparently he has been seen walking there at night. And that's not all.' He leant in even more closely. 'When he goes back to Hell, he is taking some of our girls with him!'

Lucy shifted uncomfortably in her seat. It was early evening and dinner had come and gone. The house was quiet, as Professor Lombroso and James were off on some expedition and Signora Lombroso was visiting a friend. Miss Trott and Lucy were sitting in the drawing room reading as Gina and Paola played chess. The two girls had very different approaches to the game. Gina was impulsive, hardly waiting a moment before making her decisions, whereas Paola was more thoughtful. Lucy could almost hear her thinking as she worked out every possible strategy and its consequence before finally making her move.

Miss Trott was nodding off. The book on her lap began to slip down and fell to the floor, waking her. She shook herself, presumably trying to regain her composure.

'I think I'll have an early night,' she said, getting to her feet. 'Don't be too late, Lucy dear.'

'I won't, Miss Trott,' Lucy said, watching her as she left the room. How could her companion bear her life? It seemed so very monotonous, and there was little prospect of change. Admittedly, she had travelled to Italy, which must have provided some variety, but now that she was here, all she did was sit and read, with the occasional visit to a gallery or museum. Not that Lucy's own life was so very different. Still, at least she was young and had the prospect of a future. Observing Miss Trott made her all the more determined to one day break free and forge her own destiny, whatever it took.

Paola looked up from her chess game. 'Miss Trott has left her book behind.'

Lucy went over and picked it up, intending to take it up to her. She was about to flick through it to see what it was when she noticed a small piece of paper marking one of the pages. It was folded carefully in two. Surreptitiously she took it out and examined it. The borders were decorated with a depiction of a serpent, the intricate patterns on its back picked out in red, gold and green. Written in a fine copperplate hand in the centre were the words *Serendipity – 156 Via San Pellico, Torino. Apep.*

'What's that?' Gina asked.

'Just a bookmark,' Lucy said. She was tucking the note back between the pages when Miss Trott returned.

'Ah, thank you, dear,' she said, taking the book from Lucy. 'I like to read a little once I've retired. I find it soothing. Good night.'

'Good night,' Lucy said, watching her leave. She followed her to the door to close it and noticed that Miss Trott had paused by the staircase and was flicking through the book.

When she reached the note, she nodded to herself, apparently pleased to find everything as she had left it, and headed up to bed.

For the remainder of the meal James was acutely aware that they were under intense scrutiny. It did not seem to bother either Lombroso or Ottolenghi, who tucked into their food with gusto. More wine came with their main course – agnello al forno, a fine piece of roast lamb with garlic, rosemary and white wine. It was mouthwateringly good: crisp on the outside, juicy and succulent inside. The wine served with it was a Barbaresco, one of the region's finest, according to Lombroso. It was garnet red and smelt enticingly of violets. The grape, Barbera, also formed the base of the grappa that followed, a pungent but strangely soft drink with a faint hint of juniper at its heart, a far cry from the harsh concoction James had drunk in La Capra.

Following a long lecture from Lombroso on the history of psychical research, they made their way to the abbey. It was not far – a walk of no more than about fifteen minutes up a gentle slope through some olive groves. It was chillier now, and a mist had descended, swirling round them. The clouds parted for a second, allowing him to see the thin crescent of a new moon. As they drew nearer, he could make out a large, imposing building with a tall bell tower at one end. He shivered involuntarily. It could just have been the result of the tales he had heard about the place, but then again...

The bags containing what Lombroso proudly called 'our investigatory equipment' had already arrived and were piled up outside the gates waiting for their arrival. A small, wizened figure was leaning against a wall beside them, hunched over, making him look alarmingly like one of the pictures of early man that the professor was so keen to compare to the born criminal. The man, whose name, they were informed, was Beppe, nodded at Lombroso and looked surreptitiously from side to side before opening the tall iron gates. Lombroso strode through them with great purpose as usual, with Beppe following on behind. Ottolenghi looked down at the bags ruefully, shrugged and then picked up half of them, leaving the others to James. He had no idea what they contained. He was used to the various gadgets back in the laboratory – a craniometer to measure skulls and heads, an algometer to gauge pain thresholds and an Anfosso tachianthropometer for arms, legs, feet and so on. But what equipment would be used to hunt for ghosts or the Devil? And perhaps more to the point, why was Lombroso, a criminal anthropologist, now engaged in psychical research? He still had not made his interest entirely clear. James made a mental note to ask him about it later. He imagined that there would be plenty of time. Something told him it was going to be a long night.

13

Criminal women exhibit many levels of intelligence. Some are extremely intelligent, while others are ordinary in this respect. As a rule, however, their minds are alert; this is evidently why, relative to men, they commit few impulsive crimes. Lombroso and Ferrero, 1893, p. 189

'So what could it mean?' Gina said.

After some thought, Lucy had decided to share her find with Gina and Paola. They seemed to have inherited a highly developed thirst for discovery from their father, and when she told them about Miss Trott's note, they were well and truly intrigued. The sisters perched on Lucy's bed while she paced the room restlessly. '156 Via San Pellico, Torino. Obviously that's an address, but I've no idea about Serendipity or Apep.'

'Serendipity means a happy accidental discovery. It comes from the fairy tale "The Three Princes of Serendip". The heroes were always discovering things they weren't looking for,' Paola said.

'How do you know that?' Lucy asked in admiration.

'Oh, I expect she read it somewhere, didn't you, Paola?' Gina said breezily. 'She's always got her nose in a book. The point is, why has Miss Trott written it down . . . it was her handwriting, wasn't it?'

'I think so,' Lucy said. 'And what about Apep?'

Gina shrugged. 'It's not a word I've heard before.'

Lucy wandered over to the window and glanced outside at the street below. Impatiently she tapped her fingers on the pane. 'Then of course there is the fact that all of these things are written down together. That must surely signify something.'

'Well there's only one way to find out for certain,' Paola said. 'We'll have to pay the Via San Pellico a visit.'

'How can we do that?' Gina asked. 'You know Mama would never allow it.'

'We'll have to sneak out,' Lucy said. 'After dark would be best.'

Paola frowned. 'I don't like the sound of that. We might get arrested by the carabinieri.'

'Really? What for?' Lucy asked.

'Girls found out on their own after dark can sometimes be stopped and accused of being ladies of ill repute,' Paola replied.

Gina rolled her eyes. 'Where's your sense of adventure?'

Paola was unconvinced. 'Can you imagine Papa's reaction?'

'Then I suppose we should leave it for now,' Lucy said. 'I'm sure we'll come up with something.'

She went back to the window and breathed on it, using her finger to draw in the condensation. She stood back and examined the result – a series of vertical lines. Then, smiling to herself, she rubbed them out.

As they approached the building, James felt a change of atmosphere. The closer he got to it, the more pronounced it became, to the extent that when they reached the large wooden doors beneath an arched stone cupola at the end of the drive, it was almost overwhelming. Before he had been apprehensive, but that was interlaced with anticipation and excitement at what was to come. Now all he could feel was a kind of heaviness and melancholy. He stood next to Ottolenghi and tried to discern whether he shared these emotions, but his friend's expression was giving nothing away.

Lombroso beckoned to him. 'The smaller of your two bags – could you bring it over, Murray?'

James obeyed, glad to see the back of it. It might have been the smaller of the two, but it was also the heavier by far. Lombroso took it from him and put it on the floor before opening it. It clanked as it landed. James peered over the professor's shoulder, expecting to see a camera or a piece of equipment from the laboratory. Instead the bag contained a jumble of jemmies, crowbars, spanners, screwdrivers and other similar tools, along with some lanterns and a set of strange-looking keys. Beppe picked up a slim jemmy and set about opening the door.

'You're breaking in!' James said.

'*We* are breaking in,' Lombroso corrected him.

'You never mentioned burglary!' James whispered.

'Oh, Murray, really. How else did you think we would gain entry?'

'I assumed that you had got the Church's permission.'

'I did ask for it, naturally. It was denied, exactly as I expected. They are somewhat sensitive about what happened here, which is, I suppose, unsurprising.'

'Did you know about this, Ottolenghi?' James asked.

His friend shrugged. 'No, but like the professor, I am not surprised, given the history of the place.'

'What if we're caught?' James asked, imagining trying to

explain a conviction for breaking and entering to Aunt Agnes. 'Baldovino's article makes our presence only too clear!'

'We won't be caught, as you put it, Murray,' Lombroso said. 'You have nothing to worry about. I will explain everything later. Until then, why don't you just concentrate on watching a man at his work? Beppe here is an expert – extremely skilled, in fact. We met last year in the cells at the carabinieri headquarters. He is a fine example of a born criminal. Just look at his tiny eyes and thick eyebrows! And how about those ears? '

'Sssh!' Beppe said, glaring at them.

'Yes, do be quiet, Murray,' Lombroso said. 'Beppe here needs to concentrate.'

It appeared that the jemmy was not working, so Beppe reached into the bag again and this time picked up the set of what Lombroso informed them were skeleton keys. These were far more effective, and in a moment the doors swung open with a loud and disquieting creak. They were in.

'Thank you, Beppe. I think we can take it from here,' Lombroso said.

Beppe gave a curt nod and held his hand out. Lombroso pressed some coins into it and bowed. James noted that the thief was receiving more courtesy from the professor than he himself ever had. Beppe picked up his bag of equipment and removed two of the lanterns, handing one each to James and Ottolenghi. 'You'll be needing these,' he said gruffly, and with that he shuffled off towards the gates, his night's work completed.

James and Ottolenghi lit the lanterns and followed Lombroso, who was striding ahead of them into the abbey. As they passed the roughly hewn and unpolished doors, James noticed that the locks seemed shiny and new, which was somewhat incongruous given their surroundings. He breathed in and smelt the stench of decay. The melancholy that he had experienced earlier changed to something deeper – a feeling of dread.

He heard what he hoped were Lombroso's solid footsteps to his left and followed them. Stretching before him as far as he could see was a long corridor.

'You go after the professor,' Ottolenghi said. 'I'll try the other way.'

'Are you sure splitting up is the best plan?' James asked.

'I don't frighten easily,' Ottolenghi said, although by the slight tremor in his voice, James thought he was probably trying to persuade himself of the truth of his claim.

'Right, if you say so, but we'll meet back here in one hour. Agreed?'

'Agreed.'

James made his way along the corridor, holding his lantern up to light his way. He had experienced the darkness and strangeness of such a place before. Only a few months ago, he had walked through supposedly haunted tunnels beneath the city, again with Ottolenghi. That was far from pleasant, but this . . . this was a great deal worse. Up to now, he had always been sceptical of all things supernatural, but there was something about this place. Should he be more open-minded? Shadows were everywhere, and the further he went, the more convinced he became that he was being followed. He forced himself to press on. He had to. There was no choice. The professor had come this way. He might be in danger.

That was when he heard the footsteps. They were shadowing his own. Could they just be an echo? He stopped, and so did they, but just for an instant he heard another step. But ghosts don't walk, he reasoned to himself. They float, if they move at all. He wasn't sure about demons. A breeze sprang up and he felt his hair move as if ruffled by an invisible hand. He began to walk faster. The echo of his footsteps started again and he thought he heard heavy breathing in the distance behind him. He had to find the professor before whatever it was found him.

He went on, almost running now. The corridor must be at least a mile long, he thought. The thing behind him seemed to be getting ever closer . . . then he tripped over a loose stone and was left sprawling on the stone floor, helpless as something approached him, something terrible, something deadly. With a surge of adrenalin, he told himself that he refused to die without knowing who or what his nemesis was. He turned over painfully, ready to see the face of his assailant.

14

Today the wicked man looks for a temperate woman and the depraved person seeks virtue. Evil men scout out wicked women to be not wives but only accomplices in crime. Because cruelty in women is becoming a disadvantage and compassion an attraction, women repress their wicked impulses and simulate compassion, as one sees all too frequently today in the hypocrites who behave charitably in order to seduce a man.

Lombroso and Ferrero, 1893, p. 72

Lucy sat in her room and tried to concentrate on her writing. She was finding it difficult to focus on the page before her. Her thoughts kept returning to Miss Trott's note and the strange picture of the serpent that decorated it. As for Francesco, she couldn't even begin to describe how she felt about him. Then there was the question of James and Anna and the mysterious missing husband.

She got up and went to the window. It was dark outside and the lamplight was flickering in the street. She picked up her cloak, which she had flung carelessly over the back of a chair, and left the room. The house was still quiet. She wondered what James was doing on his expedition. He had called it 'making enquiries' when she had asked him. There was no detail, of course, which was typical of him these days. They used to share so much, but now it was as if he had shut her out completely. Or was it perhaps the other way round?

His reaction to their father's death had made her so angry, almost as angry as she had been when he had abandoned her to Aunt Agnes's care without a thought for what she might want. She had hoped that they were close to some kind of a rapprochement since he had agreed to bring her to Turin. But now he was so preoccupied that she might as well not exist. Well, she would show him what happened when he ignored her, whatever the consequences. She made her way downstairs and out through the front door, closing it quietly behind her. So intent was she on getting away from the house that she did not notice the door open again a few seconds later to reveal someone else shadowing her footsteps.

Lucy wrapped her cloak closely around herself as she walked through the dimly lit back streets. The night was chilly and there was moisture in the air, perhaps because of the cover of low cloud that had descended. Or was it mist? Whatever its identity, it enveloped her in a dampness that clung to her skin beneath her clothes. She knew that she was taking a risk by venturing out alone after dark, but it seemed to her to be a risk worth taking. How else could she find out what was at the address that Miss Trott had written down on that piece of paper?

She turned down one of the narrow but fiercely straight streets that criss-crossed the city. There were not many people around. She wasn't sure if that made her feel safer or not, but at least she was experiencing something for herself, something that she could use in her stories. Wasn't that what writers did?

They drew on their own lives and used them in conjunction with their imagination. Now, for once, she would be able to do the same.

When she reached the Via San Pellico, she counted the house numbers – no easy task as many of them were missing – and soon found what she was looking for. It wasn't what she was expecting. Number 156 was a chemist's shop. Lucy peered through the windows. There was not much to see, given the late hour – just a few coloured jars. She had been hoping to find a house with people in it who might be able to shed some light on Miss Trott's interest, but for now it seemed that the mystery was resisting solution. She would have to consult Gina and Paola. Perhaps they would have some ideas about what it meant. She turned quickly. Footsteps! She had company.

'Well, well, well! What do we have here?'

Two men in uniform were standing in the doorway opposite. The one who had spoken was leaning unsteadily on the window. He was tall and skinny. The other, short and squat, had his back to her and was audibly relieving himself.

'What . . . another whore? When will they learn?' he said, shaking himself and doing up the buttons on his fly.

Both men walked over to her. 'Papers . . . You know the drill by now, I'm sure,' the tall one said.

Lucy shook her head, too afraid to speak.

The shorter man tutted. 'Oh dear, oh dear. You know what that means. We'll have to take you in. They'll check you over . . . all over, if you know what I mean . . .' He leered at her. 'All your little nooks and crannies, Bella . . . every single one.'

'I'll look forward to that. I'm sure they'll need witnesses,' his friend said, grinning.

'Come on now, Bella, if we hurry, we can have you all tucked up in your whorehouse before midnight, ready for business.' The short one grabbed her by the arm and propelled her down the street. He stank of stale sweat and garlic.

Lucy struggled. He gave her a slap. '*Puttana!* Do as you're told!'

'Don't you touch her!'

It was Sofia, Professor Lombroso's housekeeper. Lucy remembered Paola referring to her when they were having dinner.

The two men swung round. 'Oh, what's this . . . your madam worried about losing some business!'

'She is no prostitute. She is a respectable young woman!'

'If she was, she wouldn't be wandering the streets on her own looking for business, now would she?' the tall one said.

'Neither would you, come to that,' his friend said. 'Perhaps you'd better come with us as well.'

'I wonder what Inspector Tullio would have to say about this?' Sofia said. 'The two of you bothering respectable young women . . . not to mention drinking on duty.'

'You know the inspector?' said the short one.

'I work for Professor Lombroso, his good friend.' There was a pause as they struggled to take this information in. Both men seemed to grow pale. 'Well now, it was just a misunderstanding,' the tall one said. 'You go on your way, ladies. We never met. There's no need to tell a soul.'

Sofia took Lucy by the hand. 'Be careful now,' said the stocky man.

Sofia glared at them. The two officers bowed and walked quickly away.

'Are you all right?'

Lucy nodded in relief. 'Thank you. I am so glad you saw me.'

'It is just as well that I did. '

'Who were those men?'

'They were policemen . . . members of what is known as the Morals Squad. Their job is to ensure that the city's prostitutes stay in their registered brothels and do as they are told.'

'And bullying girls is part of that?'

'They would call it keeping the streets safe from unregistered whores. From their point of view an unaccompanied woman should not be on the streets at night; if she is, then she must be there for immoral purposes.'

'Gina and Paola did mention it.'

'Well you should have listened to them. What on earth were you doing?'

'It's a long story,' Lucy said.

'Then I think you'd better tell it to me,' Sofia said. 'My rooms are round the corner. We can wait there until everyone has gone to bed. If we go back to the house now, someone might see us.'

They walked together through the deserted streets. How much should Lucy tell Sofia? Was she friend or foe? Perhaps she was about to find out.

Before he could see anything, James felt a piece of cloth being thrown over his head and tightened around his throat. He thrashed around this way and that, pulling desperately on the material in an effort to free himself, but it was hopeless. He could not breathe and was losing consciousness when suddenly the grip around his throat loosened and the cloth was removed. He heard running footsteps, both away and towards him, as he tried to get up.

'What on earth are you doing down there, Murray?' Lombroso peered down at him. James took the professor's helping hand and scrambled to his feet.

'Did you see him?'

'Who?'

'The . . . the thing that attacked me.'

'Thing? What do you mean?'

'Something tried to strangle me.'

'Don't you mean someone?'

'I don't know. Didn't you see anything?'

'All I saw was you rolling around on the floor as I came up behind you.'

'I was following you! How did you get behind me?'

Lombroso tutted. 'The corridor circles the building. I thought I would do a quick tour round, but then I fancied I saw something in one of the rooms. While I was in there, I heard you lumbering past. You are so slow, Murray; it was easy to catch up with you.'

'I do not lumber! Anyway, I thought you were a . . .'

'A what?' Lombroso giggled. 'You thought I was a ghost. Is that it? Or perhaps Beelzebub himself? Really, Murray, that is most amusing. Wait till I tell Ottolenghi.'

What had the professor expected after all that talk of the Devil and girls being dragged into Hell?

'I was definitely attacked.'

'You're imagining it, Murray.'

'No, I'm not. Something . . . someone . . .' He saw Lombroso looking sceptically at him. 'There's something about the atmosphere in this place. Can't you feel it?'

Lombroso shook his head. 'Can't say I do. Have you by any chance been reading Signor Dickens's ghost stories?'

'No, I haven't,' James replied. Had he imagined it after all?

'Good. Science is what we are here for, not old wives' tales or ghost stories. Odd things do happen, but there is always some kind of rational explanation . . . well, almost always.'

'I sensed something, though, almost as soon as we arrived,' James insisted. 'I'm not saying it was supernatural, but I'm sure I saw something . . . or felt it, anyway.'

'Saw what?' Lombroso asked.

James shrugged. 'Shadows, a breeze . . . nothing tangible until I was assaulted.'

'Nothing tangible? Oh really, Murray,' Lombroso said in an exasperated tone. 'What you felt was some kind of reaction of the mind, brought on no doubt by an overactive imagination and imbibing rather too freely of the grappa! We are here to observe real phenomena.'

James was doubtful. Perhaps the professor was right and his mind had been playing tricks on him. It was easy to imagine things in a place like this. Still, it felt real enough. He rubbed his neck gingerly. If he had bruises there tomorrow, Lombroso might believe him.

'Now shall we see if we can find Ottolenghi?' Lombroso said. 'Then perhaps we can do some sensible scientific investigation. Ghosts! Beelzebub! Priceless! There really is no such—'

He was cut off by a blood-curdling scream full of anguish and fear, as if whoever it came from was being horribly tortured.

'What was that?' Lombroso asked.

'I don't know, but I think it came from the centre courtyard.'

'Well what are you waiting for, Murray? You wanted ghosts...'

Together they made their way back to the doors at the front of the building and then started to move forward until they reached a large area with a number of stone pillars and graceful arches. At the centre was a statue of an angel, its hands held together in prayer, its wings outstretched. Standing looking up at it in wonder was Ottolenghi.

'Was that you? Are you all right?' James asked.

'I am, and no, it wasn't me. I was in the graveyard outside when I heard the noise and followed it here. I think it was a fox. But look what I found.'

James and Lombroso followed his glance. The angel that he had been staring at so intently appeared to be weeping.

Before long, Lucy and Sofia arrived in a small piazza. Sofia led the way up a rickety staircase in its corner and opened a door to reveal a small room with a shabby sofa and a table and chair in the corner.

'Would you like some coffee?' she asked.

'Yes please.'

She busied herself at a small sink whilst Lucy sank on to the settee. Suddenly her legs did not seem to be able to hold her.

'I shouldn't have done it,' she said. 'I'm sorry, Sofia.'

'No, you should not... but it's done now and I think you have learnt something, no?'

Lucy smiled. 'Yes, you could say that...' Her smile waned. 'You won't tell James, will you? I don't know what he'd say. Not that he'd care.'

'I won't tell him. Do not worry,' Sofia said. 'But I think you are wrong. He does care... more than you know.'

'Are you sure? He has hardly spoken to me since we arrived.'

'He has other things on his mind.'

'Oh, you mean Anna Tarnovsky.' She had not meant to mention it, but it occurred to her that Sofia might know something.

'Madame Tarnovsky? Why would she be on his mind?'

'Isn't he in love with her?'

Lucy heard Sofia bang the coffee pot down on the table. 'What makes you say that?' Her voice had changed. Her usual husky tones had been replaced by a certain brittleness.

'The way he looks at her, I suppose.'

Lucy watched Sofia carefully. Her movements were stiff and the expression on her face was taut, as if she was restraining her emotions. 'Why did you follow me?' she asked.

Sofia hesitated. 'I did not.'

'Then how did you know where I was?'

'A coincidence, nothing more . . .'

Lucy felt that she was seeing the young woman for the first time. Before tonight she had merely been a figure in the background, but now . . .

Sofia handed her a small cup of coffee before sitting down next to her. Lucy closed her eyes and breathed in its aroma, letting it take her back to her childhood, and the coffee her mother would brew for her father; a comforting sensation of familiarity and security combined with an almost overwhelming sense of loss.

'Sofia, what do you think of my brother?'

There was a long pause. Sofia looked down into her own coffee cup as if she were seeking the answer in its fragrant depths. 'He is a good man.'

'Is he? I sometimes wonder... There are things he has not told me.'

'I do not think you should worry. To me he is someone who tries to do the right thing but sometimes lets his heart get in the way.'

'What makes you say that?'

Sofia blushed. 'I do not know. It is not my business. He is your brother. I do not know him well enough to say.'

The words seemed to tumble out as if she was powerless to stop them; an odd reaction, Lucy thought.

'Now I have a question for you,' Sofia said. 'What were you doing wandering about the streets at night like that?'

Lucy had prepared herself for this question. 'I was researching for a story that I am writing.'

'Oh, a story,' Sofia said, her eyebrows raised. 'How interesting.'

Now it was Lucy's turn to blush. 'I needed some local atmosphere.'

'Of course you did,' Sofia said. 'And I am sure you found plenty... more than enough. So you will not need to search for any further inspiration, will you?'

'Er, no... I suppose not.'

She was tempted to tell Sofia about Miss Trott's note but decided it was too soon. Sofia seemed like an ally, but Lucy could not be sure that she would not tell James, and he would be sure to disapprove.

'Shall we go back to the house?' Sofia asked. 'I think it is time.'

Lucy yawned and nodded. The evening's events were catching up with her, and she suddenly felt tired. The thought of what might have happened were it not for Sofia's timely intervention made her shudder. Still, the discovery of the address might be important, and the latter part of the evening had been interesting. There was plenty of food for thought, more than enough to keep the most persistent of detectives occupied.

15

What we have seen as true in space, among the various peoples scattered over the surface of the globe, we might view also as occurrences in time, inasmuch as belief in the spirits of the dead has never suffered an interruption, from the earliest ages down to our day.

Lombroso, 1909, p. 215

'What is this place?' James asked.

'This was known as the judgement room, where, it is said, those detained by the monks were left to await their fate,' Lombroso replied. He held his hand out and touched the liquid streaming from the statue's eyes, then put his hand to his lips. 'Interesting, it's salty... like tears.'

'What about the scream?' James asked.

'As Ottolenghi suggested, it was probably the cry of a wild animal – a vixen, I would think. We are in the countryside, after all.'

'And the statue? What could cause it to weep?'

'I don't know,' Lombroso replied. 'Perhaps it's some kind of geological phenomenon. Take a sample, Murray, could you? There are some containers in the bags over there.'

James did as he was told and placed the result back in the bag for safe keeping. 'Shall I get out the rest of the equipment?'

'Yes, good idea,' Lombroso said. 'Time to bring science into the equation.'

James and Ottolenghi unpacked the bags and stacked the equipment up against the wall. There were some thermometers, spare lanterns, two cameras and a couple of things that James did not immediately recognise but thought looked familiar. The rest was just for their comfort, it would seem – cushions, a few blankets and enough food and drink to last them several days.

'Isn't that a sphygmograph?' he asked, unravelling a set of wires attached to some small sheets of metal.

'Indeed. I see you are learning, Murray,' Lombroso said. 'And what is it for?'

'Isn't it usually used for measuring emotions through the pulse?'

'Yes, it is.'

'Who are you planning to strap it to, the Devil?'

'Certainly, should he deign to make an appearance,' replied Lombroso, apparently in all seriousness.

'I think the professor means to use one of us as his guinea pig,' Ottolenghi said.

'Ah, I see.' James nodded. 'You want to observe how we react to spending the night in a haunted house.'

Lombroso nodded. 'Correct again.'

'And this?' James asked, holding up another bundle of tangled wires and metal.

'That is my lie-detecting machine . . . or at least that is what I hope it will become once I have completed it. It is a plethysmograph – a fear detector, if you like.'

'What are you going to do with that?' James said. He doubted the Devil would agree to be interviewed, and was feeling somewhat aggrieved that he had carried all this along the drive.

'Oh, nothing much,' Lombroso said airily. 'I just brought it along to tinker with. Now shall we get on?'

James exchanged exasperated glances with Ottolenghi. He was tired and cold – the temperature outside was pleasantly balmy, but inside, the stone walls had created a persistent and all-consuming chill. He had come to Turin to complete his training as a criminal anthropologist, not embark on a new career as a psychical investigator.

'We should definitely investigate the crypt,' Lombroso said, picking up one of the spare lanterns and lighting it. 'Apparently that is where much of the activity has been reported. But first we should take a look upstairs, in the dormitory and the great hall. I understand there were sightings there too.'

To James's surprise, the damp and musty smell that pervaded elsewhere seemed to dissipate as they climbed the broad staircase. It was soon evident that this upstairs area differed considerably from the other rooms. The wooden corridors up here were polished, and there was a distinct aroma of incense coupled with beeswax. The latter reminded James of Lombroso's museum, and by association Sofia. It was where they had first met, and he still recalled his initial impression of her – all damaged beauty and pride.

There were a number of rooms leading off the corridor, and Lombroso tried one or two door handles, but to no avail.

'They are locked, and unfortunately I no longer have the means of entering. Beppe has taken my skeleton keys.'

James grinned at the irony. 'Couldn't we break in by force?' He put his shoulder to the door.

'We cannot afford to do any damage,' Lombroso said. 'Everyone in Turin knows that we are here.'

James shrugged. 'I see your point, Professor. Still, it is odd that the doors are locked, don't you think?' He looked through the small gap between the door and the jamb. He couldn't see a great deal, but there certainly seemed to be furniture, and curtains at the only window in his line of sight, which was odd.

'Perhaps I—'

Again there was a scream, followed by another. It sounded almost human . . . almost, thought James, but not quite.

'That definitely came from the graveyard! Follow me!' Lombroso said, running towards the stairs. 'Let's see if it is a fox.'

By the time they got outside, the noise had subsided, to be replaced by an ominous silence broken only by occasional rustlings in the undergrowth, no doubt made by the fox or perhaps even rats. A dense fog swirled round the gravestones, making the place resemble a scene from one of Lucy's gothic novels.

'Look! Over there!' Ottolenghi held up his lantern.

A light was drifting gently through the mist across the graveyard. It was not particularly bright, and the movement was not steady or in a straight line, but seemed to meander from side to side. Lombroso put his finger to his lips and then beckoned for his assistants to follow him as he moved towards it. It seemed to be heading for the building itself. James tried to think of a rational, scientific explanation for what he was seeing. Was it an insect of some kind – a firefly perhaps? It seemed too big for that. Was someone playing games with them? Plenty of people knew they were here, after all, thanks to Baldovino. The waiter from the trattoria and sundry diners had all heard them discussing the abbey, but there would have been little time for them to organise anything as elaborate as this. So who or what could it be?

They followed the light through the doors and towards a narrow stone staircase. The temperature seemed to drop even further as they did so.

'It's going to the crypt!' Lombroso whispered.

Their lanterns flickered, surrounding them with shadows as they approached the stairs. Then the light they were pursuing went out.

They stood in silence for a while, trying to detect any sound that the source of the light might be making. There was nothing. Then they examined the place where it had disappeared, but could see only solid stone walls.

'We might as well go into the crypt ourselves,' Lombroso said, 'since it was what we had planned.'

'What about the equipment?' James asked.

'Ah yes,' Lombroso said. 'I'm not sure what we will need. Still, better safe than sorry.'

Both James and Ottolenghi refused point blank to haul everything down to the crypt unless it was definitely going to be used. Oddly, Lombroso did not protest, agreeing that they could use their eyes and ears until anything interesting turned up. Between them they collected the necessities – cushions and comestibles. They could at least make themselves comfortable during their vigil.

The crypt seemed to be made up of a series of small rooms. They set up camp in a corner of the first one and decided to set about exploring the rest a little later.

'You said that this was the most haunted part of the abbey,' James said. 'What happened here?'

'This is where the Devil appears,' Lombroso said.

'I thought the gates to Hell were in the Piazza Statuto,' James said.

'Hell is a big place. I daresay it has more than one entrance.'

'Why here, then?'

Lombroso lifted his lantern to his face, giving it a devilish glow. 'This is where Satan was summoned by the monks. It is where the rituals were performed that brought him forth, and where the sacrifices took place. It is said by some to be like a centrifugal force: badness swirls around the sides, culminating in a heart of pure evil.'

James was sceptical. 'And the science in that?'

'Something happened here all those years ago,' Lombroso replied, 'and something is happening now, otherwise there would not be reports of sights and sounds that remind the people who live nearby of the legends and stories.'

'These kinds of stories can leave a scar on places and people. I heard plenty of anecdotal evidence of such effects when I was studying with Oskar Reiner,' Ottolenghi said.

'You haven't told us much about that,' James said. 'What was it like?'

There was a long silence. 'It was . . . instructive. He's a strange man and I learnt some strange things from him.'

'Ah yes, he has an interest in sexual murder, does he not – *Lustmord*,' James said, remembering his discussion with Reiner the previous year.

Ottolenghi was quiet, and James sensed his discomfort. 'Salvatore?'

'I cannot say . . . not yet.' Ottolenghi seemed to sigh as he spoke. 'But what I learnt there . . . has changed me.'

'We can discuss it whenever you are ready,' James said. He was perplexed. It was unlike Ottolenghi to be so reticent.

'There will be time enough for that,' Lombroso said abruptly. 'We should continue our investigation.'

They got to their feet and began to move from room to room. James could not see much, even with his lantern, but that air of malevolence was still in evidence. As he approached the final room, tucked right at the back, the feeling of dread almost overwhelmed him. He felt a draught blow around his head. The lantern flickered and then went out completely, plunging him into darkness. He felt frantically in his pockets for a match. It was difficult – his hands were trembling so much that he could hardly hold anything steadily – but finally he managed to reignite his lantern and held it high. He gasped and stepped back. The lantern swayed precariously, casting strange shadows from the macabre tableau in front of him. Seated only a foot or so away from him, dressed in monks' habits, was a row of bodies, strangely preserved, their heads drooping and their mouths hanging open. They seemed to be screaming.

He heard Lombroso and Ottolenghi come in and stand behind him. They too held up their lanterns, revealing the scene in its gruesome entirety. For it was not just the long-dead monks who were seated in the crypt. Propped up next to them was another body. A young girl, pale and beautiful, her lifeless eyes staring straight at them in a monstrous parody of her other corpse companions. Because unlike them, dressed in their coarse brown monastic robes, she was in virginal white, complete with a bridal veil, a bouquet of fresh spring flowers clasped demurely before her. If the monks were the servants of Satan, then she was his bride.

16

. . . the majority of criminals are anything but atheist, although they have fashioned their own sensual and accommodating religion, which turns the God of peace and justice into a sort of benevolent guardian for criminals.

Lombroso, 1874, p. 70

James and Tullio stood together surveying the scene as Lombroso examined the body. He had insisted that it should be Tullio who was contacted, even though it should by rights have been the carabinieri. The inspector's jurisdiction as an officer of the public security police was supposed to be confined to the city, but presumably, James thought, Lombroso could not bear the prospect of the bombastic and always hostile Marshal Machinetti attending. There was also the small matter of them having broken into the abbey in the first place. At least Tullio could be relied upon to be supportive, whereas Machinetti would only have made capital from Lombroso's wrongdoing. They had roused an irritable San Callisto postmaster from his bed to dispatch a message to the inspector by telegram, thus avoiding any unpleasantness, as Lombroso had described it, or possible arrest and imprisonment for breaking and entering, as Tullio had, on his arrival, preferred to put it instead. James noticed that he had brought a couple of carabinieri officers with him, presumably to placate Machinetti, once he was told about their find.

The professor was examining the young girl's body, lifting her hair and picking up each hand tenderly, almost as if she was one of his own daughters.

'Could it be Sofia's cousin?' Tullio asked James. 'Chiara, isn't it?'

'Didn't she give you a description?'

Tullio was shamefaced. 'We did not get that far, I'm afraid. I assumed that the girl had run away.'

James said nothing. He had thought the same at first, so how could he criticise Tullio?

'We will have to ask her to view the body,' Tullio said.

'I was hoping to spare her that,' James said. 'From what she told me, I don't think it is Chiara. The hair is the wrong colour and her complexion is too pale.'

'But you haven't met the girl?'

'No, I haven't.'

'Then I'm afraid we will need Sofia to see the body to be sure.'

James tried to imagine how Sofia would feel once she discovered that a body had been found. He was impatient to get back to the city. It was important to him to tell her himself rather than for her to hear it from an official, even it was Tullio.

'We have two bodies now. There must be a link with the missing girls, surely?' he asked.

Tullio nodded wearily. 'We have already been through this.'

'But you still don't think it worth investigating? We don't even know where Baldovino got the list.'

'James, if I investigated every case where a girl goes missing, I would do little else.'

'Really? Is the professor right, then? It is that common?'

'Yes, it is. Girls of that class disappear all the time and nearly always under their own steam. Either they find a job or take up with some man, or sometimes they are arrested and end up being sent away or working as prostitutes. We just don't have the resources to look into all these cases. I made some enquiries but I came to a dead end and was told in no uncertain terms to stop.'

'And do you think Chiara has run off?'

'More than likely, yes, but I will look at the list again.'

'Why has the body been left here, and in this pose, with the monks? It must have some significance. Remember last year?'

Tullio rubbed his eyes. 'I see what you are getting at, of course, but the body you saw this morning is at least six months old and the monks have been here for many years. Everyone in the city knows about them, though not many have actually seen them. This girl is very recently deceased and yes, the body is posed, but they are so different that to me they seem like separate murders. This might even be an isolated domestic killing. Leave it to us. I am sure that you and Ottolenghi have more than enough to do.'

Ottolenghi was also watching, his features drawn and his face almost as pale as that of the body. Normally he would be keen to assist the professor instead of staying on the sidelines. Something was on his mind and it clearly had to do with his time in Vienna, but what could it be?

The atmosphere was one of quiet reverence. Even the carabinieri officers, who were usually fairly casual in the face of violent death, were subdued and respectful in the presence of such a young and beautiful vision. The girl's features were refined and delicate. She had long fair hair, almost white, which was simply dressed beneath her veil. Her face was also a ghostly white in colour. James wanted to pick her up and take her away from her grim monastic companions. They, by contrast, sat and sagged, as if weighed down by their own evil, their heads bowed in penitence.

Lombroso strode over. 'Interestingly, this girl and the monks have something in common.'

'What is that?' Tullio asked, drawing closer.

'They have, I think, been exposed to a form of mummification.'

Tullio frowned, perplexed. 'What do you mean?'

'I mean that the monks have been here for at least a century, as we know, and for some reason, probably something to do with their physical environment, some kind of natural mummification has taken place.'

'And the girl? She doesn't look mummified.'

'She has been here for less than a day, I would guess, and . . .' Lombroso hesitated and cleared his throat, as if he was finding it difficult to get the words out. 'This young lady has been almost completely drained of blood. Given the marks on the body, I would say that at least some of her organs have been removed – an action that might well have preceded the mummification process.'

'Like the organs left by the body in the woods?' James asked.

Lombroso nodded. 'A full examination will tell us more, but there are certain similarities. I don't think any embalming fluids have been applied, so unlike the previous girl, there does not seem to be any serious attempt at preservation. It looks to me as if some kind of ritual has been performed . . . possibly satanic.'

'Still think it is an isolated domestic killing now?' James murmured to Tullio.

Tullio did not respond. 'Was she killed here?' he asked Lombroso.

'I doubt it. There are no blood deposits... unless the draining was done very carefully indeed, so as not to spill a drop.'

At Lombroso's words, James noticed that Ottolenghi was frowning. He sat down on the remnants of an old pillar, pulled out a notebook and pencil and started to write. Lombroso and Tullio carried on their conversation, apparently oblivious.

James went over and sat next to him. 'Are you all right?' His usually placid friend was now hunched over and scribbling furiously. 'Salvatore, what is it?'

Ottolenghi's face was pale and concerned. 'I'm not sure,' he said quietly. 'It has a similarity to something I encountered in Vienna.'

'Go on.'

'If Reiner was here, he would say that the draining of blood from a corpse could mean only one thing.'

'You think that whoever killed this girl might have been satisfying their lust for blood?'

Ottolenghi looked over to the body. 'If Reiner is right, then I think we might be looking for a vampire.'

17

Like criminals, prostitutes tend to lie incorrigibly and pointlessly. This habit flows partly from their disreputable position in society and partly from an awareness of the low opinion that others have of them. Moreover, they are all in fact fleeing from something.

Lombroso and Ferrero, 1893, p. 219

James had arranged to meet Sofia that morning in order to retrace Chiara's last journey before she went missing, so there had been no time to discuss Ottolenghi's observations. He had agreed not to mention them to Lombroso until his friend had had an opportunity to examine his notes and do a little more research.

'I know how it sounds – utterly preposterous,' Ottolenghi had said. 'But if you had been in Vienna and heard what I did, then you would understand.'

James wasn't entirely sure that he would, but he respected Ottolenghi and decided to give him the benefit of the doubt.

Sofia was standing in the Piazza Solferino, beneath a statue of a man on horseback. As James drew closer, he remembered something that Ottolenghi had told him about the sculpture. It depicted Fernando Duca di Genova, a prince who had fought during the disastrous first war of independence. The statue showed the exact point in battle when the prince's horse had been killed beneath him. The sculptor, a man named Balzico, had arranged for a horse to be killed just so he could witness its death throes. The sight of Sofia standing at the foot of this homage to human cruelty seemed fitting, given the news he was about to deliver.

She gave a small tight smile. 'You are late. What happened? Did the professor actually meet the Devil?'

James shook his head.

'What is it?' Sofia asked, a note of alarm in her voice.

He took both her hands in his and looked into her eyes. 'We have found a body.'

Sofia gasped and seemed to stumble for a moment. 'Is it her? Is it Chiara?'

James could not bear to see her distress. 'I do not know for sure... It is a young woman, but from what you have told me, I do not think so.'

'How could you know for certain? You have not met her.'

'I don't know, but the girl we found had very fair hair and a pale complexion. You said that Chiara was dark, like you.'

'Hair colour can be changed. You cannot be sure,' she repeated. 'How can I know that it is not her?'

James was silent for a moment. 'There is something else I must tell you,' he said.

Sofia's face, usually such a picture of inner strength, seemed to crumple and tears filled her eyes as he explained about the older body found in the woods, but even though he assured her that it could not be Chiara, she was inconsolable. 'How could you keep this from me? How could you?'

'I... I'm so sorry, Sofia,' James said, stepping towards her.

'No!' she shouted. 'Do not come near me!'

'Please, Sofia, I didn't mean to . . . I just wanted to help. We have so little information. Tullio wants you to look at the body later, then you can be sure.'

Her eyes were so full of contempt that he felt crushed by the weight of it. She held her head up high. 'I want to see it now. I cannot wait.'

'You must, I'm afraid. Tullio is having it . . . her . . . brought back to the city. It will take a few hours.'

Sofia paused. 'Then we should retrace Chiara's steps as we planned. We can do that at least.' Now her voice was devoid of anything resembling emotion. But James knew that beneath the facade was turmoil. All he could do was follow her directions and hope beyond hope that she would find it in her heart to forgive him.

They began to walk in silence along the still-deserted streets. It was almost completely light now as the sun rose over the city, whereas in early March it would have been darker. Although this meant that the atmosphere was different, it also made everything more visible.

'It is so quiet,' Sofia said, shivering beneath her shawl. It was still chilly, despite the promise of summer just around the corner. James longed to put his arm around her to warm her up, but dared not try. It was far too soon for even that level of intimacy. She still seemed slightly unsteady. The possibility, however remote, that the body found in the abbey might be Chiara appeared to be weighing her down. James felt useless. All he wanted was to hold her, support her – do something for her. He felt her rejection as keenly as if she had shouted it to him until his ears bled.

'It is not her, I am sure of it,' he said.

'James! You do not know that, and neither do I. And even

if it isn't her, she is missing and two bodies have been found. We both know what that could mean.'

'Are you still convinced that she did not run away?' James asked.

'Why does everyone always think that? If it were Lucy who had gone missing, you would not even contemplate such a thing.'

'Lucy does not go out unaccompanied.'

Sofia raised her eyebrows. 'Chiara had . . . has no choice. She has to make a living.'

'Of course, I know that. It's just . . .'

'What? Just because she is of a certain class, she is more likely to run off? She must be unreliable because she is a servant?'

'Girls like her go missing all the time,' he said, echoing the words of both Lombroso and Tullio from the night before. 'Perhaps all six have just taken off in search of a better life. One could hardly blame them.'

'Girls like her?' Sofia stopped. Her hands were on her hips and her eyes were flashing dangerously. 'We still have our own characters. Poverty does not strip us of that!'

'I'm sorry. I just want her to be safe. That's all.'

'Chiara, as I have already told you, was frightened of her own shadow. She would be far too timid to run away.' Sofia threw her arms up in an exasperated gesture and began to walk away. 'Clearly your heart is not in this.'

'I said I would help and I will,' James said, going after her. 'I have already planned the next step.'

'And that is?'

He spoke carefully, not wishing to make things between them even worse. 'The first thing is to establish who the dead girl is, which I would think will be Tullio's priority, and see if she is on Baldovino's list.'

'It would be a strange coincidence if she is not,' Sofia said bitterly. 'You said that all the girls are connected in some way to San Callisto.'

'The town, not the abbey.'

'All the same . . .'

'That is why I am planning to find out about the backgrounds of all the girls, visit their families and perhaps talk to their friends. I want to see if they had anything else in common, if there is any kind of pattern. Why have these girls in particular gone missing? Could they all have run away? If they did, then what were they running from or to?'

'What about the body in the woods?'

'No one seems to know anything about it. It is as if it appeared from nowhere.'

'I knew that something was amiss. I felt it before. So many girls . . . and now these bodies.'

There was a long pause, but James did not dare to fill it with words, even though the silence made him afraid.

'I am glad that you are here,' she said, her words almost carried away into the distance by the breeze.

James was relieved. Even if this was all she gave him, it was something.

'So you will start today? There is no time to lose,' she said.

'I can't. I have to go somewhere with the professor.'

'What! You put your work before this?'

'I have no choice. You know that. The professor is insisting that our investigation goes on. At least Tullio is working on the case now too.'

'He is not looking for Chiara,' Sofia said. 'So where is it that you go that is so important?'

James tried to think of a way of telling her that would not sound frivolous and offensive. But he could not. 'We are to go to Madame Giulia's, to do some experiments on the… girls.'

'You can say the word. They are prostitutes, as I used to be.' Sofia's expression was one of disappointment in him. 'I am not ashamed. I had no choice. But perhaps you should be, to speak of conducting experiments as if those girls are subjects in a laboratory.'

'I have a job to do,' James said. 'We are doing some work on female offenders.'

'There are worse crimes than prostitution.'

'I know, but the professor has his reasons.'

Sofia nodded. 'Well he thinks he does… One thing, though, James.'

'What?

'Take care.'

'I'm sure I can manage a few girls, no matter what their profession.'

'No, you don't understand. It's not the girls.'

'Then who?' James asked.

'Just take care, that's all.' Sofia drew closer to him and whispered in his ear. '*Prattica co'buoni, e'sta ben co cattivi.*' Visit the good and keep well with the bad.

'What do you mean?'

'You will know when it matters.' Sofia smiled her half-smile and he felt his heart lift as she beckoned to him. 'Come now. Let us go on with our journey. And, James…'

'What is it?'

'When you talk to the girls' families, I would like to be there.'

He nodded. 'Yes, of course.'

They were just about to turn out of the Via Garibaldi into the Via Po when they heard an odd sound, like a cross between some kind of steam engine and a large cat purring. It seemed to be coming from a heap of rags and papers with an old straw hat balanced on top of it, lying on the steps of a monument.

Sofia frowned. 'That's Pietro.'

'Ah, the old man from La Capra.'

'Yes. He must be sleeping it off from last night.'

'Is it worth speaking to him?'

Sofia gave a dry laugh. 'I doubt he would remember anything from last night, let alone a few months ago. Come on. There is some distance to go yet.'

'It is quite a way. Did Chiara walk there every morning?'

Sofia rolled her eyes at him. 'How did you think she got there . . . by carriage?'

They carried on through the pearly paleness of the early morning. The sun had risen now and the day had begun to warm up. James was struck by the beauty of the river as it shimmered and sparkled in the sun's rays. A few people were around now – mostly costermongers setting up their wares, and maids making their way to their various places of employment.

'It is a pity that Chiara's workmates were not more forthcoming,' James said. 'Did they give you the impression that they liked her?'

'They did not seem to have an opinion one way or another. Why are you asking that? Do you think someone there has harmed her?'

'No . . . at least it doesn't seem likely, though they might know something. We cannot rule it out, though, as a possibility at least.'

'We cannot rule anything out. That is why it is so . . .' A

look of utter despair crossed Sofia's face. She shook herself as if trying to dislodge her doubts.

He put his hand on her arm and for a brief moment she did not push it away. 'We will find her. I promise.'

Sofia moved away from him. 'How can you say that? You do not know if we will find her or not, or even if she is dead or alive. I did not come to you for platitudes.'

'I'm sorry. I was just trying to—'

'There is no point. There won't be until I find her.'

James hesitated. 'Would you like me to come to the mortuary with you to see the body?'

Sofia nodded. '*Sì*.'

'I'm sure that Inspector Tullio will help now that . . .' His voice trailed off as he saw her expression.

'You mean now that others are dead.'

He was struggling for the right words. 'I am sure he will help.'

'He did not seem so keen when I asked him before.'

'What exactly did he say?'

'Just that he was busy. He seemed a little strange. As if . . .'

'As if?'

'As if he did not want to get involved . . . No, it was more than that.'

'How do you mean?'

'I know this sounds odd, but it was almost as if he was frightened.'

That same morning, Lucy was sitting in the drawing room after breakfast with Gina, Paola and their mother, Miss Trott having gone out to run an errand. Ostensibly she was reading a book of moral tales supplied by Aunt Agnes, but she was finding them rather hard going. She would far rather read one of her host's articles. Gina had shown her one of them and they looked fascinating. Her mind wandered to the events of the previous afternoon. She had been flattered by Francesco Rambaudi's attention, but still did not know quite what to make of him. And having found Miss Trott's odd little note, she didn't know quite what to make of her either. Everything was uncertain. It was unsettling in some ways, but in others strangely thrilling.

There was a knock at the door and a maid came in with a note. Taking it, Signora Lombroso glanced at it. 'It is for you, Lucy.'

Gina grinned, her eyes full of mischief. 'Who can it be from? Do you have an admirer already?'

Lucy blushed. 'I don't think so.' She opened the note and read it. 'It is from Signor Francesco Rambaudi. He has asked if I would care to accompany him on a visit to the Museo Egizio later this morning.'

'All those mummies . . . how romantic!' Paola said.

'Don't tease our guest, Paola. It is not polite,' admonished Signora Lombroso.

'Do you think it would all right to go?' Lucy asked. 'I should very much like to see the museum.'

'And Signor Rambaudi too?' Gina asked. 'Did you not say he was handsome?'

'Your brother is not here, otherwise I would suggest asking him,' Signora Lombroso said, glancing disapprovingly at her daughter. 'But it would be an excellent educational opportunity, regardless of your escort. I don't think he would mind.'

'Oh yes, Papa took us there last year. It has some fascinating exhibits,' Paola said.

Lucy thought about the invitation carefully. James could hardly disapprove, given his own interest in Anna Tarnovsky.

She was drawn to Francesco Rambaudi and, to some extent, her initial impressions at the Galleria Sabaudi had not changed. His eyes, the intensity of his conversation when they were talking about art and his sense of humour had all enchanted her. But still, her later observations of him at the marchesa's tea party had made her cautious about allowing herself to fall completely for him. There was something about him that she did not quite trust, perhaps because he was so evidently hiding another personality behind his more public face. She needed to get to know him better before she could make a proper assessment of his character. If it came to it, she would ask Anna for guidance, Miss Trott being far too ancient to have a worthwhile opinion on such matters. But for now, meeting him as an acquaintance would surely be acceptable, particularly if Miss Trott accompanied them, as she had already said she would. In her head Lucy began to draft her reply.

As James approached the city's mortuary for the second time in as many days, it was as if he was noticing it for the first time. Appropriately enough, it was a dark, forbidding place, made even more so by the prospect of what waited inside, this time acutely personal in its nature. Tullio was in the hallway and bowed courteously towards them as they walked in. James studied him carefully. There were some signs of change. They were barely perceptible but were there nonetheless – a few extra lines, a greyness in his pallor, nothing more than that. It was probably just overwork, but the new inner confidence detected by James at Lombroso's dinner seemed to have gone.

'Signorina Esposito, thank you for coming. I know how difficult this must be for you,' Tullio said.

Sofia nodded briefly. 'Inspector, can we get it over with?'

'I understand, but first I must tell you about the procedure . . .'

'I care nothing for procedure. Just take me in, please!'

James touched her lightly on the arm. 'Sofia, listen to the inspector.'

Tullio shook his head. 'It does not matter. Follow me.'

They walked along a panelled corridor. James noticed that it was lined with portraits of portly and self-important men, some dressed in elaborate uniforms. No doubt all were playing their part in the new Italy.

At the end there was a door. Tullio stopped there. 'When we go in, there will be a body under a sheet. The attendant will pull it back for you to see. Then please tell us if it is your cousin, Chiara Esposito.'

Sofia grasped James by the wrist. Her white knuckles were straining through her olive skin. They went in. The body was on a table in the centre, a sheet draped over it. Tullio nodded curtly at the attendant and the sheet was pulled back to reveal the pale face that James had seen at the abbey. She looked even younger than when he had first set eyes on her sitting with her macabre monastic companions. Her fair hair framed her even features, making her appear at peace.

Sofia's grip tightened and then relaxed. 'It is not her . . .' she whispered.

Tullio leant forward.

'It is not Chiara,' Sofia repeated, louder now, the relief in her voice audible. She seemed to grow taller, as if the release from this terrible tension had allowed her to shake off the burden presented by the possibility of Chiara's death. James was struck by her reaction. She must be close to her cousin. No wonder she was so distraught at the prospect of her being dead. She stepped away, gave a brief nod and walked out, leaving the two men staring down at the body before them and pondering the unspoken questions it provided.

If this was not Chiara Esposito, then who was she? And why was the last resting place of this strange pale girl a crypt in a haunted abbey, full of dead monks?

18

... when two women who do not know each other meet even briefly, they look one another over from head to foot; in that glance there is almost an instinctive declaration of war. Lombroso, 1893, p. 66

The Museo Egizio was in the same building as the Galleria Sabauda. The galleria took the upper floors, leaving the museo to occupy the lower ones with its impressive collection of ancient artefacts. Lucy had been vaguely aware of its presence during her last visit, but such was her desire to see the paintings displayed upstairs that she had tucked it into the back of her busy mind for future attention. Once she was there, however, she wondered how she could possibly have walked through the entrance hall and up a flight of stairs without at least asking Miss Trott to make a detour. She stood and looked towards the doors. They had arranged to meet Francesco there at eleven o'clock. It was now a quarter past the hour.

'This is most fascinating,' Miss Trott said as she peered at a sarcophagus heavily decorated with hieroglyphics. 'Come and see, Lucy. It belonged to Butehamon, the royal scribe of the necropolis, it says here. See the depiction of the wig interwoven with flowers – these are lotus buds to signify rebirth and lilies for purity.'

Lucy glanced over and nodded. Miss Trott was doing her best, but she was no substitute for Francesco. Where was he?

'I fear we may have been abandoned, Lucy,' Miss Trott said gently, apparently noticing her increasing agitation.

'It is of no consequence. We should proceed without him.'

Miss Trott frowned. 'I don't know that it would be entirely polite. We are here at his invitation, after all.'

'It is not entirely polite to be so late,' Lucy replied. 'Let us go on. I am sure Signor Rambaudi will be able to find us.'

Miss Trott agreed, and they were examining a large Sphinx that stood in the centre of the room when a voice rang out from the staircase.

'Ah, Miss Lucy Murray and Miss Trott . . . What are you doing down here still?'

Francesco was walking languorously down the large stone staircase. Behind him was Fabia Carignano, the marchesa's niece, a smug expression on her face. She was dressed smartly in a dark blue velvet gown with a small matching hat perched on her carefully arranged hair. Lucy felt positively shabby in her own somewhat dated attire, selected as it was by the distinctly unfashionable Aunt Agnes, whose default colour was grey and who was only persuaded to purchase new clothes when old ones became so threadbare that they could no longer be decently worn.

'I . . . I . . . there must have been . . .' Lucy stuttered, blushing.

'I'm sure I said to meet upstairs at ten o'clock.'

Lucy was confused. He had said eleven, she was sure of it. Could it be that Francesco Rambaudi was playing with her?

'There has been a misunderstanding, signor . . . All down to me, I'm afraid,' Miss Trott said briskly.

'It doesn't matter, though I fear there is not sufficient time for me to show you all I had hoped,' Francesco said.

'It has been truly fascinating. What a shame you have missed so much, Miss Murray,' Fabia said.

At this Lucy recovered her composure. She was not the sort of person to be toyed with like a cat with a bird. 'Another time, perhaps. Good day, Signor Rambaudi, Miss Carignano. Shall we continue, Miss Trott?'

'Wait, Miss Murray. You cannot go without seeing the Book of the Dead at least!' Francesco said. 'Let me show you.'

Lucy paused. It sounded intriguing.

'I am not sure it is suitable . . .' murmured Miss Trott, but she followed nonetheless as the party accompanied Francesco Rambaudi up the stairs again on to the next floor. Strangely enough, Lucy noticed, the smirk had quite disappeared from Fabia's face, leaving behind her usual sour expression.

Francesco led them through the exhibits until they reached what seemed like a dead end. On closer examination, Lucy saw that there was in fact a small door cut into the wall. He knocked and entered, beckoning to them to do likewise. They walked in obediently, like children following a teacher. The room they found themselves in was unexpected in its dimensions, being large, with windows from floor to ceiling on one side. Behind a small desk in the centre sat a dark-skinned man with a neatly trimmed beard wearing a long embroidered coat and a velvet skullcap. A pair of wire-rimmed glasses was perched precariously at the end of his nose and he was writing furiously on what looked like parchment, humming as he did so. It sounded familiar – an aria of some kind, Lucy thought.

'Professor Donati,' began Francesco. The man held up a hand and continued to write.

They stood in silence as he completed his essay. As was her habit, Lucy took the opportunity to observe her surroundings. The three walls without windows held cupboards with glass doors. On the shelves was a selection of curious artefacts. It reminded her a little of Professor Lombroso's house, although there was one marked difference. His artefacts consisted mostly of primitive items such as crudely painted vases, pots and sculptures, with some bones and skulls thrown in for good measure. In Professor Donati's room the items on display were much more refined. There were pieces of parchment with complex hieroglyphics swarming over them like insects. On a shelf behind the professor's head was a carved facsimile of a boat, complete with oarsmen and other figures standing in the prow looking out to sea. At the back were some people seated beneath a canopy. A cluster of painted stones stood on another shelf, but the workmanship was far superior to the basic daubs of Lombroso's collection. Lucy's eye then went to a collection of four stone jars. Each had a different-shaped carving of a head for a lid. One was a monkey, another a wolf-like creature and another a bird. The professor looked up sharply.

'I see you have noticed the canopic vessels of Wahibra. That is very interesting.' He got up from his chair, unlocked the cabinet and beckoned to Lucy.

'Come, child. Don't be afraid.'

She obeyed and approached him. He lifted one of the pots and handed it to her. 'Be careful now. They are priceless.' Lucy took it and somewhat gingerly began to examine it. The lid was in the shape of a man's head. The eyes seemed to stare at her as if trying to penetrate her mind. She swayed slightly and felt the pot slip from her grasp. Professor Donati caught it deftly and put it back in its cupboard.

'I'm sorry . . . I could not help it,' she said. She felt a little unsteady and put a hand to her forehead. In a trice Francesco was at her side with his arm around her shoulders. 'Take care, Miss Lucy Murray,' he whispered into her ear as he led her towards a small settee.

'I do apologise,' Lucy said. 'I do not know what came over me.'

'There is no need, my dear,' Professor Donati said. 'You are sensitive to such things. It is a gift.'

'What do you mean, sir?' Miss Trott asked. 'Sensitive to what?'

'To death and its rituals, madam, that is all.'

'Go on, Professor,' Francesco said.

'The jars were made to hold the organs of Wahibra after his death and mummification. You were holding that of Amset, one of the sons of the deity Horus. His duty was to take care of Wahibra's liver and indeed his soul.'

'He seemed to be doing a good job,' Lucy said.

The professor laughed. 'Indeed. But not all have the capacity to feel it as you have. I wonder, may I try a small experiment?'

Lucy nodded. She could not wait to tell James. He would be beside himself with envy.

The professor bowed and went over to his desk. He opened a drawer and retrieved a key. 'Excuse me one moment. I will return shortly.' He slipped out of the door, leaving them alone to wait. Lucy heard him humming to himself again as he went. The tune was familiar. What was it? Something from an opera; Verdi, she thought. Yes! That was it. *Rigoletto*, 'La donna è mobile' . . . woman is fickle.

'Feeling better?' Fabia said pointedly.

'Thank you for enquiring. I am,' Lucy replied.

'What a surprise!' Fabia said.

''I do not think that I care for your tone,' Lucy said.

'Come, come, ladies. Let us not fall out over such matters,' Miss Trott said. 'We are guests here.'

Fabia scowled. 'And exactly who are you to tell me how to behave?'

Before anyone could reply, the door opened. The professor had returned. He was carrying a wooden tray with a piece of red velvet draped over it. With some ceremony he placed it on his desk and stared down at it, breathing heavily and swaying a little, as if he was entering a trance. Slowly he began to pull back the cloth.

19

Among criminal women, one thing that can be said with certainty is that, like their male counterparts, they are taller than the insane. Yet they are shorter, and, perhaps with the exceptions of prostitutes, lighter than healthy women. Lombroso, 1874, p. 57

James stood uncomfortably in the main reception room at Madame Giulia's and stared into the middle distance. He wanted to be out there investigating Chiara's disappearance. Now that a second body had been found, everything had become more urgent, and he found himself wishing that he was anywhere other than a state-registered brothel in Turin. Lombroso, however, had insisted that they continue with his latest project. He sat in an armchair in the corner and scribbled furiously in a large notebook. Occasionally he would mutter something to himself with varying audibility, so that one caught only the odd word or phrase: 'Large hips, I'll be bound!' or 'Anomalous teeth . . . that's the thing!'

James examined his surroundings. They were deceptive. At first glance they seemed plush, palatial, even regal. But when one looked more closely at the deep red velvet hangings and the gilt cherubs, the paintings and murals of gods and goddesses, a different picture altogether began to emerge. The hangings were threadbare in parts and some of the tassels were missing altogether. The cherubs were chipped and the painted deities decidedly faded. It was all for show – a gaudy backdrop to a sordid reality. Would the girls be the same?

He'd expected to be excited by the prospect of doing some real field research for a change, and to some extent he had been. But as the time had drawn ever nearer, he'd become increasingly discomfited by the thought of examining prostitutes who did not have any real choice about their participation. Lombroso, however, seemed to have no such scruples and was almost rubbing his hands in glee.

A woman came in from a hidden side door. She was pale – not in a natural way, but as if she was wearing some kind of white make-up, like a lady from the court of pre-revolutionary France. She even had a beauty spot. This colouring, or lack of it, was highlighted by her hair, pulled severely back behind her head in an unforgiving coiffure, and her plain dress, both of which were coal black. The overall effect was extraordinary – a sort of combination of prison wardress and Chinese concubine, accentuated by a crimson slash where her mouth was meant to be.

'Ah, the *expert* has arrived. *Buonasera, Professore.*' Her voice was harsh and forbidding.

Lombroso bowed, apparently unaffected. '*Buonasera,* Signora Valeria. It is good of you and Madame Giulia to allow us to visit. Are the ladies ready to receive us?'

Signora Valeria nodded and clapped her hands theatrically. James half expected a roll of drums or a trumpet fanfare. Girls appeared from upstairs – slowly at first, and then faster, tumbling down almost like a waterfall, laughing and chattering. It could have been a girls' school at supper time had it not been for the fact that clothes appeared to be almost optional.

They were all dressed to an extent, but quite a few seemed to be in their underwear.

'Dottore!' Lombroso said sharply above the cacophony. 'Prepare the instruments, please.'

James opened the leather case that he had been given and began to remove the various measuring devices and place them on the table ready for use. At the bottom of the bag was a large ledger, which he put next to the instruments.

Signora Valeria began to organise the girls into a queue, using the back of her hand on their behinds when she felt it necessary. The first girl presented herself to Lombroso, winked at him and then pulled apart her blouse to reveal a pair of small breasts. Lombroso peered at them quizzically for a moment, as if he was working out what to do with them. Then he nodded and clicked his fingers.

'The instrument, please, Murray!'

The girls continued to giggle as James handed Lombroso a pair of calipers, which he used to measure his subject's breasts as well as the width of her thighs, calves and arms. The professor called out some numbers, which James duly noted in the ledger. After her weight and height were noted, she was led over to a table where James had set out the craniograph, a metal contraption with various levers. Here she sat down and placed her chin on a small shelf against a ruler. A thin metal bar was brought down on to the top of her head and the measurement on the ruler was recorded. Then another piece of metal was swung round to obtain the circumference.

The whole process was repeated for each girl, although no more breasts were measured, and before long the page was full. The professor had not made it clear what might be significant about the data, but James was sure that he would draw some conclusions from it one way or another.

As the measuring had proceeded, James had done his best to observe their subjects in what he thought was a reasonably systematic and scientific manner. Could any of them be said to have similar characteristics to the few female criminals he had encountered either in the course of his work as a clerk for Professor Bell, or at the criminal asylum where both he and his father had worked? He thought not. Criminal women, like the girls here, were all different. True, some of the female offenders looked older than their years and sometimes had coarse features and raddled complexions, but surely that was down to the way in which they were forced to live their lives rather than their criminality. Indeed, was it not poverty and the resulting despair that led them to crime, rather than inherited characteristics?

He studied the girls as Lombroso made the final measurements. They were sitting and watching intently, occasionally speaking to their neighbours behind their hands. One of them was a statuesque young black woman, apparently named Cleopatra, to whom Lombroso had paid particular attention, no doubt hoping that he could fit her into his 'savage/primitive' category despite the fact that her features were refined and delicate and her demeanour somewhat regal. She stared back at James, her eyebrows raised as if admonishing him for looking at her. Beside her sat Ada, a petite redhead with the most extraordinary head of corkscrew curls. She shook her head now and then, giving the air of a lion displaying its mane. As he caught her eye, she grinned and pulled faces at him, which made him smile.

Not all of the girls were young. One, Nora, must have been in her late thirties, James thought. She wore a world-weary expression that seemed to indicate that she had seen and experienced it all – and no doubt she had, assuming that most of her adult life had been spent as a prostitute. There was something melancholy about her. She made James think of Sofia, who had been forced to prostitute herself as a young girl when her father had murdered her mother and run away leaving her destitute. Had it not been for Lombroso coming to her rescue, she might still be doing so, just like the women he was studying. What stories would these girls tell when they were interviewed? How had they ended up here?

Lombroso seemed to have finished his measuring. 'Thank you, ladies,' he said, bowing to them. 'Please be assured that you have made a valuable contribution to science today.'

'*Bene!*' said Ada, tossing her red curls. 'I don't suppose our contribution will transform itself into money.'

'Alas, my dear,' Lombroso said. 'I could not afford to pay you what you are worth to the pursuit of knowledge.'

'That's convenient,' noted Nora, with a wry laugh.

'However, I have given a little something to Signora Valeria, who will, I am sure, distribute it later.'

Nora snorted. 'Minus a small fee, no doubt.'

'I would also like to interview some of you ladies in a day or two. And that, of course, will be remunerated.'

Before any of the girls could reply, Signora Valeria walked between them, clapping her hands at them as if they were children.

'The professor will be in touch with Madame Giulia to arrange it,' she said firmly. She moved towards Lombroso and spoke quietly. 'Madame Giulia would be honoured if you would both join her for coffee, Professor.'

They were shown upstairs into an elegant drawing room – a complete contrast to the somewhat shabby foyer. Everything was understated and uncluttered, quite unlike most of the interiors that James had seen in Turin. The room was dark, lit only by a small gas lamp. The heavy brocade curtains were closed so that not even a chink of natural light was visible.

The door opened and a woman walked in. She was as elegant as her surroundings, and quite breathtakingly striking. Her long auburn hair was worn loose in Renaissance style, and her skin was pale, almost translucent – not made up like Valeria's, but a purely natural beauty. In fact James thought that she looked as if she had stepped from a Titian painting. But there was something else, less tangible than her appearance. One could see from the way she carried herself that she possessed the authority and certainty that came only from knowledge of her own power.

'Professor Lombroso . . . I am delighted to meet you again,' she said, holding out her hand. Lombroso took it and kissed it. 'Signora Concetta Panatti. I was expecting Madame Giulia.'

She put her finger to her lips. 'We are one and the same, but I would prefer it if you kept that to yourselves. I have a number of business interests, of which this establishment is just one, but you know all too well how quick people can be to judge.' Her voice was low and seductive. James noticed that she lengthened each 's', so that her words seemed to linger in the air.

'Of course, Signora Panatti, we will respect your confidence.'

She smiled at James. 'I gather this is Dr Murray, your assistant.'

'Signora Panatti,' James said, bowing and taking her hand. It was cool to the touch. She looked him up and down discreetly, as if performing a medical examination. Her eyes were dark brown but flecked with gold, and their effect on James was mesmerising, making him light-headed and quite unable to tear himself away from her glance.

'I am fascinated by your work,' she said. 'You must tell me more.'

Lombroso cleared his throat. 'It is mostly the professor's work,' James said. 'I am just assisting.'

'I am sure he could not do without you,' she said, smiling slowly at him.

'Perhaps in time he will become indispensable,' Lombroso said brusquely. 'But we are not there quite yet.'

'Do sit down, gentlemen,' Signora Panatti said as a maid entered and placed a tray of coffee and pastries on the table.

James watched as she waved the girl away and began to pour coffee from a silver pot. There was something serpentine about her movements, as if she was about to strike.

'Professor, tell me, what is that you are hoping to discover from my girls?'

'I am examining the female offender generally, Signora Panatti.'

'I do not think they would see themselves as criminals, Professor.' The previously seductive tone of her voice had become almost imperceptibly harsher.

'No, perhaps not . . . The thing is . . . you see we're . . . what I mean is . . .' Lombroso stuttered uncharacteristically.

'We provide a service. One for which many gentlemen are grateful. Even the state recognises this. I am surprised that you do not.'

'We are examining your young ladies as a separate entity, Signora Panatti,' James said. 'We do not consider them as criminals but as part of our society . . . a major part, thus deserving of our attention.'

'Oh, I see . . . Now why couldn't you have told me that, Professor?' she said. 'It puts your work in a whole new light. I was about to forbid any further contact with the girls, but now that Signor Murray has explained it all so eloquently, I am minded to agree to your request. Valeria tells me you wish to interview some of them.'

Lombroso gave a wan smile. 'Indeed we do, Signora. I would like to talk to at least four or five of them, more ideally.'

'And what will you be asking them, Signor Murray?' she said.

'I think we will be enquiring about their pathway to their profession,' James said. 'Is that not right, Professor?'

Lombroso nodded. His lips were pursed and his face was a picture of disgruntlement, but James could see that the only way they would get access was if he smoothed things over. 'We would like to use some new equipment that the professor has developed.'

'What kind of equipment?'

'A lie-detecting machine,' Lombroso replied.

'You think they will lie to you? Well, I am not sure I can agree if that is your view, Professor Lombroso.'

The professor looked crestfallen, like a little boy whose toys had been removed.

'That is not our assumption at all, Signora Panatti,' James said in what he hoped was a conciliatory tone. 'We all embroider the truth, though, do we not, from time to time?'

Concetta Panatti smiled. 'I would have to concede that, I suppose.'

'It is merely a way of testing our equipment. Professor Lombroso wishes to use it in years to come, in the investigation of crime. But we need to ensure that it works before we can do that,' James explained.

'Well, Professor, I will agree under those terms. It would be unpatriotic to do otherwise. After all, we all want to see criminals brought to justice.'

'Thank you, Signora. I am most grateful,' Lombroso said.

'Oh do not thank me,' she said. 'You should be thanking Signor Murray for his intervention. He seems to be quite indispensable after all, I'm sure you'll agree.'

Lombroso nodded. 'Indeed so, Signora.'

'Now if you'll excuse me, gentlemen.' Concetta Panatti rose. 'I have some important work to do.'

Lombroso bowed and made his way towards the door. James was about to follow him when Concetta held out her hand and touched him on the shoulder. It was only a light brush, nothing more, but he felt a strange tingling in his body, as if she had a put a spell on him.

'I hope you will visit me to make the arrangements, Mr Murray,' she said softly. 'I would like you to deal with them personally.'

'Of course,' he replied.

'Good,' she said. 'That will be . . .' she moved close to him and he felt her breath on his cheek and smelt her musky perfume, 'enchanting.'

20

Although the female born criminal has intensely erotic tendencies, love is rarely a cause of her crimes. For her love, like hatred, is just another form of insatiable egotism . . . The impulsivity and casualness of these women's passions are extraordinary. When they fall in love, they need to satisfy their desire immediately, even if that means committing a crime. Lombroso and Ferrero, 1893, p. 187

'This is from the Ptolemaic period,' Professor Donati said. 'Around about 330 BC, we think. Lay your hand on it, Miss Murray, if you would be so kind, and tell us what you feel.'

The papyrus was brown with age. There were some intricate borders in black and a drawing beneath. Lucy closed her eyes and touched it as instructed. She gave a sharp intake of breath at the strange sensation.

'I feel a pain here.' She touched her breast.

'Your heart?' Professor Donati asked.

'I suppose so,' she replied. 'I don't see anything.'

'No, but you are *experiencing* it. That is what is significant.'

Lucy opened her eyes. Fabia was watching, her lips pressed flat in a thin white line. Francesco wore an amused smile.

'Would you tell us more about the papyrus, Professor Donati?' Miss Trott asked.

'It is from the Book of the Dead, a compilation of spells and hymns to the gods. They were said to give you power and influence that would help in your journey to the final destination.' He pointed to the picture. 'What you see here is a version of the Netherworld. Here is the goddess Maat watching as the heart belonging to the deceased is weighed. And here is a depiction of Apep.' He indicated an elaborate drawing of a dragon in gold and green, just like the serpent on Miss Trott's bookmark.

Lucy started at the mention of the name. 'Apep?'

'An evil god, an Egyptian demon, if you will,' Professor Donati said.

Surreptitiously Lucy watched Miss Trott. There was no obvious reaction except for a very slight arch of her left eyebrow, which might not necessarily be significant. Could it be no more than a coincidence that the name appeared both here in the Book of the Dead and on the bookmark? Surely not! Mrs Paschal was not keen on coincidence, Lucy seemed to remember, and perhaps she was right.

Professor Donati turned to her. 'The pain you experienced, Miss Murray, tells me that you are sensitive to these artefacts.'

Fabia snorted. 'Or it could just be indigestion. Might you have eaten too much at breakfast, Miss Murray?'

'I'd rather it *was* indigestion,' Lucy replied.

'Why would the heart be weighed?' Miss Trott asked.

'It represents the soul,' replied the professor. 'The heart is supposed to be the seat of intelligence, so this symbolises the Day of Judgement for the deceased. It is then that the decision is made as to whether the dead person has been pure enough to travel to the realm of the gods, or whether they will be condemned to destruction by the monstrous Devourer.'

Miss Trott peered at the papyrus. 'Purity – most fascinating . . .'

'Indeed,' Professor Donati said. 'It is often depicted as a lotus flower or a lily. Internal and external purity was considered to be the highest of virtues.'

'Is it usual to have a reaction like that of Miss Murray?' Francesco asked.

'It is unusual but not unknown. The symbolism is powerful – perhaps so much so that it creates a psychic imprint.'

Francesco nodded. 'But you surely have to be a particular kind of person to experience it . . . is that so?'

'Yes, that is a fair summary.'

Francesco smiled at Lucy. 'A fair summary indeed . . . I suspected that you were a *particular* kind of person as soon as I met you, Miss Murray.'

Lucy blushed. Was he flirting with her? And if he was, why did he arrive here with Fabia Carignano?

'And now I'm afraid I must take my leave of you,' the professor said, covering up the papyrus and carefully replacing it in its box. 'Goodbye, Francesco, it has been good to see you again, and, Miss Murray, a real pleasure to make your acquaintance.'

With that he gave a perfunctory bow and swept from the room, leaving them to make their own way out of the museum into the heat of what was now the early afternoon.

Miss Trott fanned herself with a pamphlet she had picked up. 'My, my, it is very hot, is it not? Shall we find somewhere in the shade to sit and take a cool drink?'

'Unfortunately Francesco and I are otherwise engaged,' Fabia said as she put up her parasol, almost taking Miss Trott's eye out in the process.

Francesco grinned at Lucy. 'We're expected at the

marchesa's . . . May I call on you later, Miss Murray? Since you are a *particular* kind of person, I think I need to get to know you better.'

'By all means, Signor Rambaudi,' she said, smiling at him.

Fabia adopted her usual sullen expression. 'Come along, Francesco, or we shall be late, and you know how my aunt hates that.'

He was about to follow her when he stopped. A small crowd was gathering by a newspaper vendor. 'Wait a moment, Fabia. Something seems to have happened. Let me see.'

He went over to the crowd and, a moment or two later, emerged clutching what appeared to be the lunchtime edition of the local newspaper, *The People's Voice*.

'Whatever does it say?' asked Miss Trott.

Francesco scanned the front page, then gave a strange little smile. 'They've found a young girl's body, in the Abbey San Callisto.'

James had stayed behind at Madame Giulia's to pack up Lombroso's measuring equipment. He was taking apart the craniograph ready to place it in its silk-lined wooden box when he heard a hissing sound.

'Pssst!'

It was one of the girls, Ada with the red curls. She seemed nervous.

'Can I help you?'

She walked up to him and tugged at his arm. He tried to pull away, but she persisted and he realised that she wanted to whisper in his ear but was too small to do so. He bent down closer to her.

'Are you really an expert in crime?' she asked quickly.

'I'm not sure I would call myself an expert, but—'

'Can you find people . . . if they've gone?'

'What do you mean, gone? Who has gone?'

'One of the girls, Agnella. One minute she was here, and the next . . .'

'She works here?'

'Sometimes, but she works in another place as well.'

'What other place?'

'We don't know where it is. We are blindfolded before we're taken there.'

'What happens when you get there?'

'We attend to special clients . . . well, that is to say, they do . . . I have not been chosen yet. Madame Giulia picked Agnella especially on account of her looks. Signora Valeria calls her the angel. Me . . . I'm too ordinary, I suppose, too many freckles, although there is a market for that too.'

'You said special clients?'

'I cannot say more. No one is allowed to speak of the clients or the place or what happens there.'

'What happened with Agnella?'

'She was pleased to be chosen. It meant more money and she was hoping to save enough to buy herself out of here. After the first time she was a little quieter than usual, but that was all. The next time she went was the last time I saw her.'

'How long ago was this?'

'A few weeks.' Ada was crying. James gave her a handkerchief, which seemed to make her cry even more. 'Help me to find her,' she whispered through her tears. 'Please.'

'Is there anything else you can tell me?'

'Just that one of her clients had a nickname.'

She stopped, her eyes widening. The floorboards creaked overhead. Someone was coming.

'Quickly! Tell me,' James said.

Ada leant forward again and whispered in his ear. 'Agnella called him Il Professore.'

'Ada!' Valeria's harsh voice cut through the room. The effect was instantaneous. The girl leapt away from James and scuttled across the floor as Valeria strode towards her, seized her by her hair and pushed her through a door, slamming it behind her as if she was disposing of unwanted detritus.

'Time for you to leave, signor, I believe,' she said. Her lips had formed a single thin red line.

James hesitated for a moment. Was it worth asking her about what Ada had said? He began to make his way out. Valeria stood behind him as if ensuring that he was leaving. Then he felt her hand on his shoulder.

'One moment, signor. Whatever you heard, if I were you, I'd put it from my mind. It is safer that way.'

James frowned for a second and then allowed her to escort him through the back entrance on to the street. He stopped for a moment in an effort to take in what had just happened. Another missing girl . . . when would it end?

Later that afternoon, Lucy sat with Miss Trott in the drawing room, a book on her lap. She was trying to concentrate on its contents, but her attention kept wandering. There was a large grandfather clock in the corner of the room. She listened to its slow, ponderous tick. It was almost four o'clock.

'I'm sure Mr Rambaudi will call as he promised,' Miss Trott said, peering over her glasses. 'What time did he say?'

'He didn't,' Lucy replied. 'He just said that he would come later.'

What did later mean? Her heartbeat quickened at the thought of Francesco Rambaudi. She thought back to his smell – cigars and cologne – and the sensation of his breath on her ear as he whispered into it. She chided herself. The last thing she wanted was to fall in love. Well, not yet anyway. She had other plans. Besides, she had seen what love could do and she wanted no part of it. Her mother had sacrificed everything to be with her father and had been rewarded with a broken heart that had killed her in the end. No, that was not for her. Lucy wanted something different. She wanted a career, like Anna Tarnovsky. She felt a thrill go through her at the notion. Before meeting Anna, it had not even occurred to her that such a thing might be possible, but now it seemed that it might be. Obviously it would not be an easy thing to achieve, but surely James would support her, given his obvious regard for Anna. James and Anna – now that would be a marriage of equals, assuming her husband would release her.

For a moment or two she allowed herself to drift into a fantasy future where she was married to Francesco and he was praising his witty and intelligent writer wife to a crowd of Italian dignitaries. Was it possible to have love and a career? But then even if it was, Fabia was a potential obstacle. She might be sour-faced, but she was also rich and well connected – things that Lucy could not claim to be – and she seemed to have something of an attachment to Francesco already.

The clocked ticked on remorselessly. She tried to read but found herself unable to settle to anything. Perhaps he wouldn't come at all. Maybe he had just been teasing her. He seemed to enjoy doing so, after all. She knew that it should matter, but somehow his disregard for rules and constraints on polite behaviour made him even more attractive.

She heard the sound of the front doorbell ringing and voices in the hall. A wave of excitement surged through her body. He was here! But wasn't that a woman speaking? It didn't sound like Fabia. The voice was light, almost like a small bell chiming. There was a knock at the door and the maid came in bearing a silver tray and a card. Miss Trott took it.

'Signor Rambaudi is here with his sister Bianca. That is a good sign.' She nodded at the maid, who bobbed a desultory curtsey and left, returning a few seconds later to usher in their guests.

Francesco strode over to Miss Trott and bowed deeply. 'Signora, how nice. And, Signorina Lucy, a *particular* pleasure to see you again.' Lucy felt herself blushing reluctantly beneath his gaze.

'Don't tease so, Francesco,' Bianca said. She was still standing by the door, as if uncertain at her welcome. Again Lucy was struck by her plainness in contrast to her brother's striking looks. Dressed in a dowdy dark grey gown devoid of all embellishments, her hair scraped back in a rudimentary coiffure, it was clear that she had no interest in her personal presentation. Her only adornments were the lace trim to her gloves, which she pulled off to reveal stubby fingers and bitten nails, and a red ribbon round her neck, carrying a locket. Lucy wondered idly what it might contain.

'Ah, my dear sister,' Francesco said. 'Where would I be without your advice and guidance? Perhaps you should write it up as a guide to how to behave. Signorina Lucy the writer could help you, I am sure.'

Bianca gave him a thin smile. 'An excellent scheme, if only I had the time, but alas, brother, I am far too busy organising you.'

'Do be seated, signorina, signor,' Miss Trott said, ringing a bell. 'I will organise some tea. I brought some with us, you know. I'm sure you will enjoy it.'

'Tea! So gloriously English!' Francesco said, sitting next to Lucy. 'But you are Scottish, of course. How exotic.'

'I have never heard it called that before,' Lucy said, laughing. 'The weather is not conducive to such excitement. All that rain!'

'I was referring to the evident beauty of its inhabitants, Miss Lucy, not the country itself,' Francesco said. She looked away, unsure how to react to such a level of flattery. He thought she was beautiful!

'Stands Scotland where it did?' Francesco said.

'Alas, poor country,' replied Lucy, relieved that he had chosen a quotation from *Macbeth* she actually remembered. 'Almost afraid to know itself.'

'And are you afraid to know yourself, Miss Lucy?' Francesco asked. Lucy did not know how to reply.

'You are fond of Shakespeare, Signor Rambaudi?' Miss Trott asked.

'Indeed I am – shall I compare thee to a summer's day, Miss Trott?'

Bianca looked over fondly to her brother. 'Francesco has always enjoyed the sonnets. For myself I confess I favour Hamlet rather than Macbeth. He is less treacherous.'

'Quite so,' Miss Trott said. 'Although it is Lady Macbeth who drives her husband towards his crimes.'

'Quite right,' Francesco said. 'Ophelia is a dull stick in comparison to Lady M. I do so admire strength in women.'

'And murder?' Miss Trott asked.

'I believe Professor Lombroso would think Lady Macbeth was not capable of such things, being a mere woman!' Lucy said.

'Now, now, dear. He is not here to defend his views,' Miss Trott said. She turned to Bianca. 'And how is the world of commerce, Signorina Rambaudi? You run your family's rice estate, do you not?'

'That is correct, Miss Trott,' Bianca replied. 'By necessity rather than desire. Our parents are both deceased.'

'Mine too,' Lucy said, noticing that Francesco had paled at the mention of his family. 'It is hard to lose one parent, but two . . .'

'Oh, I am not sorry about my father,' Francesco said. 'He was a drunken old fool. No one will miss him. But my mother . . . now there was a real tour de force. Beauty *and* brains.'

'She was certainly clever,' Bianca said. 'Were it not for her, there would be no estate to run. My father was no help in that regard.'

'Bianca has inherited her business sense, if nothing else,' Francisco said. 'But she left me with some other attributes, though I say it myself.'

'And you do say so, dear brother, do you not?' Bianca said. 'Frequently.'

Lucy tried to imagine James speaking so candidly about their parents but simply couldn't. He viewed such things as a private affair. Perhaps it was an Italian characteristic to be so open. There was certainly something refreshing about it. It was clear that Bianca was far more relaxed here than she had been at the marchesa's, which was interesting. Lucy looked at Miss Trott, who was supervising the tea-pouring, a perplexed expression on her face – probably, Lucy thought, at the size of the tiny coffee cups provided rather than the conversation.

'So tell me, Miss Lucy, what did you think of Professor Donati?' Francesco asked.

'I thought he was fascinating, if rather fanciful,' she replied.

'You have had no visitations from Apep, then?'

'None,' Lucy said laughing. She glanced over again to Miss Trott, who appeared to be finding something very interesting in her teacup. 'But then night has not yet fallen and I imagine as a demon he would prefer the darkness.'

'Who would?' asked a voice from the doorway.

'Professor Lombroso! How nice to see you!' Francesco said.

'Well it is my house, so it can hardly come as a surprise, Signor Rambaudi,' Lombroso said, waving away Miss Trott's offer of tea before sitting down in a large armchair. 'Now who is this demon?'

'He's called Apep,' Lucy said.

'Ah yes. As I recall, he resided in eternal darkness. I believe there is some legend about him attempting to eat the Sun Boat of Ra, which would plunge the whole world into darkness.'

'I did not know you were interested in Egyptology, Professor,' Miss Trott said.

'I am interested in many things, madam.' He peered at her. 'I am sure we have met before, which in itself is interesting, don't you think?'

'I am confident that I would have remembered such an encounter, Professor Lombroso,' Miss Trott said.

They stared at each other for a moment as if neither wanted to relinquish their respective positions. Lombroso was the first to look away, leaving Miss Trott with a triumphant expression on her face.

He cleared his throat. 'Tell me, why has Apep entered the conversation?'

'We were visiting the Museo Egizio with Fran . . . Signor Rambaudi,' Lucy said. 'Professor Donati mentioned Apep when he was showing us the Book of the Dead.'

'Indeed, it was most interesting,' Miss Trott said. 'The

professor appeared to be something of an expert on Egyptian death rituals.'

'Have you been busy measuring criminals?' Francesco asked. 'I hear you are examining criminal women these days. That sounds entertaining.'

Lombroso nodded. 'It has its moments, although I was engaged in a different kind of enterprise not so long ago.'

'Ah yes. Some spiritism, according to *The People's Voice*,' Bianca said.

'Of a kind, yes,' Lombroso said. 'Though we had not bargained on finding a body, naturally.'

Miss Trott shuddered. 'This was the girl found with the monks, was it not? It said so in the newspaper.'

Lombroso tutted. 'Yes, though quite how that wretched reporter got hold of such detail, I do not know.'

'It said something about the corpse being drained of blood,' Bianca said.

'Indeed . . . quite an enterprise. It must have taken some time to produce that effect,' Lombroso said.

'Well let us not go into that, Professor,' Francesco said. 'There are ladies present.'

'It sounds like something out of Ancient Egypt,' Bianca said, ignoring her brother. 'I believe that the death rituals were quite precise.'

Lombroso looked at her thoughtfully. 'There may be something in that, signorina.'

'Well, quite, but perhaps not a teatime conversation, Professor,' Miss Trott said firmly.

'Are you scolding Professor Lombroso, Miss Trott?' Francesco asked.

Miss Trott raised her eyebrows at him but did not reply.

'You have been most helpful, Signorina Rambaudi,' Lombroso said.

'Perhaps you should pay the Museo Egizio and Professor Donati a visit yourself,' Miss Trott suggested.

Lombroso nodded. 'Perhaps I should do just that . . . Now, Miss Trott, I think I would like to try some of your tea after all.'

21

Since the origins of human life, woman has played a particularly important role in protecting the weak: that of mothering… For woman, each sight of weakness revives those tender sentiments aroused by her infant; this makes compassion a descendant of the maternal impulse… If one observes woman in her acts of compassion and charity, one catches a glimpse of the profile of the mother.

Lombroso and Ferrero, 1893, p. 70

The following day, James and Sofia started their journey in a horse and cart driven by an acquaintance of Sofia's. She sat up next to the driver, a straw hat on her back, moving effortlessly with the motion of the vehicle, as if she did it every day. He, on the other hand, was sitting at the rear, being thrown from one side to the other as they rattled along the various tracks and poorly maintained lanes that led to their destination. He let out a loud groan as the cart went over yet another of the many potholes.

She laughed. 'Poor signor, you are not used to such humble transport. What a shame.'

He grinned back at her. 'Very funny, I'm sure. We do have such vehicles in Scotland, you know.'

'*Sì*, and how many times have you ridden in one?' she asked.

'A fair point,' he said. 'Is there much further to go?'

Sofia murmured to the driver, who shook his head and mumbled something back.

'We're not far away,' she informed James. 'Look over there and you'll see. The town is close now.'

Sofia's intensity was palpable and it made him worry for her. Perhaps their investigation would bring them closer to finding out what had happened to her cousin. But surely, with the discovery of the bodies, the end result was less and less likely to be a good one. Chiara had almost certainly not run away. It was possible that she was being held somewhere, although for what purpose he did not know. The white slave trade sprang to mind. He hoped it was not that, although the alternative was even worse. Might they find her body at some point, as they had the others?

His dilemma was this: should he allow Sofia to cling on to some hope that Chiara was still alive, or alert her to the reality? Seeing her bright and eager eyes, he knew that the decision had been taken from him. He could not bring himself to take away that hope. It would be too cruel. He would just have to be ready to comfort her if – or more likely when – the horrible and what he regarded to be almost inevitable truth came out. He loved Sofia. He would do anything for her even if that meant lying to her, or at least embroidering the truth. Indeed he had not yet told her of his encounter with Ada, the girl at Madame Giulia's, in case it turned out to be unconnected.

Sofia was right about the proximity of San Callisto, and soon they pulled up in the town square. There was a tavern on the corner and James looked longingly at it.

Sofia shook her head. 'No time for a drink. We must get on. Our friend will wait here for us.'

'Where's the farm?' he asked as he helped her down. She pointed up the road. A few buildings were grouped on a small hill in the distance.

'Come,' she said. 'Follow me.'

Although it was not far, James soon had to take out a handkerchief and mop his brow. The weather was unseasonably hot and the exertion of walking even such a short distance was taking its toll. Sofia, however, seemed almost completely unaffected, probably because she had spent much of her life in physical toil of one sort or another. She strode ahead of him. Desire surged through him. But it was more than that. His sense of loss was mostly of her friendship, and his memories of their brief relationship the previous year were not just of their lovemaking but their conversations, the meals she had prepared for him with such care and all the other things they had shared. How could he have lost her when they were so clearly meant to be together? What a fool he had been. He hoped they would find some answers here, and then perhaps she might begin to forgive him.

After a while they arrived at the small, rather ramshackle farmhouse and knocked at the door. A short, plump lady answered it. '*Buongiorno.* How can I help you?' Everything about her seemed to be cast downwards, from her arms hanging loosely at her sides to her facial features. It was clear that she was grieving.

'*Buongiorno.* We have come about your daughter, Teresa,' Sofia said.

The effect on the woman was startling. Her ruddy complexion paled until she was ashen-faced, and she swayed as if she might fall. 'Teresa? Have you found her?'

Sofia shook her head. '*No, mi dispiace, signora.* But we would like to help you.'

The woman peered suspiciously at them. 'Why? What is my daughter to you?'

'My cousin is missing from the city. She is the same age as Teresa,' Sofia said. 'She used to live not far from here.'

Without another word, the woman took Sofia's hand and led her round to the back of the farmhouse. James followed in silence. He felt like an intruder. They sat in the shade of an olive tree and sipped gratefully on the cool water Signora Mariani brought for them. While she talked, she stared into the distance, as if she could not bear to look into Sofia's eyes, knowing that she would find the same emptiness within.

At the age of fifteen, they were told, Teresa Mariani had left her rural home, like so many other young women, for the excitement and opportunities of Turin. Life in the communities surrounding the city was not easy. There were few local opportunities other than working in the rice fields, which was backbreaking and poorly paid. Teresa had tried that but had found the work too hard. She had hoped that going further afield would allow her not only to make a future for herself but also to send some money back to her family.

'She did not want to go,' her mother told them. 'But she felt there was no other option and we encouraged her . . . God forgive us.' Her voice, which had been flat and emotionless, began to break with the strain of her loss. Sofia put her hand out and touched Signora Mariani's arm. She took it and clutched at it, as though by letting go of it she might lose her precious daughter all over again.

That simple gesture of support moved James unbearably. To see Sofia reach out so selflessly underlined to him how much he stood to lose if she did not take him back. He knew it was selfish given the tangible misery of the two women, but he could not stop himself. In any event, it made him even more determined to help them both.

'Tell us a little more about your daughter, signora,' he said gently. 'What does she look like?'

The woman paused, perhaps wondering if she could trust him.

'It is all right,' Sofia said. 'This man is my friend. He will help us. You can speak freely.'

Signora Mariani nodded. 'She is small and dark, like me. Such a pretty girl! Everyone said so!'

James and Sofia exchanged glances of relief. The description did not fit the girl who had been found in the Abbey San Callisto, and like Chiara, Teresa had disappeared too recently to be the body found in the nearby woods. At least they would not have to break that news to Signora Mariani.

She continued. 'Teresa was a good girl in many ways, but . . . she had her flaws.'

'Ah well, we all do at that age,' Sofia said. 'My cousin Chiara is no different.'

'What were Teresa's flaws, if you don't mind me asking?' James said.

'It . . . it seems wrong to speak of her this way,' Signora Mariani said.

Sofia patted her hand. 'I know, but it might help.'

'She was . . . well I suppose you might call her flighty. She liked the company of young men and did not hide it. It caused her father and me some concern.'

James felt himself lean forward. 'Was there anyone in particular?'

Signora Mariani nodded slowly. 'There was someone, I think, but he was not suitable . . .'

'Could she have run away with him?' James asked.

She did not reply for a second or two. 'No, she was running away *from* him, if anything.'

'What do you mean?' Sofia asked.

'She changed.'

James was going to interject, but Sofia gave him an angry look and he realised that she was in control. This was more her world than his. 'In what way?' she asked.

'She used to always be happy – or at least that was the impression she gave. And then . . .'

There was another pause. Her eyes were dull with despair.

'And then?' Sofia said gently.

'It is as I said. She changed almost overnight . . . became subdued. Before, she would always chatter . . . we used to joke about it. And then all of a sudden she stopped talking to me.'

Tears began to fall slowly from Signora Mariani's eyes.

'She abandoned her friends and would not leave the house unless she had to. I asked her many times what was wrong, but she would not tell me. At first I thought she had quarrelled with her man friend and that she would soon recover. But it went on for months.' She paused and tried to wipe away her tears with her hand. James gave her his handkerchief and she held it to her face for a moment, as if she was hiding behind it. 'We were at our wits' end. Then my sister suggested that she leave the town and take up a post in the city as her daughter had done. She said she could arrange it and Teresa leapt at the chance. It was as if she was back to her old self.'

'Then what happened?'

'Teresa would not come back here, so I would visit her from time to time to make sure she was all right. Then one day I went to see her and she was not there. The woman whose house she lodged in said that she had gone to work and had not come home.'

'This is exactly as it was with Chiara,' Sofia said to James. 'Did you make any other enquiries, Signora Mariani?'

'*Sì*, I asked at her workplace, but they did not seem to know anything.'

'What about the police?' James asked.

The woman frowned at him. 'The carabinieri were not interested. They said that she had probably found a better position, or run off with someone.'

'Where did she work?'

Signora Mariani did not answer immediately. 'She was a maid at Madame Giulia's.' She paused. 'I assume you know of the establishment.'

Sofia nodded. James leant forward again. A second girl missing from Madame Giulia's . . .

Signora Mariani continued. 'It was not what we wanted for her, but she was so eager to leave the town.'

'We are not here to judge you or your family,' Sofia said quietly.

'But it would help to know as much as you can tell us. Do you know who the man was . . . the one she was running away from?' James asked.

He looked carefully at the woman, Professor Bell's words in his mind: 'Observe, Mr Murray, observe and learn.' He noticed that her hands were now clasped in her lap, curling tightly into fists so that her knuckles were ivory pale, just like Sofia's when she was waiting for the body to be revealed at the mortuary.

'We cannot help you if you are not willing to help us,' he said.

Her eyes filled with despair. 'I cannot... I cannot... I have said too much.'

James and Sofia exchanged glances, then Sofia took the woman's hands in hers. 'Please, signora, I beg you to tell us what you know. It might help us to find Teresa, and perhaps my cousin too.'

The woman hesitated for what seemed like an eternity. When she eventually spoke, she made her position clear. 'No... there is nothing more I can tell you.' She stood up. 'You must go now. I have chores to do.'

'You know that Teresa and Chiara are not the only girls to have gone missing,' James said. 'Another girl has disappeared from Madame Giulia's place. Not only that, but bodies have been found near here – one in the crypt of the Abbey San Callisto, as well as another female who would have disappeared some time before Teresa.'

Sofia frowned at him. They had agreed not to say anything about Baldovino's findings or the bodies in case they were not connected. Sofia had said that it would be too cruel. But since it was clear that neither of the bodies belonged to Teresa Mariani, James felt it important to at least mention their existence. At first he thought that Signora Mariani was puzzled rather than horrified. Her eyes were blinking rapidly and her posture had changed. Now rather than drooping she seemed upright, tense, as if there was something she was trying to hide.

'Go now, please,' she said. Her tone was harsher, and as before, she would not look either James or Sofia in the eye.

'Before we leave, one more question,' James said, pulling Baldovino's list from his pocket and handing it to Signora Mariani. 'Do you know any of these names?'

'No,' she replied, pushing it back to him. She had barely glanced at it.

She began to chivvy them out. Clearly she could not wait to be rid of them. They heard the door slam as she went back into the house, leaving them to walk back to town in silence, each pondering what they had heard. One thing was clear. Signora Mariani was not just distraught at the disappearance of her daughter. She was afraid.

22

While the woman whom passion leads to crime is very different from the born criminal, who violates the laws of chastity from lust and love of idle pleasure, nonetheless such good, passionate women are fatally inclined to love bad men. Lombroso and Ferrero, 1893, p. 203

James and Sofia sat in silence at a table tucked away in a corner of the local trattoria. The afternoon had not been an easy one, and there were several loose ends that needed to be tied up before they could go back to the city. They had already tried to find the family of Arianna Panico, another girl on the list. But when they had got to the address that Baldovino had given, the occupant, a somewhat dishevelled old man, had denied any knowledge of the girl or her family, telling them that he had lived there for the last ten years and that he thought the previous residents had moved to the city. After that they had decided to stay the night and continue their investigations in the morning.

They both agreed that Signora Mariani was keeping something from them. As well as that, there were now two missing girls who worked at Madame Giulia's, although as Sofia had said when he told her Ada's story, it was possible that her friend had merely managed to escape from her life as a prostitute. Teresa, on the other hand, was a maid, and free to walk out whenever she chose.

And then there was the dead girl at the abbey. Why had she been left there of all places? Something about it was bothering him, and it wasn't just the possibility of a ghostly presence or two, or even the Devil walking about the graveyard. It required further investigation and he decided to make a return visit before they left. He didn't like to bring up a potential link between the dead girl and Chiara, even as a faint possibility, but he knew that if it was in his mind, then it was almost certainly in Sofia's. The strain was clearly telling on her. Her hands were clasped before her and her eyes flitted uncomfortably around the room as if she was unable to settle on anything for more than a few seconds.

There was a bar at the other end of the establishment. Several swarthy-looking men leant up against it, drinking beer. James recognised one of them, a small, wrinkled figure hunched over his tankard. It was Beppe, the burglar who had broken into the abbey for Lombroso. He raised his hand in a mock salute, then smirked and whispered into the ear of his companion, who grinned insolently at James. He considered pointing them out to Sofia but thought better of it. The less attention they got, the better.

The waiter came in with a jug of wine and two bowlfuls of some kind of stew. James had let Sofia order for him, partly because it was simpler given her grasp of the local dialect as opposed to his own ignorance, and partly in an attempt to take her mind off things.

'This looks good,' he said. 'What is it?'

'Try it first.'

He hesitated and examined it more closely. There didn't seem to be anything obviously untoward about it, but Sofia had a mischievous glint in her eye, as if she was playing with him. His diversionary tactic seemed to be working.

She shook her head and laughed. 'It is just a stew . . . a kind of bollito misto. You have had something similar before, I am sure.'

He took a forkful and ate it. It was tender and fragrant; he thought he could detect some rosemary and a hint of garlic. 'It's delicious. Now tell me what it is.'

Sofia grinned at him. 'Not until you have finished.'

James did her bidding and ate heartily. It had been a long day and he was starving, so it was not long before he had cleared his plate. Sofia had left most of hers.

'Not hungry?' he asked.

She pushed her plate away. 'No, my mind is too busy. Did you enjoy it?'

'It was very good. Now tell me what it was.'

'It is oriòn. It means large ears.'

James peered down at his plate. 'Really? Is that what I was eating?'

'Yes and no. You were eating pig's head meat cooked slowly with anchovies, onion, garlic, parsley and rosemary.'

'Including the ears?'

'Of course. We do not like to waste anything here.'

James lifted up his glass. 'Oriòn, I salute you.'

Sofia held her glass up to his. It was the closest they had been since his return to Turin. A warmth spread through him, the kind that he had not experienced for what seemed like an eternity. Might she feel the same? He thought he could see a softening in her eyes.

'James, I . . .' she began.

He reached out to her and took her hand. She left it there for a moment.

'Can I get you anything more?' a waiter asked.

'*No, grazie*,' Sofia said, pulling her hand away quickly. There was a tense silence as their plates were cleared away. 'What should we begin with tomorrow?' she asked.

'We need to find out why Teresa left,' James said. 'It may not be relevant, but...'

Sofia nodded. 'It would be a start. We should talk to her friends here. It is a small place. Someone must know something.' She thought for a moment. 'And then perhaps we should make some enquiries at her place of work. You could do that, couldn't you?'

'Perhaps it would be better if you spoke to the girls,' he said, remembering his encounter with Concetta Panatti.

'Of course,' Sofia said sarcastically. 'One whore to another.'

'That is not what I meant.'

'Did you meet Madame Giulia when you were there?' she asked.

'Yes,' James said, trying not to catch her eye. 'She is an interesting woman.'

'That is one way of putting it. Dangerous is another.'

'Really? She did not seem so to me. In fact I thought her rather charming.'

Sofia's cheeks flushed and she muttered something under her breath.

'What was that?'

'Nothing... Just... she is not what she seems.' Sofia got up from the table abruptly. 'I am tired. I must go to my bed. *Buonanotte*, James.'

He watched her retreating form and for a moment considered following her, but decided against it. He wanted to win her back, but it would take time. He just had to learn to be patient.

*

The next morning James sat in the town square and listened to the small fountain playing softly as he waited for Sofia. She was making some discreet enquiries at the guest house where they had stayed the previous night. Apparently Teresa Mariani had worked there briefly before she went missing. He had asked around but no one had heard of Arianna Panico, so it seemed the old man had been telling the truth.

Sofia was beckoning to him from across the street, her dark hair shining in the sunlight. Next to her stood a tall, thin girl with mousy hair. She was slightly hunched over, as if she was trying to deny her height. He waved in acknowledgement and went over to them.

'*Buongiorno*,' the girl said.

'This is Giovanna,' Sofia said. 'She worked with Teresa. Tell *il signore* what you told me.'

The girl looked around her at the deserted square and lowered her voice till it was barely above a whisper. 'There is not much to tell, but Teresa certainly changed as you suggested.'

'How?' James asked.

'She used to be someone you could laugh with. You need that in a place like this, I can tell you.'

'What do you mean?'

'Secrets . . . the town is full of them. Secrets and lies.'

'What kind of secrets?' James asked.

Giovanna wrapped her arms around herself. He noticed that she kept blinking, as if someone was shining a light in her eyes. 'I'll tell you about Teresa, but that's all.'

Sofia put her hand on the girl's shoulder. 'It is important that you tell us everything you know.'

Giovanna hesitated.

'Go on,' Sofia said.

'Teresa was involved with someone.'

'Who?'

'A boy from the rice estate over to the west of the town, beyond the woods. I don't know his name but I know where they used to meet.'

'Where?'

'At the abbey.'

'Tell the gentleman what happened,' Sofia said. 'As you told me . . .'

'It was last year, about October. Teresa told me that she had met her friend at the abbey and that something had happened. But she could not tell me what. All I know is that it frightened her, and it was then that she began to change. She became withdrawn. I couldn't get so much as a smile out of her after that. Not long afterwards, she went to work in the city.'

'What about the boy?' James asked.

Giovanna shrugged her shoulders. 'Teresa said that he disappeared.'

'But there is more, is there not, Giovanna?' Sofia said, holding on to the girl's hands.

Giovanna whispered something in Sofia's ear before pulling away from her and walking off.

'What did she say?' James asked.

'Il Diavolo . . .' Sofia said. 'According to Giovanna, he is the talk of San Callisto. It is said that he has returned to the abbey.'

'And what does he want?'

'Fresh young blood . . . To be exact, fresh young female blood, because apparently Hell is running dry.'

*

James and Sofia decided to make their way up to the abbey. As they walked through the countryside, they discussed what they had discovered in the hope that together they would reach some kind of conclusion.

'Everything seems to lead here,' James said. 'Teresa and her young man meet here, see something and both disappear. Then we find a body. All the girls are connected to the place. It can't be a coincidence.'

'*Sì*, but what has happened to them?' Sofia asked. 'Do you think it was the rumours about Il Diavolo that made the professor decide to conduct his psychical experiment at the abbey?'

'It would probably tempt him, but the place is well known for satanic rituals, isn't it?'

'Perhaps *too* well known. The professor likes to be different. You know that. For him to go to a place like the abbey for an investigation . . . I think there has to be something more to it.'

James thought back to the dinner where the matter of the experiment had first been raised. 'It was Father Vincenzo who brought up the investigation, though he didn't mention the abbey specifically.'

'But didn't you say that the Church refused permission?'

'Yes, that's right. The abbey still belongs to them. That is why we had to break in.'

'I don't care if Il Diavolo does walk there. I know that Chiara is alive. I can feel it, and if I have to pay Beelzebub a visit to find her, then that is what I shall do,' Sofia said defiantly, crossing herself.

'I still think you should have left this to me. Two girls are already dead. I don't want you to put yourself at risk. '

Sofia stopped. 'No, James. We are in this together.' They stood facing each other in silence. The only sound was the wind whispering in the trees. The colours of the sky and the sunlight filtered through the green canopy and seemed brighter than before. Sofia reached up and tenderly brushed his hair out of his eyes. He took her hand and held it for a moment, looking into her beautiful dark eyes, seeing all the misery and suffering that lay behind them. She leant forward and gently touched his lips with hers. Then suddenly she pulled away from him.

'What is it? What's the matter?' he asked.

'I cannot, James,' she said. 'I am sorry. We can be friends, but that is all.'

'I will wait for you until you are ready.'

'You must not.'

'I will,' he said quietly so she could not hear. 'You know that I will.'

She had already begun to walk through the woods again. He followed her, a new spring in his step. He had thought he had lost her, but that kiss meant that she must still have feelings for him, no matter what she had said. It seemed there was hope after all, and that was all he needed.

The sun went behind a cloud, plunging them into darkness. Sofia held her hand out to him. 'Let's walk together. I feel stronger when you are with me.' He took it and immediately felt reinvigorated, as if their combined will could achieve anything.

Before long the trees began to thin out and the path widened. The outline of the abbey rose in the distance, casting a sinister shadow over them. 'There's something about that place,' James said.

'What? It is just a building like any other.'

'No, I can't accept that. I don't know what happened here,

but whatever it was has left an imprint of some kind, I am sure of it.'

'You have been listening to the professor too much,' Sofia said, laughing. 'He too has an overactive imagination.'

But it seemed to James that her laugh was forced, as if she did not really believe in what she was saying. As they walked out of the woods and further into the shadow of the abbey, he sensed her foreboding. He almost suggested that they turn back, but something made him go on until he could not have stopped even if he had wanted to. Whatever it was drew him in until he could no longer resist its pull. He felt as if he was caught in a dangerous current from which there was no escape.

When they reached the gates, he recalled that they had no means of getting into the place. Last time he had been here, Beppe, the wizened burglar he had seen only the night before, had broken in for them. Perhaps he should have asked him to pay another visit.

'What do we do now?' he asked.

Sofia raised her eyebrows. 'You are forgetting my criminal past,' she said, pulling a pin out of her hair and inserting it deftly into the lock. In a moment the gates opened and they were inside. Together they walked up the wide path towards the entrance. The graveyard was at the side, its stones rising eerily out of a mist that had suddenly descended. The sky was full of clouds now, and the day seemed to have been absorbed into a strange half-light, even though it was still morning.

As they drew closer to the building, it was clear that gaining entry was not to be a problem. The large wooden doors were already open.

23

To kill in a bestial rage requires no more than the mind of the Hottentot; but to plot out a poisoning requires ability and sharpness. The crimes of a woman are almost always deliberate. Lombroso and Ferrero, 1893, p. 189

The morning was sunny and warm, though there were a few clouds on the horizon. Paola and Gina were taking Lucy to see the museum at the university in the Via Po. As ever, they were accompanied by Miss Trott, who declared herself to be fascinated at the prospect of finding out how the professor's mind worked. Paola had laughed and said there were many who would be interested in that prospect.

When they arrived, Lucy did not know what to make of it. She had been prepared for the experience up to a point. James had already told her tales of his previous trip to Turin. And of course there were quite a few of the professor's artefacts lying around at his house. But the full effect of the exhibits at the museum was another thing again.

'This is Papa's head collection,' Gina announced proudly as they walked into the first room. On one side was a wall of shelves full of skulls of all shapes and sizes.

'Oh my word!' Miss Trott said, fanning herself with a handkerchief she was clutching. 'Who do these belong to?'

Gina cleared her throat as if she was about to give a recitation. 'There are Alexandrian murderers, Sardinian epileptics, barbarians from Abyssinia, and see up there . . . that is a portrait of a criminal with the flared nostrils, pronounced jaw and cavernous eyes typical of the Mexican and/or Spanish brigand.'

The man in the picture had a large bushy moustache, waxed at the ends. His eyes were dead, as if all the fight had left him. He just looked sad, Lucy thought, not fierce at all.

'Over here are the manacles and chains from various prisons used to restrain the violent criminal, usually habitual. And in this case are daggers and other weapons taken from members of the Camorra.'

'The Camorra?' Lucy asked.

'A group of criminals who work together to do bad things,' Paola replied.

'Let's go to the next room,' Gina said, taking Lucy by the hand and pulling her towards the door. 'There is so much more to see!'

'Wait a moment, Miss Lombroso,' Miss Trott said. 'I just want to take it all in. What made your father begin such a collection?'

Gina looked at her. 'He always tells the story of the skull whenever anyone asks that question.'

'Oh not the skull . . .' Paola said, groaning. 'I have heard it so many times.'

'Do tell us, Gina,' Lucy said, sensing her disappointment.

'He was examining the skull of a brigand from Sicily, a ruthless killer, a dedicated criminal who had been executed recently. He looked closely at the bones that lay in his hands and realised something that changed his ideas about everything he had studied.'

'Ah yes, how does he put it?' Paola said. 'He holds out the imaginary skull.' She mimed his actions. 'And then he says, "I suddenly saw, like a broad plain on a fiery horizon . . ."'

Paola joined in with her sister, intoning their father's words as though they were sacred. '". . . the solution to the problem of the nature of the criminal, who reproduces in our times the characters of primitive man and even those of carnivorous animals."'

Lucy was amused and a little envious. She used to have a father who made her proud, just like the Lombroso sisters. But now that had been wrenched away from her and all she had left was the faintest of memories of his kindness and affection, overtaken by the vision of his funeral and the mourners staring at them and whispering. She felt a tear make its way slowly down her cheek and brushed at it angrily. Miss Trott came over and offered her handkerchief, but she waved it away.

'So, Miss Gina, take us to the next room, if you would,' Miss Trott said firmly.

Gina nodded and took Lucy by the hand again, this time more gently, leading her away with Paola and Miss Trott bringing up the rear.

The room they entered was similar to the first, except that the skulls were replaced by glass cases filled with alarmingly lifelike heads laid on silk, like the interior of a coffin.

'These are Father's death heads,' Gina said.

'Death masks,' corrected Paola.

'Yes, yes, she is right,' Gina said. 'Once a criminal has been executed, they use their faces to make masks by moulding plaster to them.'

Lucy watched as Miss Trott wandered about the room peering at the men's faces. They even had hair, and eyes that stared up from their cushions like those of decapitated dummies, except, of course, that these were real features. This was what criminals actually looked like. She supposed that her own father had been some kind of criminal. He had been locked away, although she had yet to find out why. But he had not been like this. His eyes were kind and gentle, not staring and full of hatred like these poor excuses for men.

'I think some of them died in prison,' Paola said.

'Prison or the gallows, it doesn't matter,' Gina said. 'They were all born criminals anyhow.'

Paola looked at her sister, her head on one side. 'Well, not *all* born. Even Papa concedes that some have been made bad by their lives.'

'This is all fascinating,' Miss Trott said, waving her handkerchief in front of her face. 'Ooof, it is getting quite warm, is it not? I wonder... would you mind if I stepped out for a moment or two? I should like to get a little fresh air.'

'Of course,' Paola said. 'We can look after Lucy.'

'Yes,' Gina said, grinning. 'We haven't shown you the skeleton corridor yet!'

'I will forgo that pleasure, if you don't mind,' Miss Trott said. 'You can describe it to me later, Lucy, in both Italian and English. It will make an excellent exercise.'

She made her way out of the building, leaving the Lombroso sisters and Lucy to complete the tour. The skeleton corridor proved to be exactly as it sounded, with the bones standing to attention like an army unit. Anywhere else this would seem very odd, Lucy thought. But here it was as natural as the dinosaur exhibits in London's Natural History Museum.

A short while later they decided to go outside to join Miss Trott. After all, as Gina said, Lucy had all the time in the world to see the rest of the museum. As they wandered down the steps, Lucy looked around for her companion. At first she couldn't spot her, but then there she was, sitting in a café on the other side of the street, a glass of iced water before her. She was not alone. Seated opposite her, talking animatedly and waving his arms around, was Professor Donati. He was shouting, though she could not tell what he was saying. He threw some papers at Miss Trott, knocking over her drink, then stood and stalked off down the street.

At first Miss Trott sat completely still. Then she picked up the papers and hurriedly stuffed them into her reticule before summoning the waiter and ordering something else. Catching sight of Lucy, she waved hesitantly and then beckoned. The Lombroso sisters were too busy squabbling about something to notice what Lucy had just seen. The question was, should she tell them or keep it to herself? As they crossed the street to join Miss Trott, she remembered a line from a book that James had given her to help with her stories, *Pinkerton's Detection Manual*: 'When observing a subject it is better to keep your own counsel.' So that, she decided, was exactly what she would do. Secrets could be damaging, but information in the wrong hands could be worse.

James and Sofia walked into the entrance hall. The light, such as it was, shone through the stone window frames, making strange shapes on the dusty floor.

'Where do we start?' Sofia said. 'It looks as if no one has been here for a long time.'

'Which is odd in itself. Where are our footprints in the dust? Ottolenghi, Lombroso and I walked through here, but there is no sign of us being present at all.'

'It seems as if someone is trying to hide something,' Sofia said.

This time James knew exactly where he was headed. 'Follow me.' He made his way through the graveyard and down the steps towards the crypt. He examined the stone floor carefully as he went. Footprints were visible, but just one set rather than three. They stopped abruptly by the wall.

'I was certain there would be a door here.'

'Oh, but there is, *caro*... look.' Sofia walked to the left and pulled at a loose stone. A door appeared as if from nowhere and swung open.

'Well that explains the light we saw disappearing when we did our investigation,' James said. 'How did you know it was there?'

'Oh, it was... how do you call it... a hunch,' she said in English.

'You are full of surprises!' James said. Ahead of him was a passage with a room off to the left. Sofia put a restraining hand on his arm.

'Wait, *caro*, we need a lantern, or at least a candle.' She beckoned to him. 'Let's go up to the next floor and see if we can find one. This way, *sì*?'

'Yes, but do you mind if we go through the crypt this time. I'd like to take another look.'

'No, I do not mind. We must be brave. There is too much at stake.'

He nodded and allowed her to take him by the hand and lead him into the damp and musty darkness. The dead girl was gone, but her macabre monastic friends remained, still seated upright in an orderly row.

'It's odd,' said James. 'We were so focused on the girl that we hardly paid any attention to these fellows.'

'That is probably because everyone else knew they would be here.'

'Yes, of course. I remember Tullio mentioning it. How come?'

'The story is well known in the city. It is said that an evil presence lives down here.'

'Don't tell the professor, but that doesn't surprise me in the least,' James said, thinking back to his first visit.

'The monks... well, abbots really... were left down here to ensure that it could not escape.'

'A monastic guard, then.'

'Something like that, yes. They have been mummified through a natural process.'

'And the weeping angel?'

'She is said to be crying because of the suffering and sinning that she has witnessed.'

James shivered. 'Shall we go and find a lantern?'

Sofia grinned at him. 'It is just a story.'

'I know, I know,' he said as he followed her towards the stairs in the corner. The monks stared back at him from their empty eye sockets. He knew it was just his imagination, but he could have sworn that one of them had moved.

Once they got up to the second flight of stairs, James noticed that there was no dust at all, adding to the mystery.

'Let's try to get into one of these rooms,' he said, indicating the double doors on either side of the corridor.

Sofia pulled out a hairpin and wiggled it about in one of the locks. The doors swung open. The room before them was large and filled with light. The furnishings were plush and the decor ornate. Arranged in clusters throughout were large overstuffed settees and chaise longues. He smelt cigar smoke, perfume and whisky with a hint of incense. It was all familiar, though James couldn't quite place it. Sofia smiled in triumph and replaced her hairpin.

'You have a light touch,' he said. 'Perhaps you should contemplate a new criminal career.'

She stepped towards him. 'And then you could reform me, perhaps? I think I might enjoy that.' She frowned. 'I am sorry. I should not say such things. It is not fair.'

Fair? How could she say that? James thought. He wanted nothing more than to pull her to him and kiss her – but properly this time, a deep and all-encompassing embrace that would show her exactly how he felt about her and how much he regretted all that had gone wrong between them. But before he could touch her, she moved away again. He sighed in frustration. She was right. It was not fair. Why was she torturing him like this?

'Listen,' she said. 'Can you hear it?'

At first James thought she meant his heartbeat, which was thudding so hard in his chest that it was surely audible. But no – she held her finger to her lips. 'Shush . . . footsteps, downstairs.'

'You stay here,' he said. 'I'll go and see if there's anyone there. Shut the door after me.'

She opened her mouth as if to protest, but he put his own finger on her lips, mirroring her movement. 'This time do as I say!' he whispered, inwardly noting the absurdity of telling Sofia what to do. But for once she did not resist. Nodding her agreement, she watched as he began to walk slowly down the stairs, then shut the door as he had asked her.

James stopped halfway down. He heard the creaking of shoes. Was it one pair or two? He couldn't see anything that would serve as a weapon. When he got to the bottom of the staircase, there didn't seem to be anyone there, but as he walked into the gloom, he noticed footprints in the dust. They seemed to be leading to the corridor that circled the entrance hall. He was about to follow them when there was a scream from upstairs.

'Sofia!' he cried, and raced back up the stairs towards her. But when he got to where he had left her, she was gone. On the floor was a handkerchief with the letters CE embroidered in one corner and SE in the other. He picked it up and pressed it to his face. It smelt of cinnamon.

He heard a noise, the creaking of shoe leather. Someone was behind him. Instinctively he put his hands up to protect himself, but he was too late. He felt a sharp blow across the side of his head and his knees buckled beneath him. His last thought before the darkness came was of Sofia.

24

A passion for evil for evil's sake is a characteristic of born criminals, epileptics, and hysterics. It is an automatic hatred, one that springs from no external cause such as an insult or offence, but rather from a morbid irritation of the psychical centres which relieves itself in evil action.

Lombroso and Ferrero, 1893, pp. 186–7

As they made their way through the Turin streets towards home, Lucy thought over what had happened that morning. It all seemed slightly unreal. One thing was sure, though. Miss Trott and Professor Donati made an unlikely couple, whatever their relationship. Lucy tried to imagine them as lovers and dismissed the idea immediately as being too absurd to consider. Once she, Paola and Gina had joined Miss Trott at the café opposite the professor's museum, Lucy had watched her companion carefully to see if she would give anything away. But Miss Trott seemed to act perfectly normally, chatting animatedly to the Lombroso sisters about their father's exhibits and ordering ices for all to cool them down in 'this terrible heat'. Except that it was merely pleasantly warm. Could it have been some kind of a ruse?

She needed to find out more about the address on Miss Trott's piece of paper. What she really wanted to do was to ask

James. But he was away on another research trip, or at least that was what he had told Professor Lombroso, according to Gina, who had overheard the conversation.

As they approached the house, Sofia crossed the road towards them. She looked strange, dazed and bedraggled, her face streaked with tears.

'Miss Esposito, whatever is the matter?' asked Miss Trott.

Sofia's eyes were wide. '*Mi scusi, mi scusi!*'

Lucy gently took her hand. 'What is it, Sofia?'

'It is Signor James! He is gone!' She sank down on to the pavement, as if her legs could hold her up no longer.

'Gone? Gone where?' Lucy asked in alarm.

'They have taken him and it is all my fault. He was helping me to find Chiara, and now he is gone too!'

Miss Trott knelt down and helped Sofia to her feet. Sofia leant on her heavily and continued to sob. Miss Trott beckoned to the sisters. 'Miss Paola, go with Gina and fetch help.' The girls obeyed, glancing back as they left.

Lucy took Sofia by the shoulders. 'Tell me what happened, quickly!'

'We were in the Abbey San Callisto. We were . . .' She paused, as if trying to find the right words. 'We were searching for clues, then we heard a noise. Signor James went to see what it was and I shut the door behind him, as he told me. Then someone came up behind me and put something over my mouth. I must have been drugged, because the next thing I knew I was in the graveyard. I ran back to find your brother, but he had disappeared!'

'How do you know that he wasn't out looking for you?' Lucy asked. 'He might have thought that you'd be here. He could already be back.'

Sofia's face was a picture of misery.

'What is it?'

'I went back to where I had last seen him . . .'

Lucy looked down at Sofia's hands. They were stained with blood.

The pain wrapped itself around James so completely that he was too weak even to cry out. And even if he had been able to, he was gagged and could not have uttered more than a grunt. His body ached all over and he had a pain in his head that felt as if his brain was being squeezed through a colander. There was some dampness on the back of his neck that might well have been blood, though he could not be sure. But all that mattered was Sofia. Where was she? What were they doing to her? He had to get out of here and find her.

He tried to calm himself by getting his bearings. He was in darkness, but he still had some idea of his surroundings. He was lying on his side. The floor beneath him was stone, and there was dust or dirt of some kind on it. He stretched his foot out as much as he could, which wasn't far given that both his hands and his feet were tied. The walls were also of stone. It was damp and musty-smelling. He might be anywhere.

Slowly and painfully he tried to pull himself upright. It was difficult to get any kind of balance, but eventually he managed to right himself and lean against the wall. He tried to remember what had happened before everything had gone black. There had been footsteps behind him . . . one set or two? He wasn't certain. He recalled the blow to his head, which presumably was the cause of the pain that he could still feel. But how long had he been here?

There was a rattle at the door, the sound of a key being turned and a light that dazzled him. He tried to get up, but it was impossible on his own. Two men came over to him and hauled him to his feet. His gag was removed.

'Who are you? What do you want?' he asked desperately. 'What have you done with Sofia? Is she all right?'

He was just becoming accustomed to the light when it went again as someone blindfolded him. The cloth smelt of mould and decay, as if it had last been wrapped around something dead or dying.

'This way, *Inglese*.' The voice was gruff but businesslike. He was propelled along at some speed and almost fell at one point.

'*Attenzione!*' This was a second voice, softer, more educated.

After a minute or two they seemed to enter another room. There was no dampness to this one. Instead he could smell wood and polish. It reminded him of Sofia, as it had done the night at the abbey with the professor and Ottolenghi. Was he still there? That might explain the contrast between the two rooms.

He was manhandled into a chair. It was wooden, but the seat was cushioned – a dining chair of some kind, probably.

'Signor Murray, you really must not interfere in matters that are not your affair.' It was the second voice again. It sounded quite gentle, almost conciliatory.

'I was not aware that I was,' James replied.

'Oh, I think you know full well . . . and you see, therein lies our problem.'

'What problem?'

'Your awareness . . . your knowledge.' The voice was regretful now. 'It is a shame really.'

'Why?'

'Because it means we must ensure that what you know goes no further.'

'I told you. I don't know anything.'

'Now we both know that you are lying. And that can only lead in one direction.'

James felt someone approach him. He was pulled off the chair and held from behind. Then he was punched, hard, in the stomach, winding him and bringing tears to his eyes. He was punched again and again until he could no longer stand of his own accord. He felt the punches move to his face. Then the blows stopped and he felt himself being lowered back on to the seat with a strange gentleness. The pain was acute and his automatic reaction was to double over with it, but he forced himself to stay upright.

He sensed that someone else had entered the room. The smell of the place altered slightly – a faint hint of a fragrance, nothing more than that. He heard a soft rustling.

'You see, Signor Murray, that is what happens when you are not frank with us,' the voice said sorrowfully.

'I told you . . . I don't know anything.'

'So you say, but how can we be sure?'

James did not reply. He heard the sound of whispering.

'Perhaps there is a solution . . .' the voice said.

'What?'

'Clearly you are unaffected by your own pain, but what of another's?'

James felt himself tense.

'Ah, I see that we have finally got through to you.'

'If you touch her . . .'

'You are hardly in a strong bargaining position, Signor Murray. But I can see that the young lady is your Achilles heel. And then there is your sister, the lovely Signorina Lucy, and your position with the great Professor Lombroso. You are a lucky man in so many ways, Signor Murray. You have so much, but also so much to lose – love, family, reputation.'

'I don't know who you are or what you are doing. I cannot harm you.'

Someone stepped closer to him and he braced himself for another beating. Instead he felt the unmistakable sensation of steel against his cheek, cold and sharp and then stinging as it sliced into his skin. He cried out in pain and shock.

'There – a small keepsake as a reminder. Perhaps you are telling the truth, perhaps you are not. The position is this. If you do anything to indicate that you are interfering in our business again, you will regret it. Do I make myself clear?'

'Yes, very clear,' James replied. A small rivulet of blood was running down his face.

'Good. That is very good. Do not take this amiss, Signor Murray, but I hope we will not meet again, for your sake.'

A command was issued in a dialect that James did not quite understand, and the next thing he knew he was being moved yet again – through corridors and then down some stairs until he felt the sun on his back and could smell fresh air. He was put into what felt like a cart, and a piece of cloth was thrown over him. It smelt of animal dung. He heard the wheels going round and felt the sensation of movement. Before long the cart stopped. He tensed himself again as the cloth was pulled away. He could not be sure that they would not beat him again, just for the hell of it, and this time there was no one to stop them from going too far. He was dragged out of the cart and thrown to the ground.

'*Mi scusi, Inglese,*' said a different voice, and then there was another blow to the back of his head. It only stunned him this time, but he feigned unconsciousness in case they hit him again. He felt his limbs being liberated.

He lay on the ground where they had left him and heard the cart drive away. He stayed there for a few moments, just to be sure, then he opened his eyes and gingerly sat up and touched the cut on his cheek. It did not seem as bad as he had feared, and at least he was free. Now all he had to do was find Sofia. Were they holding her, and if so, where? Had they harmed her? All he could do now was get back to the city and find help. Then and only then could he think about what to do next.

25

Woman's cruelty and her reactions to life's trials stem from her weakness. Because she is unable to destroy her enemies, woman torments them, pricking them with needles of pain and immobilising them with misery. Cruelty, like cunning, is a product of woman's adaptation to the conditions of life. And thus she acquired and developed her ability to torment. In sum, cruelty is a type of defensive as well as offensive reaction in woman.

Lombroso and Ferrero, 1893, p. 68

James lay in bed and looked listlessly out of the window. The sun was shining and he heard the noise of people and carriages as they passed on the street below. It was only two days since his return to the city, but he was already getting tired of being cooped up inside as if he was an invalid. There was a knock on the door and Ottolenghi came in, knocking a pile of books over as he did so.

'Oh dear, I am sorry,' he said, scooping them up and putting them back in an untidy heap on the table.

James grinned at him. 'Don't worry. I'm glad to see you.'

'How are you?' Ottolenghi said.

'I feel like a fraud.'

'Well I don't know why. That was a pretty bad beating you took, James.'

'I know, but I'm recovered now. It's mostly just a few bruises and a bit of a headache.'

'Two cracked ribs, a nasty head wound and lacerations to the face,' Ottolenghi recited. 'I think it will take more than a few days for you to recover. What did Tullio say?'

'Not much. He took my statement, though I couldn't remember a great deal, and said that he would look into it. It was odd, really.'

'In what way?'

'He didn't seem that interested. He was rather brusque, in fact, as if I was wasting his time.'

'That is strange.'

'I know he is busy.'

'Yes, but all the same . . .'

'Is Sofia all right?' James asked.

Ottolenghi raised his eyebrows. 'She's as well as can be expected, given all that's happened. She has been told to stay at home and rest, which is what you should be doing.' He hesitated for a moment. 'You told the professor that it was over between you, I believe. Is that true?'

'It was when I told him, yes,' James said.

'But you are together now?'

'Difficult to say,' James said, remembering the touch of her lips as she kissed him in the woods.

'Do you still love her?' Ottolenghi asked.

James nodded. There was no point lying. He knew how he felt about her. That had not changed. But her emotions were, as ever, a mystery to him.

'And how does she feel about you?' Ottolenghi said, as if reading his mind.

James shrugged. 'I came back here because she asked for my help. I thought it was because she loved me. I wanted us to start a new life together, but she refused. How could I be so naïve, Salvatore?'

'Love makes us all lose our heads from time to time,' Ottolenghi replied. 'Sofia knows that it might very well destroy you if you were together openly.'

'I don't care! Don't you see?' He cried out in frustration. 'Why can't two people who love each other be together?'

'Sometimes we have to make sacrifices for what we know to be right.'

'It just seems so very unfair.'

'Perhaps, but there are other things to think of now,' Ottolenghi said. 'What happened, James? Why were you taken?'

'I truly do not know,' James said. 'Whoever it was seemed to think that I had found out something.'

'What?'

'That's the problem. I have no idea.'

'And Sofia?'

'They took her in order to get to me, I think.'

'You know what to do, James. You must sever all connection with Sofia. It is the only course of action you can take.'

'I can't,' he said. 'I just can't.'

He knew that Ottolenghi was right. The sensible thing would be to tell Sofia that it – whatever *it* was – could not go on. He should stop looking for Chiara and accept that there was no possibility of a life with Sofia. It would keep her safe, if nothing else. It would be difficult. They had shared so much. James had watched his father descend into insanity and Sofia had suffered as the result of her own father's crimes. Both of them had been damaged, but they had helped one another to survive. Without Sofia, his life would have no meaning. How could he ever hope to understand and accept his past without her at his side? But she had told him already that they could not be together, and now it seemed that there was even more at stake than happiness.

'If you don't end it, you are risking her safety. And, James, it isn't just Sofia.'

'I know. It's Lucy too. They said as much.'

'Well then, what will you do?'

'There is only one thing I can do. I have to get to the bottom of this. If I don't, then we'll never be safe . . . any of us.'

Signora Laura Capetti was not, as a rule, a fearful person. Had she been of a nervous disposition, she would not have been walking unaccompanied through the Parco Valentino just as the sun began to rise. Yes, the newspaper had talked of girls going missing in the early morning, but that did not deter her from her journey, even though the solitude and silence made it an eerie experience. Every rustle of foliage, every cry of an animal or bird seemed magnified a thousand times. For Signora Capetti, such sounds held no fear. Indeed, she prided herself on being afraid of nothing and no one, and she could hardly be described as a girl.

Since the death of her husband five years ago, she had been forced to make her own way in the world, which required a certain amount of fortitude. Luckily she had found that fortitude was a characteristic she possessed in abundance. As she had often mused since the beginning of her widowhood, you never really knew what you were capable of until you were forced to find out. Her husband had been a gambler and had left her with so many debts that she had been forced to seek employment in order to make ends meet. She had therefore taken a job at a small souvenir shop in the Borgo Mediaevale, which made her just enough to get by. This was perhaps one of the stranger parts of Turin. It was a perfect replica of a small medieval town built for the Esposizione Universale in 1884. Visitors flocked to it to look at its little shops and its castle, La Rocca – The Stronghold. During the winter months it was open only at weekends, but soon the season would begin again. Today Signora Capetti had been asked to conduct a thorough stock check so that orders could be made in time for the summer, their busiest period.

Many middle-aged women would have been humiliated by such a change of fortune – from middle-class comfort to shop worker in a matter of weeks. Signora Capetti, however, had found that she enjoyed her work. It made her feel useful. She particularly liked stock-taking, as it gave her an opportunity to look more closely than usual at the many wondrous things she sold – history books that told tales of the medieval period, maps of Turin from years ago, lace handkerchiefs and hand-made silk scarves, bottles of cologne and dolls dressed up in medieval clothes. She would place these in order, and by the day's end would have a complete list of stock, and an overwhelming sense of achievement.

All of this meant that as she walked through the park towards her place of work on a warm and sunny morning, she did so with a spring in her step. Passing through the main gateway to the castle, she imagined what it might have been like to be a medieval princess wandering her own grounds. And that was when she saw it.

At first she thought it was some kind of mannequin from a dress shop, so perfect did it seem. But on closer scrutiny it became obvious that this figure had once been a living and breathing being. It was the body of a young girl, dressed in a white gown overlaid with gold lace. She was lying prostrate in the small shallow stream that circled the castle and served as a moat. Her long red hair was fanned out behind her and moved gently with the water. Her face was pale, almost as white as her gown. In one of her hands she clasped a few long-stemmed spring flowers of blue and red. More lay at her feet, caught up in the folds of the gown.

For a moment Signora Capetti stood and watched her, entranced. She looked so peaceful, almost as if she was sleeping, just like the painting of Ophelia by Millais. The only sound was the gurgling of the water as it ran gently past her.

Lucy was sitting at James's bedside, reading to him. He was perfectly capable of reading to himself, as he had made abundantly clear. But they had hardly spoken since their arrival in Turin and she was eager to make up for lost time. He had said little about the assault except to tell her in a matter-of-fact tone that this kind of thing was something of an occupational hazard when you were researching criminals. Lucy was sceptical, even though Professor Lombroso had apparently accepted the incident as a random crime. He even seemed disappointed at James's inability to describe his attackers. 'A perfectly good piece of fieldwork entirely lost because of carelessness' was how he had put it, which seemed rather unfair given the circumstances. As she had heard James say afterwards, it was as though he was expected to ask his assailants to pause while they were beating him to allow him to do a quick sketch of the shape of their heads and make some notes. But Lucy had studied the professor's expression as he spoke, and it seemed to her that he was far more disturbed by the incident than he was letting on. There was more to this than met the eye, she was sure of it. According to *Pinkerton's*

Detection Manual, the route to discovery was observation, which sounded like a good strategy.

Lucy had suggested that she should read James a novel – *The Moonstone* by Wilkie Collins was one of their shared favourites – but the book he had chosen was by the professor. She had expected it to be dry and full of scientific terms that she would find hard to understand. She couldn't have been more wrong. Instead it was full of the most blood-curdling anecdotes about this murderer or that, and the language he used was extremely engaging. It was true that he kept wandering off the point here and there, and some of the science was, according to James anyway, rather questionable, but it was a thrilling read and something of a revelation for Lucy.

'Look at these.' She held the book up to show him. '"Before and after pictures of vicious and criminal boys",' she read out. '"William Bender and Tom Wellington – a reformed gang member and a London vagabond who went to Canada."'

James peered at the drawings. 'That's interesting. A criminal can be reformed, even if he was born that way.'

'It is comforting, but there is more,' Lucy continued. 'According to the professor, the crime rate among children is extremely high. He tells the story of a thirteen-year-old who stabbed and killed a companion over some gambling winnings. He had a pointed skull, oblique eyes, protruding cheekbones, voluminous jaws and jug ears!'

'Ugly so-and-so, then,' James said.

'Apparently his brother was convicted six times for theft, his sister was a prostitute and their mother was a criminal who suffered from migraines. His father died of financial anxieties. I didn't know that could kill you, did you?

'Mmm, interesting,' James said. 'I suppose it might put a strain on the heart.'

'Oh yes, I hadn't thought of that. In addition, his grandmother died of poisoning and his brother stuttered. The professor says that is evidence of neuroses causing inherited criminal tendencies.'

'The professor isn't right about everything, Lucy.'

'Are you sure? He seems to think he is.'

'Well that is true. He doesn't do much self-doubting.'

'You are so lucky, James,' Lucy said wistfully.

'Why?' he said, shifting uncomfortably in his bed. 'I don't feel very lucky.'

'You study such interesting subjects, whereas all I get to read are dreary self-improving tomes. Aunt Agnes must have sent at least a hundred with Miss Trott.'

He grinned. 'I wondered why her luggage was so heavy. How are you getting on with Miss Trott?'

Lucy hesitated. This could be her only opportunity to tell James about what she had discovered. But together it did not seem to add up to anything much – a note with a mention of an Egyptian demon, the word 'serendipity' and the address of a chemist's shop. Even the altercation between Miss Trott and Professor Donati did not signify anything on its own, although it was something of a mystery. Besides, he had so much else on his mind with the murder of that poor girl that she really didn't want to trouble him with it now. Better to wait until she had found something more concrete and less . . . now what was the word in *Pinkerton's* . . . ah yes: circumstantial.

'She seems nice enough, if rather dull,' she replied.

'Dull? Oh, I think dull is good. I could do with some dull,' James said. 'Mind you, it would be nice to get out of this room for a while.'

'You're not well enough yet, according to Dr Ottolenghi anyway.'

The door was flung open and Lombroso bounded in, followed by a sheepish-looking Ottolenghi.

'What are you still doing in bed, Murray? Come along, come along . . . there is work to be done!'

'But, Professor, my brother is not yet fully recovered,' Lucy protested.

'I am fine, Lucy. Don't worry,' James said as he started rather gingerly to get up. 'I just need to take it a little slowly.'

Lombroso tutted. 'We cannot take it slowly, Murray. There is too much to do.'

'Why? Whatever has happened?' Lucy asked.

'There's a body, Signorina Murray. The newspapers are full of it. Another young woman, and I would not be at all surprised if she was just like the other one.'

'In what way?' Lucy asked.

'Well, I . . .' Lombroso paused.

'Please do not feel that you have to moderate your language on my account, Professor. It is not only my brother who has an interest in such things.'

James frowned at her. 'Lucy!'

Lombroso raised an eyebrow and continued. 'I expect her to be drained of blood for one thing. And for another . . .' he paused for dramatic effect, 'I'd put a wager on her being gutted, just like a hare for the pot! We shall find out more at the post-mortem. Tullio has asked me to conduct it, as I found the first body.'

Lucy noticed that he did not seem to care about the poor dead girl. She supposed it was necessary for scientists. Could she really learn to be so detached?

'When will it take place?' James asked.

'This afternoon,' Lombroso replied.

'So where are we going now?'

'Ottolenghi and I are going to the university. You are going downstairs.'

'Why?'

'Because you have a visitor.'

'Concetta Panatti is here,' Ottolenghi said. 'She wants to liaise with you about the interviews with her . . .' He paused for a moment and glanced at Lucy, 'girls.'

'Who is Concetta Panatti?' Lucy asked.

'No one you need worry about, young lady,' Lombroso said. 'Haven't you got something more useful to occupy yourself with than troubling your brother?'

'Lucy was reading to me from your work, Professor, not troubling me at all,' James said quickly, before Lucy could protest.

'Really?' Lombroso seemed to puff out a little, like a cockerel. 'Well I imagine you may wish to read through it again, signorina. It is quite complex, especially for the female intellect. But if you wish to look at some more of my work, there is plenty at the museum. You may borrow it if you like, though I imagine you may need your brother to decipher it for you.'

Lucy was tempted to mention Anna Tarnovsky, who seemed to manage very well, but saw James's expression and thought better of it.

'I shall, Professor,' she said, 'then perhaps we could discuss it. There are already one or two aspects that I find—'

'Wouldn't it be better for you to deal with Signora Panatti, Professor?' James said, interrupting her.

'In an ideal world, perhaps,' Lombroso said. 'But the lady will speak only to you. She seems to have taken something of a shine to you, so you'd better hurry. I don't want her to change her mind about access to the girls. You can meet us at the mortuary later.'

Lucy watched as Ottolenghi helped James out of bed. He was a little unsteady, perhaps unsurprisingly given his ordeal. But there was something else. Professor Lombroso might have been unmoved by the girl's death, but for James it was as if there was something personal in the finding of another body. It was touching him a lot more deeply than he wanted anyone to know. And as his sister, she felt it was her duty to find out why.

26

In the lower animal orders, where the female is more powerful than the male, love is non-existent. The female subordinates sexuality to maternity by getting rid of the male as soon as she has been impregnated. After mating, the female spider devours the male if he has not already fled. Only when the male becomes more powerful, forcing the female to submit to his domination and more ardent sexual demands, does love become linked to reproduction and maternity. Lombroso and Ferrero, 1893, p. 73

James watched Concetta Panatti through the open door. She was standing by a bookcase, peering at its contents, languidly caressing their spines. For a moment he imagined the feel of her hands on his skin and felt a stirring of desire. Her gown was dark green velvet and hugged her curves provocatively. There was no doubt that she was a beautiful woman. The redness of her hair was striking in its depth. Her features were fine, her skin flawless, pale and delicate, and her eyes . . . well, they were extraordinary: mesmerising, bewitching.

She looked up as he entered. 'Ah, Signor Murray, it is good to see you.' She approached him with a leonine grace. Everything about her was sensual. She embraced him with her presence alone. As during their last meeting, she came so close that he could hear her breathing. Slowly she peeled off her lace gloves, finger by finger, her eyes never leaving his, her lips full, pouting as if waiting to be kissed.

'Your poor face,' she said, running a finger down the cut on his cheek. Her hand lingered there and he felt the heat from it filter through his skin. He suspected that he should stand back and create some distance between them, but he found that he did not want to move. 'I do hope that it will not leave a scar.'

'It is nothing,' he said, struggling to keep his voice steady. This was ridiculous, he thought. Here he was, a grown man, allowing himself to be manipulated by a woman he hardly knew.

'What have you been doing?' she asked.

'I was attacked,' James said. She was clearly not the sort of woman one could lie to. But why would he want to? For a brief moment he wanted to tell her everything about himself, the bad and the good – to lay himself open for her.

She had a sly half-formed smile on her face. 'You must have done something very bad to provoke such a reaction.'

'I have done nothing,' he replied.

'I find that hard to believe,' she said. 'A man like you.'

What did she know about him? What did he know about himself, come to that?

'It was a misunderstanding.'

'I see,' she said, moving away from him towards the window and casually glancing out of it. He willed her to be close to him again. Then he remembered why they were here.

'I gather you wish to make arrangements for our interviews at the university.'

'Yes. I know that you were due to visit me, but I heard that you were... indisposed.' Her eyes seemed to penetrate him. 'And I could not wait.'

'Another time perhaps,' James said.

'Yes, I would enjoy that.'

'And the arrangements?'

'If you are in charge, I doubt there will be any need for arrangements.' She smiled again. 'I have every confidence that you will treat the ladies with respect. That is all I ask.'

'Of course, signora,' James said, watching her as she approached him again, this time circling slowly round him as if waiting to pounce. From anyone else this would have felt ridiculous, but with her it seemed merely playful.

'I will deliver the girls personally.' She paused for a moment. 'I hear that one of my young ladies accosted you.'

'It was nothing,' James said.

'Ada is a fanciful young woman. I do not know what she told you, but you should put it from your mind, whatever it was.'

Her words sounded familiar. Wasn't that what Valeria had told him? He shook his head. It was hard to think clearly in Concetta Panatti's presence, but he knew he must.

'Have any of your girls disappeared recently? A young woman called Agnella, for instance?'

She hesitated. There was an almost undetectable frisson of disapproval. 'They come and go all the time, Signor Murray. Sometimes they find a man to take them on, or another position elsewhere. It is just one of those things.'

'What about Teresa Mariani?'

'Ah yes, the maid. Domestic staff are no different. She no doubt found work in a different establishment. It happens.'

James nodded. 'Thank you for being so helpful, signora.'

'Delighted to be of assistance. Now is there anything else I can help you with?'

'Signora, I wonder . . .' James began. He hardly dared to ask, but he could not resist.

'Anything, Signor Murray.' She was next to him again, surrounding him with her musky scent.

'Would you be prepared to talk to us?'

She hesitated. 'I will talk to you, and you alone.'

'I will look forward to it.'

'So will I, Signor Murray. So will I.' She was almost whispering now, her lips close to his ear, her breath caressing him.

The door opened. Miss Trott came in. 'Mr Murray, I wonder if you have seen my . . . Oh, I do apologise.'

Concetta Panatti stepped away from him. She stared at Miss Trott, her eyes conveying something not far from malevolence.

Miss Trott reddened but did not look away. 'I don't believe we have been introduced.'

'No, I shouldn't think we have. Until tomorrow, Signor Murray.' Concetta Panatti held out her ungloved hand. James took it and held it for a moment. She gave him a knowing smile before sweeping past Miss Trott, passing so close to her that she almost knocked her flying.

For a moment there was silence as both James and Miss Trott adjusted to Concetta Panatti's absence.

'My word, you are a *busy* young man, aren't you, Mr Murray?' Miss Trott said.

'What was it you wanted?' James said, irritated by her comment.

'I have it, thank you,' she replied, holding up a book in triumph. She paused for a moment. 'May I give you some advice?'

'If you must,' James said.

'Take care,' she said. 'A woman like that can cause untold harm.'

'I am quite capable of looking after myself.'

'You will not be able to control her.'

'You forget yourself, Miss Trott. You are engaged as my sister's companion, not mine.'

She shook her head sadly. 'As you wish, Mr Murray, as you wish.'

James watched her as she left. He went over to the window and gazed out of it, breathing in the vestiges of Concetta's scent and thinking about what Miss Trott had said. She had no right to issue such a warning. How could she possibly know anything about a woman like Concetta Panatti? Besides, he was free to act as he chose. Sofia had rejected him, or so it seemed. So much stood in their way that any prospect of a future together now seemed utterly unattainable. Why should he not enjoy the company of another woman? He had no feelings for Concetta, but he was attracted to her and perhaps that was enough. It might even be a relief to stop thinking about a woman he could not have and focus instead upon one who seemed only too willing. But beneath his indignation there was another thought, one that he was doing his utmost to suppress but still it remained there, like a bee with a venomous sting, buzzing around his head. First Sofia and now Miss Trott had issued a warning about Concetta Panatti. Could they really both be wrong?

Lucy stood outside the building and looked up at the window. A small vase stood on the sill in the gap between the ill-drawn curtains. She thought back to last time she had been here, when Sofia had rescued her from the Morals Squad. This time she was on her own errand of mercy, or that was what she hoped it looked like anyway. There was something that had been gnawing away at her ever since her first visit, something she wanted to find out. She had even brought some gifts – a bunch of flowers purchased from a nearby street vendor and a jar of honey from a market stall. As last time, she had not asked for permission for her outing, but she had seen plenty of young women out alone during the day and had therefore decided that it would be perfectly safe to pay Sofia a visit.

She knocked on the door. The wood was of poor quality. She could tell as much from the hollow ring to her rapping. The shabby curtains twitched slightly. A few seconds later the door opened and Sofia stood there smiling hesitantly.

'Signorina, I did not expect a visit from you.'

'May I come in?' Lucy asked.

Sofia stood back and allowed her to enter, following her up the stairs.

Lucy studied the woman in front of her as they stood face to face in the tiny room. She was paler than usual, almost diminished, presumably due to her recent ordeal. Lucy thrust her gifts out before her as if she was carrying a shield.

Sofia took them. 'You are very kind, but it was not necessary,' she said, indicating for her visitor to sit on the small faded settee.

It was not particularly solid and wobbled a little as Lucy lowered herself on to it. 'My mother always taught me never to call on someone empty-handed.'

'Ah, she was Italian, was she not?' Sofia carefully placed the honey on the table and laid the flowers next to it.

'Yes, she was.' Lucy watched as Sofia busied herself opening cupboards and pulling out vessels that might be suitable for the flowers – a jar, a small carafe and so on – until eventually settling for a ceramic jug.

She paused, hugging it to her. 'Why are you here, signorina? I am just a housekeeper.'

'You are more than that, I think.'

Sofia looked down. It was only for a moment, but it was enough.

'What is there between you and my brother?' Lucy asked.

'He is helping me to find my cousin. She is missing.' The reply came quickly, too quickly for Lucy's liking. Sofia was flushed and her hands were still clasping the jug tightly in front of her.

'And that is all?' Lucy asked, her eyes narrowing.

'First Anna Tarnovsky and now me... Signorina, you seem very anxious to find someone with an attachment to your brother. I am not sure he is the catch you appear to think he is.' She slammed the jug down on the table and picked up Lucy's flowers, chopping at the stalks with a small knife.

'I would be more than happy if James and Anna were to...'

'To what?'

'To marry, I suppose,' Lucy said.

Sofia snorted. '*Madame* Anna Tarnovsky is already married. Her husband is in Prague. They are happy as far as I know.'

Lucy frowned. Prague... Not a cruel Russian count then. How disappointing! But then Sofia might be lying – though why would she? 'Really? She has no wedding ring.'

'*Sì*, you are right,' Sofia said, waving the knife around in time to her words, as if to emphasise them. 'She does not wear it. That is because she would not be allowed by the university to work with the professor if her status was widely known.'

'And what about you, Sofia?'

'I have told you... Signor James is helping me. There is nothing more between us.'

'Not from his side, of course, but you?'

'Oh, of course,' Sofia said in what sounded like a sarcastic tone as she laid down the knife. She wiped her hands on her apron and then removed it and hung it on a small hook by the door. 'I am just a servant.'

Lucy nodded, feeling foolish. As if James would be interested in Sofia – it was ridiculous. And Sofia would not allow herself to care for a man like James.

'So your cousin...'

'As I said, she has disappeared.'

'So that is why he is concerned about the second girl's body?' Lucy said.

Sofia stared at her, horrified.

'You did not know?' Lucy said.

Sofia shook her head. Scooping up her shawl from a chair, she grabbed Lucy by the wrist. 'You should go. I have something I must do.'

Firmly she propelled Lucy to the door and opened it. Standing on the threshold was James.

27

We have discovered that women are less sensitive than men, which explains their greater vitality, but contradicts both popular wisdom and clear evidence that women react more strongly to pain. This apparent contradiction resolves itself when we take into account women's greater excitability and lesser inhibition.

Lombroso and Ferrero, 1893, p. 36

James looked from one to the other. He had not expected this.

'James! What are you doing here?' Lucy asked.

For a moment he considered telling her the truth, but quickly realised that this would be the wrong strategy. 'I could ask the same of you. You know you are not to travel anywhere alone.'

Her face began to redden.

'Wait downstairs, Lucy. I need to speak to Sofia.'

Lucy hesitated for a moment, as if she was considering disobeying him. Then silently she made her way down the stairs.

'Another body . . .' Sofia said, her voice dull. 'I was on the way to the mortuary.'

Instinctively he stepped towards her as if to offer comfort, but she leant away from him. 'There is no need to put yourself through that again,' he said. 'I will tell you if there is any news. I am sure Tullio would have informed you if there was any chance . . .' His voice tailed off. He did not want to say the words.

'I will escort the signorina back to the house before I go to the museum.'

'Be careful,' James said.

Sofia gave just the ghost of a smile. 'We will be.'

When they got downstairs, Lucy was standing in the doorway waiting for them.

'Sofia will walk back to the house with you,' James said.

'Couldn't we both go to the museum? The professor said that I might borrow some books,' Lucy said.

'I don't think so,' James said. 'We are conducting interviews there this afternoon.'

'Couldn't I assist? Perhaps I could take notes, or be a second observer?' Lucy asked.

'No, I am afraid it is not suitable. You are too young, and you are . . .' He hesitated.

'Too female?' Lucy said. 'You sound like the professor.'

'Well on this occasion he is absolutely right. This is not for you.'

'What is for me, then?'

'Lucy, this is not the time to argue.'

She did not answer him but instead changed tactics. 'Please, James. I want to do something useful for once. Anna will be there to make sure I am safe. Gina said so.'

'Another time, perhaps, but not today,' he said. 'You must go home with Sofia.'

'But—'

'No buts, Lucy. Three girls are dead. I want you at home where I know you are safe.'

Lucy glowered at him, picked up her basket and stalked off, followed by Sofia. James watched as they walked away together through the busy streets. He already felt alone, but if anything happened to either of them . . . He pushed the thought from his mind and began to make his way to the mortuary.

When he arrived he found Lombroso and Ottolenghi waiting outside. 'I thought Tullio had asked you to conduct the post-mortem, Professor,' James said.

Lombroso pursed his lips. 'Machinetti was already there with that drunken fool Gallini, his favourite pathologist. Apparently the scene of the crime, or at least where the body was found, is under his jurisdiction.'

'That doesn't sound right,' James said.

'It isn't,' Tullio said as he approached them. 'I breached his territory so he is breaching mine.'

'Ridiculous,' Lombroso said. 'Well he can't stop me from watching, can he?'

Tullio shrugged. 'I suppose not.' He seemed strangely listless. Usually he would have been infuriated by Machinetti's presumption, but he didn't seem to have any fight left in him.

'Then let us go in, gentlemen, and see whether I was right about the similarities between the bodies.'

Lombroso strode into the mortuary, followed by Ottolenghi. James steeled himself for a second before pushing his own way through the large wooden doors. The body lay on a table in the middle of the room, covered demurely by a sheet. Yet again he held his breath, hoping that it was not Chiara.

Machinetti stood in a corner, watching. 'I wondered how long it would be before you poked your nose in, Lombroso.'

'It would be better to have consistency of some kind, would

you not agree, Dottore?' Lombroso said, ignoring Machinetti altogether and addressing his question to Gallini, who merely gave a non-committal grunt in reply. 'Then we can compare the state of the corpses found in the woods and at the abbey with this one. Tell me again, Tullio, how and where was this body found?'

'She was found lying in a stream at the Borgo Mediaevale,' Tullio said.

'That's quite a public place, isn't it?' James said. 'It could not have been there for long. Otherwise it would have been discovered before.'

'I agree,' Lombroso said. 'The killer wanted it to be found, I would think. Do we have any names yet?'

Tullio glanced down at the notebook he was holding. 'The girl at the abbey was a flower seller called Nella Calvi. A friend of hers came in and identified her. We think that this girl is probably another flower seller, Caterina Spirito. She fits the description. They are both on Baldovino's list.'

'Where did he get the names?' Lombroso asked.

'He told me it was from one of his informants,' James said. 'What about the other girls on the list? Have you found anything about them – Arianna Panico, for example?'

'Not much. Panico is proving elusive.' Tullio looked down at his notebook again. 'As is the last one, Susanna Russello. I told you, girls like these go missing all the time.'

Lombroso wandered over towards the body. Machinetti glared at him. 'Get back!'

Gallini hesitated, swaying a little.

'Get on with it, man!' Machinetti barked, looking threateningly at Lombroso. 'And you, keep out of the way or I'll have you removed.' Lombroso took the tiniest of steps back.

Gallini pulled back the sheet. James was relieved. The

corpse was, as Lombroso had said, similar to the one they had found in the abbey, and it was again clear that it was not Chiara. The hair was long and pale red and the skin had a waxy tinge to it, giving it a macabre air like a sinister doll. Gallini began his examination. He was still slightly unsteady on his feet, and occasionally had to stop to support himself by gripping on to the table where his subject was laid out. James watched him with distaste. He knew that the doctor was reputed to have a problem with drink. That much had become clear during the Pilgrim investigation. But he had not realised that the man's alcoholism had got so bad that he would actually be under the influence during a post-mortem. Lombroso stood next to him as he worked, his fingers twitching as if he wanted to intervene.

'What can you tell me?' Tullio asked.

'This is my case. You address your answers to me, Gallini,' Machinetti said.

'The body was found in my jurisdiction,' Tullio said through gritted teeth. 'It is linked to the others, and with regard, to the body found in the woods, I have been asked personally to investigate by the mayor.'

Machinetti scowled back at him. 'The link has yet to be established.'

Gallini rolled his eyes and continued examining. Eventually he looked up from his work, a frown on his face. 'Something is not quite right here.'

'What do you mean?' Tullio asked.

Gallini hesitated for a second. Lombroso tutted and interjected.

'After death, certain processes automatically cease and others begin. The heart stops beating and the body starts to digest itself as cells and tissues break down. This is then followed by putrefaction as the bacteria begin their work.'

'Which means?'

Lombroso strode over to the body and began to examine it closely. Gallini moved aside unsteadily.

'Here the processes have been halted. There are only two explanations for this anomaly. The first is that the place where the body was found has an unusual level of some kind of chemical compound, which has resulted in the stalling of putrefaction.'

'Is that likely?' Tullio asked.

Lombroso pursed his lips thoughtfully. 'Possible, yes, but likely . . . no.'

'And the second explanation?'

'Is equally unlikely – that somehow the body has not been allowed to begin decomposition naturally.'

'What could cause that?'

'There is only one possible cause,' Lombroso said, pausing for dramatic effect. It was an old habit, but they had all learnt that it was easier to play along with it.

'Which is?'

'Human intervention, Inspector, human intervention . . . just as in the other two cases.'

Gallini raised his eyebrows. Notwithstanding his drinking habit, he did not look like a man who appreciated drama. He nudged Lombroso out of the way and resumed his own examination.

'As I thought,' Lombroso said, peering over Gallini's shoulder until he turned and glared at him. 'It is similar but not identical to the body at the Abbey San Callisto.'

'Meaning?' Machinetti asked tersely.

'Meaning that both were drained of blood.'

Ottolenghi and James exchanged glances.

Lombroso continued. 'But in this case, rather than all of the organs having been removed, we are missing only one – the heart.'

'Perhaps he was disturbed,' Gallini said.

'Entirely possible, I would say,' Lombroso agreed.

'Anything else in terms of human intervention?' Tullio asked.

'I cannot tell for certain,' Lombroso replied. 'But there does seem to be the residue of a kind of crystalline compound. Can you see?' He took a clean scalpel from a nearby table and scraped it along the surface of the skin. Tiny white crystals were visible on the blade.

'Is that salt?' Tullio asked.

'It might be.' Lombroso rubbed his finger over the body. 'No, actually I think it is something else . . . I believe it is arsenic.'

'As commonly used in the funeral trade,' James said. 'If that is so, then clearly there has been some attempt to preserve the body.'

'Ah yes, I was waiting for someone to say that,' Lombroso said. 'I think that is entirely likely.'

'So the draining of blood and the organ removal means that there is a link between this body, the girl in the abbey and the one found in the woods,' James said.

They stood in silence for a moment, digesting this thought. There was a knock, and an officer came in carrying a bundle wrapped in a cloth. He looked first at Machinetti and then at Tullio, clearly trying to work out which to approach.

'Bring it to me,' Lombroso said.

The officer went to him and gratefully handed over the

bundle. 'This was found at the Borgo, not far from the girl in the stream,' he said, his eyes wandering to her remains.

Lombroso ushered him out, then placed the bundle on a table and unwrapped it carefully as Gallini looked on.

'What is it?' Tullio asked.

Lombroso's brow creased. 'It is a stone pot containing our missing organ, a human heart,' he said. 'And it seems that, unlike the rest of the body, this is cold, as if it has been preserved in ice. It is still absolutely fresh.'

'Of course there is another possibility,' James said.

'And that is?' Tullio asked.

'That the heart does not belong to this body at all. Which would mean—'

Lombroso interrupted him. 'There could be another victim.'

28

In the intense heat of passion, all the moral restraints that evolution has built up slowly over time dissolve in a flash, like a fine veil in the flame, with even civilised men becoming killers and cannibals. Women, in these extraordinary, transient, atavistic reversions, become the cruellest of the cruel. They tear out the tongue of the corpse, disfigure its manhood, prolong their victim's agony, and demonstrate their thirst for inflicting pain.

Lombroso and Ferrero, 1893, p. 66

Following the post-mortem, James and Ottolenghi had been sent ahead to the museum at the university to make preparations for the interviews with the prostitutes from Madame Giulia's. Lombroso had stayed behind to discuss the case with Tullio, Gallini and, at his insistence, Machinetti.

As they walked in the warm sunshine across the Piazza Castello towards the Via Po, James had the chance to observe his friend more closely. Ottolenghi had been strangely silent throughout the post-mortem, hanging back where he would usually be taking much more of an interest. James had always admired his friend's curiosity and eagerness to learn, and this reticence was out of character.

'This monster wants to get our attention, as if murder is not enough,' he said.

Ottolenghi merely nodded. It seemed that he just did not want to talk. Undeterred, James tried again. 'You have not told me about Vienna,' he said. 'Do you still think there could be a link to vampirism?'

The vestige of a frown crossed Ottolenghi's brows and he seemed to slow down a little. He paused outside the Caffe Torino. 'Do we have time for a coffee, do you think?' he asked.

'I think so,' James said. 'Let's have some lunch, too. It could be a long afternoon.'

They went in, sat down and ordered. When he had first visited the place, James had thought it splendid, with its marble pillars, elaborate murals and huge gilt mirrors. Now its decor seemed overblown. Lucy would no doubt give it a human personality, saying it was boastful and shallow like an eighteenth-century fop. In his own mind James compared it with the scene in the mortuary – the enticing aroma of coffee replaced by the smells of death and the delicate snacks laid out in glass cases by the corpse of the young girl lying on the table waiting to be dissected. Ottolenghi sat, quiet and pale, staring into a cognac purchased with his coffee, he had said, in order to steady his nerves.

'So, Vienna, then... What was it like working with Reiner?' James asked. 'It must have been fascinating.'

'You remember Reiner from last year?' Ottolenghi asked.

'Yes, I do. A queer sort of fellow, as I recall.' James thought back to his encounter with the man during the symposium on criminal anthropology that had been the backdrop to a series of horrible murders. 'He had a rather too fervent interest in sexual murder for my taste.'

'Yes, and that was the nature of his research project. But his particular focus was on the vampire aspect.'

'I don't know a great deal about vampires,' James admitted. 'They drink blood and have an interest in dead bodies, don't they? I have read a short story on the subject, but other than that . . .'

'Same here . . . or at least that was the case before I got to Vienna.'

'What's the connection between vampires and sexual murder? I mean, they're fictional, aren't they?'

'They don't rise from the dead, if that's what you mean, but they do have certain interests.'

'Such as?'

'Necrophilia,' Ottolenghi said, shivering slightly. 'Arousal by the dead body. Then there is necrophagia – the eating of human flesh – and necro-sadism, which is the abuse of dead bodies.'

James gave a low whistle. 'That is disturbing material for anyone to examine.'

'Reiner claims that a presumption of *Lustmord* – or murder out of lust – is always given when injuries to the genitals are found. The erotic attachment to dead flesh is, according to him, inextricably linked to such crimes.'

'That makes sense, but where does vampirism come in? The story I read had a supernatural element. I can't see Reiner taking much of an interest in that.'

'He claims that the supernatural has in the past been used as an explanation for otherwise inexplicable events, but the reality is more worrying. Apparently there is a long history of sexually motivated crimes where the perpetrator has an interest in the blood of the victim. You may remember the professor mentioning such a case last year.'

'Eusebius Pieydagnelle from Milan?'

'Yes, that's right. The smell of blood in a butcher's shop triggered a condition that led to him murdering six women.'

'But even he did not drain the blood from the corpse. I have not heard of anyone doing that.'

'There have been such cases, and Reiner was keen to collate information on all of them . . . very keen, in fact.'

'So are you suggesting that this is the work of such a killer?'

Ottolenghi shrugged. 'I cannot say, but it is at least a possibility that we should consider.'

'And have you told the professor?'

'Yes, after we found the girl in the Abbey San Callisto.'

'What did he say?'

'He was sceptical, as he always is about any ideas that aren't his.'

'I know, I know . . . but that doesn't mean he hasn't tucked it away in his brain somewhere, ready to dredge it up as his own theory. And of course, at that point we had no obvious link between the victims, whereas now not only is there another shallow grave but also evidence of preservation, or at least an attempt at it.'

'There was one case that Reiner told me about that does have some marked similarities, in some respects anyway,' Ottolenghi said, drawing closer. The café was crowded, but James thought that most people seemed far too involved in their own conversations to be interested in theirs.

'Go on.'

'It concerns a seventeenth-century Hungarian countess, Elisabeth Bathory. The legend has it that one of her maids accidentally cut herself and blood found its way onto the countess's skin. She thought that she detected a rejuvenation of the area affected.'

'An anti-ageing lotion of some kind?'

'Yes . . . Well you can probably guess what happened next.'

'Girls started to go missing?'

'At first no one thought anything of it. They were all girls from the town and most were thought to have—'

'Run away?' James said.

Ottolenghi nodded. 'Eventually she turned her attention to girls from noble families. This could not be overlooked.'

'But the missing village girls could?' James said. 'Nothing changes really, does it? What happened then?'

'Bathory and a number of accomplices were arrested, and her castle was searched.'

Ottolenghi paused for a moment as their food arrived – two steaming plates of pasta. James began to tuck into his immediately. It had been a long time since breakfast.

'What did they find?'

'Dead girls, dying girls, girls awaiting torture. Some were in cages with spikes on the sides. Others were just found lying on the floor. Bites had been taken out of them.'

'Horrible!' James said. 'What happened to the countess?'

'She was kept prisoner whilst her so-called accomplices were accused of witchcraft and tortured. One had her fingers severed, Reiner said.'

James paused with his fork between his plate and his mouth and stared at his pasta – penne, fat yellow tubes in a deep red tomato sauce. He put the fork down. 'And then?'

'All kinds of rumours were circulating at the time, so it is quite difficult to separate fact from fiction. There were accusations of satanic rituals and various occultists being invited to visit the castle. But none of this was actually proved.'

'And the countess? Was she tried for murder?'

'Due to her position, Bathory herself was never convicted

of a crime, though her servants were. Most of them were executed – decapitated, burnt alive, and so on.'

'Lucky for her,' James said.

'Not really,' Ottolenghi said. 'She did not escape lightly. As far as her family was concerned, she had disgraced them and put their lands and standing at risk. They walled her up in her bedroom with just a few slits left open for ventilation and food. She died a few years later.'

'That's quite a story,' James said. 'It's a very old case. What was Reiner's interest?'

'He thought it was a classic case of *Lustmord*. The mutilations of the victims suggested that Bathory and her accomplices had an interest in necrophagia.'

'So not just a beauty treatment, then?'

'Not entirely, though she *was* beautiful from all accounts. Her skin was particularly fine, apparently – very pale and pure-looking. She was said to bathe in blood drained from the girls in order to keep it that way.'

A vision of the pale body of Concetta Panatti lying naked in a bath of blood came unbidden into James's mind. 'That is interesting,' he said, blinking as if to rid himself of the image. 'We should tell the professor and Tullio. It might well be relevant.'

Ottolenghi nodded and smiled. 'James, you don't know how good it is to talk this over with someone normal.'

James smiled back at him uncertainly. He wasn't sure if 'normal' really described him, but it was good to see his friend looking more relaxed. 'I take it Reiner was . . . well, how should I put it?'

'He was very focused on his work . . . too focused, I felt. The intensity with which he told me this tale was strange to say the least. He went into every last detail, and really seemed to be enjoying himself.'

'I presume he is safely tucked away in Vienna. He couldn't be a suspect, could he?' James said, half joking.

'No, or at least I don't think so. He was due to give a paper at a conference in Salzburg. He left Vienna at the same time as me.'

'I suppose there could be something in it.'

Ottolenghi hesitated. 'I know it seems rather far-fetched, but as the professor is so fond of saying, we should exclude nothing until we have considered the evidence.'

'And that amounts to the remains of three women, at least two of them with the blood drained from their bodies, and organs removed from all three.'

'It might be someone who is aware of the Bathory case perhaps trying to emulate it in some way,' Ottolenghi suggested.

'Is that what you meant at the abbey?'

Ottolenghi nodded. 'I may have been a little melodramatic, but it seemed so similar, it shook me. I felt as if it had followed me here all the way from Vienna.'

'Perhaps we should be thinking about another question,' James said.

'Which is?'

'What happened to all that blood?'

29

The born prostitute – lacking maternal and family feeling, unscrupulous in the pursuit of her desires, and mildly criminalistic – presents the complete type of moral insanity. This fact, too, helps explain her lack of modesty, for immodesty is characteristic of morally insane women . . . The fact that the germ of prostitution lies not in lust but moral insanity also explains prostitutes' sexual precocity, which is nothing more than an aspect of that general early propensity for evil which one finds in the morally insane.

Lombroso and Ferrero, 1893, pp. 216–17

Lucy glanced over at Sofia as they walked back together to the Lombroso house in silence. Was there really nothing between her and James apart from her missing cousin? As usual James had rushed off. But, she thought ruefully, at least he was fully occupied. The prospect of another empty afternoon with Miss Trott stretched ahead.

'You seem unhappy,' Sofia said.

'I feel so . . . so . . . trapped.'

'Trapped by what?'

'By everything, everybody! I want to be free.'

'You are free.'

'How? How am I free, Sofia?' She pulled at her drab grey

dress. 'My clothes are chosen for me. My reading is chosen for me. I cannot go anywhere unescorted. I am not permitted to speak to anyone without my brother's permission. I cannot choose my own future. Where is the freedom in that?'

'None of us are really free,' Sofia said. 'You have security. You are loved.'

'What, by James? He is only interested in his own future. He cares nothing for mine!'

'As I have told you before, he cares more than you think.'

'He still treats me like a child. He thinks I am capable of nothing but marriage and children.'

'Would that be so bad?' Sofia asked.

'It isn't that I don't want to be married, but the thought of spending the rest of my days attending to domestic matters . . .' Lucy groaned. 'I cannot imagine anything worse. There is so much else of interest out there to be studied. Besides, how can I become a great writer if I am forced to spend my time choosing menus and looking after children? I would just be replacing one prison with another.'

'There is nothing wrong with marriage if you have the right man,' Sofia said wistfully.

'Is that what you would like?' Lucy asked, watching her.

'Perhaps . . . but he would have to be a certain kind of man.'

'What kind?'

'Loving, thoughtful, trusting – able to allow me to do as I wish.'

'And have you met such a man?' Lucy asked.

'I thought I had met him, but we could not be together.'

'If you love him, then you should let nothing get in your way.'

'That is easier said than done,' Sofia said quietly.

'I can make my own way from here,' Lucy said as they approached the Via Legnano. 'Please, Sofia – allow me a few seconds of my own company at least.'

'Make sure you go straight back.'

'I will.' She watched as Sofia walked away towards the museum. As soon as she was out of sight, Lucy took a detour down a side street. She had been given a gift – a tiny morsel of freedom – but she was hungry for more, whatever it might cost her.

When James and Ottolenghi arrived at the museum, they found Sofia standing outside next to a huddle of girls who were laughing and chattering amongst themselves. Their profession was not immediately obvious. They were all dressed in similar hooded cloaks, differing only in colour and the odd detail – a ribbon here and a button there. James noticed that Ada, the girl who had asked him to help find her missing friend, was not among them.

'I do not think the university will like this,' Sofia muttered.

A carriage stood by the entrance. An elegant hand beckoned to Sofia from the window as they approached.

'Signora Panatti,' Sofia said and nodded in acknowledgement.

'Signorina Esposito, how are you?'

Sofia gave a guarded smile. 'I am well, *grazie*. Wouldn't you prefer to wait inside?'

'Yes, I would. Signor Murray is late. I will have to admonish him.' James noticed Sofia raise her eyebrows slightly.

He approached the carriage and bowed. The door opened and he held out his hand to Concetta Panatti, who stepped out elegantly and made her way into the building. As they entered, James noticed the contrast between the cacophony created by the girls outside and the tranquillity inside.

A red-faced Professor Gemelli stood waiting for them.

'What is the meaning of this? Where is Professor Lombroso?'

Concetta Panatti stepped forward and extended her gloved hand towards him. 'I'm sure he will be here soon.'

Gemelli's mouth was hanging open. He took her hand and shook it.

'May I introduce the dean of the faculty, Professor Gemelli,' James said.

'I know the professor. We have met before . . . many times. Delighted to see you again,' Concetta Panatti said to a now blushing Gemelli. 'I am such an admirer of the university. I find the male intellect so attractive. I am sure my employees will be delighted to see you again.'

Gemelli paused while he recovered himself. 'I take it you are here at the invitation of Professor Lombroso?'

'Yes, the dear man asked me to bring some of my young ladies to the university to be interviewed.'

'Really?'

'Yes, Professor. I do so apologise for the noise. But you see, they are so excited to be here . . . in a seat of learning, as it were.'

'Well, quite, but they cannot stay there . . . er, here, rather.'

'Why not? They will be so disappointed.'

'Well, you see . . . that is to say . . .'

The door opened and Lombroso backed in. 'Yes, ladies, I will let you in shortly. Please be patient for a little while longer.'

He surveyed the scene: Gemelli standing next to Concetta

Panatti, with James, Ottolenghi and Sofia watching. 'What an interesting tableau,' he remarked.

Concetta Panatti smiled, though not with her eyes, James noticed. 'There! You see, I said that the professor would be here before too long, and here he is, come to rescue us all.'

Lombroso responded with a deep bow.

'That is all very well. But what of the . . . er . . . young ladies?' Gemelli said.

'That should have been dealt with when they arrived.' Lombroso glared at James and Ottolenghi. 'Where have you two gentlemen been? I distinctly remember telling you to come here directly and organise the interviews. You see, Signora Panatti, what I have to put up with.'

She nodded sympathetically. 'Indeed I do, Professor. You are both very bad!' she said, looking intently at James and smiling slyly again.

'I do apologise,' James said. He noticed that Ottolenghi remained silent.

'I will deal with you both later,' Lombroso said. 'Now can you get on with the work I asked you to do and sort out our subjects outside?'

'About that,' Gemelli said. 'Lombroso . . . a word.'

'While you two gentlemen discuss things, perhaps Signor Murray could conduct his interview with me?' Concetta Panatti said.

'Very well,' Lombroso replied. 'Ottolenghi, Sofia – can you deal with the ladies? Murray, why don't you show Signora Panatti around before you talk to her? Now, Gemelli, you wished to discuss something with me. Will it take long? I am extremely busy, as you can see . . .'

They strode up the stairs together, Gemelli trying to keep up with Lombroso and talking all the while. James could not hear all of it, but the words 'unacceptable' and 'expressly forbidden' told him all he wanted to know.

Concetta Panatti took his arm and seemed to guide him towards one of the many entrances to the exhibits rooms, as if it was she doing the escorting. Sofia's posture was rigid and her mouth was set in a grim line.

'Would you give me a moment, Signora Panatti?' James said.

'Of course, but do not be too long. There is so much for us to discuss.'

He went over to Sofia. 'It was not Chiara.'

Sofia crossed herself. 'Thank God. Who was it?'

'A flower seller called Caterina Spirito.'

'From San Callisto?'

He nodded. 'Chiara is safe, I am sure of it.'

'I hope you are right,' Sofia said. 'But none of us can know until she is found, and the other girls too. James . . .'

'What?'

'Take care.' She glanced towards the exhibits rooms for a few seconds before leaving to help Ottolenghi in his efforts to organise the girls.

Concetta Panatti swept back in. 'Signor Murray, you are neglecting me.'

'I do apologise. There was something I needed to deal with.'

'It is of no matter. I found your colleague,' she said, indicating Anna Tarnovsky, who was waiting for them by one of the exhibits. 'She has been most helpful, although I imagine she is too busy to join us.'

'Not at all, Signora,' Anna said, smiling. 'After you, James.'

He led the way through the door. 'This is the corridor of skeletons, Signora,' he said as they wandered along the passage lined with the bones of executed criminals. She ran her fingers over them lightly, caressing them as she wandered past, and again he imagined pulling her to him, pressing his lips against hers and feeling her respond to his touch. Suddenly he thought of Sofia, with whom he had had a highly charged encounter in this very place when they had first met. He felt disloyal for a moment but pushed it out of his mind. Sofia had rejected him, and although he still had hopes for them as friends, he no longer believed that anything more was possible.

'How fascinating,' Concetta Panatti said. 'What do you think, Signora Tarnovsky?'

'I agree, they are very interesting.'

'But, of course, one might ask why the professor has collected them. Should they not have been buried? What about their families?'

'They were all criminals, Signora Panatti,' Anna said. 'As I am sure you know, they would not be buried in consecrated ground.'

'Still, their loved ones might wish to remember them, for all their badness in life,' Concetta Panatti said.

'I would not have thought you would be so sentimental,' Anna said. 'A criminal is a criminal for all eternity . . . unless of course he has seen fit to confess his sins before God prior to death.'

'Now it is you who sound sentimental.'

'Not a God-fearing woman then, signora?'

'I fear no one, deity or otherwise.'

'Perhaps we should try another room?' James said, hoping to dilute the tension, though he suspected it was his alone.

'I think not,' Concetta Panatti said. 'I think it is time we started our interview.' She glanced at Anna. 'You need not trouble yourself. I am sure the Professor will have some tasks for you to perform.'

Anna narrowed her eyes. 'I will leave you to it, then.'

'Thank you, Anna,' James said. He indicated a small office. 'Shall we, signora?'

'How kind,' Concetta Panatti said, smiling insincerely at Anna.

'*Too* kind,' Anna murmured before mouthing a good luck to James.

He was relieved to be away from the crossfire. Now he just had to deal with one force of nature rather than two.

'So, Signor Murray . . . May I call you James?' Concetta Panatti asked.

James attempted a reply. 'Well, Signora Panatti . . .'

'Concetta, please.'

'I do not think the professor would approve.'

'But he is not here, James, so when it is just you and I . . .'

James nodded, making a mental note to try not to use her name at all. He could not say why, but it just seemed wrong . . . too intimate, too personal.

'Your questions, then, James,' Concetta said. She unfurled herself effortlessly on to a chaise longue until she was reclining elegantly as if posing for a portrait.

'Am I right in thinking that you have declined to use the professor's lie-detecting equipment?'

'That is so, James. I have no secrets – not from you – so I did not see the point. You can be certain that I will tell you the truth. And I am sure our relationship is such that you will do likewise.'

James cleared his throat. She always seemed able to unnerve him. 'May I ask you about your upbringing?'

'It was uneventful. My parents were unexciting people who

lacked imagination in almost every aspect of their lives, with the obvious exception of producing me.'

'Is there anything in your past that is significant?'

'In what respect?'

'In relation to your current profession.'

'I am a businesswoman, James.'

'Yes, but at least one of your business interests is considered by some to be immoral.'

'Running whores, you mean?'

He flinched at her terminology. 'You are trying to shock me.'

'I am sorry that you find my frankness disconcerting. For some reason I thought that you of all people would be more . . .' she paused, 'open. You must understand that I see what I do as more of a service to mankind. Men need physical love, James. You will know that. And that is the commodity I supply. It is no different to any of my other business concerns.'

'You say that, but you do not advertise your association with Madame Giulia's, do you?' James said.

She nodded. 'True, but that is because I prefer to maintain a certain position in society. As I have said before, people can be so judgemental.'

James hesitated. Ada's absence troubled him to the extent that he felt he could not ignore it.

'Tell me, do you have another place similar to Madame Giulia's?'

The smile froze on Concetta's face for an instant. 'What makes you ask that?'

'Oh, just something I heard.'

'Really? Well, as it is untrue, I think it better that you put it from your mind.' Her voice was harsher now, though still low and sensual.

'I notice one of the girls is missing... Ada, is it, the red-head?'

'You are very observant, James. I suppose it is because you are a scientist.'

'Perhaps,' he said. 'Where is she?'

'You would have to ask Valeria. She takes care of the girls. I did hear that one of them was... how shall I put it... indisposed? She had to leave us after she became diseased. I suppose that might have been Ada. As I have told you before, these girls come and go. Now, are you going to ask me some proper questions?'

James studied her. Her expression wasn't exactly hostile, but it was clear that the subject was closed.

'As you wish. Could we return to your past? Was there something in it that may have led to your work?'

She paused, her head tilted slightly, as if summing him up. 'I will tell you if you will tell me. What in your past provoked your interest in studying criminals? It will go no further. Just think of it as the affirming of trust between us.'

He paused for a moment. Could he trust her? He doubted it. 'I hope you do not think me rude, but I am here to interview you, not vice versa.'

There was a silence as she scrutinised him, her eyes narrowed as if she was trying her best to claw her way into his mind.

'It will be something to do with your father. It always is.'

He caught his breath. How could she possibly know? Who could have told her?

'I am right, am I not? From your reaction it must have been something extreme.'

'There is nothing to react to,' he said carefully.

'You are lying, James. I thought we had an understanding.'

'Why did you say "It always is"?' James asked. 'What did your father do to you?'

She laughed, but without humour. 'Everything and nothing.'

'Go on,' he said.

'Not until you tell me something personal about yourself.'

'What sort of thing?'

'A memory.'

'I have no memories that I wish to share.'

'Really? Then perhaps I will have to think of one for you. What about your work? I think there is a little frisson of excitement that goes through you when you see a question that needs to be answered. Am I right?'

He was unable to maintain eye contact with her.

'Now I wonder . . . your father, he is the one who taught you about desire . . . the desire to know, no matter what the price.'

'I don't know what you are talking about.'

'More lies, James. You should be ashamed.' She studied him. He could see that she was enjoying the effect she was having on him. 'I see that you *are* ashamed. What did he do, your father? Why has it had such an influence on you?'

'We must talk about you, not me.'

She shook her head in triumph. 'I think you are afraid of something or someone. Yes! You are afraid of yourself. Of what you are.'

Those words again. How should he react? He decided on caution. 'I will not say any more, signora. You agreed to talk to me. If you are not proposing to do so, then perhaps we should end this interview.' He prepared himself to leave.

'Wait!' she commanded. 'I have not finished.' She cast her eyes over him in appraisal, then smiled, but there was no pleasure in it. He thought he could detect something else. What was it? Scorn, perhaps? An underlying derision? She began to speak.

'It happened when I was thirteen. I had an encounter with one of my father's employees. He thought that I was his for the taking. I was not, as he learnt to his cost.'

'You hurt him?'

'I killed him.'

James had not been expecting that. She had spoken defiantly. It was clear that she felt no remorse. 'And were there consequences?' he asked.

'I told the truth – that it was self-defence – and no charges were brought. The man's family were paid off at my mother's insistence, but my father . . .'

'What did he do?'

'He did nothing, but he made it clear that he did not believe me. He told me that I was born bad.' She hesitated, leaning back and closing her eyes.

'And?'

'He was certainly right. In fact I have spent the rest of my life proving him so.'

'You run a brothel. There are worse things.'

She got up from the chaise longue and stepped towards him. He found himself flinching as she laid her hand upon his face, caressing it slowly before tracing the shape of his lips with her finger. Instinctively he gripped her wrist and moved her hand away. Again she mocked him with her smile. 'Oh, I have done worse things,' she whispered into his ear. 'As have you.'

She went to the door and turned the key, then walked back to him until they were so close that he felt her breath on his face – an earthy aroma like a forest after the rain. She brushed her lips lightly over his, sending a frisson of longing through him. Her response was another kiss – long, deep, sensuous. It was as if the world around them had ceased to exist. She did not want it to end there, that much was clear.

He did not love her. She was not that kind of woman. But in that instant, part of him wanted to be possessed by her. She had him now, and if he did not stop her, he knew that she would never let him go. His path to self-destruction was only too clear. He had betrayed Sofia with that kiss, but then he did not deserve her love. This . . . this was what he deserved. Because unlike Sofia, Concetta Panatti knew what he really was.

At that moment, he understood that if he allowed this to continue, then his life, all that James Murray was and could ever be, would begin slowly and inexorably to unravel. That was too high a price to pay. He had others to think of.

He pushed Concetta Panatti away.

She stood back, contempt in her eyes. 'Too late, James, too late.'

30

In England under the Restoration, masses of women assisted in the hideous tortures of the Puritans. These were acts of impotent cruelty, a type that gives pleasure without any expenditure of energy. Like all human activities in which a power outside the individual produces pleasure, so too, ferocious or cruel activities can cause delight, the delight of blood intoxication.

Lombroso and Ferrero, 1893, p. 67

Lucy stood in the main hall of the Museo Egizio and viewed her mummified companions lying snugly in their sarcophagi. It reminded her of when she and James had been taken by their father to the British Museum to see the collection of Egyptian artefacts. She had found the experience profoundly moving, and James had teased her a little for being tearful over an account of the death and burial of a young boy. Her father had been far more understanding, or so she had thought at the time. But that was before everything had changed. Lucy's memories of that period were odd, disjointed things: the sound of muffled voices raised but indistinct; her mother sobbing inconsolably and James kneeling at her feet trying to comfort her; and an overwhelming feeling that something dreadful had happened. But the worst memory of all was that of her increasing and terrible realisation that her father's absence was permanent because of something bad that he had done. Somehow she had decided that it must be her fault too, and she had tried to make amends by bargaining with God in her prayers. But it had not worked, and now her father was dead and her mother too.

The mummies, or rather their cases, were elaborately decorated with pictures and hieroglyphics. They had tried to cheat death by planning an existence in the afterworld, and they too had been let down by their gods. Perhaps that was why she felt their pain so acutely. She certainly seemed to be sensitive to such things, as Professor Donati had pointed out last time she had been here. But that was not the reason for her coming here today. Miss Trott had met with the Egyptologist and argued with him. Lucy wanted to know why.

'Signorina Murray, I am delighted that you are visiting us again.' Professor Donati was behind her, smiling enigmatically. He did not look suspicious or guilty, or even remotely shifty, Lucy thought. But perhaps that was an act in itself.

'Professor Donati, thank you for agreeing to see me.'

'Not at all. I had hoped you would come.' He glanced behind her. 'No Francesco today, or anyone else?'

'No, Professor. Today I came alone.'

She scrutinised him. When she had first met him, she had thought him dapper, but now she could see that his face was fleshy and slightly dissipated. He might have been considered handsome in his youth, but that was no longer the case, and in his heart he knew it. He stared back at her. His eyes were a deep brown and had a tendency to wander, as if he was searching for something worthwhile to focus on. Disconcertingly, once they had alighted upon her, it felt for a moment as if he was inside her mind.

'Ah, you are a modern young lady then. That is refreshing, I suppose. Have you told anyone that you are here?'

'I have not, Professor. But then I do not see why my brother can travel anywhere he chooses on his own whereas I am expected to seek company whether I want it or not.' He looked a little anxious, presumably in response to the suggestion of female emancipation. 'Perhaps modern is not strictly accurate. I see myself more as an explorer in a foreign city.'

'You are certainly that, signorina. What is it you wish to explore?'

'I wanted to discuss the artefacts you showed us last time I was here. Would that be possible?'

'I am working with some new exhibits down in the basement. Would you care to accompany me? Strictly speaking, of course, you should be chaperoned, but as you are so progressive in your outlook, perhaps you would not mind?'

Lucy hesitated for a moment, but then nodded her acceptance. 'I would think that the search for knowledge should always take precedence over niceties, Professor. Thank you.'

'Excellent. Please follow me. We will be undisturbed down here.' He started to walk down some broad stone steps into the bowels of the building, humming the same tune as when they had first met. Lucy followed him. He was not wearing his long coat or skullcap today, but was dressed in a sombre suit. She noticed that it was worn in places and the sleeves were fraying at the cuffs.

There were no windows in the room where the professor was working, so it was darker and more oppressive than the others she had seen. They were quite alone. A number of metal tools were lying on a nearby table next to some pieces of stone. Could one of them be a scalpel? Lucy started as she saw some figures staring back at her from the corner. She relaxed when she realised that it was just a facsimile of a tomb with wax representations of the participants.

'A scene from the Book of the Dead, signorina. I thought it might interest you.'

Lucy peered at the figures. 'It is unusual to find such a thing in a museum, is it not?'

The professor nodded in a not entirely convincing show of humility. 'We are the first to include waxworks, I believe. They will go on display in the next week or so. I felt it was important to give the visitor a sense of what it was like to be at such a ritual.'

'To bring it to life?'

'Indeed, though I accept that given the subject matter, the motive might be seen as somewhat ironic.'

Lucy shivered.

'I hope I have not frightened you, signorina,' the professor said. He was standing close to her now and leaning towards her. He smelt of cheap cologne. She stepped away from him and his beady eyes followed her.

'No, no. It is a little cold, that's all,' she said.

'Ah yes. We deliberately keep it cool down here in order to preserve some of our rarer exhibits.'

Lucy studied the decorations on the robe worn by the priest overseeing the ritual. There it was again, she noticed – the green and gold serpent . . .

'I see you are looking at Apep, the evil demon,' the professor observed. 'He is an interesting character. Or deity, perhaps I should say. One would not want to upset him. He is an extremely powerful entity.'

'In what respect?' Lucy asked.

'In every respect. If crossed, he has the power of complete

destruction. He is the encircler of the world, the dark demon, the spirit of evil.'

'You speak of him as if he was real.'

The professor hesitated. 'Well now, who are we to say that he is not?'

'Are there people who believe in Apep?'

'He has a following in some quarters, and his wife as well, of course – Tawaret, the demon goddess.'

'I didn't know that gods and demons got married.'

'I imagine it was a rather different institution from the one that we enjoy today.'

Lucy thought his use of language interesting. She wasn't at all sure that marriage was something to be enjoyed, particularly if you were a wife. 'So people actually worship Apep?'

'There are all manner of gods.'

'Something for everyone, then.'

'It is not a joking matter, signorina. It is entirely possible that those who follow these gods or demons, whichever you prefer, are a danger to themselves and perhaps even others.' He frowned at her. 'I do hope that you are not—'

'Oh no, I am asking merely for information, Professor. But I am interested in any rituals that might be connected.'

'And the nature of your interest?'

'Purely academic, Professor.'

'You are a very self-assured young lady.'

Lucy considered this. She hadn't felt anything of the kind when she arrived in Turin. Might that have changed? She decided to maintain her apparent boldness. 'How well do you know Miss Trott?'

'What an extraordinary question! I don't, except of course for our meeting when you were present. Why do you ask?'

There was no point in shilly-shallying. No self-respecting

detective would do that. 'I saw you together at a café in the Via Po.' Was it her imagination, or did the professor's brows furrow ever so slightly at this?

'Yes, of course. My apologies. I had quite forgotten. We met by chance. She is a charming lady.'

'You didn't seem to find her so,' Lucy said. 'In fact you seemed to be shouting at her, if anything.'

'You . . . you must have been mistaken, signorina.' He took a few steps towards her. Again she backed away, but this time he continued until she was trapped against a wall.

'Forgive me, Professor Donati, but I must go. I have to meet someone.'

'I thought you had told no one of your visit here.'

'I was mistaken.'

He hesitated for a second before standing aside. 'Then I wonder if I might escort you out. I am afraid that I too have remembered an appointment.' He moved towards the door and waited for her.

'Of course, and thank you for showing me the exhibit. Perhaps we shall meet again soon.'

'Perhaps,' he replied in a tone that made it clear that he would rather they didn't. 'But I would have thought that a young lady like yourself, with such a pure kind of beauty, should be concentrating on more appropriate matters – marriage and children, for instance.'

'There will be time enough for that,' Lucy said. 'For the present, I prefer the pursuit of knowledge to that of a husband.'

'Be careful, Signorina Murray. Too much knowledge can be a dangerous thing.'

'I am not sure that you have that quite right, Professor,' Lucy said.

Donati merely raised his eyebrows and gave a supercilious smile as he gesticulated towards the steps.

Lucy obediently followed him upstairs. At the entrance, she said goodbye and began the short walk home. She forced herself to look back and saw him watching her intently. After a moment, he swivelled on his heel and went back into the museum. Looking down, she noticed that her hands were trembling. She shook them gently and focused on the facts. What exactly did he mean by 'a pure kind of beauty'?

All in all, she felt that had discovered very little. Still, what she had found out seemed significant. Anna Tarnovsky was married, so if James was involved with her it was an illicit liaison. Sofia was hiding something, and that something was to do with James. Miss Trott was in Turin for a purpose other than being her companion, but its nature was as yet unknown, although it seemed there was some connection with Professor Donati. Whether or not it was related to Apep, the evil demon, was still a mystery, but of one thing she was sure: Donati had lied to her about his relationship with Miss Trott. In fact he had been quite menacing towards her. What Lucy didn't know was why.

As James walked into Lombroso's laboratory, he was immediately taken back to the last time he had been in Turin. Even the equipment that Ottolenghi was setting up seemed no different.

After what had just passed between him and Concetta Panatti, it was a relief to get back the comparatively mundane nature of the experiments with her girls. He could still smell her musky scent on him. It made him feel unclean. She had consumed him so completely that it was hard to shake the memory away. Something else was there too – an overwhelming sense of guilt that gnawed at him even now and could surely only become more marked as time went on. Dealing with the professor's experiments would provide a welcome distraction.

'The plethysmograph – is that your lie-detecting machine, Professor?' he asked.

Lombroso was standing next to it. The expression on his face was that of a father watching as his beloved child took its first steps. 'Yes, I suppose so, although there is a sphygmograph needed too. I have made some changes so that it is more responsive. And I would not call it a lie-detecting machine. Really, Murray . . . you should know by now that to name it so would be overstating the capability of what we have here.'

James nodded, realising that it would be utterly pointless to remind the professor that it was he who had named the equipment in the first place.

'Anyway, the most it can tell us about these girls is how their vascular system responds to various questions,' Lombroso added. 'That is what we are about today.'

'I suppose what we are really examining is the extent to which the body betrays itself,' Ottolenghi said as he tugged on some wiring.

James walked over to his friend, who seemed to be struggling rather. His face was a study in concentration as he twiddled with various knobs. It was an odd-looking piece of equipment. At its heart was a kind of airtight glove attached to a rubber membrane. This in turn was connected to a pen that rolled over the surface of a rotating drum.

'Remind me, Professor, how does it work?'

'Really, can't you remember from last time, Murray?'

James shrugged. A lot had happened to him since then.

Surely it was not reasonable to expect him to recall every last detail. But then reasonableness was not one of Lombroso's strengths at the best of times.

'Well do me the courtesy of listening now, and try not to forget again,' Lombroso said slowly, as if addressing a small child, another of his less than endearing habits. 'The speed of the pen varies with the subject's blood flow. We believe that when someone tells a lie, the stress of deception affects his or her heart rate and blood pressure. If the researcher watches and observes the deviations traced by the pen, then he might be able to tell if and when the subject is lying.'

'I see. So how do you wish us to conduct the experiment? Do you have a list of questions?'

'I do. Ottolenghi kindly worked on them before he left to study fairy tales with Reiner.'

'They're not fairy tales, Professor,' Ottolenghi protested. 'Some of what he told me—'

'Yes, yes, we don't have time to go into it now,' Lombroso said, shaking his head impatiently. 'Let's get the first subject in. Are you ready?'

Each subject had to be connected up to the machine, which was not an easy task in itself. The girls tended to wriggle about and pull off the wires if they found them uncomfortable. The machine was accurate in some cases but not in all. The results were interesting, according to Lombroso, apparently indicating that the subjects were, for the most part, lying about their pasts. They were far franker about the present, it seemed, which Lombroso said was only to be expected, given their weak moral sensitivity and lack of feeling. James was not certain that he agreed completely with the professor's summary of their findings. It seemed to him that most of the women they had spoken to were quite frank about their motivations for embarking on a career in prostitution. The only lies they told were to themselves, and related to the future rather than the past. Many seemed convinced that they would escape their situation and retire either through being rescued by a respectable man or becoming the exclusive property of a rich one.

'Women keep tears in their pockets,' Lombroso declared. 'Not only that, but they also have two sorts of tears: one for sadness and the other for deceit.'

'And are these results from previous experiments?' James asked, half joking.

'No, they are well-known Italian proverbs,' Lombroso replied, as if that amounted to scientific discovery and fact. He was very fond of proverbs, James had noticed, as well as anecdotes. But was it really science?

One of the last girls to be seen was Nora, who had been measured at Madame Giulia's. She was slightly older than the others they had encountered, and had reminded James a little of Sofia – or more accurately of what Sofia might have become had Lombroso not rescued her.

Ottolenghi showed her in and guided her to the couch. She sat down and stared at the equipment. 'What in heaven's name is that?'

'It is a device for measuring the blood pressure and so on. Murray, will you strap the lady in?'

Nora laughed. 'Lady? It is a long time since anyone has referred to me as such. And to have such learned gentlemen dance attendance on me – what a treat!'

Carefully James pushed Nora's sleeve up and put her arm into the airtight glove. 'You have a very gentle touch, Dottore,' she said.

'Now, Signor Murray here will ask you some questions. Here, Murray, take these.' Lombroso handed him a list.

'What is your name?' he asked.

'Ah – an easy one to start with. I am called Nora Santorini, these days anyway. I did have another name, the one I was christened with, but that was so long ago now I have forgotten it.'

'I find that hard to believe, signorina.'

'Yes, yes. Get on with it!' Lombroso said impatiently.

'How did you come to your current profession?'

'How very polite you are! But then that is an English trait, is it not?'

'I am from Scotland, actually. Can you tell us how you became a . . .' He paused, not knowing how to put it.

'A whore . . . You can say it, Signor Scozzese. I do not mind speaking plainly.' Her smile had left her. 'I left my home in the countryside to come to the city to find work. The Morals Squad found me on the streets and . . . let's just say they found a use for me.'

'You were forced into prostitution?' James asked. He had heard of the dreaded Morals Squad from Sofia, but had not quite believed her account. Perhaps he had been wrong to doubt her.

'*Sì*, it is a common enough story.'

'Do you enjoy your work?' Lombroso asked.

James frowned at the list. The question was not there.

'I am good at what I do. Would you like an appointment, Professor? Perhaps I could demonstrate it to you.'

'With all due respect, signorina, that is not the same as enjoyment,' Lombroso said. 'Does it fulfil you, make you happy?'

'Make me happy? You would like to believe that, I think.

All my clients would, too. But you want the truth, don't you? Now let me see... do I enjoy lying on my back for any man who wants to buy the privilege, however old or dirty, allowing him to grope and grunt, to hold me down until I bruise, to salivate over me before he mounts me or to make me kneel before him for his pleasure...' She stopped and shrugged. 'And that is a good customer on a good day. Enjoy? What do you think?'

James focused on the machine. It was a good deal easier than looking Nora Santorini in the face. If she was lying, he would expect to see the pen moving up and down furiously as she spoke to reflect the change in her blood pressure. Instead it maintained a flat and steady line. There were no lies here. Perhaps the professor's machine was more efficient at the detection of lies than he had thought. Encouraged, he decided to try something.

'Have you been chosen for the other place?'

Finally the machine responded, and yet she had not spoken.

'What other place, Murray? What are you talking about?' Lombroso asked. 'That is not a question from the list!'

'No. I have not,' Nora said.

'Do you know about it? What goes on there?'

'I do not.' The machine continued to respond.

'What happened to Agnella?'

There was fear in Nora's eyes.

'Where is Ada?'

She ripped off the wires that attached her to the equipment, got off the couch and left the room.

The few remaining interviews had taken longer than James had anticipated. He had been forbidden by Lombroso to ask any further questions; they could not, he said, afford to lose any more girls. Given Nora's response, it seemed more and more likely that Agnella had not merely run off as Concetta had suggested, and that something had also happened to Ada. For the moment, however, he was forced to concentrate on the matter at hand.

Eventually Lombroso looked at his watch. 'I have to go, Murray. I have work to do. Can you complete the final experiment?' And then, before James could answer one way or another: 'The girl is waiting outside. I'll send her in.'

James was tired and hungry. Everyone else had been permitted to leave. Ottolenghi had departed to work on one of the professor's papers. Even Sofia had gone. Now he had another girl to interview before he too could make his way home.

'*Buonasera*.' The girl slid in through the door as if she did not want to be seen. 'Are you ready for me, Dottore?'

James did not recognise her. She had not been at Madame Giulia's when he had conducted the measuring experiments with the professor. She was blonde and well built in an obvious kind of way. No doubt she would be sought after for such charms, though they left James cold. There was something about her face . . . Her teeth protruded slightly from her full lips and her eyes were narrowed and sly. He doubted that he would be hearing much in the way of truth from her.

'Sit down on the couch, if you would,' he said. 'Now, could you roll up your sleeve?'

The girl obeyed. He attached the equipment with some care. She seemed to have positioned herself so that he had to lean over her to get everything into the right place, and he was acutely aware of the rise and fall of her breasts as he tightened the various wires.

'You seem nervous, Dottore,' she said. 'Perhaps a little

tumble might relax you. I wouldn't charge . . . well, not the first time anyway.'

James gave a thin smile. 'No thank you. I am perfectly relaxed already. Now, shall we get on?'

She grinned. 'Yes, let's.'

'Name?'

'Gabriella.'

'And how did you get into this line of business, Gabriella?'

'Through my family.'

'Could you explain a little?'

'My mother was a whore, my father was a thief.'

'So you were born into it?'

'You could say that, I suppose.'

'And how long have you been in your current position?'

'About five minutes,' Gabriella replied with a raucous cackle. 'I wouldn't mind staying in it a bit longer if only you'd take up my invitation.'

She was all smiles on the surface, but there was something else there too.

'The thing is, Gabriella, I don't think you want to be what you are.'

She stopped smiling immediately. 'Yes I do.'

The pencil swung up and down.

'Why?' James asked. 'Tell me. I genuinely want to know.'

'Do you? It's all very well for someone like you. You've never had to worry about where your next meal is coming from or whether you'll have a roof over your head. You stand there all fancy and la-di-da, doing experiments on us like we're nothing.'

'So I am right, then?'

'What comes next? Don't tell me. I suppose you want to

rescue me . . . Well I've been rescued before, *caro*. It's just more of the same.'

'I have no intention of rescuing you, as you put it. I am just curious, that's all.'

'Oh, I've had enough of this.' Like Nora before her, she ripped off the various wires and stood up. 'People like you make me sick. You want to examine us, hiding behind your science, when really you're just as bad as any of our clients. '

James shrugged and showed her out of the room. She stood by the door, her hands on her hips. 'Come on then. Escort me out.'

They went into the hall together and he was about to send her in the direction of the kitchen and the rear entrance when she turned to him.

'Oh no, Dottore. If I'm good enough to be researched, then I'm good enough for the front door.'

He tried to usher her through it quickly, but she stopped and gave him a disdainful stare. '*Arrivederci, Dottore*. I am sure we will be meeting again before too long.'

She made her way down the steps and walked over to a carriage that seemed to be waiting for her. The door opened and she got in. James watched as it drove away. He thought he caught a glimpse of red hair through the window, but he could not be certain. He rubbed his eyes. It had been a very long day.

31

Prostitutes are both sexually frigid and sexually precocious. They present us with a real tangle of contradictions: an eminently sexual profession, practised by women in who sexuality has almost been extinguished; and women who, despite their weak sexual drive, devote themselves to vice at an age when they are barely ready for sexual intercourse. What, then, is the origin of prostitution? Psychologically, as I will show, it originates not in lust but moral insanity.

Lombroso and Ferrero, 1893, p. 213

At dinner that evening, Lucy was decidedly on edge. First and foremost in her mind was whether Miss Trott could be involved in some kind of criminal enterprise. She decided to observe her carefully with a view to making some notes in her journal later. That was exactly what *Pinkerton's Detection Manual* would advise, she had no doubt.

She took a sideways glance at her companion and watched as she examined her food thoroughly before taking a mouthful. Each foray to the plate began as a mere speculative enquiry as to the fitness of the chosen morsel; once satisfied that it was indeed worthy, she would put it delicately into her mouth and chew it carefully.

No one could say that Miss Trott was an obvious candidate

for criminality. Of course, Lucy could consult the work of her esteemed host to assist her. She made a mental note to re-examine the volume *Criminal Man*, which, despite its name, did have some minor references to criminal women. No doubt Paola and Gina could also help in that regard. According to them, the professor had some pictures of female criminals, which might well be useful for identification purposes if nothing else. Perhaps she should consult him. Lucy tried to imagine the conversation but somehow couldn't.

Gina and Paola were talking animatedly to one other. They were evidently having some dispute, and their mother and Anna were acting as arbiters. Gina stabbed at her food with a fork, waving it around occasionally to emphasise her argument. Her mother gently took hold of her wrist and guided it back to her plate. Paola was more thoughtful, but Lucy could see that her points, though made with less passion, were more compelling, judging from the expression on Anna's face. Gina was losing the argument and she knew it.

Ottolenghi and Lombroso were deep in their own discussion, and as she studied them, the source of Gina's passion for argument became clear. The professor also waved his cutlery around as he spoke, though his movements were more expansive and his views delivered with a confidence that Gina did not yet possess. Naturally no one dared to guide his hand back to his plate.

Ottolenghi had his own version of passion, but it was more understated than the professor's. He had seemed initially to be a quiet sort of man, but here in the middle of some kind of debate he was bright-eyed and alert. He had a habit of pushing his round wire-framed glasses up the bridge of his long nose as he listened and nodded. He occasionally paused to eat, and when he did, he attacked his food, spearing it like a hunter, and then added his view on whatever was under discussion, as if spearing ideas too.

James was seated between the professor and Ottolenghi. Their conversation seemed to ebb and flow around him while he sat like a small island in the midst of it, staring into space and pushing his food around his plate. He was hunched over it in that way he had when he was worried about something, as if the burden had become so great that he could no longer sit upright. Lucy wished that he would confide in her. She knew he still saw her as a child, but she was mature enough to understand that something was wrong. He had been so confident and relaxed when they were travelling here, delighted and excited at the prospect of a new life. But now that man seemed to have disappeared completely, to be replaced by the old James: diminishing in stature almost daily after their father's illness had begun, as if he wanted nothing more than to shrink into the shadows of anonymity for ever more.

'I think our findings will reveal some interesting traits, both physical and emotional,' Lombroso said with a self-satisfied smile spreading across his face. 'Don't you think, Murray?'

James blinked and shook his head slightly.

'What? You do not agree?' Lombroso boomed. 'Then you must say why.'

'I'm sure you're right, Professor,' James said. 'Although as there is quite a lot of variation between the subjects, I am not sure that any patterns of behaviour will be established.'

Lombroso stroked his beard thoughtfully. 'That is true. They are by their nature contradictory. Some, for example, are both sexually frigid and sexually precocious. It is a real tangle.'

'Cesare, really!' Signora Lombroso shook her head at him. 'This is not suitable conversation for the dinner table. I do not know how many times I must say it.'

'I apologise, my dear,' Lombroso said airily. 'Murray here has opened up an interesting area for discussion.'

'Well discuss it later, please.' Signora Lombroso turned to Lucy. 'Are you looking forward to the marchesa's ball?'

'Yes, I am, signora, very much,' Lucy said, not entirely truthfully. She had not given it much thought recently. Still, it would be an interesting experience. She had not been to a ball before. Aunt Agnes did not approve of such things.

'We are going too,' Gina said. 'I cannot wait.'

'We shall be leaving early,' her mother said firmly. 'And I do not want any arguments or fuss when the time comes.'

'Very well, Mama,' Gina said, though from her expression it seemed that both fuss and arguments were more than likely.

'It sounds as if it will be quite an occasion,' Anna said. 'The marchesa tells me that she has done her best to invite everyone of interest in Turin.'

'Of course, those are very subjective criteria,' Lombroso said. 'What I find of interest and what the marchesa does might well be different.'

His wife smiled. 'I imagine your guest list would include members of the criminal fraternity, and I don't think the marchesa has that in mind.'

An image flashed into Lucy's mind of various convicts in prison uniforms shuffling in shackles around the marchesa's palazzo. Now that really would be interesting.

When dinner came to an end, as it was not a formal occasion, they all gathered in the drawing room for coffee, rather than separating according to gender. This was with the exception of Miss Trott, who had retired early again, pleading another headache. Freed from her surveillance, Lucy watched Anna take out a small, slim cigar, which Ottolenghi lit for her, and sit back in her armchair as she joined her male colleagues in their conversation, every inch their equal.

'Isn't she marvellous?' whispered Gina. Lucy nodded, but she knew it was not as simple as it appeared to be. It seemed to her that equality was dealt out when it suited but could be snatched away in a moment when it did not. She moved a little closer to the group under cover of studying one of the professor's criminal artefacts, which were arranged on a small shelf in a corner.

'I think the next step is to meet tomorrow morning, pull together all we have, including the data from Prague, and think about how it could be disseminated,' Lombroso was saying.

'Could we do this in the afternoon?' James asked. 'I have some business to attend to outside the city in the morning.'

His tone was anxious. What on earth was so pressing that he would take time off from his beloved research to attend to it?

'Very well, Murray,' Lombroso said. 'I am sure we can accommodate you, but make sure you are on time. I am anxious to present our findings to the wider world.'

'It will be particularly interesting to see if the findings reflect mine in Prague,' Anna said.

'Ah yes, the question of moral insanity – I suspect that will turn out to be significant, but we shall see.'

Her attention wandering, Lucy went over to the floor-length window and looked idly out at the deserted street below as she sipped her coffee. The contrast between the darkness outside and the large bright room full of people chattering and laughing was distinctly unsettling. A figure emerged from the house on to the street and paused briefly beneath a gas lamp. It was Miss Trott. She began to walk slowly along the Via Legnano. After a moment, she stopped and glanced up at the window. Instinctively Lucy drew back, and when she looked out again, Miss Trott had disappeared.

The following morning, James was up bright and early to go to San Callisto. He had told nobody of his intentions, not even Sofia. After what had happened during their last visit, he was only too aware that this might be a dangerous course of action, and he didn't want her involved. He was convinced that the supposedly disused abbey held the key to a number of things, not least his own abduction. But before he went there, he had another call to make.

He pounded on the shabby front door, making it shake so precariously that he softened his knock in case he broke it down. The occupant would probably deserve it, but James wanted something from him, and this was almost certainly not the way to achieve it. Eventually he heard a shuffling and some swearing as the door opened.

'*Merda!* It's practically dawn, and on a Sunday too. What do you want?'

'*Buongiorno,* Baldovino. I see you're as well dressed as ever.' James pushed past the reporter and made his way into the house.

'Hey! What are you doing?'

'I'm here to get some answers.'

The door slammed behind him and Baldovino came in tucking his stained shirt into his equally stained trousers. 'I've told you everything I'm going to. I gave you the list. That was the arrangement.'

James grasped him by his shirt and pulled the man towards him until they were face to face. 'I don't care about any arrangement. I want to know how you got the names in the first place. Who tipped you off?'

'We've been through this already. I can't tell you that. It's more than my life's worth.'

'Who was it?'

Baldovino struggled until James released him, pushing him onto a grubby chair – the same one he himself had slept on when he had tried to drink his way to oblivion after Sofia's rejection.

'What's got into you, *Inglese*?'

'Let's just say I'm tired of being so damned polite. Now give me the name.'

Baldovino got to his feet and tried to square up to him. 'It'll cost you.'

'Give me the name!'

'That won't get you what you want.'

James took a step towards him.

Baldovino lifted his hands in submission. 'All right, all right! If it's that important to you . . .' He went over to a small desk in the corner and pulled out a piece of paper from the back of a drawer. 'Here, take it. I doubt it'll help you. It certainly didn't bring me anything but grief.'

'What do you mean?'

'I made a few enquiries, but then . . .'

'What?'

'I was warned off.'

'So that's why you gave me the list. You wanted me to do your work for you. How were you warned off?'

'Some bastard shoved me down some steps and told me to mind my own business.'

'Did you see who it was?'

'No, and I don't care either, though I'm guessing they were

intimately acquainted with the name on that piece of paper. Still, it's always the quiet ones, as they say.'

'Did you find out anything before you were warned off?'

'Not much, but I did uncover something about that girl in the abbey.'

'What?'

'It'll cost you . . .'

James said nothing.

Baldovino shrugged. 'Suit yourself . . . Nella Calvi was a flower seller.'

'I know that already,' James said, exasperated.

'There's more. Apparently she did some whoring on the side.'

'Really? That *is* interesting.'

'Do you know her professional name?'

'No, I don't, and I'm not sure it really matters.'

'Fair enough. Mind you, it's a shame to end our little arrangement. I thought you could give me some information in return. Some little titbit about the old professor, perhaps.'

'First tell me the girl's other name.'

'All right. You can have this one on account, as it were. As a mark of my goodwill. Nella Calvi's professional name was Agnella. Nice touch, don't you think?'

'Why?'

'Agnella means pure . . . Interesting name considering her occupation. Now, about our arrangement . . .'

'No thanks,' James said.

'Are you sure? There would be a fee. You could spend it on your woman . . . not that she'd appreciate it. Her type never does. Once a whore, eh, *Inglese*?'

James had heard enough. His frustration overwhelmed him, and he charged towards Baldovino, picked the man up and pushed him against the wall. 'If I ever hear you so much as whisper her name, I'll . . .' He let the journalist fall. Finishing the sentence just didn't seem worth it. He had got what he'd come for after all.

He made for the door, leaving Baldovino lying on the floor muttering to himself under his breath: 'You'll be sorry for that, *Inglese* . . . very sorry indeed.' He almost pitied the man. What could someone like Baldovino do to him? Threats were all he had.

He slammed the door as he left, and grinned with satisfaction as it fell halfway off its hinges and swung pathetically back and forth. He stopped for a moment and leant on a nearby wall, hunching over in an effort to gather himself. A year or so ago he would not have dreamt of threatening violence to get what he wanted, but now everything was different. *He* was different. He thought about his father and what the man had become in his later years. Was he the same now?

The chill of the early morning was seeping into his bones. He pulled the piece of paper from his pocket and read the name that was written on it. It made no sense to him. After a moment or two he straightened up and began to walk up the narrow cobbled street towards the main road to hail a cab to San Callisto, the name of Baldovino's source tucked safely back in his pocket and Agnella's real identity in his head. He was annoyed with himself. He should have worked out who she was for himself. Still, it was clear that his visit to the abbey was vital and timely. It seemed that he might be a few steps closer to solving the mystery, and perhaps even finding Chiara.

32

The scarcity of the criminal type and lack of ugliness may cause many to doubt our theory that prostitutes are not only equivalents of criminals but, in fact, have the same characteristics in exaggerated form. However, in addition to the fact that true female criminals are much less ugly than their male counterparts, in prostitutes we have women of great youth in whom the 'beauty of the Devil', with its abundance of soft, fresh flesh and absence of wrinkles, masks anomalies. Another thing to keep in mind is that prostitution calls for a relative lack of peculiarities such as a large jaw and a hardened stare which, if present, might cause disgust and repulsion . . .

Lombroso and Ferrero, 1893, pp. 142–3

Lucy sat in the drawing room pretending to read a book and watching Miss Trott write a letter. She allowed her imagination to run riot. Could it be to some criminal mastermind, perhaps, or was it a coded letter for the head of a smuggling ring?

'I am just writing to your aunt, dear. Do you have any messages?' Miss Trott asked.

Lucy was about to reply when Sofia came in. 'This arrived for you,' she said, handing her an envelope.

Lucy read the note. It was from the Rambaudis, though she suspected it had been written by Bianca rather than Francesco. It was an invitation for her and Miss Trott to take lunch with them that day at their villa on the outskirts of the city.

'I think we should accept,' Miss Trott said. 'It would do you good to venture outside the city and see the countryside. I believe there are some pretty views in that area, and the weather is perfect for such an outing.'

'It is a pity that James can't join us,' Lucy said.

'He is busy at his work, as befits a young man of his intellect.'

'He had some business to conduct outside the city. I heard him say so last night.'

'You *over*heard him, you mean,' Miss Trott said. 'Wherever he is going, that is his business. Eavesdropping is not at all ladylike, and neither is poking one's nose into the affairs of another.'

Was she trying to make a point? Her expression was still rather vague, as if she was somewhere else entirely, or perhaps wished that she was. It did not seem as if she was being pointed.

'It wasn't intentional. I just happened to hear, that's all. He's my brother. I worry about him.'

'Do you? Whyever would you do that?' Miss Trott asked. 'He is old enough to look after himself.'

'I know, but after all that business with Sofia, and being hurt by those men, whoever they were, I can't help it.'

'I suppose that is natural. But you really mustn't worry. I am sure he was simply the victim of some kind of misunderstanding.'

'That is pretty much what he said.'

'Then that is what it was.'

'Still...'

'Still nothing. He is a young man, and sometimes they get into scrapes. It is just one of those things. My advice is to leave him be. He won't thank you for interfering. Now, have you thought about what you will wear for our outing?'

Lucy forced herself to stop worrying about James. Miss Trott was right. There was no point. He would not listen to anything she said anyway. Instead she allowed herself to think about Francesco, and a shiver of anticipation went through her. Did this invitation have any underlying meaning, or was it something more casual? She tried to tell herself that it didn't matter. After all, it would be pleasant to get out of the city for a few hours on a beautiful day like this.

James narrowed his eyes in the sun. He was sitting in the square in San Callisto, considering what to do next. He thought about what he knew, trying to make sense of it. Two of the girls on Baldovino's original list had now been identified. Nella Calvi, the girl found at the abbey, had worked at Madame Giulia's as a prostitute known as Agnella. Teresa Mariani had also worked there as a maid. According to her mother she had been upset about something, possibly a boyfriend she used to meet up with at the abbey. Both were now missing. The body found at the Borgo belonged to a girl called Caterina Spirito, a flower seller friend of Nella/Agnella. That left Arianna Panico, Susanna Russello and Chiara.

He had made further enquiries and had been given a similar story each time. All the missing girls had originated in or near San Callisto but had gone to work in the city. Arianna Panico's family seemed to have left the area long ago. The other families had all been told by the local carabinieri that the girls were most likely to have gone elsewhere, either for another job or because they had met someone. They were left to hope that one day they would be contacted by their missing daughters.

The note with the name of Baldovino's informant on it was still burning a hole in his pocket, and now his mind too. Someone he had trusted had lied to him . . . but why? He pushed his thick dark hair out of his eyes.

An image of Sofia came into his mind. He had betrayed her. Even though he had not instigated the kiss with Concetta Panatti, he had responded. If Sofia found out, that would almost certainly be the end of their friendship. She had always made it clear that trust was more important to her than anything. He leant back and closed his eyes. Why did he always make such a mess of things, allowing his heart to rule his head?

Still, perhaps it was a sign. As Concetta had said, he had done worse things . . . things that would no doubt horrify Sofia if she knew. Once she discovered what he had done, she would walk away from him for ever, and she would be right to do so. All he could do now was to try his best to find Chiara for her. Perhaps it would be enough to retain her friendship. He knew now that he could not expect her love.

Later he would pay another visit to the abbey to see if he could work out why he had been threatened. But first he had to try to find Teresa Mariani's missing lover. According to her friend Giovanna, the young man had worked at the rice estate to the west of the town. James was not sure if he would discover anything there, but it was the only lead he had, so he had decided to pay a visit and ask some questions.

He chose to walk, as it was not too far. Even though it was

cooler up here away from the city, and the path led through woodland, it was still very warm for early spring, and he had taken off his jacket and slung it over his shoulder as he went. He stopped for a moment to rest, sinking down on the mossy ground beneath a tree and leaning against it whilst he took out his handkerchief and wiped his forehead. The breeze rustled the tops of the trees, making them sound like waves breaking on to a beach. Their pale green leaves were outlined against the clear blue sky. He breathed in the aroma of pine needles mingling with the scent of earth. The familiarity was comforting. Closing his eyes for a moment, he thought of Scotland, and expeditions into the countryside with his friends from medical school during hunting and fishing holidays.

He heard the crack of a broken twig. He sat completely still, listening carefully for any sound that might indicate the presence of someone else, but there was nothing. He shook his head and laughed at his folly. Perhaps it wasn't surprising that he should be sensitive to such things given what had happened during his last visit. He picked up his jacket and got to his feet. He was about to set off again when he thought he heard a rustling sound. He told himself that it was probably just an animal – a squirrel perhaps, or a fox. He returned to the path and continued his journey towards the abbey. Every now and again he thought he heard something, but dismissed it as a sign of an overactive imagination.

Before too long the woodland began to give way to sparser shrubland. As the land became flatter, he could see fields full of what he assumed were lush green rice plants divided into grids by shining lines of water. Dotted among them were women, most of whom were bent double, moving rhythmically as they planted and weeded. Mesmerised, he paused for a moment to watch them. In the near distance there was a large villa in honey-coloured stone with a number of outbuildings set slightly away from it. It seemed that he had found the estate where the missing boy worked. Now all he had to do was find out who the boy was and why he had disappeared. Had anyone emerged from the forest behind him? No, he was alone. Heartened by this, he began to make his way down the valley towards the fields and the estate.

As he walked past the fields, some of the women straightened up to watch him, calling out greetings and occasionally ribald comments. It seemed like a good opportunity to ask some questions, so he stopped by one of them and smiled at her.

'That looks like hard work, signora.'

'*Sì*, signor. I would not recommend it,' the woman said cheerfully. She was ruddy-faced from the sun despite the fact that she was wearing a large straw hat. Her skirts were tucked up, revealing sturdy legs covered in bites.

'You should get some ointment for those,' James said, the doctor in him taking over for a moment.

The woman nodded. 'I would if I could afford it. Mosquitoes and frogs . . . they won't leave us alone, whatever we say to them. Thank God it isn't for long!'

'How long are you here for?'

'A few months. Mind you, even that's too much for some. We've had a few give up on it before the season is over.'

'Hey, Perla! Who's your new man?' cried one of the women.

'Has he got a friend for me?' shouted another.

'Don't mind them, signor,' Perla said. 'Any diversion is welcome here, especially the male variety. Did you want to know anything in particular?'

'Do you know of a young man who works on the estate? He may have gone missing recently.'

Perla paused for a moment. 'Do you mean Bruno Ferranti? He worked here last season. I thought he'd moved on, but I think I caught a glimpse of him up at the house a few weeks back.'

'Did he have a friend . . . a young girl called Teresa?'

'I don't know if that was her name, but he did hang around with a girl for a while. Haven't seen her recently, though. We mondine usually keep ourselves to ourselves.'

'Mondine?'

'That's what we're called – the rice weeders. Most of us come down from the mountain villages to work at places like this in the summer. There are a few from nearby, but not many.'

'Just one more thing,' James said. 'What do Bruno and the girl look like?'

'He's handsome enough, I suppose, in an obvious sort of way, except for a scar on his cheek from a knife fight a year or so back. A bit like yours, if you don't mind me saying, only his is bigger and deeper . . . much more noticeable.'

James held his hand up to his face and felt the thin line of the mark left by whoever it was who had cut him. Perhaps Bruno had had the same experience.

Perla continued. 'He's quite sturdy . . . looks like he can handle himself. Funny, though, he used to be quite mouthy, something of a troublemaker, but then he seemed to calm down till he wouldn't say boo to a goose. Mind you, there were rumours . . .'

'What kind of rumours?'

'Some say that he got too close to the estate owner's wife

when he was still just a boy. She died a few years back. I suppose that might explain why he's not such a loudmouth these days.'

'And the girl?'

'Short, dark, pretty . . . that's all I can remember.'

James thanked Perla for her time and began to make his way towards the buildings. At last he felt he was getting somewhere with this puzzle, or a strand of it at least. He was certain that Teresa Mariani and her friend Bruno lay at the heart of it. All he had to do now was find them.

Lucy looked idly out of the window at the scenery as she and Miss Trott rattled through the countryside in their cab. The road was uneven in places, so there was a certain amount of rolling to and fro, as if they were voyagers on a stormy sea. Miss Trott bore the discomfort with fortitude, commenting only on the heat and the lack of any breeze as she fanned herself with a large straw hat.

The vista was attractive – mostly rolling green hills punctuated by woodland. As they drove, Lucy noticed a series of fields in the distance with their crops planted in straight lines. It reminded her of the old corded doormat that used to be in their summer house – a grand name for a not very grand building; more of a large shed at the bottom of the garden really. When she was younger, Lucy liked to sit and write there, pretending to be a great lady novelist. Her father would come and sit with her, puffing on his pipe and asking questions about her stories.

'I think we must be almost there,' Miss Trott said, indicating a large villa not too far away.

Lucy pictured Francesco's face with its delicate features and rakish smile, and felt a slight rolling in her stomach that she supposed must be butterflies. As they approached the gates to the villa, she peered out of the window to admire their intricate design.

'Oh look. I see we are not the only guests,' Miss Trott remarked, pointing out a grand carriage that blocked their path so that they could not drive through the gate.

The cab driver, a fat, balding man with a small bowler hat pushed to the back of his very large head, muttered something about stopping here.

'Oh really, that is too bad!' Miss Trott complained. '*Non accettabile!*' she shouted loudly, as if the man was hard of hearing.

The driver ignored her completely, looking into the distance as if hoping that she would disappear.

'Well now, come along, signor. We cannot sit here all day!' she said, poking him with her parasol.

Eventually the man alighted and helped them down on to the driveway. Miss Trott paid him, slowly and deliberately counting out the coins and refusing to leave a tip. It was lucky that Francesco had suggested in his note that he would take them back to the city. Lucy doubted their cab would have materialised for the journey home, if the muttering coming from the driver was any indication.

As they walked past the grand carriage, Lucy noticed the insignia on the door: a large flower – a lily perhaps. It matched the design on the gate. As they approached the front door to the villa, it opened and Francesco came out, followed by several dogs. One of them barked and leapt up at Miss Trott, who was slightly ahead of Lucy.

'Get down, wretched animal!' she cried, beating it off with her parasol, which was clearly a versatile piece of equipment. This merely had the effect of whipping the dogs into a frenzy of excitement, as they seemed to think that it was some kind of game, and Francesco had to restore order, clapping his hands and shouting until the dogs retreated into the house.

There didn't seem to be any real alarm in Miss Trott's face, and yet again Lucy was struck by the feeling that at least some of this was for show, although what the purpose might be she couldn't say.

Francesco gave a deep bow. 'Come this way, ladies, come this way. We are eating outside today, as we have been lucky with the weather.'

'Al fresco . . . how very Italian,' Miss Trott murmured appreciatively as they followed their host round the house into beautiful though somewhat overgrown gardens.

'Here we are,' Francesco said, indicating a large terrace with a dining table and chairs on one side and wicker chairs to the other. It was exactly as Lucy had feared. Seated on the latter, next to Bianca Rambaudi, were their fellow guests, the marchesa, Professor Donati and – in the centre, in the position of guest of honour – Fabia Carignano. She was semi-reclined on her seat and yet still managed to look elegant, Lucy noted with irritation. She was not sure what she felt about Professor Donati. He had seemed threatening last time they met, but now he was polite, giving a little bow of his head and taking off his hat in greeting. She supposed she was safe here as long as she was in company. It would be interesting to watch the interaction between him and Miss Trott.

'Signorina Murray, how nice,' Fabia said icily.

'Likewise,' Lucy replied.

Francesco beamed at both of them. 'A cool drink is what we all need, I think. Do take a seat, ladies.'

Lucy sat next to Miss Trott, who had made a beeline for the seat next to Professor Donati. He sat bolt upright and wore the hunted expression of a man who was about to be caught out at something. His eyes darted around and his brow shone with perspiration. An awkward silence descended upon them like a damp blanket.

'How are arrangements going for the ball, Marchesa?' Bianca asked.

'The invitations are about to be sent, I believe.'

'Of course, we have already asked our most intimate friends,' Fabia said. 'Francesco and Bianca received their invitations some time ago.'

'What Fabia means is that she brought them with her today because she was coming to lunch,' Bianca said. 'Isn't that right?'

Fabia blushed but did not answer.

'But we were delighted to receive them, weren't we, Bianca?' Francesco said, as a maid arrived with a tray bearing glasses of lemonade, which she passed round with great ceremony, as if distributing the nectar of the gods.

'Indeed we were,' Bianca agreed. 'It is so nice to have a real occasion to look forward to.'

'And we look forward to seeing you there,' the marchesa said. 'All of you.'

'I know that everyone in our household is excited about it,' Miss Trott said.

'Even Professor Lombroso?' Francesco asked. 'He doesn't look to me like a man who would appreciate that kind of thing.'

'You'd be surprised,' the marchesa said, smiling. 'The professor loves an audience, so any crowd is appealing to him.'

'Ah, but is he appealing to any crowd?' Francesco said, making Lucy smile.

'I have heard that he has quite a popular following,' Professor Donati said.

'Do you know him, Professor?' Francesco asked.

'We are acquainted, yes. I find his ideas very stimulating.'

'Tell me, Professor, how did the Ancient Egyptians view crime?' Miss Trott asked.

Professor Donati hesitated for a moment. 'Their criminal justice system was not dissimilar to our own, although the punishments were rather more savage.'

'As I recall, they executed murderers by impaling them on a stake,' Francesco said.

Professor Donati nodded. 'That is correct. Burning was also used, as a kind of purification, though of course it denied the wrongdoer an afterlife as there would be no body to preserve, which is somewhat ironic.'

'I have always wondered how they made their mummies,' Miss Trott said.

'It is a very intricate process, I believe,' Francesco said.

'Yes, it is, and a fascinating one. You see, the body has to be completely free of fluid,' Professor Donati explained, clearly enthused by his subject. 'That is how the purification process begins.'

'Let's change the subject to something less morbid,' the marchesa suggested hastily. 'What does your brother think of Professor Lombroso's theories, Signorina Murray?'

'He is employed by the university?' Fabia asked.

'He is assisting the professor in his research, yes,' Lucy replied. 'I believe he admires him greatly.'

'The professor must be gratified to have such a slavish follower.' Fabia's lips formed a small, tight smile.

'You make it sound as if Signor Murray is indiscriminating, Fabia,' Bianca said.

'I am sure he is nothing of the kind,' declared the marchesa.

'Professor Lombroso has many admirers, and I am among them.'

'He is lucky to have your patronage, Marchesa,' Professor Donati said, 'particularly after that business with the murders last year.'

'Ah yes, and I believe your brother was involved too, was he not, Signorina Murray?'

'That is not a topic of conversation to be raised over lunch, Fabia,' the marchesa said before Lucy could answer.

'Speaking of which, shall we eat?' Bianca waved at a manservant who was waiting patiently in the doorway. Lucy immediately wished that she had brought her notebook. He was extremely tall and broad – the word 'immense' came into her mind. His face was most peculiar in that he had a vast, domelike forehead, large ears that stuck out at right angles and slightly drooping features. He reminded Lucy of one of the pictures of criminals that she had seen in Professor Lombroso's book. She gazed past him to the interior of the house. She couldn't see a great deal, such was the man's bulk, but she was left with the impression that no expense had been spared. Everything looked new. The paintwork was gleaming and the wallpaper was vivid, one might even say garish, particularly when compared to the faded grandeur of the marchesa's decor.

'Cosimo, can you tell the kitchen that we are ready?' Bianca said.

The man grunted an incoherent reply and loped into the house. A few minutes later, the first of a parade of tempting dishes were brought out and lunch began in earnest. Lucy could not remember when she had eaten a finer meal. There was risotto, of course – made from 'our own Carnaroli rice', as Bianca announced proudly – a local speciality called risotto alla piemontese, a creamy concoction made with fragrant rosemary and veal marrow. There were delicate courgette flowers stuffed with ground beef and gelatina – or aspic, as Miss Trott insisted on calling it. There was a broth made from veal shanks and various spices and aromatic vinegar, sieved, according to Francesco, and left to set in a cool cellar. Fresh sheep and goat's cheeses were also on offer. These were milky, fresh and buttery and served with local honey to drizzle on them. To finish, apparently in Lucy's honour, which made Fabia scowl, was *zuppa Inglese*, or English trifle. Despite bearing no relation to the true English version, as Miss Trott reminded everyone, it was a delicious dessert made with layers of sponge generously soaked with a spiced Italian liqueur called Alkermes, apricot jam, and vanilla and chocolate custard.

Lucy tucked into it all with great enthusiasm. She had never been one to peck at her food, unlike Fabia, who, Lucy noticed, had the art of self-denial perfected. She ate very little and cut everything into tiny morsels before chewing each one thoroughly, whilst wearing an expression that made her lack of enjoyment clear.

After lunch, Francesco stood and extended a hand towards Lucy. 'Would you like to see some of the estate? Our gardens are renowned for their beauty.'

Fabia got to her feet. 'I should like to come too, Francesco, if I may.'

'Oh no, Fabia, it would only bore you,' Francesco said.

'It wouldn't at all!' Fabia replied. She was pouting, Lucy noticed, which made her look a little like a goldfish.

'You know it would. Last time you yawned throughout!'

'Why don't you two go ahead and then Miss Carignano and I can follow on?' Miss Trott suggested.

'What an excellent idea,' the marchesa said, which decided the matter, much to Fabia's annoyance.

Francesco held out his arm to Lucy, who took it, and together they began to walk around the grounds of the Villa Purezza.

33

Thieves, like prostitutes, covet bright-coloured clothes, necklaces, chains, and even earrings. They are the most ignorant and gullible of the criminal species. Almost always nervous about being caught, they talk nonsensically and constantly change the subject. Assuming that those who speak their jargon are worthy colleagues, they make friends hastily. They sometimes feign romantic love, but prefer prostitutes, their natural allies.

Lombroso, 1876, p. 73

James stood by the back gate of the rice estate. What should he do next? The whole expedition had taken him longer than he had anticipated, and it seemed highly unlikely that he would get back to the city in time for his afternoon meeting with Lombroso. He squinted up at the sun. It was noon already. How would the professor react? He thought he could probably guess. Lombroso hated lateness of any kind, except of course his own. Both James and Ottolenghi had been kept waiting on many occasions whilst the professor lost track of the time in the middle of some experiment or other. Then when he finally arrived, they would be told that they should be more flexible and he did not know what the fuss was about. But if they were late, he would tut and sigh and go on about it for ages. Not showing up at all might be considered a step too far, but it couldn't be helped. He would just have to deal with the consequences when they arrived.

In the meantime, he needed to work out what he should do next. The place seemed deserted, which was inconvenient, as he needed to ask some questions about Bruno Ferranti's whereabouts.

'Hello? Is anyone about?' he called.

There was no reply. He listened out for voices, but all he could hear was the birds singing. He rattled the gate for a moment, and to his surprise it swung open. He walked through into the courtyard. There were a few pieces of farm machinery strewn about the place, as if someone had been working on their maintenance but had been called away. He started to examine an old plough. He had always been fond of taking things apart and putting them back together again. Any form of mechanism or machinery fascinated him.

'Hey, what are you doing? Thief!' A man ran towards him, grabbed him by the shoulders and pushed him to the ground.

'I haven't done anything,' James protested.

The man kicked at him. 'You were trying to steal something. Well, we'll see what the boss has to say.'

'I was looking for someone, that's all.'

'I don't believe you.' The man shouted over his shoulder. 'Bruno! Cosimo! *Vieni qui!*'

Two more men appeared from another of the buildings. One of them was one of the largest men James had ever seen. The other was much younger, little more than a boy really. There was a long, deep scar on his cheek.

'Search him, Bruno,' the first man ordered.

'*Sì*, Marco.'

The bigger man, presumably Cosimo, pulled James to his

feet and held him while Bruno went through his pockets. Before long, James's notebook was found and duly handed over to Marco, who looked at the first page and nodded. 'Put him in the stables. I'll tell the boss.'

James was dragged away to a small room, where he was unceremoniously dumped on the floor in the middle of a large pile of manure. He lay there for a moment. Had coming back to Italy been worth it? Suddenly the prospect of a practice as a family doctor in a small Scottish town with a nice, quiet, undemanding wife seemed very attractive indeed. Still, he thought, as he pulled himself up and out of the manure, he had found Bruno, the missing boy. And as far as his own well-being was concerned, at least things couldn't get any worse.

Lucy was enjoying herself. The gardens were beautiful and quite extensive, even including an ice house, which Francesco pointed out to her with some pride. Indeed, the further they went, the clearer it became that the Villa Purezza's grounds were very close to Francesco's heart. Lucy studied him as he led her through the tree-lined paths to the various sections, explaining how his mother had designed them to represent different deities, each one symbolising purity. His eyes were full of passion as he related the story of the research and care that had gone into the creation of the place. The more he told her, the closer to him she felt. She had only ever seen passion like that in her father's eyes although James sometimes got near to it when he was talking about Turin. It made her want to reach out to Francesco and touch him. In fact, it was only the close proximity of Fabia and Miss Trott that prevented her from doing so. She could hear the distant rise and fall of their conversation. Although she was not close enough to make out the exact words, Fabia's irritation and Miss Trott's failed attempts at conciliation were clear. But none of that mattered. She was alone, or almost, with Francesco, and with every moment that passed, she was becoming increasingly convinced that she was falling for him.

'So you see, Lucia, how very clever my mother was,' he said. 'And the tragedy is that she had just completed it all when she was taken from us.'

'She sounds like a remarkable woman. You must both miss her terribly.'

'I do, very much, although I am not so sure about Bianca.'

'Really? What makes you say that?'

'Oh, nothing… just a feeling I have, that's all.' He stopped outside a tall wooden gate. 'This is the last part of the garden. I have never shown anyone before.' He took her hand and kissed the palm gently. It felt to her as if a feather had been passed over it. She could hardly breathe. He took a large key from his pocket and began to unlock the gate.

'Are you certain of this?' Lucy asked.

'I have never been more certain of anything.'

They heard the voices of Fabia and Miss Trott approaching. 'Quickly!' Francesco said. 'Before they see us.'

He pulled her through the gate and shut it firmly behind them. They stood away from it to one side, and Lucy heard Fabia's voice: 'Oh really, this is too much! Where have they got to?' Then a determined Miss Trott: 'Do not despair, Miss Carignano. We shall find them. Follow me.'

She was so close to Francesco that she felt his breath on her cheek. It made her feel faint with what she thought must be desire, though she had nothing to compare it to. It was a curious sensation – as if she was slowly melting from the inside out. Was that how love felt, or was it the heat?

Once the two women had passed, Francesco took Lucy by

the hand and led her into the garden. She caught her breath at the sheer beauty of what she was seeing. In front of her was a summer house built in the style of an Egyptian temple.

'Do you like the house?' Francesco asked.

'Very much,' Lucy said.

'My mother used to come here all the time. I think she saw it as somewhere to escape to. It has several rooms. There's even a wine cellar.'

In front of the summer house was a landscaped pond in the shape of a cross. It was strewn with water lilies in all shades of red, from crimson to the palest of pinks. At its heart was a small fountain with a stone statue of a young Egyptian woman holding a sceptre.

They walked towards it. 'May I introduce you to Maat, the Egyptian goddess of purity, amongst other things,' Francesco said. 'She wrote one of the spells in the Book of the Dead – the forty-two declarations of purity.'

The statue's features were perfect. Her gaze was cast down, as if she was afraid to catch their eyes.

'She is beautiful,' said Lucy. 'Did your mother commission it?'

'She did. It was her last gift to me.'

He took hold of Lucy's hands. She closed her eyes as he drew her closer, waiting for him to kiss her. It seemed like the right thing to do under the circumstances.

'Francesco? Are you in here?' There was a knocking at the gate. Francesco released her hands. 'Later,' he whispered in her ear. 'Yes, we are here. What do you want, Bianca?'

'There is some trouble at the house. Can you come back and sort it out?'

He rolled his eyes at Lucy, who smiled back. Whatever had

just happened between them could happen again, she was sure of it. The question was whether she wanted it to.

'Very well. I will be there shortly,' Francesco called.

'Don't be long!' Bianca said. 'See you in a moment, Signorina Murray.'

'Our secret is out,' Francesco said, grinning. 'Come on. We had better go.'

As they made their way back to the house, a new closeness between them, Lucy thought about all the great literature in the world, talking of love and how it could be gained and lost and found again. And yet it seemed as if she might have fallen in love without any difficulty at all. Not only that, but it looked as if her feelings were reciprocated. Was that what love felt like? Somehow it was far too easy. Surely there had to be more to it than that.

They arrived back at the house to see everyone seated as they had been before lunch. Fabia glowered at her, and Lucy couldn't help but smile triumphantly back. If this had been a competition for Francesco's affections, it appeared that she had won it. Bianca was standing to one side and whispered to her brother. He nodded and looked over to Lucy. 'Apparently we have had an intruder,' he announced.

'Really? How very alarming!' exclaimed Miss Trott.

'There is nothing to worry about, signora,' Francesco said. 'The rogue has been caught and is being brought here as we speak.'

Why was Francesco insisting on dealing with the matter in front of them all? Was he showing off a little? Lucy wondered.

'We often have problems with tramps and the like,' Bianca said. 'They think they can come here and help themselves to anything they want.'

'Indeed. Crime is a problem in this city as in any other,' the marchesa agreed. 'We must all be vigilant.'

'I am not sure that I wish to see this ruffian.' Miss Trott fanned herself with her hand. 'Is he violent?'

'He resisted, Bianca tells me, but he was no match for my employees,' Francesco said. 'I thought it might be of interest if he was asked to explain himself. It might teach him a lesson.'

'A good idea, Francesco,' Professor Donati said. 'His kind should be made to account for their actions.'

'How will you deal with him in the end?' Fabia asked.

'I am not sure,' Francesco replied. 'He will either get a whipping or, if the matter is serious, I may call in the carabinieri and have him arrested.'

'I think you should do both!' Fabia said. 'The wretch is a criminal when all is said and done.'

'What do you think, Lucy?' Francesco asked.

Lucy thought for a moment. 'It depends on what he says. But there is no excuse for breaking in, in my opinion, and if you let him go, I expect he will just do it again. Professor Lombroso calls them habitual criminals, I believe. They cannot help themselves, as they are born to it.'

'Huh! That sounds like an excuse to me!' Fabia said.

'I think Professor Lombroso knows more about criminals than any of us here,' Miss Trott pointed out.

'I do not believe the professor is suggesting that anyone can shirk responsibility for crime,' Lucy said. 'Just that they are primitive and so have a propensity for such behaviour.'

Francesco nodded. 'Sound thinking. Ah, here they come. We shall see how primitive this chap looks.'

Lucy heard a scuffling sound in the distance, together with cries of protest. 'Let me go! There's no need for this. I wasn't doing anything wrong!'

No, she thought, it couldn't be . . . It must be a coincidence.

The servant Cosimo and another man brought the trespasser towards them, holding him tightly as he struggled between them. He made a sorry figure in his stained clothes, his face covered in cuts and bruises, not to mention a layer of what looked like mud. The men finally reached the assembled party and the prisoner was thrown to the floor in front of them.

'So what do you have to say for yourself, you scoundrel?' Francesco said.

The young man got to his feet and began to straighten his clothing, before noticing Lucy.

'James, what on earth are you doing here?' she said in horror.

'You know this man?' Francesco asked.

She nodded miserably. 'He is my brother.'

'Your brother is a thief, Signorina Murray?' Fabia said, hardly managing to contain her glee.

'Dr Murray is no thief!' Miss Trott said firmly. 'There must have been some misunderstanding.'

'Well I am sure we are all waiting to hear what it is,' Francesco said, his voice heavy with sarcasm. 'This is really your brother?'

'Yes, I am afraid so.'

'Lucy,' James said. 'I can explain.'

Lucy looked at him with distaste. 'I do not want to hear it.'

'Perhaps we should go,' the marchesa suggested.

'Oh must we, Aunt?' Fabia said, looking smugly at Lucy.

'Yes, I think we must. We are taking Professor Donati home. May we do the same for you, Signorina Murray, Miss Trott?'

Lucy nodded. 'Thank you, that would be most kind.'

The marchesa glanced at James. 'We shall wait for a few moments, Signor Murray.'

'Thank you.'

Lucy turned to say goodbye to Francesco, but he was resolutely ignoring her so she said it instead to Bianca, who gave a small embarrassed nod in return. Lucy began to follow the marchesa and Fabia to the carriage, closely followed by Miss Trott. Bianca walked after them after glaring balefully at James.

'Lucy, wait, please,' James called out. 'Let me speak to you.' He tried to follow, but was stopped by Cosimo, who stood in his path as Lucy marched past.

The way she was feeling, James would be lucky if she ever spoke to him again.

34

At least half of hysterical women are normal in intelligence, but they are easily distracted. Due to their profound egotism and total self-absorption, they adore scandal and public attention. They are extremely impressionable and as a result subject to sudden anger and unreasonable likes and dislikes. Their will is always unstable; they delight in speaking evil; and if they cannot attract attention through baseless trials and outrageous forms of revenge, they embitter the lives of their associates with continuous quarrels and disputes.

Lombroso and Ferrero, 1893, p. 234

James stood before his accuser and waited to hear his fate. It was bad enough being accused of being a common criminal, but being labelled as such in front of his own sister, and Miss Trott and the marchesa too, made it a thousand times worse.

'What do you want to do with him, boss?' Cosimo asked.

There was a pause as Francesco Rambaudi viewed his prisoner with contempt.

'I didn't do anything. You must know that!' James said.

'Your sister didn't seem so sure.'

'I can see why you might want to question me, Signor Rambaudi, given the circumstances, but what I can't understand is why you felt the need to humiliate Lucy.'

Francesco gave a mocking smile and nodded towards Cosimo. 'Let him go.' The servant did as he was told and lumbered off down the hill, back to the estate.

James stood for a moment waiting for an explanation. When none came, he began to walk towards the marchesa's carriage. Francesco stood in front of him and laid a restraining hand on his wrist. 'A private word before you go, Signor Murray. What were you doing trespassing on my estate?'

'I was looking for someone.'

'Who?'

James hesitated. 'A young man who works here, Bruno Ferranti.'

'Why are you looking for him?'

'I . . . I can't really say.'

'Perhaps I should call the carabinieri after all. Then you can tell them when they get here.'

'No, no, please . . . I am just trying to help a friend. A girl has gone missing. The boy might know something, that's all.'

'I will make enquiries. If he knows anything, I will inform you.'

'Thank you.'

'Just one thing, Signor Murray. I trust that we shall not see you here again.'

James nodded his agreement, gave a short bow and left to join the marchesa. When he got to the carriage, he found that there was further humiliation to come. Unfortunately the whiff of manure he carried on his clothes was too much for the ladies. He was forced to sit with the driver, and even he leant away from him at every opportunity.

He held onto the side of the carriage as it passed through the ornate gates on to the road home. It was typical of Rambaudi to have such vulgar taste, but then the man was clearly no gentleman. He had known that James was the intruder but had still insisted on parading him in front of Lucy and his other guests. That was unforgivable in itself.

But it was more than that. Francesco Rambaudi was not to be trusted, and as a consequence, Lucy was not safe in his company.

The following day, James was summoned by the professor to his study. He had assumed that Rambaudi had complained, and was thus surprised to see Anna and Ottolenghi sitting in two of Lombroso's more uncomfortable chairs, both looking embarrassed. Ottolenghi had a newspaper in his hand, which he handed silently to James. It was a copy of *The People's Voice*. James scanned the front page and felt his stomach churn.

SCANDAL!

It has come to the attention of this newspaper that a certain foreigner currently residing at the home of one of our city's leading citizens, Professor Cesare Lombroso, has been consorting with prostitutes under the guise of university business. It is also said that the same man has been conducting a scandalous liaison with one of the professor's servants, herself an ex-prostitute.

This newspaper is not able to say at present whether Professor Lombroso knew of his guest's activities or the background of his servant. But if he did, it must surely call into question his own standing. We call upon the university to institute an immediate investigation in order to establish the facts and root out such base immorality wherever it is found. More on pages 4, 5 and 6.

He forced himself to turn the pages. There was an editorial entitled 'Clean up our city!', which discussed at length Turin's moral decline, largely brought about by foreign visitors 'coming into our midst, infecting our minds with unsavoury ideas and lax morals'. If there had been any doubt about whom this was aimed at, then it was removed by the features section and letters page. The former contained an interview with someone described as 'an employee of Madame Giulia', who described an incident at the university where a foreigner made lewd suggestions to her under the guise of conducting an 'anthropological experiment'. To cap it all, this young woman's account was endorsed by Madame Giulia herself, who described an incident in which the same man attempted to force his attentions on her. That was not how James would have described it, but none of that mattered now. The damage was done. Presumably this was what Concetta had meant when she had told him it was too late.

The letters page apparently endorsed this view, with the great and good of Turin condemning his actions and demanding everything from his deportation to a public whipping.

'I have asked your colleagues to be present because your conduct affects us all,' Lombroso said, glowering at him.

'My conduct?' James asked. 'But you can't believe any of this nonsense, surely?'

'Explain yourself,' Lombroso said.

James told them what had happened, including Concetta Panatti's kiss.

'Now that's interesting,' Ottolenghi said. 'It sounds as if you were tricked, James.'

'Ottolenghi is right,' Lombroso said. 'It seems to me that both the Panatti woman and the girl had been given instructions.'

'What kind of instructions?' Anna asked.

'Both were told to inveigle Murray into a compromising position,' he replied. 'I'd also be willing to bet that the girl was told to leave by the front door, and that somewhere down the line a witness will come out of the woodwork saying that they saw her leaving in a dishevelled state or some such nonsense.'

'So it was a trap?' James asked.

'It would seem likely,' Lombroso said. 'Perhaps Panatti is motivated by revenge. You did reject her, after all.'

'Surely she wouldn't ruin him just for that,' Anna said. 'There has to be more to it.'

'My dear Anna, you know as well as I do that women are far more vengeful than men,' Lombroso said. 'It is in their nature. They simply can't help themselves.' Anna glared at him, but he went on. 'If you offend such a woman, you may well find yourself in the hands of an almost inexorable executioner. She is quite capable of pouring torments on her victim, drop by drop and at great length.'

'That's comforting,' James said.

'We need to find out for certain if there is another motive,' Lombroso said. 'But before we deal with that, I should tell you, Murray, that I have received a further complaint about your behaviour.'

'From Francesco Rambaudi?' James asked.

Lombroso nodded. 'I see you were expecting something from the gentleman.'

'Gentleman!' James said. 'He is no such thing.'

'What is James supposed to have done, Cesare?' Anna asked.

'Signor Rambaudi tells me that he broke into his estate and was found tampering with some farm machinery.'

'What on earth were you doing, James?' Ottolenghi said.

'Rambaudi is not entirely accurate. The gate was open.'

'He insists that it was locked and that you broke in,' Lombroso said.

'He has been misinformed. I tried the gate and it opened.'

'Well, that aside, what were you doing there in the first place? If you wanted to see your sister, it would have been more sensible to go to the house, surely.'

'Lucy was there?' Anna said.

'She was lunching with them apparently, although I didn't know it. Well, not until he exhibited me in front of her and his other guests as if I was a common thief.'

Lombroso stared at him. 'So why go there at all? It is a mystery to me.'

'I was making enquiries for a friend.'

'What friend?'

James paused. 'I was helping Sofia to look for her cousin.'

'What would she be doing at the Rambaudi estate?'

'It wasn't her I was trying to find exactly.'

'Have you decided to become an enquiry agent on the side? Do I not give you enough to do?'

'As you know, Chiara is not the only girl to have gone missing. One of the others, Teresa Mariani, had a male friend who also seems to have disappeared.'

'We have discussed this before, Murray. The girls are most likely to be runaways and I daresay the boy is no different.'

'Actually I've found him, or at least I think I have, and I'm not sure he's a runaway exactly. Also, the girl at the abbey, Nella Calvi, worked as a prostitute at Madame Giulia's. She went missing from another establishment . . . a secret one.'

'So Panatti is running a second brothel. That is interesting.'

'And another of the missing girls worked there as a maid.'

'Also interesting,' Lombroso said. 'Anything else?'

'And then there are the bodies of the girls, all with organs removed, signs of exsanguination and attempts at preservation through mummification or embalming.'

'I have been thinking about that myself. It is a peculiar thing to do to someone, going well beyond the actions of any habitual criminal that I have come across. And of course we don't know if this was the cause of death, although nothing would surprise me in this case.'

'You think they may have been bled to death . . . that they were tortured . . . That is terrifying!' Anna said.

Lombroso frowned. 'Why drain the blood? That is what I do not understand. Why kill them in this ghastly way?'

'I might be able to help with that,' Ottolenghi said. He repeated what he had told James about Reiner's research.

Lombroso leant back in his chair, his hands together in front of him as if he was praying for a solution. 'Perhaps it is some kind of sect. We are plagued with them in this city.'

'But this woman, Bathory, died hundreds of years ago,' Anna said.

'The Devil is older than that, but satanists still worship him,' James said. 'What if someone has decided to repeat Bathory's work? Reiner seems to think there is a particular criminal type who is aroused by the drinking of blood.'

'I have read his case files. There are many examples of deranged killers who drink the blood of their victims,' Ottolenghi said.

James shuddered. 'Which would explain what happened to the blood.'

'It doesn't, however, explain the attempt to preserve the corpse,' Lombroso said.

James nodded. 'True, but that could just be an extension of the criminal's perversion.'

'It would certainly fit with the profile of moral insanity,' Lombroso agreed. 'But such a manifestation would be rare indeed.'

'You have said yourself that such men exist, Professor. Look at all we went through last year. How was it that you put it in your book?

'"They are born to savour evil and to commit it",' Lombroso said slowly.

'Well someone here in Turin is doing exactly that,' Anna said. 'Girls go missing, then bodies are found – and it surely can't be a coincidence that as soon as James investigates, he gets into trouble.'

'Panatti must be involved somehow,' Lombroso declared. 'We need to find out more about her.'

'And how do we do that?' Anna asked. 'The woman is devious and manipulative. I was there the day she kissed you, James. She could not wait to get rid of me. Now I know why.'

'Sofia warned me about her . . . something to do with visiting the good and keeping well with the bad,' James said.

'An old Italian proverb, and definitely a warning. Panatti is clearly known as a bad lot in certain circles,' Lombroso said.

'Perhaps I'd better speak to her,' James suggested.

'No. Keep away from her for now,' Lombroso said. 'She's obviously dangerous, particularly as far as you are concerned. We need to be careful how we deal with her. I am told she is likely to be at the marchesa's ball, so we must plan our strategy.'

'Well, I hope you all enjoy it.'

'None of that, Murray,' Lombroso said. 'You will be there too. The article does not name you. That, I am certain, will be good enough for the marchesa.'

'But after all this, surely my presence will be controversial.'

'Perhaps, and I will of course speak to the marchesa to canvass her view. But I suspect she will not withdraw her invitation. Your attendance might just give us some idea about why this is being done to you. It is an excellent opportunity to gather information. I want all of us to be alert, particularly if there is anyone of the criminal type present.'

'Any particular type, Professor?' Ottolenghi asked.

'We may well be looking for an example of moral insanity, so asymmetry in facial features, unequal ears, thick lips, large jaw and mouth, malformed teeth, perhaps with some missing, scanty beard . . .'

'Sounds like half of the carabinieri,' James murmured to Anna.

'Are these likely to be characteristics in the marchesa's guests?' she asked.

'If they are morally insane, then yes,' Lombroso replied crisply.

'Reiner says that such people are often very precocious and have a ferocious bloodlust,' Ottolenghi commented.

'Indeed, then we must be on our guard,' Lombroso said.

'And what if Concetta Panatti is the sole instigator here?' Anna asked.

'I find that an incredible proposition,' Lombroso said. 'She is a criminal woman and therefore inherently inferior in intellect. Besides, a morally insane woman would have a virile physiognomy, and we cannot say that of her at least.'

Ottolenghi grinned. 'Certainly not, or James would never have kissed her!'

Lombroso glared at him. 'That is not helpful, Salvatore, though no doubt it is true. Of course Panatti is shameless and lascivious, traits found in both the prostitute and the morally insane. Though she is not imbecilic, which is interesting.'

'Why would the marchesa invite her to the ball?' James asked.

'She is a leading businesswoman and her association with Madame Giulia's is not generally known. And I know she interests the marchesa.'

'I will watch her closely if she is there,' Anna said. 'I look forward to it.'

'Right . . . well, we all know what we are about,' Lombroso said. 'I am confident that by the end of the evening we will understand more about this whole business.'

James hoped he was right. The prospect of attending the ball had never been particularly inviting. He had always found formal occasions a little daunting, and had been hoping to blend into the background and observe rather than participate. But now he faced the prospect of being talked about and perhaps judged by people he had never even met.

What worried him more, however, was the thought of Lucy having to endure the same fate when she, unlike him, was blameless. It was ironic, really. He was accustomed to being the subject of tittle-tattle as the result of his father's actions, and now the cycle seemed to be repeating itself. It seemed that Lombroso might have been wrong to reassure him about his provenance at the end of his first visit to Turin. Perhaps he was a born criminal after all.

35

Hysterics, like epileptics, often suffer from delirium, either melancholic or mono-maniacal. The maniacal form of the disorder is accompanied by hallucinations, impulsiveness, constant agitation or a need for movement, and desires to smash whatever lies in their way. These symptoms will appear in a flash in someone in good health, last just a short time, and leave without a trace. Suddenly a person will run from a ballroom and throw herself in the river. A girl will break all the dishes and pour boiling water over her brother's head and then fly from the house to the woods, where she may be found building a stone altar for the celebration of her imaginary marriage. These crises, like those of epilepsy, come and go.

Lombroso and Ferrero, 1893, p. 236

The evening of the marchesa's ball was warm and humid. The sunshine and showers of late spring had subsided, to be replaced by a heavy dampness, and the city seemed to shine as if it was sheathed in a thin film of perspiration brought about by the anticipation of the festivities to come.

Lucy felt the same. Her gown, pale blue silk, had been lent to her by Anna Tarnovsky. Already it was clinging to her and she had not even danced a single step. Whilst she waited for the rest of her party to alight, she watched carefully as other carriages began to arrive and the marchesa's guests, also dressed in their best finery, emerged. This might be a scene in her novel, with Lydia Loveday posing as a guest in order to detect a notorious jewel thief, watching her suspects as they mingled and wove their way through the throng, waiting for one of them to make their move. Lucy was just as alert, although her targets were less obvious. Miss Trott and Professor Donati were her suspects, though their crime, if there was one, was as yet unknown. But there were, of course, other things to consider.

Overall, the last few days had been odd to say the least. James was avoiding her, which was to be expected after the incident at the Villa Purezza. But she had known that something else was going on. There were meetings behind closed doors, raised voices on occasion, and even Gina and Paola had been unusually distant, apparently concentrating on their studies according to Signora Lombroso. Miss Trott would not be drawn on the matter, preferring to try to distract her with gallery and museum visits.

Finally Anna had taken her aside and explained things to her. James had been subjected to a campaign that was clearly calculated to destroy his reputation. He had unwittingly helped it along, but all the same, most of it – particularly the most recent 'revelations' – was untrue. Fortunately the marchesa had made it clear that she had no interest in the subject, and both Lucy and James had her full support.

Everyone of note in the city of Turin would be there, and Lucy was glad of the opportunity to observe them. Somebody was doing their utmost to hurt James, and she was determined to find out who and why. Now that they were here, it was clear that the professor was of the same view. When it was time to go in, he issued instructions to everyone as if it were a military operation. Lucy heard James whisper to Ottolenghi that Garibaldi himself would not have done better.

The professor led the way with his wife and daughters and Miss Trott, followed by James and Lucy with Ottolenghi and Anna Tarnovksy in what James called a rearguard action. This had the effect of demonstrating support for James and also protecting him from the glares and whispers that surrounded them as they entered.

Lucy was familiar with this kind of thing up to a point. When their father had been taken away from them to the asylum, the entire family had become the subject of local fascination. James and Aunt Agnes had done their best to shield her from this unwanted attention, but she was still aware of it, although the details of exactly what her father had done to deserve his detention still eluded her.

Once they entered the main ballroom, she had thought they would find a discreet corner somewhere to settle, but that was not Lombroso's way. Instead he insisted that they choose a central table, and once they were seated, he took great pleasure in rising to greet people as they passed and then performing elaborate introductions to Lucy and James.

'May I present my assistant, Signor Murray, and his sister Lucy, from Scotland. He is heading up my new research project, you know . . . a very intelligent young man! We are lucky to have him in our city.'

Of course this did not stop people from staring at them, and no doubt there was plenty of gossip circulating about the newspaper article, but the professor's obvious support did seem to be working up to a point. However, it was when the marchesa actually took the trouble to come over and greet them personally that Lucy could tell the tide of public opinion was turning.

'I am so glad you could come this evening, Signor Murray,' she said, shaking him warmly by the hand.

'I am honoured by your invitation,' James replied.

'I would be interested to hear of your work with the professor. Perhaps you would visit me soon and we can discuss it.'

'I would be delighted.'

'It is wonderful that our city is at the heart of such wide-reaching endeavour, Professor,' the marchesa said to Lombroso before turning her attention to Lucy and smiling at her. 'And, Signorina Murray, how nice to see you also, my dear. I hope that you will enjoy the dancing later.'

'I look forward to it, Marchesa.'

With that, she left them to greet some of her other guests. All of this gave those attending the ball something of a dilemma. It was clear from the attention that James was attracting that most people were aware of the newspaper article. Yet he had been acknowledged by the marchesa herself, which in itself gave him a certain respectability. In the end it seemed that most preferred to ignore him, which was certainly better than being openly snubbed.

Lucy was content for the time being to sit with her party and observe her fellow guests, which was fascinating. There were many enthusiastic greetings, both true and false, the bonhomie pouring from honeyed tongues. The ladies whispered to each other about who was wearing which gown and the extent to which it suited them. Gossip was exchanged, music began to play and drinks were served. The ball was under way.

Lucy noticed that the priest who had been at Lombroso's dinner the first night they were in Turin seemed to have assumed the role of social commentator to the marchesa. Earlier she had made her grand and glittering entrance to the usual sycophantic applause, but having performed her function as hostess, it seemed that she, like Lucy, was content to observe. Occasionally those who had been chosen for the honour were presented to her, but for the most part she sat, resplendent in her diamonds, watching as a piece of theatre she herself had created played out before her.

Fabia, of course, was in her element. The ball was in her honour and she was making the most of the fact. She was dressed in a beautiful silk gown of pink and silver that sparkled as she moved. Lucy felt quite drab in comparison. Standing next to Fabia was Francesco. Lucy expected her heart to lurch when she noticed him, but there was nothing more than slight regret. He had not tried to contact her and she had assumed from this that James had offended him so much that he would not have anything to do with her. He was paying court to Fabia, watched intently by Bianca, who was standing at his side. She murmured something into his ear, and he looked over to Lucy's table. Fabia followed his line of sight and simpered. Francesco waved as if nothing had happened and began to make his way over to her.

'Signorina Lucy Murray, how nice to see you!' he said, bowing deeply.

'Signor Rambaudi,' she said with a brief nod of acknowledgement.

'Would you do me the honour of dancing with me?'

Lucy hesitated for a moment. This would be an opportunity to make amends, but it would also be her first dance at her first ball. She had attended dancing lessons, but this was different. Hundreds of people were watching. Would she remember all the steps? Fabia was frowning at her. That decided it. 'Yes, thank you, signor,' she said, and taking Francesco's arm, she followed him into the ballroom.

'A waltz, how enchanting,' Francesco declared.

In a moment she was in his arms, being expertly steered around the dance floor. It was an intoxicating experience. She had never been in such close proximity to a man. The feel of his hand in the small of her back and the lightest of touches as his fingers intertwined with hers was almost overwhelming. Perhaps she loved him after all.

'You waltz well, Signorina Murray.'

'Thank you. But Miss Trott has told me that one is not supposed to converse whilst engaged in a dance.'

'Ah, the magnificent Miss Trott. We must bow to her infinitely superior wisdom.'

'Oh, I don't mind talking. She doesn't know everything.'

'And have you informed her of this startling revelation?'

'You are teasing me, Signor Rambaudi!'

'Francesco, please. We have no need to be formal, you and I.'

'I am sorry for what my brother did, Francesco.'

'It doesn't matter. I imagine he had his reasons.'

'He was helping a friend.'

'From what I have read, he seems to be a very friendly sort of fellow altogether.'

Lucy did not reply. Perhaps Miss Trott was right. Silence was better after all. Besides, it was difficult to know exactly what to say, since James was so evidently in the wrong. Should she really have to defend her brother? They continued round and round to the music and it seemed to her that they were increasing their speed with each turn.

Out of the corner of her eye she noticed a tall, gaunt-looking man with a piercing gaze. He looked familiar – where had she seen him before? Somehow he did not seem to fit in with his surroundings. Then round and round they went again, faster and faster. Who was the man talking to? She couldn't see. He was standing behind a pillar... oh, move, why don't you... round and round again... they seemed to be having a very animated conversation... not altogether friendly... spinning and spinning... ah, he had moved... it was Professor Donati... funny how he always seemed to be upsetting people... round and round... must keep up with Francesco. He was grinning at her and she felt herself smiling back. Then it was as if they were the only people in the room. Everyone else had melted away.

Abruptly the music stopped and they came to a standstill. Francesco bowed to her, led her from the floor, and then he was gone. She stood there, confused, not knowing what to do. She had expected to be escorted back to her party, but now she had been abandoned and, having lost her bearings, did not know where they were. In an instant, James was standing next to her.

'My dance next, I think,' he said quickly, leading her on to the floor for some kind of quadrille, with the dancers lining up in rows.

''I don't know the steps for this,' she said.

'Neither do I. Let's make it up.'

'James, we can't!' Lucy said, half in alarm and half laughing at her brother's sudden carefree attitude. 'What will people say?'

'They will say whatever they want. I'm already in disgrace. I'm sure a few misplaced dance steps will not make it any worse.'

'But *I* am not in disgrace,' she protested.

'Look. We're in luck. It's a cotillion. We will be directed

in our steps.' He indicated an elderly autocratic man who had positioned himself at the head of the lines, like a general about to direct his forces into battle. 'It will be just like dancing the reel at home.'

'I'm not sure it will,' Lucy said.

'Shush now. We need to concentrate.'

'James, I really don't think—'

She was interrupted by an elegant red-haired woman in an emerald green and gold gown who, with her partner, took her place next to James, readying herself for the dance.

'Well, well, Signor Murray. I did not expect you to be here this evening.'

'Nor I you, Signora Panatti. I did not have you down as a dancer.'

'I am here as the guest of Judge Carraldi.' She indicated an elderly man with a pronounced stoop. 'I wonder, Judge, shall we wait a little until dancing again? I do not find the company to my liking.'

'Very well, my dear,' he replied.

Lucy glared at her. According to Anna, this was the woman who had claimed that James had misbehaved so disgracefully.

'Perhaps you should go,' Signora Panatti said as she was leaving the floor. 'Nobody wants you here.'

'I do not think so, Signora,' James said. 'I have done nothing wrong, as I am sure you are well aware.'

She laughed mirthlessly. 'That is not what I have been told.'

'What do you mean?'

'I have many friends, Signor Murray. They come from all over the world and they tell me all kinds of useful things.'

'I am very happy for you, Signora Panatti.'

'At least one of them knows you of old, apparently. In particular he has been very talkative about your family. In fact, I am told that he knows better than all of us exactly what you are.'

'What is this woman talking about, James?' Lucy asked.

'I have no idea.'

Signora Panatti smiled. 'I think you have some explaining to do, Signor Murray. You see, my dear,' she continued, addressing her comments to Lucy, 'even without his penchant for ladies of a certain kind, your brother is hardly a paragon of virtue.'

She leant over to him and spoke in a low voice. 'I have only just begun.'

The other dancers were staring at them and murmuring to each other behind hands and fans.

'You are despicable,' muttered James, and taking Lucy forcibly by the arm, he began to propel her from the dance floor back towards the professor, who was watching with concern.

'You can't say I didn't warn you,' Signora Panatti called after them.

Having delivered Lucy into the safe custody of Miss Trott and Professor Donati, who had joined their table, James accompanied Lombroso, Anna and Ottolenghi outside on to a nearby terrace to discuss matters.

He leant over the balustrade and peered out into the fast-approaching darkness. It had rained recently, and the raindrops were shining like moonstones in the fading light.

'What was all that about, Murray?' Lombroso asked.

James faced them. The two men were standing and Anna was seated, all of them as if frozen in time, creating an elaborate tableau depicting some kind of inquisition.

'I don't know what she wants from me,' he said, speaking slowly, stretching the words out as if they were elastic. His breath came in short bursts and he felt a small bead of sweat trickle down his cheek, following the path of his new scar.

'If it was unclear before, it is certainly clear now. Panatti definitely has some kind of agenda,' Anna said. 'She seems absolutely set on destroying your reputation.'

'We still need to establish her motive,' Lombroso said.

'Perhaps you have found something out, or she thinks you have,' Ottolenghi suggested. 'After all, as you have said yourself, James, she has an influence in all kinds of areas, many of them illicit.'

'The only thing I have been doing is searching for Sofia's cousin.'

'Then, as we have said, it must be something to do with that,' Lombroso said. 'Is there anything you might have stumbled upon during your investigation?'

James frowned. 'The trouble is, I can't remember much from after I was assaulted.'

'Try your best, Murray. This second establishment of Panatti's is the most likely.'

'It doesn't sound as if it is state-registered,' Ottolenghi said, 'so it's probably secluded. That would make it a good place to commit murder, particularly if one wanted to drain blood from a body.'

'I thought I saw Panatti speaking to the Rambaudis a few moments ago,' Anna said. 'They are acquainted, then?'

'I'm not sure,' Lombroso said. 'I know the family, but I am not aware of any link between them and that woman. I imagine they were just being polite.'

'What about their background?' James asked. He had seen that Lucy had formed some kind of attachment to Francesco Rambaudi but had assumed that it had ended after his appearance at the rice estate. After seeing his sister dancing with the man that evening, he was no longer certain that this was the case, which was a potentially disturbing development. And if Rambaudi knew Concetta Panatti . . .

Lombroso stroked his beard, deep in thought. 'The parents are both dead. The father succumbed to the effects of drink a few years ago now, and the mother more recently from some illness or other. It was quite sudden, I believe.'

'I think Panatti could be responsible for the murders,' Anna said. 'Both Nella Calvi and Teresa Mariani worked for her, which surely cannot be a coincidence. I have encountered her criminal type before, utterly ruthless and quite without conscience. I am certain she would be quite prepared to kill, if it became necessary.'

Lombroso shook his head. 'You are wrong, Madame Tarnovsky. These killings are almost certainly the handiwork of our morally insane criminal, who is obviously a man. As I have said before, Panatti, if she is involved, is just an accomplice.'

'How can you be so certain, Cesare?' Anna asked.

Before he could reply, there was the sound of a commotion from the main ballroom.

'What the devil?' Lombroso said.

Professor Donati came running on to the terrace. 'Signor, Professore . . . your presence has been urgently requested by the marchesa . . .'

'Whatever has happened?' asked Lombroso.

'It is Fabia Carignano,' Professor Donati said. 'She seems to have gone missing.'

36

To society's shame, many occasional prostitutes are recruited through violence and traded as black slaves were. They are enlisted by some scoundrel who, pretending to find them work as waitresses or something similar, takes them to foreign countries where they have neither friends nor supports. He shuts them up in brothels where everything encourages them to give in: cajolery, threats, liquor . . . Most are raped and maliciously prevented from leaving their brothel-prison. They end up by adapting to the prostitute's life, and they continue with it because escape is so difficult. Lombroso and Ferrero, 1893, p. 225

She wakes slowly. Her head is pounding. She opens her eyes, but what she sees is not what she expects. She sees that she is in some kind of cell. The walls are made of stone and she can smell dampness, though it is underpinned with something sweet . . . no, not sweet . . . overripe, decaying. Beneath her is straw. She tries to move but discovers that she is chained to a wall by her ankle, tethered like some kind of animal. She cries out in anger and frustration and pulls at her shackles as if doing so will tear them from the solid stone they are so securely fastened to. She realises that it is more of a pit than a cell, for there is no door. Above her is an iron grid through which there is some natural light. It was night when she was taken, so how long has she been here? All she remembers is getting a note inviting her out on to the terrace. Once out there, she heard someone whispering her name in the gardens and walked towards the voice. In a moment someone had placed a cloth over her face and everything went dark.

She shivers and hugs herself. She is still dressed in her thin ballgown, a magnificent creation in varying shades of pink and silver with beaded embellishments that shone so prettily in the flickering candlelight. It is short-sleeved and low-cut, and seemed so daring when first chosen. She loved it when she put it on. It made her feel like a queen. But now she is wishing that she had chosen something warmer, or at least had a shawl to keep out the cold.

She shifts around a little. She needs to relieve herself, but how? She sees a bucket in the corner. No. She is an aristocrat. She will not sink to such depths. Suddenly she is overwhelmed by fury and pride. How dare they, whoever they are, bring her to such a place? A girl – no, a woman – of her standing?

'Let me out of here!' she cries. 'If you do not, you will be sorry.'

She hears a noise from above. There is someone leaning over the edge of her prison, watching her.

'You can shout as much as you like, but no one will hear you.' The voice is strange . . . musical, like a small bell. She cannot tell if it is male or female.

'Listen to me,' she says. 'If you release me now, I will say it was all a joke. Nothing will happen to you.'

'I cannot. You must atone.'

'Atone?' she says. 'Atone for what? I have done nothing wrong! If anyone should atone it is you. You have abducted me and brought me here. The longer you keep me here, the worse it will be for you.'

'Atone... you must atone.'

The figure moves away. The light from above dims slowly and there is a scraping sound. A cover of stone or wood is being hauled over the opening above.

'No! Don't leave me here! Come back!'

But it is no use. The lid of her stone box is in place and she is left in darkness, like an exhibit in a museum. She starts to weep. Her defiance has left her. This was not how this day was meant to be. It should have been full of wonderful things – admiration, adulation and gifts. For today is a special day. It is her birthday. But if what she suspects is right, it might well be her last.

James perused the newspapers cautiously over breakfast. The events of the previous evening were covered on all the front pages and, unsurprisingly, had taken precedence over further discussion about his own activities. Clearly it was one thing for servants and flower sellers to go missing, but quite another for a member of the aristocracy to be snatched at a society event. He and many others had searched the surrounding area, but there was no trace of Fabia except for a solitary shoe found in the gardens. It seemed as if she had been smuggled through the back gates. No one had seen anything; it had been carefully planned.

Apprehensively, he opened *The People's Voice*, and there he found his worst suspicions confirmed: an attempt to link him to the abduction. Firstly it was mentioned that the ball had been attended by some foreign gentlemen who 'may be under suspicion', although that could refer to any number of people present. Secondly, in the centre of the newspaper there was a feature about him written by Baldovino. James wasn't named, but he might as well have been. There was even a cartoon depicting a scientist with a large head and a tiny body ensnaring a young woman in a butterfly net. 'Leave me alone!' she was saying. 'I don't want to go to Scotland. It's far too cold!' The headline was THE SCIENTIST AND THE MAIDENS? and the article was, James thought, absolutely ludicrous. It suggested that foreign scientists were 'infiltrating our university'. 'Who knows what their intent might be?' it asked, and then suggested that there might be some link between their 'malign presence' and the 'disappearance of a number of girls from our city'. The implication was clear. This was plumbing new depths, even for Baldovino.

As he was reading, Lombroso came in, closely followed by Ottolenghi, who had stayed with them due to the lateness of the hour.

'More nonsense in *The People's Voice*?' Lombroso asked. James handed over his copy. 'Try to rise above it, Murray,' he advised. 'In a few days it will all be forgotten. The search for Fabia Carignano is bound to take precedence, as indeed it should.'

'It is a terrifying business,' Ottolenghi said, 'but at least the carabinieri should act now.'

Lombroso nodded. 'Apparently there are to be extra patrols on the streets, and all leave has been cancelled. The marchesa has insisted on meeting the mayor to discuss the investigation.'

'It is a pity that all this wasn't put in place when the other girls went missing,' James said bitterly, looking down at the newspapers on the table in front of him. 'They're hardly mentioned except for Baldovino trying to imply that I am involved.'

'No one will take that seriously,' Ottolenghi said. 'Reporters always like to make connections where none exist. Look at how he suggested a link to the Abbey San Callisto and the monks.'

'No doubt that will turn out to be my fault as well.'

'Even Baldovino would find it hard to connect you to something that happened a century ago,' Lombroso said.

'We did find a body there,' James pointed out.

'Indeed – one of a series of unexplained events: missing girls, dead girls, missing blood, mummified monks, reports of haunting, you being beaten and threatened, and of course last night's abduction.' Lombroso looked thoughtful. 'We need to put our anthropological thinking caps on and see what we can find.' He sat down at the table. 'But first we must take a good breakfast. After all, hunger provokes crime, as the Tuscans say.'

Having no appetite, James retired to Lombroso's small library and tried his best to work, though he was finding it difficult to concentrate. All he wanted was to get out there and investigate Fabia's disappearance in the hope that it would lead him to Chiara. But thanks to that stupid article, he had been advised to stay here. Sofia had been sent home and he did not know what she had been told, although he was certain she would have read the articles. She must be beside herself.

Before long, Ottolenghi came in and sat opposite him. Lombroso had asked them to continue with the tasks he had set; he himself had a meeting with Gemelli, presumably about the articles and other matters. Ironically, they were going through the data collated from the interviews with Madame Giulia's girls, with whom James was accused of consorting.

They had been asked to pick out quotations from what the girls had said to them, in order to illustrate the truth or otherwise of their comments.

'It will be all right,' Ottolenghi said. 'The professor will sort it out.'

'I have been such a fool!'

'You are being very hard on yourself.'

'I should have listened to you when you warned me about Sofia. It would have been better for us both if I had kept away from her.'

'You fell in love. That is not a crime,' Ottolenghi said. 'And no one could have foreseen that Baldovino would have been quite so vengeful.'

'I did rough him up a little.'

'I know, but that sort of thing would normally be like water off a duck's back to a man like him.'

'It does seem extreme. And it is not just my life that is affected.'

'So you think Baldovino is acting under Panatti's influence?'

'He did mention that he had been threatened.'

'Who by?'

James looked at Ottolenghi. In all that had happened, he had almost forgotten Baldovino's treacherous informer. 'He claimed that he didn't know. Whoever it was told him to mind his own business. That was why he gave me the names of the girls.'

'You do his dirty work and he reports it. Is that how it worked?'

'Something like that.'

There was a knock at the door and a maid came in with a note for James. She handed it to him, then ran off without waiting for a reply, as if she was afraid he might attack her.

When he had read it, he crumpled it up in disgust and threw it on the fire, watching as the flames flared up and consumed it

'Who was it from?' Ottolenghi asked.

'Baldovino. Apparently he has some information for me.'

'Will you go?'

James hesitated. 'I suppose I'd better.'

'Are you sure that's a good idea? The professor told you to stay here. It might make things worse.'

'How could they get any worse, Salvatore? My reputation is in ruins, not to mention that of my sister. I might lose my job and I've almost certainly lost Sofia. Do you really think I should just sit here and wait for it all to blow over? Baldovino might know something. At the very least, he could tell me who's behind these stories.'

'Do you want me to come with you?' Ottolenghi asked.

'No,' James replied. 'This is between me and Baldovino. Just cover for me if you can.'

'I will. But be careful. Whoever threatened Baldovino is dangerous.'

James acknowledged his friend's warning as he left, but he knew it would make no difference. He had to solve these riddles before anything else happened. He remembered the words of his captors when he had been abducted. They'd told him he had a lot to lose and they were right.

Then there was that Panatti woman. 'I have only just begun,' she had said at the ball. At least some of this was her doing, but why, and how much? Perhaps Baldovino held the key. He was certainly involved. James knew it was risky, but too much was at stake. He had to find out.

*

Baldovino's broken door was still hanging off its hinges, as it had been the last time James was here. He pushed it open.

'Baldovino, are you there?'

There was no reply. He stepped inside, then stopped to take in the scene. The place had never been particularly tidy, but now it was completely wrecked. Pieces of china were strewn around. The windows were smashed. Every stick of furniture had been pulled apart. Even the shabby sofa had been slashed with a knife. He heard a groan from behind it and went to investigate. It was Baldovino. He had been stabbed as well as severely beaten. His blood seemed to be everywhere. James knelt down beside him and opened his collar. He was still breathing, but only just. Something was tucked underneath him. James lifted his coat and pulled it out. It was a large knife.

'What do we have here, then?' said a voice from the doorway. James stood up quickly, the knife still in his hand. Two carabinieri officers walked into the room.

'Put it down, son. You've done enough.'

'You can't think that I did this.'

'Drop the knife,' the second man said, stepping towards him.

James obeyed and held up his hands in surrender. The first man knelt down by Baldovino and felt for a pulse. He nodded at his colleague.

'You're under arrest for attempted murder,' said the man, handcuffing him.

'I did not do this,' James protested.

'Funny, that's what they all say . . . to start with, anyway.' He escorted James out of Baldovino's room and into the street.

'I need to get home,' James said.

'The only home you're going to is jail,' said his captor. 'You won't be seeing anywhere else for a while.'

James had been told that if he interfered he would regret it. He had chosen to ignore the warning and he had been wrong. The threat had been carried out, and regret it he certainly did.

37

Every mental abnormality makes its own contribution to criminality. The idiot is given to explosions of rage, assaults, murder, rape and arson for the mere pleasure of seeing the flames. The imbecile and feebleminded, succumbing easily to their first impulses or the suggestions of others, become accomplices to crime at the slightest prospect of gain. Lombroso, 1889, p. 275

Lucy sat at the breakfast table, still thinking about poor Fabia. Where was she now? Was she even still alive? Gina and Paola were poring over the newspaper, much to Miss Trott's disapproval.

'It says here that the carabinieri are questioning everyone who attended the ball,' Paola said.

Gina sighed. 'I wish we had not left early. We might have seen something.'

'If you'll excuse me,' Miss Trott said, 'I have to go out shortly. I have some things to do. I doubt I'll be back before lunchtime. I am sure you can occupy yourself until then, Lucy.'

'Do you think you should, Miss Trott?' Paola said. 'The editorial warns against going out unaccompanied. It says here that no one is safe.'

Miss Trott glared at her. 'I think that young ladies should not be reading at the breakfast table!' She got up, snatched the newspaper away and stalked out.

Gina watched her leave. 'I wonder where she's going.'

'Probably shopping or visiting a gallery or something,' Paola said as she nibbled delicately at a pastry.

'She might be going to the Via San Pellico,' Lucy said. 'Let's follow her.'

Gina waved her butter knife enthusiastically. 'That's a very good idea.'

'But what about the warning?' Paola said. 'Won't Mama object?'

'She won't mind if we don't tell her. Besides, we'll be together.'

Lucy nodded and got up from the table. 'We should hurry. We don't want to miss her.'

The girls waited in Lucy's room until they heard the door to Miss Trott's bedroom open and close. The game was afoot.

Miss Trott was a fast walker. The day was warm and humid and the sun was unrelenting, so keeping up with her was no easy task. *Pinkerton's Detection Manual* was, as ever, invaluable in its advice, giving ten tips for successful pursuit of suspects:

1. Keep your distance.
2. Ensure that you are never directly behind your subject.
3. Be discreet.
4. Wear a disguise where necessary.
5. Do not make loud noises.
6. Do not lose sight of the subject.
7. Carry a newspaper so that you have something to hide behind if your subject suddenly stops or you are spotted.
8. Do not under any circumstances run.

9. Carry a likeness of your subject so that you can ask passers-by if they have seen him in the event you lose sight of him.
10. Always carry a notebook, pencil, a map and pocket watch.

They had all agreed that most points were rather obvious and that number 4, although inviting, was likely to be a recipe for disaster. Gina was tempted to dress up as one of her father's criminal types, but this was rejected because, frankly, it was far too warm. They were going to take a newspaper, but Professor Lombroso was reading it. However, they did manage to equip themselves with a notebook, and Lucy said that she would use her silver propelling pencil, a gift from her mother. The only map they could find was not of Turin, and the pocket watch and likeness of Miss Trott were equally elusive. In fact they spent so long trying to get ready that they almost missed their quarry altogether. Had it not been for the fact that Miss Trott had evidently forgotten something and was forced to return to collect whatever it was, they would have failed before their mission had even begun.

Despite the teething problems, they managed finally to follow Miss Trott, and a merry dance she led them. It was odd, Lucy thought, that she did not seem to be going to one particular place to conduct her business. Instead she meandered through the streets, turning down alleyways and even at one point doubling back on herself, forcing her pursuers to take evasive action that involved ducking into a millinery shop, where they examined the merchandise with some care. In fact, such was Paola's attention to detail that she had to be almost dragged away from a pretty straw summer bonnet and reminded of their aim.

Eventually, after an exhausting hour, Miss Trott seemed to be walking with more purpose, and it was not long before she began to slow down and examine the buildings she was passing with more care. Then, quite suddenly, she stopped. Fortunately the girls were able to slip into an alleyway and observe her from a distance. She stood and peered at the building for a moment as if undecided. Then she drew herself up, put her shoulders back and her chin in the air and marched inside.

'Let's see where she went,' Lucy suggested. 'Then we can decide what to do next.'

'No need. I know where she has gone,' Paola said. 'Papa has pointed it out on more than one occasion. It is the headquarters of the carabinieri.'

Baldovino lived only a few streets away from the carabinieri's headquarters, so James had to suffer the ignominy of being escorted on foot. A crowd made up mostly of small boys began to follow them, jeering as they went. There were also a couple of enterprising street pedlars who supplied snacks where requested. It was, after all, not every day that a gentleman was arrested, and the officer seemed to take great pleasure in slowing their progress at every available opportunity. After what seemed like an age, they arrived at their destination, and their followers melted into the background as if they had never actually been there. When James made as if to go through the front door, he was directed round a corner.

'Tradesmen's entrance for you today,' the officer said firmly.

He was taken to a shabby reception area, and then to a holding cell, where he was shoved onto a bench and told to wait until someone came for him. There were a number of other prisoners also waiting, and a motley crew they were.

Two of them had obviously been in a fight and were nursing various wounds and glaring at each other. Another was clearly drunk and sat in a corner moaning to himself, a pool of vomit at his feet. A woman with heavily rouged cheeks and a large feathered hat winked at James and blew him a kiss. James began to think that perhaps Lombroso had a point in his description of the criminal type. They certainly resembled some of the photographs he had seen in the professor's study.

'Wait here. You will be taken through to be interviewed when someone is available,' the officer said.

'Who?' James asked.

'Whoever is here.'

'I want to see Inspector Tullio.'

'Oh do you?' said the officer. 'And will he want to see you?'

'Yes,' James said decisively. 'He will. I am innocent.'

'Oh, I see. Well that makes all the difference,' the officer said sarcastically.

'Please . . . the inspector will understand.'

'He's a busy man. The marchesa's niece has been abducted. The whole city is up in arms.'

'I want to see him now. I did not do this.'

'So you've said, but that's for the courts to decide. Maybe he'll come and see you in jail.'

'Please. Just tell the inspector that I am here.'

The officer shrugged and walked away, leaving James trying to avoid the glances of his companions and contemplating what Lombroso would say when he heard about this. As for Aunt Agnes . . . He sighed in frustration. He should be out there looking for Chiara and Fabia and the other girls, not stuck in a cell.

A few minutes later he heard the sound of a key in the

outer gate. The bars rattled ominously. Was he about to be taken to prison? A familiar face came into view.

'Tullio, thank God!' James said.

Tullio, unsmiling, nodded at the man who had opened the gate, who pointed at James. 'You, get up and follow me.'

James did as he was told, and soon he was sitting in a small room with Tullio. It was almost normal except for the fact that he was shackled to the table and the inspector, rather than sitting, was standing uncomfortably in a corner looking anywhere but at him.

'We need to get the professor on to this first of all,' James said, 'and Ottolenghi. If you can bring them to the scene and then to Baldovino's bedside, that would be best. Once he comes round, it should be a simple matter, but I don't know when that will be. How is he?'

'He is in a bad way. He may not recover at all.' Tullio's voice was cold.

'I feared that might be the case. He was badly injured when I found him. Well, we will just have to examine the scene carefully. It will exculpate me soon enough.'

'The evidence is damning,' his friend replied.

'You must know that I did not do this, Tullio!'

Tullio shrugged. 'I cannot help you, James.' He looked pale, and new lines seemed to have formed around his mouth and on his forehead.

'Is it because it was you who tipped off Baldovino?'

Tullio's eyes darted towards him. 'I don't know what you mean!'

'I think you do. You gave him the names of those missing girls. What I can't work out is why.'

'Whether I did or didn't makes no difference to this. I

cannot change the evidence. There is a clear motive, and you were found holding the weapon.'

'What? You think I half killed a man just because of a few stupid newspaper stories?'

'Men have been murdered for less.'

'Perhaps, but not by me! You know me better than that.'

'I will make sure that the professor is informed. But that is all I can do.'

'Is that it? Tullio, what is wrong with you?'

'I'm a policeman, James. I have to do my job. It isn't personal.'

The inspector got up to leave, but then hesitated briefly. Just for a moment James thought that he would go back to being the old Tullio, but he was wrong. He opened the door and called the jailer back before walking quickly away. James stared at the grey walls and wondered how on earth he was going to persuade a jury that he was innocent if could not convince his friend of the same thing.

Lucy, Gina and Paola stood in a huddle wondering what to do next.

'What could she be doing there?' Lucy said.

'Giving herself up?' Gina suggested. 'I still think she might know something about the abduction.'

'That doesn't seem very likely,' Paola said.

'It is possible,' Lucy said. 'She must either be reporting something, or she's witnessed a crime.'

Gina groaned. 'So we are no further forward.'

'We will be if we go inside,' Lucy said.

'How can we do that without being detected?' Paola asked.

'We can't, but it may not matter. Follow me.'

'Are you sure this is a good idea?' Paola said, her voice quavering.

Gina gave her a withering look.

Paola tutted. 'All right . . . if you really think it will help.'

They walked into the building. Miss Trott was standing at a counter having a heated argument with a carabinieri officer.

'I do not wish to speak of these matters here. I want to see someone in authority!'

The officer gave her a puzzled look. His mouth was open. 'Signora, you need to tell me first. Then I will decide.'

Miss Trott tutted loudly. 'Really, that will not do. It is a confidential and important matter.'

The man shrugged and began to speak slowly and carefully, as if addressing an idiot. 'You tell me what it is, then I will decide.'

'No, no, no! Is Marshal Machinetti available? It is vital that I see him. Or perhaps Inspector Tullio.'

'He might be,' the officer said hesitantly. He was clearly impressed that she knew both of them.

'Then I suggest you find him immediately!'

'There are other people waiting,' the officer said, gesturing towards Lucy, Gina and Paola.

Miss Trott frowned at them. 'What in the world are you doing here?' she said sharply.

'We happened to see you come in, Miss Trott,' Lucy said. 'We were concerned and thought we might be able to help.'

For a brief few seconds Miss Trott narrowed her eyes, then suddenly, as if she had remembered who she was, her manner changed completely. 'Oh . . . good gracious me . . . how kind of you. It is nothing really.'

The officer looked confused. 'Not vital, then?'

'Just my parasol... I left it somewhere and wondered if it had been handed in.'

'You wanted the marshal for a missing parasol?' the officer said.

Before she could answer, there was the sound of a door being unlocked in the corner.

'Stand back, ladies, please. A prisoner is coming through.'

Lucy was interested at first. She had little experience of criminals. But then she saw James being led through a barred door, handcuffed, surrounded by carabinieri officers, his face a picture of misery. At first she was paralysed with shock. She could not believe what she was seeing. Wasn't he meant to be working in the professor's study? How could he be here, and chained up like that? Had Francesco got him arrested? She took a step towards him. 'James...'

She felt Miss Trott's restraining hand upon her arm.

'Don't you worry, Dr Murray. Clearly there has been a terrible error. I will ensure that this is sorted out straight away.'

'Tell the professor, please,' James said as he was propelled firmly through another door. 'Lucy...' he began. But in a second he was gone, and Lucy sank onto a nearby bench feeling lonelier than she had ever done in her entire life.

38

Maintaining the death sentence does not mean using it often. It is sufficient that it should be suspended like a sword of Damocles over the most terrible criminals, those who have attempted to kill innocent people. This removes the last justifiable objection to capital punishment, that it is irreparable. Lombroso, 1896–7, p. 348

There was an expectant hush as James appeared in the dock. The courtroom was large and suitably imposing, with a preponderance of wood panels and red leather seating. He blinked as his eyes became accustomed to the comparatively bright light.

It was hard to believe that he was here. He had been held at the police station over the weekend, and during that time he had tried again and again to explain his presence in Baldovino's rooms, but nobody believed him. His attempts to contact Tullio had been fruitless, which was perhaps not surprising. He had been seen with a knife in his hand leaning over a stabbed man. Not only that, but he had ample motive given the articles that had appeared in *The People's Voice*. And if Baldovino died, well then, that was the end of that. They still had the death penalty here, although it seemed likely to be abolished soon, if Lombroso was right. But how would that help him?

Lombroso was sitting at the front of the public gallery with Ottolenghi beside him. The professor lifted a hand in acknowledgement. It seemed that James had not been completely abandoned. But he was going to prison, at least until trial. There appeared to be little doubt about that. At the back was a flash of red hair. Concetta Panatti sat and smiled at him – not in greeting, but in satisfaction. She was almost certainly behind his downfall, but why? What had he ever done to her to warrant this? And who else was involved?

There was absolutely no sign of Sofia. She had probably given up on him altogether. He thought of her half-smile and felt an ache of longing. If only he could see her, even if it was for the briefest of moments, just to tell her how much she meant to him. But there was little chance of that. He would be spending a good few months in prison before his trial, he imagined. By then, even if he was acquitted, which in itself seemed unlikely, she would have moved on. He had tried his best to find Chiara for her, but he had failed comprehensively. He deserved to lose her and she was better off without him.

James stood as the judge came in – a small man with a pinched face and a mouth that looked as if it was permanently pursed. The proceedings were brief, as he had expected. The prosecution's lawyer read out the facts of the accusation against him. The charge was attempted murder. His lawyer, an elderly man appointed by the court, seemed to be dozing throughout and had to be poked by his clerk into responding.

'The matter of bail, your honour?'

'Under the circumstances, I do not think that is appropriate. Given the facts of this case, the prisoner might as well accustom himself to custody.' So much for an unbiased hearing. The judge's voice was thin and reedy and his expression dour. James imagined him sitting with Aunt Agnes, comparing sins or something similar. They would get on like a house on fire.

There was some rumpus going on in the public gallery. A note was passed down from Lombroso and eventually found its way to the judge, who tapped his long, thin fingers impatiently as he waited for it to be delivered. He opened it and his eyebrows shot up in surprise. After a long pause he spoke. 'The prisoner should stand.'

James got to his feet and braced himself.

'It appears that you have influential friends. A bond has been lodged with the court, which, given its provenance and size, is enough to persuade me that you should be released until your trial. It is conditional on your residence at the home of Professor Cesare Lombroso in the Via Legnano. If there is the slightest hint of any misbehaviour, then to prison you will go. Have I made myself clear?'

James could not quite believe what he had just heard. He had thought that prison was inevitable. He hesitated as he took it in.

'Well?' the judge said impatiently.

'Yes, your honour.'

'You may go.'

As James was released from the dock, he noticed that Concetta Panatti's seat had been vacated. Whoever his influential friend was, it certainly wasn't her.

Lombroso approached him and shook his hand warmly. 'Come this way, Murray. We are taking you home.'

As James walked through the courtroom to freedom, a feeling of dread overcame him. He would be seeing this place again, he had no doubt. And the next time perhaps he would be leaving through another entrance altogether.

Lucy was whiling away the morning by trying but failing to read one of the books that Aunt Agnes had sent with Miss Trott. The last few days had been almost unbearable, but despite all she had been told about the accusations that James faced, she was absolutely certain of his innocence. He just didn't have that level of violence in him.

There were sounds from downstairs. It seemed that the professor and Ottolenghi had returned from court. She hoped they would not come in here. She knew the outcome of the proceedings. It was inevitable. But she did not want to hear those words – *James is in prison*. She could imagine it only too well: his pale and handsome face peering out at her through bars. He would try to smile, not wanting to upset her, but she would know. How could she not? His eyes would betray him, as they always did, and she would see in them his abject misery and fear of what the future held. The question was, did she have the inner strength to support him, or would it be too much for her?

Then she heard the sound of someone bounding up the stairs. The door flew open and, by some miracle, there he was, standing in front of her and grinning like an idiot. James was home.

39

Another, and very serious indication of moral insanity is the lack of maternal feelings that makes the born prostitute the twin sister of the female born criminal. Lesbians, especially, are completely indifferent to maternity and indeed terrified of pregnancy.

Lombroso and Ferrero, 1893, p. 214

'The only way we can prove that you are innocent, Murray,' Lombroso said, 'is to find the real culprit.'

'I know,' James said. 'But how can we do that unless Baldovino recovers and identifies him?'

He was sitting with Lombroso, Ottolenghi and Anna in the professor's study after lunch, enjoying a glass of grappa. Given what he had been through, and the prospect of what might be in store for him, it seemed to James that everything tasted a little sweeter.

'Surely this is all part of the same mystery,' Anna said. 'James has been framed for this assault by the people who threatened him before. Their identity is the key to everything.'

'Anna is right,' James agreed. 'That is what I need to focus on. Anyway, at least I'm free to investigate. Thank you for the bond, Professor.'

'It wasn't me that bailed you out,' Lombroso said. 'You have Sofia to thank for that.'

'But she has no influence.'

'No, but the marchesa does,' Ottolenghi said. 'Sofia went to her and asked for help.'

James could barely contain his joy. Sofia cared! She still cared after everything.

'That is very good of the marchesa, considering that her niece has been taken,' Anna said. 'She must be beside herself.'

'Well, it was not entirely altruistic,' Lombroso said. 'Both Sofia and I have spoken to her about your enquiries, Murray, and she believes that you may be able to help in finding her niece. Any ideas?'

'If Teresa Mariani's friend Bruno Ferranti is working on the Rambaudis' rice estate, then we should talk to him,' James said.

'*Eccellente!* We can talk through criminal types on the way.'

Lucy stood on the grand Renaissance steps of the Duomo and watched Sofia walking across the piazza towards her. She wanted to help James, but since he was clearly keeping things from her, she had concluded that it was time to get some answers from the only person she thought would not lie to her. It had not been easy. James had made it clear that she should not leave the house unaccompanied, given Fabia's abduction. But he had gone straight into the professor's study after lunch and Lucy had taken the opportunity to slip out, hoping that he would not notice.

Sofia smiled hesitantly as their eyes met. All Lucy knew for certain was that there was something between James and Sofia. The part Sofia had played in freeing James proved that. And if they were as close as Lucy was beginning to suspect, then he would have told Sofia about his past – that was the sort of man he was.

'Signorina, I am here as you asked,' Sofia said when she reached her.

'Thank you for coming. I know it must be difficult for you at the moment, with Fabia being taken.'

'Your brother is free now and he will help, I am certain of it.'

'I am sure you are right. It is my brother I have come to talk to you about. Shall we walk?'

Sofia agreed, and together they went into the cathedral. It was quiet. There were just a few people there, dotted about, looking at the interior or praying. Lucy had selected it as a venue because she wanted somewhere calming, and it seemed that she had chosen well. They began to walk along the main aisle until they reached a small chapel. Lucy followed Sofia in and watched as she gazed at a statue of a woman at prayer.

'I need you to be truthful with me.'

Sofia's expression was difficult to read, but there was something. It was no more than a flicker in her eyes, but it was enough for Lucy.

'Tell me, Sofia, do you love my brother?' she asked in a low voice.

Sofia hesitated for a moment and then nodded slowly. '*Sì, sì*. You must believe me when I say that I have always loved him. But . . .'

'But what?'

She had tears in her eyes. 'As I have already told him, we cannot be together.'

'I know about your background, and it will be difficult, but if you love him . . .'

'It is not enough.'

'Why not? Is it James that you do not love enough?'

'No, it isn't that. But I have others to think of. I cannot say more.'

'When you were with him, I imagine you shared a lot. You must have done, to love each other so much. You know he still loves you, don't you?'

Sofia nodded. 'It would be better for us both if he did not.'

'Did he speak about our father?'

'Yes, he did often, and it troubled him. We found that we were very similar . . . Our fathers both sinned in the worst way possible and left us with the consequences.'

'How did James describe our father's sins?'

Sofia paused. 'I do not know that I should tell you. It should come from him.'

'He will never tell me. He thinks I cannot cope with the truth, that it will hurt me to know what our father did. But not knowing is far worse.'

'Your father became obsessed with his work.'

'I have seen that in James too,' Lucy said.

'He fears that in himself, I think.'

'So what happened?'

'Your father operated on someone using experimental techniques and it went horribly wrong. James found out; they argued violently. After that, your father took to drink. He got involved in a brawl, stabbed someone and ended up in his own asylum.'

Lucy felt faint and held onto the wall for a moment. She had not expected Sofia to be so direct. 'Father killed someone? Why didn't James tell me?'

'He didn't want to hurt you . . . and also . . .' Sofia hesitated.

'What? What is it?'

'For some reason he blames himself for your father's

downfall. But it is not just that. He is afraid that part of your father lives on in him. That is why he came here to the professor . . . to see if it was true.'

'To consult him, you mean?'

'Yes, though I am not sure that he got the answers he was looking for.'

'What did the professor tell him?'

'I think he reassured him, or tried to, but James was still not sure. His fear is lodged too deeply inside him. I can tell that it is still on his mind. He is very troubled.'

'And someone is using that uncertainty to destroy him,' Lucy said.

'I think so too. I am sure that Panatti woman is involved, but there is more to it than that.'

Lucy grasped Sofia's hand. A memory had come to the forefront of her mind – a gaunt-faced man and what had seemed like a strange comment to make at a funeral. 'I have to go, Sofia. There is someone I must speak to.'

'Will it help James?'

'I hope so.'

'Then you must try.'

'I must succeed,' Lucy said firmly.

In its introduction, written by Pinkerton himself, the manual stated that any good detective must be resolute and persevere until the investigation was complete. She would follow the instructions to the letter. Nothing less would do.

James looked wearily out of the window as the carriage jolted its way towards the Rambaudi estate. Lombroso was holding forth about his profile of the killer.

'He is a morally insane epileptic, of this I have no doubt.

We are looking at someone with a number of telltale physical characteristics.'

'Ah, yes,' Ottolenghi said, still very much the student at the feet of his master. 'I have taken the liberty of noting these down, Professor, as you have mentioned them throughout the investigation.' He took his now battered notebook out of his jacket pocket and consulted it. 'Our killer has asymmetrical facial features, a big jaw, jutting cheekbones, large mouth, thick lips with malformed teeth. If he has facial hair, it will be scanty. He enjoys sexual perversion of all kinds and the drinking of blood. He is intelligent but unable to tell the difference between good and evil.'

'Could the killer be a woman?' Anna asked, holding onto the carriage door as they went round a corner at speed.

'No,' Lombroso replied. 'Not enough physical strength and, besides, a woman would not be intelligent enough to do this.'

'There are plenty of female killers,' Anna said, clearly unwilling to let the possibility go. 'You have seen my own photographs and read my research.'

'No, I do not think this killer is a woman,' Lombroso said firmly.

'But my data reflects yours, Cesare!' she protested. 'I too found asymmetry of the face. Remember the two women who killed their husbands? And the others . . . the demi types who did not fit the profile completely but still had big jaws, deep-set eyes and dark hair.'

Lombroso gave her a patronising smile, and she pursed her lips as if with the effort of not interrupting. 'These are domestic murders, though, my dear Madame Tarnovsky, quite different from our man – and it is a man, I am sure of it.'

'Your description is very precise, Professor,' Ottolenghi said carefully.

'Quite!' Lombroso said, beaming at them. 'A man like that shouldn't be too hard to find.'

'Aren't we concentrating too much on these characteristics? Because frankly . . .' James hesitated. He did not know exactly how far he should go with this, but he was becoming increasingly frustrated by Lombroso's fixation on appearance.

'Out with it, Murray! If you have an idea, we should hear it, you being such an expert.'

'I just think we would be better served by examining what this person has done and trying to work out why,' he said.

'Studying the description of the location where the bodies were found and the state they were in might well be helpful also,' Ottolenghi said.

'I don't doubt that both of these approaches might be of use, and I commend you for your attempts at adding something to the investigation.' Lombroso's face was reddening with each word. 'But may I remind you both that my theories have been tried and tested over many years, so I think we will stick with them if you don't mind.'

James did not trust himself to reply. Instead he merely nodded and allowed Lombroso to continue outlining his increasingly outlandish ideas as the carriage took them, he hoped, nearer to finding a solution. They passed through the imposing wrought-iron gates resplendent with their fleur-de-lis design. Why could his colleagues not see what was staring them in the face? The answer to this mystery was not in criminal types but criminals. Lombroso's talk was merely a distraction. James was convinced that Bruno Ferranti held the key, and he hoped that he would shortly have the chance to question him in person.

40

Female criminality increases with the march of civilisation. The female criminal is an occasional criminal, with few degenerative characteristics, little dullness, and so on; her numbers grow as opportunities for evil doing increase. The prostitute, on the other hand, has a greater atavistic resemblance to the primitive woman – the vagabond Venus – and thus she had a greater dullness of touch and taste, greater fondness of tattooing, and so on.

Lombroso and Ferrero, 1893, p. 148

Lucy studied the wooden sarcophagus in front of her carefully and scribbled some notes down in a notebook she had purchased on her way to the Museo Egizio. The artefact was the same one she had seen on during her first visit with Miss Trott. It was magnificent, highly varnished and covered with elaborate depictions of rituals, animals and gods. She started to sketch it, wondering if it might be a good place to hide a body for Lydia Loveday to discover. She noticed that there were several other scholars paying similar attention to various exhibits. Clearly if one wanted to study the history of Egypt, this was very much the place to come. They were mostly much older than her, and male. The only exceptions to this were a couple who had arrived at about the same time as she had.

He was a handsome young man with a shock of dark hair that he kept pushing impatiently out of his eyes, just as James did. She noticed a deep scar running down his face and wondered idly if it bothered him. The girl was short and dark. She was studying a statue of Sakhmet, a fire-breathing goddess with the head of a lion. Lucy had wanted to examine it herself, but the other girl had got there first. The pair certainly seemed to be together, and Lucy soon concocted a fledgling romance for them: love amongst the dead, or some such. There might be a short story in there somewhere, although she doubted she would ever write it. Detective rather than romantic fiction was her forte.

She rubbed the bridge of her nose to relieve an itch. It was important to blend in when conducting surveillance of any kind, which was why she was wearing a pair of wire-framed spectacles borrowed from Paola, who with Gina had helped her prepare for her visit. The sisters had wanted to accompany her but she had managed to dissuade them, quoting from *Pinkerton's*, which claimed that 'the best surveillance is carried out alone'. The spectacles were perched uncomfortably on the end of her nose. She hoped they would make her look learned and perhaps a little older than her years, but now she wished that she had left them at home. Still, no one seemed to be taking the slightest notice of her, which was the main thing.

Lucy could see the steps down which Professor Donati had led her during her previous visit. Her intention was to confront him in his lair. She had to know what he had been discussing with that man at the ball, the same man who had made such a fuss at her father's funeral. Who was he, and what was he doing in Turin? With luck, Donati would at least be able to name him.

She stretched and feigned a yawn. It would be only natural

to take a break and look at the other exhibits, wouldn't it? She wandered over to an impressive Sphinx by the stairs and pretended to examine it closely. Her scholastic companions did not seem to have noticed her. Satisfied, she made her way down the stairs towards Professor Donati's workshop.

Striding along the basement corridor of the Museo Egizio, she was pretending to be a good deal braver than she actually felt. The place was deserted, and every now and then she would catch a glimpse of a statue of a god or a frieze with Egyptians solemnly standing in a line, arms raised, worshipping something or somebody. Eyes seemed to be everywhere, but none of them were human, or alive at any rate. Finally she reached the room where Professor Donati had been working. The door was open, so she went in. There were the waxworks, looking even more eerie and lifelike than on the last occasion, but of the professor there was no sign. Lucy decided to wait for a few moments in case he had stepped out for a moment.

She examined a piece of papyrus that was lying on a table. Clearly Donati had been looking at it recently. Next to it was the sheaf from which it seemed to have come, neatly rolled and lying in a box decorated with gold and turquoise. On a piece of paper were some scribbled notes. The heading was 'APEP: Book of Spells'.

She leant forward and squinted at it in the half-light, trying to make sense of what was written beneath. So intent was she on deciphering Professor Donati's script that she did not hear someone approaching her from behind. Suddenly a strong arm grabbed her and a hand clamped a cloth over her mouth and nose. The smell was chemical, but with a strange sweetness to it. She understood immediately what was happening and attempted to prise the hand away from her mouth, but the grip was too strong. She tried to hold her breath, all the while struggling as hard as she could, grabbing at the face behind her, hoping to get her fingers into his eyes, and pulling at his hair. All she could think was, no! This must not happen to me! I must survive! But it was hopeless. Her assailant was too strong for her. The last thoughts that went through Lucy's head before the blackness descended were firstly regret that she might never know the solution to the mysteries she had encountered, and secondly that her life might be over before it had scarcely begun.

'How strange to see you here again, Signor Murray,' Francesco Rambaudi said as he lounged elegantly on a wicker chair in the courtyard of the Villa Purezza. He had not even bothered to stand up in order to greet them, which, given Anna's presence, was unforgivable.

James tried to put his personal dislike to one side, the better to assess Francesco's character.

From his expression, it was clear that Rambaudi was amused. 'I thought we had a gentlemen's agreement on the matter. But then of course you are not really much of a gentleman, are you? Or so I have heard. What is it you are accused of? Oh yes – a serious assault, perhaps even attempted murder. Well, my personal knowledge of you would certainly seem to confirm your propensity for both dishonesty and violence. I will, of course, testify to that effect at your trial. It should be a most interesting experience. And let's face it, prison is where you belong.'

James tried to keep his temper. He knew that Rambaudi was goading him, and that if he responded, he would play into his hands. Ottolenghi's comforting presence was there behind him, but nonetheless it was going to take a supreme effort of will to maintain his equilibrium.

'Signor Rambaudi, thank you so much for seeing us. Please be assured that we will not detain you for long,' Lombroso said. 'We merely wish to question one of your staff.'

'Well, Professor Lombroso, do you know, I am not minded to allow it.'

Lombroso raised his eyebrows. He was not accustomed to people saying no to him in such a forthright manner. 'May I ask why?'

'I rather think that is my question.'

'This particular young man has been reported as missing but has been seen here.'

'I assume that your assistant is your witness. Hardly a reliable source.'

Lombroso continued. 'The young man's name is Bruno Ferranti. Can you confirm that he is employed by you? Then we could at least reassure his family. His mother, in particular, is worried about him.'

Rambaudi hesitated, as if he was summing up the pros and cons of being difficult. 'Very well, Professor. I agree that family is important, especially mothers. Yes, he does work for me. Strange, though. I was told that he did not have any family. Still, I must take your word for that.'

'May we speak with him?'

'No, you may not. He is busy working for me. He does what he is told, as all servants should. But then . . .' Francesco smirked at James, 'it is so difficult to find obedient, law-abiding staff, don't you agree, Professor?'

James stepped forward but Ottolenghi placed a restraining hand on his shoulder.

'Yes, that's right. Always best to keep servants and animals restrained in company,' Francesco said. 'How's that sister of yours, Murray? A pretty girl . . . such a pity she's not from better stock.'

A light voice came from behind them. 'I do hope you are being hospitable to our guests, Francesco.' Bianca walked over to her brother as if in solidarity.

'I have done my best under the circumstances, sister dear.'

'Signorina Rambaudi,' Lombroso said, bowing. 'We have no complaints.'

'To what do we owe this pleasure?' Bianca asked.

'We just had a business matter to discuss,' Lombroso replied.

'I usually deal with such things,' Bianca said. 'Francesco has no head for business. He is far too sensitive.'

'They were enquiring after Bruno,' Francesco told her.

'I think he is working away from the estate today. I will send him to you, though, if you wish to speak with him.'

'That is most kind, Signora,' Lombroso said. 'Well, I think that concludes our business here. We shall leave you both in peace.'

With that they began to walk up the drive to where their carriage was waiting. James paused and took a last look at the house. He doubted he would be able to visit again. There was something forbidding about it despite its golden stone – a kind of coldness, perhaps. Unhappiness almost seemed to seep from its walls.

'That was interesting,' Lombroso said as they reached the end of the drive, 'although not particularly helpful.'

'I agree,' Anna said. 'There was very little of consequence that was actually said. Signor Rambaudi seemed to be interested in insulting James rather than anything else.'

James was silent. He had found the conversation far more illuminating. As he knew only too well from Professor Bell's own techniques in the analysis of conversation, it was not always what was said that was important. Sometimes what was left out was far more significant. Francesco knew of his interest in the servant from their last encounter, but neither he nor his sister seemed remotely curious about why Ferranti had been reported missing or what reason they had for wanting to speak with him. As Professor Bell often said, the only reason for a lack of curiosity was surely that the facts were already known.

41

Even born criminals for whom sex is not all absorbing are livelier before puberty than normal women, but their vivacity gradually disappears. Almost all of them begin their careers by fleeing with a lover; and prostitution is always one of their many sins, although not the most serious. They feel a strong attraction towards men and are more curious than other women about the mysteries of sex.

Lombroso and Ferrero, 1893, p. 172

When they arrived back at the museum, they found Machinetti waiting for them in one of the exhibits rooms. With him was a tall, pale girl with long fair hair tightly plaited and wound so closely around her head it looked like a bid to prevent it from escaping. She stood next to the marshal, glancing uneasily at both him and the walls, which were lined with various artefacts including some of Lombroso's death masks and jars of pickled human remains.

'Ah, Lombroso, at last,' Machinetti said. 'I have someone here who may be of interest to you.' He pushed the girl forward. 'Tell them your name.'

'I am Susanna Russello.'

'Well go on, girl! Tell them what you told me,' Machinetti said.

'I have been working in Vercelli recently, but I came back to see a friend. She told me that a policeman had been asking about me. Until then I did not know that anyone was looking for me.'

'And there we have it,' Lombroso said. 'This, Murray, is why we should take care not to leap to conclusions about these girls, Sofia's cousin included.'

'But we have three dead bodies, and I don't suppose Fabia Carignano has run off to work in Vercelli,' James pointed out.

'We are looking carefully for the marchesa's niece, of course,' Machinetti said.

'Fortunately, so are we,' Lombroso said, glancing at the marshal. 'The bodies are a matter of concern. All I am saying, Murray, is that we should be focusing on those and the abduction of Signorina Carignano and not worrying too much about the Esposito girl.'

'Which is what I have been saying all along,' Machinetti said smugly. 'Now I must go. I have an appointment with the mayor.' He swept out, leaving Susanna Russello standing awkwardly in the middle of the room.

'I will see you out, signorina.' Anna began to usher her towards the door.

'No, wait,' the girl said.

'What is it?' demanded Lombroso.

'Before I went to Vercelli, something happened to me. I was frightened and that's why I left Torino.'

'Go on, signorina,' James said.

Anna led her over to a chair and she sat down on its very edge, her hands clasping and unclasping in front of her.

'It was on the first of November. I was walking to work at the market at the Porto Palazzo so it was early . . . about five o'clock, still dark.'

'Was there anyone around at that time?' James asked.

'No, it was deserted as usual . . . well, mostly. But I could hear a carriage behind me. It was driving slowly, as if it was following me.'

'What did you do then?' enquired Anna.

'I began to walk more quickly, but it seemed to gather speed. Eventually it drew up beside me.'

'Did you see anyone in the carriage?' James asked.

'I could not see clearly. It was still quite dark, though the street lights were gone. But it looked as if a woman was sitting inside.'

'Did you see her hair?'

'Not really. It was covered, I think. There was a flash of something red, but . . .'

'What happened then?' Lombroso asked.

'I heard someone walking behind me. Then I felt someone try to grab me . . . but an old man came out of an alleyway and started shouting and waving his hat around. Bits of straw were coming off it and flying everywhere. The carriage drove off. I think someone jumped onto it, but I could not be certain.'

'Did you notice anything else?' James asked.

'No, I'm sorry. It all happened so quickly. The old man might be able to help, if you can find him.'

'That is unlikely, I'm afraid. It is a great pity that you did not come forward earlier,' Lombroso said, peering at the girl over the top of his glasses.

'I . . . I did not know . . . I was frightened.'

'Never mind,' Anna said firmly. 'You have been most helpful, signorina.' She took the girl by the hand and led her out, giving Lombroso a look of disapproval as she did so.

'Well it seems pretty clear to me, whatever Machinetti

thinks,' James said. 'Somebody is abducting girls and killing them.'

'A morally insane epileptic, I'll be bound,' Lombroso said.

'Perhaps . . . but it would help to look at the victims. I'll try to be as organised as I can . . . by date is probably best.'

'That sounds like an excellent plan to me,' Anna said as she came back into the room.

'May I?' James picked up a piece of chalk and walked over to a blackboard in the corner. Lombroso pursed his lips as his assistant rubbed off his drawings and began a list of the missing girls, reciting it as he wrote.

1. Body in the woods – unidentified. Signs of attempted preservation. Organs removed. Missing for at least six months.
2. Teresa Mariani – San Callisto. Maid at Mme G's. Missing from city – 1 October.
3. Agnella/Nella Calvi – body found at Abbey of San Callisto. Prostitute at Mme G's. No sign of attempt at preservation except for organs removed. Missing 1 January.
4. Chiara Esposito – maid at marchesa's. Missing 1 March.
5. Caterina Spirito – flower seller, friend of Nella Calvi. Body found in the Borgo. Signs of attempted preservation with arsenic, and organs removed. Missing 1 February.
6. Arianna Panico – missing 1 December.
7. Susanna Russello – maid. Attempted abduction 1 November.
8. Fabia Carignano – marchesa's niece. Missing mid-April.

'We can see from this that the disappearances took place on a monthly basis,' James said. 'In fact all the girls, except for Signora Carignano and possibly the body in the woods, went missing on the first of the month.'

Anna tapped a pencil on the table in front of her, deep in thought. 'There must be some significance in relation to both the date and the frequency.'

'Why does he choose those particular girls?' Ottolenghi asked.

'There is some variation in appearance, so that doesn't seem to be influencing him,' Lombroso said.

James looked at the blackboard. There was something bothering him about the list. He breathed in sharply.

'What is it, Murray?'

'We have only found three bodies so far.'

'So where has he left the others?' Anna asked.

'Nowhere, yet.'

Lombroso looked at him in surprise. 'What do you mean?'

'They are not dead.'

Lombroso shook his head. 'Nonsense! Just because we haven't found them yet doesn't mean that they are still alive.'

'He is keeping them,' James said. 'Whoever is abducting these girls is holding them somewhere. That is why there is a gap between the abductions.'

'But what about the bodies?' Anna asked.

'He kills them eventually, but not until he's ready.'

'And the state of the bodies?' Lombroso asked.

'He tries to preserve them using various techniques, then he leaves them to be found – posed. Which means . . .' James hesitated for a second.

'He is a morally insane epileptic!' Lombroso said. 'There, you see! I knew I was right.'

'Which means that he is a curator,' James said, ignoring Lombroso. 'The killer is abducting girls and putting them in his collection.'

'And the killing only happens when he is ready to share,' Anna said.

'Yes, that's right. He is not just leaving the bodies for us to find . . . he is putting on a display.'

'But didn't you say that the first body was laid to rest?' Lombroso said. 'Really, Murray, as I am always telling you, a scientific approach means that consistency must be maintained.'

James exchanged glances with Ottolenghi and Anna. Lombroso had his own unique way of dealing with such matters. If something wasn't consistent, he would simply go back and alter data until it was. 'I have considered that. Given the state of the body, it is likely that it belongs to a much earlier victim. I think at this stage he was still practising his art. Preservation of a body is not a simple task, particularly for an amateur. He would need to learn by experience.'

'That would explain how the bodies were found – the embalming, the draining of the blood, the removal of the organs and so on,' Lombroso said.

Ottolenghi nodded enthusiastically. 'That would fit in with the mummification . . . Weren't organs removed during Ancient Egyptian death rituals?'

Lombroso beamed. 'Well done, everyone! I knew you would get there eventually. It is so very gratifying to see one's protégées shine.'

'So you knew already, Cesare?' Anna said, giving James a sideways glance.

'Of course, although I have to concede that Murray here filled in some of the detail.'

'Very generous of you, Professor, I'm sure,' James said.

'Not at all! Now, of course, we have to fix these theories to something a little more solid.'

'Meaning?' James asked.

'Meaning – where might we find a morally insane epileptic with an in-depth knowledge of Ancient Egyptian death rituals?' Lombroso smiled. Clearly he knew the answer to his own question. 'There is only one person in Turin with those credentials. Although come to think of it, I don't know if he is an epileptic, or morally insane . . . though he could be both.'

There was a sharp rap on the door and it opened to reveal an agitated Miss Trott accompanied by a tearful Paola.

'Mr Murray, a terrible thing! Oh, I have been so lax!' Lucy's companion could hardly get her words out, she was so breathless. 'We came as soon as I realised.'

'Realised what, Miss Trott?' James said. 'You're not making any sense.'

'Paola, what is it?' Lombroso asked.

'I am sorry, Papa, Signor Murray. But it is Lucy.'

'What about her?' James said.

'Apparently she went off on her own on some silly mission after speaking to Sofia.' Miss Trott glared at Paola.

'She said she knew who had been trying to hurt you, Signor Murray,' Paola said.

'She must have meant Concetta Panatti,' James said. 'The woman made it clear that she had more planned for me. Did Lucy go to Madame Giulia's?'

'No. She went to the Museo Egizio,' Paola said. 'She said that she had to see Professor Donati.'

42

The graffiti I have collected from women's prisons and hospitals for syphilitics indicate an excessive libidinousness in four out of seventy-eight examples. For example, one graffito read 'Dear dickybird'; another said 'Always thus' under a sketch of an immense penis; and a third said, 'Bring me a bird to my taste and I'll bring one to you, and when I am free you will find that I am just as hot and tight as you want . . .' But these graffiti were created by prostitutes who were also born criminals. In the graffiti of others, insofar as it exists, eroticism is latent, as in 'I kiss my little brother', or else the writings express only sentimental love or desire for revenge.

Lombroso and Ferrero, 1893, p. 173

The movement of the carriage was bumping Lucy up and down, this way and that. They had travelled some distance, she thought, given the length of the journey. Whatever had been used to drug her had quickly worn off, perhaps because she had held her breath. Despite this, escape was impossible, as her hands and feet were now both tightly bound. She had to content herself with feigning unconsciousness and trying to work out where she was being taken. The terrain was smooth to begin with but then had become rough, which meant, she assumed, that she was being transported from the city to the countryside. But just as she was becoming accustomed to travelling, they came to a halt and she was lifted and thrown over someone's shoulder as if she was a sack of potatoes. She risked opening her eyes for a few seconds and managed to catch a glimpse of what she thought were farm buildings. She tried to look further but she could hear another person approaching so she had to shut her eyes again.

'Put her in number three. That's free now.'

The voice belonged to a woman – youngish, Lucy thought. Number three? That meant that there were at least two more.

She heard something being slid back; it might be a stone or a piece of thick wood. It was hard to tell. Then she was put in some kind of a basket and lowered down into a hole or a pit. She started to panic. What if she was being buried alive? No, someone was coming down after her. She could hear them. There must be a rope ladder, she thought, as she couldn't hear any scraping sounds. Rough hands pulled her out of the basket, laid her down and untied her. It was a man, she was certain. He set about shackling her to the wall by her ankle. He slid his hand surreptitiously up her leg. She tried not to flinch.

'Stop that!' The voice came from above – a different sound, softer. The man straightened up and cursed softly, then pushed Lucy roughly aside with his foot as if she was a piece of meat before starting back towards the ladder. Lucy opened one eye and almost gasped when she recognised him. It was the young man from the museum. He must have been watching her – the girl too, perhaps. But surely they couldn't be in charge. They were too young.

'I see you are awake already,' said the second voice. It was light-sounding, as though it was chanting a mantra. Not real, Lucy thought. Someone was disguising their voice. But why?

'It will do you no good, Signorina Murray . . . no good at all. Deceit is not what is needed here. Only humility will help you. You must atone.'

'And if I don't?' Lucy asked.

'Then I will kill you sooner rather than later . . . and that would be a shame.'

'Who for?' Lucy asked. 'You or me?'

The voice laughed. It was like little bells, the sort you might find on a sleigh at Christmas time in the snow.

'For that, my dear, you can go hungry. A little suffering will speed up your repentance. You will be pure enough before you know it.'

The lid or grid or whatever it was began to move, and soon she was plunged into darkness. Frustrated at her helplessness, she pulled on her shackles. But they were of thick metal and could not be shifted. She sat back against the cold stone wall. A solitary tear slid down her cheek.

'No!' she said. Then more loudly: 'I am Lucy Murray and I will not be afraid!'

'Lucy? Is that you?' The voice was muffled. It sounded as if it was coming through the wall.

'Fabia?'

'Yes, it's me. How long have I been here?'

'Two days,' Lucy replied, thinking how typical of Fabia it was to put herself first.

'Really? It seems like more.'

'Are you hurt?'

'No, not hurt, but, Lucy . . .' There was a pause. 'I'm so frightened. I keep hearing noises.'

'What kind of noises?'

'Crying mostly, some talking . . . but screams, too.'

'From one girl?'

'I don't know. I just don't know.' Fabia's voice trembled. 'Who are these people? Why are they doing this?'

Lucy closed her eyes and leant back against the wall. She felt like crying too, but she knew that she had to be strong. 'Fabia, listen now. This is important. You said you heard talking. What was said? Tell me exactly.'

Fabia sniffed and Lucy pictured her wiping away her tears. 'When the girl was crying, he told her to stop and that she had to atone.'

'That's what was said to me.'

'Me too,' Fabia said. 'But what are we atoning for, and how are we supposed to do it?'

'I don't know,' Lucy said.

'Perhaps if we ask them and do what they want, they'll let us go.'

'Maybe.' Lucy was doubtful. No one else had been released, and she had a terrible feeling that unless they were rescued, whatever they said or did the end result would be the same.

'Someone will come for us,' Fabia said. 'My aunt will make sure of it.'

'Perhaps,' Lucy replied. 'But we don't know how much time we have.'

Fabia cried out. 'Don't say that!'

'I just mean that we need to find our own way out of here. Let me think.' She began to go through escape routes in her mind, each less possible than the last. As she did so, she heard someone crying.

'Fabia, is that you?'

'No . . . it's that other girl.'

'Hello! Can you hear me? What's your name?' Lucy called.

The crying stopped. 'Arianna . . .'

A noise came from above. Someone was coming. There was talking. It was quiet, but Lucy could just about make out what was being said.

'I told you, Bruno. We cannot wait. Those that have failed the test must be purified.'

The voice was familiar, but she could not place it. It was too quiet.

'We can't do them all together. Start with December. The latest one is a replacement for November. She has yet to be tested. We'll wait for that and then you can do April.'

'I want to do April first. If I have to listen to her complaining just one more day . . .'

'Sssh, Bruno, just follow the path. That is all we ask.'

'What about March? Isn't she ready yet?'

'No. Her atonement is incomplete. It is December's turn.'

'Do we use the drugs?'

'No. Do it without this time. There aren't enough left.'

'She's going to be awake for everything? Won't someone hear?'

'Foxes scream all the time, don't they?'

At James's insistence, Sofia was sent for and told to meet them outside the Museo Egizio. He knew that meant they might be seen together, but frankly he had ceased to care. As soon as she saw him, she came to him and took his hand in hers. 'We will find her.'

'I haven't found Chiara. What makes you think Lucy will be any different?'

'Have faith.'

'In God? That hasn't worked out well so far.'

'In yourself, James, *caro*.'

He allowed her to lead him into the museum. Lombroso and Ottolenghi followed behind at a discreet distance. Anna and Miss Trott, both of whom had insisted on accompanying them, waited outside.

'Lucy told me that she had been to see Donati before. He took her down to a workshop in the basement,' Sofia said.

'That sounds like the right place to go,' Ottolenghi said.

'Yes,' Lombroso said. 'He would need somewhere secluded where he could easily subdue his victims and do whatever he liked without detection.'

Sofia squeezed James's hand. 'Do not listen to him,' she whispered. 'You know how he likes to dramatise.'

James nodded. He couldn't really blame Lombroso. It wasn't as if similar thoughts had not entered his own head on the way there.

The museum was almost empty. A few scholars remained, but they were far too caught up in their own studies to notice the party as they made their way down the broad stone steps to the basement. Once down there, they began to walk slowly and silently along the main corridor, Lombroso inevitably taking the lead. There was no evidence of anyone else being down there, as far as James could tell. The passageway was lit by gas lamps, but they were few and far between. There were rooms on both sides. Were they cells? Was Lucy tied up in one of them? Ottolenghi peered in each as they went, shaking his head as he found them to be uninhabited.

Lombroso held out his hand and stopped them. The sound of whistling was coming from one of the rooms further along. The tune was familiar. James was certain he had heard it before. Where was it from? An opera, he thought. Ah yes, 'La donna è mobile', the aria from . . . *Rigoletto*, was it?

The whistling grew a little louder, and in a moment Donati

was standing in the corridor staring at them, his eyes darting about in alarm. The whistling stopped.

'Ah, Professor,' Lombroso began. 'We thought that we'd pay you a visit.'

Donati ran. James went after him. Ottolenghi was behind him, huffing and puffing as he tried to catch up.

All at once Donati seemed to disappear. Had he gone into one of the rooms? James slowed down to a walk and made his way into a large chamber. Sarcophaguses lined the walls. Some of them had depictions of people on the front. Their eyes seemed to follow James as he walked slowly round. He stopped and listened carefully. Was that breathing from one of the coffins? He put his hand up to remove the lid.

'Murray, did you have to go so quickly?'

James was briefly distracted by Ottolenghi, who was almost bent double near the doorway. The lid pushed into him, making him stumble, and Donati ran past him, shoving Ottolenghi aside as he went.

'Are you all right?' James asked his friend.

'Yes,' Ottolenghi said, picking himself up. 'Go after him! I'll search the rest of the rooms.'

James ran back out into the corridor. Donati was just visible in the distance. He went up some more stairs and James followed him through what appeared to be a back door. On they went, right round the museum towards the front entrance, Donati gaining the advantage by taking short cuts. Miss Trott and Anna were standing outside at the bottom of the steps. Miss Trott went towards Donati as he ran past and gamely did her best to tackle him, but he swerved and she missed him, though only just. James went after him but was so far behind that he couldn't catch him.

Ottolenghi came down the steps. 'There is nowhere for a

girl to be kept in those rooms. But I did find these.' He held up a pair of spectacles. 'They were on the floor underneath a table in Professor Donati's workshop.'

'Those are Paola's!' Miss Trott said. 'Lucy must have borrowed them as a disguise. Such a resourceful young woman!'

'So it seems there is little doubt that she was taken from here against her will,' Lombroso said.

'But where to?' James stood there hunched over as Sofia tried to comfort him, but even that could not help assuage his guilt. He had been so concerned with his own affairs that yet again he had let Lucy down, and now he felt utterly powerless. A chill spread through his body. What if he could not save her? What if he had lost her for ever?

Lombroso strode over to him, making Sofia step back in surprise. He took James by his shoulders, forcing him to straighten up. 'Now listen to me, Murray. We are experts in crime and criminals and we will not be beaten by the monster that has done this. We will go back to the museum, sit down and do some hard thinking. We shall not stop until we have solved this and found both your sister and Sofia's cousin.'

Before James could reply, Tullio arrived. He was slightly out of breath.

'You have heard about Lucy?' James asked. 'We think Donati has taken her.'

Tullio shook his head. 'That is not why I'm here.'

'What is it?' Lombroso said sharply.

'Machinetti is on his way.'

'Good. We need the carabinieri to start searching,' James said.

'No,' Tullio said. 'That's not it. He is coming for you, James.'

James looked at him in confusion.

'The girl in Baldovino's article. Gabriella.'

'What about her?' Lombroso asked.

'She has gone missing and James is a suspect. Machinetti is coming to arrest you. Your bail has been revoked.'

43

One essential trait of the most serious cases of moral insanity and epilepsy in women is premeditation. The crimes of insane women are sometimes even more remarkable than those of ordinary female offenders in terms of skill, premeditation, steps taken to establish an alibi, and efforts at covering up. Lombroso and Ferrero, 1893, p. 228

Lucy looked around her. Escaping from her cell pit, as she had begun to think of it, was clearly going to be no easy task. The walls were steep and at least twice her height. But as *Pinkerton's Detection Manual* was fond of saying, 'There is always a method – it is just a question of finding it.' She thought back to her arrival. She had been lowered down in a basket, and there was also a rope ladder allowing access. That meant that all she had to do was get up high enough to pull either the ladder or the basket down. Then she might be able to climb out. Hopefully she would be able to push the lid aside far enough to escape.

The first thing to do was to get out of her shackles. That shouldn't be too much of a problem, if her memory was accurate. She had researched this problem for an early Lydia Loveday story called 'The Captured Orphan', a complex tale in which an evil aunt engineered the abduction of her niece in order to get her hands on a substantial inheritance.

She put her hands up to her hair, which was held back by a large decorative clip given to her by Miss Trott. She pulled it free and examined it carefully. If she bent part of it back, it would leave a sharp point. She began to wiggle it in the lock on the chains, just as the orphan had done in her story. To her amazement, the lock sprang open. She was free. At least the first stage in her plan had been accomplished. Now for the rest of it, which, she had to admit, might be rather more difficult to put into action.

She began to scrape at the wall with her fingernail. A small cloud of sand came out, making her cough. This confirmed her suspicion that some of the bricks were loose. Might it be possible to work enough of them loose to enable her to climb up using the gaps as footholds? She did some more scraping, but it was hard work and before long her fingers were red raw. She pulled at the brick. It was definitely looser, but not by much. It would take forever to get just one of them free. She slumped back against the wall and stared miserably into the darkness. It was hopeless.

She pulled herself to her feet and walked around a little. As she did so, her foot hit something small and hard. She bent down and picked it up. A smile spread slowly across her face. It was a spoon. It wasn't exactly a pickaxe, which was what she really needed, but it might speed her bid for freedom up a little. She moved back to the brick that she had been working on and began to scrape again. This time her new tool meant that she made more progress. As she worked at the brick, a chilling thought came to her. How had the spoon got there? Had another captured girl had the same idea as her – Sofia's cousin Chiara, perhaps? Could she have left it there in a bid to help her successor? If so – and this was the worst part of it – where was she now?

James stood in the shadows and tried to catch his breath. Tullio had turned a blind eye, allowing him to leave before Machinetti arrived to take him in for questioning. Everyone had pledged their support and promised to do their best to help him, but he could not go to the museum, the Via Legnano or Sofia's place for fear of being found. It was imperative that he remain free to search for Lucy. Whoever had framed him for Baldovino's assault would clearly not be satisfied until he was behind bars. He was a wanted man with no safe haven. All he could do was carry on looking for his sister and hope that he would not be detected.

With that goal in mind, having recovered a little, he continued to make his way along the back streets, walking with his head down and hoping not to bump into any carabinieri officers. Soon he found himself in the small courtyard outside the back entrance to Madame Giulia's. A figure came out, her identity almost obscured by a large basket of washing. Seeing the red curls bobbing above it, however, James knew immediately who it was.

'*Buongiorno*, Ada,' he said gently, taking the basket away from her.

She stepped back and peered at him fearfully, her eyes darting this way and that. 'I cannot talk to you. Gabriella—'

'Do you know where she is?'

She did not answer. Her arms and face were covered in scratches and bruises. 'Did Valeria do this?' James asked.

'*Sì*, and if you do not go, she will do it again. I have already been turned into a scullery maid. I don't want any more trouble.'

'What about your friend Agnella?'

Ada shook her head. 'She has not returned. I don't think I will see her again.' There was a noise from inside the house. 'Please go. Leave me alone. I don't know anything.'

'I will, but first, is there anything else you can tell me about your friend's client . . . Il Professore, wasn't it?'

She hesitated for a moment as if weighing up the risk of saying more. Then she picked up her basket again. James thought that was that, but he was wrong. 'Agnella gave him that name because he was so clever. He used to talk of faraway places and their history – Egypt and suchlike.'

'Why did he choose Agnella?'

'He said that he liked pale girls because they were untroubled by sin.'

James thanked her and carefully laid some money on top of the washing.

'Wait . . . one more thing,' Ada said in a whisper. 'The other place . . . it smelt strange. It reminded Agnella of going to church.'

There was the sound of footsteps coming towards the door, so James quickly walked around the corner so that he was out of sight. As he moved away, he heard the unmistakable harsh tones of Valeria scolding poor Ada. He resolved to ask Anna to help the girl. It was the least he could do.

As he turned into the main street, Sofia ran towards him. '*Aspettami!*'

'What is it? What's happened?' James asked as she reached him and grasped his arm, catching her breath.

'We need to find the old man.'

'What old man? You're not making any sense!'

'The woman who came to see you . . . the one who was nearly taken.'

'Susanna Russello?'

'*Sì*, that's the one.'

'What about her?'

'According to Madame Tarnovsky, Susanna said there was an old man who saw it happen.'

'I know that, but we don't know who he is. It could be anyone.'

'No. That is what I am trying to tell you. I know him!'

He hesitated.

'What is it, *caro*?'

'Sofia, if you are found with me, you will be locked up too.'

She checked that no one was near and he thought she was about to leave, but then she pulled her to him and kissed him. It was all he needed.

Sofia set off across the street with James behind her. They could not be seen together. It was too risky. Fortunately she had brought an old hat and a large overcoat for him to wear, which helped to disguise him. As they rushed through the city, one question preyed on his mind. What was it about all these girls, Lucy and Fabia included, that had made them targets for this monster?

Lucy was working harder than she had ever done in her life. But then this was the first time that her life and those of others had depended on her industry. She scraped away with her spoon at the grouting holding the bricks together, desperately trying to forge sufficient hand- and footholds to allow her to climb up and escape. She knew it would be difficult. The walls were high and there was no guarantee that she would be able to get enough purchase to get to the top. But she knew that at least she had to try. From what she had heard, it was obvious that they were running out of time.

She had to work harder. She scraped with renewed ardour. She had already removed two bricks, although they had been loosened already by the passing of many years, no doubt. Now she was working on a third.

'What are you doing?' Fabia asked.

'My best . . .' Lucy replied, wiping the sweat from her forehead.

'They've taken the other girl away. Did you hear?'

Lucy could hardly have missed it. Arianna had wailed and screamed and it sounded as if she was putting up quite a struggle. In the end, her increasingly desperate protests had suddenly stopped. Someone had evidently hit her with such force that they had either knocked her out or subdued her. Then she had been dragged away to her fate, whatever that was.

As if to underline the desperation of their predicament, there was a scream – or the vestiges of one. It came from outside but was still loud enough to make the suffering that had caused it only too clear. Lucy stopped for a moment to inspect her handiwork. She wiggled the brick – it was definitely loose. If she could just . . . She moved it up and down and then . . . there! She finally pulled it free. Time for the next one. She put the spoon in her mouth and began to climb. This time of course she had to go higher, and so had to rely on the holes she had already created. She clung to the sides of the wall and pulled herself up until she was in position. As she took one hand away to get the spoon out of her mouth, she lost her balance and fell back on to the hard floor.

She lay there for a moment, winded by the impact. Every muscle and bone in her body felt as if it was bruised. She looked up miserably at the stone that was her makeshift ceiling. It wasn't going to work. Soon – it could be minutes, hours, days or even weeks – her captors would come, and she and Fabia would be dragged away to suffer the same horrible fate as Arianna was enduring. Part of her wanted to weep and wail at the injustice of it all. What had she done – what had any of them done – to deserve this torture? But another part of her was furious at whoever was depriving them of the life they had yet to live. She sat up. Giving up was not an option. She had to fight on, even if it proved to be fruitless.

She was about to pull herself to her feet when she realised that the darkness was becoming lighter. She looked up. The stone was being pulled free. She was too late. It was her turn to die.

44

Nymphomania transforms the most timid girl into a wild and shameless reveller. She looks at every man with longing and flirts outrageously, even to the point of violence. Often she is extremely thirsty, with a dry mouth and bad breath, and she swings her hips almost as if in intercourse. She tends to bite everyone she meets, as if rabid, so much so that she is sometimes repelled by liquids and feels that she is being strangled.

Lombroso and Ferrero, 1893, p. 229

James and Sofia were still searching for the old man, who was proving elusive. According to Sofia, it was almost certainly Pietro, whom they had seen sleeping off a night at La Capra when they were trying to trace Chiara's last footsteps. The day was coming to a close and the shops were shutting. Sofia had said that as far as she knew, the man lived on his wits, or what was left of them, and did not have a home as such. Occasionally he was arrested for loitering, but usually the carabinieri just ignored him, preferring to avoid the bother of taking him to a cell and filling in forms.

'I think it was around here that Susanna Russello says they tried to snatch her,' James said as they reached an alleyway off a winding cobbled lane near the market.

'Yes, this is certainly one of the old man's haunts,' Sofia said.

They moved up the narrow passage. The height of the buildings on either side had made it dark despite the fact that the sun had not yet set, and even though it was in the middle of a busy city, it was quiet and secluded.

'This would be a good place to snatch someone,' James commented.

'Look, I think that might be him.' Sofia indicated a pile of newspapers in a doorway with a battered straw hat balanced precariously on top of it. They approached quietly. The papers rustled gently in the breeze and the telltale sound of snoring emanated from beneath the hat, which now had a jaunty striped ribbon tied around it. A wrinkled, liver-spotted hand held a half-full bottle of cheap brandy.

'Hey, *svegliati*! Wake up!'

The snoring continued. James poked the body gingerly with his foot. The snoring stopped for a moment and then went on.

Sofia shrugged, knelt down beside the apparently sleeping form and snatched the bottle from its hand. The body seemed to erupt like a small but contained earthquake, newspapers falling left, right and centre until a small, shabby figure emerged.

'Eh, give it back!'

'*Un attimo!*' Sofia said, and held the bottle aloft, forcing the old man to struggle to his feet and stretch up in an attempt to get it away from her. He began to leap up and down, desperately trying to get hold of it.

'Wait, signor, wait!' James said. 'Answer my questions and you'll get it back with interest.'

The old man grunted and stopped jumping. He gave James a bleary-eyed stare. 'What do you want to know?'

'It's Pietro, isn't it?'

The old man nodded suspiciously.

'A friend of ours told us that you saw someone try to snatch her off the street near here.'

Pietro's eyes widened in fear and he shook his head vigorously. 'She is mistaken.'

'Are you sure? She was very certain.' James got some notes out of his wallet and waved them under Pietro's nose. The old man paused and peered at them, his nose twitching as if testing their scent. He tried to snatch them from James's hand, but he was not quick enough and could only watch as they were held aloft, out of his reach.

'La Capra,' he said, and pausing only to pick up a tatty woollen blanket that he wrapped around him like a cloak, he stomped off in the direction of the bar.

Sofia looked heavenwards and began to follow him, James running to catch up. 'Why do I always end up at La Capra?' he said.

'It is Hell's back door,' Sofia said, as if it was obvious.

'No wonder I never leave there sober.'

In a few moments Pietro was slumped at his usual table nursing a large glass of grappa. James had been forced to lurk in a corner while the drink was bought so as not to be recognised. Gambro, the barman, gave him a curious stare when he came across to collect some dirty glasses, but then simply shrugged as if to accept him into the criminal fold that made up his usual clientele.

'You have your drink, Pietro, and you will have your bottle back. So tell me what you saw,' James said.

There was a pause. 'A carriage. I saw someone try to pull the girl into a carriage.'

'Who was there?' Sofia asked.

'A man . . . a young man . . . he tried to grab her. I shouted . . . I wanted him to stop . . . Leave her alone!'

'What did the young man look like?'

'Dark, he might have had a scar. He was driving the carriage.'

'Who was in the carriage?' James asked.

'A woman . . . that's all I know. I just saw her gloves . . . lace . . . very fancy.'

'What about the carriage itself?'

'That was fancy too . . . had a picture on it . . . Some kind of flower . . . white, I think.'

'Did you see the woman's face?'

Pietro hesitated and looked down into his drink. He was wheezing, as if the effort of remembering was impeding his breathing.

'No . . . not her face.'

'Her hair, then?' James asked urgently.

Pietro shrugged.

'Did you see red hair?'

'Can I have another drink?'

'In a moment . . . Did you see red hair?' James repeated.

Pietro nodded. '*Sì*, I think so . . . something red anyway.'

'So the man tried to snatch the girl,' Sofia said.

'Yes. She struggled, wriggling around, kicking and screaming. He was trying to get his hand over her mouth, but she bit him. Don't take her! I said . . . then he dropped her and jumped into the carriage, which went off.' Pietro's eyes widened again and he peered into the distance, as if he could see the scene right in front of his eyes. 'It was the same the second time.'

'Second time?' James said, leaning forward.

Pietro nodded. '*Sì*, a couple of months ago . . . but that one did not get away.'

Lucy stood up tall and straight as she waited for the inevitable. Whatever her fate, she was not going to make it easy for her tormentors. The lid was slid back with relative ease and light flooded into her cell.

'Do exactly as you are told and you won't get hurt.'

She winced as the light hit her unaccustomed eyes. She shaded them with her hand and squinted towards the voice. It was high, but definitely male. She could not place it. 'Who are you?' she asked in confusion. 'Why have you brought me here?'

'Silence. Do not move until I tell you.'

The rope ladder was thrown down.

'Climb up slowly.'

She hesitated for a moment and then obeyed. After all, what other choice did she have? At least she would get out of this pit.

'Lucy, what's happening?' It was Fabia.

'Be quiet. Your turn will come soon enough,' the man said.

When she got to the top, he pulled her out. A second figure stood in the shadows. Lucy was pushed roughly to the ground, her wrists were bound and a blindfold was put on. She struggled.

He pulled her hair with one hand. 'Keep still or your friend will get a visit she won't forget. Understand?' Lucy nodded. He pulled her to her feet. 'Come on, *puttana*. Time to go for a little walk.' She felt herself being dragged along by a rope like an animal being taken to market. She had no idea where he was taking her, but wherever it was, it seemed as if she would not be returning.

45

Among the morally insane, Krafft-Ebing has observed early signs of sexual perversion and sexual overindulgence followed by impotence, a phenomenon I have seen in criminals. 'The sexual impulses of the morally insane,' Krafft-Ebing continues, 'are often precocious or unnatural and preceded or accompanied by a ferocious bloodlust.'

Lombroso, 1884, p. 215

James and Sofia left a happy Pietro in his usual corner in La Capra. He had been well paid for his information and had already begun the process of drinking his earnings.

'That must have been Chiara's abduction he saw the second time,' James said. Sofia was crying. He took her in his arms and she leant against him, convulsing as she wept. Now it was beyond question. Chiara had been taken just like the other girls . . . just like Lucy. But she had been missing for two months, which meant that she might well be dead already. He could not admit that to Sofia, though, and take away her last vestiges of hope.

'She is gone! She is gone!' Sofia said through her tears.

'Sssh now, *cara*. We don't know that for certain. Think about it. If she is dead, where is her body? We must not give up on her . . . or Lucy.'

Sofia wiped her eyes and nodded. 'You are right. There is no time to be lost. We must tell Tullio and the others what we know.'

'I can't . . . not yet. Machinetti might be waiting there for me. You find Tullio. I am going where no one will look for me.'

'Where?' Sofia clung to him. 'Will you be all right, *caro*?'

'I need to rest and think. It is better that you do not know where I am.' He took her hand. 'As I said before, you're just going to have to trust me. Can you do that?'

She nodded. '*Sì*, but then what choice do I have?'

She kissed him on the cheek and left him. He watched her as she hurried through the dying light of the terrible day. When she was out of sight, he took the risk and hailed a cab. Walking would take far too long. He had lied to Sofia. It was not rest that he needed. James had to act now and hope that he would be in time.

Lucy was tearful with pain and humiliation. The man was dragging her along some kind of track, but he was going so fast she was finding it almost impossible to keep up.

'Please stop,' she begged. To her surprise, they came to a halt. This was it, her only chance.

'Can you loosen the blindfold a little? It is hurting.'

She heard a sigh. Her captor came up behind her and began to fumble with the knot at the back of her head. Sensing that he had released the tether, Lucy gave him an almighty shove. She heard him stagger back. She managed to pull off the blindfold and began to run for her very life, desperately trying to loosen the rope around her wrists as she did so.

She was on a rough farm track leading towards fields. Some labourers were finishing work and making their way towards a group of buildings, presumably to eat and then sleep in readiness for another day. Should she try to make it there, or might the workers be party to whatever dreadful plan was being enacted?

Beyond and to the left was a wood. If she could get there, she would find cover at least. She knew where she was. She recognised Francesco's rice estate. Should she make her way to the Villa Purezza? No, it was too far. She hoped the town was nearer. Yes, that was the best plan.

She looked behind her. No one appeared to be in pursuit. She allowed herself to slow down and catch her breath a little. It seemed strange that she had not been followed. She made her way through the damp fields to the wood. Someone was standing there, hands on hips. He moved towards her. Lucy hesitated for a second and then began to run sideways in a bid to avoid him. Her skirts were sodden with water and mud and weighed her down so she could barely move. In a moment he was upon her. She tried to move away but stumbled. He took hold of her and punched her to the ground, where she lay in a damp mass, frogs leaping around her and mosquitoes buzzing round her tear-stained and throbbing face.

He stood over her and laughed. He was close enough for her to see his scarred cheek as he stared at her. 'That was your last journey, Bella. I hope you enjoyed it.' Then he pulled her up and began to drag her again by the rope back towards the stony track, where a cart was waiting. She tried to resist, pulling away from him, but he grabbed her and held her to him, his lips close to hers. His breath smelt of garlic and stale tobacco. 'Try that again, *puttana*, and I'll have you right here. You never know, you might enjoy it.'

She turned away from him.

He grabbed her face and twisted it towards him. 'What's

the matter? Too fancy for the likes of me? Well you wait and see what's in store for you. Then you'll be begging me to end it.'

Lucy summoned up her courage. 'How dare you! Wait till I tell Signor Rambaudi. He'll have you flogged.'

The man laughed again.

'What is so funny?'

'Wait and see, *puttana*, wait and see. Let's go.'

When they reached the cart, he put her in the back, tying her to its barred sides.

'We're going on a mystery trip. I don't want to spoil the surprise,' he said, before blindfolding her again and throwing an old piece of sacking over her. As they drove, she tried her best to push it off so that she would be visible, but to no avail. He had tucked it in around her and she just could not shift it.

After a short journey, the cart stopped. Lucy strained to hear something, anything that might provide a clue to where she had been taken. There was the sound of running water. After she had been untied, her captor led her into what felt like a hallway and down some stairs. He took off her blindfold, tethered her to a door and went over to light a series of lanterns.

As her eyes adjusted to the candlelight, she could see shapes emerging from the shadows. To one side was a beam with some manacles. The floor surrounding it was covered in bloodstains. There were a number of large glass jars with liquid in them. On a shelf were more jars, but these were smaller and made of stone, with carvings on them. They looked familiar. When Lucy remembered where she had seen them, her blood ran cold. They were like the canopic vessels of Wahibra that Professor Donati had shown her, designed to hold organs removed from a body in Egyptian death rituals. But that was not all.

In the centre of the room was a table. When she saw what was on it, she had to use every ounce of will left in her to fight her instinct to cry out. It was a girl, naked and pinned out as if she was a butterfly in a natural history museum, her skin peeled back in two neat flaps like one of the illustrations in her father's anatomy books. The girl's face was pale – translucent almost. Her mouth hung open as if in a silent scream and her lifeless eyes stared into the distance. Underneath the table was a bucket of blood, and a tray containing a pair of kidneys and a human heart.

As the cab made its way out of the city towards his destination, James considered what he knew. Professor Donati had a workshop in the basement of the Museo Egizio and Lucy had clearly been there. He had met her there before, and had also been at the marchesa's ball from which Fabia had gone missing. He had expertise in Egyptology, and when they had found him, he had run away. All these things suggested that he had to be involved, although James suspected that someone else was in control – and he had a good idea who that was. The question was, where had Donati and his employer based themselves? To keep several girls at one time you would need space. It would need to be somewhere secluded. If they were being tortured, they would be making a noise. He pictured Lucy covered in blood, screaming in pain, crying out for him. It felt as if somebody was ripping his heart out of his chest. He leant forward, urging the cab to speed up.

46

Paradoxically, in some cases maternity and sexuality, instead of working against one another as usual, join together in incest, and the mother becomes the lover of the son, adoring him partly as a son and partly as a lover.

Lombroso and Ferrero, 1893, p. 186

'Soon that will be you,' said the man as he pushed Lucy into a small room with a bucket of water in the corner. He threw in a parcel and locked the door behind her. 'Wash yourself and put this on. Your hair should be loose.'

'No, I won't!' Lucy said.

'Want me to come in and undress you myself? It would be a pleasure.'

'Turn your back.'

He gave a sly smile and obeyed her. Quickly she slipped off her clothes. In the parcel was a long white robe, Grecian in style. She put it on and took her hair out of its pins, shaking it out until it tumbled down her back. Was there any chance of escape? Might it be worth keeping hold of one of her hairpins? After all, it had worked before.

'I'll take those,' the man said holding his hand out through the bars. She gave them to him and he pocketed them, still smiling soullessly at her.

'What happens now?' she asked.

He was silent for a moment, then he said simply, 'You won't have to wait long.'

'Why are you doing this?'

The man did not respond.

'Tell me.'

This time he spoke. 'I am doing it for her. She was there for me when I needed someone. This is my way of repaying her.'

'Who?'

'You'll find out.'

There was a noise from above. Footsteps. Someone was coming.

'It's time.'

Lucy readied herself. Her only chance was to make her escape once she was released from her cell. The man turned the key and pulled her out.

There was a sharp rapping sound above. Someone was knocking at a door. Was it James? Had he managed to find her? The footsteps stopped. The rapping began again. Whoever was upstairs went to answer it. The man held her tightly against him, his large sweaty hand over her mouth and his other arm round her neck so she could hardly breathe. She knew that she had to get away from him and run upstairs, but the more she struggled, the tighter his grip became. She heard the door opening.

James stood outside the door. He had knocked but there was no reply. He considered trying to break in, but the place seemed to be almost impregnable. He knocked again. Were those footsteps he could hear? His hands tightened around his cane. The door started to open.

*

Lucy relaxed in the man's arms in the hope that he would loosen his hold, but instead he whispered into her ear: 'One word from you and I'll break your pretty neck.'

She heard a muffled voice as the door was opened. It sounded as if whoever it was had been asked to come in. The invitation had clearly been accepted, because the door was shut firmly behind the visitor. Had James come to rescue her? She hoped so. Be careful. Please be careful, she pleaded silently.

'Yes, that's right . . . down the stairs. Watch yourself. They're quite steep.' She thought she recognised the voice, but surely she must be wrong.

There was creaking as the visitor negotiated their way down. Then they seemed to change their mind and went back up. Lucy brought her heel down hard on her captor's foot, and as his grip was momentarily loosened, she wriggled free and made a break for the stairs. He came after her and caught hold of her skirts. She tried to cry out, but he had his hand over her mouth again before she could.

'Oh my word. What is that noise? Do you have an intruder?'

'It is nothing,' Francesco said. 'Now tell me, how can we help you, Miss Trott?'

James stood and stared in consternation at Beppe, framed in the large wooden doors of the Abbey San Callisto. 'What are you doing here?'

Beppe raised his eyebrows. 'I could ask you the same thing, *Inglese*. Aren't you on the run? What's up? Looking for somewhere to hide? It'll cost you.'

James lifted his cane in what he hoped was a threatening gesture. 'Stand aside.'

Beppe shrugged and did as he was asked. 'No need for that. I'm just the caretaker. You can pay me later.'

James walked in quickly and stood in the hallway, listening, but there was only silence.

Beppe followed him and shut the door behind them with a crash. 'There's no one here. The whorehouse is closed until later. The girls haven't even arrived yet.'

James ignored him and ran up the stairs to the room that he and Sofia had broken into just before they had both been taken away. This time the door was wide open. There it was again – the faint aroma of incense and beeswax polish. Beppe was right. It was deserted.

He walked in and wandered around the room. Its purpose was clear. Couches and chaises longues were arranged artfully about the place. There were paintings on the walls – classical depictions of gods and goddesses, but engaged in distinctly ungodlike pursuits. Various doors lined the room, and he opened one. There was a bed, a dressing table and an armchair. It would have seemed perfectly normal were it not for the rack of fearsome-looking leather riding whips, manacles and chains on the walls. Beppe had joined him and was leaning on the doorpost leering at him.

'Like what you see, *Inglese*? Want to bed down here? I could arrange some company for you.'

James frowned. 'I take it that when you broke in for Professor Lombroso, that was just a performance?'

Beppe laughed. 'The boss knew he was coming, so they cleared out for the night. I just hung around in the right place and there he was, asking me for a bit of help. Did you enjoy my lantern show, by the way?' He grinned and waved his arms in the air, moaning softly.

'What about the girl's body?'

'Don't know anything about a body.'

'And who is your boss? Donati or Concetta Panatti?'

'None of your business, and if I were you, I'd keep it that way. Now, signor, it's time to go. I don't think it's worth the risk letting you stay, you being a fugitive from justice and all. Besides, sooner or later the boss will be back, and then you'll just get another beating, like the last one, and maybe a scar to match the one you've already got.'

Ignoring Beppe, James ran down the stairs until he was near the crypt. There was the door that Sofia had found. He knew it led to underground rooms. That must be where Lucy and the others were being kept.

'Lucy! Fabia!' he called.

'What are you doing, *Inglese*?' Beppe had joined him.

'Let me in,' James demanded. 'I know the girls are there.'

'What are you talking about? I've told you. No one is here.'

'Open up.'

Beppe did so grudgingly, then stepped back and bowed. 'Be my guest, but you won't find anyone.'

James barged past him and walked along the stone corridor. It was musty and damp. He stopped. Silence. 'Lucy?' he called again.

He walked on. There were several rooms branching off the corridor. Most seemed to be used for storage. One had a desk and a couple of chairs. He noticed dark red marks on the floor and bent to examine them. They were drops of dried blood – hardly the pool that one might expect if someone had been exsanguinated. But the room felt familiar. He winced as he remembered the feel of the knife slicing through his cheek. Was this where it had happened? He wondered if the girls had ever been here. Certainly there was no evidence to suggest that anyone was here now.

He heard a noise. Beppe was standing behind him. 'Time to go, signor.'

James followed him out. When they reached the front door, Beppe held it open for him. 'If I were you, signor, I'd keep quiet about this place,' he said as James walked past him. 'They don't take kindly to interference, as you know.'

James waved a dismissive hand at him and left. He had no time to lose. He knew now that Concetta Panatti's unregistered brothel was at the abbey. Presumably Agnella had never left after her second visit, ending up in the crypt with the mummified monks. Had Panatti been responsible for her murder? It seemed likely. But why drain the blood from the girl's body? Was she trying to cover up something by making the death look like the work of a lunatic? He still could not be certain that she was responsible for the missing girls, or Lucy and Fabia's abductions. But if it wasn't her, then who had taken them, and where?

He thought back to the old man Pietro and his description of the woman in the carriage. Had he actually said that she had red hair? He couldn't recall. He did say something about the carriage, though. What was it? Something about a picture – a flower of some kind? Where had he seen something similar before? When he remembered, a cold shiver went down his spine. He had been so convinced that Panatti and the abbey were at the heart of all this that he had ignored everything else the old man had said.

As he ran down the hill, a carriage seemed to come from nowhere and overtook him. Then it stopped. The door opened. Someone stepped out and began to walk towards him.

47

If one goes back over reports of female cruelty, one can detect a common element, whether they be about epidemics or individuals, the demoniacal atrocities of certain queens and criminals, or the smaller vulgarities of spitefulness and daily persecutions. That common element is woman's tendency to inflict the largest amount of pain – not to obliterate her enemy but to martyr him slowly and paralyse him with suffering.

Lombroso and Ferrero, 1893, p. 68

It was dark now, and the moon was obscured by cloud. A tall, shadowy figure was getting ever closer. 'James!' it hissed.

'Ottolenghi? Is that you?'

'Yes, hurry! Before you're seen.'

'Ah, there you are, Murray,' the professor said as James climbed in, having given instructions to the driver. 'We were beginning to think that you'd gone back to Scotland.'

'Where is Sofia?' James asked as the carriage bumped along the rough road.

'She guessed that you had gone to the abbey, so we came to find you. She and Anna will follow on once Miss Trott has reappeared. Apparently she had yet another errand to run. Odd timing, but there we are, that's women for you. Now tell me what on earth made you go back to the abbey, and where we are going now.'

'It's a long story . . . but never mind that. I know where the girls are.'

'Indeed. Well, better late than never.'

'The insignia that the old man saw was almost certainly a lily, which symbolises purity . . . hence the Villa Purezza.'

'Really? You think young Rambaudi is responsible? I was beginning to think that he might be a mattoid.'

'What does that mean?' James asked.

'A mattoid is another variant of the insane criminal. They are prophets of a kind . . . self-appointed, naturally; revolutionaries who rise up from the lower classes to spout utopian ideas.'

'How does that fit with Rambaudi?' Ottolenghi asked. 'I thought you said the killer was a man with large ears, a scanty beard and a propensity to write erotic poetry?'

Lombroso shook his head vehemently. 'No, no, no, Ottolenghi! I do wish you would listen! Rambaudi sees himself as someone who has a profound moral insight. His actions reflect that. It is his way of spreading ideas.'

'He is certainly courting public attention,' James said, 'but I would hardly term him a revolutionary.'

'Perhaps you are right,' Lombroso conceded. 'I did think he fitted the hysterical criminal type – egotism, self-preoccupation, leading to a desire for scandal and public attention – but that can't be correct.'

'Why not?'

'Because they are almost always women, Murray. And I knew all along that this was the work of a man.'

'See. There it is,' James said, pointing out the lily on the gates as they approached the entrance to the Villa Purezza.

The place was in almost complete darkness except for some gas lamps by the house.

They alighted from their carriage and walked up to the front door. 'Should we ring, do you think?' Ottolenghi asked.

'We don't want to alert him at this stage,' Lombroso said, pulling the bell rope. 'We are merely paying a call, finding ourselves in the area.'

James could not quite believe what he was hearing. 'Why aren't we tearing down the door? We're here to find Lucy, Fabia and Chiara, not make a social visit!'

'I think it best if I do the talking,' Lombroso said, frowning at him. 'We must be careful. Lives are at stake.'

The door opened to reveal Cosimo, the enormous servant who had dealt with James during his last visit. He gave James a hostile glare.

'Would Signor or Signorina Rambaudi be at home?' Lombroso enquired politely.

'I'll see,' he said and slammed the door in their faces.

'A certain lack of finesse there,' Lombroso said. 'Probably a born criminal of the most basic type. All the primitive atavistic features are present.'

The door opened again. 'This way,' Cosimo said, ushering them into the hall. 'Signor Rambaudi is out, but the signora will see you in the library.' He pointed to a room in the corner and left them.

Lombroso shrugged and walked over to the door. He knocked and entered, James and Ottolenghi following behind. Bianca Rambaudi was sitting in an armchair reading. She stood up to greet them. 'Ah, Professor, an unexpected pleasure.'

'I do apologise... Your manservant...'

'Not at all, Professor. Cosimo is a little rough and ready, I know. But he is obedient and loyal. What more can one ask in this day and age? Were you and your colleagues here for anything in particular?'

'It is a rather delicate matter.'

Something of an understatement, James thought, but it had to be said.

Bianca raised her eyebrows. 'I see. Then you had better all be seated.'

'It is about your brother. I am so sorry to have to say this, but it appears that he may be responsible for the abduction of a number of young girls.'

There was a long pause as she assimilated this information. She seemed oddly composed, although James thought that her eyes told a different story.

'Exactly what evidence do you have for that outrageous suggestion?' she asked eventually.

'A witness saw a carriage with your family's insignia at the scene of two abductions,' Lombroso said.

'That does not mean Francesco is responsible.' She spoke precisely, positioning her words like a medieval typesetter.

'Nonetheless, we would like to speak to him. If he is not responsible, he might be able to help us find the real culprit. Whoever it is has almost certainly murdered at least two young women, and others are at risk.'

Her hands were folded primly in her lap. The left forefinger had been rhythmically tapping her wrist. When murder was mentioned, it stopped.

'It is true that my brother has been behaving erratically since the death of our mother. They were very close.' She stared into the distance, as if she was seeing something that was hidden from everyone else. Her whole body had stiffened. 'I suppose that grief might have clouded his judgement. But he would not abduct anyone, let alone harm them. He doesn't have it in him to do such a thing.'

'Perhaps, but we are searching for the girls. Do you know where he might have taken them?'

'I do not.'

James had had enough. It was all too damn polite and it wasn't getting them anywhere. He raised his voice. 'He *has* taken Lucy, and you know where, don't you?'

She blinked at him, her face still devoid of expression.

'Is there a place that is special to him?' Lombroso said with a sideways glance of warning at James.

She thought for a moment and nodded. 'Follow me. There is only one place I can think of.'

'Lucia, you look even more beautiful each time I see you,' Francesco said. 'That dress suits you. It fits exactly. Bruno, release her immediately!'

'What if she runs off again?'

'She only did that because she didn't understand. Isn't that right, Lucia?'

Lucy nodded. Miss Trott stood and watched in silence.

Bruno shrugged and obeyed. Francesco held out an arm. 'You will join me for dinner, won't you, Lucia? I have some guests who are dying to meet you.' He paused for a moment. 'Just think of it as a test. If you pass, you will live here with me, happily ever after.'

He turned to Miss Trott. 'I do hope you will join us. Our guests will be delighted to meet you.'

'I came only to retrieve my parasol, Signor Rambaudi,' Miss Trott said, her eyes flicking to the body lying on the table. 'I came here because I could get no answer at the house. It is of sentimental value, you know. My dear late father gave it to me as a gift. However, I can see it is not here, so I will not trouble you further.'

'Not at all, Miss Trott. I would not hear of it,' Francesco said, standing in her path, preventing her from getting to the stairs. 'You will join us. Then you can see if Lucia passes her little test.'

'And if I don't?' Lucy asked. She forced herself to walk over to Francesco and take his arm, knowing that she had no choice. Her skin crawled as he patted her hand.

He glanced at the body, the beam with the manacles, the bloodstains, and smiled sheepishly at her. 'Then I fear you will follow the same path as Arianna, and you don't want Miss Trott to witness that, I am sure.'

He led Lucy carefully up the stairs, followed by Miss Trott escorted by Bruno. Lucy didn't know what the test might be, but one thing was for sure: she had to pass it to survive.

As they emerged from the cellar area, she finally realised where they were – Francesco's summer house, or rather his late mother's. The statue of Maat was gleaming even in the darkness.

'Now let me look at you. I want to make sure you are presentable.' Francesco arranged her hair and straightened her dress a little before standing back to admire his handiwork. 'Yes, I do believe you are ready. Follow me.'

They stepped out into the garden in front of the summer house. There a table was laid with crystal glasses and fine white linen. Candles were lit, and baskets laden with bread and fruit waited for them. A heavily veiled woman dressed in white was seated at the head of the table. Lucy presumed that she was the guest of honour. Miss Trott nodded at her charge almost imperceptibly, as if telling her to play along with their host, not that she had much choice.

'Of course if you are to be my consort, then you will need servants.' Francesco indicated a young woman in a maid's uniform. 'Curtsey, girl!' he said sharply. 'Show some respect to your new mistress or you know what will happen.'

Lucy gasped. It was Fabia. She looked both terrified and crestfallen. She bobbed to Lucy. 'Good evening, madam,' she said shakily.

Another girl dressed as a maid was at the far end of the table, pouring wine. She was small with dark hair and looked uncannily like Sofia.

'Chiara?' Lucy said. She nodded and curtseyed too. At least they were alive, Lucy thought. Now all she had to do was work out what this test was and ensure that she passed it. It would buy them some time at any rate.

Francesco led her with great ceremony to the head of the table, where the guest of honour was sitting. As he gently drew aside the woman's veil and bent to kiss her cheek, Lucy recoiled in horror. The figure before them was not a living woman but the mummified remains of one. Her leathery brown skin was stretched over the bones of her face and her mouth was set in a ghastly parody of a smile.

Francesco pulled her closer to the figure. 'Now, Lucia, I don't believe you have met my mother.'

48

While the woman whose passion leads to crime is very different from the born criminal who violates the laws of chastity from lust and love of idle pleasure, nonetheless such good, passionate women are fatally inclined to love bad men. They fall into the hands of frivolous, fickle and sometimes depraved lovers who later abandon them, often adding to betrayal the even greater cruelties of scorn and slander. Lombroso and Ferrero, 1893, p. 202

James stood at the entrance to the storage barn. 'Why here?'

'It is where Francesco spends most of his time,' Bianca said. 'He is usually with Bruno.'

He walked over to one of the grain pits, pushed aside the lid and looked down into it. There was a bucket and some scraps of food on the floor. 'This is where he keeps them?'

Bianca came over and looked down. 'So it seems. I had no idea. Still, it does not mean that he has hurt anyone.'

She was standing next to him, completely still, her hands clasped loosely in front of her. As before, she was hardly reacting at all. Her voice was neutral. Her face was devoid of expression. There was not even a raised eyebrow. Did she not understand, or was it that she didn't care? Perhaps she was in shock. She unclasped her hands. There were small red crescent-shaped marks where her nails had been digging into her flesh. She both understood and cared, it seemed, but did not want to show it.

James and Ottolenghi went to each pit in turn to see if anyone was still there, but they were all empty.

'There must have been some indication,' Lombroso said.

'There have been one or two incidents with girls from the area. He and Bruno would befriend them, and sometimes we had to make payments to smooth things over when they got out of hand.'

'Teresa Mariani, for example?' James asked. 'You paid her mother, didn't you?'

'Yes,' Bianca said. 'The girl works for me now, so she did well out of it.'

'What happened to her?'

'Bruno violated her. But we sorted it out,' she said casually, as if it was a trifling matter. 'We have to beat her now and then, sometimes put her in a pit for an hour or two. But she usually does what she's told.'

James looked at her in disgust. 'Where else might he have gone?'

'I don't know of anywhere else . . .'

'Yes you do. I can see it in your face. You're lying. It would be better for him if you told us. We need to find the girls before . . .' James could not bring himself to say it. 'If you tell us where they are, I will do all I can to help Francesco.'

She hesitated for a few seconds. 'Follow me. It is not far.'

A few minutes later they were standing at a small wooden door encircled by roses. James could smell the sweet scent of them in the still warm air. Bianca took a key from her pocket and opened it to reveal a garden with a large pond in the shape of a cross. A statue of a young woman stood in the centre in front of a small fountain. Beyond it was a summer house, built in the classical style, complete with fluted pillars and frescoes. The murmur of conversation wafted over the water with the chink of glasses. Someone was laughing. Bianca stopped for a few seconds, as if halted by the sound, then beckoned to them. They followed her in silence towards a terrace at the front of the house.

At its heart was a large table, laid for dinner. Two maids stood by. One of them appeared to be Fabia Carignano and the other also looked familiar. Might it be Chiara? The young man James assumed was Bruno Ferranti watched as two of the diners appeared to lean in and whisper to each other like lovers. James felt his heart lurch. One of them was Lucy, ashen-faced, her eyes full of fear. Francesco had his hand clamped over her wrist. Miss Trott was sitting uncomfortably next to the fourth figure in the flickering candlelight. She gave him a small, tight smile.

He looked more closely at her companion. Repulsed, part of him wanted to turn away, but the sight was so strange and so terrible that it was oddly compelling. Seated at the table between Francesco and Miss Trott was the mummified corpse of a long-dead woman, her silver hair still strangely intact and held up with pearl combs like a macabre Miss Havisham. Could this be Francesco and Bianca's dead mother? His thoughts scrambled around in his mind in an effort to make sense of what he was seeing.

'Bianca?' Francesco said. 'I wish I'd known you were bringing guests. I'd have had the servants lay more places.'

Bianca moved towards him, as did James. In one quick movement Francesco pulled Lucy to her feet and held her, his arm across her chest. In his other hand was a knife.

'I didn't want her bled like the others, Bianca. I really think that she's the one.' He spoke in a strange sing-song voice, as if mimicking his sister.

Again James made as if to go to Lucy, but Ottolenghi pulled him back. Miss Trott edged away as Bianca continued to move slowly towards her brother.

'What's that?' Francesco said, looking towards his mother. 'Are you sure?' He flinched slightly. 'Yes, Mother, if that is what you want.' He spoke quietly to Lucy. 'Mother doesn't think you are suitable after all, Lucia.'

'Then let her go, Rambaudi,' James said. 'She has not harmed you.'

'I must kill her, Bianca,' Francesco said. 'Mother wants me to.'

He lifted the knife and brought it down on to Lucy's throat. A few drops of blood trickled down towards her collarbone. She looked back at James, her eyes wide. He couldn't lose her!

Francesco laughed. It was a light sound, almost musical. 'Oh, she is wicked. Mother says so. She is mocking me, and what is worse, she is mocking my dear sweet mother. She is just like all the others.'

'Francesco, hush. You do not know what you are saying.' Bianca took another step towards him.

'Lucy is different,' James said carefully. 'She would never mock your mother. She has lost her own.'

'Don't come any nearer, Bianca,' Francesco warned, 'or I will tell them everything.'

'There is nothing to tell,' Bianca said.

'Go on, Signor Rambaudi,' James said. 'We are listening.'

'Mother wants me to find a wife. Isn't that right?' He looked at Bianca, who did not respond. 'But I haven't found the right girl. There were plenty of candidates, but none of them were pure enough.'

'Tell me why not.'

'How could any woman measure up to Mother? Lucia here is no different.'

'Please, Francesco!' Lucy said.

'Hush, Lucia, hush. You see, that has always been your problem. A woman should be strong, and from that inner strength comes purity. That is the mistake they all made, with their childish pleading and crying. How can a woman be considered pure if she does that?'

'How did you find the girls?' James asked, hoping to divert Francesco's attention from Lucy.

'Usually Bianca found them. Some were from the estate, some from San Callisto itself. Then when that got too risky, we took local girls that Bruno knew who had moved to the city, to make sure they would not be missed.'

James was curious. 'Why did they have to be local?'

'Purer stock. One always needs to check pedigree if one wishes to breed.' Francesco glanced down at Lucy, who shifted slightly. He responded by moving the knife a little so it was resting against her neck. He went on. 'Eventually Bianca decided that the experiment was failing because of class, so she selected some more upmarket fillies, as it were – Fabia, and then Lucia – although Bruno and I found the girl from the abbey. I really thought she was special. She was so pale already, and so submissive. She used to call me Il Professore... I liked that.' He sighed. 'But then she ruined it all by asking me for money. We gave her the chance to atone, but it did not work. How could it? She was just a whore, when all was said and done. They all are at heart, even my dear sister.'

'What form did this atonement take?' James asked.

'We kept them until they were cleansed outside and in.

Then they were introduced to Mother. If they were polite and she accepted them, they would live here as my bride.'

James imagined that the likely reaction of any girl in that situation would be one of horror. No wonder they didn't pass the test. 'What happened if they did not atone?'

'After Bruno and I had amused ourselves, Bianca took them away.' Francesco tightened his grip on Lucy. 'Now, I think we have had enough of talking. The time has come for Lucia here to bid you all goodbye.'

Lucy's eyes were full of terror. He had to do something. He could not let her die. But if he made a move, Rambaudi would kill her. The knife touched her throat.

'Stop there, Mr Rambaudi!' A voice rang out from behind them. 'If you move an inch, I will shoot you!'

Miss Trott was standing next to Ottolenghi, her legs apart, her arms raised, a determined look on her face. She had a derringer pistol in her hands.

'I am a very good shot, Mr Rambaudi. I will not miss. Move away from Lucy and drop your knife.'

'Euphemia Trott,' Francesco said, still smiling dreamily. 'I just knew you and Mother would get on.'

He lifted his hand again. Miss Trott braced herself.

'What is it, Mother?' Francesco said, bending towards the corpse. He loosened his grip on Lucy for a split second, but it was enough for her almost to wriggle free. He still had hold of her dress and for a moment it seemed as if he would drag her back, but then a shot rang out. He glanced up in shock, and Lucy pulled away and ran to Miss Trott. Francesco fell to his knees and looked down at his stomach. Blood seeped from it.

There was a scream. Fabia had been seized by Bruno Ferranti. He dragged her away through the garden, holding her in front of him as a shield. James blocked his path and grabbed the struggling girl, pulling her free. Then he launched himself at the man, knocking him to the ground. They wrestled for a moment, but Ferranti escaped, leaving a dazed Fabia sitting nearby. Ottolenghi chased after him.

Francesco was lying in Bianca's arms. The knife was in her hand. As James walked towards her, she held it up in warning. 'Stop, Signor Murray.'

James did so. Lombroso slowly walked over and stood next to him. 'You must leave him to us, signorina,' James said gently. 'You have done all you can for him.'

'You don't understand. He must die.'

'If you allow me to stop the bleeding, then he can be saved.'

'No.'

'Why?'

'Because I love him.'

'Despite all he did to those girls?' Miss Trott said quietly.

'He just played with them a little. The rest was down to me.'

Miss Trott looked at her, aghast. '*You* murdered them?'

'Many years ago, Francesco and I were close. We barely spent a minute out of each other's company. But when he was about seven years old, our mother, Sylvana, began to take an interest in him.'

'What kind of interest?' Lombroso asked.

'The kind that my father denied her. Francesco knew no better. She told him it was a special kind of love that only a mother and son could share. He believed her. Why would he not? He worshipped her.'

'And how did that make you feel?' Miss Trott asked. Taking advantage of this attempt to distract Bianca, James tried to move slowly away. He wanted to see if he could approach her from behind and get to Francesco that way.

'Lonely, neglected... second best. She would flaunt their relationship, leaving doors open so that I could see everything they did together. Then, when I turned away, she made me watch.'

This time Lombroso asked a question. 'When did she die?'

Bianca's face slid into an insincere smile. 'A few years ago. A wasting illness... a terrible thing...'

'Poison will do that,' Lombroso said.

Bianca laughed. 'How clever of you, Professor. Yes, but she had to die. You do see that, don't you?'

'How did Francesco react?' Miss Trott asked.

The smile left Bianca's face in an instant and she looked down at her brother. 'He was devastated, inconsolable. I offered myself to him but he was not interested. I told him that she would have left him soon anyway. I could see the signs. She wanted the boy, not the man. But he would not accept it.' She looked up. 'If you could have seen him... He was distraught, dying of grief. I could not lose him like that, so I tried to preserve Sylvana for him. I even kept her heart in our ice house.'

'The heart that was found at the Borgo?'

'Yes, that's right. A nice touch, don't you think? A heart was the one thing my mother never really needed.'

'And after Sylvana?' Miss Trott said.

'Francesco was grateful at first, but then he wanted more, so I found him a girl – one of the mondine.'

'Teresa Mariani?' Lombroso asked.

'No. She's just Bruno's little plaything. We kept her alive to amuse him. The mondine come and go all the time, so I knew that no one would miss them. When I got him the first one, he toyed with her a little but then he discarded her. He said she did not measure up to Sylvana because she was not pure enough.' Bianca ran her bony fingers across Francesco's cheek. 'I wanted to please him, so I locked her up in the grain store and told her to atone. I waited until she had her monthly visitor so she would be clean, and then I drugged her and purified her for him.'

'Purified?' Lombroso asked.

'The Egyptians bled their dead and removed their organs to cleanse them for the afterlife. We learnt this from Francesco's tutor, Professor Donati. So I did the same, though of course I did not wait for death. To achieve real purity, one needs to conduct the process while the subject still lives. I hung her up, with the help of dear Bruno, then I bled her, removed her organs and embalmed her. I wanted to see if I could preserve her beauty better than I had managed with my mother, so I tried a different technique, but it didn't quite work.'

'So you got Bruno to bury her in the woods,' Lombroso said.

'Yes. I gave him the exact specifications for where to dig the grave. I wanted to be precise. It is very important, don't you think?' she said, her head coyly to one side. 'Francesco thought so. He could see what I was trying to do. He and Bruno, my mother's other little pastime. So I kept doing it, and I gave the bodies to Francesco to play with. Chiara's monthly visitor never arrived – I think she was too young – so we kept her as a sort of pet.'

James thought of the anguish that Sofia had gone through. Bianca was a monster, whatever the cause, and her brother was no better. Still, he should not be allowed the solace of death. He inched closer as the questioning continued.

'What about the girls in the abbey and the Borgo?' Lombroso asked.

'Francesco was bored. He was becoming more interested in

living girls, like Lucy here. But I had grown attached to my work. I was getting quite good at it, you know. I decided to put it on display. I selected my subjects carefully. Bruno gave me their names. Then once I had created my pieces, I wanted to share my first collection. Did you like it?'

'And Lucy and Fabia Carignano?' Miss Trott said. 'Why did you take them?'

'As I said, my brother needed a wife. It was going to be Fabia due to her stock. We thought that made her pure enough, but she was so objectionable we decided on Lucy. Francesco made Fabia wait on her. Don't you think that was amusing? He knew it was the thing that would hurt her most. He was always inventive in his cruelty. He learnt that from my mother. I would have killed Fabia for him when he tired of her . . . Lucy too if he'd wanted me to.'

'I do not think it was love for your brother that made you kill,' Miss Trott said. 'Now was it, dear?'

Bianca smiled her dead smile.

Miss Trott went on. 'First he took your mother's love from you, and then when she was gone he rejected you. You never forgave him. Poor Bianca . . . always the odd one out. They loved each other but never had time for you, even when one of them was dead.'

James had almost reached them when Francesco stirred. Bianca kissed her brother's forehead. Then, without warning, she lifted her arm and brought the knife down on his throat, slicing through it from side to side. Before anyone could act, she did the same to her own. The blood poured from their wounds and mingled on the ground beneath them, uniting them in death.

James heard shouting in the distance. Anna, Sofia, Tullio,

Ottolenghi, Machinetti and a crowd of carabinieri ran through the gate towards them. Bruno Ferranti was in handcuffs.

Sofia broke away from Anna and embraced Chiara as if her life depended on it. James waited for Machinetti to approach him. He knew he would be arrested, but now that Lucy was safe and Chiara found, it didn't seem to matter. He would be taken to prison, which after all was where he had always belonged.

49

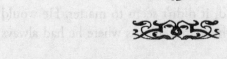

The chief motive for female crime is vengeance. The inclination towards revenge that we noted even in normal women becomes extreme in criminals. Because their psychic centres are irritated, the smallest stimulus can provoke an enormous reaction. But usually the female born criminal revenges herself more slowly than men. She has to develop her plan little by little because her physical weakness and fearful nature restrain her even when her reason does not.

Lombroso and Ferrero, 1893, p. 186

At the marchesa's private dinner, held to mark the return to her care of her niece, the mood was subdued rather than celebratory.

As they took their seats, she remarked pointedly, 'It is hard to believe that so many girls could be taken and so little was done.'

Lucy noticed that the fat little policeman, Machinetti, had the good grace to blush at this at least. He had taken great pleasure in arresting James at the Villa Purezza because of a girl who had apparently gone missing. It had looked for a while as if James would have to await trial in custody. Fortunately his friend Tullio had received a tip-off and the girl was found at Madame Giulia's, claiming that she had never been missing in the first place.

All involved with the Rambaudi case, as it was now known, had been invited to the dinner, including Chiara and Sofia. Lucy noticed how her brother made sure that they did not feel uncomfortable, including them in the conversation whenever he could and discreetly demonstrating how each course should be tackled. It was clear how he and Sofia felt about each other. He would touch her affectionately on the arm or hand at every opportunity. Sofia was less openly demonstrative, but her emotions were clear. Chiara was watching them carefully, just as Lucy was, and now and again they would catch each other's eye and exchange knowing smiles.

James was still tense, of course, though he was doing his best to hide it. His freedom was in question. The trial would be upon them soon enough, and Lucy could only guess how apprehensive he was about its possible outcome. Baldovino was still unconscious, and much of the evidence was damning. The professor seemed confident that they would win, but Lucy could see that James did not share his certainty.

Fabia was quieter than Lucy had ever known her, which was not surprising, considering her ordeal. Thanks to James's intervention, she had largely escaped physical pain. But she had been humiliated, and that, for Fabia, was a form of torture in itself, as Francesco had known so well.

Perhaps they were all dreaming in the same way, reliving their experiences. Sometimes it happened even when Lucy was still awake. Just closing her eyes could conjure up Francesco's face and the expression on it as Bianca had sliced through his throat, or the sight of his mummified mother seated at the head of the table. She had already decided to write it all into one of her stories. She would never show it to anyone, but she was finding that pouring her feelings onto the page in the form of fiction was comforting, and comfort was exactly what she craved.

She observed the remaining guests with care. Tullio, the other policeman, looked pale and tense as he listlessly pushed his food around his plate. His eye would twitch occasionally and his smiles were strained. Every now and then he would glance at James and close his eyes as if he did not dare to look at him directly. Why was he so worried? The case was over and it was not he who was about to stand trial.

Miss Trott was the opposite. She was relaxed and chatting animatedly to the marchesa and Anna. Her eyes were shining as if a burden had been lifted. Nothing further had been said about her part in the rescue. Lucy had thought her companion to be so dull. Who would have thought that she would save the day, and with the help of a derringer too!

After dinner, they all gathered in the marchesa's drawing room. Professor Lombroso was going to address them about the murders, and 'other crimes', as he had put it. He said that it would help them all to understand what had happened, and Lucy was inclined to agree.

'Francesco Rambaudi was not a born criminal, but his immorality became instilled in him at an early age due to the attentions of his mother, Sylvana.'

'Should the young ladies be hearing this?' Miss Trott asked.

'Thank you for your concern,' the marchesa said. 'But given their ordeal, I think it appropriate for them to hear the background from experts in the field, assuming they wish to stay. As the professor says, it may help them to understand it, insofar as it can be understood.'

Lucy nodded vigorously, as did Fabia and Chiara. Lombroso continued.

'As his sister told us, Rambaudi developed an obsession with Sylvana, both physical and sexual. When she died at Bianca's hands, he needed to find a substitute. This was the motivation for his actions. Assisted by Bruno Ferranti, a young man with overdeveloped sexual impulses, he began his search amongst some of his employees.'

'The mondine?' James asked.

'Correct, Murray. As your research led me to that conclusion, perhaps you would care to continue.'

James got to his feet, his face serious and intense. His tone was measured and authoritative. Lucy didn't think she had ever felt as proud of him as she did at that moment.

'The mondine are the itinerant seasonal workers who come to labour in the rice fields of the region, planting, weeding and harvesting the crop. They live and work together, but that work is hard, back-breaking in fact. I questioned one of them, a woman called Perla, and she confirmed that girls from surrounding villages came to work there but that the turnover was high. For many of them the work was too unpleasant and they left. This means that no one noticed when some of them disappeared. Everyone just thought they had gone to work elsewhere.'

'What happened to them?' Ottolenghi said.

'The first was a young woman called Teresa Mariani,' James said. 'Sofia, you remember how her mother reacted strangely when we talked to her?'

'*Sì*, she did not seem surprised about the finding of the bodies.'

'That's because she knew Teresa was not dead. Bruno Ferranti chose and befriended the girl. But after a while she became frightened of him and wanted to leave him. He threatened her, so she ran off to the city. But he found her and took her back, forcing her to work for the Rambaudis. Her mother knew this but was too frightened of what they might do to her to intervene.'

'Was she the girl with Bruno at the museum?' Lucy asked.

James nodded. 'Yes, but it was not her choice. She was as much a victim as you.'

'What will happen to her?' the marchesa asked.

'She is helping us with our enquiries,' Tullio said. 'I doubt she will be charged, unlike Bruno Ferranti.'

'What about the body in the woods?' Anna asked.

'May I?' Lombroso asked. James nodded graciously and sat down. The professor was treating him as an equal, Lucy thought. Good for him!

'This was the first victim. She was abducted, murdered and then some form of experiment was performed on her by Bianca, assisted no doubt by both Francesco and Ferranti. Francesco was always interested in Egyptology, so he no doubt influenced Bianca as she tried to re-create their death rituals in order to preserve her handiwork.'

'So Professor Donati had nothing to do with it?' Lucy said.

'He gave some advice but we cannot be sure that he knew its purpose.'

'I'm sure he did,' Anna said. 'Why else would he run away from us at the museum?'

'Yes, he must be guilty of something!' Lucy declared.

'We will hear more of him in due course, dear. Be patient,' Miss Trott said.

'This led to the forming of a pattern of behaviour. A girl would be abducted, an experiment conducted, and then she would be kept at the summer house as an exhibit before being disposed of. Moral insanity at its most extreme.'

'Where are their bodies?' Anna asked.

'I am guessing that a search of the woods and perhaps even the grounds of the estate would be fruitful,' Lombroso replied.

'I have sent men to do just that,' Machinetti announced.

'It is a wonder you did not do so when the first body was found,' the marchesa said, looking on disapprovingly as Machinetti flushed and shifted in his seat.

Lombroso continued. 'The bodies at the abbey and the Borgo were left there for us to find. As you may remember, Baldovino helpfully publicised my investigation. Bianca had tired of keeping her experiments to herself and was also aware that rumours were beginning to circulate amongst the mondine. She needed to target a different set of victims and so took the opportunity to develop a new approach, which she wanted to show off.'

'How did she select her victims?' Anna asked.

'By name,' James said. 'All the girls had names that signified purity in one way or another. Chiara means clear bright light, Lucia means graceful light, Susanna is graceful lily, Ariana is chaste and holy, Caterina means pure and so does Agnella.'

'Why did Bianca arrange for Agnella to be left at the abbey?' Ottolenghi asked.

'She worked at the abbey as a prostitute and Francesco was her client. He told Bianca that he wanted her, so she complied, then exhibited the body where she knew we would find it.'

'What does Fabia mean?' Chiara asked.

'Bean farmer, I believe,' the marchesa said with an affectionate glance at her niece, who was scowling.

No wonder she didn't pass Bianca's test, Lucy thought. And it might even have been her own name that saved her.

'How did Baldovino find out about the missing girls?' Anna asked.

'I told him,' Tullio said.

'What?' exclaimed Machinetti. 'You passed on information to a reporter? You will answer to the mayor for this!'

'Why, Tullio?' James said.

'I was getting nowhere and he has certain contacts. I thought it might assist. Sometimes you have to use unconventional means to achieve a result.'

'As you did in relation to Concetta Panatti,' Lombroso said.

'Please tell me you have not been using her as an informant!' Machinetti said.

'We have been investigating the abbey for some time. The suspicion was that Concetta Panatti was running an illegal brothel there. The mayor and Father Vincenzo asked me to be discreet, as a number of establishment figures are implicated, including members of the Catholic clergy. I asked the professor to go up there and look around under the guise of one of his psychical investigations.'

'Is that why we had no relevant equipment?' James asked.

Lombroso looked sheepish. 'Yes . . . well, actually, other than a camera and a thermometer, there is no equipment for such an enquiry.'

'For the avoidance of doubt, the rooms on the first floor are where the brothel is,' James said. 'Ada, one of Concetta Panatti's girls, told me about its existence, and about her missing friend Agnella, or Nella Calvi, who worked there.'

'Can you bring Concetta Panatti to justice?' Lombroso asked.

'Not yet . . . perhaps not ever,' Tullio said. 'It has been difficult to prove anything because of all the vested interests involved. She has kept her association at arm's length.'

'I went there looking for Chiara,' James said. 'My visits and

Ada's information were enough to ensure that I was threatened and beaten. Why didn't you warn me, Tullio?'

'I couldn't,' Tullio said. 'It would have ruined the investigation. And . . .'

'You were being threatened too?' James asked quietly.

Tullio nodded. 'I was told that my family would be harmed if I did not stop investigating.'

James was looking at his friend's face, pale and strained, and Lucy could see that he understood the stress that Tullio must have been under. 'Is Panatti behind the assault on Baldovino and the supposedly missing Gabriella?' he asked.

'It is possible, but again we cannot prove it,' Tullio said. 'No one will speak up, such is her hold.'

'She is a blackmailer,' Lombroso said. 'An unusually intelligent example of female criminality.'

'I thought you said that women were incapable of such things, Professor,' Lucy pointed out. 'What makes Concetta Panatti so exceptional?'

'An excellent question, Lucy!' Anna said. 'What is your answer, Cesare?'

'She is of course physically incapable of satisfying her perverse instincts. However, superior intelligence in a criminal woman can be explained by two things – the fact that she is a born criminal and the originality of her crimes. She has combined prostitution, pandering and blackmail with legitimate business interests – a lethal mix that makes her almost invincible.'

'And she is ruthless,' Ottolenghi said. 'Look at what she has done to James. First she flirts with him, and when that doesn't work, she has him physically assaulted. Then she tries to seduce him, attempts to discredit him with that nonsense in *The People's Voice* and frames him for an attack on Baldovino.

When he gets bail, thanks to the marchesa, she cannot allow him to be free, so she arranges to hide Gabriella so he will be arrested.'

'Do you agree, Tullio?' Anna asked.

Tullio nodded forlornly. 'I do. It was one of her girls who told us about Gabriella's whereabouts.'

'Ada?' James asked.

'I cannot confirm that for security reasons,' Tullio replied. 'Panatti's influence cannot be underestimated. She has collated information on so many members of the establishment, particularly in high places. I am sorry, James. I wish we could do more.'

'I understand,' James replied.

Lucy was confused. He was being framed for a crime that he had not committed. Why wasn't he shouting out his innocence for all to hear?

'We can only hope that more is revealed at the trial,' Lombroso said.

'Indeed,' Miss Trott said. 'I am making my own enquiries. I am confident that they will be fruitful.'

'Ah, the redoubtable Euphemia Trott,' Lombroso said. 'But we have met before, have we not? You were a nurse at St Euphemia's Hospital in Pavia when I was working there all those years ago.'

'Indeed, Professor, you are correct. I took my pseudonym from the hospital. You stared at me so when we first met, I thought my cover was blown right at the beginning of my mission.'

'What is Serendipity?' Lucy asked.

'It is the code name I am known by at the agency.'

'Agency?' James asked. 'Is that where Aunt Agnes found you?'

'Hardly,' Miss Trott said. 'It is a detective agency. My name was given to your aunt by Professor Bell, who happens to be my cousin. Both of them wanted some protection for you and your sister, so I was asked to watch over you.'

Lucy gazed at Miss Trott in admiration. It was ironic. She had been writing about a lady detective when all the time there was a real one in their midst. No wonder she kept disappearing. 'That wasn't your only brief, though, was it, Miss Trott?'

'No, dear, it wasn't. As I was coming here anyway, my agency asked me to look into another matter.'

'Professor Donati?' Lucy asked.

'A thief,' Miss Trott said. 'That is all there is to say really. He stole from the British Museum what is reputed to be the demon god Apep's book of spells. It was not his only acquisition. Scotland Yard have been after him for some time. He operates from an address in the Via San Pellico, a chemist's shop.'

Lombroso beamed at her. 'I knew it! An expressive face, manual dexterity and small wandering eyes . . . all classic signs of the criminal type.'

'Perhaps, Professor,' Miss Trott said. 'But generally speaking I prefer to use more old-fashioned methods – intelligence from fellow criminals, surveillance and, naturally, deduction. It is, after all, what led me to both Donati and Francesco Rambaudi.'

'Your methods certainly seem to be effective,' James said.

'They played their part, Dr Murray,' Miss Trott said. 'But let us not forget that your detective work also took you to the Villa Purezza.'

'Eventually, though I allowed my suspicion about Concetta Panatti to divert me from the truth. I was so intent on catching her that I heard only Pietro's mention of seeing something red through the window of the carriage when he witnessed the abductions.'

'You thought he was talking about Panatti's hair,' Ottolenghi said.

'But what was it?' Anna asked.

'It was the red ribbon round Bianca Rambaudi's neck!' Lucy said. 'I noticed it when she came for tea because it was so unusual. It holds a locket.'

'Bravo!' Miss Trott said. 'You have excellent observation skills.'

'You put me to shame, Lucy,' James added, looking downcast. 'If only I had been as astute.'

'You saved Fabia from that man Ferranti, Signor Murray,' the marchesa said. 'I will be forever in your debt for that.'

'Yes, well done, Murray,' Lombroso said, shaking his hand. 'And I have to admit that I was wrong about Donati.'

'You were wrong, Cesare?' Anna said. 'Can we have that in writing?'

'Very droll, Madame Tarnovsky, very droll,' Lombroso said. 'But I still think that Francesco Rambaudi suffered from epilepsy . . . the hidden variety, of course. It is difficult even for me to distinguish such criminals from the merely morally insane, so I can understand Murray's mistake.'

'So in fact you were right?' James said.

Lombroso nodded. 'Quite so, Murray, quite so. I knew you'd get there in the end. We'll make a criminal anthropologist of you yet.'

James grinned. 'Oh I do hope so, Professor, I do hope so.'

50

Contradictions within the legal system lead to trials marked by wasted money, scandalous publicity and uncertain outcomes . . . Numerous cases demonstrate the complete ignorance of most jurors.

Lombroso, 1896–7, p. 335

James sat in the dock and tried discreetly to observe the jury. They did not seem to like him, and based on what they had heard so far, who could blame them? Not only had he been discovered standing over the victim, Baldovino, with a knife in his hand, but he had also been the subject of critical pieces by the man in *The People's Voice*, giving him motive, means and opportunity. In addition, the clothes taken from him at the police station had been produced, now covered in blood, even though James was sure that there had been no more than a few drops when he had been arrested.

Despite the fact that the marchesa had paid for an expensive lawyer and that Lombroso himself was about to give evidence on his behalf, it was not looking hopeful. Having seen the expression on the judge's face, he had resigned himself to a good few years in Le Nuove at best, and at worst . . .

James's lawyer, a serious grey-haired man with a monocle,

asked the professor his first question: 'How long have you known the accused?'

'Almost a year. He has worked as my assistant.'

'And during that year, what impression have you formed of this man?'

'I have found him to be extremely sound. He is honest, intelligent, hard-working and an excellent employee.'

'He is accused of a violent crime. Is he capable of such an act, in your expert opinion?'

The prosecution lawyer, a sharp-featured younger man, sprang to his feet. 'Is this witness here to speak to character or expertise?'

'Both,' replied James's lawyer.

The judge peered down his glasses and indeed his nose at Lombroso. 'I will allow an answer, but keep it brief.'

'So is he capable of this crime?'

'No.'

The defence lawyer sat down and the prosecution stood up. James wanted to shout: *Is that it?*

'Professor Lombroso, as you have given evidence relating to your expertise in crime and criminals, I wonder if you could tell us about heredity in crime?'

'That is a most interesting question. The main thing to note is that criminality can be hereditary.'

'I see, and how does this relate to alcoholism?'

'Oh, that is a fascinating phenomenon, for I have found that parental alcoholism is an important factor in inherited propensity to violence.'

James put his hands over his eyes in despair as Lombroso warmed to his theme, bringing his conviction closer with every sentence that he uttered.

'I studied a boy with thick dark hair and pale skin whose

father was an alcoholic and a killer. He himself was only twelve years old when he committed his murder. And of course the ferocious Galetto of Marseille was the grandson of Orsolano, the cannibal rapist, Dumolard was the son of an assassin, and the Cornu family was filled with murderers from father to son, and those are just a few examples.'

'Thank you, Professor, that is most helpful. Can you also confirm that the father of the accused was confined to an asylum for the criminally insane after he stabbed someone to death in a bar brawl?'

There was a long silence. Lombroso fiddled with his glasses, and his beard twitched as if a small animal was living in it.

'Professor, can you answer the question,' the judge said impatiently. 'Was the father of the accused a killer?'

'Yes, I suppose he was.'

'Thank you, no further questions.' The prosecution lawyer sat down with a satisfied grin on his face. The jury murmured to each other and the packed public gallery did likewise.

James sat there helplessly, watching as Lombroso left the witness box. It was all over. He was going to prison. His career, Sofia, Lucy . . . everything was to be taken from him, and all for something he had not done. But it didn't matter. It was better for everyone if he just accepted his fate. He might not be guilty of this crime, but he had committed another, just as heinous.

He saw a flash of red hair in the public gallery. Concetta Panatti gave him a smug smile. Next to her was a gaunt man wearing a scarlet cravat.

'I know what you are,' he had said when they had first met. And now he was about to get what he had wanted all along: revenge.

*

The speeches had been made and the jury were out. James was waiting in a tiny room with a barred window for his fate to be announced. He had asked to see Lombroso, Ottolenghi and Anna, and before long they were ushered into the room. He felt calm. He knew what was coming and it was almost a relief. Finally he would get the punishment that he truly deserved.

'I have something to tell you,' he said. 'Something that I think may explain what has happened and why I deserve my sentence even though I did not commit this crime.'

'You do not know that you will be convicted, Murray.'

James gave a wan smile. 'I am certain that I will be, but it is all right.'

'It is nothing of the kind! I am so very sorry, Murray. I had no idea they would bring your father's case up. I do not know how they found out,' Lombroso said.

'I think I do,' James said. 'Do you remember last year when I first told you about my father?'

'Indeed I do. He performed illegal brain surgery on a young man in the asylum where you both worked, did he not?'

'Yes. I told you that I was assisting at the asylum on an ad hoc basis in order to gain some experience in the field.'

'Yes, I remember.'

'Sir Henry Gadd, the father of the young man who was operated on by my father, is here today.'

'And what business does he have with you?'

'As you know, the operation was not a success. Richard Gadd was transformed from a patient troubled by hallucinations and blackouts into little more than an idiot.'

'What does that have to do with the trial?' Ottolenghi asked.

'Richard committed suicide earlier this year.'

'I can see why Sir Henry would be angered, of course, but this was due to your father's actions, surely,' Lombroso said.

There was a silence as James closed his eyes and wished that he was anywhere but there. His shoulders dropped and he began to stoop as if a burden had been placed on his back. 'I was there.'

'You were present at the operation?' Ottolenghi said incredulously.

'Yes.'

'You lied to us, then?' Lombroso said.

'I lied to you and I lied to myself. I did not condone the operation but I did assist. I tried to prevent my father from conducting it, but . . .'

'But what, James?' Anna said gently.

'He was adamant. I thought that at least if I was taking part, I might be able to ensure Richard's safety.'

'But you were not able to do so?' Lombroso said.

James shook his head. 'I was not sufficiently experienced to know how. I was arrogant. I thought that I knew more than I did. It seemed to me that it went well, or as well as it could do.'

'And when you discovered the consequences?' Anna said.

'I argued with my father. There was a terrible row and the rest is as I have already told you.'

'And now?' asked Lombroso.

'Sir Henry holds me responsible for the death of his son . . . and he is right.'

'So he has engaged the services of that Panatti woman to assist in this?'

'It is more likely that she has her own reasons. First I visit the abbey and find the brothel, so she has me abducted, beaten and threatened. I persist in my enquiries, so she tries to seduce me in order to control me, and when that doesn't work, she manipulates Baldovino into writing those pieces in *The People's Voice*. Finally, perhaps encouraged by Sir Henry, she frames me for murder by forging a note from Baldovino getting me to visit him. She wanted to discredit me and found the ideal way to achieve it. It is clear that she did her research. No doubt Sir Henry was happy to assist.'

'Then the trial must be stopped. We must tell the authorities immediately,' Lombroso said.

'No. I deserve this. What you said in court was right. I have inherited my father's morals and his propensity for violence. Look how I threatened Baldovino.'

'This is nonsense, James,' Anna said. 'You tried to stop your father. And threatening a reporter is hardly demonstrative of a propensity to violence.'

'It's done. I'm going to be locked up where I belong. I could have saved Richard but I did not. I am a born criminal like my father before me. I need to be put away before I do more damage. I deserve this.'

'Don't be ridiculous, Murray,' Lombroso said. 'You are no more of a born criminal than I am. You must believe me. I know what you are!'

James flinched at the irony of the words.

'But James—' Anna began. She was interrupted by a knock and the door opened. 'Time's up,' the jailer said. 'The jury is back.'

'Take care of Lucy, Anna,' James said. He watched calmly as his friends were shown out. Anna gave him a tearful wave before she disappeared.

Back in the dock, he watched as the jury filed into their seats. Sir Henry sat in the gallery, still smiling.

The judge strode in and shuffled his papers about before

nodding at the court clerk. He in turn nodded to the foreman, who stood to deliver his verdict. The jury refused to look James in the eye. His fate was sealed.

Outside there was a kerfuffle and some shouting. Then the door was flung open and a small rat-like man in a bowler hat limped in with the aid of crutches, closely followed by Miss Trott.

'What is the meaning of this interruption?' the judge said, glaring at the man.

'I am the victim, your honour, Baldovino of *The People's Voice*, and I demand to be heard.'

There was a pause as the judge pursed his lips. 'Very well, swear him in.'

Baldovino took the oath. Would he tell the truth? It was impossible to tell from the look on his face. The prosecution lawyer got to his feet. 'Can you identify the man who attacked you?'

Baldovino paused and looked round until he found James, then he smiled and gave a mock salute. 'No.'

The prosecutor frowned and tried again. 'Is the man who attacked you sitting in this court?'

'No.'

'Who was it who attacked you?'

'I don't know who they were, but it was not James Murray.'

'Are you sure?'

'Yes. I *was* there, you know.'

The prosecutor scratched his head for a moment and then had a whispered discussion with the man sitting behind him. It seemed to go on forever.

'Well, what do you want me to do?' asked the judge.

The prosecutor shrugged.

The jury began to talk amongst themselves, then the foreman stood.

'Yes, what is it?' enquired the judge.

The foreman looked over at James. 'We find the prisoner not guilty, your honour.'

The court erupted. There were cheers from the public gallery and James was patted on the shoulder as he was released from the dock. In all the chaos, he noticed one face focused unerringly on his own.

'I know what you are,' Henry Gadd mouthed at him. 'I know what you are.'

51

Woman's sensitivity is notably different from man's, as the anatomy of her organs itself suggests. Her eye is smaller and more on the surface of the head; her nose and ears are shorter. Lombroso and Ferrero, 1893, p. 58

'You know why I am here,' James said as he walked into the kitchen at Lombroso's house. Although it had been a few weeks since the trial, he was still coming to terms with his freedom. Lombroso had given him some more work to do to keep his mind occupied, and that had certainly helped, but he knew that there were matters to resolve. The marchesa had visited that day and made it clear that she would do anything she could to assist him. She held him responsible for the return of her niece, chastened a little by her experience, but unharmed.

'How can I help you?' she had said, and he had told her.

Sofia was baking bread, as she had been when they shared their first kiss. He realised now that they were destined to be together no matter what. He was here to claim her and make her understand that he would fight for her until the day he died.

'We can't keep pretending,' he said. 'It is meant to be. I think you know that.'

She sighed. 'I have to be honest now. I know this, *caro*. There have been too many lies already. I do love you. I have never stopped loving you.'

He pulled her to him and held her. 'Then I will ask you again. Will you marry me?'

She did not move away from him, but she did not respond either.

'I cannot.'

'You can, Sofia. We can be together. The marchesa has arranged everything.'

Sofia shook her head. 'No, I cannot.'

'I have a teaching position in America. Lucy can come too. I want you to be my wife.'

She shook her head again and pulled away from him. 'I cannot do that. I want to with all my heart, but I cannot.'

'Why not?' James asked. 'There is no reason for us to be apart.'

Sofia's tears were dropping onto the loaf she had been kneading. He took her in his arms again. 'We can't keep saying goodbye,' he said. 'What is stopping you? I know our lives, our backgrounds are different, but we can get over all of that. We love each other and that is all that matters. We have a future.'

She put a hand up to his cheek and caressed it before leaning forward and kissing him. As he held her to him, for a moment it felt as if nothing could touch them as long as they were together. But then the dampness of the tears on her face told another story. 'What is it, Sofia? Tell me!' he begged.

'Chiara,' she said.

'I got her back for you. She will be all right now.'

'I know, and I will never forget what you did for us.'

James held his hands out. 'So, what then? We will ensure

that Chiara is in good hands. Your cousin has a position with the marchesa.'

Sofia paused. 'Chiara is not my cousin, *caro*. She is my daughter, and I must put her first.'

'Are you sure you have to go, Miss Trott?' Lucy said as she watched her companion pack her things into her carpet bag.

'Yes, dear, I must. I have been called back to my agency. Apparently they have another assignment for me.'

'What's it like?'

'What do you mean, dear?'

'Being a detective. Is it exciting?'

'It can be. But it can also be monotonous, tiring and dangerous. I would not recommend it unless one had no choice.'

'And did you? Have a choice, I mean?'

'Yes, I suppose I did. I was to marry, but my fiancé died. Once he had gone . . .' She looked wistfully into the distance as if he was waiting there for her. 'No one could replace him, so I did not even try. Besides, I wanted to make my own way in life. And it turned out that I had particular talents.'

Lucy looked at her in admiration. In a way, she envied Miss Trott. She knew where she was going and what her place was in the world. Lucy herself had no such certainty. After her experience with Francesco, she had no interest in love . . . not for the time being. She too wanted to make her own way. The only question was how.

She had been working closely with Anna in the months since her abduction, and had found it both stimulating and fulfilling. Indeed, Anna had asked her if she would consider continuing their work back in Prague. But before any decisions about her future could be made, she had to sort out

James, who had been miserable ever since his trial despite his exoneration by Baldovino.

Chiara knocked on Miss Trott's door. 'Signorina Lucy, I am here as you asked.'

Miss Trott looked up from her packing. 'Is there something I can assist you with?'

'Yes,' Lucy said. 'There is. We are both worried about James and Sofia.'

'Ah yes. I understand that your mother has told Mr Murray she cannot go with him to America.'

'It is so wrong!' Chiara said. 'She is giving up everything for me when I do not want her to!'

'Then you must tell her,' Miss Trott said.

'I have tried, but she will not listen.'

'I see,' Miss Trott said. 'Then perhaps you need to tell her again but in a different way. Let me explain.'

James was sitting in the drawing room looking disconsolately out of the window. He had thought that everything was about to change, but it was not to be. Sofia's confession had seen to that. In some ways it was a relief. It explained why she had rejected him. She had other responsibilities and had been left with little choice. She had given birth to Chiara when she herself was scarcely a child, and the baby had been looked after by a family member who lived in San Callisto. When the woman had died, Chiara had returned to Sofia, who had explained to her who she really was.

'I want to be with you, *caro*,' she had told James. 'But I cannot abandon my daughter again.'

Now he had nothing, or at least that was how it felt. He would still go to America, and hopefully Lucy would go with him. But he was done with love. No one could ever take Sofia's place.

There was a knock at the door and Lucy came in. Behind her were Chiara and Sofia.

'Sofia, would you sit down?' Lucy asked.

Chiara nodded at her mother and sat next to her.

'Chiara and I have been talking,' Lucy said to James. 'There are a few things we need to explain.'

James frowned. 'You do not need to worry. Sofia is to stay here with Chiara. You and I . . . well, I have some plans for us.'

'No, James. I am afraid that will not do. Chiara and I have plans of our own.'

'*Sì*, we have,' Chiara said. James could see the likeness between her and Sofia now. She had a way of half smiling that was almost identical to her mother's.

'Plans . . . what sort of plans?' Sofia said, looking mystified.

Chiara turned towards her. 'Mamma, you must go to America with Signor James and be happy.'

'I cannot leave you,' Sofia protested. 'We have only just found each other again.'

Chiara took her mother's hands and held them tightly. 'Don't you see? I want you to be happy, and I know that this is the only way.'

Sofia hesitated and looked carefully into her daughter's eyes. 'Really? Are you sure, *cara*?'

'I have never been more sure of anything,' Chiara said. 'The marchesa has offered me a new position and I have decided to accept it. It will be quite challenging and will involve some travelling, but I think it will be very fulfilling.'

'It won't be dull, that's for sure,' Lucy said.

'No, indeed,' Chiara said, smiling. 'I am to be Fabia Carignano's companion.'

'*Santo cielo!* Are you certain? She is a handful, that one,' Sofia said. 'You'll have your work cut out.'

Chiara laughed. 'Remember, I have seen her in a maid's uniform, curtseying to Lucy. If she gets too much, I will remind her of that.'

'But what about Lucy?' Sofia said. 'Perhaps she is not so sure?'

'I don't want to go to America,' Lucy said, 'if that is what you were hoping for, James. Because I too have been offered a position, of a kind.'

'What position? You're not thinking of going back to Scotland, surely!' James said.

'Certainly not. I have changed, James. You must see that. I'm not sure Aunt Agnes would approve of the new me. The thing is . . .' She paused, as if she was trying to find the right words. 'Anna is going back to Prague. She has decided to conduct her own study on women and crime, inspired by what happened here. She has asked me to go with her to assist. She wants me to use my experiences to further her knowledge on the subject. I will stay with her and her husband, so I will be well looked after.'

'So there you are,' Chiara said. 'We have made our arrangements; now you can make yours. We will visit, though. You can be certain of that.'

James held out his hand to Sofia. She walked over to him and took it. 'Signora Murray,' he said. 'I like the sound of that.'

'If we are going to America, then it will be Mrs James Murray,' Sofia laughed. 'I like the sound of that even more!'

Seven months later

Mr and Mrs James Murray stood on the deck watching the famous Statue of Liberty come into view as they approached New York. He kissed his wife and breathed in her scent of cinnamon and lemons – still there even though they had left Italy weeks ago.

Saying goodbye to their friends and family had been hard for both of them. They had married in a quiet but beautiful ceremony, surrounded by those who were dearest to them. Lombroso, who had given Sofia away, had seemed quite tearful, though he claimed to have something in his eye.

James noticed that the professor had wasted no time in replacing him at the museum. A serious and studious young man called Guglielmo Ferrero was to take his place on the research project. Now there was a new case to write up, that of Francesco and Bianca Rambaudi and their mother Sylvana. It seemed that Lombroso had been right after all. Women could be crueller than men, and none more so than the two who had manipulated Francesco until he was nothing more than a shell of a man completely at their disposal.

That was all in the past. Now James Murray was the happiest of men. He had everything he wanted: the woman he loved at his side, an interesting new position in a thriving and exciting place. It was all going to be perfect. He squeezed Sofia's hand and she laid her head on his shoulder as they looked out across the harbour to their new life.

But on that harbour stood a familiar figure, smiling with satisfaction at the prospect of the Murrays' arrival. It was a year or more since their encounter in Turin, but he had not forgotten them. The epitome of a well-to-do American, he carried a silver-topped cane and wore a distinctive coat, smart and elegant, with an astrakhan collar. He watched as the ship came closer, but before it reached the harbour, he turned and walked away. It would wait, he thought. *They* would wait.

Because murder should never be rushed.

Author's Note

Cesare Lombroso (1835–1909) is known as the father of modern criminology. His theory of the born criminal dominated thinking about criminal behaviour in the late nineteenth and early twentieth centuries. Essentially he believed that criminality was inherited, and that criminals could be identified by physical defects that confirmed them as being savage throwbacks to early man.

Lombroso and women

In 1893, together with his assistant Guglielmo Ferrero, Lombroso wrote *Criminal Woman, the Prostitute and the Normal Woman*. Here he applies his ideas about the born criminal to female offenders, and in doing so tries to explain the nature of female crime by applying his born criminal theory.

However, this was not a straightforward perspective. Lombroso had already made his view of women, whether criminal or not, quite clear in *Criminal Man*, claiming that they were inferior, less evolved and in some cases no more than 'big children'. Surely it would follow that they would have more of a propensity to commit crimes?

The problem was that female criminals were then, as they are now, a relatively rare phenomenon. Once his critics had pointed this out, Lombroso and other criminal anthropologists were therefore forced to argue that women were less criminal than men *because* they were inferior to them, being essentially too weak and stupid to be bad. Women were so passive that they were incapable of reaching either the intellectual and moral heights of men, who were normal, or the primitive, atavistic depths of the male born criminal (Gibson, 2002, p. 68). Such female born criminals that did exist were much more savage, morally deficient, vengeful, jealous, inclined to refined cruelty and possessed more evil tendencies, as well as being physically scarred with imperfections and abnormalities.

Criminal woman, Lombroso insisted, was a true monster. This viewpoint was not easy to maintain. Lombroso turned to science, and was one of the first criminal anthropologists to use a control group of 'normal' women, and to try to define deviance in a scientific manner and to identify the boundary between normality and abnormality (Gibson and Rafter, 2004, pp. 7–9).

One might assume in the light of his theories that, like many men of his era, Lombroso was something of a misogynist. The views expressed in *Criminal Woman* certainly seem to suggest that this was the case. In his private life he was surrounded by strong women. Both of his daughters, Paola and Gina, were academically gifted, and it is likely that they were influenced by Anna Kuliscioff, a socialist feminist and physician and a regular visitor to the Lombroso home. Russian physician Pauline Tarnowsky was a fellow criminal anthropologist, on whose work with Moscow prostitutes Lombroso drew heavily. (The character of Anna Tarnovsky is fictional but loosely based on an amalgam of both of these women.)

Interestingly, Lombroso's translators, Nicole Rafter and Mary Gibson, speculate that Lombroso was apprehensive about his daughters' growing independence, and that this might explain in part his irritation and frustration when writing about woman's nature. They point out that he also apologises for his harsh words about women, perhaps because he was mindful of arguments at the family dinner table about the roles and status of women and wished to keep the peace. It is worth noting that although both daughters were well educated, arguably neither reached their full potential, being held back by the ideals of their time (2004, pp. 13–14). Paola organised a series of children's books, thus buttressing the family and Gina became her father's secretary (Gibson 2002, p. 89).

The 1880s and 1890s saw the beginnings of the formal Italian women's movements, which Lombroso found troubling, notwithstanding his relatively liberal political stance. Perhaps that is why, as his translators Rafter and Gibson suggest, he was so dismissive of clever women and insisted that maternity was their proper aspiration. I know that while I was researching this book by reading his works, there were many times when I would have cheerfully slapped him. However, I also had to remind myself that despite his attitudes, which did after all reflect the times in which he lived, and his somewhat slapdash research methods, Lombroso was creative, passionate and influential.

Lombroso's influence

Given his sometimes eccentric views, it is easy to dismiss Lombroso as being ridiculous and therefore unimportant. This is, to my mind, a simplistic viewpoint. His theories were certainly flawed but, as Rafter points out, he was responsible for transforming criminology into a fully-fledged science (2008, p. 84). The impact of *Criminal Woman* was far-reaching, particularly as a version was published in English in 1895. It was the first book to focus on the causes of female crime and remained so for many years. As a result, the idea that women who commit violent crimes do so for biological reasons is still with us.

Lombroso and the paranormal

Another of Lombroso's interests was paranormal investigation, particularly ghost-hunting or, as P. J. Ystehede puts it, 'going around the town on the lookout for ghosts' (2012). Essentially, like many others of this period, Lombroso wanted to prove that crime had its roots in the possession of such things as malign and evil spirits. He even studied ancient and modern witchcraft in the hope that his work would help to gain acceptance for the idea that the supernatural did exist.

Lombroso the man

Lombroso was an ebullient, enthusiastic, energetic and provocative man with an interest in many things. I particularly liked the description of a typical day in his life written by his daughter Paola (cited by Nicole Rafter 2008, p. 79):

> ... composing on the typewriter, correcting proofs, running from Bocca (his publisher) to the typesetter, from the typesetter to the library and from the library to the laboratory in a frenzy of movement ... and in the evening, not tired and wanting to go to the theatre, to a peregrination of two or three of the city's theatres, taking in the first act at one, paying a flying visit to another and finishing the evening at a third.

Rafter also cites the historian Delfino Dolza, who writes of Lombroso's almost total inexperience with the practical aspects of existence, his childlike innocence and a gullibility so extreme that his children felt a need to protect him.

Lombroso's museum

A born collector, as his daughter Gina would later describe him, Lombroso began to assemble artefacts when he was still a student himself in the 1850s. These included skulls and brains and other pickled body parts, death masks, skeletons and examples of prisoners' art (Montaldo, 2012) all of which he brought with him to Turin and kept in his house. One can only imagine his wife Nina's reaction to that! Eventually, and no doubt much to her relief, he moved these items to his laboratory at the University of Turin. In 1892 it opened to the public for the first time, and although it closed again in 1914, the museum reopened in 2009.

Sources

I have drawn on a number of academic sources in my research, most of which are listed below. If there are factual errors then they are, of course, mine.

Bibliography

Gibson, Mary (2002), *Born to Crime: Cesare Lombroso and the Origins of Biological Criminology*. USA: Greenwood Press

Gibson, Mary (2006), 'Cesare Lombroso and Italian criminology: theory and politics'. In P. Becker and R. F. Wetzell (eds), *Criminals and their Scientists* (pp. 137–58), New York: Cambridge University Press

Horn, David (2003), *The Criminal Body: Lombroso and the Anatomy of Deviance*. London: Routledge

Lombroso, Cesare (2006), *Criminal Man* (M. Gibson and N. H. Rafter, trans.) Durham and London: Duke University Press. (Original work published 1876–97)

Lombroso, Cesare and Ferrero, Guglielmo (2004), *Criminal Woman, the Prostitute and the Normal Woman* (M. Gibson and N. H. Rafter, trans.) Durham and London: Duke University Press. (Original work published 1893)

Montaldo, Silvano (2012), 'The Lombroso museum from its origins to the present day'. In Paul Knepper and P. J. Ystehede, (eds), *The Cesare Lombroso Handbook*. (pp. 98–112). London: Routledge

Rafter, Nicole (1997), *Creating Born Criminals*. Chicago: University of Illinois Press

Rafter, Nicole (2008), *The Criminal Brain: Understanding Biological Theories of Crime*. New York: New York University Press

Ystehede, Per Jorgen (2012), 'Demonising Being: Lombroso and the ghosts of criminology'. In Paul Knepper and P. J. Ystehede (eds), *The Cesare Lombroso Handbook* (pp. 72–97). London: Routledge.

Acknowledgements

The Devil's Daughters started taking shape at an Arvon course in Moniack Mhor, Scotland. My thanks go to the staff, all of the 'Arvonites' and our tutors Val McDermid and Andrew Taylor for an inspiring and joyous week.

The writing of this book would have been a much more difficult task had it not been for the advice of my PhD supervisors from the University of Southampton, Rebecca Smith and Professors Peter Middleton and David Glover.

Thanks as ever both to my editor Jemima Forrester, who has again guided me through the writing process with her customary intelligence and charm, and my lovely agent Luigi Bonomi for his invaluable guidance and support.

Fellow writers are always a great source of comfort in those darker days when you just can't finish a chapter or sometimes even a sentence. Thanks for being there when I needed you Will Sutton, Tessa Ditner, Tom Harris, Matt Wingett, Christine Lawrence, Zella Compton, Sarah Baxter, Carolyn Hughes and Claire Holland.

Thanks to Nicole Hahn Rafter and Mary Gibson for allowing me to quote from their translations of Lombroso's work.

My colleagues at the Institute of Criminal Justice Studies at the University of Portsmouth have again been a great source of expertise and support. Thanks in particular go to Dr

Paul Smith and Jenny Weaver for some informative if rather hair-raising conversations about forensics, blood draining and female sex offending, among other things.

Thanks to my husband David for reading drafts, offering advice, solace, tea, cake and white wine, always with patience and love.

And lastly, to my wonderful mum, without whose influence and encouragement I would never have become a writer in the first place. I miss you.

HIGHBRIDGE

Phil Redmond is best known for creating three of Britain's longest-running drama series *Grange Hill*, *Brookside* and *Hollyoaks*. Redmond came up with the concept for *Grange Hill* in 1978 and has written extensively for TV, radio and stage, running independent company Mersey Television for 20 years until 2005. A fellow of the Royal Society of Arts and made a CBE in 2004, Redmond was appointed Deputy Chair and Creative Director of Liverpool's time as European Capital of Culture in 2008. Since then he has worked pro bono in the public sector, being influential in getting David Cameron to launch the ill-fated Big Society in Liverpool.

Praise for Highbridge

'A high-octane journey through many touchstones of broken Britain . . . Highbridge sees Redmond repurposing those TV writing techniques. Each chapter is a melange of storylines building to an end of chapter cliffhanger that hooks the reader as firmly as Brookie's go-to-ad-break jeopardy. Dialogue is freighted with sass and politics. There's a splashy, violent denouement. We're back in Redmondshire.'
Guardian

'Gritty, pacy and populated with memorable characters.'
Good Housekeeping

'A state-of-the-nation novel.'
Samira Ahmed, Front Row

'True to form, this book has a plethora of viewpoints, punchy plotlines and twists before we get to the crunching finale . . . everyone packed into these pages is a real as if you've just passed them by on the street.'
Crime Fiction Lover

PHIL REDMOND

HIGHBRIDGE

arrow books

1 3 5 7 9 10 8 6 4 2

Arrow Books
20 Vauxhall Bridge Road
London SW1V 2SA

Arrow Books is part of the Penguin Random House group of companies whose addresses can be found at global.penguinrandomhouse.com.

Penguin
Random House
UK

First published by Century in 2016
First published in paperback by Arrow Books in 2017

www.penguin.co.uk

A CIP catalogue record for this book is available from the British Library.

ISBN 9780099569176

Typeset in Ehrhardt MT by Palimpsest Book Production Limited,
Falkirk, Stirlingshire
Printed and bound in Great Britain by Clays Ltd, St Ives Plc

FSC www.fsc.org MIX Paper from responsible sources FSC® C018179

Penguin Random House is committed to a sustainable future for our business, our readers and our planet. This book is made from Forest Stewardship Council® certified paper.

To those who know how long this took and helped it along its way – especially Mrs. R who has had to cope with rediscovering what it's like to have a writer in residence.

Prologue

Like most people, Janey knew she was going to die. But like everyone else she just didn't know when. She never imagined nor expected it to be outside the Co-op.

Like a lot of people she was simply looking forward to a great Friday night out with her sister-in-law and gang of mates, so had stopped at the cash machine. She had just got back to her car and was fumbling for her keys when she felt the shove that sent her one way and her bag and keys the other.

Lying sprawled on the ground she saw the indicators flash, heard the doors unlock, and realised she was being mugged. As the engine started she pushed herself up and leaned over the front of the bonnet holding her hands out, instinctively, perhaps in the vague hope that whoever it was would stop before running her down. But when her eyes locked with the wild, dilated ones peering over the nodding Buddha she kept on the dashboard, she knew there was no hope.

The Peugeot 207's low-profiled front end did what it was designed to do and scooped her up to prevent her being run down. Before the car swerved right to throw her off – where she smashed her skull against the car park wall. This in itself might have been fatal, but the carjacker couldn't know this.

But those wild eyes had seen hers. And her eyes had seen the face that contained them. That was why the car stopped. Then reversed. At speed. To run her over.

Then, just in case, the car jumped forward and crushed any remaining life out of Janey. Then, again, to make sure, reversed. Then leapt forward over what was now nothing more than a lifeless shape. To escape. Swinging out into the High Street and off into the night.

The withdrawal receipt from the cash machine fluttered and blew in the backdraught, coming to rest against the lamppost that illuminated the place where Janey had died. The latest random casualty of the so-called war on drugs.

The receipt was for £45. It was all she had had. Just enough for a night out. Or a night's supply.

Janey never knew her killer. Neither did Buddha. Three years on, nor did anyone else.

1

Coming Home

The trouble with living in a mediocre town is that you end up having to support a mediocre football team. Something might happen every forty years when, somehow, they get to something like the semi-final of a cup competition. Everyone gets excited. Mayors make fatuous speeches about it being an historic day. Then 95 per cent of the fans are disappointed because the ground is too small to hold them all. Then they get whacked and everybody goes back to sleep for another forty years. But at least they tried. Typically British tosh.

Well, it used to be like that until Sky Sports came along. Now you can see Arsenal and Chelsea shirts in every High Street. And even Man U in cities like Newcastle and Liverpool. At one time that would have been like wearing a suicide vest. These days, it's just kids following the telly, isn't it?

It was one of Joey Nolan's recurring themes as he drifted in and out of consciousness, during his weekly journey home. Back to Highbridge. Where once was a rural village with rural villagers with rural mentalities is now a sprawling urbanised place on a map. A collective of urban dwellers. With urban dwellers' mentalities. Home is where the Internet is.

The town owed a lot to its inn, the Lion, still at its centre but once a famed stopover for its game pies. Then the canal came by and after that the railways, which took the pies the length and breadth of Britain and then the four corners of the Empire. In Rawalpindi and Christchurch they knew of Highbridge pies. And in return people came to see for themselves. This tiny village that supplied the Empire with pies. And so the street market that sold the pies grew. To become a thing in itself.

Joey grinned when he recalled this bit of history. How where he lived was because someone, at some time, made a great pie. But everything has to start with one idea, he mused, just as the train crossed the motorway. The latest transport revolution, with the strings of pearls and rubies of commuter traffic stretching into the distance. No time for buying pies or napping in that lot, he thought, starting to stir himself as he knew it was now only a few minutes to where the Romans once paused, as did the Saxons, long before it had become the site for a new town, complete with its own industrial estate built not on any entrepreneurial instinct, like that of the piemakers, but from a post-Second World War recovery plan and managed economy.

Out went rationing and dried bananas and in came nylons and the transistor. Gone was rural deference and knowing one's place, replaced by the promise of a welfare state and the white heat of technology where people never had it so good. Or so everyone thought.

For a decade or two they made white goods, nuclear components and secretive parts for the military. But with old technology. And an increasingly expensive as well as increasingly unwilling workforce. The signs of decline were there but nobody wanted to look. Nylons and fresh veg were gradually squeezed out of the market by tights, bin bags and previously owned DVDs. The pies of Empire are still sold in the supermarket where the cattle market used to be, but now they come in artificial atmosphere packaging, delivered by tailored Euro-lorries from the factory in Kent which is owned by a secretive family from Wisconsin who promised to protect jobs but never said which or where.

The factories were razed. Industrial estates became business or retail parks and every now and then money arrived from various European social funds to build inappropriate leisure facilities in inappropriate places. Rural idyll replaced by political ideal. But there are only so many discount three-piece suites you can buy and only so many hours at the health club when either you don't have a job or spend all your time commuting, thought Joey, watching the metal lattice of the railway bridge glide past the window as the train slowed on its approach to Highbridge Station.

He once asked his dad why it was called Highbridge and was told it was because it was higher than the old road bridge. For years he believed this, until Sister Maria had pointed out that it had been called that in the Domesday Book, long before Robert Stephenson and his dad George gave railways to the world. Amazing what you take off your dad when you're a kid.

Joey stood and stretched his aching six-foot frame, then reached up for his holdall. It wasn't there. What the—? He looked up and down the carriage but half were asleep and the others a thousand miles away, tethered to the Internet or their iPods. Then he saw it. The luminous logo. Passing the window.

He grabbed his coat and went up the carriage in the same direction, hitting the platform just in time to see his oversized sports bag heading up the stairs, across the bridge, over the track and towards the station exit. With the weary commuters and weekenders congealing on the stairs and the train still blocking the route across the tracks, Joey decided to go under them. Over the fence into the overflow car park, down the slope and through the underpass.

As Joey turned into the underpass, a couple of miles away, on the hill overlooking Highbridge, his lifelong friend and brother-in-law, Luke Carlton, was pressing his weather-worn face against the buffer, looking down the scope of a Barrett M82A1 suppressed sniper rifle. 'Where'd Billy get this?' he asked.

'Where'd you think? He's just got back home.'

'God Bless America. God Bless al-Qaeda,' whispered Luke, as he turned the ring on the Leupold scope to bring the fat target in the chippy into sharp focus. Nearly a mile away. One squeeze. No frying tonight.

Just under a mile from Luke, on the other side of the hill, Joey's brother Sean was coddling his suntanned face in thick Egyptian cotton as he emerged from his waterfall shower. As always, Sean took too long in the shower for the environmentalists but he reckoned he'd already put in a life's worth of sacrifice as a child, when he, his brother and sister were allowed just one bath a week and then only after the immersion heater had been on for twenty-five minutes. No more. No less. Regardless of time of year, regardless of the water temperature. Now he enjoyed the luxury, probably indulgence, of having constant hot water, his conscience salved by the fact that the water came from a water butt, was heated by solar, used less than a bath and was more fun for two to share.

That would be part of the theme of his speech tonight. Another after-dinner. He'd talk of those memories. The clichéd tales of waking up to iced-up toilets and curtains frozen to the windows. But as he always said, clichés were only clichés because they were truisms. Like, how do you break the chain that stretches from childhood poverty to adult crime?

Yes, he'd give the tale another outing tonight. How he and his siblings had started in deprivation but by their own endeavours were now doing relatively well. How their friends all took different routes but only a few followed a criminal path, and even then often through circumstance rather than choice. And now, how he is wealthy enough to have constant hot water and a body dryer, despite the angst around global warming competing with that instilled by the Christian Brothers, and how the Venerable Bede, the patron saint of writers, taught him to fight for the things you think are important. The things you cherish. Like your life. On the number 10 bus. A memory that took him to where he didn't want to be. Remembering what had happened to his sister.

It was that same early education in survival that drove Joey, as he came out of the underpass and vaulted the fence into the car park opposite the station exit. He came up behind a parked Audi Q7 and, as he passed, tapped on the window and dropped his shoulder bag on the bonnet, nearly causing his wife Natasha to spill her cappuccino into her lap, but then watch, first puzzled, then with rising alarm as she saw her husband slip into that all too familiar purposeful swagger. Even under the bulk of the CAT insulated twill jacket that masked his fit but slender body shape, she could see him stiffen. Shoulders back, arms at his side, fists clenching and unclenching. Then she saw the spin of his hand. She started up and waited. For trouble. For someone.

Two miles further on, three girls were walking down the appropriately named Hill Street towards the equally appropriately named High Street.

'I'm just saying, he's a psycho.'

'You think everyone's a psycho.'

'Five per cent of people are psychos.'

'You just hate him because he's foreign.'

'Christ, will you two give it a rest.' It was the tall one, Tanya Nolan, Sean's niece, Joey's daughter. The one with the ASOS oversized bucket bag. She was walking between her two friends, Becky, the short one, with the now scuffed Stella McCartney Python tote bag, and Carol, the medium one, with a leather Topshop slouchy holdall. All were in jeans. Parkas pulled tight and arms folded, huddled against the cold. They were all in boots. Tanya and Carol in worker's. Becky in biker's.

'It's five per cent are deviants. Not psychos,' Tanya added as she hit the pedestrian crossing button but didn't stop to wait for green.

'Well, he's a deviant, then,' insisted Carol, following automatically.

'What about hating foreigners? That's deviant,' countered Becky, as she hesitated and looked right, left and right again. But quickly.

'It isn't. Deviancy is when you stray from the norm. Right, Tan?'

Tanya refused to comment. She, like her dad, always seemed to end up playing the role of mediator. And like her dad, sometimes wished other people would sort out their own issues.

'You saying that being racist is the norm?' Becky fired back at Carol.

'No.'

'You just did. You said hating foreigners is normal.'

'I didn't.'

'You did.'

'What am I supposed to do now? Say "didn't"? And then we grab hair and have a catfight?'

'You said—'

But Tanya cut across them. 'Will you stop it? It's like a bad version of some big celebrity reality slag-off.'

Back at the station, two other deviants from the norm were about to collide as Joey's bag came out of the door. The guy carrying it was busy checking back over his shoulder so had no idea that Joey was about to stand in front of him; no idea that Joey was pulling his beanie down to cushion his own forehead, nor any warning that Joey's head was about to hit his own. He went down under the force and a cascade of sincere-sounding apologies from Joey.

'Sorry, mate. Really sorry. You OK?'

This had the desired effect of guiding the slowing onlookers on their way. Especially as Joey knelt down as though to administer further aid. The guy looked far from OK. Groggy. Blood running from his nose.

'Don't move too quickly. Take it easy.' Then, more quietly, 'It's not like on the telly, is it? It really hurt, yeah?' Then quieter as he leaned in. Closer. And flicked the bagman's nose. 'Like that. Looks broken. Hope so anyway.'

Bagman was now starting to look more wary than shocked.

'Yeah. Weren't expecting that, were you? Like I wasn't expecting you to carry me bag off the train for me, you thievin' get. Now go, before I break every other bone in your body.' Joey leaned back, with a cheery smile for the benefit of the last onlookers. 'You'll be OK, mate.'

Bagman hesitated, but saw the cheery smile fade and didn't like what replaced it. He rolled to one side and was already up and running as a jobsworth approached from the station.

'Oi. Did you just go over the fence on the other side?'

'Yep. And?'

'Do you have a ticket?'

'For what? Jumping the fence?'

'Don't get smart with me, lad.'

'OK,' said Joey, handing over the ticket.

'Then why did you jump the fence?'

'Never been one for sitting on them.' Joey turned and walked away towards the car park. He never saw the bag snatcher again. He didn't want to and he didn't care. His body loosened. His smile returned. His mind had already moved on. To Natasha. As she brought the Q7 alongside.

Sean was standing under the body dryer for a last blast of warm air to help dry his hair and beard, looking across to the floor to ceiling mirror. Sandra's right, he thought, we shouldn't have that mirror there. There are other ways of demonstrating success than carrying round a pot belly, even it was all paid for. She preferred jewellery. He liked having a body dryer in his bathroom. The eco-warriors and anti-carbonists would hate it, though. Having an electric heater to save drying yourself with a towel is a bit OTT, he knew. But it was fun.

Perhaps I should include that in the talk tonight, he mused. How the carbonists had started to make everyone feel guilty about switching on anything electrical. And never mind all the talk of asking the Indians and Chinese not to follow the same path to industrialisation that we had trodden, it's hard enough for people like himself, who had had to develop mountaineering skills to traverse from the bedroom he shared with his brother Joe to the kitchen. Every morning. Clothes bundled in his arms he'd go down the wooden banister, then use the skirting boards to shimmy his way along the hallway before swinging on the kitchen door to land on the seat near the cooker. All to avoid having to walk on the glacial surface of the quarry-tiled floors. He'd light the grill to warm up the kitchen while he got washed and dressed at the sink, using the pan of water his mother had boiled before heading off for work as a cleaner at the local Comp where Joe and Janey ended up going.

Those skills were learned because he had passed the old eleven-plus, which meant he had to go to the grammar school across town. Which meant he had to get a bus. Which meant he had to leave the house by 7.30 and be in school at 8.30, while the others fell out of bed to a warmed-up house at 8.30 to walk the 300 yards to the Comp. And they would be home at four, while Sean had to battle his way back across town to get back by five. His parents might not have named him Sue, but they certainly sent him out with a target on his chest. That badge of St Bede on his blazer pocket.

The childhood memory, like all the others, had started to become bittersweet, taking on the rosy tint of lost innocence. A time before responsibility pressed in and grief started to visit. Like every child who wakes up suddenly an adult, he had come to accept that one day he would lose his mum and dad – but not his sister Janey. Even the cat and dog fights he and Joey had had with her were becoming cherished memories. Which was why he was now spending less and less time fretting over trying to persuade the Chinese to buy an extra sweater rather than build another power station, and more and more poncing about, as his brother Joe put it, with after-dinner speeches on the charity circuit. If they couldn't stop people like Janey being killed on their own streets, then what was the point of everything else?

'What was all that about?' Natasha asked as Joey dropped into the car and leaned over to kiss her. She smelt good. She always did.

'Mediocre dickhead in a mediocre town. Product of what our Sean calls the cycle of deprivation.'

She knew better than to take the bait, so pointed the car in the direction of home, via the underpass Joey had just run through. He looked at the graffiti and piss stains and smiled as he let his mind go back to the time he kissed Margi Hewland under there when he was fourteen. That's the thing about kids today, he thought. They never get to learn the shortcuts. No need. No hot pursuit. No door to door. No reading the clues trying to track the gang. Now it was all precision rendezvouses by GPS. Live feeds from their mobiles.

'You have to break the continuum, don't you?' It was Luke's spotter, Matt O'Connor, lying next to him. And, like him, wearing black Gelert packaway waterproofs over his Helly Hansen jacket and jeans. Equally effective in the dark, cheaper and less conspicuous than cammos. Matt rolled to one side, reached down and massaged the scar on his inner thigh. He'd started to notice that the pressure cramps were coming more frequently, a consequence of age. And weight. Although medium build, he'd always been referred to as stocky in youth, then as a bull of a man, but now he was veering towards rounded. One of life's natural sociologists, always quick to find the black humour in life, believing it was naïve to be surprised by anything people do. They are, as he often says, only human, but Matt also believed that every day is a crossroads and it is up to everyone to decide which turning to take next. Some choose a selfish route, others tend towards helping others. Each is a choice. Each comes with its own consequences.

'Take out all the warlords at once,' he continued as he shifted his weight from the scar. 'Otherwise, pop one, another steps up. Slot 'em all. Or, give their women the vote. They'd soon be bogged down putting up shelves and decorating instead of blowing up marketplaces. Democracy. They're going to have it whether they like it or not.'

'Great idea. And end up like us? Not having a clue who or what we are voting for?'

'You never voted.'

'That's not the point.' Luke turned, his tall frame extending a foot or so beyond Matt's boots. He was still trim, almost angelic looking. When he chose to be. More often the angel of death, but the transitions were getting harder as the ageing cracks started to multiply. If Matt was the sociologist, Luke was the philosopher. Which made him one of life's squad leaders, but also deepened the cracks. Understanding why people committed evil did not prevent it. Or excuse them. But it made killing them easier.

'In a democracy, O'Connor, you're supposed to ask. Not sit round carving it up for yourself. The political class we now seem to have are as bad as the herders round their campfires.'

'What did you expect? They'd phone you up or something?'

'Why not?' Luke went back to his scope. 'They've got my mobile. They've got all our mobiles. No point havin' GCHQ, MI6, Echelon or Homeland Bloody Security if they haven't.'

Matt laughed. 'They could just send out a sort of national emergency text, like: Do you, or do you not, agree with nuking Europe. Text one for yes. Or three for no.'

'I vote we focus on tonight's target and sort out the voting system tomorrow.'

Matt rolled back to his spotting scope to see the chippy owner getting into his daily opening routine. 'I know I've put on a few ounces, but he's like a bin bag full of balloons.' Then, without a pause, 'Are we going to slot him?'

'Dunno,' Luke replied and then grinned. 'Do we get to vote on it?'

'Do you care?'

'Gave up caring in Somalia.'

'We weren't supposed to be there, remember. And Janey definitely wasn't there, Luke.'

'But we were. And I was. When it happened.' It was as harsh as it was still raw.

Matt had learned over the past three years that, unlike

his thigh, this was an open wound, but he never gave up trying. 'You couldn't have done anything. It was just one of those crap wrong place, wrong time things.'

Luke knew his friend was right, but it never made it any easier. Why should Janey have been in the wrong place at any time? Just because of pieces of filth like the one in his scope right now. He tightened his finger. One small squeeze. Then he felt Matt's version of the Vulcan nerve pinch on his shoulder.

'He's the bait. Bigger fish to fry.'

Luke hesitated for a moment, but then relaxed his finger. 'Was that an attempt to defuse the moment with humour, Dr O'Connor?'

'Only following orders.'

'I hate democracy.'

'That is the point, mate. It makes it inconvenient for psychos like you.'

The girls were heading along the High Street. In silence, heading for Sanderson's, one of the few remaining independents to survive the supermarket wars, passing the local hoodies loitering with intent outside the Lion. Intent on doing what was always open to question, but typically one detached himself from the pack to stand blocking their path.

Tanya instinctively reached for her phone. Becky and Carol instinctively stepped off the pavement to walk round. The hoodie instinctively turned and watched them, with a power grin. Until he suddenly felt himself knocked sideways. He spun round ready to confront whoever it was but hesitated as he took in the big brown eyes, big lashes and bigger hair as Tanya, apparently busy texting, looked up from her phone, and was right in his face. 'You're in the way.'

Another instinctive reaction, as Hoodie stepped back. Meekly. The ASBO manual didn't tell him how to deal with Barbie on steroids.

'No need to apologise.' Tanya threw the comment and her hair back over her shoulder as she strode away, leaving Hoodie to sidle back to the pack, all of them obviously enjoying his moment of discomfort.

'If anyone's a psycho, it's you,' said Becky as she looked back at the brooding hoodie, kicking out at one sidecrack too far.

Tanya just grinned as she strode on. The young lioness. Her father's daughter. And like Joey, she never realised how much she intimidated people. She was also her mother's daughter and, like Natasha, she never realised that a lot of it was because of the way she looked. Just as she still couldn't accept that she had been in real danger a fortnight before when she was clawing and scratching at some randomer who had tried to snatch not hers, but Becky's bag. And why Joey had gone over the edge.

'Do you know why each generation is taller than the next?' Joey was still musing as Natasha guided the Q7 on to the so-called expressway.

'Am I supposed to say nutrition?'

'You are, but it's communication. Each generation learns how to communicate better so they don't wear their legs out looking for each other.'

'Is that the sort of thing you think about on that train every Friday night?'

'Nah. I have much better things to think about than that.' He reached across and felt for the telltale bump under her thick woollen skirt.

'I don't know why you like these stupid things. They're freezing in this weather.'

'And I don't know why you keep asking. You know I'm damaged. Sexually abused as a kid.'

'Oh, you think being seduced by the woman next door amounted to sex abuse, do you?'

'It'd count now. Just a male fantasy then. But that's it, isn't it. It left me vulnerable. Conditioned. Well, it'd be groomed now. Susceptible to manipulated media images of sexuality.'

'Spent all week looking at pin-ups in the mess room, more like.'

He turned and grinned. 'Exactly. Only that lot can only dream. I've got the real thing.'

She laughed. She always did. Just as she always denied her own looks. Something Joey put down to his mother-in-law, which she would tacitly admit on the rare occasions he could get her to see how she had everything other women paid good money to achieve.

A childhood spent learning to be self-deprecating. A childhood that led to a life of self-criticism. A childhood conditioned by the manipulations of a demanding mother.

Even when she had lived up to the expectations of doing well in her A-levels, her mother had criticised the fact that she only got one A while her friend got three. Because Natasha was brighter. Which she was, but suffered the irony of a proud mother suffocating her by being over-demanding. She had decided not even to try for university, opting instead for one of the new regional colleges of further education, where she studied graphic design. Her mother, being a nurse, had wanted Natasha to do better and become a doctor, although her father, on being told of her plans, was delighted, having always regretted becoming a quantity surveyor rather than an architect. He wanted someone to take up his lost spark of creativity.

Unfortunately, his untimely death from cancer meant he never lived to see her achieve her degree, and was probably also a reason why she took up with Joey. He was strong and supportive when she needed someone to fill the gaping hole in her life. She stayed with him because she got to lean on him, not his reputation. And discovered the man she then fell for. And he had been smitten from the moment she showed any interest.

Joe squeezed her thigh and looked across. Like him, she was buttoned up, head to toe against the cold. But instead of Screwfix work gear, an All Saints Fin jacket masked the heavy, but practical sweater and skirt, creating an almost androgynous shape. Only the waves of perfume and hair suggesting what may lie beneath. The deep brown hair she had passed on to Tanya, but because of which, she was always threatening to cut it short. The eyes. Also brown, but always bright, sharp and mischievous that pointed to her Irish ancestry. As did her tongue. Never short of an opinion on anything and everything, but usually correct, and an ability to talk to anyone, about anything, which was probably one of the main things Joey admired about her. He preferred to keep his opinions to himself and couldn't see the point of small talk, accepting that if it were not for Tasha, their social life would be extremely limited.

This train of thought looped back to his mother-in-law. 'How's your mum been this week?' he turned and asked.

Natasha gave a weak, sad smile. 'OK. Just OK. Sometimes she's as bright as she always was. Then . . .' She gave a sad shrug. 'But it's only going to get worse. And I'm still learning to go with the flow, as the doctors said. Correcting her all the time only makes things worse.'

'They sure she's losing it? My mum's always been scatty. And she's nursing people with dementia.'

That started to bring the smile back to Natasha's face, helped by Joey reaching across and stroking the back of her neck. 'I love you, you know. Especially for coping when I'm not here to share the load.'

She didn't reply. She didn't really want appreciation.

She wanted him home. But she didn't want to tell him that. They had made the decision for the future. So she just reached up and held his hand in acknowledgement.

This was something else her mother had drummed into her. Almost contrary to the self-deprecation. Independence. An independence that made her more than a mental match. He could quite easily have ended up on the wrong side of the law, if she hadn't been there to drag him back and keep at him to finish his electrical qualifications. She earned enough working at the local newspaper to allow him time to go on the training courses, until it was bought by a national group and things were rationalised. Which meant she was out of a job, but fortunately just when Joey started bringing in cash. She did the books during the first pregnancy, with Tanya, and had done so ever since, with a bit of coaching from her brother-in-law Sean. That developed into doing the design work for the garden centre promotional literature, which in turn led to a few other small contracts and from that she started selling cards and wall prints on Etsy.

Joey was still looking at her with all this running through his mind. Brains and beauty. It didn't get much better. She could easily have won the last Rose Queen title, before it was hounded off the social calendar by the townies, just as much as his sister-in-law Sandra, Sean's wife, but Tasha never had any interest. Unlike Sandra, who still thought she held the title, which she did in a way, so appeared to dress the part. Joey sometimes thought it would be nice if Tasha dressed more girlie, but always ended up smiling. If she put herself out more she wouldn't do this for him. He ran his fingers over the armoured cloth that disguised the suspender clasp again, causing her to glance across with a knowing, wicked grin. She could turn it on when she wanted to. But only for them.

'You'll have to control yourself tonight, though. Tanya's having a gathering.'

Joey groaned. 'What happened to wanting her freedom and individuality? And staying out later than I say she can?'

'Something to do with them all wanting to protect Becky from some bloke who's been pestering her.'

'Oh great, not only babysitting but we're likely to have a bunch of blokes round on the sniff.'

'Think it's a bit heavier than that. And anyway, thought you always wanted to know where she was.'

'I can know without having her in the house on a Friday night. They must have figured that out by now. Alex and Ross go to their mates. Lucy goes to ballet. Tanya thinks she's sneaking off to the pub without me knowing. That's what Friday nights are about. It's taken quite a bit of logistics to get that organised.'

'Calm down. Another few hours won't kill you. And as far as the kids are concerned we don't do sex. Urrghhhh. Gross.'

Joey smiled. Another of life's great truisms. And,

unfortunately, more and more so as the kids got older. Kids really are life's natural contraceptives.

Breaking the chain. Yes, that would be the theme for tonight, Sean thought as he reached for his dress shirt. How we need to break the cycle of deprivation that leads people into petty crime and anti-social behaviour, that in turn condemns them to a life of missed opportunity and social prejudice. Once branded, how do you redeem yourself?

Yes, he'd talk about his own life, and perhaps that of his siblings. How they had come from the wrong side of town but had taken different paths. Both he and his younger brother Joe had passed the old eleven-plus and while he thrived at St Bede's, Joe didn't. Despite what Joe said about not hacking the academic bit, long disproved by breezing through his electrical qualifications, the truth, as Sean had included in his Best Man's speech at Joey's wedding, was that he dropped out because he was a randy sod and didn't fancy turning gay.

His sister Janey on the other hand, he had found out later in life, had pre-empted any such decisions by deliberately failing the eleven-plus so she wouldn't be separated from her friends. All of whom she stayed in touch with and all of whom turned up at the funeral. Who was really the brightest of them all?

Yes, Sean thought, his own life story, from college-pud, uni-geek and accountant to hippy garden centre owner has always gone down well at the charity dinners, especially since his sister Janey's senseless death. Tonight was about yet another anti-drugs initiative. How many had he been to? Better detection. Better prevention. Better education. Better medical help. Better counselling. He'd given up counting, but the emerging pattern was obvious. Whatever people tried, it didn't seem to work. Usually because of two things. Short-term thinking and independent action. Not thinking far enough ahead, and therefore not providing adequate funding, and trying to work in isolation. But there was never one reason for people getting into difficulties, so how could there be one solution?

Tonight, it was Stepping Stones. Or 'stepping on stone-heads', as Joe called it, but in reality a charity that wanted to give ex-offenders somewhere to go. Where they could get help with their particular problems and avoid slipping back into the drug culture. Not to find an immediate answer, but to be guided towards people who might have one. Sean got it. Give them a stepping stone. A place they can gather their thoughts and get themselves together. To work out what to do next and not, as brother Joe was quick to point out, where to get their next score.

Sean knew that his brother was playing back popular sentiment, and within it a fundamental truth – most ex-offenders did reoffend – which was why tonight he would float a new idea. Instead of wasting time constantly trying to raise money, like tonight, to help the charity, so they could go on trying to persuade employers to take on ex-offenders, why not make it a statutory obligation? Part of the rehabilitation ethos of the judicial system. All local authorities must give ex-offenders a job on release. It was simple. If any organisation should have the capacity to handle ex-offenders, it should be the public services. But another great public truth stood in the way. Would any politician have the guts to do it? Probably not. Sean zipped up his trousers and fastened the waistband. Tighter than last time. When it came to diet, he too was a recidivist.

'You have to break from tradition, see, Luke. Tradition encourages traditional thinking that leads to risk aversion and then inertia.' Matt was also still musing as he prepared to slip out on the daily coffee run. The one operational luxury they permitted themselves.

'And this is more of you trying to manage my PTSD and steer me away from my particular problem, and grief, is it? Engage me in the more general scenario relating to the global drugs trade?'

'Yep. But it's not just drugs, is it? It's like all crime. Or conflict. Or corruption. Like when we went over to Basra. Round 'em up. Explain that there's a better way to make a buck than turning over the neighbours. And if, or when, they didn't embrace democracy, hand out a good smacking. If we do it over there, why don't we do it here?'

'Which, I think, is why we are here,' Luke said. 'How far do you reckon that is?'

Matt brought the spotting scope up to his eye. 'Twelve

hundred. Downhill. No wind. Back soon.' He pulled off his waterproofs and slid out of the hide.

The Barrett is generally considered an anti-material weapon with an effective range of 1800 metres but a maximum range of around 6800 metres, although at that distance it was more for harassment than accuracy. At 1800 metres its job was to stop vehicles by punching a hole in an engine block. But that took a bit of time as the fluids leaked and the engine seized. Unless you got lucky and took out a steering rod or ball joint. Every sniper knew that the best way to stop a vehicle was to kill the driver. For that Luke would have preferred an Accuracy International L115A3, but at 1200 metres a No. 1 Sniper, like Luke, could use the Barrett to kill the fat lump he now had centred in his scope. It did not have to be a precise head shot and he could also do it with much less remorse than he had when shooting at the Taliban. At least, he thought, they were fighting for something they believed in, no matter what you made of it, but as far as Luke was concerned, the guy running the chippy was nothing. A parasite feeding on the community. A canker or cancer to be taken out. Maybe not tonight. As tonight was about the explosive force the Barrett could deliver. The shock and awe of blowing things apart. One night, though. Soon. Perhaps tomorrow.

'His face, though.' Carol was scanning the pizza across the self-service till. 'He probably thought it was Buffy Croft, the Hoodie Slayer or something.'

Becky laughed, then reverted to default anxiety. 'But, what if he'd been like that loser with the knife the other week, Tan?'

'As if. That 'tard was Barry Lupton's little brother. He probably hasn't even got hairs between his legs yet.'

'Probably about all he's got down there,' said Carol. 'We can't have this one.' She was reading the ingredients on the pizza box. 'The chicken's reconstituted.'

'How do you know?' asked Becky, taking the box from her.

'It says "made from" not "made with". If it's "from" that means it's mushed up bits pressed into a shape. If it's "with" it means whole pieces.' She headed off into the shelving maze.

Becky waited for her to disappear between Meals and Soups before she turned back to Tanya. 'What do you really think? About Huz?'

'Do you really want to know?'

'I'm asking.'

'I know, but do you really want to know the answer? Or do you just want reassurance that Carol's got one of her things going about him? Did you put this Cookie Dough in?'

'You sound just like my mum.'

'Did you?'

'Er, yeah. Sorry. It's just that . . .'

'What, missing your Pharaoh and need some comfort food?'

'I'll put it back.'

'No way. It means I can keep my Cookies 'n' Cream.'

'You didn't answer my question.'

'You didn't answer mine.'

'You sure you really want to know?'

'Well, yeah.'

'OK. He's creepy.'

Tanya was right. It wasn't exactly the response Becky was hoping for.

'Is she in all night then?' Joey finally asked, as the Q7 came across the old Victorian swing bridge into Highbridge. He had been sitting brooding, trying to figure out how to salvage something of his planned evening. He'd been thinking it through since Wednesday when she told him both the boys were going to be going on sleepovers. With Lucy out at ballet, for the first time in God only knew when they would have the house to themselves for most of the evening. They usually only had an hour by the time they got back from the station, before he had to start his regular Friday night taxi collection service. Stay by the corner. Don't speak. Just drive. He knew the drill.

'Don't know. She just said that she and Carol were trying to keep Becky occupied and away from some bloke.' Natasha leaned over and squeezed his thigh. 'But thanks for the flowers.'

'Why, though?'

'Because yellow roses are my favourite. And because I love the way you love me.'

Joey looked across and she had that wicked grin again. 'And I love the way you love me too, but why is Tanya keeping Becky under house arrest?'

'She'll tell me tomorrow.'

Joey gave an exaggerated exhale of breath. Fed up. 'My daughter's sabotaging my homecoming and you haven't even got the inside track to gossip about. Should have agreed to go out with the lads over to—' But he was interrupted by a sharp blow to his right biceps as Natasha's left arm lashed out, just as he spotted something, or someone, on the side of the road. 'Pull over. Just for a sec.'

'What for?'

As soon as she stopped he was out of the car and moving towards the Costa. Natasha turned to see Joey hand-clutching and shoulder-hugging Matt who was now carrying a couple of to-go's and a panini bag.

'How's it going?' Joey asked.

Matt glanced across at the car and waved to Natasha as he spoke.

'Does she, er, know anything?'

Joe just looked at him. Get real.

Matt nodded. 'Friggin' freezing up there in the wind, but we've got the fatty's POLO down to the minute. We know more about him than Tesco do on his Club Card.'

'Er, what's his POLO?' Joey asked, once again bewildered by jargon.

'Pattern of Life Operations. Another yankism,' Matt explained.

'You positive it's happening?' Joey asked.

'Positive,' Matt confirmed. 'He slips the gear in with the fish and chips. Just have to know the right combo to ask for.'

'What? Fish and chips with salt, vinegar and throw in a bit of crack?'

'It's slightly more subtle than that. But, basically, yeah. Cod is coke. Has a "C". Haddock has a "H". For smack.' Then in answer to Joey's puzzled look, 'Yeah. Smack. Heroin.'

'What would I get if I asked for jellied eels?'

'Funny looks. You been down sarf too long,' Matt replied.

'Tell me about it,' Joey replied with a giveaway glance at the Q7. An obvious raw nerve. 'But how's it work?'

'Like all scams.' Matt grinned. 'Dead simple when you figure it out. They have their own currency.'

'What?'

'Druggie meets the banker round the corner. Druggie hands over cash. Banker hands back note. Any note. Fiver, tenner, whatever, right? Druggie then gets back same note with a C or H or whatever on it.' He held out his arms. Simple. Then chuckled again. 'But not J. And they couldn't do cockles either. 'Cos that'd have to be C too.'

'Could be an E, though,' Joe offered. 'For eels.'

Matt nodded, taking the point. 'Or E for Ecstasy, I

suppose. Anyhow, druggie then takes marked note in to Fatty, say, one with a C. "Cod and chips" he asks for, but Fatso waits until he sees the C note. Recognises a real customer and gives him a special.'

'Neat. But how does he pass over the goods without others seeing him?' Joey asked.

'We haven't got that next link in the chain. But we will,' he added with a grin as he directed Joey's eyes to the Q7. 'Haven't you got things to do?'

Joey glanced back at the waiting car. Like Natasha earlier, he could see a familiar look and read familiar body language. Even at 20 yards. 'Er, yeah. I'll catch you tomorrow.'

Sean was looking for his cufflinks. He wore them so infrequently he never remembered where he put them. And he couldn't ask Sandra because she would remind him of the fact. Sod it, he thought, and as usual folded back the cuffs. He spent a fortune on Sandra's jewellery but never bothered much himself. He liked watches, though. She had bought him a gold Longines out of their first year's dividend from the garden centre, but he got so fed up taking it off every time he had to roll his sleeves up properly that it stayed in the drawer for five years. Then one Christmas she surprised him with a Jaeger-Lecoultre Polo. It was, he had discovered, originally designed in 1931 for actually playing polo. As such, the watch could slide and be swivelled in its case to show only the steel back and protect it from stray mallet attacks. It now very rarely left his wrist, and the back plate displayed both the scars of history and the practicality of the design.

It was something Sean had come to appreciate more as his wealth grew. That the things often seen as the symbols of wealth usually started life with a very practical purpose. True, there was very little demand for playing polo in Highbridge, but the watch survived the rigours of potting conifers, even if the straps didn't.

'I need a new strap for my watch,' he called out to Sandra.

'Right now?'

'Next time you're in having your jewellery serviced.' Then his mind changed tack. How ridiculous was all this? How ridiculous is life. From peeling icy curtains from frosted windows to living in a six-bedroomed house with constant hot water, and wanting a new strap for a watch that was worth more than a few months' pay for most of his staff, simply because he was too sentimental to take it off.

Sandra emerged from the dressing room looking, as she always did, as though she'd stepped off a fashion shoot but immediately picked up his now pensive mood. 'C'mon. You know why you got into all this anti-drugs stuff. Although I don't know why you bother. Dressing up for dinner isn't going to change much. But if we are, do you have to wear that suit?'

Sean turned to look at himself in the mirror. Automatically

sucking in his stomach. 'What? This is my favourite suit.'

'Which is why it's worn out. Too small and . . .' – she playfully prodded him in the stomach – 'ten years old. Wear the blue Gieves and Hawkes.'

Sean let out a resigned sigh. He knew she was right, so turned back towards his wardrobe. 'OK. I give in. On the suit. But as for tonight, everything starts with someone thinking they can do it better.'

'And that's you, is it?' she asked, smoothing down the lines of the Anglomania Taxa dress. She'd also put on a few pounds since she bought it.

'Someone has to try,' Sean replied but wanted to move on. It was a recurring conversation. 'Er. . . But if I'm changing, what happened to the red dress you showed me earlier?'

'Too low.'

'That's why I like it.'

'But not for a bunch of do-goody druggie-huggers. Or having Rupert Bronks from the Golf Club's nose in my cleavage all night. I'll feel better in this.'

'Then why ask my opinion?'

'See if you can make the right choice. And if you still fancy me.'

'You're still here, aren't you?'

'And God only knows why. Do this up for me then.'

He crossed to help her fasten her bracelet but held her hand for a moment. 'The cost of that could fund this whole drug rehabilitation programme for three years, you know.'

'And we didn't work for twenty years to give it away. Now come on, we're late.'

'What's with the we . . . ?'

'And don't go on about your mountaineering skills being honed by deprivation, again. Hard times are affecting everyone at the moment.'

'Says the woman in the megabucks bracelet.'

'And the guy with the Lecoultre watch? A lecture on poverty would sound rich, coming from you.'

Sean laughed at the barbed pun. 'Good one, that. But we worked for it.'

'Exactly. We didn't get here by shoving stuff up our noses, sponging, or mugging other people. We worked bloody hard. And God knows, some days I feel like part of a persecuted minority. Doomed to solve all political issues by paying more and more taxes. Don't we do enough, spending it to keep the economy going? Mind you, I know that's not going to get any sympathy votes, is it? Just as I know you'll want to recount your adventures from the most deprived council estate in the world. But stick to what happened to Jane. And what we need to do to stop it. Cut the liberal tolerance crap and get them into jobs. OK. Let's go.'

There. She'd done it again. Found the nutshell. It was what attracted him to her in the first place. Just after her breasts. And her legs. And her sense of independence.

He had met Sandra while auditing an engineering factory. While he was employed by an independent firm of accountants and was there on a four-week assignment, she worked through an agency and was on a six-month maternity cover. To Sean, out of the two of them, she seemed to have the better idea. She basically worked for herself and could come and go and dress as she liked, which often hardened opinions and various other male body parts. Although he also moved from company to company he still had to conform to the sombre suit and sensible shoes dress code of his almost Dickensian accountancy practice.

Everything about her used to fascinate him. He was captivated by everything from the works of art she would often dangle from a swinging crossed leg to the speed she pounded away at what was probably one of the last old-fashioned electric typewriters. Then there were the looks on his colleagues' faces when he told them how much she earned for preferring not to have a proper job and the fact that, as a temp, he could chat her up without risking a sanction for fraternising with the clients. However, it was only when it was time to wrap up and move on that he realised he wanted more than the office banter. That coincided with a small retirement party for one of the older secretaries and that led from one thing to another and one room to another until he and Sandra found themselves well and truly caught beyond fraternising.

While Sean moved to another job, Sandra simply never went back, continuing to see him until the inevitable consequence. He fell in love with her and out of love with being an auditor. It was not long before they had moved in together, into a dingy flat above a dingy shop, and despite Sandra's ability to see things coming and his ability to add up, it wasn't long before one and one made three and what would become known as Noah was on his way.

That wouldn't have been so bad if it had not been for the night when Sean was so depressed and tired with all the travelling and sleepless nights that he found himself almost hitting Sandra when she insisted he got up and looked after their increasingly noisy second child, Megan. It was the lowest point in their relationship but the starting point of their future strength as Sandra took him once again to find the nutshell: life should be better than this. They should stop living as everyone expected them to live; stop trying to meet or feel guilty about not meeting the so-called standards that everyone else set. Sandra, with her own previous nomadic lifestyle, gave Sean both the confidence and support to decide to live his life for himself not for what his father, mother, teachers or employers expected of him.

They agreed it was daft paying dead money in rent, or even accepting the life sentence of a mortgage as, after working out how much it cost them both simply to go to work, they figured out they could live on less, bought a motorhome and decided to travel the world. They could live, work and eat wherever and whenever they wanted. So they did.

Yes, that was why she was still here. He'd be lost without her. He followed her out, grinning.

So how does he pass the gear over? Luke was wondering as he watched Fatchops go back and forth preparing for the night's business. Same routine. Fresh white warehouse coat: fryers on; warmers on; check the wrappings; stock up drinks cabinets; float in till; shouts at the part-timers to get the food on the go, and then the bit that Luke always found curious. Fatchops would meticulously wipe down all the surfaces. Here was a bin bag of balloons, dealing drugs in a chippy, but with an obsession with cleanliness.

They'd been watching him for about two weeks now and he never varied. The first thing he did when opening up and the last thing he did when closing. Wipe down every surface. He never left it to anyone else. It was his job. His pride and joy.

Luke's train of thought was interrupted by the vibration of his phone. He looked. Matt was on the path on his way to the hide. A moment or two later he slid in and handed a latte and panini to Luke. Luke nodded thanks and then nodded towards the Barrett. 'Do you think Fatso's ambition, when he was growing up tending chickens or goats or sheep or whatever his family did back in the Albanian mountains, was always to run a chippy in a crappy northern British town?'

'Probably lay on a hill not unlike this one and longed

for it,' Matt replied, as he rolled over to reposition the spotting scope.

'Yeah, like I always wanted to run a hamburger stall in Rhyl.'

Matt had now refocused the scope. 'He does take a pride in his work though, doesn't he?'

'Yeah, but he didn't get that scar down the side of his face because he missed a grease spot somewhere. Saw a few of those in Kosovo, which is just across the border from where Mr Sheen there was daydreaming about having his own chippy.'

'So what was that about. Back there.'

'Oh, just asking what Luke was up to over the weekend.' Joey replied, then quickly added, 'He wants me to look at the electrics up at the cottage.'

'How long's he staying then?' Natasha asked.

'How'd you mean?' Joey tensed, having known this moment would come.

'Luke never usually hangs around this long. Comes back for the anniversary then goes.'

'Yeah. Don't know. It's been three years now. Perhaps he's getting over it?' Joey offered, hoping it would satisfy her curiosity.

'Have you? She was your sister,' she asked.

Joey didn't answer. He knew he didn't have to. It was more of a statement. But also a question he had continually avoided. Who felt the loss more? The brother or the husband? When the husband is the best friend of the brother.

Natasha knew the inner conflict. Just as she had her own. The wife and sister-in-law. Yet they had been through it so often before. Let it go. But how did you do that? She knew Joey had been trying. Luke had. They all had. But now she sensed something else was going on.

'Just seems odd. Him and Matt both here?' She tried to make it casual.

'I think they're between jobs. And Matt just tagged along.' Joey did sound casual but he was making it up as he went, knowing he would have to stick as close to the truth as he could otherwise she would sense something was wrong. She had always been as good as his mum for knowing when he was lying. 'I, er, don't really know. Think they've been working together. Since they were all made redundant in the cutbacks.'

'Doing what?'

'Do you fancy going to the Palace, if the house is occupied?'

'Sure. Or we could go gatecrash your Sean's do.'

'What's he doing tonight? Strategy, selling or syringes?'

'Stepping Stones.'

'Those stone heads again. Have they got something on him? Or hacked naked pictures of Sandra, or something?'

'You know why. He's trying to do something. He's got a social conscience.'

Joey bristled at the implication that he didn't seem to

care as much as his brother. He was doing something. But something he wanted to keep away from her. 'I've got a social conscience. And we won't solve the drug problem by turning out in penguin suits and having raffles at the Golf Club.'

It was a bit too forceful. Natasha looked across. But he was staring out the window, chewing on his lip. What's he up to? she wondered, but knew now was not the time. Instead: 'It's at Treetops.'

'Then the Palace it is.' He reached over and felt for the bump.

She put her own hand on his and glanced across. What was going on in that head tonight? She had learned to give him about an hour after he came off the train. Whether it was the journey itself or the week away, but apart from the sex, which she looked forward to as much as him, he was always fixated on something. Whether they were acting as good role models for the kids? Was the separation worth the material returns? Whether society had its priorities right. How come the town had gone downhill? Should they just take the kids and go on a gap year? She knew tonight's brooding was all connected with the third anniversary of Janey's death and, like Luke's guilt, his own anxieties about being away so much. Especially after Tanya being threatened with a knife the week before last.

And when he came home he tried to cram everything into the weekend, but then became too tired to really enjoy it. He'd always put the hours in, something she admired about him. But at least he used to see the kids passing in the hall every now and then when he was home. The older the kids got, the more independent they became and the less he saw them at the weekend.

'How long do you reckon this London job will go on?'

'Dunno. Another few months. If they don't stop frigging about and adding things. Why?'

'Just wondered how long I'd have to put up with this on a Friday night?' She pushed his hand on to the suspender clasp.

'You're stuck with them, I'm afraid. As long as you're married to me.'

'I could end it that easy, could I?'

'Yep. But it'd be over then anyway.' She looked across at him. 'Because if you ever left me, you'd be dead.'

'Why don't I doubt that?'

'Because you know me. Where I come from. And how much I adore you.'

And she did. Ever since the day he had pulled her out of the snow. It'd taken a couple of years to finally get together but she had known from that day. 'Do you remember that day down in Bottom Edge?'

'When I saved your life?'

'I was only stuck in the snow.'

'You could have frozen to death.'

'It's a five-minute walk back to the High Street.'

'Not in heels. Anyway, how could I forget? Why?'

'Just remembering. I did get stuck with you, didn't I?'

At last the smile came back to his face.

'What do you think the white coat's all about?' asked Luke watching Fatchops buttoning up the warehouse coat.

'Obviously to give the place a bit of class,' Matt replied, before switching track. 'You can tell a lot from a good scar, can't you?' Almost instinctively, he reached and rubbed his own scar before adding, 'Initiation rite, perhaps?'

'Initiation rites are supposed to be secret. Which is why the Yakuza wear suits to hide their tattoos.'

'They do that Yacobutsomething-or-other though, don't they?'

'Yubitsume.'

'Yeah, chopping off bits of their little fingers so everyone knows when they've screwed up,' Matt replied. 'I reckon Fatty's mates done him for something.'

'I was thinking it being some form of accident,' Luke said.

'Nah. Too boring that. Gotta be some form of ritual thing. They like their feuds over there. Remember that tale that squad in Cyprus told us about their tour in Serbia? About the fella who had kept an old wood saw in his house for fifty years waiting for the collapse of Communism. So he could use it to saw the head off the bloke who had used it to saw his own dad's head off? Fifty years. Guess Balloon Boy got off light then, if that scar's some sort of feud thing.'

'If,' Luke said. Matt nodded, conceding the point. Or perhaps not, Luke continued the thought. The real scars are mental. Seen a few of those, even my own. Still, no matter what brought that and what it has or hasn't done to you, mate, even if you did or didn't deserve it, you shouldn't be doing what you're doing now.

To Luke, it was as simple as that. Now. There had been a time when he had tried to rationalise and understand what made people turn to crime or killing or terrorism. Before he met Janey he knew he was on some form of destructive path that he couldn't alter. It seemed that life had dealt him a particular hand. A poor one. He couldn't change his circumstances, no matter what they said in school. He knew at an early age he was already tagged and bagged. Factory fodder. Except that there weren't any. So what do you do then? What countless people had had to do in the past. Live for the day. Enjoy the moment. And fight. Not for what you want, or even need. But just to stand still. Upright. Whether that was walking the streets or leaning against a bar. Always someone wanting to prove they were bigger, harder, tougher than you. They had all come through it. But he had felt trapped by it. Until Janey. And even that had been a fight.

It was like a classic teen movie. It wasn't Janey's dad he had to get permission from, but her brother. His best mate. Joey. Perhaps that was why Janey had been attracted to him. Living, not with Joey, but under his protection. Anyone who went near her was quickly frightened off. Big brother was always watching. Until Joey's fourth child's, Lucy's, christening and Janey had kept on and on at him to dance. She wanted to have fun. Enjoy life and she wanted him to do the same.

She told him she had always enjoyed him coming to the house. Ended up longing for it and then, without Joey realising it, engineering it. You could get Luke to help. You could ask Luke. Luke wouldn't mind. And he didn't. Whatever it was. She was the first person who saw just him. Not a label. He was neither a tearaway nor a hooligan. Just a nice guy looking for someone to love him. And she did. She told Joey before she told him. She then gave him a reason for living. A belief that he could after all, like Joey with Natasha, change things. They could change things. And have a great life together.

Four years of being an item, three years of marriage and then she was snatched away. Senseless. Painful. Agonising. And the reason for living was replaced by a reason for killing.

After that, he'd finally decided that life, as his dad had always told him, just wasn't fair. Now, it was just good guys and bad guys. And bad guys were the ones who made life unfair. He'd also recognised that he'd always known this. Even at school. Then it was your mates against the psychos. The older he got the more he realised that there were psychos everywhere, but you couldn't just round up the posse and sort them out in a four o'clock ambush. They were often your bosses so you got sacked for fighting back. That's why he'd joined the army. See the world. Get a trade. Meet and sort out more bullies.

And, after Janey, he'd given up the rationalising. While those behind the gunsight provided the motivation for what he did, those in front of it gave the outlet for his frustrations. They got what they deserved. Nor did he any longer deny that he had found a home. A camaraderie he had not had since the old gang at school. With Janey he sometimes wished the trade he'd been given was something a bit more useful. Like fixing cars or plumbing. But afterwards he accepted that there didn't seem to be much call for No. 1 Snipers down the Job Centre. But he didn't care. Not the army's fault. He knew what he was getting into and now acknowledged that he actually enjoyed it. The covert positioning. Scoping. Picking the shot. The evac while avoiding detection. He also acknowledged that it was a deliberate choice. Being able to operate at distance. Know and pick his own targets. So he hadn't had some of the trauma he's seen in others who have gone through both sides of the friendly fire scenarios. On the other hand, he knew he had been desensitised to the obvious product of his job: killing. Now he had no compunction, worry or anxiety about taking out anyone he thought deserved it. Like this fat so-and-so in his reticule.

'All right then. If it wasn't some homeland feud. What about the riots?' Matt asked.

'What?'

'I'm just trying to come down to your rather mundane take on life. So, if it was just an accident, perhaps it was during the 2011 riots, when he got it . . .' Matt hesitated for a second or two to build up the expectation. 'He got it . . . On a smashed shop window when he was nicking some trainers.'

Luke started to laugh. 'What? Does he look like he's ever gone looking for trainers?'

'Just a thought,' Matt replied.

'And we could lie here all night dreaming up daft ideas but in the end he's still what he is.'

'A thievin' drug dealer?'

'Which is probably all the explanation you need. The druggies like their knives too.'

Finally Matt seemed to concede the boring point, as Luke went back to wondering, once more, why life was like this.

'Why do we have to do this anyway?' It was Becky, moaning again as she threw the Sanderson's bag on to the central reservation and set the oven to warm up while unwrapping the pizzas.

'Why can't we just get a takeaway?'

'Because it's healthier,' Tanya responded.

'And,' added Carol, 'we know which takeaway you would want to go to.'

'No I wouldn't.'

'Yes you would.'

'Enough,' Tanya cut across again, throwing the ice-cream tubs to Becky. 'Freezer. Carol, plates. And why does he hang out at that place anyway? It's horrible. That fat fella who looks like he's eaten all the pies.'

'Oh God, yeah. And in that creepy doctor's coat he wears. What's that about?' Carol gave an exaggerated shudder at some obscure thought. Although she didn't share it, the others exchanged a look of not knowing exactly what she thought, but assumed it was from one of the freaky downloads she would later try and get them to watch.

'He's his uncle or something,' Becky offered. 'He's letting him stay there for a while.'

'Why, though?' asked Carol.

'Dunno.'

'You don't seem to know much about this great love of yours.'

'It's . . . It's something to do with his parents not liking his lifestyle.'

'What? Like going out with white girls?'

'You're being racist again.'

'No I'm not. You read about it all the time. They want them to marry their own. Me dad's just as bad about wanting to know the ins and outs of everything and everyone I go out with.'

'Tell me about,' Tanya added as she started to chop the now washed salad.

'At least he'll be glad you're at home tonight.'

'It's Friday night, Carol.'

'Oh yeah.' She and Tanya exchanged a grin and then another exaggerated shudder at the thought of parental sex.

'What?' asked Becky.

Tanya exchanged another look with Carol. She is clueless.

'Is that why you find him attractive then, Becks,' Carol asked to get back on subject. 'That you are his forbidden fruit?'

'Well if I am he hasn't had a bite, yet.'

'But you're thinking about it?'

'No, well . . . No.'

Tanya dumped the salad on the table. 'Anyone want dressing?'

'Are we allowed, Mum?' Carol asked as she went to the fridge, synching her phone with Tanya's wireless speaker on the way.

'It's your figure you're jeopardising, my girl,' Tanya responded in mum mode. 'And not that playlist you had at Jules's party last month. It's all old people like Take That and I'm not quite my mum yet.'

'She's into old people, aren't you, Becks?' Carol grinned.

'Oh My God. Will you stop? You're obsessed.'

'You're the one obsessed with the Pharaoh.'

'And will you stop calling Husani that? He just happens to be Egyptian. And he's about twenty-six.'

'That's older than Mr Hibbert in History and you wouldn't go out with him.'

'Mr Hibbert wouldn't buy me a Chloé bag.'

Tanya laughed. She couldn't help it. 'It's one of Bobby McBain's fakes. You can get one for about twenty quid at the end of market day.'

'Mr H. wouldn't even buy me one of those,' Becky protested. Lamely.

'No, because at twenty-five he's not sniffing round a sixteen-year-old schoolie either, is he?' asked Carol.

'What's wrong with him giving me things?'

'It's what he thinks he's paying for.'

'I don't know why you two are so down on him.'

Tanya started slicing the first pizza. 'I told you. He's creepy.'

'Why, why do you say that?'

'It's the way he looks at you.'

'You mean, never stops looking at you,' added Carol.

Becky turned to Tanya. 'Like you never get that everywhere you go?'

'He's different, Becks. The others try sly looks, but he's, he's . . .'

'Blatant?' offered Carol.

'Even more than that. Like, you know, he's just constantly sizing us up.'

'What? Don't treat me like a sex object!' Becky shot back defiantly.

'I can't quite explain it, but he's like the dog when we're eating.'

'Yeah,' Carol agreed. 'And that's what makes him creepy.'

'How, how can you say that? You've never spoken to him.'

'We don't need to. We don't like him, OK?' Carol shot back at Becky, patience finally strained.

Becky turned and headed out of the kitchen, slamming the door behind her. Carol turned to Tanya, anxious, but Tanya carried on switching pizzas in the microwave. 'She's left her fake Chloé.'

Carol looked across to where Becky had indeed dumped her bag, and relaxed.

'Don't kill yourself, Cags,' Tanya said, as she dug out the pizza cutter and designated Carol as slicer. 'She needs to hear it.'

'I know, but I think we made the same mistake my dad always does.'

'Unsuitable boyfriend syndrome?'

'Yes, Mum. Any ketchup?'

'Yes, darling. In the fridge. Get it yourself.'

As Carol opened the fridge, Tanya opened Becky's bag and removed the Samsung. She killed it and frisbeed it into the mound of old blankets that covered the dog's bed. With a bit of luck he'd eat it.

*

'You may be right,' Matt conceded.

'I am.' Luke was his usual dogmatic self. 'No matter which way you go at it, it always comes back to the one answer. Unemployment. They never really focus on that in films. Do you remember *Rambo*?'

'Brilliant film. In my top ten. The first one.'

'Yeah, but if they'd only given John Rambo a decent job when he came home . . .'

'They wouldn't have had a movie?' Matt interjected.

'There is that. But it's like the 2011 smash and grab riots. Whenever you see something on the telly about the bad guys terrorising people on council estates . . .'

'Projects, they called them in things like *The Wire*.'

'Thanks. But are you still trying to defuse any potential build-up of psychotic stress-related blame tendencies?

'Is it working?'

'No,' Luke replied. 'I'm not blaming anyone. Except those clowns on TV who are quick to blame the cops. And the politicians. They haven't got a clue. Never have had, especially as most of them didn't come from the estates.'

Matt just nodded. He knew where Luke would go next. He'd heard it all before. There was no point debating, because he agreed with it. It was the reason he was lying on a freezing hill beside his mate. A reason the politicos would never understand. Because they were definitely a world apart.

They blamed their predecessors and drugs and failing education and, well, almost anything and everything they could crap on about, except the one thing they could do nothing about. Jobs. What happens to 30,000 people when their main source of income, their employment, just ups sticks and walks away?

Luke was definitely on a similar track, as he panned the Barrett to look down over what was laughingly called Meadow View. It used to be called Butler Fields after some long-forgotten councillor but became known locally as Butcher's Field when things started to fall apart in the 1980s. Luke adjusted the focus on the scope to take in the empty concrete slabs where the industrial park used to be.

'What've you seen?' Matt asked, suddenly alert.

'Nothing. Just history.' Luke panned back on target. Noting again the array of domes clustered on the corner by the alley. All-round view. Way over the top for the average chippy. His mind went back to the consequences of the global tides of change that send manufacturing overseas. The local factories are closed, dismantled and shipped overseas too. More shipwreck than train wreck, but they still should have seen it coming. The companies sail away leaving their workforce behind. Marooned. Marooned on concrete islands once built as so-called new towns of opportunities and amenities. Sometimes referred to as overspill estates as they socially cleansed the inner cities to get rid of the Victorian slums or Second World War bomb damage. When the Council did more damage than Hitler, as his mum and dad often said.

'Do you think politics is war by other means?' he asked Matt.

'You what?'

'Never mind.' He went back inside his head. How

many times had he heard that one about the Council doing more damage than anyone while he was growing and fighting for his life on the walkways and underpasses of Butcher's Fields? He saw it coming. At thirteen. When he opted out and left school. Voluntarily excluded himself. They didn't like that. But back then they didn't really give a toss. Well, no one carved themselves a nice little earner and gold-plated pension pot by caring or siding with the people.

It was also another reason why he joined the army. They liked that. Get him off their statistics on to someone else's. Hopefully one of the casualties. But something the politicos always forget. People. Punters. Voters. They don't just read the papers. They live, breathe and create the stories that go in them. Politicians read about life. Real people live it. They also do another very dangerous thing. Well, some of them do. They read books. No wonder the first thing any puffed-up dictator does when they try to grab power is stop people reading. These days it's cutting off the Internet, but it's the same trick. Stop people getting ideas.

'You think too much, Luke. Always been your trouble, mate,' Matt said, puncturing the thought bubble Luke, as Matt had often pointed out, always retreated into. 'There's nothing you can do about the shifts in global capitalism mate, so why bother yourself?'

'What? Get pissed or get something from the likes of that fat bastard down there?'

'No. But you could spend a bit more time trying to fill that bloody black hole left behind by losing Janey.'

Luke turned ready to have another go, but saw Matt was waiting for an outburst. It had been a deliberate shot. Bang on target. You see. People. They get ideas. Uncomfortable ideas. Right ideas.

'You should have stayed at that seminary, Father O'Connor. Priesthood lost out when you decided to join our band of homicidal maniacs.'

'Better than ending up a kiddy fiddler.'

'Welcome, Mr Joe. And Mrs Nolan. You well tonight?'

'All the better for seeing you, Lin.'

'Yes. Those Chinese people in London. Not real thing. Usual?'

'Yep. You know me. No imagination.'

'You just have excellent taste. Be right back.'

Joey flopped into the seat. The adrenalin from the station now subsiding.

'You didn't answer my question,' Natasha said as she picked up the menu.

He didn't need a reminder about which question. He knew when he changed the subject in the car, just as he knew she wouldn't let it pass. But at least it had given him a bit more time to think. 'They're doing private security work.'

'What? Group 4 or something?'

'Don't think they're nursemaidin' prisoners back and

forth to court, or sitting as cocky watchmen outside some factory somewhere.'

'They're mercenaries?'

'Close Quarter Operatives, they call it.'

'Where?' she asked, but Joey just stared back at her. Don't ask.

'What? You'd have to, or they'd have to shoot me if you tell me?'

'I don't know. All I know is that they left the army, well, got their P45s in the last round of cuts. Apparently Matt was one of the ones who had to finish his medical rehab before they binned him. Bit like those old movies isn't it, where they patch people up and get them fit so they can hang them.'

It was Natasha's turn to just sit and stare. And wait. She wasn't going to let him drift off this time. 'So what do you do when all you know how to do is kill people?' Joey asked. Eventually.

'Oh for God's sake, Joe. Don't be so dramatic.'

'I'm not. That's what Luke said to me. They had a look around at life outside the services and decided it wasn't for them. So went back out and signed up with one of the security firms offering close quarter protection. Four times their army pay.'

Natasha nodded now. She seemed to get it. 'And I suppose with what happened to Janey . . .'

'Exactly. What has he got to come back for? Not sure why Matt's in it, though.'

'You're joking, aren't you? He's (a), a lazy sod so where and how's he going to get a decent job. And (b), he's a basket case.'

Joey had to concede with a slight nod. Typical. She had always had them all sussed, which is why he'd been constantly walking on eggshells since agreeing to bankroll Luke. It was true that he had come back to see his mum. But he had carefully never said why they had stayed.

'So, they would shoot people if necessary?'

'What?'

'Your mates. As, what did you call them, Close Quarter Operatives?'

'Er, yeah, they provide close quarter protection as Private Security Operatives.'

'Mercenary bodyguards, in other words.'

'If you like.'

'And they'd shoot people.'

'If necessary.'

'And who decides when it's necessary?'

'Er, whoever pays them, I suppose.' Which was suddenly a very uncomfortable thought. He hadn't reasoned it through before, but if he was bankrolling Luke, that probably meant it would be his call as to whether they killed the fat fella in the chip shop. Shit.

2

Catch-Up

Joey was at the kitchen window with his thumb hovering over the send icon, watching the dog tripping the passive detectors on the garden lights as he went on his morning bladder patrol. Every week he meant to turn down the sensitivity, but every week something else took precedence. It was usually something like replacing the wattle fence panels, now just visible in the spill from the path lights, not whether he would be asked to pass a death sentence on some fat bloke in the chippy. The microwave pinged. He turned and as he did his thumb stroked send and the progress bar started to fill. U R NOT ACTUALLY DOING HIM R U? was on its way. Unstoppable. Damn.

He walked across, took out his World's Best Dad mug with the warmed milk and put it under the built-in coffee maker. Part of the Saturday morning routine. He'd get an hour or two to himself before taking the boys to swimming and football practice, while Natasha got those few hours in bed after a week of school runs. He was always still too wired and tired to lie in. Especially today. Especially now. He looked at the green text bubble on the screen. It was the one thing he hated about the iPhone. The send icon being too close to the keyboard layout for work-thickened thumbs like his.

He'd had a fitful night pondering that text message. Even the sight of Natasha unclasping her stockings had done little to lift his sense of anxiety which, thankfully, she put down to Tanya's counselling session with Becky getting in the way of their usual Friday night routine. He took his pre-brewed, pre-frothed coffee back to the window. He used to spend these quiet hours catching up on the local newspapers, until the kids bought him an iPad for his birthday, just like their Uncle Sean's. It had been Lucy's idea, mainly because she wanted to play Angry Birds but then became one herself when she realised he would take it to London every Monday. That's how he now kept up to date with the local news and saved a fortune on newspapers. Sean was always going on about how daft the newspapers were for giving away their stuff online. Like him offering free compost to everyone, and then chuckling when he said, as he always did, not much difference really. Then again, Sean had said those wattle panels would last about ten years when he and Joey had put them up. Had they had the house ten years already?

Must have, he thought. Lucy's nearly eleven and Nat was pregnant when we moved in.

As the dog came back with a much more relaxed swagger, Joey opened the door and felt the sharp edge of the cold. He wondered if Luke was up on the hill now. I should have thought it through. What else would Luke and Matt do? He kept telling me. That's what they were trained for. Was Fatchops already a dead man walking?

'Hey up. Side alley.' Matt was refocusing the spotter scope.

Luke directed the Barrett's scope on to the alley. Two young girls were being let out of the reinforced side door at the back. It was difficult to make out who was helping them in the gloomy morning light. Could be male or female. 'What do you reckon?' he asked Matt.

'Someone up to something they shouldn't be.'

'That your professional opinion, Sherlock?'

'Yep, but someone else's mission.' Luke responded and eased the Barrett back on to the chippy. Which was still in darkness. 'No target.'

'I'm only here, you know.'

'Old habits.'

Matt nodded. As he kept the spotting scope on the young girls. Just in case. He could already feel his heart rate increasing along with the pulse below his scar, indicating that his anxiety level was rising. Slow it down. Just another reminder. Stay on mission. Push it back, he told himself as he watched the girls until they reached the end of the alley, took a cautious look out and then scurried off away from the chippy. Away from the target. Old habits, indeed. But the anxiety diminished. The old memory dealt with. Controlled. As he put the scope back on the chippy, he grinned. 'I'd never have hacked it as a priest.'

'What?'

'Old habits. Monks. Priests. You rabbitin' on before.'

'Have you thought of donating your brain to science?'

'Nope. Nor could I have dedicated my life to celibacy.'

'You'd have found some young nun to look after your needs. Locked in a conspiracy of guilt and silence. But great sex every Saturday night.'

Matt rolled on to his back again and grinned. 'Sunday afternoon more like. State of grace after eleven o'clock Mass.'

'See. You've got the mind for it,' Luke replied, as he scanned the street outside the chippy. Just for something to do. Until he came to rest on the AMG Mercedes SL500 they'd seen arrive in the early hours. 'What do you reckon that's doing round here?'

Matt immediately rolled back to his own scope. 'Courier?' he suggested. 'But defo someone else up to something they shouldn't be. Won't get one of those on the Mobility Allowance. No wheelchair access.'

Luke panned back to the chippy, just as Fatchops came from the back with another man, both just visible in the blue light from the bug zapper. They hovered in the doorway. 'Door.'

'Looks family.' Luke was watching Fatchops unlock the shop door and then go into the now almost obligatory male gripped wrist and body hug parting. He then relocked the door and went back through the shop as his visitor headed down the street, head bowed in the typical religious pose of a serial texter. Towards the Mercedes. Opening it and starting up without fumbling for keys.

'Keyless entry and quick getaway. Invented for the bad guys those things,' Matt said, as he watched the car speed away. 'What d'you reckon? Asian or East African?'

'Does it matter?'

'Nah. That's the beauty of globalisation. No one cares who kills who.'

Sean tapped the code into the garden centre alarm system, then stood back to let Glynnis enter. She was always there before him. Often there after him. He watched her wander off towards the café, pulling her coat tighter against the cold. Within half an hour she would have the café open and ready to start serving the first breakfast of the day. His. One of the perks of owning the place was every day having a Full Welsh, as Glynnis insisted it be called, as he skimmed through the news headlines on his iPad before going through the previous day's takings, or sorted out any changes to the coming day's work patterns. Today it was the switch from Halloween to Christmas and he'd been pondering on where best to place the Singing Santa Gnomes.

He knew they'd be a winner because Sandra hated them. She'd almost kicked the sample over the fence when it started singing 'We Wish You a Merry Christmas' as she arrived home from her tennis lesson. Fortunately she was better at tennis than football so she'd sliced her shot, and Santa had only gone into the box hedging. Still singing. A testament to its build quality. He'd wondered about putting that on the display sign, 'Will Keep Singing If Kicked', but decided he'd probably end up with too many warranty claims.

As he settled in to the corner table he used as his early morning office, Glynnis arrived with the Welsh. Fried egg, two Red Dragon sausages, bacon, beans, fried tomato, Welsh black pudding, one piece of brown toast, to show willing, a glass of orange juice and a pot of tea. 'Where do you think I should put the Santa Gnomes, Glynnis?'

'Anywhere except in here.' She went back towards the kitchen with a just perceptible shake of her head. Then stopped. 'But I'll have the nodding polar bears.'

'I was going to put them in the entrance as a come-on.'

'That's daft. If they're at the door they've already come. You need to get them in here and spend some money. My mark-up's better than out there.' She straightened a chair, went a few more steps and stopped again. 'You doing that Santa Shed thing again this year?'

'You mean the Grotto?'

Another slight shake of the head. 'Well, if you are doing it, you should put a Christmas garden outside. It could be where he grows sprouts and cranberry and has free-range turkeys. All the Christmas food. Like where he has his allotment.' She turned and left with a parting shot over her shoulder. 'Everyone knows it's a shed.'

Sean watched her go. Late forties, single. Not unattractive even though she never seemed to be bothered about her appearance. She always looked like she ran her fingers through her hair every morning and seemed to have only seven different outfits. All a combination of black trousers with black tops. It was as though she was in a constant state of mourning. She lived alone. No family. And didn't appear to have any other life except work. Sean suspected there had been some tragedy in her past and had tried several times over the years to tease it out of her, but she never responded, always changing the subject. He'd long since stopped being surprised by her. The only thing that still amazed him was why she was like she was. She was the best employee he had, yet she couldn't read or write.

He assumed that was why she didn't mix. It was an avoidance strategy. The less she mixed with people, the less chance of being forced into a situation where she would be found out. She didn't speak much, but whenever she did it meant something. Like the Santa Shed. She was right. And the garden idea was great.

He switched to email and sent a note to himself. REMEMBER SANTA SHED + GARDEN + TURKEYS. He then turned back to dissecting the black pudding. He'd put the Singing Santas near the tools. Like the old Big Mouth Billy Bass singing fish, it'll be the guys who will go for the laughs.

Joey looked at his phone again. Nothing. Radio silence, he thought. He hoped. He raised his mug to drain the coffee, but nearly dropped it as a pair of arms came round his waist. Jesu. It was Natasha.

'You OK?'

He turned and put his arms round her, went to kiss her but she turned away. 'You stink of coffee.'

'You're not usually up.'

'You're not usually so preoccupied. What's wrong?'

'Nothing. Everything's fine.' He pulled away. Immediately confirming that it wasn't. 'Want a tea?'

'Rather have an answer.'

He could already see the corner he was being boxed towards. 'Just missed our weekly catch-up last night because, you know, Tanya and her counselling session.'

She looked at him, now with his back to her, in only boxers and T-shirt, his strong legs and shaped back still trim enough to suit the fitted tee. He'd always been sensitive about sex with the kids in the house, but she could see the tension in his shoulders. 'It's something else, Joe.'

It was. She saw the shoulders drop.

'It's not. Everything's fine,' he lied. But she was silent. Still. Waiting. He was already in the corner. He tried a feint. 'Well, if it's anything. It's about Benno.'

'Benno? Why? What's wrong with him?'

He sensed the slight gap he could spin through. 'I can't remember leaving his envelope.' Joey raised his phone. 'Been trying to get in touch.'

It seemed to work. Benno was the guy he worked with down in London. 'You shouldn't be doing that, Joe,' she said as she headed for the toaster. 'If the tax catch up with him you'll get it too.'

Joey shook his head. 'It's a gift. On top of what he gets off the job. I'm just helping out a mate because he watches my back down there. But I must be getting old to forget leaving his envelope.'

'Or too tired.' She smiled, turning back for the expected riposte and defence of his hunter-gatherer virility, but instead caught the pensive look on his face. 'What?'

The look was quickly replaced with one of attempted reassurance. 'Nothing.'

'C'mon Nolan. How long we been together?' She broadened her grin as she pulled him towards her, hooking a leg behind his. 'You still in a state over last night?'

Another opening. 'Well . . . Mother Teresa and her gang do tend to dampen the mood.' He nodded at the yellow roses as the toaster donged to tell them it was ejecting the toast. It always made Joey smile.

'You sure it was just that? And not the money again?'

Another of their recurring topics. Was travelling to London worth the money? It was good. Daft, even. Even after paying out for the train and digs, he was still pulling in three times what he could locally. Provided he didn't get sucked into the card school and avoided the traditional and so-called swift one on the way back after work or any other overheads. He couldn't believe how so many of them just blew what they were earning. Might as well stay at home on the crap jobs and go home to the missus every night. He looked across at Natasha. She was wearing the red silk dressing gown and matching strappy nightie he had bought for Valentine's Night. As she buttered the toast every movement accentuated her shape. 'Nobody butters the toast like you, do you know that?'

'No one else wears this sort of thing to butter toast, I know that?'

He knew it was a weekend gesture as her preferred choice was passion-killing winceyette floral pyjamas. Perhaps that was it. The others didn't have a missus like his so they enjoyed living the life down there. Or perhaps they did and it was him who was being daft. 'I couldn't make the sort of money I do now up here. Not enough oligarchs or sheiks trying to outdo each other. The bloke we're doing this house for, well knocking all three into one.' Joey shook his head. 'The stuff he has installed then ripped out when he goes somewhere and sees something he likes better. He's changed the M&E spec three times.

Ivantmoreofich we call him. Now he's discovered he's the only one in the street not to have a three-floor basement. So he's got them digging out another floor. They're insane.'

'They're running away. They don't like their own country so they spend most of their time flying round the world looking for something better. It's not about money, Joe. It never is.' She offered the toast and squeezed his hand as she said it. And the big brown eyes said everything else. We made the decision.

'I know. But, well, I just need a bit more time. Get finished on this job and we'll have enough to last about six months, I reckon.'

She leaned up and kissed him. 'You sure? Is it the right decision?' I hate you being away, but . . .'

'You like Friday nights too?' The impish grin was back on his face.

'We can still have all that. But we agreed for you to do it until you had at least a year's worth of work.'

'Stop.' He put his arm round her shoulders as he leaned against the granite worktop next to her. 'It's the right decision. I'm coming back. I don't want to miss the kids growing up just so we can have a self-loading singing toaster.'

He didn't have to mention that it was also a result of the recent scare over Tanya with a knife and that he would never be able to cope if something did actually happen to her when he was away. He knew what it was like to be the brother. Had seen how it chewed up Luke as the husband. No matter what sort of world-weary faces they had put on over Janey. What would it be like as the father? Instead of mentioning this, he simply tightened his squeeze on Natasha's shoulders.

She grinned and pushed her body more into his. 'It does match the food mixer, though.'

'It does. And it makes us smile.'

'Especially if we can still have our Friday nights.'

She pulled herself round, into his chest, never appreciating that her hair nearly suffocated him every time she did this. But he thought it would be a nice way to go.

'We've got a couple of hours before you have to go and get the boys.'

'What about the girls?'

'They won't surface until at least the shops open.' She reached up and kissed him quickly. 'But brush your teeth first.'

She turned and headed out the door, he ditched the coffee down the sink then turned to follow but saw her quickly return with a frustrated grin on her face as Tanya came hurrying into the kitchen, still in a hooded jersey sleep shirt, and across to the dog basket. 'Move, Roscoe.'

Joey looked at Natasha, who was now trying to suppress a giggle, then back at Tanya. 'What are you doing?'

'Becky's phone.' She waved it as she went across to switch the kettle on while flicking through the phone and apparently deleting text messages.

'Should you be doing that?' asked Joey.

'Should you two be walking round in your undies with the house full of my friends?'

It was a more pertinent point. Joey turned to Natasha, now really struggling to contain herself. She grabbed his arm and dragged him to the door as Tanya curled her lip and threw a parting shot. 'And remember. There's only a stud and plaster wall between you and us.'

Out in the hall Joey turned to Natasha. What now? She just giggled again and dragged him upstairs, towards the spare room. At the far end of the landing. No, Joey thought, life is not all about money.

'It just takes one.' It was Matt, breaking open a fruit breakfast bar from the Vestey Army Ration Pack they had brought with them. 'One bad apple. The whole barrel's toast. Toasted apples, I suppose. Do you want the porridge?'

Luke took another sweep along the street. All quiet. He glanced at his watch. It would be another half-hour before the van that dropped off the spuds and stuff. Every day. 10.30, give or take a minute or so. They had been eyeballing Fatchops for three weeks now. Clocking his lifestyle POLO. His timings. His habits. And he had them. Most people do and they don't even know it. How they get up in the morning. Which ball or breast they scratch first. Which curtain they open first. Whether it's tea or coffee. Whether they get dressed and eat, or eat and dress. Whether they pick up a newspaper before breakfast, or on their way out. Once you have it clocked it's just a question of waiting for all the other stuff to fall into place. Whether the postman, milkman or paper lad delivers on time. Is early or late. Too early and they might knock the routine. Too late and they discover the body and it all kicks off too early. He rolled to face Matt.

'Yep. Creature of habit. We all are. Even your toasted apples. Clock their habits. And here we are. Same brekkie every morning.'

'Not much choice in these things,' Matt countered. 'But doubt anyone'll slot us if we opt for the Chicken Masala before sun up. And if these packs weren't so bloody expensive I'd probably just live on them at home. Always had a ten-man box in me dad's shed. Before he popped his clogs. Just in case. Got a new one every summer and me and the old fella would scoff the old one when we went fishing. Especially after me mum went and he didn't have anyone nagging him.'

Luke looked across and saw the watery eye and the habitual rub of his scar. He was not as hard as he tried to make out, so decided to move the conversation on. 'I thought you told me not to worry about the shifts in global capitalism.'

'It's not global capitalism I fret about, mate.' Matt sniffed, pulling himself out of his memories. 'It's the greedy gets in the union suits who have worked out they can bring the country to a standstill by stopping the overnight deliveries. Imagine if Fatty down there didn't get his regular supply of spuds?'

'People could be healthier?'

'It's not his spuds that's killing people. Otherwise we wouldn't be up here freezing our nuts off.'

'You reckon a ten-day box is enough, do you?'

'Yeah. Two days of posturing. Two days to mobilise the troops to step in. If necessary. Two more of huffing and puffing. Two days for some sort of deal to be made. Two days to get back to normal.'

'Still a bit tight.'

'Nah. You're forgetting the panic buying. Shops'll know before anyone that a strike's on its way. They'll overstock because they know the public are stupid. Whack a couple of pence on here and there. Get rid of everything in the panic buying running up to the strike. Big boost to profits. Then, lay off all the casuals for a week. Saving on wages. Only ones who lose, as usual, are the ones in the front line. Not the suits. It'll be the bloody delivery drivers. But hasn't that always been the way?'

Luke looked across at Matt finishing off the breakfast bar. He never ceased to amaze. 'This the sort of thing you think about when we go dark?' he asked.

'I'm always dark me mate.'

'True. But is it?'

'Actually, it's usually only when I'm lying frozen in a tank track for fourteen hours trying not to be seen by some goatherd with his standard issue AK-47 and pondering on what service I am actually doing for our beloved country, while some dickhead with a company credit card is swanning round the country trying to get paternity leave or something for his members. Things do tend to come into focus then. Until the sun goes down. And we take off again. And I know why I chose what I do. Did. Just wish they'd be a bit more grateful. That's all.'

'Part of the deal though, isn't it. Keep them safe in their beds?' Luke asked.

'Oh yeah. So they can get their legs over and have more kids so they can get more paternity leave. All coming into focus now. Democracy.'

'Never have so many been so lucky because of so few?'

'You got that off the bog wall in Helmand.'

'I did.'

'How long d'you reckon? Before we pop Fatty?'

'As soon as we find out how he's passing the stuff over.'

Tanya heard the creak of the ceiling boards as she finished cleaning up Becky's phone. She let a slight sigh escape as she shook her head. Typical. They sneak along to the guest room, forgetting it's above the kitchen. She brushed Becky's phone across the butter, tossed it over to Roscoe who initially eyed it with suspicion until his nose, then tongue, registered the butter. As he licked away Tanya reached for her own phone, then smiled at a message. T'HOUSE? 9-ISH? It was the local name for the pub now known as the Sandstone Box. Originally called T'House at Cross it was a 500-year-old former coaching inn that marked the eastern approach to the town. It was built in sandstone blocks that matched the cross opposite its front door, the monument to the old Abbey that once stood on the site.

In the late 1990s old Jim Mulligan, whose family had owned T'House for three generations, finally decided he had had enough trying to scrape by as an independent and sold out to the brewery. Five hundred years of history was immediately absorbed by the marketing machine and turned into yet another themed outlet, the new name aimed at the transitional youth market. Somewhere 'between the sandpit and thinking out of the box', the Planning Committee was told. They didn't really care so long as old Jim got a decent price for his service to the community and the community itself got to keep their pub, with real ale and a bronze, not cheap brass, plaque on the wall outlining the site's heritage.

Everybody seemed happy, especially in refusing to call it by its daft new name. It was, is, and always will be T'House. If you didn't know that, you weren't local. And there was some value in knowing that. Especially as Billy and Shirley McGuire, who now ran it, interpreted the brewery's transitional youth policy as any local over sixteen, as Billy and Shirley knew who they were and knew their families would appreciate knowing where they were.

Which was exactly where Tanya would be tonight.

However, MIGHT B, was all she texted back as she heard a hollow thump from overhead and decided it was time to go back to bed, trying to blank any images of parental sex.

*

Even Sandra, who could talk the leg off a chair, had not got far with Glynnis, telling Sean that the only thing she found out was that Glynnis had moved into the area about twenty years ago. So whatever it was had happened before that. The only other thing Sandra suspected was that Glynnis had 'a thing' for Sean. Initially, like the rest of the staff, she thought it was a crush, but it became more than that. Not romantic, more protective. She would do anything for him. And only the three of them knew why. She had become dependent on him.

Sandra had suggested they try and get her to learn to read and write, but Sean said he had tried when he found out but she reacted so badly that he had to work hard not only to stop her moving on, but also to convince Glynnis that her secret was safe with him. Which is why he had really laid down the law with Sandra, and even then only told her when she was getting a bit too pointed in asking him what the attraction was with Glynnis. Since then, and to his great delight, she had been true to her word and had even helped work out strategies to protect Glynnis.

It was Sandra who suggested they always had a junior member of staff working with her to keep all the paperwork up to date, as it was Sandra's idea to present the menu in pictures, an idea picked up when they had been to Japan during their travelling years. It was supposed to be for letting kids pick their own meals, for which it had been a great success, but it was really to allow Glynnis to put up the Specials Board. And in this she had blossomed to become both photographer and graphic artist as she herself took the pictures when they changed the menu, then imported them to the graphics package, manipulated the menu style and printed out the new versions. Even words like Menu, Starters, Mains, Puddings, Service, VAT and everything else that creeps on to menus she recognised by the font design and word shapes rather than the cluster of letters.

Sean was reflecting on this as he finished the last bit of Red Dragon, then wiped the runny remnants of egg, beans and tomato sauce from his plate with a piece of toast. Something Sandra wouldn't let him do at home. It was another of life's great mysteries still to be solved, why no one had yet been able to bottle that extraordinary culinary mix that remains after a runny egg breakfast. Probably linked to individual preferences, Sean thought as he got up to go. One person's amount of egg against another's beans and sauce. These are the things that make us unique. As a species we tolerate conformity but we desire individuality. It is also what makes us survive. What makes someone at some time, somewhere, decide that enough is enough and go after change.

It was, Sean thought as he headed off, like his brother Joey's dog Roscoe, for the daily toilet patrol, what allows people like Glynnis to slip through the education and social net. Non-conformers who are either tolerated because of a uniform understanding of difference or, more likely, dismissed for not conforming. You can be tolerated outside the system if you don't make trouble for the system. That was what Glynnis had opted for. Something had set her apart from the herd but if she didn't make trouble, the herd would leave her alone. But what a waste of human potential. What a waste of a life.

As he ticked the inspection sheet on his way out of the toilets he realised he was back on the same theme he had finished up talking about the night before, after his tales of boyhood mountaineering: wasted potential. His idea for local councils to take on recidivists had gone down, as expected, like the proverbial lead balloon, although, Sean smiled, at least he had left them with the question: how do local towns face the challenge, perhaps curse, of modern life and find local solutions to their local problems when everyone seems to be focused on national targets and benchmarks?

He had talked about the issue of teenage unemployment being, as he thought, high on the list as a root cause of all the town's social problems. Boredom. Teenagers bored with nothing to do or look forward to, but with an almost irrepressible energy and need to explore the world around them. That was what they were genetically programmed to do. If they can't do it legitimately, then they will find other ways. Like the drugs problem the town was currently facing. Why had it got so bad in recent years? And why did he always finish his breakfast with these sort of thoughts? Better get on and get Santa's Garden on the go.

It was such a good idea he would tell Byron that it was Sandra's. Byron had a real soft spot for Sandra. Well, so did most men of a certain age who still recalled her time as Rose Queen, but Byron was also one for his own ideas. Sean had appointed him as Manager of Rock 'n' Shrub not for his people skills but because he was as straight as a die and a stickler for detail, process and procedures. Every bulb, cutting and bag of peat would always be meticulously documented and every timecard stamped, checked and kept up to date. He was, as everyone said, anal.

It always made Sean smile. The five-foot illiterate café manager and the six-foot-five anal-retentive garden centre manager working alongside each other. If only he could blend them and split them down the middle. But as he couldn't, he knew it wouldn't be a good idea to tell Byron that the Santa Garden was Glynnis's idea. Glynnis would understand. So would Sandra. She'd lost count of how many good ideas she had supposedly had, as well as the amount of times, as a consequence, Byron had told her she should be running the place, not Sean. He picked up his plate and took it over to the counter and shouted thanks to Glynnis as he went off in search of Byron, nodding to the wannabe Mohican haircut who was talking to the Coy Carp, as he did every morning. Where would life be without its dysfunctionals? Sean mused, as he spotted Byron heading into the Salvage Barn.

Joey deliberately and noisily scuffed his feet as he went past Tanya's room, not wanting anyone else to wander out after bumping into Carol on his way out of the guest room earlier. He went down the stairs two at a time, staying on the edges so they wouldn't creak, heading for his North Face All Terrain jacket hanging on the rack near the garage door. As he pulled it on he took a look at his phone. Nothing. He tapped in the code to unlock the garage and just as he opened the door he nearly jumped out of his skin.

'Morning, Mr Nolan.' It was Becky, halfway down the stairs on her way to the kitchen in search of her phone, with that similar knowing but slightly embarrassed smile Carol had upstairs. She was also, like Carol, only half dressed in a tight tank and boxer-type shorts. He had once asked Tanya if she paraded round her friends' houses like that, but was, he thought, given a backhanded compliment by being told no, only in their house. There were no adolescent predators and he was, well, her dad. Which obviously meant Alex and Ross were still babies and he was no threat, but equally was a constant source of embarrassment. A role in which he appeared to be excelling this morning. He grinned, as he always did, when he turned the key in his pride and joy. The boys hated it and usually refused to go out in it. But this morning they would have no choice if they wanted to get a lift a home. He pressed the fob to open the garage door and checked the phone again. Still nothing.

The Mark 2, 3.8 Jag was politically incorrect in every way, according to all the family, except one. It was part of Britain's past and future. It was part of the manufacturing heritage that had built the country, a symbol of its past loss, while emphasising the need for recycling. At least that is how Joey defended it during the family dinner arguments. But in reality he just loved it. It had been built ten years before he was born but he could actually fix it if anything went wrong, unlike the Q7, which required a man with a white coat and a laptop. He also loved it because he had taken it in exchange for the outstanding account on the golf club job, when Rupert Bronks had run out of cash, or so he said. Unlike Sean, Joey was a bit wary of Rupert. Under the country squire act there was some form of scrap merchant, in all ways. Something in that 2 second 7 second thing: 2 seconds to decide if you like someone or not, 7 seconds to confirm. Rupert was about 3.5. Meaning Joey was still not convinced.

He turned into the car park opposite the Michael Greeves Memorial Playing Fields, named after a young lad who had collapsed and died during a school football match ten years earlier. Something to do with his heart. He'd just got taken on at Stoke and was destined for big things, so they said. Tragic. But every year at the town festival they held a football tournament named after him. His dad used to come and give out the cup, but stopped about two years ago, saying it was getting harder to take the longer it went on. So much for time being the great healer.

Suppose that's part of the reason I took up the offer from Luke, Joey thought as he wandered over to the touchline. There's enough ways for parents to lose their kids without scum like him in the chippy. He had wanted to drive past it on the way but had resisted, taking Luke's advice not to be seen anywhere near Fatchops and a CCTV camera at any time. Especially in what Luke called, disrespectfully, his bucket of bolts. Joey glanced down at his phone. Nothing. He glanced up at the hill dominating the town. Nothing. He went over to the touchline. Half-time. No score.

'There's Joey in his pride and joy.' Matt had him in the spotting scope. 'Talk about conspicuous.'

'He's not supposed to be trying to hide anything.' Luke stayed on target, watching the chippy.

'True.'

'And here comes the spud man to give us our daily spuds.'

Matt moved his scope back to the chippy. Luke glanced

at his watch. 10.30. Every time. Give or take a few minutes. The van pulled up in the side alley. As usual. Monitored on the CCTV. The steel side door opened immediately. As usual. Fatchops was out organising things. As usual. Lots of waving arms, but never actually lifting a finger. As usual. Until the end. The smallest box was always his. Wouldn't break any sweat. As usual. Take the box from the front seat. Sign the chit. Dismissive waves. Van away. Fatchops back inside. Barred and bolted. Everything as usual. But not quite.

As the van driver came back from the front of the van he slipped or tripped or stumbled, but even before he did Fatchops moved with a speed they had never even imagined he was capable of thinking about, never mind achieving. He had the box in his hands before the driver knew he was falling. Which he probably wouldn't have done if Fatchops hadn't kicked him in the knee, following up with a hefty toe poke to his back.

'Do you reckon that counts as negative customer feedback?' Matt asked.

'Hmmm. Beats phoning a helpline.' Luke shifted the Barrett to put the scope on the driver. 'He looks terrified.'

'So would I be, delivering to a customer like Fatty.'

'That's it, isn't it? Who's working for who here?'

'The answer to that is probably in that box.'

Luke nodded and went back on Fatchops, refocusing the scope on to the box, now locked tightly under a fat right arm. He just had time to make out some of the lettering before the box and arm and owner disappeared behind the steel door. 'Something . . . t – i – c?' Luke asked Matt.

'Is that something, then t – i – c? Could be attic?'

That'd be something, something t – i – c. Just three letters at the end.' He tapped the scope. 'Like, Op-tic? Drama-tic?'

'Mas-tic? Fantas-tic? Could be anything. Could be just any old box he picked up to use.'

True, thought Luke. He glanced at his watch again. 10.41. Time to go and catch up with Joey. And figure out how to get eyes on that box.

'Why's it all sticky?' It was Becky, still busy trying to clean her phone with the remnants of a tissue previously used during some emotional tragedy in the distant past.

'I told you. Roscoe was guarding it for you,' Tanya replied, as she scooped up the train tickets from under the bullet-, terrorist-, drunk- or irate-passenger-proof protective barrier that kept the station staff safe, and headed for the platform, careful to avoid Carol's eye – she was trying to focus on Twitter, desperate not to smile.

'Urgg. It's disgusting. He's disgusting.'

'You should be used to sloppy dogs slobbering all over you.'

'Don't start again. OK? I hate dogs. Why'd he do that anyway?'

Carol was unable to resist joining in. 'He was probably guarding it in case Pharaoh texted. And he'd have barked if he did.' Carol threw a conspiratorial look to Tanya. 'He always texts, doesn't he?'

Becky shook her head, deflated. 'Not last night.'

'That's it, then,' Tanya said quickly. 'Must be over.'

'You wish.'

'I do, yeah. He's bad news, Becks. Have I mentioned that?'

'Only as often as he usually texts her,' Carol added.

'That's why he gave me this one. He said it would always work.'

Carol shook her head. 'You're hopeless, do you know that?'

But Becky was more focused on Tanya. 'Don't give me that look, Tan. You don't know what it's like to be in a proper relationship.'

'Neither do you. Relationships are not just about someone having a flash Mercedes or giving you a real designer handbag. And don't you think giving you a phone is, well, creepy?'

'Why? He likes giving me things. What's creepy about that?'

'It's what he thinks he's getting in return. What he's paying for.'

'Like what?'

Tanya held back for a moment. Was Becky being deliberately obtuse? Or just stupid? 'He is twenty-five, isn't he?' she finally asked.

'Urghhhh.' Whether she was being obtuse or stupid,

she was now getting annoyed. She bit her lip for a moment but then said. 'And?'

'And,' Tanya repeated. 'Why's he sniffing round a fifteen-year-old then?'

'Will you stop? You make him sound like that stupid dog of yours.'

'That's what he's like,' Tanya hit back. Slightly harsher and louder than she intended. But she too was getting annoyed. 'You can practically see him salivating. Like when we give Roscoe a Dentastick. In the Pharaoh's case it's probably more Rent-a-dick.'

Becky went to respond but Tanya was in full flow. 'And you're already in a deep and meaningful relationship.' She gestured to herself and Carol. 'With friends who care about you. It's nothing about him being foreign or even the money, Becks. He's just, well, creepy. But you've heard that a million times too, haven't you. Come on, here's the train.'

Tanya and Carol moved towards the edge of the platform. Becky had one last forlorn look at her phone. Nothing.

Neither was there anything on Joey's phone as he joined the other assorted waterproofed and anoraked dads clustered against the wall of the Community Centre that served as a windbreak and took the edge off the hailstones that were bouncing off their tightly pulled hoods. 'I hated playing in this.' A voice came from along the line.

'I loved it,' a second voice responded, with a deep growly laugh.

'You would,' said a third voice, which brought another growly laugh from number two, but a few nervous titters from the hail-battered hoods as number two, in what looked like an Alexander McQueen leather parka, was Bobby McBain, who was actually number one in the Highbridge villain stakes. His seemingly pebble-dashed face a road map of how he got there. He was generally regarded as OK, if you didn't get too close to him. Or antagonise him. Which was about to happen, because Joey knew that growl.

'You loved it because the Ref couldn't see you doing everyone else,' voice number three added. This brought instant silence as every eyeball swivelled towards Bobby, now leaning forward to look up the line.

'You talking to me?'

Hearing the classic challenge, voice number three pulled his hoodie forward and leaned back, making it harder for Bobby to see him. 'If I was, I'd have whistled first. Like you do for any animal.' It was Joey.

The line of assorted dads collectively reached for their assorted phones to check the time or texts, collectively realising they must have assorted things to do elsewhere. Most headed back to the touchline, preferring the skin-lacerating hail than anything that might follow as Bobby weighed up his challenger, now nonchalantly looking at his phone too.

'You looking up your doctor's number?'

Joey ignored him.

'Hey, gobby, I'm talking to you.'

Joey waited a moment, then pulled down his hoodie to reveal the huge grin on his face. A crack also appeared in the pebble-dashed face. 'I might have known it'd be a headcase like you, Nolan.'

The two men closed the gap and wrist-gripped, but didn't hug. Old acquaintances. Not friends.

'You still scrounging for work in London?' Bobby asked, with more than a ring of disdain as he fell back against the wall.

'You still scrounging and scamming back here?' Joey asked as he turned back to watch the boys trying their best to play while hunched up and shivering against the hail.

'Doing me best with the hand life dealt me.'

'Still a victim of circumstance then?'

Bobby shrugged with a wider grin. 'Like you'll be filling in your VAT and tax returns as diligently as the vicar.'

'He probably doesn't need one.'

'True. He gets everything he wants off everyone else. And you know what, Saint Joe, I bet I pay more tax than anyone else in this town.'

Joey looked across to see that Bobby was also staring out across the field to where some older boys were playing. He was now pensive. This was not just banter. 'Go on then. Enlighten me.'

'VAT. Fuel duty. Stealth taxes. Every pound I spend the government gets 20p, doesn't it. Every time you tank up your car, ker-ching, they take their cut.'

'You shouldn't have such an expensive lifestyle, Bobby.'

'You mean my ex shouldn't. She's unbelievable.'

'You still paying, then?'

'Too right. Got me by the plums, she has. Every six months she threatens to go to court to get – get this – proper maintenance. She knows she gets more than any court would give her. Just as she knows she gets it because I can't go in there and declare all me earnings.'

Joey nodded. He knew that too. Everyone did. Just as everyone knew how Bobby got his cash. Any way he could. And as Tanya, Becky and Carol knew, nearly everyone in Highbridge had a fake designer logo courtesy of Bobby.

'Sounds like you're about to have that six-month chat, then?'

It was Bobby's turn to nod. Then another nod towards the football pitches. 'Got the lad for the weekend, but the wicked witch says we'll have a chat when I drop him back tomorrow.' Another growly laugh. 'You know the daft thing, Joe? I could have her topped for five hundred.'

'You what?'

'Yeah. Could get it done for less than fifty by some of the smack street brigade, but for five hundred? Job well done. And it'd all be over. Imagine that. I've told her, too. But she just laughs. She knows me too well. I mean, what would it do to the boy. Plenty of other reasons to top people. Plenty of people willing to do it too. But, I suppose it's a bit over the top for a bit of alimony.'

'Suppose it is.' It was all Joey could manage to say as their attention was caught by the noise of many whistles sounding across the different pitches. He glanced at his watch, too early to finish. Seems odd to have a foul on every pitch at the same time, he thought, as he looked across to see something even more odd. Both referees and various helpers and coaches were shepherding the teams off the pitches. No one seemed to need a second coaxing as the mad scramble began to get to the changing rooms, piles of bags and cars before the hailstones took the skin off the players' bones. What was going on?

The answer came when Alex, Joey's fourteen-year-old son, came trudging over. He looked every inch a potential Premier League prima donna although now tinged slightly blue with cold. Behind him came his bag carrier in the form of his twelve-year-old brother Ross.

'Cameron Gordon went to retrieve the ball from the bushes and found a dead body.'

'And they wouldn't let us go and see it,' complained Ross.

Joey exchanged a concerned glance with Bobby, who just shrugged. 'Another smackhead sniffs the dust?'

Joey gave him a do-you-have-to look, with a glance at the boys. Bobby just gave another shrug and then turned to Alex. 'Better tell your old man what's been going on while he's been away earning enough to buy those Nike Mercurials for you.'

He held out his hand to Joey for a fist bump and moved off. They could already hear the emergency sirens on their way.

Joey headed for the Jag, wondering what Bobby was alluding to but not getting much time to dwell on it as the boys were already moaning about the Jag and how long the heater took to warm up.

'Can we go with Noah, instead, Dad?'

Joey turned to look where Alex was pointing. It was a two-year-old VW Golf and Noah was seventeen. A couple of years ahead of Alex as school sports hero and Joey's brother Sean's eldest. 'I'm sure Noah has got other things to do than run you two back to the house.'

'I'll ask him,' said Alex, as he dashed between the cars that were slowly starting to dissipate. 'Bring the bags, Ross.'

Joey turned to see his younger son, still carrying his puppy fat but dragging the sports bags out of the car, as Noah was giving an OK signal.

'You're twelve now, Ross. You don't have to do everything he does, you know.'

'No, but your job's to be understanding, Dad. He'll just give me a right hard time later.'

True, thought Joey, as he scooped up the boys' sports bags and walked Ross over to join his brother and cousin. 'You sure you're OK with this, Noah?'

'Yeah Uncle Joe, no worries. We might stop off at Maccy D's on the way back.'

'OK.' He took out a £20 note and handed it to Noah. 'Thanks, and tell your dad I'll call him later about lunch tomorrow.'

'Er, you could text him yourself.' It was Alex, now busy bluetoothing his phone to the car's radio, which burst into life as Noah pulled away.

Joey watched them go. What would he have given for such a car when he was seventeen, something else he would soon be facing as Tanya counted down the months. That's a few more grand I'll have to find, he thought as he made his way back to the Jag, stopping to let Bobby McBain's gas-guzzling but tax-delivering Range Rover Autobiography pass with a flash of its headlights. Black on black.

'Can't help himself, can he?'

Joey turned to see Chief Superintendent Hilary Jardine standing behind him, in uniform but holding a golf umbrella as a shield against the hail, a wry smile on her face. 'Never could resist flashing the cash, could he?'

It was a reference back to their shared youth. When they had all been at the Comp together. She held out the umbrella so he could join her. Whereas many would baulk at being so close to a police officer, Joey accepted the offer without hesitation and saw that although the years had left a few lines around her eyes, she was still recognisable as the fit hockey player they used to lust after, and still stood and sounded like the head girl that terrified them. Well, most of them.

'You here because of that?' Joey asked as he nodded over to where the police and paramedic vehicles were congregating.

She nodded. Then the smile faded. 'Young lad.'

'Druggie?' He was close enough to feel the warmth of her breath.

'We don't know yet. Probably.'

'Sounds a bit matter-of-fact, Hilary. Common event, is it?'

'Better to say not uncommon.'

'Oh yeah?'

'Yeah. Like fights in the Lion.'

Joey let out a sigh. 'Bit below your pay grade, isn't it?'

She nodded. 'But spotting patterns isn't.'

'Like?'

'Like, we're getting too many of these tragedies.' She nodded over to the congregated vehicles where a forensic tent was being set up and the area cordoned off. 'And like,' she continued, but turned to face him. Close enough to indicate that she felt safe with Joey. Close enough to betray a past intimacy.

'. . . you seeing more of Luke Carlton. Like Matt

O'Connor being home at the same time. Bit like the old gang. Fighting at the weekends. And then I see you and McBain in a huddle?'

Joey didn't respond. He just stared at her and waited. But she was giving nothing back.

Eventually he smiled. 'You used to do that as head girl, you know.'

'Do what?'

'Widen those big hazel eyes. Pretending you knew more than you did, until someone told you what you needed to know.'

She turned away, slightly embarrassed but amused by his recollection of their past. But the professionalism returned quickly. 'And is there anything I need to know?'

'You asking officially, or as a friend?'

'Can I say, both?'

Joey nodded. Then, 'But there isn't much to know.' He turned away and looked at the now emptying car park as the last of the frozen footballers were being rescued. 'You probably know that Luke has been brilliant at holding me together after what happened to Janey.'

'I do, and I don't know how often I can say it, but we are still trying to find . . .'

Joey waved it away. 'He's also been good at making me accept the shit happens thing. Christ, some of the things he's told me. Or, like that.' He nodded across to the now officially designated crime scene. 'But, that fight. It started in the Co-op car park where some, some . . . idiot was pissing against the wall where Janey died. Not just that. But it was the anniversary. Did you know that?'

She shook her head. Then waited for him to continue.

'Anyway, Luke had put some flowers there earlier. And . . .' Joey didn't have to finish. She nodded, now getting it.

'It spilt over into the Lion?' she asked.

Joey nodded. 'It was just verbals in the car park, but when we went in the pub later he was there. Few mates. Started sounding off about why we shouldn't be intervening overseas. Creating psychos like Luke coming back. And, well, he just lost it. I was actually fighting to stop Luke killing the guy more than anything else. So, if you came to warn me about it, Hilary, it's done.' He turned and leaned forward to make eye contact. 'We've got a lid on it. OK?'

She stood, considering it for a moment or two. 'And Matt being back is no more than a coincidence, is it?'

Joey shrugged. 'They do happen, you know.'

She nodded. Considered it for a moment before saying, 'OK. But keep the lid on, eh?'

She touched his arm briefly. 'Please'. Then she headed off to her assembled troops. She still had it, Joey thought as he flopped into the Jag. He watched her stride across the playing fields, remembering how her chest bounced and her hockey skirt flounced as she ran rings round the others on those same pitches. Christ, he thought, with a last look back. Coincidences? How come one of my schoolmates is the top cop and another is the top gangster who tells me it'll only cost five hundred quid to have someone topped? Properly.

Luke, now wearing a Berghaus Ulvetanna parka, was half a mile away from the hide before he switched on his phone. It vibrated as soon as he did. Damn. Same old security issue. What was the point of them going dark to make sure the cell data couldn't put them close to the hide if Joey sent stupid texts like that. Right then, though, his immediate concern was the weather. If it kept up like this nothing would happen this weekend, Luke thought as he saw Joey heading up the road towards him.

'You know, most of the people we take down is not because of surveillance, but because they can't help broadcasting what they are doing.' He waved his phone at Joey.

'I know, I know. I didn't mean to send it but . . . Sorry.'

'OK. So, who am I supposed to be "doing" then?'

'What?'

Luke waved the phone again. 'It's deleted off here, as I hope it is off yours?' He saw Joey nod. Apologetically again. 'And although I very much doubt our chums at GCHQ have us tagged, if it ever comes to someone wanting to take a peek at our data, who am I supposed to be "doing"?'

Joey looked at a loss. But Luke turned to the cottage. 'Well, as the cops have a log of our anti-social behaviour the other week, I suggest we need to have a reason why we are in each other's pockets at the moment.'

Joey finally nodded. Then added, 'Hilary Jardine cornered me earlier.'

Luke returned a vindicated, but wary, look. 'What's she guessing?'

'Just thinks we are up to something. Because Matt's back. And I was talking to Bobby McBain.'

Luke's expression changed to one of amusement. 'Typical. Too busy looking for the conspiracy that they miss the obvious. It's true, you know.'

'What is?' Joey asked as he followed Luke up the cottage path.

'Hide in plain sight. Can't see what you don't know you're looking for.'

Joey twisted that round in his head and thought he got it, as Luke carried on.

'All the more reason we need to have ourselves covered. Got to be something to do with the electrics on this place. What do you reckon?'

'Er, yeah, but . . .'

'What's the usual way you get done in your game, Joe?'

'Some prick undercuts me.'

'Exactly. So, if I give you the estimate I've just had from that guy on the industrial estate to rewire this place, we . . .' it was emphasised, 'We . . . could "do him", couldn't we?'

'Er, yeah, I suppose . . .'

'And that look and sound of your voice makes me think you are uncomfortable with such, what, unethical practice? Which is exactly what your text meant to me. Oh, Luke, surely you couldn't "do that" to a fellow tradesman?'

Joey nodded. He used to run with Luke and Matt. He could handle the clowns on any building site. Or stand up to guys like Bobby McBain, or that skag bag on the train, but when he brushed up against Luke and his world he always felt like some gawky kid.

Luke recognised the look. 'It's OK, mate. Our game's about mindset. It takes years to get into it. Then you never lose it. Someone's always watching.'

Joey nodded, then turned to the cottage. 'You really got a quote for the electrics?'

Luke nodded in return as he opened the front door. 'Promised Janey I'd do a bit every time I came home. Just want to finish it now.'

'Why? It must, well it must do your head coming back all the time?'

Luke gave a wry smile. 'My head's well done in, Joe. And what else am I supposed to do? Move on? That's what Matt's always banging on about. Get on with my life? She was it, Joe. Besides, what else would I do with the cash? Put it in a zero-rate savings account? Or spend it? On what?' He didn't wait for an answer. There wasn't one. He just headed for the cottage door. 'Do you want a coffee, while you give me a quote to undercut the other fella?'

'Is it Colombian?'

'Most of the good stuff is.'

As Joey followed Luke into the living room, straight off the street, as all good artisan cottagers used to do, he saw nothing much had happened since Luke had hacked back to the brickwork and exposed the floor boarding. The old rubber-sheathed cables hung from the exposed first-floor joists.

The kitchen was the only room in the house that not only looked like part of a house, but was actually fully fitted and fully working, as Luke demonstrated by taking a couple of clean mugs from the Neff dishwasher that was colour co-ordinated with the combination oven, hob and microwave.

Joey was already compiling a mental estimate. He couldn't help it. 'Do you want sockets in each corner. Lights switched from either side?'

'Whatever. So long as it's cheaper than that.' Luke offered him the estimate he had stuck behind a fridge magnet on a brand new Smeg fridge. He then went over to rinse out the cafetiere, tapping the head of a nodding Buddha on the windowsill as he did. A Buddha that matched the one Janey had on her dashboard. It had gone when they eventually found her car. Something that added to Luke's sense of loss. Sense of violation.

They had bought them on a trip to Thailand, after she flew out to meet him on a 72. All that way for three days together before he was deployed again. He thought it was precious at the time. For three days they lived the dream. Then it became priceless. Three weeks later she was dead. Crushed with her own car by some druggie looking for the next score.

After all this time. After all the verbiage he had spent and wasted, the questions were still always there. Especially at night. Lurking in the dark. Refusing to be dislodged by the cold light of day. Why? The question. The one he and everyone else kept coming back to. Why did it happen? And why her? Why did she go out that night? Why didn't someone help? Why didn't the police catch him? Why, why, why? And the biggest why always came back to why wasn't he there to protect her? Why was he even in Afghanistan supporting the Yanks? What was that all about, anyway? What's changed? He knew it was irrational. Shit happens. None of it made any sense. It never would.

'You still do that?' Joey asked, having noticed Luke tap the Buddha.

'Yeah,' Luke smiled. 'We used to say if Buddha was laughing, so were we. Been everywhere with me, this fella. This, and her voicemail on my real phone. Which is backed up to a USB in my lock-up. She was so excited about this kitchen, Joe. We'd just been on a two-week search and destroy. The Yanks lost a couple of guys and that voicemail . . . The sound of her being so happy . . . Better than all the debriefs and shrink stuff. Makes you realise . . . Well, did at the time. Thought I was doing it to protect, what, our way of life? Keep her safe . . . Then she gets killed back here.'

Luke turned and handed Joey his coffee. 'There you go. One dose of Colombian. We drink this drug. And another killed Janey. One farmer may have provided both. What do we make of that then, eh?'

The following day, the question still hung over Joey as he pulled the Q7 into the Old Mill car park, stopping right by the restaurant door so Natasha and the kids didn't have to fight the driving wind and rain. Another druggies' den that had been socialised and formalised over time but at its heart was one of history's greatest killers, alcohol.

'Don't start, Dad,' Tanya said as she slowly, delicately, started to climb out of the back seat.

'Start what?' Joey asked, looking at her in the rear-view mirror.

'Your sermon about drinking. It's all over your face.'

'Don't have to. Looks like you've got the hangover that proves my point.' Tanya just threw him another teenage lip curl of death. 'At least I'm here, aren't I?' It was her parting shot and, as if to illustrate the point, she slammed the door and then swung her bag at her two annoying brothers, while protectively escorting her younger sister towards the restaurant door.

Joey turned back to a grinning Natasha. 'Aye, at least she is. Heavy night up at T'House was it?'

'Heavy date more like.'

'Not surprised after what she was nearly wearing when she went out. Or is that a typical dad-like comment?'

'Yes. Especially thinking about what you'd have me wearing, given your own way.'

'Ah – and you were, are, someone's daughter?'

Natasha grinned and leaned over to kiss him. 'And remember whose daughter she is. If she goes off the rails it's . . .'

But he'd been through this one before. 'No. It's your fault. You seduced me, remember. Laid a trap for me with that see-through chiffony blouse . . .'

'It was not see-through. That was the wind, but if that's what makes your memories better. So don't go on about it over lunch and don't get your Sean started.'

Joey followed her look to see Sean's Mercedes 500S indicating to turn into the car park. 'But ask him when he's delivering those panels for the back fence.' She jumped out and hurried in against the rain to join the kids.

Joey moved the Q7 to park up and let Sean stop by the door. As he walked back Sandra was already out trying to shield her hair from the wind, as she dashed inside followed by the new teenage queen, daughter Megan.

'Why couldn't I have come with Noah?' Megan was back on another familiar item.

'You know why,' Sandra responded.

But Megan pointed at Joey. 'Uncle Joe lets Alex and Ross go with him.'

As Sandra guided Megan towards the door she smiled back at Joey, but remained focused on Megan. 'Uncle Joe allows a lot of things that your father and I don't agree with. So for the last time: you are not travelling in your brother's car until he has done twelve months on the road without killing himself. Especially in weather like this.'

'She off on one today then?' Joey asked Sean as he made his way back from the car.

'My fault. Jumping ahead of myself again, with an idea for sprucing up the restaurant – sorry, café – at the garden centre.'

'Oh. Fence panels.'

'What?'

'Nat told me not to forget to mention them.'

'Right.' The two brothers hugged and stepped under the entrance porch out of the rain.

'And we're not to talk about alcohol being a drug and all that,' Joey added with a laugh.

'It's cannabis this week.'

'What, like Disability Week or something?'

Sean laughed, then took a quick look through the glass door as though he didn't want Sandra to hear him. 'I'm hosting a CAD event next week.' Then, in answer to Joey's quizzical look, 'County Against Drugs, CAD. It's a private–public anti-drugs partnership and they've got some new idea about showing people what cannabis plants look like. So if they spot any growing where they shouldn't . . .'

'They'll suddenly lose all fears of being kneecapped by the local druggies and turn in their neighbours, will they?'

'No. But we've got to start by educating people.'

'You should start by doing something more useful. More direct.'

'Like what? Beating them up in the Lion car park, perhaps?'

Joey held up an apologetic hand. But then added, 'Although it would be cheaper.'

Sean gave a slightly nervous glance at the door. 'You're sounding like Sandra now.'

Joey grinned. 'Go on then. How much is this spot the pot plant campaign going to cost? Couple of grand? For a few weeks? A few posters, leaflets, talks and visits to schools and then on to something like "get your three, oh no, five a day"? And when they want to waste more of our cash they change it to seven a day?'

'I get it. But most of it has been raised through private donations.'

'Still a waste of money. They'll never solve anything like that. The druggies, Sean,' he nodded inside to make the point, 'are like the brewers. They're out there 24/7. To fight it you have to meet it with a similar level of resource. And commitment.'

'Which is exactly why we need things like the CAD Partnership. To backfill. Plug the gaps in awareness.'

'It's not awareness you need to worry about, Sean. It's taking away the opportunities. And those who will exploit those opportunities. And other people.'

Megan came out of the door. 'Come on Dad, or Mum will make me have that salad thingy.'

'On our way.' He then turned back to Joey. 'Sandra hates me spending money on these things, but,' he shrugged. 'It'd only go on a necklace or something. And, well, this might help. A bit. So, why not?' He let the question hang in the air before following Megan back inside.

Joey waited for a moment and looked out at the hill dominating the skyline. Why not, indeed. It was his money that was funding Luke and Matt while they waited for their opportunity. It was money he was hiding from Natasha. And how long would he have to keep that up? Luke had told him that it definitely wouldn't be this weekend. They wanted the right opportunity. At least three settled days so that the wind and rain wouldn't compromise what they were doing. They wanted a few good clear nights. The weather forecast was crap for the whole of next week. Fatchops might be a dead man walking, but he might just see another weekend. The thing is though, thought Joey, as he went inside to join the now traditional family Sunday lunch, can I hold it together for another week?

3

First Contact

By the time Joey settled into his seat on the Monday 5.36, he knew his daughter had become the target for some young buck's raging hormones; her mate Becky was being stalked by some foreign bloke; his brother Sean was as idealistic as ever; there'd been three drug-related deaths in the past six months; Fatchops was still alive, and he still hadn't fixed that fence panel. Just another typical weekend at home really. He took a quick glance round the carriage. The usual weekly nomadic tribe of mixed gender and skills heading off as latter-day hunter-gatherers to the richer pastures, or jungle, of London. He nodded to one or two he had shared the journey but nothing more with over the past year or so and flicked open his iPad to catch up on the news. It wasn't long before his mind drifted away from the irrelevant world of sports headlines, political adultery and celebrity trivia.

Would Luke stick with the agreement simply to scare off Fatchops, or would he take it further? Joey just couldn't call it any more. When they were young bucks cruising the streets he'd seen what he thought was a killer look in Luke's eyes many times. When the adrenalin was pumping and he was itching for a fight. Yet, over the past few weekends he'd seen glimpses of something else. But as Joey had told Hilary Jardine, it was Luke who had been acting as the calming influence on him. Until that night at the Co-op and the Lion. That was when it changed, Joey thought. That was when the look in his eyes had changed. He'd heard about the thousand-yard stare. About guys having it after battle. Becoming detached from the reality of war. But Luke now seemed far from detached. It was almost the opposite. Luke was totally engaged. On a mission. And that, Joey reasoned, probably proved he was detached from reality.

He automatically reached for his phone but knew he couldn't contact Luke. He'd have to wait while everything took its course. He'd have to wait for the updates. Instead he scrolled to Natasha's number. Another weekly ritual. ON TRAIN. MISSING YOU. SPEAK 2NIGHT. LXXJ He then went back to the iPad and opened the latest revision to the electrical layout he'd downloaded the night before. The steam shower had been doubled in size, the spa had got bigger, again, and now Ivantmoreofich wanted the mood lighting in the pool to be co-ordinated with the cinema, and a separate ring main installed in the kitchen to run at

110 V so he could bring over appliances direct from the US. That, plus the mark-up on the transformers would go a long way to buying a car for Tanya. Keep it coming. Live the dream, mate. And let Benno scavenge at the weekends.

His concentration was broken as the train cruised through Stafford, momentarily projecting an image on to the reflective black of the windows. Another hour for the sun. Instead of refocusing on the drawings, his mind went back to Fatchops. From somewhere on the hill that dominated the town, Luke and Matt would be watching, waiting for that one static moment. When the conditions were just right to take the shot. Or take him out? Christ. The usual nagging question. How did he get involved? Well, he knew that. The typical pub chat about something needing to be done. And Luke saying he knew how to do it.

Joey glanced down the compartment. There were several guys about his and Luke's age. City warriors suited and booted with their laptops out and smartphones at the ready. Most slightly overweight. Some with the polished and honed look that only comes from the controlled conditions of the gym culture. They could probably run a marathon and bench press double their own weight but how many could sleep for ten days on the hill overlooking the town? How many would he want to be standing next to him on a Saturday night, or on the site in London, protecting his back? He reflected again on the ironies, perhaps cruelties of life that determined who and what you became almost as soon as you were born. We all start from different places but the rules of the game never change. Learn to blend in and survive.

He knew he could no more hold his own in whatever corridors of power, meeting rooms or conferences the suited brigade were heading off to face, just as he doubted he could survive something like Iraq or Afghanistan, as Luke appeared to have done. But then again, Joey thought, one of life's biggest ironies was that Luke probably wouldn't last five minutes on a United Nations building site. A bit like a cop being thrown into prison. Without the authority of greater firepower, he'd soon become an Equal Opportunities or Health and Safety casualty. That was something Joey was determined never to become. Which was how the catch-up conversation had turned to why, in all walks of life, someone usually needed to give someone a good slapping. When you couldn't turn to, or rely on, the so-called forces of law and order or the rules and regs that governed life. When Health and Safety could stop you climbing a ladder, but offered no guidance on what to do when you were shoved into a room by three guys demanding a commission on everything you earned or they'd kill you, your wife and kids and dog. Or when everyone knew who the druggies were but kept saying they had to have proof.

That was the common bond, from battlefield to playing field. When natural justice had to take second place to bureaucratic process. That was what had pushed them over the line. Especially when it came too close to Joey's own front door. When it put Tanya in danger. That's how he had got involved. When Tanya, like Janey before her, had found herself fighting off some knife-wielding druggie. When Luke asked if it was time to act. Would he like him to sort it out? It was one simple word. Yes. That was it. That was how it all started. That one word. And what he was keeping from Natasha.

His phone vibrated just as the train hurtled into the Kilsby Tunnel, the twin vibrations causing Joey to jump. He looked at the text. Natasha's reply. YOU 2. MORE EACH WEEK. MUST TALK TONIGHT. LXXT. Must talk? He looked at the time. 6.15. Too early for the school run, he thought. Guess I didn't hide things too well after all. He went to reply but whilst the tunnel was one of the engineering wonders built by Robert Stephenson on the London–Birmingham line in the mid-nineteenth century, with the gradients, bends and railway bed still able to facilitate today's inter-city flyers, Stephenson never envisaged mobile phone signals. Joey stared at the No Service icon. At least it would give him time to think.

'He's up to something, Sean. I know your Joey. And his mate Luke. He's always been trouble. He was only back five minutes and he and Joey were in the police station.'

Sean was trying to keep up with this trail of feminine intuition as he dried off after his morning waterfall shower. He was going in late, to give Sandra a lift. 'Is all this coming from seeing Joey talking to Luke in Sanderson's car park the other day?'

'It was the way they were talking.'

'Which was?'

'The way the kids do when they don't want us to know what they're up to.'

'Right.'

'Is that it?'

'Yes. I could throw you a "so what", if you like? But what's really going on here is displacement.'

'Enlighten me.' Sandra stood, with her old Armani trouser suit in one hand while she held in her stomach and looked in the mirror wall that lined their dressing room. If the Anglomania had been a bit tight, what was this going to be like after a couple of years?

'That.'

'What?'

'You having to go in and see the VAT man. So you think you have to squeeze into your old business suit. That's what's getting to you.'

Sandra let her stomach go. He was right. 'You want me to look the part, don't you?'

'You do in whatever you wear. Anywhere. Any time. And,' he added, slightly wearily, 'we do own the place. You can wear what you like.'

'I know. But I also know,' she added, pulling her stomach in again, 'I want to look the part.'

Sean put his arm round her waist and pecked her neck.

'I love every bit of you. Every inch means a special memory.'

'That's the trouble. Too many memories. And I've always hated this wall of mirror.'

Sean didn't want to remind her that she designed the dressing area, so tried more displacement theory. 'I don't know why you don't just buy yourself a new suit. I'm sure no one would notice you've gone from size 12 to size 12.5 or whatever size you've ballooned to over the past fifteen years or so. What time's he coming?'

'Nine. And that's another thing. It's not a him. It's a "Miss". Bound to be some size 8 stick insect.'

'What time will you be free, then?'

'Fancy taking me to lunch?'

'In that old suit? Not anywhere public, but er, I was wondering if you'd fancy dropping in to something at lunchtime.' He saw that she had picked up his hesitancy, although, fortunately, a mark on the Armani sleeve had her full attention so he tried to make it sound as casual as he could. 'You know, I'm letting the anti-drugs partnership use the demonstration area to show people what cannabis plants actually look like.'

A lick and dab at the sleeve. 'Why?'

'So they know what they are looking for. And can spot the decoys. We're going to put the real ones in among a few others like tomatoes or lupins. And a few more exotic varieties like Cleome or Castor Bean. To see if people can actually spot the real thing.'

Having salvaged the Armani sleeve, Sandra had moved to the shoe museum, as Sean called her racks of shoes, so he felt confident enough to continue.

'There's a great tale of an old couple in Bradford who bought what they thought was just a nice little plant from a car boot sale. A few years of TLC and they had a lovely bush outside their window. And armed cops demanding to know why they were growing cannabis in their garden.'

'Don't tell me. They got sent to prison, or something?'

'Not this time. Genuine mistake. But they got their bush confiscated.'

'And I suppose while you're donating our premises, staff and no doubt lunch, everyone else there will be being paid by the taxes we also pay?'

Sean sighed. She'd found the co-ordinated shoes so he now had at least 25 per cent of her attention.

'It's a public–private partnership. You know. Business in the Community and all that?'

'Where was the public bit of the partnership when we needed planning permission to turn that muddy field into a car park?'

Sean thought about replying along the lines of water under the bridge but saw that Sandra was about to try on the trousers. 'Spending our taxes saying no, Sean.' One leg. 'That's where they were. And why are they having this session today?' Other leg. 'The Council and police are supposed to be being paid because they know what they are doing.' She was delaying trying the zip.

Sean wondered if he should make his escape as Sandra rattled on, building up the momentum to try the zip. 'Like, perhaps, anti-drugs people knowing what the drugs they are anti-about actually look like?'

Her mood suddenly changed. Lifted. The zip had closed easily. 'I don't mind writing cheques to good causes, Sean, but a free lunch for people who should know what they're doing comes way down the list, for me. Sorry.'

'You sure you didn't vote UKIP?'

She ignored the gibe, as she twisted and turned in front of the mirror wall and held in the slight bulge above the waistband. 'I'll keep the jacket on.'

'So, it's safe to give your seat to someone else, then?'

Sandra nodded. 'I think I'll give this one a miss.' But I'll check out the lupins in Mum's garden, when I drop in there later. She often talks about how people should be allowed cannabis for pain relief.'

'That's just to save the surgery's drug budget.'

'If it makes sense and saves money?'

'Your mum's a receptionist, Sandra, not one of the medics.'

The look was all Sean needed to know that it was time to drop the subject or go. He was already dressed in his Barbour Countrywear shirt and moleskins, which he felt gave the right image at the garden centre, as well as the fact they were comfortable. He reached over for the Gieves and Hawkes suit and shirt that was hanging in a suit carrier, which in turn was hanging on the towel rail radiator. This was for lunchtime and, as Sandra had said, looked better than his favourite. But Sandra wasn't finished yet.

'But . . . that's part of the issue, isn't it? You're always saying most crime comes from social deprivation not criminal genes, so isn't the drugs issue a social issue as much as a medical one? Why don't we just let anyone who wants to do what that old couple in Bradford did, do it?'

'Grow their own?'

'For their own personal and private use. Then you handing out free lunches might be worth doing.'

'Bit radical coming from you. Thought you were in Joey's camp. Shoot druggies on sight?'

'If they are dealing and wrecking other people's lives.'

'I might just suggest that over lunch. Especially the shooting bit.' She shot him another sarcastic look, then turned back to the shoe racks. He stepped forward to nuzzle her neck before heading for the door, but she turned and pointed a Manolo Blahnik left foot at him.

'I bet that's what Joey and Luke are up to.'

'What? Growing or shooting? And I think your L.K. Bennett flats should be about right for the VAT Goddess.'

But Sandra was too focused to joust. 'They're growing stuff in that old cottage of Luke's.'

'Our Joe? No way.'

'OK. But he could be putting in the electrics for all the hydroponics and growing lights. Well? Couldn't he?'

Sean was about to say it was ridiculous, but there was that intuition thing. Joey and Luke had looked a bit odd in the supermarket car park the day before. And that business at the Lion. And, he had to concede, Joey often walked too close to the line.

'Joey won't be doing the drugs bit, Sean.' She'd read his mind. 'But you know what he's like. Anything to help a mate. Ask him what's going on. There's something.'

Sean nodded. He knew they'd be up to something. But drugs? No. Joey wouldn't do that.

By the time Natasha heard the shower pump signal that their elder son Alex had finally dragged himself out of bed, Joey's train was just passing the Roundhouse on its final glide down into Euston and he knew he might have something else to tell her tonight. He had almost made the decision to go back. Almost. When at that moment his phone vibrated. OUTSIDE. USUAL SPOT. It was from Benno. Waiting in Drummond Street just across the road from the side entrance in Melton Street. From there they would be on site in what had become known as the Billionaire's Bunkers within a matter of minutes.

Joey left the train and the travelling herd behind, turning right instead of left as he came off the platform ramp, and strode out through the loading bay to see Benno sitting in the old ambulance he used as a travelling workshop. He had long ago given up driving a white van mainly because he was fed up having it broken into overnight, despite fortifying it to a level Luke and his team wouldn't have objected to in Helmand, but mainly because even the traffic wardens who were paid per ticket usually ignored the ambulance. According to Benno. However, according to Joey, although Benno looked the part, especially in his dark overalls, hi-viz vest and the two old paramedic jackets he had hanging behind the seats, he usually remained untroubled because he had a face anyone would think twice about aggravating. In comparison, Bobby McBain's pebble-dashed features looked like an ad for Botox.

Benno was around five foot three of sinew and scars with a face that not only looked like the proverbial bag of spanners but looked like it had been formed by being hit with one. Which, in a way, it had been. When, thirty or so years before, he fell from a scaffolding, right on to his own bag of tools. He had told Joey he couldn't remember much about it except waking up to discover that as well as not being paid while he was off work, his then employers said he wasn't covered by any insurance because the accident had been his own fault. He had used the scaffolding, rather than the provided ladder, to take a shortcut to get from one floor to another. Everyone did it. In the time before Health and Safety became a religion and ladders were deemed instruments of the devil.

He was philosophical about it, as cases like his were now part of the chanted creed, just as he was philosophical about hitching the site fuel bowser to the back of his van one night. If they wouldn't give it to him. He'd take his own compensation. Everyone did that. In many ways it was a much fairer system. Everyone took what they thought they were owed, instead of some bean counter or computer calculating what some tax table said they could have. It was the face and the philosophy that had watched his back the past couple of years.

As Joey got closer to the ambulance he could see Benno in that all too familiar slightly bent forward position, staring at his lap. For most it would be taken as the BlackBerry Prayer position and he was checking his phone. With Benno it meant he was busy manufacturing one of his foul-smelling rollies. Sure enough, as Joey pulled open the door he had to clear the seat by scooping up the old Oxo tin that contained Benno's Rizlas and baccy.

'Do you have to light up every time I arrive?'

'Do you have to arrive every time I light up?' Evidence of which was slowly being dragged along Benno's bottom lip.

'How old is this thing?' asked Joey as he dropped the tin between the seats and wound down the window.

'Older than me.'

'Antique, then?'

'Probably. Me ma gave me that for me snap when I started out. You can get two rounds of cheese and pickle, a pasty, apple and a biscuit in there. As she did. Every day. I ended up hating cheese and pickle.' Having lit up, Benno started the ambulance and moved off, the rollie dangling from the corner of his mouth.

If you put Benno in a line-up with Luke and Matt and asked people to vote out the mercenary, tiny Benno would win hands down. He was, in a way. Like Joey, he was going from job to job, away from home and family, following the money. Which was how they'd met. Working on a hotel refurb in Luton. Then being asked by the builder to do some work on his own house in Borehamwood. From there one of his rich mates had asked them to work for him and before long they had formed an informal partnership, moving from one bling merchant to another. The houses and jobs getting bigger and more lucrative. Joey – well, Natasha – took care of all the paperwork and Benno pulled on a network of contacts they had built up over the past few years. Even as Benno exhaled and filled the cab with another cancer-inducing cloud of pollutants, he was someone else Joey would always want on his shoulder when things got tricky. As they seemed to be doing more often these days. That was why it was so hard making the decision to go back home. What would Benno do without him?

'Then what was up with Dad over the weekend?' Tanya asked, making herself a cup of coffee in her Starbucks to go mug. 'I mean, I know he does the Neanderthal thing because he thinks he has to, but he was a bit excessive on Saturday night.'

'How do you expect him to react after what nearly happened to you the other week?'

Tanya let out a long sigh. Not this again. 'Oh come on,

Mum. I nearly got killed like Aunty Janey? Really? She got jumped from behind by some mugger and run over.'

'That lad had a knife out at you, you said.'

'Yeah. And, like, right outside the garage with a million CCTV cameras. Not in the empty car park of the Co-op.'

'He had a knife, Tanya. And if he was crazy enough to do it outside the garage, then he was crazy enough to stab you.'

That point, along with her mother's obvious anxiety, was enough to at least make Tanya hesitate. 'OK. But he didn't, did he?'

'No. thank God.'

Which was enough to allow Tanya to swing back into gear. 'He was crapping himself more than we were. Well, except for Becky. And what would you have wanted me to do anyway, Mum? Let him rape me or make me go down on him, or something? Without a fight?'

'He was probably only after money,' Natasha replied quickly. She didn't want to contemplate anything else.

'Yeah. Exactly. And when I told him he wasn't getting any he backed off. Went looking for someone he could intimidate. Don't make yourself the victim. Isn't that what you and Dad have always said?'

'And which is why your father is probably being over-protective.'

'OK. I get that. Just as he has to get the fact that he can't be away all week and then come home and come over all heavy handed at the weekend.'

Even though she agreed with her daughter, and it was what had got her up so early, Natasha didn't want to get into family politics when she still had to get Lucy and the boys out the door. 'Can we talk about it tonight?'

'Sure, no big deal. Do you want a coffee to go?'

'Please. But how was Becky after not hearing from her Egyptian prince?'

'Don't let her hear you say that, Mum.' Tanya laughed. 'His name's Husani.'

'OK. I'm still getting used to every second person in town being an immigrant.'

'That is so racist.'

'It's not. It's a fact. Well, perhaps an exaggeration. But you know what I mean anyway. So how's Becky after not seeing Humani?'

'Husani. He still hadn't phoned her up to last night. After we cleared her phone he was probably giving her the silent treatment back, thinking that she had blanked him all Friday and Saturday. So, she's still devastated.' Tanya put the back of her hand to her forehead for the melodramatic effect. Then: 'God knows how Dad'd react if I came home with one of Hus's friends.'

'Actually, he'd be OK. Provided you weren't showing as much as you were on Saturday night. You can do short or low cut. But not both.'

'You mean Dad doesn't like me dressing the way he'd like to see you dressed?'

'I'd never be able to dress the way your father would like. And that's the point. He is your father. You're his daughter. And he knows there's too many blokes like him out there.'

'Which blokes are like Dad?' It was a bleary-eyed Ross heading for the cereal cupboard.

'None you know,' replied Natasha to prevent any potential Monday morning conflict. She picked up her phone and saw the text from Joey. OK. I'LL CALL WHEN FINISHED.LXXJ. But then noticed the time. 7.45. 'Any signs of your brother, or Lucy, Ross?'

'Someone's in the bathroom, which I guess won't be Alex.

Pass us the milk.'

'I hope you're not talking to me,' his mother replied.

''Course not. Her.'

'And who's "her"?'

Ross picked up the motherly tone, let out a huge symbolic sigh and trundled over to the fridge. Natasha headed for the door in search of the feet-draggers, but stopped as she passed Tanya. 'Tell Becky to be careful, though. Racist or not. I don't like the way they treat their women.'

'Point's already been made.'

As Natasha left, Tanya instantly replaced Sky News with *Friends*, while Ross unscrewed the top of the milk carton and tipped almost as much on to the table as landed in his cereal bowl.

'Look at the mess you're making, moron.' Tanya moved quickly to scoop up a sponge to wipe it up.

'I don't buy these big cartons, do I?'

As Tanya tried to work round Ross, and his namesake on screen was about to deliver his punch line, *Friends* was replaced by the planner and a nanosecond or two of Ross's favourite programmes until he settled on *Embarrassing Surgical Mishaps*.

'Don't move whatever you do,' Tanya growled.

He raised his bowl so she could wipe underneath. Then increased the volume on the TV. She reached over and turned it down. He turned it up. She snatched the remote and hit the standby button. He looked at her for a moment. She looked back, waiting for what he'd try next. It came.

'You're hormonal.'

'What?'

'You got a new boyfriend?'

'What?'

'It's not time of the month, so . . . ?' He let it hang with a shrug. Then: 'That what Dad was giving you a hard time about? You putting it out for this new bloke?'

'You're watching too much MTV.' With that she turned to go, but stopped. 'And how do you know when it's "time of the month"?'

'Apart from you being a right pain. Every four weeks or so, isn't it? Two of our ten-day timetables. It's week two. And I've seen the wrappings in the bin.' He gave another shrug and then grabbed the remote and turned the TV back on. 'I don't tweet about it or anything, though.'

'Thanks. You're such a comfort.'

'Is it him that's like Dad, then? This bloke?'

'Eat your breakfast. Like a good little boy.' She put the emphasis on little, but as she swept out the room she wondered if she'd been as grown up at his age.

And while Natasha was on the school run, Matt had left Luke in the hide and was on the scenic route home. Past Fatchops's chippy. Everything looked as it always did. Shuttered, barred and bolted, like almost every other shop along the High Street. Sign of the times, Matt thought as he ambled along. Almost. But no one else had so much CCTV and closed shackle hardened steel padlocks on their shutters. Supposedly bolt-cutter proof, they also had the highest insurance rating. Seemed a bit excessive to protect a few spuds and mushy peas, Matt thought as he went past, turning up the side alley where they had seen young girls being let out of the yard behind the chippy.

What were these characters actually up to? Matt pondered again as he felt the pulse in his leg quicken. Another reminder. Stay on mission, he thought as he carried on walking. Aware that someone would be watching the CCTV monitors, he was careful not to be too obvious while taking another long look at the steel door that must have opened into the yard. Double keyholes. One top. One bottom. Typical. No matter where they went they found similar scenarios. The bad guys thinking in fortress mode. Determined to keep everyone out, they concentrated on defending one entrance, forgetting that it also meant there was only one way out. Rats in a trap.

He hesitated just past the door, reached for his phone and adopted the BlackBerry Prayer position. He moved his thumbs but never touched the keypad. After a moment the phone screen lit. *J@% Random characters. It could be a pocket dial. But it meant Luke had been watching from the hill. It would mean nothing to anyone else. Especially to those who later might want to construct an incriminating timeline.

As Matt wandered on his way, Luke eased away from the spotting scope and ran over things again. They now knew what the chippy gang were up to. How they distributed. How they would try and escape. All we need now, Luke told himself, is how they are getting the stuff in and out.

Then he began to wonder if that mattered. The next link was the delivery guy. Follow him. Find the next real link. But, he thought, better to bring them to us. He put the scope back on to the side door to the chippy. He knew Fatchops would be out later to take the regular delivery. Luke's money was still on the delivery guy. Especially the way he had seen Fatchops react when the driver had dropped the box.

Perhaps we'll get a bit more when Matt does his return trip, Luke was thinking, when his train of thought was broken by something obscuring the scope. He looked up to see a stray Sanderson's shopping bag snagged on the gorse bush just in front of the hide. Before he could reach out to move it, it billowed and was lifted away on a passing swirl of wind. Luke watched it fly higher and higher, then dip and dive over the town as it was carried on the wind to land serendipitously who knew where, another symbol of the transient, disposable society that had both created and condemned towns like Highbridge to an uncertain future. Economies built on passing fashion rather than heritage. It also reminded Luke of the days he, Joey and their crowd used to come up to the top of the hill and set fire to the paper potato sacks they nicked from Sanderson's, when it was still a proper greengrocer's. Long before the Chinese lantern craze, if the wind was in the same direction as today, they would watch the sacks float towards the town, betting on how far they would travel. Until one came down in the cornfield behind T'House. And set the whole field alight.

Brilliant to watch, but leaving a long-lasting regret when they discovered it was the final nail in the coffin of Holt's Farm. The lost corn was the difference between survival and bankruptcy. They had not spoken about it much, either then nor recently, but he and Joey had learned one of their first big lessons about consequences, and they still felt some form of obligation to their old community. Hard to express, but it was there. He put the scope on where that cornfield had been – now, of course, covered in housing – and wondered how much old farmer Holt lost, how much he'd sold up for and how much whoever bought it made from selling it for houses. And would it still be full of crops or cows instead of houses if they hadn't set that paper sack on fire? Or, his thought continued, if they had used plastic sacks instead.

He allowed himself a nostalgic sigh as he turned the scope back to the chippy. And then he made the connection. Plastic bags. Ends in t-i-c. Plastic. The chippy used plastic bags to put stuff in. But they would need more than one box. What came in a box? He focused the scope on to the chippy counter and panned along. Then. There it was. Best place to hide anything is in plain sight. Plastic forks. That's how they did it. It was the forks. Now they had it all. As soon as the weather settled, it would begin.

'But why bother? That's what I don't understand.'

'You're not going to give me a hard time about the free lunch too, are you, Glynnis?' Sean asked, as he came into the demonstration area still fastening his tie while shouting thanks to young Ben, their online wizard with a sensible haircut, now scurrying away with the cart he had used to bring in the chairs.

'It's your money so you can waste it any way you like, Sean,' Glynnis responded, more focused on straightening up the back row of chairs. 'If people want to grow drugs and kill themselves, then why stop 'em? It'd save us all money in the end. All that policing and hospital bills when they OD or whatever they do. And you'd sell a lot more compost.'

'Have you been speaking to Sandra?'

'Why? She saying how daft you are too? Although Byron seems to be enjoying himself at your expense.'

Sean followed her eye line to see Byron coming in with Gill Hawkess, the Project Co-ordinator of Working Together Today, or WTT as she referred to it. She was, as usual, perfectly coiffured and manicured, the flowing coat giving glimpses of her figure-sculpting but strictly business suit. Byron had a schoolboy's entranced grin on his face, as he pushed a plant trolley full of Gill's promotional material. Sean couldn't quite remember exactly what WTT actually was, beyond the fact that he knew they were some regional organisation that helped facilitate community action. Gill was always talking about the quest to train community organisers, which Sean found a difficult concept to grasp as he felt people were either organisers or not. Still, a lot of people in council and police circles must think that Gill and WTT were wonderful, as they kept giving her money to facilitate things, which, in itself, seemed to prove something, although Sean was still struggling to understand what.

'Surprised you know how one of them works, Byron.' Glynnis nodded towards the trolley, pressing on before

Byron could reply. 'Like a cup of tea?' That one was aimed at Gill.

'Oh, only if it's not too much trouble.' Gill flashed a professional smile that was supposed to convey how approachable she was. It merely bounced off Glynnis.

'Not for me it's not. And it's his money we're throwing away, isn't it. You can have a biscuit too if you like.' She turned to Byron. 'You can get your own.'

With that she wandered off to the café, leaving Byron to control his obvious irritation. He knew she was deliberately baiting him. As she always did when Sean was around.

'I'll, er . . . leave you two to it, then. Nice to have met you, Miss Hawkess,' he said.

Gill flashed another smile. One of charmed gratitude. 'Thanks for the help bringing them in.' As Byron left, Gill turned to Sean and dropped the smile. 'She's a bit of a character.'

It was a statement that didn't need a response, issued while she unpacked her portable pull-up banners. One about the CAD partnership: County Against Drugs. One about the local partnership. One about WTT. Of course.

Sean looked at the local banner. HAD: Highbridge Against Drugs. She caught his eye. 'Good, isn't it? HAD – following the CAD line. Each town across the county will have one.'

Sean looked at it again. 'Does that mean Barnfield will be BAD? Sandwalk will be SAD and Templeton a bit TAD?'

There was a moment's hesitation and uncertainty before another smile. This one of amused tolerance. 'That's the point about doing a pilot. Canvass views and opinions.'

Sean nodded but continued to stare at the poster. Gill's smile slipped again. She sensed there was something else. 'And?'

'Oh, er, I was just wondering, Highbridge Against Drugs, well, whether it looks a bit like a poster for a referendum? That there could be an opposition view. Highbridge For Drugs? Vote Yes or No?'

The smile of tolerance was replaced with one of polite bemusement. It was an adaptable weapon. 'Not really. We are all against drugs, aren't we?'

'Er, yes.'

He didn't get the chance to develop the argument as he saw that Gill was again reaching into her quiver of smiles. This time it was welcoming, as her attention had turned to something over his shoulder. He turned to see that she was now heading, hand outstretched, teeth flashing, to greet one of her benefactors, Chief Inspector Hilary Jardine.

As they went into a full networking exchange, Glynnis returned with two teas on a tray. And a plate of biscuits. 'I figured out what WTT means.'

'Go on,'

'Witches' Tittle Tattle.' With a nod at Gill and Hilary, Glynnis went off chuckling at her own joke.

Sean looked at the two women. One perhaps tittle-tattling, the other, he knew, more used to trials and tribulations. As Gill was busy searching her smartphone for something obviously important to pass on, Sean raised a teacup to Hilary, who glanced at Gill then raised her eyebrows and grinned in return. Obviously not one of the faithful. But all part of the job.

What was not part of any job, at least as far as Joey was concerned, was people taking advantage. As he was now witnessing outside the container that served as the mess room on site. The Italians were walking out grumbling, while the Chinese were lining up to pay. It was theoretically known as the Workforce Weekly Lottery Ticket, for which everyone was supposed to contribute £10. No one ever saw a ticket, nor doubted that tickets were ever bought. But Gustav, Ivantmoreofich's East European project manager, or all-round enforcer as the other site managers referred to him, sat at his table every Monday collecting the contributions for the kitty. From everyone. Except Joey and Benno.

'Hey Joseph,' Gustav called.

Joey ignored him, going to the tea table to make a brew.

'Joseph? Why do we have this conversation every week? You the only one not paying.'

'Then as I say every week, Gus, I'm the one missing out on the chance, aren't I.'

'And what about your friend. Doesn't he deserve the opportunity?'

Joey was going to ignore him again when he saw Gustav was deliberately looking out the window, up towards the third-floor scaffolding. He went to the door and looked up, and his heart sank. His back stiffened and his hands started to clench and unclench, as he saw Benno obviously cornered by two of Gustav's known associates.

Joey turned back to Gustav. 'Going to have a nasty fall, is he? If I don't pay up?'

Gustav just shrugged. Then gestured out across the site. 'These places can be very dangerous. Yes? But you buy ticket. Good luck comes.'

Joey looked up at Benno, holding a half-metre length of rebar and ready to try and give as good as he would get, but Joey knew that, whilst he had the heart, the years would let him down.

'So you reckon it's the forks then?' Matt asked.

'Got to be,' Luke answered. 'He's been in and done his usual Mr Sheen act. Everywhere spotless.'

'Make even RSM Bronson smile, that would.' Matt grinned. 'Squeaky clean and free of any traces. Of anything, yeah?'

Luke nodded, slipping back to the Barrett as Matt continued, now convinced by Luke's logic. 'Which is why he puts a new box of forks in there every night. It's not just out with the old evidence but in with the new supply.'

Luke refocused the scope on the box. It was all so

obvious. Now. When someone passed over a marked note, Fatchops gave them a wrap. But his wrap contained a plastic fork wrapped in cellophane, inside of which were the drugs. Neat.

'What do you reckon?' Matt then asked. 'If Fatty doesn't take the bait, we go after the delivery driver? Weather's looking good for it, right?'

'Right,' Luke agreed as through the scope he picked up Fatchops bringing in a bucket of fish from the back. He put the Barrett right in the middle of his chest as he watched him start to batter the fish. The .50 cal round would blow him apart. Shock and awe. He held his breath and counted. At this range, the bullet would take around one and a half seconds. But it would only take a second for a stray head to bob in and out of the reticle. They needed five. The five seconds it would take someone coming in from the front or the back door to reach the counter. Five seconds when Fatchops would be standing still and no one else was likely to step into the shot.

Five seconds was a long time in a busy chippy so Luke knew they were unlikely to get that clear a shot until the mid-evening lull. Like the changing of the tide. When all the people coming home from work had been fed and just before the pub exodus began. Then, with luck, Fatchops would once more be battering the fish. Luke started breathing again. And let Fatchops continue to do the same.

'Do you think she ever stops to take a breath?' Hilary Jardine asked Sean, as she nodded towards Gill Hawkess.

'Nose breather. Like the Aborigines. Circular breathing. In the nose, out the digee. Hum-da-hara-hum-da-hara.

'Done a bit with your didgeridoo, have you, Sean?'

It was the sort of risqué remark that never ceased to amaze Sean, coming, as it did, from the lips of Chief Superintendent Jardine. He was never sure whether she meant it or just had the knack of triggering something in his own brain. He knew there was gossip about her and Joey once, even though everyone said she was out of his league. Middle class. Posh. But then, they said Natasha was out of his league too. Joey and Hilary had always denied it, but everyone knew they had something going. Whatever it was, it was short-lived as she surprised everyone by leaving before her A-levels, refused to go to university and joined the police. She was head girl. She was supposed to become a doctor like her father. But she had moved to Manchester and become a copper.

No one could ever quite read Hilary. Especially when she had that mischievous glint in her eye. As she had now, while they stood waiting for the Chair of the County Council to arrive to anoint the initiative and probably drone on about the increasing importance of public–private partnerships in an age of austerity.

Sean took a look around. The usual shirt and tie brigade scoffing his sandwiches and tea. The Chair of the Town Council, Harold Peagram, was present. One-time carpet king on the High Street, now retired and enjoying restoring classic tractors. He had probably only turned out because the Chair of the County Council was coming. At the moment he was swapping stories with the Secretary of the Round Table, Jason Charles and the guy who ran the tyre outfit behind the railway station, whose name Sean could never quite remember. Brenda Hodgson from Pets Parlour was talking to Samir Khan who now ran the Trading Post, the only real local shop for local people left on the High Street he kept telling everyone, deliberately ignoring the fact that he had only arrived five years earlier.

The current Head of the Comp, Julia Erskine was there, as was the Vicar, Deborah Joynston, known as Dibley after her TV counterpart, talking to Lady Winifred Garstang, or Winnie to the locals. Pushing ninety, now a bit unsure on her feet but still sharp as a razor. She seemed to have been around for ever and been on every committee, and had been a governor on the Comp while Sean was still there. Her title came from her deceased husband, who had been knighted for services to a military charity. Although neither talked about it, he was something of a war hero with the RAF and they had lost two sons to military action during the slow dismantling of the British Empire. The only clue left was the commemorative plaque in the porch of the parish church, a porch paid for by Sir Dennis and Lady Garstang.

All this was something of an irony as while Winnie

was very happy to chat to Dibley she had refused to set foot in the church since her arrival. It wasn't that she didn't agree that women should be ordained, but it was ridiculous that any woman would devote herself to the idea that God could have been a man. Men worshipping men was one thing. She could tolerate that. Women did that too. But to see another woman worshipping at the altar of what was nothing more than the creation of a serial adulterer and wife Killing King was too much. Now that Dennis had passed away she had no one else to pacify.

Hilary's grin had widened as she looked across at Gill Harkess, in full networking mode, offering her card to the Director of Public Health.

'She's certainly one of a tribe. Still, I suppose we need them. Get between us and the people we need to reach. Just a pity we seem to spend more time talking to them than doing the day job.' She paused for a moment, then asked, 'But what about you, Sean? Why are you doing this?'

'You're the third woman to ask me that today,' Sean said.

'Oh dear. And?'

'And . . . You probably know the answer, Hilary.'

'The Nolan equivalent of the Armalite and the ballot box?'

Sean turned, genuinely surprised. And irritated by the inference.

'Sorry,' Hilary said. 'Too long in counter-terrorism,

perhaps. But you favour politics over, I'm guessing, Joey's and Luke's desire for direct action?'

Sean's irritation was turning to anger. 'God, Hilary. Talk about two and two make five. If Joey and Luke wanted to take "direct action", as you term it, do you think they would have waited three years?'

She went to respond, but Sean could feel his blood pressure rising. 'No, hang on. And this . . .' He waved his arm round. 'Well, what? My sister gets killed by druggies, so I want to try and do something about the growing problems? Doesn't take much police work to figure that one out, does it?'

Hilary was starting to feel uncomfortable. But Sean kept going. 'So what's the issue here? I don't know what Joey's up to, if anything, but if I don't support this sort of thing, who will?'

'I'm sorry, Sean. I never really meant anything. It's just . . .' She looked and sounded full of regret. 'OK. Sorry. You heard what happened in the park at the weekend?'

Sean started to nose-breathe. Calming down. 'Noah gave me chapter, verse and every social media posting.' His anger was now displaced by curiosity.

'Oh, I put my foot in it with Joey too,' Hilary explained. 'Grilling him about what his friend Luke Carlton is doing home.'

'And?'

'Two and two make five. Anyway,' she added, 'keep on

doing what you are doing. We do need and appreciate it.' She offered a weak, almost apologetic smile as she moved away.

Sean watched her go, recognising that it must be difficult policing a community of old friends, but wondering as much about his own reaction as hers. Joey and Luke both had bad reps. He accepted that. And she was, when all was said and done, a copper. But why did it cause him to react so forcefully?

Joey was still looking up at Benno, cornered on the edge of the scaffolding. Remembering the fall he had had in the past, he turned back to Gustav. 'OK. Call off the dogs and I'll sort something out.'

He stepped back from the window, boiled up the kettle and started making a fresh pot of tea.

Gustav weighed Joey up and down. He was still not sure how to read him. Most would have buckled a long time ago.

'It's only ten pounds, Joseph. Not a lot. I offer you five. And you still refuse? What is the point?'

'That is the point, Gus. It doesn't sound much, but from one hundred blokes?'

'Ah, you jealous?'

'No. I just think you're a parasite.'

Gustav laughed. 'We don't have to get married.' Then his voice became more threatening. 'Just help out your friend.'

Joey nodded. He could see he didn't have much choice, dug into his pockets, pulling out a few coins. He counted them before putting them on the table. 'Two pound forty. All I got on me. Until tomorrow.'

Gustav looked, gave a smirk of derision, then turned to the window and gestured for the others to let Benno go. 'That will be twenty pounds tomorrow. For you both. This I keep as interest.'

Joey glanced out to see that Benno was now safe and coming down the scaffold, before picking up the teapot and then suddenly kicking the edge of the table so it rammed into Gustav's stomach. Then he reached over and pulled his head down hard on the table. Holding it there, with the teapot hovering just above, he leaned over him.

'Listen, you. I don't care what you and the others do. But I'm telling you now, once and for all. I'm not interested. And neither is Benno. And if you get any ideas of coming after us again . . .'

He poured the tea across Gustav's neck, causing him to yell in pain. Joey held him down for a moment or two before letting him pull his head up.

'You're right, these are dangerous places.'

'I kill you.'

'You can try. But first, you'd better get that under a cold tap. Or get to a hospital.'

Gustav shoved the table aside as he made for the door, pushing a surprised Benno out of his way.

'What's going on?' Benno asked.

'Tea?' Joey said, offering up the teapot.

Benno looked out to see Gustav being bundled into a car. 'Looks like he's off to A&E.'

Joey glanced up at the clock. 'Let's hope the waiting time's still around four hours, then. We'll be away by then.'

'And what about tomorrow? You know he'll be back.'

'I do,' Joey replied, calmly pouring the tea. 'And as James Bond said, Benno: tomorrow is another day.'

4

Certainty

The buzz had already gone round the site. Joey had put Gustav in hospital. It both enhanced his reputation and increased the chance of retaliation. It was now also one of the key factors Joey was considering while trying to make up his mind about going back home, while, at the same time, figuring out how best to run the 110 V ring main Ivantmoreofich wanted.

He wondered if it would make it easier if he told Benno he could keep all the stuff they had stashed. Or reclaimed, according to Benno. The idea had been that they would use it for refurbs instead of buying new, and they had around £10,000 worth in a lock-up in Camden. If I let him have that, Joey thought, it would give him a bit of a head start. Or would it? Would it only help ease Joey's conscience? Initially Benno had been the one who had taken Joey under his wing and found the work, but recently his age had been catching up with him and, as the incident with Gustav had demonstrated, Joey was now his minder.

Sean was still pondering on what had triggered his anger with Hilary Jardine earlier. He knew everything had been heightened when his niece Tanya was threatened and he had spent a lot of time after that, like Luke, talking Joey out of going hunting with his baseball bat. But it was deeper than that. The attack had tapped into something else. Something deeper.

A growing desire to try to do something to make things happen. He was getting more and more fed up listening to everyone complaining about why things never got done. Whether it was emptying the bins, fixing the street lights or clearing out the druggies from the park. It was always the way. Why can't the Council do something?

He was never quite sure what had initially fired him up, but knew it had started with the fight over planning permission. All he and Sandra had wanted to do was expand the business, create more jobs and sort out the parking issues with the neighbours. He couldn't understand why, when the local paper's letters pages were constantly full of people moaning about his customers parking on the grass verges, the planners took such an intransigent line. The muddy field, as Sandra constantly referred to it, had suddenly become an important wet meadow, which just happened to be right opposite one of the local councillors' houses.

At first Sean had taken the line that that was just local gossip until Sandra came home from tennis one day to tell him that Dorothy Mathis, whoever she was, had confirmed that it was indeed the Executive Member for Tourism and Business who lived directly opposite that muddy field. Not only that, but after googling it on her phone while changing ends, Sandra had galvanised Wendy, who apparently ran what was regarded as the militant wing of the Mums 'n' Tots Club at the community centre, to organise an online petition while Nicky, who knew the mother of Arthur Young, the local newshound, soon got him on the case. Within a week a perplexed and bemused councillor was in the local paper sweeping aside any misunderstandings or objections to the excellent plan to resolve a long-standing community issue while helping a local business to thrive. That was, after all, why he was elected, the quotes said.

While it all worked out well in the end and Sean made a point of throwing a Christmas party for the Mums 'n' Tots militant brigade, he, like many others, was left wondering why it always seemed to be like that. Why was the community always fighting the Council? A lot of it could be put down to the fact that the Council had to do what was for the good of the many over the needs of the few, but Sean sensed it was deeper than that. He'd sensed it as soon as he and Sandra had come home from their global wanderings. Having experienced the 'why not?' atmosphere of the greater global emerging economies, even in parts of the USA where 'why not?' still trumped 'why?', he had found the restrictive, rule-driven, jobsworth psychology of Britain oppressive.

Had it got worse while they were away? But thinking back he had concluded that there were now more rules because there were now more things to do in life, and therefore to regulate. If you didn't have anything to do you didn't need a rulebook. It was a legacy of the aristocratic feudal system that the country had still not quite shaken off. Everyone, as far as officialdom was concerned, was still expected to know their place. That was the trouble with politics. Before they were elected, candidates wanted to be representatives. Once elected, they became leaders. And leaders expected people to, well, follow. Follow their lead. Be told what to do. Didn't they?

And to do that they needed a way to control things. Rules. Regs. And the police. Was that what Hilary was querying? Why was he stepping out of his place? Not leaving things to them to sort out. All this was going through his head as he heard the Chairman of the Council thank him for his support and hospitality and ask him to come forward and say a few words.

'Thank, you Mr Chairman,' Sean began. 'It's a pleasure to do whatever I can to help our local community.' He turned back to the assembled community representatives in front of him only to focus on Glynnis apparently chasing Arthur Young away from the food with a shake of her head as she started to quietly clear the buffet.

That was it. No more. She was protecting her profit margin. His eye caught Hilary Jardine's and he saw she was smiling at him. A supportive smile that would have made Gill Hawkess proud. It was the old friend again. Not the rule enforcer.

He returned the smile, and then heard himself say, 'This is the bit I always like. When I find out what I am going to say.'

'Run it past me again.' Luke was trying to absorb one of Matt's latest ideas.

'The average smoker costs the NHS about thirty or forty grand over their lifetime, especially at the end when they're coughing their guts up. OK?'

'So you tell me,' Luke responded. 'And this is one for the list, is it?'

Matt nodded. 'One hundred and one things to do with a sacked sniper.' He had started compiling the list when they had heard that they, like many others, were being 'released to pursue their careers elsewhere', as some suit had told them at the debriefing. Funnily enough, as Joey had told Benno, they had not found many jobs advertised for their skill sets once they were out of the services.

'I haven't started ranking them yet. Just, you know, brainstormin' the ideas and that. But I think stopping smokers beats shooting badgers and foxes.'

Luke conceded the point with a nod. 'It certainly takes things up a level or two.'

'OK,' Matt continued. 'So how much does a bullet cost?'

'What calibre?'

'It's supposed to be theoretical, Luke. But, OK, let's say we'd use a standard H&K PSG1. So, 7.62, right?'

'About three dollars a box or something. Or what was that gear we used on the last job?'

'Er, Tulammo. Yeah. Around 25 cents that Canadian guy said. OK, bulk buy. We'd probably get 'em for less than 15p.'

'So, your argument is, we just shoot smokers and instead of the thirty grand it costs to treat them, it only costs 15p to waste them?'

'Yeah.'

'I can see some people voting for it.'

'And I know what you're going to say next. Win the war, lose the peace, right? How do we win the minds and hearts beforehand?'

'Something like that,' Luke conceded again.

'OK. The thing that's always missing. Fairness. Give everyone a chance.'

'What? Arm the smokers so they can shoot back?'

'Now you're being ridiculous.'

'Oh, sorry.' Luke slid back into the hide. Nothing would happen until tonight. He reached for the boiled sweets in one of the ration packs. 'Go on then. Win my heart and mind.'

'We set up on top of a high building. OK? Good angles.

All-round vision. We spot a smoker. Red dot them. Bit of a jiggle until they see it. They get thirty seconds to stub out. Or be taken out. Their choice, isn't it?'

'If they know what the red dot is.'

'Labels on all ciggy packs. Red dots can kill. Something like that.'

'Education. Always the key. But, that's it? One chance? What about, I dunno, someone who's short-sighted or colour-blind? Or am I just being a woolly liberal?'

'No, it's a perfectly valid democratic argument. Which is where we nick the three strikes rule from the Yanks.'

'"We" do, do "we"?'

'Yeah. So they just get a warning for the first offence, right? Blam. Fleshy bits around the armpit. You know the way smokers hold their arms when they light up.' He had put the Barrett's scope on one such target about to light up, watching him raise his arms slightly to shield the lighter from the wind. 'They get that fixed and, here's the clever bit . . .'

'It all sounds very clever to me so far.'

But Matt was winding up to his really clever bit, so missed the sarcasm. 'During the patch-up, the medics stick in an RFID implant. Use radio scopes that get a return path from the implant, right? Second-time offender. Blam. Opposing upper body shot.'

'And we fix that. And put in another implant?' Luke asked and saw Matt nod with a grin of delight. He knew he was being drawn in, but when Matt started on one of his theoreticals, it was like approaching a black hole. Once over the event horizon there was no turning back. 'So the next time they get tagged. Two return signals. Third offence. Kill shot?'

'But don't forget the thirty-second warning. It's their choice to stub out, or –'

'– be taken out,' Luke finished it off for him.

'Three shots. 45p.' Matt beamed.

'Er . . . what about the cost of the operations to patch up their armpits?'

'Less than five grand, on average, apparently. For a straightforward in and exit repair. We'd be using balls, remember. So, on average, three at five is fifteen plus the 45p for the ammo, right? Couple of grand for us and overall it'll save the NHS between ten to twenty grand. And don't forget, that's only for the right stubborn so-and-sos. I reckon most would jack it in after the first shot.'

'Or before. With enough publicity. We could get that Ross Kemp to do a show about it.'

'Right. As you pointed out. Education. Always about educating people. And multiply it all up by the millions of smokers we'd take out of the system. Money that can be better spent on roads and education and other health problems.' He held out his hands. 'Simple, yeah? But the best bit is that it gives people like us something to do with the skills the government has spent years giving us, but then doesn't know what to do with when we've finished killing on their behalf. So. We just carry on doing it for them. In a new way, with a renewed sense of purpose, while saving the taxpayer a fortune in the long run.'

'I get it. Stub out or be taken out. It's catchy. And you have thought it through, haven't you?

Matt nodded, as he slid back from the Barrett, while adding, 'And I've got the perfect name for it.'

'Go on.'

'Surgical Strikes.'

Luke couldn't suppress a laugh. It was so daft. So macabre. But made so much sense. As much as it did them lying in a hide waiting to take a shot at a fat bloke in a chippy.

'Never happen though, would it?' Matt grinned as he reached across for a granary bar.

'Something tells me not,' Luke replied.

'We'll just have to go back and work for the Yanks. Be the ones that the locals whinge about. They come over here. Take our sniper jobs. Kill our enemies. Kill our friends. Should be local killing by local people. That's what they'll mutter into their beards. And exactly what everyone's muttering here, isn't it?'

Luke looked across at Matt, now rummaging in the ration box for another granary bar. Sometimes he was never quite sure. The line between genius and madness.

'What you looking so glum about?' Benno suddenly asked as he wriggled out from a service duct dragging the 110 V cable behind him. No one else was small enough to fit.

'Oh, usual. Why life has to be so complicated.'

Benno just cackled. 'Keep telling you, Joey, lad. It ain't. Do unto others and all that. If everyone's OK, it's fine. But if they're not, then you have the right to slap back.' He held up one end of the cable. 'You figured this out yet?'

'Nearly. Get the return to behind that worktop.'

Benno nodded and started to pull the cable from its reel, as Joey mulled over Benno's words. It seemed like such a simple code. Much simpler than the turning the other cheek line. It was that simple but markedly different interpretation of the Christian ethic that had got him into so much trouble during his life. Especially the bit about not taking matters into his own hands but letting others like the school or the law do it for him. Problem was, they never did, really.

'It's probably the reason that mate you were telling me about can't settle after leaving the forces,' Benno offered. 'A lot of them can't. If someone sticks a gun in your hand and the authority to use it, must be a bit hard having to deal with the jobsworths you meet back home.'

Joey had been telling Benno a bit about Luke. You got to know someone very well when you slept in a sleeping bag side by side. Luke may have been on some mountainside with Matt, but Joey had spent many a cold draughty night with Benno, kipping down on site to save spending money on digs.

Joey had also told Benno that life seemed to be falling

into place for Luke when he met and married Janey. He had only a year left on his term before they would buy one of the small cottages on Top Road that, as its name suggested, looked down over Highbridge, and then start a family. How Luke then went to Afghanistan and while scraping the remnants of his colleague from the remains of a Snatch Land Rover he got the call to say Janey was dead. A relay of transport legs got him back for the funeral but 48 hours later he was back hunting the Taliban with a renewed vigour his commanders were concerned about but couldn't fault.

But, Joey explained to Benno, they had offered him all the usual psychobabble counselling, as he referred to it, but fell back on his own self-diagnosis. He had had only two things in his life and one of them was now dead, killed for no purpose other than becoming another statistic. It was not long before the disillusionment mounted alongside the body bags.

While the cause was worthy, Luke had repeatedly told Joey, the resources and political will were, as usual, lacking. Politicians always seemed to want to fight a civilised war. But, Luke kept asking, what the hell was that? The locals never appeared to mind blowing up their own, whether kids, women or passers-by. So why not let our lads get down in the gutter with them and rip 'em up?

They all knew it was about politics and opinion polls. And risk aversion. Just the system. But Joey also knew that, like Luke, Benno understood the real cause of disillusionment. Being screwed by that system. Just as Benno had become a victim of Health and Safety, so Luke became a victim of austerity cuts. Having decided to re-enlist he discovered that, despite his past service, he was, like so many others, no longer required. So he joined one of the American companies that provided what was euphemistically called 'additional security'. Luke knew he was following one of the oldest traditions of warfare, from the Roman legions through the Crusades and into Afghanistan. History's hired guns. Of course he was never allowed to use the term 'mercenary', but as Natasha had said, that was exactly what he was. And whatever he did, he made sure he was paid. Handsomely.

'So why'd he come home?' Benno had asked, going straight to the point.

'Dunno, Benno. Just dunno,' Joey had responded after deciding that despite how close they were, he wasn't going to say it was because after a late-night chat at the cottage, the obvious conclusion they had reached was to use the skills Luke had been given. And shoot the sort of people who had caused the death of Janey.

It was all this and the sense of camaraderie Joey shared with Benno that was going through his mind when Benno asked him why he looked so glum. To help one friend he would have to let down another.

Sean had been speaking for about ten minutes on the theme of how most people have strong opinions on what needs to be done but feel powerless to influence anything. A feeling that no one in authority listens or is in touch with them. Looking round the room he noticed how this just bounced off the seemingly impervious skin of officialdom. A sign that he was right? Or simply that they'd heard it all before?

He decided to ramp it up a bit.

'But, well,' Sean continued. 'We lost another of our young people at the weekend. Another senseless death. We probably all have our own individual opinions on what we should and shouldn't do. But that is always tempered, perhaps restrained, and constrained, by what we can do. I mean, what we are allowed to do.'

He turned and looked deliberately at the County and Council Chairmen and then towards Hilary, the major power brokers in the room. The Chairs remained impassive. Did they really have an opinion, Sean wondered, or was this just something they had to do as part of the role? But from Hilary there was a slight nod, although that, Sean knew, could simply illustrate either an understanding that people will take things into their own hands if frustrated enough, or her own desire to be let off the leash. To hang 'em and flog 'em. It did, however, give Sean his next line.

'But does that mean more draconian action? Zero tolerance? Round 'em up?' He looked at Hilary, then to Arthur Young who was now taking advantage of Glynnis heading off to the kitchen to work his way through a plate of mini chocolate éclairs. 'Hang 'em and flog 'em? Or, as we've tried that for years, decades, perhaps centuries, do we look for a new strategy?'

'And when that fails, yet again, is it any wonder that people are looking to fringe politics? If they think those in the traditional parties – those in power – don't listen or seem powerless to act, is it any surprise they start to look for answers elsewhere?'

He hesitated for a moment. Wondering how far he should push his own ideas today. Or should he just play the polite host? He noticed Arthur was now being joined by a few other grazers who had spotted the cakes. Sod it, Sean thought, I am paying for this. Taking a deeper breath, he raised his voice above the growing gabble.

'But do you know what I really think? We should stop messing about with all this.' He waved his hand in the direction of the CAD pop-up displays. 'All this partnership stuff is great, but what is the point?' He saw Gill's teeth immediately retract behind stiffening lips. A smile of apprehension. This could be bad.

'I don't mean the partnership bit. That's fine.' The lips remained tight. 'But what are we really working towards? Teaching people what cannabis plants look like? For what? So they can spy on their neighbours? Or worse, as someone has already pointed out to me, they turn informant on the local drug gangs and then get knee-capped, or worse, for doing it?'

Gill was slowly moving towards the County Chairman.

He might need some support, but Sean noticed he had a smile on his face. Did that mean he agreed? Or that he enjoyed someone making an idiot of himself? But the smile didn't match the one that now spread across Hilary's face, although Sean noticed her eyes were not on him but on an almost panicky Gill heading towards her main funder. Even the newshound was grinning as he put down his plate and reached for his iPhone.

'I don't mean to be controversial,' Sean continued, 'but surely the answer is in education.' He looked over to find the Head of the Comp, who had frozen, chocolate éclair almost in her mouth. He saw the expression on her face. Oh God, she was thinking. What's he going to blame me for now?

'Not in school,' Sean quickly added. 'As the kids probably know as much, if not more than any of us about the "drugs bad" philosophy, but real education about what drugs – any drugs – do to you.'

The éclair disappeared into a relieved and grateful mouth.

'We spend time teaching our children the dangers of things like bleach under the sink, don't we? We practically educate them on how to handle two other major killers: alcohol and nicotine. But on other things we remain silent. We don't even try to find out, if we are honest, because we feel it isn't, well, it doesn't feel right. Is that simply because we think that if something is illegal we shouldn't? Somehow we feel we are not allowed to learn more about it.' He emphasised it again. 'Or, is it because we are not encouraged, perhaps allowed, to discuss these things openly?'

Despite the now almost tolerant smiles from the Chairman and Hilary and the look of glee from the newshound, Sean could almost feel the temperature in the room drop. Vicar Dibley's lips were pursed. Almost as tight as Gill's. This isn't what they came for. It should have been a nice pleasant lunch. Not a seminar. Or a debate.

'I know that's not what I was supposed to say.' Sean was now almost apologetic. 'But, well, you are eating my sandwiches and what do they say: there's no such thing as a free lunch?'

It got a few weak smiles. But a lot more nervous glances towards Hilary and the Chairman, both having regained their impassive public personas.

'You calling for legalisation, then, Sean?' It was Arthur the newshound, now sensing if not a possible front page, then a definite spark for the letters page.

Sean glanced across at Gill. Eyes wide, head shaking slowly, lips forming the word noo-o-o. There was no grant funding in legalisation. His eyes flicked to Hilary. Her face rigid but her eyes smiling. Go on, you dug the hole. The Head was trying not to catch anyone's eye, while Winnie Garstang was beaming. Another man making an idiot of himself?

'No, Arthur,' Sean replied. 'But what about regulation? We do it with cigarettes and alcohol. Why not other drugs, like cannabis?'

'So you're saying cannabis is no worse than booze and fags?'

'Nice try,' Sean countered. 'But that's one for the medical professionals to answer, actually. There's a debate going on about whether terminally ill people should be prescribed cannabis as part of the end of life palliative care.'

'All cancer patients should be encouraged to smoke, then?'

'Now I know you are being provocative.'

'It's what I get paid for.'

'OK. One last thing, then I'll let everyone get on with the cakes, tea and learning how to spot the pot.'

There were a few relieved faces as Sean paused to try and put things simply and quickly. 'As a society, we have learned how to control alcohol and tobacco. No one really thinks of injecting pure alcohol or nicotine, as they would die. We have learned how to use those drugs by diluting them: 3–4 per cent alcohol. Dangers of tobacco. And so on. We teach our children these things. Why shouldn't we do it with other things? And, Mr Chairman, we have also learned to tax the use of those drugs. Taxes that pay for a lot of the services your authority delivers.' He turned to Hilary. 'I know we still have crime attached to their use, but at least the money that taxes raise helps provide the resources to fight it.'

As both the Chairman and Hilary gave a nod of concession Sean decided to quit while he was, if not ahead, then at least climbing out of the hole he had dug. 'OK. That's it for me. Except to remind you of the first public consultation up at Treetops tonight at . . . er . . . 7.30?' He looked across to Gill, who had a smile ready. Confirmatory. Supportive.

'So, sorry if I went off on one, but please support CAD whenever and wherever you can . . . And . . . have a browse round while you are here and spend a bit to help me pay for the sandwiches . . . And . . . everyone can have a 10 per cent discount for being so polite. Thank you.'

The last bit at least got the applause going and Sean headed off to get a cup of tea trying not to look at either Glynnis or Byron, who was now clearly in Glynnis's camp. Ten per cent discount?

Luke was alone in the hide. Matt had gone on the Costa run, leaving Luke mulling over the point that local people should kill local people. Another bit of perverse logic. But one that avoids the bit everyone forgets. Not the people doing the killing, but the ones who see the horror. He had no qualms or doubt that Fatchops deserved what was coming. Like his suppliers. If a half-inch piece of steel blew your head apart you wouldn't know it, but everyone standing around you would never forget it. Did they deserve that? Did everyone else deserve what happened to Janey?

He looked at his watch. 17.55. Then panned the Barrett along the street. The guy with the silver Transit would be arriving any minute. Silver was the new white van around Highbridge, Luke had noticed. Then the old boy from No. 78, who always struggled to get his wheelie bin out through the front of the house, would hobble along and wave to Silver Van Man. Then the kid on his mountain bike. The woman in the hi-viz jacket on her way home from the Community Centre. And all the other regulars would come and go. Habit. Routine. POLO.

Eventually the scope came back on to its intended target, now finishing off his nightly cleaning routine and, yes, putting out his box of special forks, just below the counter, below the one already open on the countertop. No one was going to help themselves to the specials. Another hour and the banker would arrive to stand in the alley with the stack of marked notes and the users would start arriving to convert their hard-earned or easily stolen cash. Luke put Fatchops's head in the cross hairs. It would blow apart like a ripe melon. If the bullet hit him. The problem was that it was going to have to be a cold snatch shot. No chance to readjust. When they had those five seconds they needed to make sure he was stationary and no one else would walk into the shot. He moved the scope down to Fatchops's torso, then grinned. That's too big to miss. Just as he did, the hi-viz jacket of the woman from the Community Centre appeared in the scope. Exactly what they wanted to avoid.

If he had squeezed the trigger then, the woman in the hi-viz jacket would have arrived just in time to see

Fatchops's head blow apart. She might even have ended up with some of his brains mixed in with her nightly cod and chips. And be traumatised for the rest of her life. Luke had long since been desensitised. He'd actually been trained, perhaps indoctrinated, to accept it as simply a natural outcome. They all had. And in the age of the Internet he couldn't understand how some still arrived in the so-called theatre of war and were shocked at what they saw. It was all over the web. If YouTube didn't let you see it there were plenty of other ex-military, soldiers of fortune or wannabe sites that had all the graphic detail, including, because of smartphones, the soundtracks.

That was the real difference, Luke remembered. The sound. They had all gone through the live fire drills with instructors yelling their lungs out, but unfortunately the targets and their families had not been on the induction courses. A dickhead pretending to be a bad guy was nothing like the wailing grief and eyes of pure hatred that came at you when things got really hot. Like the first time you get whacked in the school playground. It isn't play fighting. It hurts. And it's a big shock. And the bigger the whacking, the bigger the trauma. No, Luke thought, while Fatty deserved everything he had coming, that woman in the hi-viz vest didn't. And neither did her family, who would be left having to cope with her, perhaps for the rest of her life.

A low whistle brought his attention back to the hide entrance. It was Matt warning him he was on the way in.

'Whoa, you look like you've been brooding,' Matt said without any greeting but handing Luke his latte and panini.

'Yeah, I was just . . . You know . . .'

Matt was expecting another round of counselling about Janey, but was surprised to hear Luke say, 'I'm not sure we should slot Fatty.'

'You want to cut and run?' Matt asked. 'I'll do it if you don't feel—'

But Luke cut across him. 'No, it's not that. It's just . . . Do you think Joey could handle it?'

'Ah. I thought you'd been there and got past it.'

'So did I, but . . . They don't really know, do they? Ulster was the worst for me. Young, keen, thinking I was going there to help. And they were just like us, weren't they? Until you were told to kick in their doors and drag their men away. And raised on folklore that romanticised the struggle, they then came into direct contact with a size ten boot or rubber bullet. I hated that. I never believed in what we were doing.'

'Never our job, Luke. It was a civilian issue that they should have sorted politically before putting us on the streets. Last resort, we are, remember. Like now, probably. Why don't the cops just go and take this fat bastard out?'

'Why indeed?'

'So, do you want to scrub it?'

Luke hesitated for a moment. Matt already knew the

answer and waited for the shake of the head. 'Just change the scenario.'

'Nice one, Sean,' Arthur Young said as he shook Sean's hand on the way out. 'Great when someone stirs it up a bit.'

'Sells papers, does it?' Sean replied, with a laugh.

'Yeah. And you won't mind if we splash you over the front page? Local Boss Blasts Bureaucrats?' But he grinned as he saw Sean become anxious. 'No worries, Sean. You're one of the good guys. Who else would give this lot a free scoff?'

'That include you?'

'Of course. And much appreciated. Nah, you won't be on the front page. Not up to me anyway. The editor sent me here to get something on the dynamic duo there, wasting our money.' He nodded across to where the Chairs of County and Town had colonised a table and took out his phone to take a shot, just as the Town Chair was stuffing another custard slice into his mouth. 'Let them eat cake, eh? Yeah, it'll be those two. Something about fat cats and cream. Put money on it. It's that and good local celeb stories that sell the paper, Sean. So who've you got opening your grotto?'

'Well, I hadn't really thought of—'

But Arthur was already conjuring up a story. 'Have you tried Craig Harlow? My mum knows his mum, Wendy.'

Sean laughed. 'Your mum seems to know everyone.'

'Why do you think I came into this game? Long line of nosey parkers. Straight, though. He's often back on the quiet to see his mum and I bet he'd pop in one day and play Santa. Great front page that would be. Anyway, got to go. Apparently someone saw a ghost up at the war memorial last night. Always gets the letter pages going, that one. I'll send you Craig's details. Stay sharp.'

And with that he was off, leaving Sean to ponder on Craig Harlow. Local celeb. One-time boy-band member now Hollywood A-list actor. Would he actually do it?

'This is really about your girl, isn't it?' Joey heard Benno ask as he dropped to the floor to started fishing the 110-V cable behind the worktops. Once more going to the point. Joey had told him about the skirmish Tanya had found herself in a few weeks ago.

'Yeah, suppose so,' Joey responded, hoping not to have to go any further. Some chance with Benno.

'You have to do it, Joe.'

'What?'

'Go back.' Benno said, as he reappeared above the worktop. 'You have to.'

Joey knew Benno was trying to make it easier for him. Although he wasn't expecting the next bit.

'Besides,' Benno said, 'I'm off tomorrow anyway. Before Uncle Gus comes back.'

'What? Where?'

'Remember that job up in Borehamwood we knocked back for this? Still got a spot for me.'

'How? When did you fix this?' Joey asked.

'It's been brewing for a while now, hasn't it. Not letting me get to sleep having to listen to all your troubles.'

Joey laughed. That was a good one. But he appreciated what Benno was doing. Leaving him no excuse to stay.

'So, no point you hanging about fretting down here,' Benno continued, then fixed Joey with a hard stare. 'Or fretting about me. I can look after meself. You do what you have to do, lad.'

With that he disappeared into the service duct again, leaving Joey to finally make the decision. He bent to the service duct. 'OK, oh wise one. But I'll stay until the end of the week while we clear out the lock-up.'

'So you make sure you get your proper share?' came a cackling reply.

'There is that.' Joey grinned. But at least now he had something concrete to tell Natasha later.

'What's wrong with your face?' Natasha asked her daughter, as she stacked the dishwasher following the evening food fest. No matter how much she used the mantra, 'straight in please', somehow everyone always seemed too busy to bend down and open the door.

'Just got another message from Carol. Becky's gone missing again,' Tanya replied as she retrieved her jacket from the couch. Roscoe immediately saw it as a cue that he might be going for a walk, but was soon deflated. 'Not now, Roscoe. Mum'll take you later.'

Roscoe doubted that as he slumped back into his basket. He'd be lucky if he got a quick round of the garden, when he'd be under pressure to perform before being sent to bed for the night. At least though, he knew he'd get a Dentastick from the older female.

'And where are you going at this time?' Tasha asked.

'It's only nine, Mum. I'm just going to meet Cags and see if Becky is hanging out with Hus.'

'I'm not sure I like the sound of all this.'

'That's why I'm going. Don't worry, I won't get involved if she's with him. I'll text you later.'

'Be back by ten, young lady.'

But the door had been slammed. Natasha looked at the clock. That's when she was going to speak to Joey. She'd been worrying all day about what might be going on in his head.

At 21.30 Luke and Matt lay prone, watching the tide of customers starting to ebb. The earlier teatime rush had slowed and Fatchops was now getting everything ready for the late-night snackers. Luke had him framed in the scope as he was again meticulously cleaning the countertops to remove any traces that might have fallen from his box of special forks. Matt was slowly sweeping the street through the spotting scope. It was time.

'Still clear.'

Luke widened the scope to take in the whole shop. It was empty except for Fatchops and one of the two spotty helpers placing a bucket of chips beneath the mushy peas and curry table at the back, ready for the next incoming tide. As soon as Spotty went back to chipping more spuds, Luke would take the shot. If he still kept getting Matt's all-clear reports.

'All clear bottom end.'

Luke put the Barrett onto Fatchops. Slight refocus. He began to settle and steady his breathing. He just wanted those five clear seconds.

'All clear top end,' came from Matt.

Luke flicked off the safety and moved his finger to the trigger. He was just about to start the squeeze when Matt spoke again.

'Hold. That Merc SL is back.'

Luke flicked the safety back on and slid round to pan the Barrett, almost at the edge of its sweep on the tripod, and picked up the driver as he got out of the car, chattering away into the Bluetooth link in his ear. He walked round to the passenger side and opened the door, gesturing for someone inside to get out. Luke wasn't so much worried that they would arrive after the shot as that they would see the muzzle flash.

They had decided that the risk of anyone seeing the flash was small, as most of the residents of Highbridge would neither be expecting it nor recognise it for what it was. If anyone did see it they would probably assume it was kids messing with fireworks. Unless, of course, they saw it and then walked in to find their mate or relative spread all over the back wall. Unless, of course, they were up to no good. With no-good people who carried guns. Then they might put it all together.

However, the driver's demeanour caught Luke's attention. Suddenly his cocky swagger dropped as he spun round to focus on something further down the street. Through the scope it looked as if someone had called to him, as he seemed to wave, but hesitantly. Behind him, a mane of teenage hair appeared out of the Mercedes, followed closely by another.

'Amazing what a nice car will do for you,' Matt said as he turned his scope back down the street to see what the driver was waving at, and picked up another girl walking up towards him. 'And looks like he's ready to party.'

'If he is, we'll see the children's entertainer arrive next, judging by the age of those two.'

Matt panned the scope back to the Mercedes trio and let out a low growl. Luke could feel the tension. But Matt had spotted something else. 'Hey up,' he said. 'Isn't that Joey's girl, Tanya?'

Luke moved the Barrett. 'Yes. What's she doing here?'

He shifted slightly to pick up the girl as she was about to pass the alley beside the chippy. But she seemed to hesitate when she saw the other girls getting out of the car. Matt and Luke watched this silent movie play out in their scopes, watching Becky spin round as Tanya and Carol crossed towards her, obviously angry and agitated as they started dragging her away, shouting back up the street at the driver now holding out his hands in a form of protest. What could he possibly have done?

'Kiddy fiddling, that's what you've done, mate,' Matt muttered as he watched Tanya and Carol drag Becky away. He then went back to the driver and the girls who, now out of the car, looked in their early teens trying to look in their late twenties and curious about what was going on. The driver waved a dismissive hand in the direction of the retreating Tanya, Becky and Carol and then put his arms round the girls' shoulders and guided them towards the alley.

'Might be his sisters or cousins?' Luke suggested.

'Like the ones we saw being let out the back the other night? And if they are, why don't they go through the shop?'

Luke agreed as he watched the driver escort the girls down the alley to the rear fortress door, where he banged on the door, all the while talking into his phone. He could hear Matt's breathing deepen. Troubled. He knew why. And why he didn't want to go there right now.

'Let's stay on mission. Someone else can sort that one.' He moved back on to Fatchops and zeroed the scope once again. 'Shop's still clear. How's the street?' There was a hesitation as Matt was still brooding on what he'd just seen. 'Matt?' Luke hissed.

'Top clear. Bottom clear,' came the response.

Luke settled himself. Matt pulled the spotting scope back to cover the area outside the chippy. A five-second kill zone. Luke slowed his breathing. Moved his finger back to the trigger and put the cross hairs exactly where he wanted them. Cold shot or not, the target was big enough to make the mess he wanted. Breath. Hold. Squeeze.

'Hold,' Matt suddenly said. 'Tanya and her mates are heading back.'

Too late. The ball was in flight.

5

Changed Scenario

'Oh, and what? You've been one day away and now you're sure are you?' Natasha asked. It had that tone. The one that warned him she was not the little woman. The one who could be told what to do.

'I'm not saying my mind's made up, Nat,' Joey said, as he took a quick glance back through the window. He was out on the scaffolding. Above the skips that filled the yard below where he and Benno had colonised as their sleeping quarters. Builders' squatters in billionaires' bunkers. It was where he could be out of earshot. Although he needn't have worried as Benno was already cocooned in his sleeping bag and snoring for Great Britain.

Natasha, though, was going up a gear. 'Will we be able to manage?'

He held back. He was about to remind her that it was she who said life was not all about money, but he didn't want to enter the maze of female logic just yet. Especially long distance. He wouldn't stand a chance. So, instead, he tried a softer, more diplomatic line. 'All I'm saying is that I want to talk to you about it properly and I'm telling you now so you can think about it over the week. That's all.'

It seemed to calm her down. 'Oh . . . OK. I suppose we can . . .' But then her tone changed again. Concerned. 'Oh . . . Oh my God. I'll call you back.'

Joey was left staring at his disconnected phone. Natasha sounded really distressed. Which she was, as she rushed towards her daughter, who was helping a sobbing Becky and extremely distressed looking Carol through the door.

'What, what has happened?' Natasha's maternal eyes went straight to the cut and rapidly swelling bruise around her daughter's right eye, before darting to Becky then Carol and back again, as her brain ran rapidly through the index of potential parental horrors.

Tanya saw the worry in her mother's eyes. 'No . . . no . . . It's nothing like that. But oh my God, Mum. It's mad . . .'

'What? What's happened?'

The identical thought was going through a very nervous Mercedes driver who had rushed through from the back with two other men, shouting and gesticulating for them to secure the door and get the young counter servers out of the shop to the back. The one at the door was now shoving a couple of surprised Bingo goers outside before locking up. The other was scampering and squealing back and forth behind the counter, trying to scoop something out of the boiling oil in between yelps of pain. It was the special forks box.

Mercedes was still shouting for him to stop shouting so that he could make himself clear as he shouted for the one by the door to lock up and kill the lights. As some form of control returned, Mercedes stepped towards the counter. The soft drinks cabinet was wrecked, its door hanging open and the floor covered in sticky liquid, which he assumed must be from the shattered bottles. The fork box and wrapping paper had fallen from the counter but nothing else appeared to be damaged. He looked over the counter to see the prone legs of Fatchops. Lifeless. What had happened here?

Up on the hill only Matt and Luke knew as they watched through their scopes, their breathing slow with relief after witnessing the nightmare scenario almost play out in front of them. Fortunately the Barrett's 50 cal bullet had slammed into the chippy drinks cabinet seconds before Tanya and her posse arrived at the door.

Luke had automatically chambered another round ready, as he would later tell Joey, to take a shot if he felt Tanya was in any real danger. As it was, he had calmly watched as she was backhanded and brutally shoved out of the door just before the Bingo couple. It was only when Carol had pulled both her and Becky away and down the street that Luke had taken his finger off the trigger. She'd survive.

*

Natasha's phone was vibrating on the table. Joey was trying to get an answer. As was Natasha herself, now forcing a sandwich bag of ice on to her daughter's forehead above her swelling right eye. 'Slowly. Tell me slowly.'

'It was mad, Mum. Wasn't it, Cags?'

'Yeah,' Carol confirmed. 'We were just going back to see if Hus was there, and—'

'Going back where?'

'He was parked up the street. With two other girls, right, Becks?' Carol looked to Becky, trying to make the point, but all Becky could do was nod and reach for another tissue. Then hug Roscoe as he came over to offer support.

'The chippy,' Tanya said, beginning to regain her composure, taking over the sandwich bag as she stood up and went to the sink to get a drink of water for Becky. 'We were just about to go in and there was this, well, sort of huge bang. Right, Cags?'

'Yeah. Just really loud and then they all came rushing out the back shouting and screaming.'

'At each other. And then us,' Tanya added as she gave Becky the water then wrapped a piece of kitchen roll round the sandwich bag. 'They just shoved us into the street.'

'What do I want this for?' Becky asked.

Tanya looked at the glass. Good question. It must have been something she'd seen on the telly, but she added with a hint of her old sarcastic self, 'To replace the fluids you've lost on the way home?'

'That one with the beard really hurt my arm.' Carol was pulling off her jacket to examine it.

'Er, hello?' Tanya snarled, pointing at her eye. 'He did this to me.'

'Who? Why? What was it about?' Natasha asked, more in hope than anything else as she could see the teenage fright was now being pushed aside by exuberance, as they realised they were safe. Even Roscoe thought it safe to leave Becky and return to his bed.

Back in the now quiet chippy, the one with the beard had been the one at the door, who had backhanded Tanya, but was now switching off some of the lights, while the one without a beard was nervously guarding the rear door, nursing his burnt hands inside a dirty tea towel, as Mercedes slowly rounded the counter to approach the prone lump that was Fatchops. He was still not moving and his head was covered with the pile of wrapping paper he must have pulled down on himself as he fell. That was probably how the forks had ended up in the fryer. Mercedes stepped forward and delicately, nervously, kicked the lifeless legs. Nothing. He took another look around. At the counter. The drinks cabinet. The floor. What had happened? Beard and Beardless shrugged. Both still apprehensive. They were all tense. They all knew what the real trade was that went across the counter. They all knew they could come under attack. At any time. But was this it? There'd been nothing on the CCTV monitors.

Mercedes looked back at the lump. Was he dead? How did you tell? He'd seen the movies where they touched a place just below the ears. But did that really work or was it just a Hollywood thing? He stooped down, being careful to keep his Prada jeans dry, then reached out and shoved Fatchops's back. It wobbled. But was he breathing or was that just fat sloshing around? He shuffled closer, carefully, still trying to avoid the liquid. Was it blood? He reached down and wet his fingers. Smelt it. But what did blood smell like? Cherries? He hesitated but then tasted it. Sugary, sweet? He'd heard that somewhere. But decided it was more likely to be from the soft drinks bottles. He did another duck shuffle to keep his Pradas dry and was just about to try and find Fatchops's neck when the lump moved, and as it did Mercedes fell back in fright and felt the sugary liquid soaking through his Pradas. He swore. Then kicked out at the prone body. Fat idiot!

'It's not marketing, Sean, it's throwing money away,' said Sandra.

'Bigging myself up, as you put it, must by definition fall into the category of letting people know about the business.' Sean was trying, but even though the VAT Goddess had turned out to be a mumsy size 18, he knew he had lost the argument as soon as he'd mentioned the 10 per cent discount offer to Sandra.

'Marketing is supposed to be about getting real people

in to spend real money. Not a bunch of freeloaders who then end up getting a discount.'

When she put it like that, as she always had the knack of doing, Sean knew it was time to retreat.

'How'd the rest of your day go, anyway?' He gestured to the TK Maxx hooded top and ruched leggings that had displaced the Armani.

'Mum and Dad are well, thanks. But I assume you want to change the subject because you've realised how daft you are?' He didn't answer, but went across to the boiling water dispenser.

'Do you want tea?' It might be taken as a peace offering. It wasn't.

'I'll do it. You might waste two teabags as we'll probably have to start economising soon if you keep throwing money away.'

He went across to the table, knowing he would have to take what was coming to him.

'And do you think it made any difference?'

'And that's what I'm trying to say about it being like marketing or advertising,' said Sandra. 'You never quite know what works, do you, except it does. You can tell by seeing the results.'

'What results?' She put the tea on the table and sat down opposite him. 'Go on, how will you be able to judge?'

But Sandra didn't get to answer. A third voice entered the debate.

'Hear you want to teach kids how to use drugs, Dad.'

'What?' Sandra turned to face Noah, who was coming into the kitchen dangling his car keys from his finger while treading his usual path to the fridge.

'Yeah, Dad ripped into the chatterati or something. Said we teach kids how to use tobacco and alcohol so we should do it with drugs. The Head was all over it this afternoon.'

Noah re-emerged with what appeared to be a piece of ham wrapped round a chunk of cheese. Then grinned at his mother's obvious discomfort. 'She asked me if I had "any worries" at home.' He then turned to Sean. 'Good one, Dad.'

'So now you know which part of your so-called marketing worked,' Sandra shot at Sean. Then back to Noah. 'She wasn't serious, was she?'

'As serious as any retard can be.'

'Don't use that word.'

'It's OK, Mum. You'll still be able to walk down the High Street without people pointing at you. They think it's Dad sniffing the plants in the greenhouses. And everyone knows the Head's a trembler. First sign of any controversy and she panics. Anyway, I'm just going to Josh's for a bit. See you later.'

'We should have put you on that curfew insurance scheme. I don't like you driving at night.'

'Except when you two have been on the drugs, you mean?'

'What?'

'Dad'll explain. Socially acceptable, but still a drug, isn't it, Dad? Alcohol?' With that he threw a sarcastic smile at Sean, received one back and left. His job there was done.

Sean started to smile. Pleased. Imagining the whittering that must have gone on after his speech.

'See,' he said to Sandra. 'That's a result.'

'It's not funny, Sean. The Head of the kids' school thinks you're some kind of druggie?' But she noticed he was drifting on to something else.

'Remember that motorhome we had? And we ended up travelling because you were always asking that sort of question. Well, it was more "who are they to judge"?'

She finally grinned as she accepted her own words thrown back at her. He had that impish, mischievous glint in his eye that she had fallen for all those years ago. Mr Goody Two-Shoes who was desperate to be a rebel like his little brother Joey. The Mr Perfect who loved being top of the form but hated being called a spod. Who loved being deputy head boy but hated not being able to kick a ball straight like little brother Joey. Who could talk for Britain with every girl in the school but was always too shy to ask for a date. The Mr Clean who never traded in cash and hated drugs. How could anyone think he was some form of closet druggie? Not her Mr Softie.

'Wish we'd just kept going sometimes,' she smiled.

'Nah, there was never enough room for the kids.'

'Is it that, then? All this, throwing our money at community causes because you worry what they think of you?'

'Bigging myself up, you mean?'

'Go on, how much did it cost us?'

'Sean spotted the emphasis on "us". He let out a sigh of surrender. 'Probably around five hundred for the food and lost business.'

'And the discount.'

'Yeah. But that lot wouldn't have spent much anyway. They wouldn't have been there in the first place, so whatever they spent we made.'

'You're too soft a touch. Do you know that?'

'Better than bigging myself up?'

'Probably. At that price though I wish I had come now. I'd have loved to have seen Julia Erskine's face. And that prat Harold Peagram.'

'You could always come to the CAD consultation tonight. I'm, er, we're not paying for that.'

She shook her head. 'Same old, same old. Having Rupert Bronks staring at my breasts all night?'

Sean grinned. 'I had noticed, but I can't really blame him. Even in that top.'

She ignored the comment as she stood to go. 'But you know what, Sean. If you really want to do something, do it. Don't mess about. If you're going to waste our money on good causes, pick something that will really make a difference locally.' She headed for the door, but stopped and turned back. 'Or go into politics for yourself. I'd also love to see Peagram's face if you announced you were standing in the election. I'm going to see how Megan's getting on with her homework.'

Sean stared at the door. Was she really serious? Go into politics? After everything they had both said about politicians in the past? What everyone seemed to think about them at the moment? He had toyed with the idea before but always wondered if he could do any good as an individual councillor. He quite liked the whole networking scene, but getting anything done would mean he'd have to work his way in and then up one of the main political parties that seemed to dominate everything. More and more their idea of a good local candidate was a good national party member, which made it all feel close to the sort of nationalist totalitarian state parties that democracies were supposed to counter. Sean knew he would not be seen as one of the club so had always pushed the thought away.

He picked up his mug and went across to put it on the drainer, but then decided he didn't want another ear-bashing about why he couldn't put it actually in the dishwasher. He put it on the top rack and let the door swing up. Yes, he grinned, he might not make a difference outside the political clique, but, like her, he'd love to see Harold Peagram's face.

'No, they're all fine, Joe.'

Natasha was on the house phone as Joey had got

frustrated trying to get through on the mobiles. But his frustration was nothing against Natasha's.

'It's those swines down at the chippy, Joe,' she said.

Joey had already processed that Luke and Matt had done something. But as Tanya was safe he wasn't concerned about that. It was the vehemence that took him completely by surprise, as did the speed at which Natasha was winding herself up.

'You may have been away, Joe, but you must know what's going on down there. Those guys. The drugs. The girls. Something's got to be done. Someone's got to do—'

'Hold on. Wait. Hang on.' Joey was scrambling to catch up. Was this just mother's talk or was she winding up to telling him she knew what he and Luke were up to? 'Nat, Nat. Slow down. Talk to me. What guys? What drugs? And what girls?'

'Everyone knows, Joe. The so-called parties. Getting young girls off their heads with—'

'What?' This was something new to Joey. 'Are you saying Tan was—'

'No. No. She was just there looking for Becky's boyfriend and—'

'Is she involved?'

'Joe, look, accept that you're not here. You don't know. And you're not going to catch up over the phone. God only knows what happened down there tonight.'

Joey had some idea, but couldn't share it with her.

'OK. Yeah. But. You sure Tan's OK? Definitely?' He

heard himself still trying to sound calm while his mind was in overdrive wondering what the hell Luke was thinking, doing something when Tanya was around.

'Yes. Yes,' Natasha replied, causing Joey to relax slightly, but not for long. 'She's got a bit of a bruise . . .'

This additional bit of news immediately heightened Joey's anxiety about what Luke might have done. And what might have happened to his daughter. Again. But Natasha immediately sensed his anxiety coming down the line and knowing she was stepping into an area she'd prefer to keep from Tanya, she said, 'I'll call you back on my mobile.'

With that she hung up the house phone and looked across at Tanya, who, still holding the improvised ice pack to her eye had moved on from water to making hot chocolate, while Carol was at the toaster and Becky was scrolling her phone. They seemed to be getting back to normal.

Natasha was already pressing Joe's icon as she stepped out on to the patio, quickly closing the sliding door and not realising she nearly decapitated Roscoe who was on her way to join her. He pulled back just in time, then sat wondering what was so secret even he wasn't allowed to hear.

'She's OK, Joe. Honestly. Sounds like they walked into some kind of aggro going on inside the chippy.' She stopped talking and listened to his breathing. It was slow but hard. She knew he was trying to keep himself in check. Just as she knew he was probably rerunning what he had been saying to her over the weekend.

'You couldn't have done anything, Joe,' she quickly added. He didn't respond. She sensed he was fighting a similar thought. 'You can't follow her round all the time.'

'But,' he finally replied. Now calm. Cold and determined. She could imagine his back stiffening, hands clenching and unclenching. 'I could be down that chippy now, though, couldn't I?'

'And back in the cop shop again. What good would that do us?'

She could hear the breathing getting lighter. He was trying hard to control his frustration. 'Why are you so calm, anyway?' he asked.

'I'm not,' she replied. Making a greater effort to calm her own breathing. 'I'd like to go down there myself right now . . .'

'Nat, don't you even—' But he heard her voice go up a pitch as she cut across him.

'I'm just telling you how I feel. How everyone feels, probably.'

'About what?' Joey asked. Now cautious.

'Haven't you been listening to what your Sean and Sandra have been banging on about all these months? Or their Noah's campaign to clean up the park?'

'I try not to.'

'Don't be flippant, Joe.' She paused, realising she was getting wound up again, before adding, 'Something does need to be done. Somebody needs to sort them out, Joe. If the police won't do it. Someone has to.'

This took him completely by surprise. This was not like her. She usually dismissed Sean's rants as naïve do-gooder ramblings. 'Er, what exactly are you saying, Nat?'

'I'm saying, Joe –' Natasha explained. Slowly, deliberately – 'that you're not the only one who has time to think when we're apart. I know you, Nolan. And I know Luke Carlton.'

She let it hang in the air. Waiting for his response. He stood staring at the occasional electrical flashes that came from the overground electric rails. She always used his surname when she was making the point of where he had come from. Who and what she had married. Did she really know? Was she fishing? Or was this just something she'd dreamed up herself?

Before he could decide which one to bet on, he heard her voice again. She had turned to see Tanya and the others getting up as though they were getting ready to go out again. Damn.

'Look, I'll have to call you back.'

'Why?'

'Because I'm freezing. I'm outside on the patio.'

'That's why they're called mobiles, Nat. You can keep talking as you change locations and—'

But she was in a hurry to stop Tanya from leaving. 'Yeah, I know, but I need a sweater too. Call you back.'

Joey was left hanging in cyberspace. Not even a quick luvya. What's she keeping from me, he wondered. What did she mean about girls and partying? He stood looking at the urban skyline, thinking it through. Had Luke taken the shot? If he had, surely Tanya would have seen something? But would Luke really do that if Tanya was around? No, not if anyone was around. He'd told Joey about waiting for that clear five seconds. No witnesses. So, what had Tanya walked into? Whatever it was, it was a reminder that within a couple of weeks the apple of his eye had twice come close to being badly hurt.

He tapped the messages icon and scrolled to Luke's number. But he knew he couldn't text. He'd just have to wait. Which only lasted about five more electrical flashes on the horizon before he climbed back through the window, threw his stuff in his bag and was out the door. He'd call Benno in the morning.

Everything in the chippy was now calm, relatively. Fatchops, far from being splattered all over the walls, was leaning against the counter wheezing as the bearded one held a few pieces of crumpled wrapping paper against a cut on his forehead. The beardless one still appeared agitated by the rear door, while Mercedes was calming down as he twisted and turned, trying to gauge how bad his sticky Pradas were. He then went to examine the drinks cabinet but feeling the stickiness seeping between his legs he turned and aimed another kick at Fatchops.

Kicking 'must be a family thing,' Matt said, with a chuckle as, up on the hill, he pulled away from the spotting scope and prepared to pull out. Luke waited another second or two then slid back himself with a sigh of relief. He and Matt had remained motionless as they waited for the bullet's impact, thankful that at 900 metres per second it easily outpaced Tanya's run. She had arrived after its kinetic energy tore through the glass door of the drinks cabinet and blew six 2-litre Coke bottles apart with enough explosive force to set off a chain reaction of bursting cans as they flew off the shelves. The bullet had then passed through the cabinet, coming to rest embedded in the damp plasterwork behind. It was the impact noise that had caused Fatchops to turn, startled, and then slip on the cascade of Coke foam erupting from the shattered cabinet. He started to slide sideways, tried to stop himself by grabbing at the counter but only managed to spin so that he cracked his head on the way down, clutching and clawing at the wrapping paper. That was the moment Tanya had arrived, closely followed by Becky and Carol, only to be met by Mercedes and his associates rushing from the back of the shop. It had got a bit rough and heavy handed, but at least the bearded one had shoved them out of harm's way. That might help him later. But for Luke and Matt, it was time to move on.

They slid out of the hide, with the broken-down Barrett split between Matt's guitar case and Luke's backpack. They would have preferred to just go. With the collectors coming later. That way no one is connected. The shooters have no weapons and the collectors can claim they stumbled across it all. Using women and kids was even safer, as every rebel force in history had learned. Democracy's greatest weakness was its most valued principle: civil liberties.

Still, no one should be looking, but to help cover their activities they tipped out the contents of a bin bag. Their own ration pack boxes were replaced with a mixture of crushed soft drinks, lager cans, a collection of sweets, fast food and tobacco packaging. They wanted it to look like a temporary kids' hangout.

While they were clearing up, so too were Mercedes and Fatchops who were in the back of the shop trying to figure out what had happened. The counter servers had been sent home, as had the guy in the alley who acted as banker, along with a few disgruntled customers hoping for either their special forks or sausage curry.

After fifteen minutes or so of going over and over the fact that there was no one else in the shop, no one else in the street except for those stupid girls looking for Husani, and no other damage anywhere, they had all concluded that perhaps it was just a bottle exploding. Especially as they had retrieved one of the soggy labels to discover it was from the fake batch they had bought in from India.

Any further investigation was abandoned when the bearded one came through from the house with one of the young girls who was obviously wondering what Mercedes was doing. Immediately he lost interest in Fatchops's sensory powers or where the drinks came from, and went back to the real reason he had turned up tonight, but not before he reached over and picked up a few special forks that had avoided being deep-fat fried. He then waved for the bearded one to help Fatchops clear up, as he led the young girl back inside. Maybe she could help him out of his sticky Pradas.

All this was still being watched by Matt through a small night-spotting monocular as Luke finally gathered everything together.

'Looks like they bought it,' Matt said as he set up a huge commercial firework rocket and tube. 'We could have done with a few of these when we got caught in that goat market ambush.'

'They're probably banned under some goat protection convention,' Luke responded as he started off down the hill. After a moment or two to allow him to get a safe distance away, Matt did one last 360 with the night scope. All seemed clear so he lit the long fuse of the rocket and a couple of other ground-based fireworks before, as the instructions said, retreating to a safe distance, going the opposite way to Luke. Up the hill. By the time the rocket roared and soared skyward to explode with a sonic boom and brilliant starburst that would be heard and seen all over Highbridge, Luke was on his way down the hill, silhouetted against the Golden Rain that was spewing out behind him.

Now, if anyone had seen the Barrett's muzzle flash and bothered to climb up to investigate they would leave thinking it was 'just kids' messing about with fireworks. Like the initial reaction in the chippy. They would assume what they were already expecting. Job done. Get gone.

'Quiet, Roscoe,' Natasha soothed as she stroked his head, stepping out once again on to the patio. 'It's only a firework.'

She waited, as did Roscoe, head up, ears primed, but after a few minutes both assumed that was it. They then turned and looked back into the kitchen, now a scene of typical teenage occupation. Natasha had managed to talk Tanya's friends into staying put, so Tanya was handing out the hot chocolate. Carol was fighting someone in a distant multi-room, probably Ross, for control of the Sky EPG while Becky was thumbing her way through her phone menus. Natasha and Roscoe exchanged looks. Neither really wanted to go back but both thought they should.

'So, excitement over for the night then, boy?' Natasha asked as she stepped back inside and went to make herself a cup of tea, while Roscoe headed for the treats cupboard. He had, after all, warned them of the firework. However, as no one was paying attention he went and flopped back into his basket. Natasha realised she was unlikely to get much more out of her daughter as she was now preoccupied, reconnected to her digital universe, so she turned her attention to Carol, still trying to get control of the Sky Box. She stepped across, took the remote and pressed 204. There was no counter entry. 'If they see that, they know I am looking for something to watch.'

'I can't wait to be a mother,' Carol said as she went across to the table to join the others.

Natasha smiled as she collected her tea, not sure control of the Sky Box was worth going through childbirth for but it could be classed as an unforeseen benefit. She decided to try again, quickly, as she saw Carol picking up her phone, heading for the digital exit. 'So what do you think was going on down at the chippy, Carol?'

'Dunno. They were really freaked out by something, though.'

'Fridge exploded,' Tanya announced without looking up from her phone. 'According to Henry.'

'And Nisha's just tweeted: Dad's got me behind counter. Big Bingo rush. Chippy closed. He owes me,' Becky chipped in.

Carol had by now also gone digital. 'Holly's saying: Fatman Flops on Fridge.' She scrolled down the thread. 'Mia reckons Fatty fell over and smashed into the fridge and shattered all the bottles.'

'Wouldn't want him falling on me,' Tanya added. 'And that firework came off the hill, according to Zolly. Reckons it'll be someone off the Riverbeck estate.'

Natasha looked at the Sky remote and then back at the digital news service around her kitchen table. Who needed the TV news? She passed the control over to Carol and headed for the door with her tea. 'Wait about five minutes as I'll tell him he should be asleep.' Then, to Tanya, 'You all OK now?'

Tanya stood up and hugged her mother, then sat down, without taking her eyes off her phone. Natasha smiled again. And was that worth going through childbirth for? But seeing they were now all relaxed. And safe. Yeah, she thought, it was. And she'd get the full story from Tanya in the morning.

'But that's not the full story, Rupert and you know it.' Sean was on his way out of the public consultation, pleased with the number of nodding heads he had noticed while repeating almost word for word the speech he had given at lunchtime. He was now speaking to Rupert Bronks, local Golf Club owner, part-time scrap merchant and full-time cleavage gazer.

'It was a good speech, though. Really. And I liked that answer you gave about "if politicians can't find jobs for people they should find something else to keep them occupied". That makes sense.'

'And I believe it. Redefine our values so that what we consider "work" is also about what we do with our time, rather than just working for money.'

'That's where you lost me,' Rupert replied, nearly losing Sean as his gaze wandered towards the ladies' toilet where another cleavage had just appeared, but he didn't lose his thread.

'Seems to me,' he continued, as he turned to watch the cleavage head back to the function room. 'That the trouble is too many of them do that already. They want someone else to give them the money so they can have a good time without working for it. But no doubt that's too simplistic again, is it?'

'No. Not really,' Sean responded, waiting for Rupert to turn back. Which didn't look like happening. So he prompted. 'It's about balance, Rupert.'

This seemed to do the trick. 'Ah, balance,' Rupert commented as he turned with a smile on his face. 'Must be some sort of politically incorrect joke about balance and breasts, eh?'

'Or perhaps not?' Sean offered, wanting to neither agree nor subscribe to this male-bonding line.

Rupert just snorted. 'Being PC, are you?' But he didn't wait for a response. 'That's like balance. I hate that almost as much as I do "impartiality". I don't want to be impartial. I don't want to be balanced. And I don't want to be a reconstructed metrosexual, whatever that is. I want to do and think what I believe in. And that's not buying someone a new suit to go for an interview who could get a job digging ditches and save up for a suit. And they're only a few quid down the charity shop. Plenty of my old things in there, I can tell you.'

'I'm not really asking you to buy them a suit, Rupert.'

'I know, Sean. I know you're not that daft. Just as I'm not as daft as I make myself sound. You want me to look at the reasons they're like they are. Why they take to drugs? Why they become homeless? Become unemployable?' Sean nodded. Rupert leaned forward and prodded him on the shoulder. 'Then you'll have to adopt them all at birth. Think Sandra would go for that?'

'I know, I know.' Sean accepted this, but started to guide Rupert towards the door as he saw another group of women heading for the Ladies. 'But I'm trying to talk about what we do right now.' He continued: 'about helping the ones already caught up in it all. Give them a hand to try and do something else with their lives. Give them an option other than the street corner dealer.'

'And how many addicts do you have working your tills down at the garden centre?'

Sean gave a nod of defeat. He knew that simplistic truth was the killer point. If he didn't want to take the risk, why should others.

'Exactly. The approximate number I have at the Golf Club. Might have them among the membership, mind, but I'm after their cash, not letting them get at mine. Sorry, Sean. I never had anything when I was growing up. And I never turned to drugs.'

Rupert headed off for his car but stopped to shout back, 'Probably because I was too pissed to find them. But, er, not tonight of course.' He nodded over Sean's shoulder to where Hilary Jardine was heading towards them. Out of uniform but appropriately dressed by John Lewis. No cleavage. 'And give my regards to Mrs Nolan. Tell her I missed her. 'Night, Inspector.'

Hilary smiled a goodnight as Rupert headed off and she crossed to Sean. 'We'll have to stop meeting like this, or something like that?' She continued walking towards the car park.

Sean followed. 'Do you think you can get addicted to anti-drug get-togethers?'

'I get paid for it. Although,' she hesitated, before saying, 'And don't fly off the handle at me . . .'

'You're still wondering why I bother?' Sean finished the question for her. 'You and Sandra,' he added, waving to Rupert as he drove away in his old Jaguar XJR. 'Someone's got to try and do something. And if only it was as easy as getting a job digging ditches. Been there and done that. It's got to be how we think about work, hasn't it. In an area like this. Where so many people work for the state in some form or other.'

'Like me?'

'Yeah. And most of them at lunch. And here tonight. All getting cash from the state, just like people on benefit. I mean, you're a job creation scheme really, aren't you?'

'Never saw myself as that, I have to admit.' Hilary started fishing for her keys as they had reached her very sensible Skoda Fabia.

'No, because your job was created a hundred years or so back. When "we", society, decided we'd rather pay other people to keep the law than have to worry about it ourselves. But, if you think about it, you lot, and nurses, doctors, teachers, the fire service, are all there because we, society, or communities, decided to create those jobs. We didn't decide to create the job of shoemaker or baker or banker or blacksmith. Or people like me selling plants. They all came because individuals saw a demand and wanted to make a living out of it.'

'You're going to end up in politics if you're not careful,' she replied, but now with a real smile on her face.

'You are sounding like Sandra now.'

'Bet she's not encouraging you.'

'And you are?'

'Well,' Hilary hesitated, before adding, 'We could do worse. We probably are doing. And although you'd probably make our life a bit more difficult, we could do with a few more like you.'

'That sounds like some form of backhanded compliment.'

'You care, Sean. And that could get us all into trouble.'

Sean smiled. 'Think you're mistaking me for my son. Or my brother?' He saw the smile stiffen again. 'You don't seriously think Joe's up to something, do you?'

He was relieved to see the smile relax again.

'No. He's not trouble. Never was, really. Thinks he's Jack the Lad, but he's only a statistic. I get paid to sort out the likes of your Joe every now and then. But . . .' she let it hang, not sure whether to go on or whether she was adding two and two to get five.

'But?' Sean prompted. Then took a guess. 'Luke is from a different set of statistics?'

Hilary nodded. 'I know his history. Even before. And

although Joe has told me he has been a calming influence . . .' She let that thought hang with a shrug as she changed tack. 'Just ask Joey to make sure neither of them becomes another statistic I have to deal with. Which also applies to Noah. Goodnight. Love to Sandra.'

With that she drove off. Leaving Sean to ponder the female hive question. How did all the women in his life seem to say the same things? Was it that intuition thing – or did they really converse telepathically?

By the time Luke arrived back at the cottage, Matt had showered, changed and was taking the clothes he had been wearing earlier out of the washing machine. As the clothes were the only real chance of anyone tying them to the vicinity of the hide, they were now destined for the charity shop. If they burnt the clothes and the cops did happen to come knocking, then they would find that suspicious, but it was highly unlikely they would go rummaging through the charity shop just on the off-chance of finding a particular colour of jumper that matched a witness description.

Luke immediately started stripping off and loading the washing machine as Matt was searching the fridge.

'You should have popped in the chippy on the way back,' Luke said with a grin.

'Funny that,' Matt replied. 'It was closed for some reason. Get the Barrett stowed?'

Luke nodded. 'I'll have scrambled.'

'You'll get, as my old mum used to say, what you are given.'

That would be one of the one-pan meals Matt had mastered on their global excursions. Whether Palau or Risotto. Or Paella or Ragù. Or Scouse or Cawl. Matt started to slice and dice. 'You reckon it's safe under that bridge?'

Luke nodded and reached over for a bottle of water, then nicked a tomato from Matt's ingredients pile, just dodging a flick from his Blackhawk folding and barely legal Hornet knife. Another souvenir from his time as a US contractor.

'There's a local gun club not far down the track. If anything gets found the cops'll waste a day or two making two and two equal six and harass the law-abiding membership while they hunt for some imaginary gun freak.' He bit into the tomato. 'But they'd have to know where to look. We used to hang out up there. It's a small gap where the bridge supports meet the bridge itself. Some kind of bearing or shock absorber that cushions the load. You'd only know it was there if you worked on building the bridge. Or were bored out of your teenage brain and looking for things to do.'

'Boldly going where no one else in their right mind would go?'

'Probably. But then Joe and I did a lot of things out of sheer boredom.'

'Which explains a lot. And why Fatty and his gang have

them queuing down that alley. We going to hit him again tomorrow?'

'See how bright he is. Whether he figures it out and calls in the troops.'

'Let's hope he's brighter than he looks, then. How'd you want your eggs?'

'Just as they come?'

'Good answer.'

Which was something Fatchops hadn't found. He was still searching for an answer while throwing his clothes into a washing machine: it was part of his POLO as he was actually more concerned about his own forensic residue than that of Luke and the others, as it was more durable than that left by firing a weapon. For this reason he always appeared to wear the same clothes, having a cupboard capable of providing three changes a day. For the lunch, dinner and chucking-out time waves. He walked back into the now spotlessly clean shop and stood looking at the damaged drinks cabinet once more, not quite convinced that a bottle of fake cola could do so much damage. His head was still pounding from the fall. He'd take an over-the-counter drug, not one of his own, and figure it out in the morning.

6

Build-Up

By the time Fatchops began his search for the real answer to what had happened the previous night, Joey had visited Luton, Birmingham, Stoke-on-Trent and Crewe, reinforcing his twin beliefs that modern transport enabled people to make journeys undreamt of in his grandparents' age and that they were designed to make Londoners feel safe in their beds, certain that no provincial hordes could descend on them overnight in an orderly manner. Similarly, it was virtually impossible for anyone to escape the outer reaches of the capital beyond 23.30, when all long-distance trains were suspended, unless they already had an escape plan in place. Joey had three. He always had. Ever since starting the weekly commute he had wanted to know how fast he could get back to Natasha and the kids if wanted to. Like now.

The full-on emergency option was taking Benno's ambulance, but that would mean returning it. And right now Joey didn't think he would be coming back. By the time he left Benno going after a new world record for snoring, his options had been reduced to one of the other two. The 23.30 overnight bus to Liverpool had gone. That left the half-past midnight service to Manchester, but looking at his phone he knew it would be touch and go whether he could get to Victoria Coach Station in time. Its second stop at Golders Green was also on the edge. He could, however, get to its third stop at Luton Airport by 01.40 by taking a direct train from Blackfriars. After that he'd have to change buses at Birmingham, then drop off at Stoke and catch a train to Crewe, then home. It was part of his weekly routine to check the timetables in the hope of finding a more direct route, but there never was. At least this one allowed plenty of time at each changing point for delays. And pondering. On what he would be walking into when he got home.

Once at Stoke he knew Natasha could collect him within forty minutes, but that would mean her getting up early, not being able to do the school run, and that would escalate her anxiety. Better, he thought, to jump on another local train to Crewe and be home before she got back from the school run. Then he would be able to calm her down face-to-face. So at 07.00, just after purchasing his ticket to Crewe, he sent a holding text.

HOPE THINGS BETTER THIS MORNING. TRAVELLING. TALK LATER. LXXJ. He then tapped his favourites and found Benno's number. Time to tell him what he was up to.

Neither Mercedes nor Fatchops were in the best of moods as they came through from the back of the chippy. Fatchops was fiddling with a large crêpe bandage that was now wrapped round his head. Mercedes was fiddling with the drawstring on a pair of definitely non-designer baggy, and chequered, catering trousers. Their depression was deepened by the knowledge that no matter what had happened last night, they had lost most of their product to the deep-fat fryer and while that had had to be cleaned out, the money for the product would still have to be accounted for.

Waste was a term with only one meaning in their business and if they didn't pay up it would be applied to them. While a grumpy Fatchops moved to start getting things ready for the day, a sullen Mercedes unlocked the external door then threw both the keys and a killer look back at the counter. Giving a last irritated look at the baggy trousers, he opened the door and stepped out, pulling his coat around him against the wind as he hurried to his car, grateful for the keyless entry that would allow a quick exit before anyone with any fashion sense could see him.

Whether Matt had any real views on the subject was open to question and if he did they were probably directed more towards Joey's tales about his scruffy London companion Benno, but the sight of Mercedes scurrying up the road made him laugh.

'He doesn't look like a happy bunny this morning,' Matt's voice announced in Luke's ear. They were now using Motorola MT352 walkie-talkies with voice-activated headsets held securely in place with surgical tape as they were wary of using the pay-and-throws for extended periods, or of relying on the vagaries of the mobile networks for instant communication. The Motorolas had an advertised potential range of 35 miles across 22 channels, each with 121 privacy codes. The 35 miles claim was always followed by an asterix, of course, meaning don't rely on it, but they would cope with a few miles round Highbridge. And they might not survive being dropped out of a helo or Warrior, like their usual comms kits, but they came with a few other advantages. They were really cheap, licence free and could be bought for cash. And while their expensive encrypted kit was designed so no one could eavesdrop, that always assumed someone was trying to listen. The other great advantage of the MT352s was that their frequencies were illegal in the UK, so the chances of someone else having one and stumbling across which of the 2,662 potential channels they chose to use was remote.

While Matt was back on the hill, Luke was sitting in an old Transit van just down the street from the chippy.

It was parked so he would have a clear line of sight from its side door, although at the moment it was closed and he was sitting watching the Mercedes start to move away on a small colour monitor he had taped to his thigh. It may not have been as sophisticated as the chippy's CCTV, but the small inspection camera at the end of the flexible optic tube they had wedged into the door seal gave a clear view of the whole street.

'It's not bad, this. How much was it?'

'Seventy quid in a sale from Maplin. Got it for sixty-five for cash,' Matt replied. 'Says it'll do night vision too. But only at 1.5 metres.'

'Useful to see who you've tripped over, then?' Luke asked as he slid back behind the Barrett.

'Think they had inspecting your drains or hidden wiring in mind, rather than target spotting, actually, Carlton. And something you might find in a crappy builder's van.'

Luke had the Barrett on a tripod so he could shoot from a sitting position. He was wedged between side racks of chaotically stacked trays filled with electrical fittings and plumbing pipework, along with all the screws, nails and general bits and bobs that make up the organised chaos of any typical builder's van. To the casual eye. To the more experienced viewer it would look exactly what it was. A collection of junk and scrap. For two weeks, alongside scoping the chippy, they had been scavenging skips, taking full advantage of the throwaway society.

After running a vehicle check paid for with a prepaid

credit card, they had bought the van on eBay for £300, complete with eight months' MOT and one month's tax by phoning the buyer direct. They had turned up, paid cash and given the address of a Domino's pizza outlet in Birmingham. Neither should have done that under eBay's terms, but then again, neither should people be selling illegal drugs. Nor other people planning to shoot them. By the time the DVLA V5C form had worked its way through the system, Fatchops and the Transit would be history, someone at Domino's would probably return the V5C to the DVLA and the seller would be an innocent victim of who knew what. All in all, eBay would probably never find out. Especially that its one-time listing was now parked up in a northern town as a sniper hide posing as just another builder's white van. To the casual eye.

And it was casual eyes they were depending on, as they had agreed that, although it was a long time to sit and wait for the spudman to make his delivery, parking up early was the best option. Most people are half asleep on their way to work or school, so they wouldn't notice Matt park up and leave a white van with a tool bag. Just another builder doing a job somewhere. But a guy sitting in a van for three or more hours would attract attention. Even to a casual eye.

As a result, Matt was now halfway up the hill watching through a pair of birdwatching binoculars. Just another middle-aged bloke filling his unemployed time, but he could be back at the van within minutes. As soon as he saw the spudman approaching.

'They do make me laugh, these characters,' Matt continued. 'They live among the world's filth but are always so flash – no, fastidious, about their appearance.'

'Playing the part,' Luke responded. It's like the footballer's manual. Tattoos. 4x4. Big headphones. These guys think it's designer clothes and cars.'

Matt chuckled again. 'He's probably got a gold-plated phoney AK under his bed too.'

'Is anybody likely to walk past and see you talking to yourself?' Luke replied.

'That Lukey for shut up and wait?'

'It is.'

'OK.'

It was also Luke's way of keeping everything as normal as possible. Ordinary. It's often not what's in front of people that matters but what they pick up or sense. Even if a passer-by saw Matt chuntering away to himself they would probably just think he was talking on his handsfree. But perhaps not if he was animated while looking through his binoculars. Joining dots that are sometimes not obvious. Like peripheral vision and the reason they kept their eyes moving, from point to point, as it's the peripheral vision that picks up movement. Or like the lines they had sprayed on the road the week before. There for everyone to see. White, like the ones councils spray round holes instead of fixing them. One circle with an arrow pointing to the kerb. Another arrow on the kerb pointing into the road. Few would even notice, never mind wonder what they were, but when the Transit parked with the arrows lining up with the two mud splashes below each door window, Matt and Luke knew that when the side door cracked open a few inches it would present a perfect shot. Like the previous night. Straight through Fatchops's front door. It's all in the prep.

'Tell me what really happened last night before the beasts come down,' Natasha asked, as she leaned across to examine Tanya's now badly bruised eye. 'You'll need to cover that a bit more.'

'Why?' Tanya asked, defiantly. 'If anyone asks I'll tell them what happened.'

Natasha sighed. Knowing she had already lost the argument about not provoking more trouble. But she had a maternal duty to probe. 'Well, you could start by telling me?' she asked. More in hope.

Now it was Tanya's turn to let out a long sigh. She had a teenager's duty to evade. 'Just Becky still not getting it.'

'What?' Natasha couldn't follow the logic jump. 'Last night it was all about things exploding and guys pushing you about?'

'We were only there because Becky can't get what that guy's after.'

'Which is?'

Tanya just looked. 'Er. . . Where've you been for the last few years? White girls are easy?' With the faintest shake of her head she took her tea and headed for the door.

'Is that it?' Natasha called, but got no answer. Obviously it was no longer a trending tropic, but at least Tanya appeared to have her head screwed on about sexual predators. That just left Joey to update. She headed across to the patio doors to let Roscoe in after his morning patrol and pulled her phone from the pocket of the fleece Joey really hated. One of the advantages of him not being around in the week. She could grab whatever was still on the bedroom chair, like every other school run mum. She saw his holding text then replied. WHAT TIME TALK? LX2T The text went the three miles to the nearest phone mast, then the ten miles to the nearest exchange, 200 miles to the central server then back, to be delivered to Joey's phone half a mile away, as the cab that was ferrying him from the station turned off the High Street towards home. By the time he got there, there was only Roscoe waiting with a happy but confused look on his face. It couldn't be the weekend already!

'Aye, lad,' Joey said as he grabbed Roscoe's nose and gave him a playful to-and-fro. 'New routine.'

Roscoe just stood. Waiting. As a puppy he used to like this game that would end up in a fun fight round the kitchen, but as he got older he had adopted a resigned tolerance, knowing that it wouldn't last long. He was right. Joey gave him a head rub, then went to the coffee machine as he texted Natasha. AFTER SCHOOL RUN? LMOREXXXJ Natasha looked at the text from Joe, but was too preoccupied trying to keep up with her mother's spiralling conversation.

'I'll follow you, then.'

'Mum, you gave up driving five years ago.'

'Did I?'

'Yes,' Natasha confirmed, trying to keep the frustration out of her voice. It only made matters worse. 'Remember, you had that funny turn when you ended up nearly driving into the canal?' How could anyone forget that, she thought, but the mind is a mysterious thing, especially when it starts to fail.

'Not really. You sure that was me and not . . . er . . . not . . . ?'

'Who?' It was an automatic response, but Natasha was still coming to terms with her mother, Grace's, early signs of dementia. Or perhaps not coming to terms with it, as Joe was beginning to say.

'You know. Oh, what's her name . . . ? You know. She's always at the doctor's. Practically lives there.'

'I wouldn't ask if I didn't . . .' But she bit her tongue. Go with the flow. That was the advice. She drew breath. 'Give me a clue?' she smiled and squeezed her mum's hand.

'Oh, I am getting forgetful these days. I know it must be difficult. I was only telling Pamela yesterday that I can't remember from one minute to the next at times.' She stopped and squeezed Natasha's hand harder. 'I do have a friend called Pamela, don't I? She's still alive and living close . . .'

Natasha couldn't help but laugh as she interrupted the flow. More out of relief than the dark humour of trying to keep up with the short-circuiting that was starting to happen in her mother's brain. Sometimes she felt like she was carrying on three separate conversations at once. 'Oh, Mum. Yes. Auntie Pam, as we all grew up calling her. And you were at the baking club with her yesterday.'

'I knew that bit. Just had to check whether it was real or not. I'm getting confused more regularly these days, aren't I?'

Natasha just nodded. It was true. Even if it was difficult to admit. Like this morning. She still hadn't found out why her mother had called to ask her to come round straight away.

'Bound to happen. Seen so many of them down at the hospice,' Grace continued. 'Can't remember their own names, some of them. Remember the one who used to live next to the garage off Market Street? Had a snake tattoo. On her arm. Oh, what was her name? Began with the same letter as the shop over the road. You know, from where the vet used to take the horses.'

Natasha just stared. Trying not to look concerned. Go with the flow. But now totally lost. 'I er. . . I don't remember anyone with a tattoo, sorry Mum.'

'I'm not surprised,' her mother said. Then started to laugh and point at Natasha. 'Your face. Had you there, didn't I?'

'Mother! It's bad enough without—'

'It's all right, love. If I can't laugh at it, who can? And at least I still can. Anyway, it was Betty I was thinking about.'

'Betty?'

'Who drove into the canal? Remember?'

'Are you still winding me up?' Natasha asked warily.

'No, I meant before. When I was trying to remember who I thought had driven into a canal. I was thinking of your sister-in-law, mother. Betty. The doctor's receptionist. But she reversed into a paddling pool, didn't she? At Joey's brother Sean's lad's birthday party. Noah. And it wasn't his paddling pool but the younger one's. Megan. She did that around the time I went through that fence and nearly . . .' she emphasised it again, 'when I nearly, went into the canal. So, I just got the two things mixed up, didn't I? But, you see, I can still remember things.' She gave Natasha a broad smile, then sighed. 'Just not every now and then. Or in the right order.'

To stop the tears welling, Natasha squeezed her mum's hand again, then started to gather the teacups. 'Well, while you're remembering, you stopped driving after that.'

'I remember it was you who stopped me,' her mum shot back. 'And leave those. I can still manage.'

'It was actually Joe. And it was the right decision.'

'I know,' her mum conceded. 'He's usually right, your Joe. I've always listened to him.'

It took all Natasha's strength to resist asking, since when? Just as it was fortunate her mother stood up and started gathering the teacups. Otherwise she would have seen Natasha's jaw hanging with incredulity. Her mother never listened to anyone, never mind her son-in-law. She was still telling anyone who would listen how Natasha had wasted her life on him. Go with the flow, she told herself. 'So you still can't remember why you asked me to call round. Urgently?'

Grace slowly shook her head. 'But you did say to dial Star 6 if I needed you. Perhaps I should write things down first. So I won't forget.'

'Yes, perhaps,' Natasha agreed, thinking how long it had taken to get her to remember the speed dial function on her phone. 'Was it something to do with lunch over the weekend?' It was a wild guess, but she had learned that Grace was entering that stage when food became the focus of life.

'Yes. Yes, that was it. Was it? What time will we be eating, do you think?'

'The usual time. As always. And we'll pick you up and take you to the restaurant.' She stood up and tried again to take the cups from her mother. But Grace held on. Slightly defiant.

'I'd better go,' Natasha said, to avoid the confrontation. 'I left Roscoe in the house.'

Grace nodded, put the teacups back on the occasional table and walked her to the door. 'Give my love to er. . . er. . .' But seeing her daughter's expression, not amused, she smiled. 'That bloke you've been married to for seventeen years. Text him my love or whatever you do these days.'

'I will. Bye, Mum.' She gave her mother a last hug and left, sending the text to Joe straight away. MUM SENDS LUV. GETTING WORSE, MAKES ME MISS YOU MORE. SPEAK LATER LXXT No sooner had she pressed send when a text from Tanya arrived. GOING BECK'S AFTER SCHOOL HOME 9ISH.XX THAT WOULD MEAN LESS ARGUING AT HOME. OK XXX It would also give her a quiet hour to speak to Joe, as although he said he wanted to talk, she knew he found it difficult while at work.

What she didn't know was that he was beginning to pace the kitchen wondering where she was. What he didn't imagine was that she was cursing her long-gone dad, as she always did when she had to ease the Q7 round the walled flower bed he had hand-built right opposite the front door, but smiling at the memory of how proud he was of it. He had no idea at the time that his daughter would at some point be driving a civilian troop carrier. Once clear of the wall and pointing towards the gate she turned to wave back at her mother who was, as always, standing in the window waving.

Time and age, Natasha thought as she gunned the Q7 down the road, it gets us all in the end. Something similar was going through Grace's mind as she watched her daughter drive off, too fast, as always. She turned away from the window and felt in her cardigan pocket for the card she had folded inside. Typed in bold were three words. Time. Clock. List. Beneath them Grace herself had written Betty – Sean's mum. Sandra – wife. Noah – oldest. Megan. She sighed, looked across at the clock on the mantel. What should she be doing now? She headed off towards the kitchen to look at her list, leaving the teacups where they were.

'If you want to change anything, Sean, you should run for mayor or something. At least get it out of your system.' It was another of Glynnis's throwaway lines as she manoeuvred a Christmas tree through the entrance of the café. Stopping when she had another idea. 'You could get your sister-in-law to design your electioneering pamphlets. People'd like that. Local jobs for local people.'

She then left him with that thought and he was more convinced than ever about the female hive. Or that Glynnis and Sandra either talked every day or were separated at birth. It was almost word for word what Sandra had said to him the night before when he had tried to recount his after dinner chat with Hilary Jardine. Followed quickly and emphatically with a reminder that they had put their time in building the business and all she now wanted was to enjoy the last few years they'd have with the kids before they all flew the nest.

His phone chirped as a text arrived. It was Arthur Young passing on Craig Harlow's contact number. He chuckled at the thought of a global rock star turning up to play Santa. But stranger things happen, he thought. And if Craig could win a Grammy, then why couldn't he himself win an election? Then he chuckled again as he wondered what Sandra would make of her soulmate Glynnis's idea of him running for mayor, even though Highbridge was too small a town to have an elected mayor.

Yet, he wanted to do something and as he liberated the Santas with a last slash of his retractable knife, he looked at his watch. Just time to get the Santas deployed before lunch. He grinned. Perhaps he could start his own party and take over the whole process. Local politics for local people. His grin morphed into a laugh. The idea of revolutionising local politics was probably not what Sandra would consider a way of enjoying the last few years with the kids. His laugh then developed into a chuckle. If he became some sort of party leader, though, it would be a good excuse for her to renew her wardrobe.

Joey walked along the landing to the spare room, now changed and his hair wet after a quick shower. He looked in to see their weekend sanctuary, away from Tanya and her friends, was now doubling as Natasha's work space. Printed copies of inspirational quotes she would sell on Etsy were strewn across the bed and what looked like a half-finished design was still drying on the printer. He was now beginning to feel a sense of anticlimax. The hero's overnight odyssey battling the creatures of the night to be by the side of his princess was rapidly feeling like a sad over-reaction.

Where could she be? Joey wondered as he made another coffee. Anywhere, he concluded. Another reminder of how they led separate lives during the week, and while he imagined what lay behind the weekly headlines he never quite knew. Another side effect of mobile phones. You never had a clue where anyone was these days. Should he text again? But that would probably get her going. Then again, he'd said he'd call after the school run. She'd expect him to call around now. 'What do you reckon, Rosk? I travel all night to get back and support her, and she's nowhere to be seen. Any clues?'

But as usual Roscoe opted to not get involved and went to the patio door to be let out. As he closed the door behind him, Joey reached for his phone. CAN YOU TALK? But no sooner had he pressed send than he heard Natasha's phone chirp, accompanied by a loud OMG of surprise. He turned to find her in the kitchen doorway holding both phone and hand to her chest.

'What the hell are you doing here?'

Not quite the heroic welcome he had expected. 'Yeah. Sorry. Didn't want to worry you last night, so I—'

But she cut him off as she crossed over to hug him, causing her hair to nearly suffocate him once again. 'You scared the . . . Jesus, Joe.'

At the end of his lung capacity he eased her back and

kissed her. This was a bit better. 'Sorry for giving you a shock but I thought . . .'

She hugged him again and then stepped back. 'No need. It's why I love you. You always know when I need you.'

As she took off her fleece Joey watched her closely. His attention on the frown across her forehead. He guessed his instinct had been right. Something was going on here that she'd been trying to keep from him. But she was recovering.

'What . . . What about the work?' she asked.

'Not important. Benno's sorted it. Just jumped the overnight bus.' It was all she needed to know at the moment. He'd tell her about the wino at Birmingham and psycho at Stoke some other time. 'So. Go on. I'm here. What's going on?'

'Don't know where to start, really.'

'How about something typical? Cup of tea and begin at the beginning. Just ramble.'

And so she did. For the next hour.

'Cracklin' cocaine,' Luke suddenly heard in his headset. He didn't respond, just waited. He knew one of Matt's philosophical ramblings was on its way. 'There's Crack Cocaine, isn't there? Fatty's just invented another variety. Deep-fried? Crack-ling? Cracklin' Cocaine.'

Luke managed a smile as Matt chuckled at his own joke. Then carried on. 'I mean, it's priceless isn't it. Why put the stuff so near to the fryer in the first place?'

'Because he's at the bottom of the food chain?'

'Yeah,' Matt agreed. 'And looks like he's working out all his inner tensions on that countertop this morning.' His tone changed as something in his binoculars caught his attention. 'Now then, what's Fatty doing now?'

Luke couldn't make out the detail on the monitor but Matt relayed how Fatchops was struggling to drag an old fridge from the back room towards the damaged cold drinks cabinet. He then started to pull the cabinet away from the wall to make space for the fridge. And as he did he noticed the damage the 50 cal round had made in the plasterwork.

'He's found the impact point.'

Luke leaned on the Barrett but kept an eye on the monitor while listening to Matt's commentary as Fatchops eased the cabinet forward, to see the hole in its back lined up perfectly with the damage to the wall. They both waited. Tense. It was too early for him to discover what was going on. After a moment or two of fingering the damage, perplexed, wondering whether an exploding bottle of cola could do such damage, he backed away. They relaxed. His body language said it all. What else could it be? Even if he knew what he was looking for he wouldn't be used to seeing – never mind expect to find – the damage from a 50 Cal. Luke heard the relief in Matt's voice as he described Fatchops giving the damaged drinks cabinet one last shove to make space for the old fridge.

'Do you think he's wondering if that's a design fault and it's still under warranty?' Matt asked.

Luke smiled as he checked the Barrett one more time. It would be another cold shot, but from this distance he could probably just point and shoot. Still, they had already laser-ranged the distance so he was ready. The closer distance reduced the margin. No flight time for people to accidentally step into the shot. This time, almost as soon as Luke squeezed the trigger the target would be destroyed. In one way it was easier. But in another way much more dangerous, as they would be in close proximity. Even with a suppressor the noise would be noticeable.

Again they were relying on the unfamiliar and unknown. And that there would not be many folk around at the time. However, there was always the chance of a passing smartphone and the chance of getting on the evening news. Unlike the previous night, this time they would have to get the job done and get gone, sharpish. Luke glanced at his watch. 30 minutes.

'We've only got half an hour before we have to be back for that stupid enrichment lecture,' Carol shouted from behind the toilet cubicle door.

'He said he would wait for me until lunchtime,' Becky countered as she continued her pleading to get Tanya and Carol to go to the chippy.

'Listen to yourself,' Tanya counter-countered, while

looking at her bruised eye in the mirror. 'If you did you'd realise how pathetic you sound.'

'I only want to find out where he is.'

'God, Becky. How many times. Look at this!' Tanya pointed to her bruised eye, as Carol emerged from the cubicle. 'And he was with two other girls last night.'

'He said he was only giving them a lift. But you wouldn't wait to find out, would you?'

Tanya turned to Carol. Help me out here.

Carol tried. 'But why was he giving them a lift to some greasy chippy?'

'I don't know. You'd have to ask them.'

'Don't want to know, you mean,' Carol fired back. 'You've read Lizzie Peterson's feed about the parties,' she made the quotation marks gesture to emphasise the point. 'The parties where they all get off their heads. He was probably rounding them up for his mates.'

'Lizzie Peterson's a skank,' Becky tried to protest. Lamely.

'And?' Carol asked incredulously. 'I don't think it's her social standing they're after. They don't even want her standing.'

'Look,' Becky was becoming tetchy again. 'I know you hate him. But you don't know what he was up to any more than I do. So he might have given a couple of girls a lift to help out his friends. It's their choice and . . .' she turned to Tanya as she saw her about to come back in. 'They go to that chippy because their parents don't approve of, well, you know.'

'What? Him salivating over white girls?' Tanya asked, her exasperation getting the better of her. 'And he's probably already engaged to some fat cousin he's never seen in some village he's never heard of back home.'

'Don't be so racist.'

Carol pushed between them. Sensing Tanya's impatience would cause Becky to stomp off by herself. 'C'mon Becks, he's twenty-five or something, isn't he? And still worrying about what his parents will say about who he dates?'

'It's . . . It's some kind of religious thing. He doesn't want to upset them.'

'So who's being racist, then?' Carol asked.

'It's not racism. It's religion,' Becky responded as she headed out of the door.

'Oh, so that's OK then? Selective prejudice,' Carol called as they followed her out.

'And like religion hasn't led to people killing each other all over the world?' Tanya chipped in again.

'All right, all right. I get it,' Becky fired back. Now getting angry herself. 'It's not just because you don't like him. You don't understand his culture.' She strode away from them. But towards the Sixth Form Centre.

Carol turned to Tanya. 'Well, at least that stopped her going out.'

'Why can't she see it, Cags?'

'Now listen to yourself!'

Carol headed off after Becky, leaving Tanya chewing her lip. She had spent most of her life sidestepping predators, but for Becky this was the first big thing. Why couldn't it have been that moron in her geography group who kept buying her cupcakes?

It took a moment for the motor to get going, but it wasn't long before Byron had to jump aside to avoid the spray of artificial snow heading his way.

'Careful, Sean!' Byron called as he took a long arc to come up behind the snow machine. Sean was trying to position it so that the artificial snow would fall directly in front of the entrance doors. 'Are you sure it wouldn't be better over the exit?'

'Byron, the whole point is to get people in the Christmas spirit on the way in. So they will spend more inside.'

'Well who's going to clean it all up when people traipse it inside?'

'It dissolves, like rain. And most people are like you. They'll dash through it. But hopefully it will make them smile. Especially if they've got kids and are coming to see Santa's Garden.'

Byron didn't look too impressed. He didn't have kids. 'If, and it's a big if, they actually know it's here. I don't care what young Ben says about social media, it's only like being in the pub. If you're there you can join in the conversation. But if you don't even know where the pub is, how can you? We need to spend money advertising. Telling the real people. The old people—'

'Older people,' Sean interrupted.

'The people who can come in here on a wet Tuesday afternoon.'

'They those wet people who traipse in, in their wet and muddy wellies?'

'Touché. And I know it's one of Sandra's ideas so it will probably work, but you can tell the staff they will need to clean up.'

'Do you really think so,' Sean replied with a huge grin, as he nodded over Byron's shoulder.

Byron turned and let his shoulders sag as several of the staff were already running in and out of the snow, scooping up handfuls and throwing them at each other.

'I think it's a primeval thing. And . . .' Sean said and then indicated a young lad standing under the snow shower taking pictures on his phone and then putting his thumbs to work, 'I think Ben's already got the digital gossiping going.'

He began to walk away as Byron fired one last shot about doubting that Ben had their customer database in his favourites list before going over to remind everyone that they still had work to do. Which Sean also had to do. He pulled out his own phone and pressed redial.

'Hi. It's Sean Nolan for Craig, again. Any chance?

OK. Yeah, understand. Fine, no problem.' He then went on hold and listened to Craig's latest single, wondering exactly what were the chances of getting Craig Harlow to open Santa's Garden. Probably two. Slim and fat. But just as he was starting to tap along with the music, he was back on with Craig's PA. And his mood soared.

'Really? He's considering it? Great. Yeah, I'll be here all afternoon. Thanks.' He was about to ask what the hold music track was but the line clicked off. His face started to beam in a broad smile. Their local pop star was considering opening Santa's Garden. However, he didn't get much time to dwell on it as his phone sounded the klaxon alert that meant one of the kids was calling. It was Noah. Speaking at light speed as Sean put the phone to his ear.

'Noah, Noah. Slow down. You're going too fast.' Sean was standing surrounded by Singing Santas, once again speaking into his phone, knowing that Noah was extremely upset not just by his voice but by the fact that he had actually called. This was way beyond the power of text. 'Tell me again, from the beginning.'

By the time Natasha had talked Joey through everything that had been happening with Tanya and Becky over the past few months, he had gone from thinking they had just wandered into something outside the chippy by accident to worrying that his own daughter was slowly being pulled into another modern horror story of drugs and sex abuse. To be fair to Natasha, she had got it all out in about five minutes but he had kept asking her to go over and over the details, trying to make sure he wasn't simply reacting to media perceptions and local prejudices. He was not alone in regretting the way Highbridge had changed through an influx of outsiders, or offcomers, as the old locals called them, but he had always parked that as a natural resistance to change. Until it came close to his own. Then it became nothing more and nothing less than a threat.

'So, you reckon Becky's being groomed by this Egyptian bloke?' he asked again.

'Tanya certainly does. And as usual she is getting herself involved too much.'

'Wonder where she gets that from?' he smiled.

She returned the smile, appreciating that he meant them both, but then it hardened. 'So, as you came back, you obviously feel something needs to be done too?'

'What? Like asking Luke to go and sort them out?' He said it facetiously, expecting her to treat it as a throwaway, but was completely caught by her response.

'Well, it wouldn't be anything he's not used to. And what's he doing here? He's never hung around this long before.'

Joey now decided to deflect. Worried by where this was going. 'Do you think he might just want to take a break?' He then tried to use the same line he had with Hilary Jardine. 'Spend some time at home? On the anniversary of Janey's death?'

Natasha considered this, but shook her head. She knew Luke almost as well as Joey. Not just from personal experience, but from all the tales Joey had told her. And since he had married her sister-in-law. 'He's been running ever since Janey. So I don't see why he'd suddenly decide to settle down. Here.'

'He might,' Joey offered, still trying to steer her away from where he thought this conversation would inevitably end up.

'Yeah. Like getting you into a fight down the Lion?'

'OK,' Joey conceded. 'He might still be a bit messed up, but what I'm more concerned about is why you are suddenly wanting to go to war.'

'I . . . I dunno, really. Last night. God, if you'd seen them when they first got back. In fact when you see the bruise on Tanya's face. If you'd been here then, as I said, I'd probably be still trying to bail you out.'

He got up and squatted next to her, hooking his arm round her shoulders. 'So? I'm here. As you said. When you need me. But . . .' he hesitated before posing the question that would take them over a line. 'What do you really want me to do?'

She held his stare for a moment. His eyes had gone cold. She knew he wouldn't have come back if he wasn't really concerned. Which meant that no matter what he said, he knew more than he was admitting. Which meant he was ready to do something. He was really asking her permission.

Her own eyes hardened. 'You're already up to something, aren't you? You and Luke?'

Joey hesitated. He wasn't sure how she would react. But she had asked. 'You don't need to know.'

Suddenly she felt cold. Perhaps the shiver people often spoke about going down the spine. Although she had asked the question, she hadn't really expected that answer. She'd always known who and what Joey was. How he'd changed or, more correctly, held himself in check. For her. So she should have expected something like this. But hearing the words brought it home. It was too easy to constantly say something needed to be done about this, that or the other, but only a few people would have the nerve to actually do anything. She knew he had. But was that what she really wanted? She stood up and walked across to the patio doors to let Roscoe back in, partly to give herself a moment or two to think.

Joey stood and leaned against the table. Waiting. Watching. As she stood looking out across the garden where the kids had grown up. Where they had had many a BBQ. A happy lifestyle perhaps about to be put in jeopardy.

'How risky will it be?'

'You don't need to know that either,' came the matter-of-fact response. In fact, too matter-of-fact.'

'Christ, Joe. It's not some game or street corner brawl we're talking about.'

'And what are we talking about, Nat?'

He was pushing. She knew. He was pushing to get that permission. He didn't want her involved in the details but he wanted her to be aware of what he might get involved in.

'I . . . I don't know, Joe.' She turned back to face him. 'Perhaps it's all . . . Last night. The way my mum is. That's where I was before.'

'Is she really getting worse?'

She nodded. 'And something else to deal with.' But then she brought them back to the point. 'Perhaps all I want is what you've just given me. To be back here. With me. Sharing the load?'

'OK. You've got that. But . . .' He hesitated again. Not sure how far to go. But, as always, he needed to go the extra step. 'That wasn't how it sounded on the phone last night. Or before.'

'I wanted them dead last night,' she admitted. 'Which is probably why it is best to sleep on these things.'

'And having done that . . . what do you want to do?'

Natasha could only chew her lip. The line was right in front of her. Did she really want to cross it?

Forty-five minutes after taking the call from Noah, Sean was in the Custody Suite standing in front of a custody sergeant who looked younger than Noah and wondering why life did this. One minute he's on the phone ecstatic because Craig Harlow is considering opening Santa's Garden, yet without giving him any time to really savour the moment that same phone is informing him that his son has been arrested for public disorder. Fifteen minutes later they were in the garden centre Land Rover heading home with Noah trying to explain to his father why they should sue the police for wrongful arrest, harassment, entrapment and brutality while disrupting a perfectly peaceful protest in the park.

By the time they reached home, Sean was trying to explain to Noah that the police were not victimising him and his friends but trying to act on behalf of the whole community by preventing him and his co-protesters from coming to any harm.

It was met with a typical teenage 'as if' look. Followed by, 'And I don't need the Mark Twain quote about how much I'll realise how wise you are by the time I leave university.'

'The point, Noah –' Sean toughened up as he brought the car to a stop outside the house – 'is that it stays with you for the rest of your life. On a file somewhere. Never mind all this stuff about spent convictions and sealed files. They never delete anything. And you don't know where you will want to be in the future. And how it might count against you.'

'Oh right. "Teenage kid arrested for trying to save a children's playground." Definitely be on the US Homeland watch list with that one.' With that parting shot Noah went to get out of the car, but Sean put his hand on his arm. Just enough to stop him.

'No, but "organising protests against the state" might. It depends who writes the report.'

'Yeah, and history is written by the victors, Dad. But our democracy is about controlling the report writers, isn't it? And the only way we can do that is to make them and everyone else aware of what is going on. Evil prospers when good men remain silent and all that?' He gathered his stuff ready to bail out, but turned back to face Sean. 'Er, I think someone in this car once told me that.'

With that verbal dig he was out and on his way into the house, ignoring the Singing Santa trying to wish him a Merry Christmas, as Sean sat reflecting on hearing his own words thrown back at him. Hire a teenager, he concluded. While they know everything.

As he got out of the Land Rover, Sandra's Mercedes SLR 300 swung into the drive and she emerged, still in her tennis gear.

'Have you heard what he's been up to?' Sean called, hoping for some support.

'The whole town has,' she replied, holding up her phone as she swept past to find Noah, which she did at the fridge. 'I had to leave when we were 5–3 up in the final set for this.'

'Sor-ree. But I didn't organise the timings. And that's another thing.' Noah turned back to his father. 'Invasion of privacy.'

'What?'

'They must have hacked into our accounts or something to get there that fast. We were only there five minutes before the riot squad turned up.'

'You mean this account?' Sandra offered her phone and then did what everyone does in times of crisis: put the kettle on. 'I suppose you'll want to eat now you're here.'

As neither responded she took that as consent and started to drag the necessary components out of the fridge.

Noah had looked at the phone, passed it to his father and flopped on to the bench that wrapped round the kitchen table wall. Deflated. Sean was now looking at the phone and grinning.

'Who needs Big Brother's surveillance society when we've got social media?' he asked as he waved the phone at Sandra. She nodded towards her handbag and Sean dropped it in.

'Who came up with the Kids for Kiddies Facebook page?' Sandra asked.

'Does it matter?' Noah sighed. 'Just one of the group. And I told them not to post until we were actually there and established.'

'And . . . Dump the Druggies?' Sandra asked.

'That was me. It's the way to beat them. Name and shame. Drive them out. Social media is the new public protest.'

'Or village mob?' Sean asked.

'Or posting a target on your back?' Sandra asked, the scathing edge slightly softened by a mother's concern.

'Don't you think your druggies will be online too? As well as the police? And who would you have rather got to you first?'

Noah glared at her. Wanting to fight, but caught by her logic.

Sean couldn't suppress the wide grin on his face. Nor resist saying, 'That could be Mark Twain's missus, that.'

'You can be such a dick sometimes, Dad.' And with that he got up and went out. No doubt to reconnect with the group.

'Language,' Sandra called, more from habit than anger. That was directed at Sean. 'Did you have to?'

'No. But I don't really appreciate being dragged away from work to collect him from the police station.'

'Well you can't say your family hasn't had experience of that in the past. So let's hope he hasn't inherited the wrong Nolan genes.'

Sean took the barb. This might be rites of passage stuff, but he too hoped his son hadn't inherited any of the more aggressive Nolan genes. Like his Uncle Joe.

'Ten minutes,' Matt announced from his position halfway up the hill.

Luke glanced down at the monitor again. The street was quiet. As expected.

'You can record on that monitor as well you know,' Matt added, assuming Luke was watching.

'You know where that can end up,' Luke replied as he

arranged the black weed matting he had got from Sean. It was supposed to be for the cottage garden, but before that it had been commandeered to act as blackout inside the van. Even when he slid the door back to take the shot, anyone who happened to be looking in the direction of the van would find it difficult to make him out. 'Bad enough when we had to do it. Ended up collecting evidence on ourselves.'

'Yeah. Perhaps not the best of ideas. Hey up. Spuds on the horizon.'

Luke watched the monitor as the delivery guy's van came down the road towards the chippy. He then settled back down behind the Barrett. It was already chambered and ready to fire. He pushed a foam earplug into his right ear. Even with the suppressor the muzzle blast inside the van would be enough to cause temporary deafness. He tugged on a cord attached to a pulley system rigged to the side door. Just enough ease it back a few inches. They had taped and wedged the door lock to make it easier, and quieter, to slide open and if they had lined up the van properly with the marks on the road, then pointing the Barrett at the scratch mark on the inside of the door would line it up exactly on the open chippy door. And zero it in on where they had expected Fatchops to drag in a replacement fridge. It was. Spot on. Luke flicked off the safety.

'How close?'

'Twenty seconds,' Matt replied. 'Take the shot.'

Luke pushed the other earplug into his left ear and started to steady his breathing. Clear shot. Squeeze.

The old fridge exploded before the trigger finished travelling. Fatchops was once again diving for cover. Even before he hit the ground Luke had panned left a few degrees, sliding the bolt to reload, then steadied and the back wall turned green under a fountain spray of mushy peas. Luke came back right, now lined up on the delivery van.

A second later the driver discovered what the anti-material weapon was really designed for when he was thrown forward into his windscreen as a shattered engine block brought the van to a juddering halt. At such close range, without armour there was no need for luck. The 50 cal round had probably pierced the aluminium block, to smash a connecting or push rod, immediately causing the engine to seize.

Luke had already slid the door closed and was looking for the discharged cartridge casings as he felt the Transit rock, then start to move. Matt had arrived, as planned, just after the second shot, to drive them away, past Spudman, who was getting out, nursing his head, to inspect the steam, water and oil pooling beneath his now immobilised vehicle. As Matt turned the corner he could see Spudman was recovering the usual box of forks from the front and heading for the chippy, with an occasional glance back, wondering what had happened.

Inside the chippy, Fatchops was now getting to his feet and making his way to the old fridge. This time he could see the entry hole in the buckled door and, not having had the time to fill it, he could also see the exit hole at the back. He pulled the fridge out and saw the damage to the wall. Not too far from and not too dissimilar to the damage caused the night before. It took another second for it to register and another one for him to drop to the floor again. Now he got it. Someone was sending a message.

7

Follow-Up

When was the last time we did this?' Joey asked, pouring water into two glasses as Natasha put the reheated chicken casserole meals on the table.

'What? Have lunch together in the week? Or plan on attacking someone?'

'Well, I do that bit quite regularly.'

'Don't, Joe. It's not something to joke about.'

He nodded to accept the rebuke. And acknowledge that what Luke termed a proportional response did not come naturally to her. After a moment of guiding the chicken pieces round her plate she pushed it away and sat back in her chair. She had no appetite. For food.

'Go on then. Tell me.'

'Really?'

'Just what or how you are involved.'

Joey still hesitated. He didn't want her to know much, just in case it blew back. He wanted her to be ignorant. So ignorant the cops couldn't charge her with anything. Just as Luke kept telling him to keep out of the details. The operational logistics, as he put it. He'd given Joey the talk about the law of conspiracy. Just talking about doing something illegal was enough in itself, without actually committing the crime. For murder the sentence was mandatory life. As it was for conspiracy to murder. So, how far was he involved? And how far could he allow Natasha to go?

'OK. I'm going to try and pick my words here,' he began. 'I don't know what Luke is up to. He won't tell me because he doesn't want me involved. Because I can't be involved. OK?'

She nodded and waited. She had had the conspiracy chat too.

'All I'm doing is helping a mate working on his cottage. And lending him a few quid here and there. OK?'

'Bankrolling him?'

'Helping a mate with his cashflow.'

'How much?'

'About five grand so far.'

'What? And where's that coming from?'

'Stuff Benno scavenges from the skips every weekend. Stuff that rich Russian fella keeps throwing away.'

'But . . . But that's supposed to be going to set you . . . set us up back here.'

'I know, I know. And Luke is going to pay me back when he gets his next job sorted. It's just that he hasn't got it at the moment, to pay for – well, whatever he needs to do.'

Natasha was silent, her brain trying to process how Joey seemed to be using their cash to bankroll a couple of mercenaries. 'How?' she finally asked.

'How what?'

'How did you get involved?'

'I'm not involved.'

'How did you start lending your mate money, then?' She tried hard to take the edge off the sarcasm. But the irritation remained.

Joey now sat back in his chair. 'The night that prick took a knife to Tanya.'

'What? You just went to Luke and said, "Someone's just threatened my little girl, will you sort them out please?" Really sounds like you, Joe.' No effort to hide the sarcasm this time.

It brought an ironic smile to Joey's face. 'He's already told me it's nothing to do with me any more. 'He's just found a way to get some sort of payback for Janey. The bloke who killed her is probably long dead. But he, well, he just wants to take this lot out so they won't kill anyone else.'

'And he actually believes that?'

'No. 'Course not. Just wants the excuse.'

'Why? He must know the police will come after him.'

'Doesn't care. Said he's screwed up mentally anyway. Walking dead.'

Natasha took a moment to digest this. She could believe it. 'He always was off his head. That's why Janey was so good for him.'

Joey reached over and squeezed her hand. 'Like you and me. You pulled me back. And that is the real issue. If he was on the edge before. She pulled him back. So where do we think his head is now?'

'God, Joe. You seem to be so, I don't know . . . matter-of-fact about it all. He's your best friend. You can't just give him a few quid every now and then and wait for him to do God only knows what.'

Joey was trying to remain calm, but was becoming exasperated. This was his world. Even if it was one he tried to keep from her. 'Nat, look. Do you trust me?'

'What kind of stupid question is that?'

'No, it's not. I mean. You do, don't you?'

Natasha nodded but didn't comment. She did trust him. She trusted that all of this would have been thought through long and hard. And she wanted to know where it was going.

'So you'll know that whatever Luke is up to,' Joey continued, 'I know it's not something he suddenly decided last weekend. It's not something he decided after that fight in the Lion. Up to that point it was him who was holding me back.'

'What?'

'No, listen. We've both wanted to rip the town up ever since Janey's funeral. But . . . we held each other back.

By telling each other that I'd already lost a sister. He'd lost a wife. And the kids had lost their aunty. I didn't want them to lose their uncle. Just as I didn't want to lose my best mate. So by holding me back he was also, actually, holding himself back. Yeah?'

'So far,' Natasha said.

'And it was working, Nat. I kept feeding back what he had always told me about how random shit like that happens. Random shit. That was always his phrase. His stock in trade, he told me. So I fed it back. Over and over. But every now and then it would boil over. Like in Luke's head when that idiot desecrated where Janey died. Then later on started mouthing off about us only having jihadists running amok because of what guys like Luke were doing in Iraq and Afghanistan. I could have punched him myself, I tell you. If—'

'So,' Natasha finally cut in. 'So what happened to this great pact of self-control?'

Joey emptied his lungs with one huge sigh. This was the bit he didn't really want to get to. 'Me. That's what happened,' he said but held up his hand so she wouldn't ask anything else while he pulled the words together. 'I lost it.'

She gave him a look that asked what else was new, but he slowly shook his head to signify that this was a bit more than usual.

*

'Human beings, that's why. After all we've seen and done, does anyone have to ask why there are bad guys. Adam and Eve. The serpent and temptation. Sin. All that.'

'You fantasising about Sister Frances, again?' Luke turned to Matt as they settled back into the No. 2 position overlooking the chippy. Halfway along the Hilltop Walk, from where they could still look down on the chippy.

They had not long visited the fifth skip they had used to dump the last of the stuff out of the van. Each one at the back of a factory or industrial unit where guys dumping building waste from a Transit would be too common to notice. Now it was in the car park of the Hilltop Walk, stripped and cleaned. In case someone had said they'd seen a builder's van outside the chippy. It was now just another white van.

They held on to the Motorolas as with no data records anywhere they were just tools of their offshore trade. Another piece of typical British logic. Ownership in itself was not illegal, but using them was. The Barrett was left under the railway bridge, from where it would be retrieved by Billy Higham, once they told him what weapons they would like next.

'Now Sister Frances was sent by the devil. Defo,' Matt continued as he trained his birdwatchers on the chippy. 'Did I tell you she used to stroke my backside?'

'Once or twice. And, if I remember, you only made that

up after Joey told us about getting his leg over the woman next door.'

'Er, I think you mean I felt safe enough to confide in you.' He drifted off into some real or imaginary memory. 'Pity I was too young to realise what was going on.'

Matt let out a long, regretful sigh at the distant memory and opportunity, in his mind, lost, while Luke had a more immediate thought in mind as he started to dig out a ration pack from the rucksack. Fatchops too was overseeing the lunchtime trade, but also staring at the piece of plastic that had just cost him a sausage dinner. He had been given it by the guy who had come in ranting about reporting him to the Trading Standards people after finding it in his mushy peas. Normally Fatchops would've argued, too used to people trying to get anything free, but the last thing he wanted was to have anybody official poking around inside the shop. Especially as the shard of plastic looked like a piece of the shattered drinks cabinet. He went across to the peas and gravy counter tubs and started fishing. It only took one swirl before he was reaching for his phone.

'No, Nat. When I heard about Tan being threatened with a knife I just . . . After Janey. I went hunting. Down the Riverbeck estate.'

Now Natasha became alarmed, but Joey was staring hard at the table, avoiding eye contact. Which worried her more.

'It wasn't hard, tracking him down. I got enough out of Tanya to get the rest out of one of the street corner gangs. He had one of those daft tidal wave style haircuts. He'd be in the park. Behind the precinct or up on the old bridge across the railway. Third time lucky.'

He then fell into a reflective silence and used the arrival of Roscoe, who plonked his head on Joey's thigh, to avoid looking at Natasha again. Perhaps Roscoe had sensed the need for moral support, but it gave Joey an extra moment or two before having to answer the next obvious question.

'And?' The anxiety was equally obvious.

Joey carried on ruffling Roscoe's head for a moment until the question came again. More insistent. And in a tone that made Roscoe decide it was time to slope back to his basket. Out of harm's way.

'And? What happened, Joe? Or is this something else I shouldn't know? Or something you can't trust me with?'

Joey looked across at her. A slowly brewing and volcanic mixture of concern, anxiety, irritation and anger. Trust her? With his life. But admit his failings? Face up to his own imperfections? He couldn't hold her stare.

'For Christ's sake, Joe. Cut the macho numb act. Just tell me what you did. Or what you shouldn't have done. I've worked that bit out.'

'I didn't finish the thing,' he responded, his own sense of frustrated anger erupting. 'I had him hanging off the railway bridge ready to drop him in front of the next train.'

Natasha physically recoiled. Whatever she was expecting, it was not this image he was conjuring up.

'All I had to do,' Joey continued, 'was wait. Wait for a train to come through and . . .' He tailed off again.

Natasha waited. Hoping for the 'but'. It didn't come. Nothing did.

'He's moving,' Matt announced. The food was forgotten and five minutes later the Transit was slowly cruising behind Fatchops, who was scuttling down the High Street.

'Absolutely classic,' Matt said as he watched Fatchops turn into the park and head for the playground area. 'He's heading for smack alley.'

'Double bluff, so he thinks,' Luke replied. 'If the users think it's safe, so will he.'

'What do you reckon, then? Don't want to be sitting in this thing for too long looking at the kiddies' playground.'

Luke nodded. No one would think they were planning to shoot someone, but plenty would immediately identify them as potential paedophiles. He started to edge the Transit away, watching Fatchops flop on to a bench on the far side of the park. Away from the playground, but right next to another entrance. 'Let's go round the other side. They'll probably come down Waters Street.'

Which they did. A BMW X5 came to a stop outside the park entrance and three guys got out and headed towards Fatchops. Just as Luke and Matt arrived to watch. One was white, undercut and windswept top hair, wearing a heavy leather duffle-style coat and leather ankle-strap boots. Expensive. From that, and the way the other two – one Caribbean, one Asian – had shaved heads in mid-market designer sweat pants and puffas, obviously not yet earning real money. They let Leather Jacket go out in front suggesting he was Fatchops's next link in the chain, and confirmed by the way he greeted a now nervous but grateful-looking Fatchops. A quick head butt, punch to the side of his head and a push back on to the bench. The sweats and puffas took up positions at either end.

'Another classic. Don't look at us folks, whatever you do,' Matt chuckled. 'Easto, like Fatty, you reckon? Looks like he grew up where the hard men wore leather. Stasi. KGB.'

'Russian Mafia chic?' suggested Luke. Then added with a grin, 'Or subscribes to Bobby McBain's counterfeights catalogue.'

Matt nodded. 'Interesting thought. Although the other two probably nicked a box set of *The Wire*.'

They sat watching as Fatchops appeared to be talking eighteen to the dozen, finally showing them the piece of shrapnel he had fished from the mushy peas. Leather Jacket took it and turned it over in his hands. Eventually he nodded, but then leaned in to Fatchops with a pointing finger to emphasise some form of motivational message along the lines of, if this happens again you're dead. It seemed to work, as when he flicked a dismissive hand Fatchops was up and scuttling away, once more at a speed no one would have thought possible.

Leather sat for a moment, leaning forward, examining the piece of plastic. That, the fridge and hearing about the Spudman's engine meant someone was sending them a message. But who? And why? He stood up and headed back to the BMW, with the other two hurrying to get there first. One to open the door for him, the other to get into the driver's seat.

'Follow?' Matt asked. Luke just nodded. Matt started the Transit and followed the BMW as it pulled away and headed back out of town along the expressway.

'Until?' Natasha finally asked, still hoping. 'For God's sake, Joe. Who? What?'

'Someone grabbed me from behind.'

He finally looked across at her and saw the fear as she was running through all the possible scenarios. Joe dropping the boy. A train hitting him. His friends gabbing. The police? What? What? What?

Quickly he reached across and grabbed her hand. Reassurance. 'It was Luke. He pulled me and the kid back.'

'So . . . So you didn't . . . ?'

Joey shook his head. 'Luke had tracked me. Pushed me to one side and got hold of the kid himself. Pulled him back up. Calmed him down. Then asked him, really calm, did he understand why I was after his skin? The kid was terrified but nodded. Luke then asked him if he would tell anyone about it. Kid naturally said he wouldn't. He'd have said anything to get away.

'How . . . how old was this "kid"?' Natasha suddenly asked.

'Younger than Tan, not much older than Alex. And I know what you're thinking. He had a mum and dad. Perhaps even together. Probably. Brothers. Sisters. I dunno.'

'Christ Joe, and you . . .'

'Yeah, I know. I know. I was only going to smack him about a bit but he was such an arrogant . . . He'd told me whatever I did to him he'd do to Tanya . . . Which is why I lost it. He wouldn't be able to do anything if he was dead, would he? So right then, right there, when he was screaming for his life, I didn't care if someone, somewhere loved him.'

He elapsed into numb macho mode again, until Natasha prompted him.

'And would you? Really?'

'I've gone over and over it . . . And honestly. I'm just glad Luke turned up. Then turned it all back on me. Fed everything I'd been feeding him. How it would be you and the kids, and Sean and his lot, who would lose if I got put away.'

While Joey continued to unburden himself, Natasha started to realise how close all this was coming to her family. Her sister-in-law. Her daughter. Her nephew. Now Joey getting involved. How pervasive it was becoming. No wonder people talk about it as some form of virus-borne disease. Or even cancer. And Joey and Luke were trying to cut it out.

'Jesus, Joe,' she interrupted. 'You can't take this on. Shouldn't it be the job of the police?'

Joey couldn't help but give a derisory snort, then leaned forward in his seat. Challenging. 'Hang on. Last night you wanted them dead. That's why I travelled all night.'

'What? Who will rid me of this meddlesome priest?'

'Er, that from one of those period dramas you watch without me?'

'History GSCE,' she corrected. 'Henry II said something like that about Thomas Becket, which led to him being killed. It's more about being careful what you wish for. And that was last night. In the, I don't know, heat of the emotion, I suppose.'

'And that's what it takes to deal with these people. When they attack you. You fight back. There and then.' He was vehement. Driven by emotion. But seeing the worry and anxiety still on her face, he softened again. 'And I took it that you obviously needed me here.'

She reached forward to him and clasped his hands. 'I do, but not running round on some vigilante mission.'

'At least it's in a language they understand.' He sat back again, his impotent frustration still dominating.

'Oh, like what?' she threw back, equally frustrated. 'Asking some stupid teenage kid to promise to play nice in future?'

'Making him aware what will happen if he does it. Sean craps on about making people aware of the consequences of doing drugs. But what about the consequences of selling them?'

'I know, I know. But isn't that what the laws, and the police, are for?'

She knew she said it more in hope than conviction as she was wrestling with her own position as much as Joey's, so was not surprised when he gave another snort of derision. But then he added, 'It used to be. But now we have a so-called justice system where everyone has rights. Including the right to feed off other people.' His mind was back on his confrontation with Gustav on the London site the day before. 'They're everywhere, Nat. Lowlife. Parasites.'

'So your response would be to just let Luke kill them all?' she kept pushing. While still fishing.

'They're killing people!' But he immediately held up his hands in apology, realising they were starting to go round in circles. He had also noticed the slight flicker of suspicion pass across her eyes, which was quickly followed up when she asked him about Luke and Tanya's attacker.

'You talked about consequences. What did he do?' she asked.

Joey broke eye contact. Which told her there was more.

'What did he do, Joe?'

Joey let out a resigned sigh. 'He told him he wanted to give him something to remember us by.' He hesitated. She waited. He finally continued. 'Then he held out a folded hand. You know, the way you give something to someone. Kid holds out his hand. Luke just grabs his thumb . . . and breaks it. Crack.'

Natasha winced at both the thought and this further image.

'He just did it. To a kid. So he is right. He is screwed up. He used to be . . . He used to be a real laugh. Do anything for you.'

'For you, you mean. And your Janey,' said Nat.

'Yeah, but . . . Anyway, we know all this, but . . . he also made me aware of what he'd been going on about. About his tradecraft. What he did, still does, for a living. And from that moment everything turned over. He was no longer holding back but, well, protecting me. He'd found what he had been looking for. The excuse. To do some hunting of his own.'

'And where's that going to lead?' she asked, still horrified.

'I honestly don't know, Nat, but, remember how you felt last night? With your daughter injured in front of you? Keep that right there.' He tapped the front of his forehead. 'Don't let go of that. Otherwise, they win.'

Before Natasha could even assimilate that thought,

never mind respond to it, her phone rang. She looked. Then stood up, alarmed.

'It's Mr Bryce. He lives next door to Mum,' she quickly told Joey as she answered, listened and then let her shoulders sag in relief as she thanked Mr Bryce. She ended the call and turned towards the door. 'C'mon, she's locked herself out again.'

'Up and over?' Luke asked. Matt nodded. They waited until the BMW X5 passed the exit lane before they pulled off and Luke accelerated up to the junction roundabout that flew over the expressway. He timed the gap in the oncoming traffic to slot in, drive across and go straight back on to the expressway, now several more cars behind the BMW X5. If they were watching they would probably have seen the white Transit go off and then relaxed, or if they weren't watching, another white Transit joining the expressway wouldn't register. Probably. But just in case, Luke kept a five-car separation.

It was not long before they saw the X5 indicate and turn off, heading down what looked like an old country lane that had probably, at one time, been the main link between the outlying villages but now, a mile or so along, it became a back route into a sprawling post-war housing estate. The X5 stopped outside what appeared to be the original old farmhouse, now sitting on the edge of what was officially called Downside, although it had become known locally as Downer-side until some 1980s regeneration plan had renewed the street lights and pavements and renamed it Orchard View. Everyone now knew it as The Spew.

The farmhouse had been upgraded and sold off privately, but the social housing came right up to one side of it. The back and other side still sat in a field, but the front looked on to the road, probably widened to allow access to the estate.

'Good 3G signal,' Matt announced, checking his phone as they cruised past. 'Very nice property too. Shame about the neighbours.'

'Probably more customers,' Luke added as he looked in the nearside wing mirror to see Leather Jacket get out of the X5 and head into the house. The X5 then carried on, now following them, until Luke spotted a cul-de-sac sign on his left and indicated to turn in. The X5 drove past. With an exaggerated gesture of having made the mistake of turning into a dead end, just in case anyone was watching, Luke turned the Transit and went off after the X5 once again, just in time to see it pull off into a pub car park.

As they approached they could see that, like the old farmhouse, the pub had been chosen for its prime location. One way in. One way out. And nothing else around but cleared sites where houses used to stand. And nothing but clear sightlines. No one could approach without being seen. No one should be there who wasn't welcome. These were the situations Luke dreaded most. He'd rather run across a moonlit fire zone than walk a hostile urban landscape where the only people watching his back would be the ones getting ready to kill him.

The pub was called the Spotted Greyhound. No one knew why. No one cared. The locals called it the Fast Dog. The two shaved-headed minders were out of the X5 and exchanging fist greetings with two other guys sitting astride quad bikes. All eyes turned to watch the Transit go past and, while being a white van man provided a certain degree of invisibility, Luke and Matt decided this was not the time for surveillance. They would come back later.

'This happen often?' Joey asked as Natasha got back into the Q7, having retrieved her mother and got her safely home.

'Not that often. But more and more, recently.'

'Do you think it's time for a care home?'

'I think we've got a bit more on our plates at the moment, Joe,' she snapped back and sank into silence as Joey eased the Q7 round her dad's raised flower bed, waving to Grace now standing in the window.

'What did she say about me being back?'

'I told her you were the taxi driver.'

'What? Why?'

'Because she's losing it. Which I think I am at the moment.'

Joey knew he'd get a more coherent answer later, just as he knew now was the time to leave Natasha to let her work out what was in her head. She turned and watched the countryside go by, still struggling for a real answer. Struggling with the images Joey had planted at the front of her head. She knew she could easily repeat the mantra. Leave it to the police. But she was feeling uncomfortable. No matter how unpalatable it was she knew she was facing another moment when she had to reaffirm both the reality and the strength of her relationship with Joey. As it often did. As it always had.

She had always prided herself on having been the one to get him from the wrong side of the tracks. Back on the rails. Defying everyone. Her parents. Friends. Defending him against everyone. You don't know him. He's changed, she would say. Then, later, what a great dad he was. And all the rest. And when it came to her own lioness moment, seeing her cub under threat, she felt she was capable of doing what many always said should be done but never had the bottle to do themselves. Perhaps when it came to the crunch, she wouldn't actually be capable. But she knew Joey would. Just as she knew that was why she loved him. He made her safe. He had bottle. To defend his own. No matter what the risks. And that was why she wanted to remain strong. Play her own role in their relationship. Protect him from himself.

At home she got out of the car and went straight inside. Joey sat for a moment wondering where she was up to. He knew he had pushed their relationship a few times in the past, but she had always been there. Right behind him.

Or dragging him back. But this was different. How would this one go, he wondered, but decided that the only way to find out was to go after her and force the issue. She was starting to clear the table when he reached the kitchen and asked the question.

'I'm not sure what I'm thinking,' she began. 'Part of me, I don't know whether it's the maternal thing, whether it's right or wrong, wants to just tell you to get on with whatever you and Luke are up to. Another part is saying I'm losing my mum, so sod it. Who cares about those scum? Another, probably the sensible grown-up part, is with your Sean about trying to sort it out through some form of community action or . . .'

She saw him react negatively at the mention of this huggy-feely stuff, as he always called it, but she palm-punched his shoulder and hardened her eyes. 'You are going to listen. Especially if you are home for good,' she continued.

'I am,' Joey immediately replied, holding her shoulders, gently. For reassurance.

'Then perhaps you will have more of an influence on Tanya, like you've been saying. Getting her to be more careful.' She cradled his face in her hands. This time asking for reassurance. But it wasn't coming.

'And what happens when the boys get older? It's touched us twice. I don't want a third time.' And to emphasise the point he took her hands and intertwined them with his own. 'It is like some form of cancer, Nat. And someone's got to cut it out.'

There. He'd said it again. The line to be crossed. It was now up to her whether she wanted to take that step. They both stood holding hands. Silent. Natasha still assimilating the journey Joey had just taken her on, while he waited for the decision. Eventually, it came. As she pulled away and went to the table to collect their now congealing dishes. Wanting to start retrieving some sense of normality.

'You're right. I don't want to know any details. Except one. You are only helping a mate with a bit of cash? That's it? Nothing else?'

Joey nodded. Then put his arms round her as she placed the dishes on the worktop above the dishwasher. 'It's the only thing I'm allowed to do. Deniability, I think they call it.'

He felt her body relax slightly as she turned to face him, smothering his face with her hair again and mumbling something into his chest. He pulled away and asked her what she had said.

'We should be careful what we wish for.'

Immediately, Joey thought that if he was still of the faith he'd probably say Amen to that.

'Thanks for coming back, Joe,' she said.

'Well,' Joey grinned. 'I knew you'd never ask.'

Joey grinned as he felt her smile against his chest. Then, as she hugged him more tightly the pheromones flowed and his second thought was about whether he could get away with suggesting something else he often wished for.

But he decided against it. He didn't want to lose this moment. The hero's real return.

Matt had taken delivery of a Ford Focus hire car when he had handed over the Transit to be kept out of sight. In a lock-up they had been using for the duration. One that they could just walk away from. No connection. Just as they could from the Ford Focus, hired in the name of Elsie Jordan, a resident of the Pines Care Home who, despite being bedridden, still held a clean driving licence and a Gold credit card. Her son, Terrence, was down as a registered driver so if stopped, Matt would have seven days to produce his documents, while Terrence could prove he was in Amsterdam at the time.

Even before he had slowed to a stop at the traffic lights, Matt could see it coming towards him. The window wash hustle. One window washer. One flower seller. He had pulled up in the outside lane as instructed. The flower seller came to the driver's window to block the view while negotiating, while the window washer stood by the passenger door and covered one side of the windscreen with suds, totally blocking any view from that direction. By the time the window washer had moved round to the driver's side the flower seller had gone, leaving a fairly large bouquet. Matt handed over a £20 note and got a theatrical protest in return, along with two £5 notes. The same trick Fatchops was using. Each note had the not uncommon random numbers scribbled on it. Different colours. Different writing. A legacy of someone's petty-cash counting system.

On one, the writing was in purple ink and circled. 3–24. He glanced down at the bouquet now on the passenger seat to see the top of a set of registration plates at the centre of the bunch. They would be from another Ford Focus matching the one he was driving but, like the Transit, now sitting in a lock-up somewhere, off the road. Out of sight. The cloned plates would pass unchallenged through the number-plate recognition system that was on all major roads. The numbers on the £5 note meant they had it for three days.

Pulling away he marvelled once again at the way Billy and many like him around the world could deliver. On both sides of the line. Operating in the twilight world often referred to as Black Ops by the media, without which many covert things could not be done in the name of democracy. Don't ask: don't tell. But it didn't stop Matt wondering how Billy and his team knew the registration number was safe for three days. Was it stolen to order? In a garage for repair? Sitting in a long-term car park? Or did it come from a black database at the DVLC?

Whatever it was he never dwelt on it, just accepted that it was what they did. He always wondered more about when someone would finally wake up and recognise two things. One was that the bad guys didn't play by the rules. So things like ID cards and number-plate recognition systems only worked if no one cheated. The other was that formal education had no link to intelligence. If entrepreneurship thrived on opportunity, then opportunity wasn't restricted to purely legal activities. At one time getaway cars and drivers commanded a premium. Just as safecrackers were like gold dust. Now it was all cyberwarfare. All about computer hackers and cloning.

For the next three days Elsie's car would not be tracked. Everything would be logged against the one sitting out of sight somewhere, and provided they didn't go through any speed cameras no one would be the wiser. With that in mind, Matt headed back to Highbridge. With their new 72-hour cloak of invisibility.

'So, what do you reckon? Got time before the school run?' Joey asked, hopefully as he held her round the waist and nuzzled her neck.

'Oh yeah. Let's decide to bankroll a bunch of mercenaries to run amok round the town and then jump into bed. Great turn-on, that is.'

'Power's supposed to be an aphrodisiac, isn't it?'

'Power is. Losing your mind isn't. Ask my mother.'

Joey relaxed his grip and arched back to examine her eyes. Anxiety. Second thoughts? She saw his concern. 'I'm OK. Really. But I meant it. All we are doing is helping a friend with some cash. Nothing more. Clear?'

He nodded.

'Say it, Joe.'

'I'm clear. Nothing more. No details.'

She then sank back into his chest, giving him just enough time to find a breath hole.

'Promise?' she asked again.

'Promise,' he reaffirmed.

'And I can feel where your mind is going,' Natasha said, as she pressed her groin against his, then pulled away. 'But I do have to go, as I want to look in on Mum before picking the kids up. So calm down.'

'What about tonight, then?'

'You'll be out.'

'What? Where? I'm not supposed to be here.'

'But you are. And now you're here, you can do the taxi run tonight.'

'Where to?'

'Oh, Tanya's off on one because I've said we won't let her go on holiday with this new boyfriend of hers.'

All thoughts of a romantic night evaporated. 'What new boyfriend?'

'Exactly.'

'But . . .'

She started gathering her handbag, phone and car keys. 'The compromise is that she can go to the student night at some new club they've been badgering me about for ages. Provided that I – well, you now – can drop her off and pick her up. And that she stays with the girls.'

She gave him a quick kiss as she headed for the door.

'Hang on. Why's she going out on a school night? And where is this club?'

She finally smiled. 'Warrington.'

'What? That's an hour each way. And how were you going to do this if I wasn't here?'

'Er. . . Alex is fourteen.'

'You leave them on their own?'

'Joyce pops in from next door. Welcome to the world of shared parenting, Joe.'

With that she left, leaving Joey realising how much she had kept from him while he was away. What else did they all get up to when he was trying to stay awake listening to Benno's stories? But then his phone vibrated on the worktop ALWAYS 2MORO. GET SLEEP. I'LL WARN KIDS YOU HOME. LXXT Joey grinned. Tanya's going to love me being here to hound her, he thought, but his mind soon went back to his main concern. Who is this boyfriend?

'Oh My God, you're trending,' Megan announced to Noah, scrolling through the Twitter feeds as they walked in from school.

Sandra had insisted Noah came straight home. And stayed home.

Noah instantly snatched Megan's phone to look. Which she instantly snatched back. And then had it instantly snatched by Sandra.

'Mum!'

Sandra then handed the phone back. It wasn't her daughter she was getting angry about. 'Look. The pair of you.' But she focused on Noah. 'Today was not your

Mandela moment. No matter what your father said about peaceful protest. OK?'

'So how many dead kids does it take, Mum? Someone's got to do something,' Noah shot back, obviously liking the Mandela reference no matter how pejoratively Sandra meant it.

'But not you, Noah. It's bad enough having your father banging on, without you getting yourself arrested for fighting with the police.'

'I wasn't arrested . . .' Noah countered. 'We were just protesting. Remember?'

The sarcasm could not be missed. It just bounced off Sandra, who was straight in Noah's face. 'Did you get permission?'

'Permission to protest? That's an oxymoron.' But he stepped back a little as he said it. Just in case.

'The only moron around here is you.'

'I'll go with that. I'll tweet it,' Megan offered unhelpfully.

'Don't you dare, young lady . . .'

The tone was enough to cause Megan to put her phone down and move to the kettle. 'Tea, anyone?' she asked. Sweetly. Proto-teen sarcasm. Also not missed, and she turned away sharply to sit at the kitchen table in response to her mother's glare.

'Well?' Sandra demanded.

Noah flopped into a seat opposite Megan. 'I told Dad. I told the plod. We were talking about next Saturday's match and how we're fed up with having to get there early to help clear up all the mess the druggies leave behind on Friday nights.'

'What sort of mess?' Sandra asked, deciding to follow the logic chain. 'Syringes and things?'

Noah exchanged a quick glance with Megan. Eyes and ears wide open. 'It's not *Trainspotting* or whatever movie you grew up with, Mum.'

'Like sex, is it?' Sandra asked.

'What?'

'Drugs are something else your generation discovered?'

'I didn't mean it like—'

'Your look to your sister did,' Sandra shot back, which was a reminder that thirteen-year-old Megan was at the table. 'Megan. This has nothing to do with you.' Sandra pointed to the door.

Megan thought about making a symbolic protest but knew that's all it would be, so huffily stood up, grabbed her stuff and headed for her room, stopping just outside the kitchen door to try and listen. Until.

'All the way. Go. Now.'

She gave an exaggerated eye roll and headed off. She'd find out all about it later. Online.

Sandra refocused on Noah. 'Continue with my education.'

'There's an occasional syringe.' Noah started. 'But it's mostly wraps. Bottles, cans.' Then, with a glance over his shoulder to make sure Megan wasn't still lurking,

'Condoms. Tampons. Although finding a dead body was a first.'

Sandra gave him a disapproving glare. Enough. But her revulsion remained.

'And you have to clear all this . . . mess up before you can play football?' Sandra asked.

Noah nodded. 'For some reason they always use the goalmouths,' he added.

'That's because the trees shelter them from the wind.' Sandra said. Authoritatively. Which was not missed by Noah.

'Oh yes. And, how do you know that?' he asked. Grinning. Intrigued.

Sandra couldn't help but grin herself. 'I told you. Your generation didn't invent everything.'

'Moth-er!' Noah said. Surprised.

'Anyway,' Sandra said. Realising it was a detail too far. Wanting to get back to the point. 'What's any of that got to do with being arrested?'

'Well, why should we be forced to do the clearing up? The teachers used to do it while we were too young to see life's dirty little secrets. But now we are apparently old enough, we can help share the burden of protecting our young.'

'So you decided to organise a protest?'

'Er . . . yeah. I think that kid's death took it to a whole new level. We only wanted to highlight the point that it's getting worse. It was supposed to be peaceful. Until the robocops arrived.'

Now having a bit better understanding, Sandra tried to offer some support. 'Everyone's a bit sensitive about that area at the moment. Not just the drugs but whether they're going to sell the playground. So I suppose the Council and police are getting a hard time about anything that goes on down there.'

'So they end up giving us a hard time?' Noah asked. The irritation returning.

Irritated by his irritation, Sandra toughened up again. 'And you end up giving us a hard time by making a show of yourself.'

Noah stood up to gather his stuff. Obviously he'd had enough. 'Oh, what? All the gossip in the hairdresser's, is it?'

Sandra rose to meet him. Enough was definitely enough. 'It's more the way you went about it. And yes, you do have to have permission to protest, Mastermind.'

Noah tried to end the lecture with a dismissive shrug and turned towards the door. Until—

'Stay.' He stopped. Recognising the rising but controlled maternal anger. Sandra continued. 'Since our generation invented not only sex, drugs and rock'n'roll, but raving. They passed laws making it illegal for any more than half a dozen people to gather in one place outside.' She paused to increase the emphasis. 'Without a licence. It was to stop people turning up spontaneously and taking over fields for rave parties. And, yes, that means we invented flash mobbing too.'

'So what, Mum? So you were all teenage rebels. Great. But so what?'

'The "so what" is because . . .' She was trying to hold on to herself as well as her son. 'Because some people acted irresponsibly, laws were rushed through that in the end caused people to fret about whether they needed a licence to have a barbecue in their own gardens. Imagine how that would have affected the business.'

'But that's a stupid law,' Noah responded. Voice rising.

'A lot of laws are,' Sandra shot back. Increasing the decibels to match. 'Because some people act stupidly . . .' she said as she tapped the side of his head, invading his personal space as only a mother can. 'And then so-called intelligent people try to be too clever trying to stop them. Instead of everyone talking to each other first.'

'So, we're supposed to go to the cops and ask permission to protest against them not doing their job?' His frustration was building again.

'In a nutshell, yes,' Sandra said. 'It's what's called democracy.'

'Then it's wrong.'

There it was again. Teenage perception. Black. White. No greys.

'Yes,' Sandra replied. 'And you can do the bull elephant thing with your father, but don't try it on with me.'

Noah held her eyes, but not for too long. Even if it wasn't fair, he knew she was right. He could have a real fight with his dad but that mother thing . . . A lifetime of obedience and gratitude for the pain of childbirth. He reached for his only defence.

'Can I go now?'

She nodded, accepting the capitulation, but couldn't resist her maternal right to dispense advice. Although she softened her tone once more. 'What I'm really annoyed about, Noah, is that you didn't think it through.' She tried to take his hand, but he pulled it away.

'You can do the wise oracle thing, Mum. But don't patronise me. OK? I don't need anything kissed better.'

She gave another nod. This time accepting the point. He took it as a concession. A small step in acknowledging that he was growing up. She took it as a need to defuse the situation.

'You don't have to ask permission to protest about the police not doing their jobs. But they'll have all the excuses lined up for that. You should protest about politicians not giving them the resources to do their jobs. Then they'll see you as being on their side. Not as the enemy. Then they'll help you. Not arrest you.'

'That it? That the end of today's life lecture?' But as her face tightened and eyes flared, he grinned. 'I get it. I do.'

Instinctively she reached out to stroke his forearm in maternal acknowledgement. This time he accepted it, as it was also a sign that he could go. At the door, he stopped. Unable to resist a final shot.

'It's bullshit though, Mum. Someone's got to do something. And not sitting around chatting like Dad.'

'Go,' Sandra snarled. A verbal flash of the claws.

He did. And she was left recalling that Sean had told her to try and go easy on him. He was a good kid at heart and all that proud dad stuff. But it's always the good kids who can't spot where the real trouble can come from.

Six hours into their 72-hour window, Luke was heading for the Fast Dog, having just dropped Matt in the lane about 200 metres from Leather Jacket's farmhouse. Matt was now working his way along the field, behind a hedge that kept him screened from the road. He was in full blacks: boots, coverall, turned-up beanie, Motorola in place, and carrying a backpack. When he reached the corner of the field that touched the front of the farmhouse fence, he swung the backpack off and settled down. Listening. Apart from a passing car, there was nothing. All quiet on the other side of the fence. Satisfied that no one had seen him approach he took out his phone and rechecked the 3G signal. Still strong. He squawked the Motorola to advise Luke, then opened the backpack and started setting up the drone.

Outside the pub, Luke had never felt so exposed. As Matt's squawk came it faded. He had tried re-squawking but had no response. He was out of range and he'd just been marked. One of the quad bikes they had seen on the recce had followed him into the car park. With the

Motorola useless he reached for his pay-and-throw. No signal. No backup. He was on his own. With only his good looks and smooth tongue, as his mother had often said.

While Leather Jacket had demonstrated his desire to remain below radar, Luke knew from the lack of helmets and registration plates that law enforcement, never mind Health and Safety, was not something the two young bucks riding the quad were concerned about. They only had one thing on their minds. Him.

'Oh, I love him. You will bring him in here for a cup of tea won't you?'

Sean had just told Glynnis that he'd had another call from Craig Harlow's PA. He would come along on Saturday and take a look at what Sean wanted, when he visited his mother. Her surprise at this was beaten only by Sean's over her excitement.

'It is still up for discussion, Glynnis.'

'If he's coming here because his mum says so, it's a dead cert.'

'Perhaps, but . . . it's supposed to be a quiet, private visit, Glynnis. He, er, we don't want too many people to know just yet so we can make a big splash in the paper later.'

'Have to put a bag over his head then. Cos as soon as he steps through that door, word'll be round town like wildfire.' The surprises then kept coming. 'Hey, if he's not coming into the café, will you introduce me? Do you think he'd sign a menu for me? Or have one of those pictures I can put up on the wall? I might even get a mobile phone so I can get a selfie.' Without waiting for an answer she then went off, with an excited grin across her face that Sean had never seen before. 'Can't wait to tell our Hilda.'

That was something else new. He had never heard Glynnis refer to anyone in her life before. No family. No friends. So who was Hilda?

'No idea,' Byron replied when Sean asked him later. Nor did he have any idea who Craig Harlow was, but he still agreed to be sworn to secrecy.

Luke sat slowly tapping the steering wheel. Fight or flight? He knew they couldn't match him for speed, just as he knew that if he pulled away it would confirm whatever was in their heads and from that moment he would be a target. The quad had shot past and spun to a stop right in front of him. Headlight to headlight. Luke wondered what, or who, might come next. That came in the form of a small van, speeding into the car park and stopping within six inches of his rear. Blocking any thought of reversing.

No one moved. Luke knew this game. They were waiting to see what he would do. The driver had a retro skinhead and parka look. The rider looked more Ragged Priest with long, lank hair. They were probably a bit older than he was when he first signed up. Still just kids. Playing at cops and druggies. If they had weapons they would have showed them by now, so Luke assumed they were in the van. Out of sight but ready. He looked in the mirror but could only see two heads against the panel obscuring the back. The same reason they had chosen to shoot from a van. How many more could be inside? He knew that in the car he had a chance. Out of the car he had none. They would have to come to him. So he sat and waited. And waited. His cold stare matching those of the quad riders.

After a three-minute staring contest, the Ragged Priest slowly dismounted and walked up to Luke's window. He lowered it. Only partly. Waiting for the challenge.

'You lost, then?' The global question. The same neutral non-aggressive tone. The one he had heard the world over, no matter the dialect or language. It wasn't an offer of help, but a probe. To get a response. In many places, from Belfast to Helmand, a response in the wrong accent would have meant a death sentence, but at least here he wasn't already tagged as an enemy combatant. Or at least he hoped. Just someone who had strayed where he shouldn't. He looked in the mirror again. No movement, but also no way back. Only forward. So forward it had to be.

He slid the Motorola under the seat out of view and ran through the cover once more. He was looking for the David Lloyd Sports Centre. He'd clocked it on the way in. Part of the routine. Keep logging. A nearby location. Close enough to be easily missed. Stay as close to the truth as possible. The rev of the quad engine informed him their patience was running out. Time to play. Luke got out of the car, a move that made the Ragged Priest step back. He wanted the swing space but looked nervously at the van, confirming Luke's early assessment. If it kicked off that was where help would come from.

As he straightened, Luke held up the pay and throw with a useless shrug. 'David Lloyd Centre? Satnav's useless.'

'Signal's crap round here,' the Ragged Priest responded.

'Right. Do you know where it is?'

'Yeah.' But nothing more.

Luke held his stare, knowing it was part of the anxiety test. 'And?'

'You passed it on the way here.'

This was the all-important moment. The one when the van men would decide whether he was a potential threat or just some random idiot.

Luke tried for the idiot badge. And idiot's ramble. 'Oh, really? Damn. Must have been looking at this and not the road. Then it, well, the Maps app just seemed to stop and I couldn't figure out where I was, so I decided to pull in and ask. And then you . . .'

It seemed to do the trick as the Ragged Priest let out a sigh of frustration, while distracted by a commotion near the recycling bins. Three men were dragging another, followed by one more, that Luke immediately recognised. Leather Jacket. The Priest was obviously as curious as Luke and wanted to go and see what was happening.

'OK. It's back that way,' he quickly announced. 'At the end turn right.' Then, with heavy irony, 'You can't miss it.'

'OK. Thanks. Thanks for that,' Luke responded.

The Priest waved to the van. All OK. Then started to walk towards the action over by the recycling bins. But stopped as Luke made a show of locking his car and heading for the main pub door. The Priest's acolyte jumped off the quad and stood in front of him.

'Where you going?'

'Er, been on the road a bit. Just thought I'd er . . . use the er . . .'

The Priest felt he should tell him to wait until he got to David Lloyd's but knew that might get the idiot, whoever he was, either too curious or so irritated that he might start something at what was supposed to be an ordinary pub. The sort of ordinary pub to be found in many inner cities where men dragged other men around the car park. So he nodded to the acolyte to let Luke pass. He was also too curious about what was going on over by the recycling bins.

As the van headed back to its watch position and the quaddies headed over to the action, Luke went into the pub, gave a quick résumé of his story to a barmaid and was pointed in the direction of the toilets. Once there he checked the pay-and-throw again. Still no signal. He took out his real phone. No signal. He tried to make a call. No network. Then it dawned on him. They were jamming. Anyone unlucky enough to be categorised as suspect, enemy or traitor wouldn't be able to dial a friend. They would find themselves dragged out to that recycling bin. Not a black spot. A black hole.

8

Let's Chat

Inside the black hole, Luke had managed to get the toilet window open slightly, just enough to use his phone camera to watch Leather Jacket overseeing some form of kangaroo court around the recycling bins. From what he could see and hear, or figure out, the guy they had dragged out was pleading that they'd got it wrong. What he had or hadn't done Luke couldn't determine, but it amounted to the same thing: insubordination. And as with every armed militia everywhere, the code was the same. Zero tolerance. The outcome inevitable. And like every legally constituted judicial system it relied on precedent. Broken code. Broken bones. Summary justice.

What Luke hadn't expected was the form of summary justice, although it was clear that the transgressor had, as the wet stain that appeared on the front of his trousers indicated when he heard the deep roar and burble of a heavy diesel engine start up. From where he was, Luke couldn't see the source, but turning the camera to follow the terrified look of the transgressor he saw a crane hook descending above him. The guy made an attempt to run but was soon caught and pinned over the recycling bin. A flexible bike lock was then wrapped round his ankles and in what looked like a well practised drill, an extender cable was looped through, hung on to the crane hook and the still screaming and protesting guy was yanked into the air, swinging wildly to and fro.

As the assembled group separated and stood back, more to get a better view than to keep out of the way, they looked across at Leather Jacket, now leaning on the front of a Porsche Cayenne Hybrid. That caught Luke by surprise. But then he checked himself. Why not? Drug lords can have an interest in saving the planet. If only for themselves. From his display in the park with Fatchops, and now the cold detachment he was showing here, it was clear that this was no mere link in a chain. Here was someone who controlled the summary justice system. He was the kangaroo judge, jury and executioner.

The signal came as the judge looked up at the now dangling and slowly rotating figure rapidly running out of energy even to plead for his own life. After savouring this for a moment, Leather waved his arm towards where the crane must be parked. The hoist brake was released and the jib given a slight nudge so that the figure was flicked to one side as it crashed to the ground. Another well practised move so that the hook itself would not hit whoever had been unfortunate enough to be dangling from it. That way the injuries were consistent with a fall from height. Not being crushed by a heavy metal object. Falls are common. Being crushed by a crane hook isn't.

'I like this lot,' Matt said, as he reviewed the recording on Luke's pay-and-throw before deleting it in the car on the way back to Highbridge. 'In a certain way, right?'

Luke knew what he meant. They were efficient. Down to the guys waiting with a hose and gardener's pressure spray knapsack ready to cover the impact point with bleach before they hosed it down. Kill the guy. Kill the DNA.

'Wonder if they dumped him in one of the recycling bins?' Matt asked. 'But what do you do with a dead druggie? Compost heap would be better.'

'I didn't wait for that bit. How'd you get on?'

Matt nodded. 'Good. Should have plenty. If that night vision camera worked.'

The drone had been on Billy Higham's shopping list. Along with full blacks and the weapons. Aware that Joey's budget probably wouldn't stretch to a full spec Reaper with Hellfire or Sidewinder missiles, Matt had asked for a DJI Phantom so he could rejig the provided camera. You could run a small war with an Amazon account. Except for the weapons. That was the bit Billy did. Don't ask, don't tell. Just use and return in good order.

As they came off the expressway, Matt was still mulling over Leather Jacket's style of execution. 'Probably got the crane idea from that *Homeland* series.'

'Or YouTube?' Luke offered, being careful to slow down for a speed camera. Even if they had cloned plates, it didn't seem fair to leave someone else to pick up the bill. Apart from the risk that the camera might be linked to a live control room and a mobile police patrol might decide to ease their boredom by running a spot check. 'Plenty of footage from Iran or Saudi.'

'Or,' Matt said, 'the tale of Mary the Tennessee Elephant.'

Luke emptied his lungs in an exaggerated sigh. But knew it was unavoidable. 'Go on.'

'She was hanged by a crane,' Matt continued. 'But I'll keep that for another day when you are in a more appreciative mood.'

'I am now.'

'No, you're not. I know that sigh. You're only doing it to humour me.'

'You could be right.'

Matt nodded. As they reached the swing bridge into Highbridge, he switched back to the mission. 'You want to hit them here?'

Luke nodded. 'Yeah. Main route in and out of town. Choke point.'

Matt nodded. It was. He was looking forward to it.

*

An hour later Joey was not looking forward to his dad taxi night as he cleared the choke point and directed the Q7 towards the expressway. Joey could never persuade Tanya and her posse – unlike the boys – to go out in the Jag.

'So, you sure you don't need ID to get into this club?' It had been his last hope of opting out of a five-hour drop, wait and return evening.

'One of the guys knows the owner.'

'Which guy?'

'You don't know him.' And the bit about not needing to know him was implicit in the tone, reinforced as Tanya spun in the passenger seat to share some latest digital headline with Becky and Carol.

It was also the signal for him to adopt the learned routine of going deaf and just driving, but as he did he glanced in the rear-view mirror to see them all suited and booted and excited at their first, he assumed, big night out, remembering how he, Luke and the others had always been on the hunt for such conquests. The thought immediately put him back into dad mode as he glanced across to the apple of his eye, thinking again how stupid, yet apt the phrase was. Another relic from the nuns. The apple being the eye and the eyelid being God protecting such a precious thing. Or so they said. Anyway, Tanya was precious to Joey and the thought of the sort of thing happening to her that had happened to Janey was what had driven him to agree to fund Luke's plan.

He was not naïve enough to think that Luke was doing it out of pure altruism. He knew it was all wrapped up with looking for some form of revenge, or closure about Janey, but he was also not blind enough to think that Sean and his windbag mates would ever find a political solution. Better people had tried and failed in the past, just as equally arrogant folk would try and fail in the future. At least this way, Joey thought, guiding the Q7 on to the motorway for the short leg to Warrington, we can chase them off for a while and give Sean's cronies a chance to get their act together.

He took another quick look at Tanya. Although the skirt was shorter than any dad would really like, she was, at least, fully covered on top. A bit of her mother there, he thought as his mind was dragged back by a shriek.

'He's coming! Oh My God! He's coming!' It was Becky. Now even more excited.

'Tell me it's not true.' That was Tanya.

'Afraid so.' Carol confirming.

'I didn't. I didn't think he would,' Becky said as her thumbs battered her screen to reply.

'Why did you tell him where we were going, Becks?' Tanya again. Not pleased.

Joey was trying to stick to the rules and not get involved in the conversation, but he guessed this must be the mysterious Egyptian Natasha had told him about.

'We were supposed to be having a night out away from

him,' Carol moaned. 'I don't want to be spending my night watching you making an idiot of yourself.'

'You don't have to.' Becky. Defiant.

Joey was fighting hard to remain in role, something obviously sensed by his daughter as she put her hand on his arm. 'It's OK, Dad. Just teen stuff. We're cool, really.'

'I hope so,' Joey replied, trying to make it light but with the perceived fatherly warning.

She flashed him a smile. 'And you'll be in the getaway car outside, won't you?' She patted his arm again and went back to the backseat conversation.

'You're your mother's daughter all right, my girl.' Joey laughed as he checked the satnav against his own, probably out of date, local knowledge and a short while later pulled the Q7 in to a bus stop opposite the old supermarket that had been converted into the latest techno music palace. Almost before the car stopped Tanya was leaning over to kiss him on the cheek before getting out to join the others.

'Park down the road, or something.'

'Well I can't stay here. Text me just before midnight.'

'What?'

'The time you're leaving.'

'Yeah, right.' And with that she was out, flicking her hair back over her head as she linked Carol's arm for mutual support as they guided their seven-inches across the road.

Joey waited to watch them get across safely, only to find

a 4x4 pull up next to him and block his view. Who's this clown, Joey thought as he started to move the Q7 forward, but turning to try and see Tanya he saw the leather parka behind the wheel and realised the 4x4 was Bobby McBain's Range Rover out of which was pouring a male posse. As the lads headed across the road to join the girls in the queue, Bobby eased forward and lowered the passenger window.

'Hey up, Joey lad? One of yours going in there?'

'Aye. Tanya and her posse.'

Bobby nodded. 'Hold up.' He turned and whistled out of his window. One of the lads looked round and Bobby waved for him to come back. He then parked in front of Joey, got out and put his arm round the lad to say something in his ear. The lad nodded as Bobby pointed over to the club. At Tanya.

Joey's heart sank. It couldn't, could it? he thought as he watched Bobby nod and then point to Joey, pull the lad closer and speak to him before giving him a hug and a small shove off towards the club. He then walked across to the Q7 with a huge grin on his face.

'What you doing here? Thought you lived with your other family mid-week. Lots of cock and knees and all that?'

'Don't give up your day job for the comedy club circuit, Bob,' Joey flashed back, but took the proffered high five hand-clamp.

'Never had a day job, mate. Fancy a quick coffee?'

*

Luke was also preparing a coffee as Matt loaded up the video from the drone's SD Card. They were back at Luke's cottage.

'Nice old farmhouse. Plenty of outbuildings. Got himself a pool out back. Away from the road. Overall. Not flash. Not run down. No one would take much notice. Unless you look here. And here.'

He pointed to the screen as the video showed them an aerial view of the house and grounds, before homing in on the CCTV cameras. Then the solid fence. And re-inforced back door.

'Looks very quiet,' Luke commented.

'It was. Watch.' Matt pointed back at the screen and the video image widened to hover over the farmhouse. After a few seconds all the security lights came on to give a much cleaner picture.

'I threw a piece of wood over the fence to see if there were any movement detectors.' He nodded at the screen. 'Obviously. But no action. No one home.'

'Unless they were watching the cameras.'

'True,' Matt conceded. 'But no cars.'

Luke conceded that one with a grunt. He knew exactly where Leather Jacket had been.

'What about kids? Any signs?'

'Unlikely.' Again he gestured at the screen. 'After getting no reaction to the lights I took the drone lower. No bikes, swings or trampolines. But. A big doggy bowl.' He pointed to something on screen. 'I mean big.'

Luke grunted again. But it wasn't anything they hadn't tackled before. Matt paused the video and switched to a Google satellite view.

'We can come across this field. Right to the back fence. We can access down this road here, to what looks like another pub or restaurant.' He zoomed the image.

'We leave the car in the car park. Go behind this shed or whatever it is, through this bit of a wood and cut straight across. Five minutes. Ten, tops.'

Luke leaned forward to study the satellite image, wondering how old it was. Anything could have been put in their way since it was taken. Nothing beats a live feed. Sensing his friend's concern, Matt switched back to the drone video. From hovering over the farmhouse it turned away and swept across the field, took in the pub car park and then made its way back across the route Matt had mapped. It was clear. Luke turned and grinned.

'No more than 300 metres. Or the drone would have done a GPS auto return.' His grin matched Luke's. 'So all we need now is: go or no go. And when?'

'Usual knockin' hour,' Luke replied immediately. 'Tomorrow. Keep the pressure on. Billy do the exchange?'

Matt nodded. 'Checked when I picked up the B-Kits. Two H&K MP5s. SD3s with suppressors and red dots. And a dozen mags.'

While the MP5 was one of the most widely used law enforcement submachine guns, the B-Kit was a term they had coined for a full blackout kit of boots, coveralls, gloves, balaclava and body armour. It wasn't meant to completely obscure their identities, just provide a temporary disguise in low to medium risk situations. For anything higher they went for an A-Kit: A for anonymous. Head to toe covering. Nothing in, nothing out except what was filtered through their face masks.

'We'll use one MP5 for the stand-off,' Luke said. 'Pick it up on the way.'

'Going live?' Matt asked, already suspecting he knew the answer.

Luke just shook his head. 'Poke and provoke tonight.'

'You sure? They're likely to be.'

Luke shook his head again, thinking back to his encounter at the Fast Dog. 'They keep the guns mobile.'

Matt was still a bit apprehensive, but at the same time relieved that Luke was calm enough to stick to the plan. And it was his call. Bring them back to the choke point. 'OK. Natural charm it is then. Tonight.'

He then woke up the laptop and pointed at the farmhouse fence on the satellite image. 'Any clues as to how we get over that?'

'Improvise. And hope he's at home when we come calling?' Luke responded, but Matt was ahead of him again as he tapped away at the keyboard. A new window opened with a live stream from the farmhouse parking area.

'Someone is,' he said as he pointed to the screen where a Mini Cooper convertible sat parked. 'Must have come home while we were on our way back.'

They were watching a feed that was coming direct from a battery operated 3G camera. Matt had hooked it over the fence, right next to one of Leather Jacket's own, so the risk of detection was small. Just as peripheral vision catches sudden movement, familiarity overlooks small changes. Things hidden in plain sight. Especially in the dark. The battery would last around ten hours and provide a constant stream that could be accessed from any phone with the app. It would also detect any new movement and send a text alert.

Another grunt from Luke. 'He's got a Porsche Hybrid.'

'Bit of a tree hugger then?' Matt asked with the same level of interested surprise Luke had checked himself on earlier. 'What do you reckon? WAG? Boyfriend? Cleaner? Cook?'

'Don't say bottle washer,' Luke quickly cut in.

Matt ejected the drone's SD Card and put it in the microwave, ready to nuke just in case they got a call during the knockin' hour. The usual pre-dawn raid when no matter what social habits people have they are likely to be at home, having been out and returned to the nest, or getting ready to leave it for the day. Since the dawn of warfare, the time when people were still slightly groggy.

'Time for a nap, I think,' Luke said as he looked at the time on the computer screen. 'We'll go at 0430 regardless of what we see there. If he's not in, we'll let him know we have been.'

Matt smiled broadly as he headed for the fridge to crack some eggs. At last. If he wanted to be a spook he'd have joined MI6, but this was what he signed up for. Cracking heads.

'What's worth more, Joe? What you know or who you know?'

'Which is why she didn't need ID,' Joey replied as he offered a Costa latte to Bobby, busy on his phone.

Bobby took the mug and gave a deep gravelly chuckle, but never deviated from his phone as he replied, 'Pal of mine owns it. I've told him to keep an eye on them. There'll be no funny stuff inside. And, as I can see that dad look in your eye, I've told my lad there's two things I'll kick the shit out of him for. Hitting a woman and getting one pregnant.'

It was some comfort. But not enough. 'There's a lot more in between, Bobby.'

Bobby laughed, the pockmarked pebble-dashed face cracking as he glanced up from his phone.

'He's a good lad, my Max, Joe. Really. Sometimes I think he might be a bit of a shirt-lifter, but . . .' he shrugged.

Joey couldn't help but smile as the irony of Bobby wearing Alexander McQueen struck him, but Bobby didn't notice as he swept on.

'At least he's not a tranny, like that bloke in the optician's. Suppose he thinks folk won't notice his five o'clock if they need specs.' He went back to the phone. 'I'd have to love him though, wouldn't I, even if he was. And I'll tell you what. These kids aren't as rampant as we used to be.' Then the gravel rattled again. 'No one is.' He put his phone down for a moment. 'I mean. Would you have ever imagined, when we were out marauding . . . that we'd be ferrying our kids about and then sitting having a coffee, while waiting for them to whistle?'

Bobby shook his head as he sipped the froth from his latte, at both the realisation of what he'd said and the memory of what his dad would have said if he'd even asked for a lift anywhere. His phone vibrated. He picked it up, looked at the message but this time didn't respond.

Joey grinned at his own memories of his youth and how he never even had the option of asking for a lift. 'I guess not.' He raised the latte in a mock toast. 'But er, how long have they been . . . ?'

Bobby just held out his hands and shrugged. 'That's one thing that hasn't changed. Did we tell our parents anything? Christ, I don't even tell them what I do now.'

'I think they might have guessed, Bobby.'

Again the deep gravelly chuckle that developed into a gurgling laugh. 'I guess you're right. At least about some of it. But they're all Facetwitters anyway, aren't they?' He waggled his phone. 'Not that hard to guess what they're up to. Unlike those that don't put it all out there. Like you?'

Joey felt this wasn't a casual question. It was leading somewhere.

'And how do you know that, Bobby?' He nodded at Bobby's phone. 'You posting now?'

The gravel rattled in his throat again. 'Weekly sales reports. Can get anything you want through these, can't you.' He leaned back in his chair. 'Except what Lukey Carlton and merry Matthew are up to?'

That was where he'd been heading. Joey tried not to react, but could see Bobby was reading his body language. A predator hunting.

'Go on. You must know,' Bobby pushed.

'Know what?'

'You're doing some work up at his ghost house, aren't you?'

'Don't call it that.'

'It's what it is, isn't it? A shrine to his dead missus?' Then added, to emphasise the family connection, 'And your sister, of course.'

Joey didn't rise to the bait. 'The only thing he's shared with me is where he wants the sockets and switches.'

'Bollocks.' Bobby crossed his fingers. 'You and him were like that. If he'd tell anyone it'd be you.'

'And why do you think he's got some big secret?'

'He might come back every now and then to keep the flame burning, but what's he brought his Matty for?' Bobby asked, fastening his predator's eyes on Joey. Probing. Joey decided to leave the question hanging in the air. He wasn't going to become the prey. He matched the predator's stare. After a moment it was Bobby who blinked. Perhaps aided by another vibration from his phone.

Bobby leaned across to pick it up. 'You know what I reckon?'

But this time Joey didn't need to think about a response. That moment had passed and Bobby was off on his own track. 'He's always wanted to find the smacko who did his missus. He's always come back hoping to stumble across him. And if he has Tonto with him, I reckon he's found out who it was. Am I right?'

He then made a quick response on the phone.

Joey smiled. He knew his body language couldn't possibly betray him now. 'I really don't know that, Bobby. Honest. You'll have to ask him.'

The predator sniffed. But seemed satisfied. 'He won't tell me. But you can tell him something for me. If he wants a hand with anything. He's only got to ask. And I mean anything, Joe. Right?'

'That be one of those fifty quid contracts you can organise? Or, what was it, five hundred for a proper job?'

The pebble-dashing cracked again. 'Daft, isn't it. But true. And if you ever want anything, Joe . . .' The crack widened even further. 'As we may be father-in-laws soon.'

'God, I hope not.'

'Thanks.'

Joey laughed. 'That came out wrong. I meant, she's too young.'

'She'll always be too young, Joe.' Bobby's phone

buzzed. A call. 'But I mean it,' he continued. 'If you ever need anything.' He looked at his phone and stood up. 'Have to take this one. Suppliers. Want another?' He pointed at the latte cup as he started to walk away.

Joey nodded and started to ponder why Tanya had to go for Max McBain. She could have the pick of the town, even if that was, like Bobby, only proud dad thinking. So why the town gangster's son? Brought her up too well, perhaps. Too much telling her to take no bullshit and take people as she found them. All that stuff about people having to live with what fate gave them. Good and bad in everyone. Why didn't he just tell her to be more picky?

'Because she wants someone with a bit of edge, Joe. Like I did with you,' Natasha said on the other end of the phone.

Joey had called her as soon as Bobby moved away. 'I get that. But why didn't you tell me it was Bobby's lad?'

'Er . . . perhaps because I didn't know. Exactly.'

'And what does that mean?'

'She only said it was someone you'd throw a strop over.'

'Me?' He felt offended. More that his daughter could so easily read him.

'What you doing now?'

'Confiding my concern?'

'Could be a strop. Anyway, it'll blow over soon enough. She's too young for anything serious.'

'You're not exactly,' he emphasised the word, '*comforting* me here.' But all he got back was the sound of her giggling.

'Oh, Joe, you're so funny when you get like this. She'll be fine. Just think how safe she will be with no one daring to try anything. Not even the poor lad himself, if what you said Bobby said is true. So . . .' she giggled again. 'Enjoy your dads' night out with Bobby.'

At least she was a lot lighter than when he left her, Joey thought. 'I'm sure I will. Now that you've comforted me. As if.' Then instinctively he lowered his voice. 'But er . . . You still OK with what we talked about?'

There was only a slight hesitation before she replied. 'Yes. You know I'll back you. Always.'

'Yeah. And . . .' Now he hesitated as he felt his eyes mist slightly as an emotive mix of gratitude, admiration, pride and appreciation swept over him. He was unable to put it into words. It was at times like this that he wished he'd stayed at St Bede's longer. No matter what he said about surviving the Comp being the best education anyone could want. All that now came out was 'I really love you, you know.' He might always be ready to take on the world, but it was a lot easier knowing his soulmate would always be there. Right behind him. No matter what. 'I really do,' he added. Unnecessarily.

'I know,' Natasha replied, referring more to Joey's typical macho male inability to vocalise his emotions. 'As I love you.' Then came the quick caveat. 'But . . . just like we said. Yeah?'

'Yeah. Yeah. Promise.' And he had to say it again. 'I do really love you. And thanks.'

'Love you too. But stay safe,' Natasha replied. He could hear the emotion in her own voice even though she was doing her best to sound matter-of-fact. It was one of those calls when neither side knows how to end. Mainly because the one thing you couldn't send over the phone was the very thing they both needed. A hug. Time to end the call.

He looked across to see Bobby, still on his phone, dropping some money on the counter with a keep the change gesture, and heading back across to Joey. 'Anyway, he's on his way back,' Joey said. 'I'll see you later, eh?'

'You may see me but I'll probably be asleep when you get back. But look forward to tomorrow, eh?'

'Absolutely. Love you.'

'Love you too' came the automatic response. But this time held for that extra second or two, before Natasha added, 'No matter what. 'Bye.'

As Joey watched the call end on his screen he knew that, despite the reassurance, they would, no doubt, revisit everything in the morning. He looked back at Bobby and wondered what sort of sales figures he was receiving now. But whatever they were, Bobby's body language suddenly changed. He ended the call, turned and waved to the girl behind the counter, pointed over at Joey and received a nod.

'Sorry.' He waved his phone. 'Got to go. But I've ordered you a raspberry slice as well.'

'No problem,' Joey replied as Bobby turned away, but then stopped. 'You coming to watch the game tomorrow? Now you're back.'

'What game?'

'God you are out of touch, mate. School match. Your Alex plays for the Under-15s, doesn't he? Used to do them on Saturdays in our day but . . .' He shrugged. 'They either won't pay the overtime, or they're all too busy getting excees for the community teams. So they miss Maths and English instead. No wonder the BRIC economies are racing ahead, eh, and buying up all them London mansions you make your cash out of.' His grin broadened. 'Give my love to Anastasia. And my future daughter-in-law. See you at the footie tomorrow?'

Joey refused to rise to the Tanya crack but nodded agreement on the football. But then asked, 'What about Max? I could give him a lift back.'

'What? And watch the two of them snogging in your back seat? Er, awkward. As they say.' Then he let out another deep, gurgling laugh at Joey's obvious discomfort thinking about it. 'Honest, Joe. You've got a real dad's face on you tonight.'

Joey shrugged to acknowledge that he had, as Bobby swept on.

'But thanks. Although there's no need. The only benefit

of still having the ex on the scene is that he stays with her midweek. I don't mind dropping him, but she'll have to turn out later. Give him a lift home on her broomstick. But I best be gone.'

The phone back at his ear, he waved to remind the counter staff not to forget Joey's latte and raspberry slice. Joey watched Bobby's rapidly departing back, thinking there was more to this parenting than he remembered. He checked the time and wondered whether to call Nat back, but decided that might kick them both off again. He then checked his texts. One from Benno. ALL GOOD. LOCK-UP STUFF TOP PRICE. ON NEW JOB. OLD MATE. CATCH UP WHEN. That sounded good. Joey had told him to sell everything from the lock-up after moving on. Without him Benno would soon become another target for the bully boys. You always needed someone watching your back.

There was nothing from Luke. Joey wondered what he and Tonto, as Bobby had called Matt, were up to at that moment, but knew he wouldn't let him know. Then something else caught his eye. Outside. Bobby was walking rapidly towards an old boy who was sitting on what was some public artiste's interpretation of a bench. As he finished his call, Bobby pulled out what looked like a £20 note, wrapped it round the phone then neatly dropped it into a shopping trolley by the side of the bench. Nothing more than a faint grin passed between the two as Bobby headed off to find his Range Rover.

Now Joey had something else to wonder about. The mysterious world of pay-and-throw phones.

Sean had just entered the code for the alarm and picked up the plant tray Sandra had selected and asked him to bring home in the Land Rover, when his phone went. He hadn't bothered putting in his Bluetooth earpiece for the short walk to the car so thought about ignoring it, but then wondered if it might be Craig Harlow calling back. Or worse: Noah in trouble again. He put down the box, fished out the phone and saw it was Joey. Yo, bro, he heard, as he tried to wedge the phone into the crick of his neck and pick the box up again so he could talk and carry the box, but as usual found it wouldn't stay in position. So he put the box down again.

'Don't you wish these so-called smartphones had rubber grips or something round the edges?' he asked Joey.

'Er, not something I spend that much time on, to be honest.'

'You can't wedge them into your neck, like the old ones with buttons.'

'That's true but, er, have you tried those little things that go in your ear and connect . . .'

Sean sighed. He'd asked for it. 'What's up?'

'Where you now?'

'Where do you think I am?'

'Either at some charity do annoying Sandra or locking

up. But . . .' Joey let it hang, to egg Sean on. 'Guess where I am?'

'How many guesses do I get? Seeing as London is such a big—'

'Warrington,' Joey cut across.

'Why?'

'Because I love my wife and kids. And want to be near them in their hour of need.'

'OK,' Sean said, getting the gist. 'But when . . . ?

'Last night. Well, this morning. You heard what happened to Tanya outside the chippy?'

'Had Sandra in my ear all morning. She's my personal social networker. Then had Noah all afternoon.'

Sean brought Joey up to speed on that, trying to keep his temper under control as he relived the trauma before eventually asking him what he was doing in Warrington.

'Taxi duty,' Joey responded. 'No point going home. By the time I got there I'd be on my way back. So been hangin' with Bobby McBain.'

'What'd he try and sell you?'

'Reassurance. About Tanya and his lad Max.'

'What about them?' Sean asked, surprised. And intrigued.

'Boy/girl stuff. I've been told not to fret about it.'

'I would.'

'I'm not you, though.'

'True,' Sean responded. Recalling his earlier thoughts about hoping Noah wouldn't turn out like Joey.

'So what else should I know about Bobby?' Joey asked.

'Oh, he's winding everyone up with a makeshift car park off the High Street.'

'When you say winding people up do you mean real people or—'

'Or my do-goody council mates, you mean?' Sean felt the spike of annoyance he always did on hearing his little brother's dismissive tone.

Joey felt the resentment. He'd done it again. Pressed the insecurity button. He tried to row back. 'I didn't mean . . . But, well, it's the same with his counterfeit stuff, isn't it. Everyone says it's disgraceful. But everyone's got one. He'll say it himself, Sean. He just offers what people want.'

He had a point. As did Bobby, but right then was not the time to get into a semantic argument about market forces and social policy. 'Can we argue this over dinner or something? I've got to get home.'

'Things to do, you mean. Instead of chatting to your brother who is trying to while away a few hours waiting for his daughter?' But it was light. Banter.

'How about I call you back when I'm in the car. And bluetoothed?'

'Great. You struggling with something?'

'Yeah. Box of winter greens to spruce up Janey's grave.'

'Ah yeah . . . and er . . . as usual, big bro. Thanks for doing that sort of thing.'

'No worries. It's Sandra actually. But part of what we do. So what you after?'

'Feel a bit crap now, but was going to ask if you had the trailer hooked up?'

Sean hesitated. He knew it was a hook for something. But in the end he had to fill the silence. 'Go on. Yes, so what?'

'The one you could sling on those fence panels you promised me?'

Sean let out another sigh of frustration and glanced back at the now bolted and alarmed compound. 'How about we sort that tomorrow, now you're home?'

He could hear Joey laughing at the other end.

By the time Sean drove home, Joey had driven back to park outside the club, using the travel time like he did on the train, to catch up on things so he could thoroughly impress his big brother by knowing who Craig Harlow was. Being Joey, he had crossed paths with nearly everyone from Highbridge during his own rites of passage years, but he'd duly agreed to be sworn to secrecy about Santa's Garden. Due to his own history he was also able to calm Sean down over thinking Noah was going off the rails, then arranged for Sean to drop the panels the following day, confirmed arrangements for a family lunch at the weekend and explained why he was back. Fed up with London. Missing the kids' growing up. Eventually getting to the part about realising that, although she would never admit it, perhaps everything might be putting too much stress on Natasha, especially with her mother deteriorating. And how he was grateful their own parents still seemed fit and well. He decided not to mention the bit about bankrolling Luke to sort out the chippy crew.

Instead he switched the conversation to whether Sean knew anyone who needed work doing. Now he was back, he'd have to start building up his business.

'Well, there is one thing you could do for me, actually,' Sean replied. 'Santa's illuminations?'

'Will I be able to tell anyone about it?' Joey laughed.

'If they work. Catch you tomorrow.'

'You will.' But before ending the call, Joey fired another question. 'Hey, Sean. Bobby told me there's a guy in the optician's who's a tranny.'

Sean immediately brightened. At last something Joey didn't already know. 'Everyone knows that, Joe. Well, those who live here.' He couldn't resist the barb. Nor the follow-up. 'But that's a double hit.'

'What is?'

'Well, Martin or Marian as he, or she calls herself must be the only thing in a dress you haven't tried to bed.'

'Oh, nice one, Bro.'

'Tomorrow,' was all Sean said before ending the call. But Joey heard him laughing at his own joke. That made him chuckle, wondering how early the optician had started and, if he was even half decent, whether he might have tried to pull him at some stage. He decided not to go too far down that memory lane as he swiped the phone to check his messages just in case there was anything from Luke. There wasn't. But he was getting a visual message from the two piles of muscle outside the club. Being suspicious was part of a bouncer's job description. He might be just another dad waiting to pick up the kids. But he could be an illegal taxi driver who would kick off a fight with the licensed guys. Or he could just be a perv on the prowl. No matter, they now had him on their threat assessment list.

As he washed the dishes after their meal, Luke was also thinking about tomorrow. Going through the operational plan, such as it was. Get in. Poke the nest. Get out. Matt had already lost himself on his laptop, alternating between cookery, military forums, property, cars and porn, noting wryly to himself how his preferences had changed over the years. A few years back, porn would have been first on the list, but there was only so many times you could get excited about some MILF flashing her bits.

Luke took the opportunity to reflect on whether it was time to sell up and move on. He knew everyone else had their own theories as to why he kept the cottage, and most had some validity. It was unfinished business. A reminder, like the nodding Buddha, of happier times. Or tragedy. It was a foothold back home. But above all, for him, it was a safe bolthole. Somewhere to aim for when things got too hot elsewhere. Where he could find a friend like Joey. And, as he had told him, what else would he do with his cash?

It was the same reason Matt was constantly trawling

estate agent websites, searching for somewhere to buy. Matt's trouble, though, was that since splitting from his wife before any kids came along, then losing his parents, he didn't have any roots from which to grow. Luke had thought of selling up and buying something closer to his own parents, but the idea of an apartment on the Costa del Pensions didn't exactly do it for him.

He picked up the nodding Buddha and gave it a tap. How long was it since he had felt real happiness? He rolled on his bed to look at the picture of himself and Janey on the bedside cabinet. It had been taken on the Thailand trip after she flew out to meet him on that 72. To stop his mind going down the blind alleys he had explored too often he rolled away from the picture and got up. He'd go over the plan one last time. The plan for payback. And that, he knew, was the real reason he kept coming back.

Joey was scrolling through the radio station list, another reminder of the lack of choice once outside the capital, when a text message popped up on his phone. HELP. It was Tanya. A microsecond later Joey was out of the car and heading for the two suits on the door, more High and Mighty than Jacamo and who, rightly, didn't know what this potential madman had on his mind. Until he held up the phone and pointed to the door, where Tanya was rushing out frantically looking for her dad. The bouncers hardly reacted at this all too familiar scene. Just another kid discovering reality is different from expectation and comes running for Daddy to sort it out. Still, before any of them had to do something they might later regret, Tanya, relieved at seeing Joey, pointed to the door and ran back to help Carol, who was struggling with a drunken Becky while trying to fend off the ever pursuing Husani, who'd swapped his Prada for a D&G look.

'Let go. I'll take her home,' Husani was saying. 'She's safe with me.'

'Oh yeah. She looks it,' Carol shot back.

'Here,' he tried to pull Becky away from Carol. 'I will take her.'

Which was when Tanya flew into the fray. Shoving Husani backwards. 'We're doing it, Hus!' she shouted.

The bouncers exchanged looks, then stood back and flicked their heads for Joey to pass. They had seen all this before too and knew it was best to let the domestics sort themselves out. Apart from which, they knew what might come next. As it did. As Becky attempted to empty the contents of her stomach on to the pavement between them all. While Joey was not quick enough, it had the effect of disentangling Husani's arm from between Carol's and Becky's. Joey looked down at his sick-splattered trainers then, fighting to control his irritation, gestured for Tanya to get Becky over to the Q7, while he turned to Husani.

'Who you?' came straight at him.

'I'm the guy who's taking them home.'

'No need. I do it. I'm with Becky.'

'Not any more. Tonight.'

Husani just grinned and went to step past Joey, but Joey leaned sideways, jamming him against the wall. He reacted by shoving Joey away. The bouncers took a step forward but Joey held up his hand. No trouble. Then leaned back in to Husani.

'Now, what you lot do tomorrow is between you and them, but I think it's best if I take my daughter . . .' Joey hesitated to make the point. Which Husani took. Hell's fury over a scorned woman had nothing on a protective dad. He stood back. Slightly.

It was enough for Joey to continue. 'So I'll take her and her friends home and you can go and finish your night. Somewhere else. Yeah?'

Husani held Joey's eye for a moment, then looked across to where Tanya was pushing and Carol pulling Becky into the Q7. He didn't seem to want to let her go and stepped forward once again. Joey blocked his way. The bouncers went on alert again, but this further flash-point was defused as another well-cut suit came out of the club. Joey's age. Very smooth manner but the fresh scar across his forehead suggested he had recently seen the sharp end of life. The bouncers nodded deferentially and made sure he avoided the souvenir from Becky. A man of influence.

'Er, anything I can help you gentlemen with?'

Both Joey and Husani turned to the new arrival. He

immediately sized them up, turned to Joey and then nodded at the girls. 'That your daughter?'

'The one pushing, yeah.'

Husani immediately realised that his age and the numbers were against him. 'I text you, Becky!' he shouted and started to back off towards the club.

The bouncers looked to the man in the suit. He shook his head, so they indicated that Husani should carry on walking, which he did, towards his Mercedes SLG, throwing a dismissive wave over his shoulder.

As the bouncers watched him go the suit turned back to Joey. 'Sorry. Bobby McBain . . . ?' He searched Joey's eyes for recognition. Then continued when Joey nodded. 'Bobby asked me to keep an eye on them.'

'You own this place?'

'And a few others. We did watch them. Even checked when he showed up, but they said they knew him.' He glanced at Husani and shrugged. What could they do? 'But then they started to look a bit uncomfortable,' he continued. 'Which was when your girl probably decided to call for Dad's army.'

Joey grinned but it faded quickly as he turned to see Tanya suddenly leap backwards, as Becky vomited out of the side of the Q7.

'And er . . . I'll leave you with that, shall I?' the club owner asked.

'Er . . . Yep. No problem,' he replied as he started towards the car.

'Oh,' the club owner called after him. 'You will tell Bobby we looked out for them?' His voice was edged with concern.

'Oh yeah. I'll give you a five-star rating.'

The club owner hesitated. Was that good or bad? Still, as he couldn't influence anything he continued to be as good as his word. And left Joey to deal with the vomit. Which he had to do again ten minutes into the return journey.

'Stop. Stop. Stop!' Tanya screamed from the back seat and started hauling a retching Becky over her lap to the door in the hope of escaping potential contamination. It was a good move. Joey brought the Q7 to a stop, but not in time to get Becky far enough across to miss the door. He just sat, eyes fixed ahead. He didn't have to look. He'd been through the scenario before. Already he could hear Natasha having a go at him for letting it happen. In her car.

Joey waited until they were fifteen minutes down the motorway before glancing into the rear-view mirror and saw the now mopped and wiped Becky across Tanya's lap, asleep. Carol was snoring as good as anything Benno could manage, while Tanya was staring out of the window, preoccupied about something.

'You OK?' Joey offered.

'Yeah. Sorry about . . .'

'It's OK. It's your mum we have to worry about.' He saw that at least that made her smile.

'Didn't turn out like you expected?'

'It did, actually. She's such a retard.' Her voice was laced with venom, but she stroked Becky's forehead at the same time.

'Who was the bloke?' He tried to make it sound causal, but she knew he was fishing.

'A bigger retard.' It was accompanied by a huge sigh that signalled the subject was probably off-limits to parents.

Joey decided he'd make one last attempt.

'No sign of Bobby's lad, though?'

'If you mean why wasn't he looking after us' – the sexist implication was clear – 'he had to go home early when Mummy came to get him. OK?'

Joey understood. Just drive. And then took another glance in the mirror. Tanya was still stroking Becky's forehead, but had gone back to sharing her thoughts with the window. Joey smiled. Bobby had been right. His ex must be a right dragon.

A few hours after Joey had delivered the girls home and cleaned up the Q7 as best he could, Luke and Matt were once again on the expressway. Matt had got the text alert on the way. At 04.47 and on checking the feed, saw that Leather's Porsche Cayenne was now parked outside the house. They'd had nearly six hours' sleep. It was time to go knockin'.

Matt was monitoring the live 3G feed on his personal smartphone, accepting that this was the most dangerous bit. Transporting weapons. Overseas they slept with them. But back home, no amount of blarney, Irish or other, would get them off a firearms charge. If they were walking down Highbridge Hill they could claim to have found it and were on their way to hand it in. But driving down the expressway or in a pub car park there could only be one conclusion. They were up to no good.

To create some form of alternative script Billy had delivered the weapons, as usual, unassembled, wrapped and bagged as replacement parts. Matt had taken one of the MP5s and further separated the components into different bin bags, ready to be discarded if they thought they were about to be pulled. If they couldn't dump the bags they would argue that they were only carrying spare parts. Not a weapon. No ammo. And hope for an importation offence. Back from overseas. A bit of black market on the side. Add a dash of remorse and naïvety and with the right lawyer that was probably a fine or six months inside. Perhaps both. But that was better than the potential seven years for possession of a firearm. And six months in a British nick was not as daunting as a few of the tours they had been through.

It was all probably academic though, as they knew the chances of being pulled were low at this time of day, when austerity cuts had trimmed police numbers. But they were prepared. As always. To improvise. Which they did by commandeering two metal rubbish bins from the side of the pub across the field from Leather's farmhouse. Matt pulled on his gloves and reassembled the MP5. If they were caught exposed he would ditch the gun. Nothing on him. Nothing on the gun.

They then checked the feed from the 3G camera. All quiet. Leather's Porsche Cayenne was still parked up. Time to go. They calmly walked the 200 metres to huddle against the farmhouse fence. From this viewpoint it looked exactly like what it was. A fenced compound.

Luke lifted his phone to the top of the fence, once again using its camera to scan the other side. All quiet. One last look at the feed. No change. He then set off round to the front of the property. Down the side where Matt had fixed the camera earlier. Matt followed.

Two-thirds of the way down the fence, when they were just in front of the farmhouse, they upended the rubbish bins but Matt carried on to the corner of the field where he had been earlier, loosening his backpack as he went. He reached up, unhooked the camera, dropped it in his backpack and went back to Luke. He dropped the back-pack as Luke made a hand step to boost him on to one of the bins. Matt in turn held out a hand to help Luke up on to his bin.

They then checked every angle and listened to the sounds of the night. Background traffic hum. A far-off blue light siren. A couple of animals talking to each other or shouting at perceived threats. Luke turned to Matt. Go? A confirmatory nod came back, so he finger-counted down from five and went over the fence. The movement detectors immediately picked up his presence and the security lighting illuminated the entire area inside the fencing, accompanied by the instant sound of a large dog barking inside the house. Luke grinned. All as predicted. So far.

Leather Jacket wouldn't want to attract too much attention from the outside, but would want to be in complete control inside. Luke looked across to the parked Cayenne and Cooper convertible. Knowing that anyone now up and watching the CCTV screens would see him clearly, Luke deliberately ducked low as he hurried across to the Cayenne and tried the doors. Then moved towards the Cooper. He wanted to appear as, hopefully, perhaps, just another opportunistic car thief. Even better, a stupid car thief. The only type who would have a go at the local drug lord's car.

They had reasoned that the house would be another typical drug fortress, so without resorting to the standard entry procedure – of blowing a hole in the wall quickly followed by a few flash bangs – their best bet was the same as the choke-point plan. Get anyone inside to come out. Right now, Luke hoped, Leather Jacket would be looking at the CCTV monitors, outraged that some idiot was trying to snatch his car. The more outraged he became, the more careless he would become.

Luke was right. After a moment or two the front door flew open and the dog that belonged to the bark rushed out. A German shepherd. Followed by Leather Jacket, but now in sweatpants and hoodie. It looked like he had hurriedly pulled it on, as it was unzipped, exposing the kaleidoscope of body art across his chest. He looked like he worked out a lot. It also looked like Matt had been right. There was now a Beretta Over-Under shotgun pointing directly at Luke. This could get a bit tricky.

9

Go Or No Go

Matt was now ruing his decision to go along with Luke. He had been tempted to slip one magazine into his backpack, just in case, but accepted the associated risks of being found in possession. They agreed they would use live ammunition only when they knew they were on their final exit plan. Which included fighting their way out. Right now, he thought, it wasn't going to be down to natural charm or blarney, but sheer bottle. And spotting an opportunity.

That came in the form of the dog doing what he had obviously been trained to do: attack. In its rush to get at Luke it brushed against Leather's legs, causing him to sidestep and take his eye and shotgun off Luke for a moment. Which was just enough time for Luke to turn and use the Cooper's bonnet as a step towards the Cayenne's roof. The dog tried to follow but slipped off the Cooper, went to try again but was stopped by a whistle from the front door. Luke looked across to see what must be the WAG, also in sweatpants and hoodie, but in pink and designed to show more the results of working out than the working out itself.

'He's goanna' scratch me car, soft lad!' she shouted at Leather in pure Scouse. But stopped dead in her tracks as a flash of red went across her eyes and a red dot bobbed across her breasts.

Immediately the dog turned its attention to this latest intruder but before he could even attempt a lunge up at Matt, now leaning on the fence behind the MP5, he was halted by another whistle from Leather, who had the Beretta back on Luke. The dog looked confused. What was the point of being trained to attack people if they kept stopping you? It sloped over to the WAG and sat beside her, obviously knowing who was its real best friend.

As Luke had earlier, Leather decided to buy time while he figured out was what going on. The all blacks. The red dot site on what looked like an automatic with a silencer. This was no random carjacking. This was an organised team and he was caught in a stand-off, out in the open with a useless dog and his equally useless WAG, now a bargaining chip. But a bargain can only be concluded if both sides play. It was a game he needed to control.

He shouted over his shoulder at Matt. 'You hurt her and—' He didn't finish. A jab of the shotgun towards Luke made the threat clear. The accent was thick, but to

Matt and Luke's surprise it was more East Manchester than Eastern European. A mixed marriage.

'And you,' he jabbed at Luke again. 'Tell your mate to back off. Or we start a shooting war. And this is legal – his isn't.'

'Yeah, but you'll be dead before the cops even get here.'

Luke saw the flicker. Leather now knew they weren't cops. Just as Luke intended. But it did little to dent the bravado.

'And you won't be?'

'Maybe,' Luke said, making a play of holding his hands up as he sat down, crossed-legged on the car. Leather might have thought he was capitulating, but he was actively reducing his size as a target while putting more flesh between the Barrett and his genitals.

'But,' Luke continued, 'you that accurate? You're going to have to hope you hit me here' – he framed his face with his hands, making it look like a small target. 'His will go where that red dot is. You might make a bit of a mess of me, but I'll live. She'll be burying you.'

It was the tone. The calm detachment. The way Luke spoke, rather than what he said, that put the doubt in Leather's mind. He looked across to Matt. These guys looked and sounded like pros. Or total headcases. Which was worse. What was he up against? He needed more time. Needed an opportunity.

'Nice cozzies,' he said. 'What is it? A Terrorist-a-gram? Trick or treat for Halloween, or something?'

'Not bad, that,' Luke chuckled. 'But let's not turn it into a Halloween movie, eh?'

'So what is it you want? Before I tell you what you can expect.'

Luke pointed first at the shotgun. Put it down. Then at the dog. Send it inside. Leather held his ground. Luke then directed Leather's attention by pointing to the WAG. Matt moved the red dot across her eyes and steadied it in the middle of her forehead.

'For Christ's sake, just give them what they want.' She was terrified.

Leather sighed. He could have done with a little more resilience, but he laid the shotgun down. Carefully. It was expensive. He then turned to the dog. 'Inside. Go.'

The dog looked totally perplexed. This game was supposed to end with him ragging someone's arm then being thrown a steak, or at least a sausage. Not this. He hesitated for a moment. Just in case. Until—

'Go!' It was harsher. Temper being controlled. Not to be ignored. The dog slowly skulked across to the front door.

'Now, back up and close the door,' Luke said to the WAG. 'Arm's length. Don't step too close or it'll be the last step you take.'

Meekly she did as she was told, all the time looking at the red dot that was now back on her cleavage. As she reached back and pulled the door closed it immediately deadlocked. The dog wouldn't be coming out again.

'Well trained,' Luke said to Leather, not differentiating between WAG and dog.

'As you are, by the looks . . .' Leather snarled back. As Luke had witnessed earlier, he was used to being in control so was struggling to contain his anger. 'So what the frig do you want?'

'Not a lot,' Luke answered as he slid off the Cayenne's roof to stand square on to Leather, side-kicking the shotgun out of reach. 'Just you out of Highbridge.'

Leather half smiled. This was now becoming more than irritating. It was becoming ridiculous. Who did these guys think they were? Or were dealing with?

'Really?' he asked. It said it all. No way.

Luke returned the half-smile. 'You may think you own the town, but you don't. The people we work for do. And they want you out. No matter what it takes.'

Leather once again looked Luke up and down. Deliberately. Then back to Matt holding the red dot on his woman. Still trying to buy time. Trying to think of a way out.

'Tell them who you are, Peter!' the WAG screamed, desperately hoping his reputation would frighten them off.

'I think they might already know,' he replied. Calmly. This was, he now thought, strictly business. 'You do Fatty's place the other night?'

'I heard about it,' Luke replied. Equally calm. 'Town's getting dangerous for those who shouldn't be there.'

'And what if I tell you to go and f—' Leather started again, winding himself up, but stopped as a red glare caught his eye. Then he noticed the red dot dancing on Luke's chest. Then move down on to the ground and across to him. Up his legs, circle his crotch and settle in the centre of his chest. His anger was simmering at his own impotence. Luke nodded towards Matt, then tapped Leather on the chest. Twice. The double tap of death.

Luke noticed Leather's fists clenching and unclenching. Just like Joey did when he was either winding up for a fight, or keeping himself under control to avoid one. It meant Leather was now on a very short fuse and could kick off at any moment. He was probably also trying to decide whether he could dodge the red dot long enough to grab Luke as a human shield, so Luke took a step away, towards the shotgun, but the meaning was obvious to Leather. He'd never make it.

'You can have this week. But after that . . .' Luke paused, leaving the thought in the air, before adding, with heavy emphasis, 'Pete.'

Although he returned a caustic glare, Leather took the point. They did indeed know who he was, and didn't seem to care.

Luke picked up the shotgun. 'Nice gun,' he said, as he broke it slowly and took out the two cartridges while backing away towards the perimeter fence. 'After this week, Highbridge is off limits to you and yours.'

There was neither humour nor threat. The neutral tone

was enough for Leather to conclude that this was, as he thought, strictly business. There was no further attempt to argue. He just wanted to get the situation over so he could regroup. And get back in control. To do that he had to stand and watch Luke drag his patio table and a chair to the fence, then watch as he placed the Beretta on the table, stepped up and over. Improvising.

The woman immediately hurried over to join Leather as the red dot danced between their chests. The warning was obvious. But just as Matt turned away and was about to drop out of sight, Leather called out. 'Oi. You do know what to expect, don't you?'

He took Matt's slight hesitation as acknowledgement of the threat. He couldn't see the smile beneath the balaclava as he dropped from view. The bait had been taken.

Joey was also up early as usual to let Roscoe out on his morning patrol, and when he'd made sure that the boys were up and ready for school he had gone out to check on the Q7 after its emergency clean-up from the previous night. But he knew human vomit was second only to spilt milk to make a car uninhabitable. He'd take it in to Glass & Shine and see if they would do a valet while he waited.

He was just taking his morning Colombian from beneath the coffee dispenser when Becky came into the kitchen, hunting for her stuff, still in the clothes she had been wearing the night before. Like many, she had suffered the nightclub exchange rate. Going in looking a million dollars: coming out a million lire. It might even be drachmas these days, Joey was thinking, as he heard the kitchen door open.

'Oh, sorry, Mr Nolan. I er . . . I wanted to be gone before anyone . . .'

'It's OK, Becky. You're not going into school with—'

But she hurriedly interrupted. 'My mum's in the car outside.'

'OK. But remember, it happens to us all every now and then, you know.'

'Yeah. But not, like, spewing over someone else's car.' She had gathered up the abandoned shoes and bag from the stagger-in, so headed for the door. It was only when the front door banged that Tanya came hurrying into the kitchen, pulling on a thick tartan dressing gown.

'Was that Becks?'

'Think she was off to find a hole to crawl into.'

'Why? What did you say? You didn't have a go at her for—'

'No.' Joey cut across her. 'I know it's part of my job description to take the blame for everything, but this time: no. Think it might have had something to do with leaving her scent on your mother's car?'

This seemed to calm the lion cub, for she walked over to the table, dropped into a chair and took her phone from her pocket. Her thumbs got to work as she spoke. 'God, Mum doesn't know, does she?'

Joey shook his head and sat down opposite his daughter. Every week he noticed a change. Each week losing a bit of his little girl, as the woman emerged. Nat was right. He had been missing the kids growing up. Not that such things were on Tanya's mind.

'She is such a retard.'

'Are we still on your mother now, or—'

'Becks. That bloke, right. God, what was she like?' She put her phone down and leaned forward. There was still a bit of his little girl wanting to share a secret with her dad. 'He's the one that keeps stalking her. He's really creepy, Dad. I'm sure he spiked her drink.'

'That's some accusation, Tan.'

'Then why'd she start behaving the way she did?'

'And I don't suppose they gave out any discounted shots?' He was, after all, still the dad trying to guide his daughter towards the realities of life.

She considered it for a moment. 'Well, yeah, but we all did the same.' She saw his eyebrow move. Even if involuntarily. 'But I suppose we're, well, Cags and I, are more used to it.' She saw his eyes harden. The little girl retreated, to be replaced by the cub. 'And don't look like that. I'm nearly seventeen.'

'You're supposed to be eighteen to drink.' But Joey knew he had slipped too far into protective dad mode and was losing the moment.

'Yeah, right.' Her phone lit up. She looked. 'She's going

home to clean up. Why didn't she do that here? You sure you didn't say something?'

'No. But what I should have said to her, and I'm now saying to you, is that you are all still too young to be hanging around in clubs owned by the likes of Bobby McBain. Or going out with his son.'

'God, you're so hypocritical. It was OK for you to hang out with his dad when you were our age, but I'm not supposed to see Max? He's really sweet.'

'Sweet?'

'Yes, he is, actually. Just because his dad's some big gangster, doesn't make him one.'

'It's not him. It's where he'll end up taking you.'

'And where's that?'

'I don't know.' Joey instantly knew that was a stupid thing to say. To anyone, never mind a teenager.

'Oh, right,' Tanya said as she stood up. The moment was definitely moving away from Joey. 'You haven't got a clue what you're talking about but you want me not to see Max, just in case there might be something, but you don't know what?'

Joey tried to recover. 'OK, put like that it sounds daft. But—'

'It doesn't sound daft, Dad. It is.'

'I can always ground you, you know.'

'Oh, great. You haven't been around for God knows how long and now you come swanning in thinking it's all going back to walks in the park and teddy bears, or something. I don't think so.'

With that she was gone. His little girl had definitely morphed. That was the real killer. He had missed that happening.

'They're all trying to get in on the act now,' Glynnis said, as she delivered Sean's Full Welsh to his corner table in the café. Sean glanced up from his Google search. He thought he had better know a few of Craig's chart hits before he met him. He saw Glynnis standing, tight lipped, arms folded, glaring out at Santa's Garden where there was a small army of little helpers tidying and primping. Sean smiled, but couldn't keep the quizzical look from his face.

'Don't look at me,' Glynnis quickly said. 'There's where you want to look.' She nodded out to the hive of activity, where Byron was directing operations with all the aplomb of a concert conductor. 'He's probably been and goggled or boggled or whatever you do on those things –' she pointed to Sean's iPad. 'And now he knows what a big cheese is coming. He'll be trying to be first in line, you know.'

She used it as her departure line, but the meaning was more obvious. *She* wanted to be first in line. Sean chuckled as he dissected the egg to start creating the glue for the egg and bacon sauce, as a text message popped up on the iPad screen. Sandra. WHAT TIME CRAIG DUE? Sean nearly choked on the first piece of bacon, sausage and black pudding. They were all trying to get in on the act.

Luke and Matt were now naked. They were going through the drill of loading their mud-splattered blacks into the washing machine to clean them up and get rid of any superficial dirt that could link them back to Leather's farmhouse. Not that they expected Leather to call it in. The concern was always dog walkers. Or joggers. See something suspicious. Call the police. The nation had been inculcated in this mantra. A couple of guys in black cover-alls and balaclavas carrying bins across a field might fall into that category. The idea that it would be Leather who pressed charges was a fallacy imported from American crime shows. In Britain it was the cops who decided whether you needed lifting.

Having set the washing machine going they went upstairs for a shower. If they had just got back from a firefight they would have changed, burnt their gear and wiped down not far from the scene, so they could travel home relatively clean. They knew that forensics might always find something, but that was when they were looking and after they'd picked up any superficial clues. Matt had switched the car registration plates as soon as they got back, feeding the cloned car set into the incinerator Luke had installed as part of the eco-heating system. It burnt all household and garden refuse to provide the hot water that was now running over their backs.

They had talked through the likely scenarios on the way back. About how Leather would probably assume it was a land grab. So he'd come looking for who was likely to gain, not some old school chums out for revenge. That would go one of two ways. He looked the type who would want to react quickly to stamp his authority – yet, the execution by crane suggested a man of detail and planning. Who needed to be in control. That suggested he would wait until he felt the time was right.

Either way, they agreed that he would come after dark. More creatures of the night. They might be brazen enough to act in daylight on their own patch, but not in Highbridge. Yet. That was why they had to be stopped. Before they did.

The plan was to stop them at the choke point. The swing bridge into town. If the bridge opened at the right moment they would have to stop. And once stopped, they would be fixed targets. There for the taking.

'We going to be ready at the swing bridge every night from now on, then?' Matt asked, as Luke came into the kitchen still pulling on a sweatshirt.

Matt was now showered and throwing together another one-pot dish. Paella.

Luke nodded. 'You sure you can get all the cameras to work?'

'Don't see why not. Four cameras. Four IP addresses. Four feeds,' Matt responded, but then added, 'You sure Billy couldn't just swing a drone for us? A proper one.'

Luke laughed. 'I'm sure if the price was right. Although someone in Nevada might query the idea of targeting that chippy.'

Matt shrugged, accepting that was probably a fair observation, which was why they were going with Plan B. Supplementing the 3G camera they had used at Leather's farmhouse with three more, each positioned on the expected route to Highbridge. Each of the four cameras would be mounted inside what looked like a standard bird nest and feeder box, the sort that often have a camera rigged inside so enthusiasts can watch the birds feeding and nesting, and the chicks growing. However, with Matt's boxes the camera was pointing outward. Each had a small power pack with a long trailing power cable. Each was painted in British road sign grey. They also had large zip ties attached so they could easily be strapped tightly to any one of the many road signs that cluttered roadside landscapes. They would look just like any another piece of kit some jobsworth somewhere had put up to monitor only they knew what.

'How long will it take to rig everything?' Luke asked.

'Couple of minutes each, tops. Travel out. Back. I can set up the laptops on the way back. Couple of hours, say three tops?'

'We'd better get them rigged this morning, then. Rest up this afternoon.'

'OK,' Matt replied, reaching over for two plates. 'Get the water. And did you find out about the bridge?'

Luke nodded, putting two water bottles on the table. 'Found out that it only opens on demand, though.'

'How's it work? Can we rig it?'

'It's electric. Operated from a control room overlooking the canal.'

'So,' Matt concluded, as he scooped out the paella on to two waiting plates. 'All we have to do is hot wire it?'

Another nod from Luke. 'And if we can't, I think we know a man who can.'

Matt grinned. 'I think we do. But er . . .' He stopped for a moment. Not sure whether he really wanted to bring up the subject. 'But er . . . We – or you – sure about Joey? I know you had another word, but . . . Is he still up for it all? I mean, frightening Fatty's one thing, but we know where this is going, don't we?'

Luke acknowledged the point with a nod. 'And that's something else I'm going to ask him. Go or No Go.'

'And what happens if it's a No Go? If he can't live with it?'

Luke pondered for a moment. The same issue. Easy to say people should be shot. Different doing it. And different living with the trauma of feeling responsible. 'Let's see what our man says first.'

That man was now walking down the High Street looking for Bobby McBain's controversial car parking scheme. Joey was curious and had time to kill while the guys at Glass & Shine removed the stench of Becky's stomach from the rear door side panel of the Q7. With a bit of luck they'd all get away with Natasha thinking he had had the car cleaned as a surprise.

It didn't take him long. He just followed a convoy of cars that turned off the High Street into Saddlers Street. As he rounded the corner he saw they were then turning into a wide open space, that once housed the junior school. On one corner was a small shed, outside which a young lad with a shock of red hair was collecting money. Joey walked over and asked the lad if he knew where Bobby was. A phone came out and within five minutes Bobby's Range Rover arrived.

'You trying to scrounge another coffee, Nolan?' the gravel voice called as the driver's window slid down.

'If you're buying.'

'Get in.'

Another five minutes and they were walking into Costa. Again. And for once, Bobby had turned off his phone.

'Politicians are like ex-wives, Joe,' Bobby said. 'Never know what they want and when they get it they're never satisfied.'

'What you on about now?'

'You asked me about the car park. They carp on about wanting inward investment and businesses to invest in the community. When you do, they start harassing you.'

Joey laughed. 'I don't think they had you squatting on their land in mind, Bob.'

'Er, careful, Joe. It's not theirs. It's ours. The people's. That's what they don't get. And that carrot head manning the car park? Slung out of school because of his "anti-social" behaviour. His dad's inside. His mum's got something missing upstairs and he's number nine out of, er, twelve I think. That's conjugal visits for you. So no wonder he's anti-social, eh? But he's a brilliant lad. Hard worker. Because I give him what he wants. A bit of love and respect.'

'So you're Uncle Bob, are you?'

'I am more than the Council lot, but . . . That's all I wanted, you know. Bit of encouragement. Want to grab a seat? I'll sort out the order.'

Bobby then walked to the front of the queue to give the order to the young lad on the till. Joey looked round. Every seat seemed to be occupied. Until Bobby noticed him, still hovering. He walked over and gave an exaggerated sigh of disappointment, which was immediately picked up by a group by the window and one near the toilets. Both stood up and offered Bobby their seats. He pointed Joey towards the window group then, with an appreciative wave, he went back to collect the coffees. Joey, slightly embarrassed, eased himself into the still warm chairs.

There was no such embarrassment from Bobby as he came back with napkins and cutlery. Still in full flow about the Council.

'They're supposed to be there for us, aren't they. Not themselves.' The pebble-dash cracked again. 'That's our job, isn't it. Looking out for us and ours.'

Joey gave a nod of agreement. He couldn't fault Bobby's logic.

'Anyway,' Bobby continued. 'They knocked down the junior school, right? Guffing out some tosh about falling school rolls while the population's actually increasing. How'd they get away with it, eh? But they did, and created that big open site. So, I moved a few lads in there and we charge a quid an hour or a fiver for all-day parking. And on market day. Coining it, mate. Coining it.'

'Haven't they tried to move you off?'

'Oh yeah.' The gravel laugh again. 'They hate me. Hate me. I'm even worse than the travellers, aren't I? I'm never going to move on, am I? But in terms of investing in the community I may be trespassing, but I'm not asking for water and 'lecky, and I'm providing a much needed service: cheap parking and a little haven from the traffic wardens. Everyone wins.'

'Except the Council.'

Bobby just gave a dismissive shrug. And then surprised Joey by adding, 'Doing it for my own lad, actually.'

Bobby saw Joey's curious look. 'Got a few legit things building up to pass on to him. That's why I sent him to Hazelhurst like your Sean's kids. Give him a better education than the one we didn't get.'

'We learned a lot more on the streets,' Joey agreed. 'And at night school.'

The gravelly laugh. 'Didn't we just. But it wouldn't be

so romantic in that park these days, having to step over dead smackheads.'

'How'd it get to that stage, Bob?'

'Life doesn't change, Joe. Just the illegal highs. In our day it was send someone into the offie to get the booze, and then back to the swings to split it up before coming down the cut and through the fence at the back. We learned a few things in those goalmouths, didn't we?'

We did indeed, Joey thought back, as the lad from the till brought the coffees over. Bobby gave him two £20 notes.

'Keep a fiver and put the rest towards what they had,' he said as he nodded over to the previous window group now standing near the toilets finishing their drinks.

'So now it's drugs instead of drink?' Joey asked as the lad left.

'Both. It's never either–or, Joe. People want it all.' Abruptly Bobby switched tack. 'They'll have to find a new playground, though. When they turn that old one into houses.'

'Er, how's that go?'

'Everyone knows what's going on. Council. Cops. They can't stop it. So they reckon that if they get rid of the playground there'd be one less place to hide.'

'Just move the problem somewhere else?'

'But it might stop my Max and your Alex discovering they've got a dead druggie in goal.'

‘When do you reckon that’ll all happen?’ Joey asked, completely surprised by the news.

‘Soon as the Council can fiddle the planning. The real reason they demolished the old junior school, and the reason they really hate me, is that it’s right behind the playground. One big plot to sell off. And I’m the poison pill in the middle.’

‘How do you know all this stuff?’ Joey asked. But didn’t get an immediate response as one of the previous window group came over and thanked Bobby for covering their drinks. Joey smiled. Amazing. He walks in, throws them out of their seats and they end up thanking him. Did people respect or fear him? He remembered him always being in trouble. And saying that if they treated him like a gangster, then he was going to be the best Highbridge had ever seen. No doubts on that score.

‘Go on,’ Joey continued. ‘I keep up with the local paper while I’m away. So how’d you know more?’

‘This stuff’s never in the papers, Joe. Cops are a good source of stories and the Council’s a big spender on ads. Why would the paper really want to upset them by asking awkward questions? Like why the Council is demolishing stuff so they can sell off the playground for houses? You should check it out. Someone will want a sparky if the house deal goes through.’

‘And will it? As you seem to know everything.’

Bobby just cracked the pebble-dash. ‘My business to know, Joseph. Talking of which. How’s your girl’s mate today? Sounded like a right slimeball trying to get in her drawers last night. Want us to give him a seeing to?'

Joey felt his back stiffen. A reminder. He was, after all, supping with the devil. And his daughter was going out with the devil's son. No matter what Joey wanted, the devil would protect what he thought was his own.

Joey just grinned and shook his head, no need. He also wanted to steer the conversation back to Bobby.

'Anyway, did you talk to them beforehand?' Joey asked what he thought was a perfectly obvious question. 'They might have let you do it?'

Bobby shook his head. 'Trouble is, Joe, it's like being back in school. They never let you stand up, do they? Never let you get back on your feet. Always waiting to knock you down because of what they think you are.'

'I remember,' Joey said, thinking back to the way he'd been treated differently to Sean. He was the swot. Joey was the scally.

'I'm branded so can't change, even if I wanted to. So they won't even talk, never mind listen to me. Which is OK, because I can play them. Like the travellers. I'm forcing them to go through proper processes and all that bollocks. That'll drag on so long and get so heavy-handed that local support'll force them to let me keep the site. Or find me another one. That'll make it legit. The lad'll then have a car park business to keep going. Just have to keep one step ahead of the buggers. And, I don't know why I'm telling you all this.'

'Because you're leading up to the real point?' Joey asked.

'Rather than distracting me with some tosh about worrying about your kid's inheritance.'

He knew Bobby too well.

Matt was nearly right. It had taken only two hours to recover the Transit, travel to Leather's and set up three of the four cameras on the way back. At each location, Matt had jumped out the side door, rigged and positioned each camera, then set up a cheap but clean laptop on the way back with a 3G dongle. Like the cameras, it too was disposable. They had already placed the camera outside Leather's gates and two on the speed limit signs without any trouble. Apparently two council workmen rigging monitoring equipment. Hiding in plain sight. Invisible.

Unfortunately, when they got to the preferred location of the fourth, the lamppost next to the Welcome to Highbridge sign, they discovered real Council workmen. Not hiding. Actually in plain sight. The lamppost was undergoing routine maintenance. That was ninety minutes ago and there were only so many times they could drive past to see how things were going. The cloak of invisibility would only last so long. Especially since Billy had told them that their new cloned registration plates only had a life of six hours as the donor was in having an MOT.

'Let's hide the van, then come back to this one,' he suggested to Luke, who then pointed the Transit in the direction of the swing bridge.

*

'Fantastic. No. Saturday's great. Thank you. Please tell Craig how delighted we all are,' Sean said as he ended the call and allowed himself a smile. A more demonstrative gesture would have been to punch the air, or go into a semi-crouched position while thrusting his clenched fist forward. However, with young Ben and Deborah on the tills he felt the need to maintain a certain managerial decorum. Nevertheless, he was pleased.

'He's still coming then,' Glynnis asked. She had been hovering while he was on the phone.

'Yes, Glynnis,' Sean replied, his smile broadening. 'Saturday morning to take a look round.'

'Brilliant. I knew he would. Once his mum asked him,' Glynnis responded, a smile also spreading across her face. 'Oh, it's exciting, isn't it?' This was aimed more at Ben and Deborah.

'My mum will be excited,' was all Deborah said.

'Can I tweet it yet, Mr Nolan?' It was Ben, the resident social networking expert.

'Er . . . No, not yet, Ben,' Sean replied. 'Let's wait until he confirms the real thing on Saturday.'

'But you'd better have your thumbs on standby then,' cautioned Glyniss. Cos as soon as he walks in it'll be all over town. I'm telling you.'

Sean shared a knowing smile with Ben. Typical Glynnis – until she turned her attention to him.

'And here's something that might wipe the smile off your face. Remember that 10 per cent discount you gave away to that druggie lot. Well, a couple of your councillor mates are coming in to use it later.'

Glynnis was right. The smile had disappeared, as she continued. 'You know, the ones that are married and claiming two sets of expenses. They phoned up to ask if it applied to lunch as well.' Glynnis's distaste was obvious.

'Oh, what did you tell them?'

'I said, you're a man of your word. And if you're daft enough to offer it in the first place, then you'd be daft enough to give it on lunch as well.'

And with that she headed back to the café.

'Can I tweet that, Mr Nolan?' Ben asked. 'About the councillors coming in?'

'No. I'm giving them enough without the publicity.' He tried to make it sound light. But he was already wondering how much it would cost him in the end.

'Probably scare off people as well,' Deborah suddenly chipped in, before turning to help a woman unload her trolley.

But if they do come in, Sean thought as he headed for his office, at least I can tell them about the business with Noah. And ask what they are doing about it all. That should be worth 10 per cent.

'There, that's it,' Bobby said, sitting back in his chair. 'It's just a, what do they call it, a hypothetical.'

Joey knew it was more than that. If Bobby did, as he claimed, know everything that went on in town, then he was now fishing. The devil was after the detail. And the last thing Joey wanted to do was help him get it.

'So, your plan—'

'Hypothetical,' Bobby corrected.

'Your idea is to round up a few of us and sort out the fat get in the chippy?'

Bobby nodded. Casually. 'Like we used to.' But then it came. Casually again but as Joey knew, fishing. 'Or would you use Carlton and his oppo for that?'

As he'd been expecting it, Joey was able to look surprised. 'Go on, then. What's that mean?'

Bobby leaned forward in his seat. This was not for everyone's ears. 'Just that they like a bit of aggro those boys, don't they. Sign up for it. Get used to it. Must be hard holding back when they know they could sort out stuff like this with a well-timed knock on the door in the middle of the night. Bag over the head. Off the viaduct and into the river. Who'd know?'

'You. As you apparently know everything,' Joey replied and leaned in closer. 'And the police, perhaps?'

The pebbles rattled in Bobby's throat again. 'Now you're winding me up. Or getting confused about policing and justice, Joe. The cops know. Well, most things. Trouble for them is that that isn't their job. Their job is to prove things. Knowing isn't enough.'

'But good enough for you?'

'Natural justice. The only justice people like you and

me believe in. The way they did things in the old days. With strangers' fields.'

'Which was?' Joey asked, intrigued.

Bobby edged even further forward. 'In the old days, villagers sorted things out themselves. Any stranger giving aggro would be taken down to a field. The strangers' field. And sorted out. One by one, each villager would land a blow. Weapon or fist. Didn't matter. Then everyone took a turn in digging the grave. Everyone had to take part. Everyone culpable. Everyone knew everything, so nobody spoke. Mutual responsibility. Mutual respect. That's how we should handle things. People like me and you, Joe.'

Joey was about to protest, but Bobby came back with a quick jab. 'And don't try and give me some old bollocks. I know . . .' he emphasised it. 'I know. You'd soon give someone a good smack if they came near you and yours. Like you would have done last night at the club? Eh? Your trouble, Nolan, as it's always been, is that you can't just walk away. Damsel in distress. Someone getting a hard time. Get yourself involved in things when you don't have to. Max tells me your Tanya's the same.'

The comment stung. Unintentionally. And ironically. That was exactly the opposite to the way Joey was feeling at the moment. He shook his head. He was thinking that he hadn't been doing much getting involved lately when they were interrupted by a voice from behind.

'You two look like you're up to no good.'

They both turned to find Luke standing behind them, a coffee to go in his hand.

'That a bit of the old SAS training? Creeping up on people?' Bobby asked.

Luke shook his head as he joined them. 'Not necessary when people get locked in to their own little worlds.' He indicated how close they were sitting, then pulled a chair round to join them.

Joey noticed he was now, like himself, in a more lightweight jacket and jeans, obviously not having come straight down from the hill.

'So what you doing?' Bobby asked, with a glance to Joey. 'Still hanging round?'

'Just needed a chat with Joe about some electrical work I want doing.'

'Up at your ghost house?'

Luke just grinned. Refusing to be baited. 'Where else?'

It was enough for Joey. There was something else. Otherwise he would have just agreed. The devil also picked up the detail. It was a probe. What did he know? So he fired one back himself.

'Thought your services would be much in demand in this troubled world we live in?' he asked.

Luke followed Bobby's quick glance to Joey, as he also reached to pick up his phone. Luke's arrival had served as a reminder to Bobby that he had been out of touch for too long.

'You going to record this bit, Bob?' Luke asked. It was

a deflection, but a grin showed he was joking. Bobby's counter-sneer showed he wasn't impressed.

'Bobby reckons you and Matt could solve the town's drug problem by throwing people off the viaduct,' Joey said, trying to sound casually incredulous.

It didn't go unnoticed by the devil. It was a heads up on the conversation.

'Ah. How much?' Luke asked Bobby, believing the best form of defence is always attack.

'Where's your community spirit?' Bobby asked with a throaty laugh.

'Expended on some far-flung foreign battleground. Go on, how much?'

'Bobby told me last week he could get it done for fifty quid,' Joey said. 'Or, five hundred for a proper job?'

Bobby took a quick look round in case the wrong sort of ears were within range. Too much detail even for the devil. It was Luke's turn to laugh.

'And how many of these proper jobs end up with the executioner in jail?'

Bobby just shrugged. Like Joey, no matter how tough he felt, there was something cold and measured about Luke that made him feel, if not inadequate, then slightly out of his depth.

'Enough to make it not worthwhile. There's three kinds of crime the cops take seriously. Multiple rape. Serious fraud. And murder. They'll verbal a lot about everything else, as we all do, but when it comes down to it it's those three that frighten the powers that be. Those three that get everyone agitated. Worrying that it could happen to them. Or get people asking questions about why they should keep paying taxes and keeping them in jobs. Why? Because people do a lot to protect their lifestyles.'

He focused on Joey. 'How long you been going up and down the country for a decent job?'

Joey conceded the point, as Luke pressed on. 'And Hilary and her gang aren't really interested in your fake knock-offs, Bob. Or clocking someone doing thirty-five in a thirty. They want to be doing the serious stuff. And so long as they do a good job we put up with all the pettiness that comes with it.' He grinned at Bobby. 'So, five hundred quid? For ten to fifteen years inside?' Shook his head. 'Need to multiply it by a thousand to make it worthwhile.' He then grinned. 'To do a really proper job.'

This time Bobby appeared to miss the look that went between Luke and Joey as he was now scrolling through his accumulated text messages. The look that reminded Joey what he was getting for his money. Something more than community spirit. Revenge for Janey.

'Well, that takes me out of the frame,' Bobby said with another throaty chuckle, as he stood up and waved the phone. He had to go. 'But if you drop your rates, I might have a list you could work your way through.'

With that he headed for the door, then across the street to where his Range Rover was parked half on and half off the pavement.

'Do you really have a job for me?' Joey asked Luke.

'I'm thinking of adding a steam generator to the shower. If anyone asks. But I'm also interested in learning more about the way electricity works. Like you told me how you can always get power from street lights.'

'Go on.'

'Just wondered how, for instance, someone could rig the swing bridge to open. For a prank, say?'

Joey shook his head. 'That'd be a bit of work. You'd have to, I'm guessing, be working with any number of combinations from 11,000 Volt multi-poles, 415 Volt AC, 240-Volt three-phase down to 12-Volt DC control systems. That's why I've got certificates.'

Luke looked deflated. Until Joey grinned. 'But there's an easier way.' Then added, in answer to Luke's curious look, 'Remember Gary McClintock? The guy who used to come to school on his trail bike?'

Luke nodded. 'Got expelled for tearing up the running track doing wheelies or something?'

'Doughnuts. Anyway. He's got the keys to the castle.'

'What?'

'He lives in the old cottage on the towpath. Just along from the control box. Where he . . . ?' He let it hang for Luke to pick up.

'Operates the swing bridge?' Luke asked. Intrigued.

Joey nodded, but noticed that as Luke took this in he seemed a bit more preoccupied with something else. 'And?' he asked.

'One last question from me.' He leaned forward and brought the coffee cup up to his mouth, obscuring his lips, just in case. 'Go or no go?'

'What's that mean?'

'We're trained for point and shoot. In, out, job done, get gone. Someone else always has to consider the consequences. It's always someone else who has to make the final decision.' He left it at that. For Joey to think about. To think through the consequences.

Joey did. For him, Natasha and the kids. Of him getting caught. He had thought of little else since his chat with Natasha. But he'd also thought a lot about Janey. About what had happened and nearly happened to Tanya. And about the young lad found dead on a sports field named after another young lad who'd died tragically from a heart condition. That was a waste. But how much greater waste was it for someone to be killed by drugs?

'If you mean can I live with the consequences of . . . what? Whatever you want to do with your body warmer? Then, yeah. I can.'

The two old friends held each other's eyes for a moment. Understanding. It was go. Before their attention was drawn to the window by the sound of the horn on Bobby's Range Rover, as he roared off.

'Hilary was right. Can't help himself,' Joey laughed. But then turned back to Luke. More serious. 'Do you think he knows anything? Or just guessing?'

Luke remained unfazed. 'Even if he does, he's not going

to talk. The real question is, why is he letting this bunch from out of town operate on his patch?'

It was a good point. And one Joey had completely overlooked. If Bobby did know everything that was going on in Highbridge then he'd know exactly what was really being sold at the chippy. And, much more to the point, was he in on it? Was the devil really fishing to protect his own?

Over by the gas heaters Sean was in deep discussion with Mr and Mrs Councillor.

'Yes, we heard all about the demo. But that is not the way to go about things. There are procedures.' It was Mr Councillor, Malcolm Sawyer, Chair of Education.

'And as for the playground itself, Sean, it's been debated and agreed. It's for the good of the town.' Mrs Councillor, Sarah Sawyer, Chair of Planning, declared in a tone that she expected would bring the conversation to an end.

'Who by?' Sean replied with an incredulous edge that seemed, to the Chair of Planning, to be challenging the very principles of democratic government.

'By the elected members of the Town Council, Sean,' Mr Councillor, Chair of Education, replied on behalf of both himself and his spouse and fellow Chair.

'And did they consult anyone who might be vaguely interested? Like the public they are supposed to represent?'

'We are elected to do the job on their behalf,' Education

responded. 'You know how it works. If you don't like it, you can easily vote us out.'

'Oh come off it, Malcolm,' Sean responded. 'All I'm asking is whether it's true, or not, that you lot are flogging off the kids' playground.'

'It's your tone we are finding objectionable, Sean,' Mrs Councillor, Chair of Planning, replied. Firmly.

Sean decided to take a breath. Count to ten and continue. But he only got to three before Education had had enough of this intrusive invasion of their shopping trip.

'Look, Sean, we are out trying to enjoy ourselves by spending money here, with you. If you feel so strongly about this matter, then write to us formally.' The Chair of Education then took the elbow of Planning to guide her away. Obviously the meeting had been declared over. But Sean stepped in front of them. With Any Other Business.

'Hang on,' he said. 'All right, I might have been a bit harsh, but what is that political saying? If you can't stand the heat, get out of the kitchen?' He glanced round, and smiled, hoping it would defuse the obvious tension. 'Or greenhouse, perhaps?'

'Your apology is accepted, Sean,' Planning responded. 'But Malcolm is right. If you feel . . .'

It hadn't worked. 'I didn't apologise, Sarah. I've . . .' He emphasised the point. 'I've done nothing to apologise for.'

'Are you implying that we have?' Education suddenly blustered.

'Well,' Sean commented, slightly surprised by the vehemence of the reaction. 'What's that other saying about he who protesteth too much? Have you Malcolm? Is there something going on that we, the electorate, should know?'

'How about this, Sean? We won't tell you how to grow plants if you don't tell us how to run the Council. Now, are we still welcome to buy a spot of lunch?'

'Look Malcolm, I know you see yourself as part of some sort of local political dynasty, following on from your dad and granddad, but you are there to represent everyone, remember, not just the ones who voted for you.'

'Well if more people bothered to turn out and vote . . .'

But Mrs Councillor recognised that this was drifting towards a typically male, locked-antlers confrontation so demonstrated why she had become Chair of Planning, and intervened.

'Sean, if what you are asking is, are there any plans under consideration for redeveloping the playground area, then the answer is yes. We have a preferred developer, but all is being done above board and under the EU Procurement Rules. Which we have to abide by, of course, whether we like it or not.'

She succeeded in making the two stags back off, but only long enough to allow Sean to draw breath and come back with another question. 'If that's the case, then how come the public and local media don't know anything about it?'

'Sometimes we have to act, on behalf of the people if you like, under a cloak of commercial confidentiality.'

'And what does that mean?'

'You know as well as we do about all the problems attached to that playground.'

'Yes. Including the young lad who was killed there the other night,' Sean countered.

'We don't know if he was killed,' the Chair of Planning shot back. No doubt as a Point of Information. 'Only that he died. Tragically, perhaps, but we mustn't jump to conclusions. About anything.' It was her turn to emphasise a point.

'Sarah, look . . .' Sean was trying to remain calm in the face of this political stonewalling. 'He died of a drugs overdose. Those who sold him the drugs killed him, in my book. And those who allow that to happen should be . . .' He hesitated as he could see her lips beginning to purse and the Chair of Education's complexion changing to a ruddy hue as his blood pressure was obviously creeping up. 'Should be challenged.'

'Through the proper procedures,' the Chair of Education replied, clearly thinking he needed to educate Sean on the workings of the Council. 'As I said at the outset. And if you have any trouble with that, I suggest you take it up with the Chair of the Council, Councillor Peagram.'

'The Chair of the Council? Why are you being so formal,

Malcolm? What happened to the spirit of public–private partnership?'

'Because, Sean, that only goes so far.'

'As far as a free lunch, perhaps?' Sean regretted it as soon as he said it. He had thrown them a way of getting off the hook. Dignified outrage. Something they appeared well used to deploying.

'Is that really the way you see public service, Sean? Scratching backs and feathering nests?' Education enquired. Loftily.

'None of us enter public service expecting gratitude or favour,' Planning added. For information.

Sean now appreciated how good and formidable a pair they were as he tried to recover. 'I didn't mean . . . That came out wrong. I'm just trying to find out what's happening.'

'Then I suggest that the first thing you find out is how the formal procedures should be followed. But if it suits you better, if you don't like what we say, then, by all means, talk directly to Harold. Now, may we go for lunch?'

Sean knew when he was being stonewalled, or ignored, but tried to smile graciously as he stepped to one side and offered a guiding arm towards the café.

The Chair of Education headed off gruffly, without another word, but the Chair of Planning, the real politician of the pairing, leaned closer to Sean. He thought she might be going to offer some word of political advice. He should have known better.

'I hear Craig Harlow's going to open your Christmas attraction. How thrilling. And we'll be here to support you. I'm a big fan.' She almost sounded guilty, as she gave a hunched-up smile and headed off.

Perhaps he should listen to Glynnis and Sandra more. Especially about running for the Council himself. If he had had any doubts before, he didn't now. Even if it was just to see the look on their faces as they discovered that, in the end, there was no such thing as a free lunch. But, right now, he thought, if word is creeping out I'd better make sure everything works properly for when Craig arrives. And I can throw a bit of work Joey's way at the same time.

Joey had just finished replacing the wattle hurdle fence when the call came from Sean. Could he come over the following day and check the wiring for Santa's Garden as a celebrity was visiting on Saturday?

'That'll be Craig Harlow,' Natasha said when he asked her if she knew anything.

'How'd you know that? Sean just said it's a secret.'

She gave him a look. 'But not from Sandra?'

Joey nodded, then added, 'As you know everything. Is there a tranny working in the optician's?'

'You mean Marian?'

'If I knew I wouldn't be asking, would I?'

'Everyone knows that. He's a bit weird but seems very efficient. So everyone says.'

Joey was about to ask whether he wore a dress to work or not, but noticed the number of plates Natasha handed him.

'What are all these for?'

'It's pizza night. All the kids bring friends over.'

He had no need to say anything. His face said it all. Another of life's rituals he had missed but would have to start getting used to.

'How much else have you not told me about while I've been away?'

She leaned over and kissed him on the cheek. 'Only the stuff you didn't need to worry about. I just set the plates and cutlery. They do the rest online. And I settle down to my spinach and apple salad in front of *Eastenders* and stare at my phone, hoping you will call.'

'Oh yeah? Like the good little wifey?' he teased.

'But I've got you here tonight, haven't I?' Then, with a mischievous seductive laugh, 'In the flesh.' She pulled down her cowl-necked sweater to reveal the Elle Macpherson bra he had bought her for, as she kept reminding him, his last Christmas present. It took him by surprise. Something else his face gave away.

'What's wrong?' she asked.

'Nothing,' he said quickly. Instinctively. Then corrected himself. 'Didn't think you'd be, well, in the mood, after . . . You Know.'

'What? After you confirming what I'd been suspecting for the past month or so? C'mon, Joe. So long as you promise me you won't get directly involved. And it doesn't affect the kids. I don't care . . .' But she hesitated. Correcting herself. That wasn't exactly the way she felt. She did care. About Luke as her brother-in-law. But not for the ones who didn't care about her kids. They were due anything that was coming to them. 'I don't care what happens to the people Luke is after. So long as you keep your promise.'

He reached out to pull her closer, but she resisted the full engulfment. She wanted to look him directly in the eye. Knowing that she would see any nanosecond of doubt. There wasn't any. So she let herself be engulfed. They were, as always, locked together.

Matt and Luke were, if not enjoying, then finishing off another ration pack. Italian Tuna Pasta. Matt had opted for the cherry flavoured isotonic drink while Luke had gone for the lemon. Matt was looking at the empty sachet.

'How come we get Italian pasta from a company in Denmark that has it made in Thailand? Shouldn't they be making Thai curried chicken or something?'

'Italians probably doing that,' Luke responded.

They were sitting in the Transit watching the four camera feeds on the four cheap laptops. Matt had got back to the Highbridge sign and fitted the last camera as soon as the maintenance team moved on for lunch. Thanks to Joey's earlier seminar on tapping into a lamppost's power supply, each camera would be permanently on, even though they expected Leather and his gang to appear mid- to late evening when there would be people around to squeeze. They would use the same global drill. What have you seen? What do you know? Any strangers in town? Who's been here you didn't know? What did they look like? A robust mix of coaxing, cajoling and outright torture, if necessary. The aim was twofold. Gather information. Spread fear.

The laptop was cable-tied to the loading rack just by the side door, and had its power pack connected to a power inverter linked to a deep charge 12-Volt car battery. It would run for the hours they needed it and be rotated with a replacement battery each day, if required. They didn't need a seminar from Joey on that one.

'So Gazza lives down in the old towpath cottage now, does he? Come with the job?' Matt asked.

'Don't think so. But he was mad on fishing, wasn't he?'

Matt nodded. 'And he gets to walk two minutes to work. How'd we contact him?'

'Three rings on his Emergency line. No pick-up. And he'll pop down and open the bridge. According to Joe, he reckons if it's after midnight and we can be in and out within a few minutes no one will kick off. Between about half nine and midnight it'll be fifty-fifty. Any earlier we'll have to break into his cottage, drag him out and make him do it.'

Matt spluttered out half a pack of a fruit and nut mix.

Luke just shrugged. 'That's what Joe said.'

'Does this sound like he's done it before?' Matt asked. 'Or am I being paranoid?'

'Stag do's, apparently! I didn't want any more details,' Luke responded. It was all Matt needed to know.

They sat for a moment dividing up what remained of the ration pack, while going over what each had to do when Leather's crew arrived. They both knew that this time it was not going to be about front. Or bottle. It was going to be win or lose. Nothing else.

'One thing,' Matt suddenly said. 'When this is done . . .' He didn't finish the sentence. He didn't need to. The reflective sadness in his voice was enough.

'OK,' Luke said. 'I know.'

Matt held out a wide five. Luke clasped it. The pact was sealed.

A few hours later they were both asleep. Matt had checked the feed from Leather's house as soon as they got back to the cottage, but there was nothing in the log. No activity. So they had done the only thing they could do. Recharge their own batteries. The old maxim. Sleep when you can. It was something many took to the ultimate level, even sleeping on the helos on their way into a hot zone. Matt was never that relaxed. With the pact agreed, he couldn't wait to get into the fray.

10

Consequences

Although having to sit through *EastEnders* was not what Joey had in mind for a regular regime, sharing a settee with Natasha was a lot better than a boil in the bag supper with Benno. As the drum fill sounded on the theme music he took advantage of the cowl neck to slide his hand inside to cup her breast. She took it out. She wanted to return to the conversation they had been having before she'd shushed him so she could focus on that night's hook.

'The biggest surprise in all this, Joe, is actually you wanting to be involved with Bobby McBain.'

'Oh, the family's good enough for your daughter is it, Nat, but not for me?' Joey protested, tongue very firmly in cheek.

'There's not much we can do about who Tanya fancies,

although from the picture she showed me he does look quite cute.'

'Well he didn't get that from his dad, did he?' Joey said as he continued to tell Natasha about the conversation with Bobby. How he was trying to set up a few legit businesses to, if not leave his own past behind, then at least give Max a better chance. How it was something all parents wanted and who were they to pre-judge him like everyone else did? And how, once branded, it was difficult to shake off the reputation.

'And what makes you think people still don't ask me why I ended up with you?' she asked, but was smiling.

'He's going to send me a copy of the Council's confidential briefing for potential developers.'

It worked. She was immediately intrigued. 'And how'd he get that?'

'Apparently . . . He knows everything that goes on in town.'

'Which is exactly why you shouldn't get involved. He'll only be getting that briefing through some dodgy dealing.'

'But it would keep me home more.' He slid his hand across to cup her breast again.

'If you don't end up in jail.' But she didn't remove his hand this time. Which was when Tanya came in, just in time to see her father's hand rapidly retreat from inside her mother's top.

'Oh, sorry. I forgot, you didn't get any last night.'

'Tanya!' Joey spat out. In instinctive father mode. As

was his look to Natasha. 'Is this what she's like when I'm not here? As well as out clubbing on a school night?'

'Oh don't start again. Tell him, Mum.'

'I think you're quite capable of telling him yourself,' Natasha replied, not wanting to get involved. It would help Joey catch up if she left him to fend for himself. She stood up and collected the plates. 'Tea, darling?'

Joey nodded, noting the grin. As did Roscoe, who probably decided Joey could cope as he followed the carbonara plates out. Joey turned back to Tanya. 'Look—'

'Don't be so patronising,' the return came back, with power.

'What?'

'People who start by saying "look" are like teachers or politicians who think they obviously know better than the lowlife they are deigning to talk to.'

'OK. I get that. All I was . . . am trying to say is that Bobby and I go back a long way. So, I know what he's like.'

'I'm not seeing him. How gross would that be?'

'I know, but—'

'Dad, look—'

'Deigning to talk to me, are you?'

She gave him the lip curl, folded her arms and bit her lip. The point was obvious. Was there any point talking to him?

'All I'm trying to do is advise you. OK? And you were right, I can't ground you if I'm not here. And I'm not up here because I spent too much time on street corners with the likes of Bobby, and so I am now trying to catch up, to give you all a better choice. A better choice than hanging round street corners and getting up to mischief and . . . you know.'

'What? Get pregnant to get a council house or something?'

'No, of course not. I'm just nervous that Max might end up like his dad.'

Tanya couldn't contain her anger any longer. 'And I get all that. But for God's sake, I've been out with him a couple of times and one of those he had to go home early because Mummy said. You've already done your job, Dad. I can tell the difference between a lad who thinks and one who thinks it's all about what's between his legs.'

He was about to try and recover, when Tanya's friend Carol came bursting into the room.

'Tan, Tan. Oh sorry, Mr Nolan. She's gone.'

Tanya started towards the door. 'What? When?'

'She got a text and then just went,' Carol explained, as she followed, smiling apologetically at Joey, just as Natasha came in with two teas.

'What? What's happening?' she asked, as they heard the front door slam.

Joey shrugged. 'Sounded like the other one's gone AWOL, or something.'

Outside, Tanya and Carol were hurrying to try and catch up with Becky. They ran to the end of the cul-de-sac, but by the time they reached the corner by the main road Becky was climbing into a parked and familiar Mercedes. Too late. Becky was gone.

'And, apart from having a free house tonight, where did that come from?' Sean asked, stroking Sandra's hair as she lay across his chest.

'Dunno, really. That business with Noah. The young lad in the park. The greenery for Janey's grave?' She looked up at him – then kissed his chest. 'Just made me think how lucky we are, really.'

Sean squeezed her closer. 'True. But saying Janey was run over is a bit of a euphemism. Bloody psycho off his head on drugs.'

'That's what made me think about it, I suppose. And, how I like how you get so concerned about things. No matter how daft, or sad, you get about them.'

'I'll take that as a compliment,' Sean responded.

'You can. Just this once. But is Craig Harlow definitely coming tomorrow?'

'So his manager said.'

'Believe it when I see it.'

'Don't think he has a choice. His mum is a big mate of the local paper's editor's mum, apparently. Make a great front page, apparently. So Glynnis tells me.'

'Ah, now I'm beginning to believe,' Sandra commented.

'It's a powerful thing this mums' mafia,' Sean added, with a smile.

'We do have our uses.'

'So I just witnessed.' Sean laughed, until he saw a maternal flash of admonishment. 'Or was that me being useful for you?'

'Good recovery,' Sandra grinned.

'And Craig on the front page will be better than "local businessman says legalise drugs".'

'Indeed.'

Sean kissed the top of her head and wondered how long he could lie there before she would let him go.

'You can go if you like. Now you've had your wicked way with me.'

'Er . . . who was being wicked with who?'

'I know you want to go and do something else. I can hear your breathing.'

'What's my breathing got to do with anything?'

'You're not relaxed.'

'That was very relaxing, actually.'

'But you want to go and phone Harold Peagram.'

'Who said anything—'

'Sean. How long have we been together?' She pushed herself up and kissed him. 'And why did I say I loved you before?' She then rolled over on her back. 'You can either take me as I am, or make me a cup of tea.'

'Cup of tea?' He'd been with her the same length of time.

'Good choice. As I know you're incapable of anything else.'

He thought of trying to respond but knew he'd lose. So he leaned over, kissed each breast, then her lips, and got up and started to dress.

'I might just see if Harold is in. As you mentioned it. You coming down?'

'Think I'll stay here. Catch up on my Sky box.'

He nodded and headed for the door. 'I'll bring it up in a minute but er . . . what about that snow machine? I think it should be in Santa's Garden.'

'Anywhere you want it, babe.' She was now flicking through her planner. 'And I wouldn't mind a bit of toast.'

'Now that you've burnt off a few calories?'

She hit play and the voice of Benedict Cumberbatch as Sherlock Holmes filled the room. Time to go.

'Are you sure?' Luke asked. One final time. 'Point of no return?'

Matt just nodded. 'I knew where this was likely to end up when I signed on. And if I'm going down, this time I don't want to be caught with nothing more than an expensive club in my hand while some clown is pointing a loaded shotgun at me.'

They were in the back of the Transit, assembling the MP5s. This time with live magazines. There was now no point of separation or ambiguity. No legal eagle on the planet would talk them out of this. Especially with six body bags in the back. They were definitely going out equipped to do serious harm. It was win or lose all round. But they had no intention of losing. Anywhere.

Although they had prepped and were ready to come back night after night, they had read Leather as a man of action. It was shortly after ten, when Gazza had predicted they'd have a fifty-fifty chance of no one complaining about the bridge, when a text alert told Matt there was movement outside Leather's house. Sure enough, on the 3G live feed they saw the gates open and a figure come out, just as the BMW X5 they had followed came into frame. It stopped momentarily to pick him up, then sped off. Several minutes later they saw it come up on camera 2, and a short while later on camera 3. They were on their way. Time to call Gazza.

By the time the X5 passed the Welcome to Highbridge sign, Gazza was in place, Matt was standing at the field entrance, his hi-viz jacket slung over his shoulders to mask both his body armour and the hanging MP5. His task was to walk out into the road in front of the X5, so Gazza could see him and start opening the bridge. At the same time Luke backed out the Transit. At speed. Causing the X5 to slide abruptly to a stop. The internal hand gestures at odds with the politely waved apology from Matt as he guided the van back into the field, then followed with another apologetic arm raise.

Leather and his crew were still gesticulating as they attempted to carry on, only to find the red traffic lights flashing, the barrier dropping and the bridge slowly opening and in doing so masking them from anyone stopping on the other side. There was, as yet, no traffic coming up behind, not that they noticed, as they were too busy trying to top each other's cracks about country yokels. Nor did they notice Matt fling the hi-viz jacket into the field, pull down his balaclava and follow Luke out of the field.

There were four occupants, but none of them noticed Luke slide round the back of the X5, to come up on the rear passenger door. They didn't notice because at the same time Matt was tapping the X5's passenger window with the MP5's suppressor. They all turned to see the red dot dance around the car as the muzzle of the suppressor steadied then gestured for the passenger door window to slide down. All the city-slicker street bravado dissipated. There was the expected moment of hesitation as they tried to figure out what was going on. That was a serious piece of kit pointing at them. Leather said something over his shoulder to the back seat and made a play of putting up his hands as he got out.

As he did, the rear offside passenger door opened quietly, slowly, and a Skorpion machine pistol emerged slightly ahead of its handler, who yelped in pain as the stock of Luke's MP5 hit him hard on his wrist and his hoodie was yanked backwards, fast, down, to the tarmac. Hard. A kick to his side forced the remaining air out of his lungs.

Luke side-footed the Skorpion under the car and

towards the kerb. He then stepped back, put his red dot on the driver's head and gestured for him to get out. It was one of the shaved heads that helped terrorise Fatchops in the park. But now the swagger was gone. Glancing nervously at the writhing figure still gasping desperately for breath, he meekly followed Luke's gesture to pick up the other guy and take him round the back of the car. Luke followed while doing a quick 360 check. Nothing else on the road. Yet.

On the passenger side, both Leather and the fourth occupant had taken in the full blacks, military stance, and the rapidness with which the others had been neutralised. Whatever, or whoever, these guys were, they were serious players. Leather's next assumption, on taking in the MP5s close up, was that it was some form of police SWAT team. An occupational hazard, but at least they would have to play by the rules.

'What the . . . ? We haven't done . . .' was about all he managed to say before Matt's left hand chopped his throat, causing him to gag, gasp and be unable to resist being propelled towards the back of the car where Luke had the other two at the end of his MP5, but with an angle ready to cover Matt. This didn't feel like part of the rules. The fourth occupant, the biggest of them all, obviously the muscle, remained defiant until Luke put his red dot on his chest, with a slight slant of his head. Do you really want this?

Normally, they would be barking commands, using the

most disorientating weapon they carried: their voices. Like all animals, humans are programmed to fear loud noise. Loud voices startle. But not tonight. Tonight was do not attract attention night. Gestures were enough. The guy turned and followed the others towards the field. Once inside and out of sight of the road, Mr Muscle's legs buckled under the force of Luke's boot. As he went down, everything went black as a hood came over his head. He then felt the weight of Luke's knee in his back as his hands were pulled back harshly and zip-tied. The other three soon joined him in a line, on their knees facing the hedge. Tagged and bagged. Out of sight. All now starting to feel real fear. No, this was definitely not part of the rules.

Luke gestured for Matt to go along the line to make sure they were not carrying anything else. And collect their mobile phones. With a nod to Luke to say they were clear, he then went back to check the X5, scooping up the Skorpion as he did, wondering if that too came into the country as parts. Opening the tailgate he found a holdall. By the weight he suspected it was the weapons bag. He hoisted that on to his shoulder then headed back to the field, noticing that the swing bridge was already closing and a car was approaching. He glanced at his watch. Three minutes. Hopefully still on the good side of Gazza's fifty-fifty bet.

Luke had already bundled the driver and the now whimpering Skorpion handler round to the open back doors of the van. Matt put the holdall on the passenger seat and then grabbed Mr Muscle, immediately feeling resistance – he was primed, ready to fight. As was Matt. He spread his legs slightly, so if the guy lunged back he wouldn't be knocked off balance. He then leaned forward.

'Do it,' he said. The challenge unambiguous. Goading.

Immediately Luke sensed the danger. From Matt. Win or lose.

'Problem?' he asked.

Whether it was the proximity of Matt, with his hot, adrenalin-pumped breathing, or Luke's warning tone, the guy unwound and allowed himself to be dragged up and pushed to join the others by the van doors. Matt slowed his breathing and gave a nod to Luke. No problem. Luke returned the nod, but was not fully convinced, as he tugged at Leather's collar to get up.

'You're dead,' Leather hissed at Luke as he begrudgingly allowed himself to be forced towards the van.

'You got that one wrong. I died a long time ago,' Luke replied. Then added. 'Peter.'

At the sound of his name Leather spun back. Now he knew what this was. The guys who had tried to warn him off. But he was roughly turned back to face the van. Then the hoods came off. Suddenly Leather felt weak. In front of him on the floor of the van were the body bags. He realised that was the point. They wanted them all to see the bags before the hoods went back on and they felt themselves being pushed into the van, the doors slammed and the engine started. Leather now felt more than weak. He felt vulnerable. As it sank in. He was inside a steel box. An execution chamber.

'I understand all that, Harold. Yes . . . I do . . . But all I'm saying is that if we, the community, don't do anything then some hothead is going to take it into their own hands. And none of us want that, do we?'

Sean was sitting at the kitchen table, in the Paul Smith black dressing gown Sandra had bought him for his birthday, still talking to Harold Peagram, but was beginning to lose his thread. Sandra was taking advantage of the free house and, having paused Benedict Cumberbatch in mid-sentence, she came gliding in, wearing the Jane Woolrich negligee set he had bought for their last anniversary. She was also looking for the promised cup of tea. Sean mouthed sorry and pointed to the phone.

She pointed to the Jane Woolrich. Which is more important? He knew it was no contest, but had to finish listening to Harold repeating the proper procedures line as he watched Sandra seeming to float around the kitchen, the long silk train appearing to act like a hovercraft skirt. Or a Dalek, he thought. Good job she was anal about keeping the floor clean. But Harold broke through again.

'Well, yes,' Sean switched his attention back to the phone. 'I might. I might even consider running for election myself. I am that serious. Yes.'

He managed to carry on the conversation with Harold

even when she came over and mischievously nuzzled his neck, but with tea made, she playfully scooped up the negligee and let it glide across his head as she left the kitchen. The sensuality of the silk combined with a waft of her perfume was too much.

'Er, Harold, I'll have to call you back.' He was tempted to say that something had come up, but decided against it. 'Yes, I'm free for lunch on Tuesday. Great.' He put the phone down and headed after Sandra. The Council could wait.

Whether it was the sight of the young girls being spit roasted, or the dog attacking the young boy, or the guy being dropped from the crane that sent Matt's pulse and anxiety level off the scale, Luke couldn't be sure. Matt would later say it was the sound. The cries of those being tortured against the sound of Leather laughing, that acted as the tripwire. Whatever it was, they were now looking down at Leather crumpled in a heap in front of them. Put there by several wild strikes of a baseball bat.

It had only taken a few minutes to reach the old chemical quarry. The name was a historical reference. It was in fact a toxic lake. The quarry had originally been used to extract stone but the chemical industry had appropriated it as a convenient and unregulated waste dump. The result was that after a century of dumping no one now knew exactly what was in there. And no one wanted to carry the cost of finding out. Building was prohibited anywhere near it and, although slowly rusting away, the signs on the fence made it clear that you were risking your life by venturing beyond the perimeter. It was a conveniently overlooked legacy of the industrial revolution and, as every local scally knew, the perfect place to get rid of evidence.

It was highly unlikely they would be disturbed while interrogating their guests. They had dragged them out one by one, into the old weighing-in station, to be stripped naked and forced to stand in the stress position. Legs back and spread to put all their weight on their fingertips. Luke and Matt stuck to the drill. Keeping their balaclavas on at all times.

By the time they had brought the last one in, the Skorpion handler, the other three were starting to shiver, while Skorpion was sobbing almost uncontrollably. Mainly through fear but also the stench of his own embarrassment. He had made such a mess of his jeans that Matt doubted any amount of washing would get them fit enough for a charity shop. When he was told to strip, Luke and Matt exchanged surprised looks. They could see this was a young body, still forming, but the back and sides were covered in slowly healing knife slashes. Despite the smell, Matt stepped closer, made him turn round to get a better look, then angled the guy towards Luke. Someone had carved 'For Pete's Sake' on his back. That was the first trigger point.

Matt slammed the stock of his MP5 into Leather's

lower back. Not enough to put him down, but enough to arch his back in pain. Yet, it was the lad that protested.

'Don't. Please. Don't.'

Matt couldn't believe it. He whipped round and yanked the hood off the lad's face, so he could eyeball him. 'You what? You pleading for this . . . this . . .'

But Luke stepped across and physically pulled Matt away. He knew what would now be running through Matt's adrenalin-fuelled mind. The brutalisation of the innocents. But he didn't want that to take control right now. Because he also recognised the lad. It was the Ragged Priest from the quad bikes. Now, with tears running down his face, and legs covered in his own excreta, he looked about twelve but was probably in his mid-teens. And far less threatening than he'd seemed before.

Always the same, Luke thought. Always the kids. He was the only one actually carrying a weapon. The others would try the same line of fiction he and Matt had off pat. Been away. Just back. Not knowing what was in their mate's car. But the naïve, impressionable kid would get a juvenile sentence and be back with the troops in a year or two. Same the world over. The so-called hard men hide behind the kids.

'Please don't hurt him because of me.'

'Why? Got brothers, have you? Said he'd do the same? Or a sister he'd do worse to?'

Even though Leather was still winded, facing away from him with his hood on, the lad was terrified. Luke had been there before. He knew it was hopeless trying to break through a lifetime of conditioning. No matter how short that lifetime had been. He just gave the lad a tap on the shoulder, put the hood back on and put him in the stress position. He was already in his own hell. A bit more suffering wouldn't matter. And it was safer all round.

He then backed away, taking up the watch position. Matt, now calmer, stooped to open the holdall from the X5, into which he had tossed the mobile phones and wallets he had taken off the drug crew. He lifted out three aluminium baseball bats, two cut-down shotguns, the traditional close-quarter weapon of choice, another Skorpion, and a Glock 21 .45 – The higher-calibre handgun of choice for many of the world's more macho law enforcement organisations. Very nice, thought Matt, as he removed the clip and lifted it to show Luke.

'Like your guns, then?' Luke directed at Leather. But received no reply.

'Our guys get banged up for bringing souvenirs like this home. Did you know that?' Matt shouted across to the four naked shiverers. 'Criminal that, I'd say. What do you say?'

Again, no one answered. No one knew how or whether they should risk it.

Luke was also watching Matt. Looking for any more signs of volatility. He still looked calm as he lined up all the six mobile phones the drugs team had had between them. Two – the Samsung Galaxy and iPhone 5 – would probably be their legit domestics. The others a collection of throwaways. He then noticed Luke watching him.

'I'm, OK. OK?' he said.

Luke nodded and watched as Matt stood, made sure his MP5 was on safety and at his back so couldn't be easily grabbed, before going down the line.

'Now,' he started. 'I'm guessing we've all seen the box sets of *The Sopranos* or *The Wire* or *24*. And what Jack Bauer can do to people he doesn't like. We don't want to do that. Well,' he leaned closer to Leather. 'In your case we do, to be honest, but we won't if . . .' he paused for the emphasis. 'If . . . If you just tell us, first, the unlock codes and then, for bonus points, everything else we want to know. OK?'

The two foot soldiers agreed immediately, as they probably only had the throwaways. Mr Muscle told Matt what he could do with the phone, which didn't sound too comfortable, so he edged his feet further from the wall.

Matt then moved back to Leather. 'Well?'

Once again. No response. Which was when Matt took out his Blackhawk folding knife and quickly rammed it into Leather's hand, catching Luke as much by surprise as it did Leather, who let out a squeal as Matt twisted the knife, before yelling out his unlock codes. He was obviously a Jack Bauer fan. Matt looked across to Luke. Did it work?

Luke held his stare for a moment. What was that? Matt

shrugged. He didn't care. Did it work? He nodded towards the phones. Do the codes work?

Luke thought back to seeing Leather drop the guy from the crane. Matt was right. He didn't actually care either. He tried the codes. Then nodded. Leather's phones opened. With pictures of the dog on both. Snarling. So much for Leather's Scouse Spouse. He then disabled the lock codes so they would stay open.

Matt smiled, pleased his tactic had worked, and backed over to Luke who was now scrolling through the Samsung's heavily populated address book. A gold mine, if they knew what they were looking for. He then opened the photo library and among all the usual family, dog, holiday shots he found a video folder named Stuff. He opened it and started looking through the content, his face hardening. Matt leaned over to take a look. And that was the second trigger. When it had really kicked off. What put Leather into a heap on the floor. It didn't explain why they were now searching for him, and the Ragged Priest, in the dark.

Since watching Husani's brake lights slide round the corner at the end of her road, Tanya had not heard or seen a thing from Becky. She was now sitting in Becky's parents' kitchen trying to calm them down while wondering if she should really be doing this role reversal thing. She was even more suspicious of Husani than they were, but here she was with Carol trying to reassure two parents that their daughter was probably safe and just infatuated by some rich guy in a flash car.

When they asked her whether they should call the police she wanted to scream, yes, do it, but when she glanced at Carol she could see her wide eyes were expressing exactly what was going on in her own head. No-o-o. How embarrassing could that be? She'd go crazy if her own mum and dad called the cops if she went off with a new guy. But that's if they knew, she thought as she looked back at Becky's mum now desperately chewing her lip and looking to her husband for support as she was replaying all manner of horror news stories in her head.

'And you think this lad's been stalking her?' she asked.

Another look to Carol who was also beginning to pick up the anxiety and focus her attention on Becky's dad, himself trying to erase the media images from his mind. They had to call the police. It was seeping from every pore. They couldn't just sit and hope, could they? It was conveyed in a look towards Tanya. This isn't fair, she thought. I am just a kid. Really.

And in that moment she decided to do what kids often do. Phone the ones they often ridicule. Their mums.

It had only taken Luke a moment to get across and grab the baseball bat, to stop Matt cracking open Leather's skull. It wasn't that he was fussed one way or the other about what happened to him. The images on his phone had already condemned him. What he was fussed about was having traceable DNA splattered all over the place. It had only taken a moment, but that was all it ever took. One lapse. And from then on you're on the back foot trying to catch up. Like now, out in the dark, without night vision. He never envisaged they would need it and they were, after all, operating on someone else's budget.

After pulling Matt off, Luke had put his fingers on Leather's neck. He had found the pulse. At least he was still alive.

'You should have let me finish him,' Matt whispered as they peered into the darkness. 'While I was in the grip of the beast.'

It was a phrase Matt had adopted to explain the surges of rage. It was part of the post-traumatic stress litany. Matt knew that. As he knew that it was never a problem in normal civvie life. At least not in the parts where people didn't go round terrorising others. Especially kids. That was always the trigger. He knew that too. As did Luke. Ever since the snatch and grab just outside Basra. Going house to house to find the target, they had come across a group gang-banging a small girl. It was outside their rules of engagement so they were backing away, until the rapists sent an eleven-year-old boy old after them with a suicide vest. The boy died, as did the rapists. They'd made a mistake. And given due cause.

Matt had then carried the young girl ten miles to

the field hospital with a shrapnel wound to his thigh. They were both treated, but she later died of her injuries. There's always one moment that does it. Imprints a memory impossible to dislodge. For Luke it was Janey's death. Nothing could dislodge that. And looking across at Matt, now squatting against the opposite wall, working to keep himself under control, Luke knew those memories were why they were both here. Wondering what to do next.

Originally the idea was to snatch them, slap them around, and terrify them to the point that they would agree to move on. But it didn't seem to be going down that route. As soon as he had seen Leather order the crane execution he knew these weren't just street corner dealers. They had, he thought, not missing the irony, stepped into a war without proper intelligence and without a plan for its execution and aftermath. If that is the case, his thoughts continued, we will have to do what we have always done in such circumstances. As they had done at Leather's farmhouse. Improvise.

It was why he was surprised, but not shocked, when Matt stuck the knife into Leather's hand. After how they'd seen him treat the young kid he could have ignored anything Matt wanted to do to him. The next stage of the improvisation was to see what deal could be struck.

'OK,' he had suddenly announced, as much for Matt's benefit as for the drugs crew. 'Let's see where we're up to? I told you to stay away. You didn't. Now, we have you bollock naked. We have your phones. On which are all your contacts and photos. We have your weapons. All of which constitutes enough evidence to put you all away for a very long time. We also have body bags. So, we have a few choices.'

He looked across to Matt who seemed to be in agreement, if curious as to where Luke was going.

'We could leave you all here and call the blue lights,' Luke continued, but saw that didn't particularly appeal to Matt. 'We could simply slot the lot of you and leave you in the body bags.' That got a more considered nod.

'Or,' he continued, looking at Matt, expecting a reaction. 'We could call it a truce and all get to go home.' Matt didn't disappoint. His eyes flared. No way. But Luke held up his hand. 'And never come back.'

Matt was shaking his head. Why was Luke offering a way out? Not only had they seen what Leather was capable of but he would be running the same scenario as Matt was in his head. Say yes. Get home. Recover. Come back better prepared.

But it was Mr Muscle who broke the silence. 'Tell him to go piss—' But it was all he got to say, as Matt placed the muzzle of the MP5 on his back. Shut up.

The driver tried next. 'Say, yes, Pete.' He didn't have to add the begging please.

Eventually. It came. 'OK. OK. Deal.'

Luke turned to Matt. Matt shook his head again. You

can't. Luke nodded. He wasn't. 'Not you,' he then said to Leather. 'But the rest of you can go home tonight.'

He stepped across to Mr Muscle. 'Even you.'

But that was the moment.

Perhaps it was because he was deliberately goading Mr Muscle into action, Luke had just got careless, but the result was the same. Mr Muscle answered as he had all night. With defiance. A pure attack dog. Even though still hooded he pushed himself back from the wall and swung out, just catching Luke a glancing blow. It wasn't enough to knock him down, but it pushed him across Matt's line of vision. By the time it cleared, Mr Muscle had his hood off and was grabbing the driver and pushing him towards Matt. He then turned and ran for the door, but Matt had sidestepped, grabbed another of the baseball bats and cut him off at the knees. He then dropped his weight on to Muscle's back, yanked his hands round and zip-tied them again. This time attaching him to the remnants of the old cast iron heating system. After putting the hood back on he looked across to see Luke doing the same to the driver. But Leather had gone. Along with the young kid.

A moment. That's all it takes.

'There's coppers all over the place, Joe.'

It was Gazza. Calling Joey. Telling him what had happened at the bridge.

'Do they know the bridge was open?'

'No, don't think so. Just saw them talking to a couple of wrinklies who got stuck behind a car.'

'OK, then go home. And Gaz . . .'

'Yeah?'

'Thanks. But don't call me again on this number. OK?'

'Er . . . yeah. OK, Joe. And er . . . We quits now, yeah?'

'No problem.' Joey ended the call and turned back to the house, only to find Natasha leaning on the open patio door.

'Who was that?'

He just looked at her. She nodded. Remembering. She didn't want to know. 'Although,' she then said, 'I would like to know what's going on with Tanya.' She turned back to the house, but stopped. 'Is that a new phone?'

'Er . . . yeah. Something I picked up from Bobby.'

She turned as her own phone rang inside. Going to answer it she shouted back, 'I hope it wasn't one of his knock-offs.'

Joey followed with a wry grin. He hadn't been referring to the phone itself. Only its disposability.

'There,' Matt hissed. Directing his hand and Luke's eyeline to a small weed-covered mound about 30 yards to their right.

Luke nodded when he saw the small movement. A sniper's target. A geometric shape in amongst nature's chaos of weeds. A head. Trying to determine where they were. Despite having neither night vision headsets nor sights on the MP5s, they did have one small advantage. The pasty white skin of the young kid. While their blacks would make them hard to see, even in a half-moon naked flesh would jump out. Matt had rolled off to his right to try and work his way round to their left side, while Luke moved to the left, to come up on their right. At least they didn't have any weapons. Luke had checked they were all still in the holdall and that was now locked in the van.

Coming level with the mound, Luke could see Leather and the kid had run out of places to go. They were on the edge of the quarry.

Luke waited until Matt's red dot danced across the crouching figures. He then stood up and flicked on his own, so that it was clear they were now caught in a crossfire. Slowly Leather stood up. Again the hands were up in surrender. He was still hoping to deal his way out. Slightly more nervous, the young lad looked up at Leather, who flicked his head to tell him to give up. He too started to rise slowly, until he was quickly grabbed by Leather, who twisted his arm behind his back and held his throat, to use him as a human shield.

'What's the point?' Luke called. 'You're not going anywhere.'

But Leather thought he had a bargaining chip. Their emotions. He had noted their reactions to seeing the cuts on the kid. He'd use that as a way out. He tightened his grip on the lad's throat, causing his eyes to widen in pain and confusion.

'That deal you offered. I'm up for it.'

'It's not on the table any more,' Matt said, as he moved closer, maintaining an arc of separation so that Leather had to keep glancing from side to side.

'I'll toss in the kid.' He then laughed at what was coming. 'Either in the deal. You lay down your weapons, let me walk away . . . Or . . . I'll toss him over the edge.'

'What sort of daft offer is that?' Matt asked. 'You'll be dead then.'

The young lad was sobbing again. 'Please. Please,' he kept repeating.

'I was dead inside there, wasn't I? But I'm here now. And . . . I'm guessing – but I don't think you want this fella to die, do you?'

Luke glanced at Matt. He was fifty-fifty. But Luke could see the beast emerging.

'Go on,' Leather continued. 'You'll get what you want. I won't come back. I can't, can I? You've got all that evidence. Like you said. And the kid lives.'

He squeezed again. The lad gagged.

'OK. OK,' Luke called and lowered his weapon, gesturing for Matt to do likewise. 'OK, Deal. Let the kid go . . .'

Leather, more suspicious of Matt, turned to take a quick look at what he was doing. It was all Luke needed. To quickly bring the MP5 back up. Just a moment when enough of Leather's head came into Luke's reticle. Just enough for the kill. Two quick *phludffers* and it was done.

The force of the double-tap took Leather back towards the edge of the quarry, but to Luke and Matt's horror the young lad went with him. He hadn't been hit. Leather had died instantly so was no longer holding him. The horror was that the young lad had lunged and grabbed him, to try and save him going over the edge, but his weight had pulled the lad over as well. By the time Luke and Matt got to the quarry top, all they could see were the ripples spreading across the moonlit caustic pool.

Natasha had only been on the phone 30 seconds when Joey heard her tell someone to stay where they were. She was on her way. He was then designated babysitter as she scooped up her handbag and keys to the Q7. Before long she was at Becky's house, where, having been brought quickly up to date by Tanya, she had turned to Becky's mum. 'I wouldn't risk Becky's safety because we all feel embarrassed.'

This was all Becky's dad needed, and he went to the phone. 'But you are sure she went off with this Husachi, fella?' he asked. It was directed at Tanya.

She nodded, but corrected the name. 'Husani.'

'Jesus Christ,' Matt said as he and Luke watched the ripples starting to fade away. 'I thought I'd seen it all . . . But what was that about?'

Luke didn't have any immediate answer. He could say they'd seen tortured hostages trying to protect their tormentors before. But that was usually in fear of the future. This one had none. He'd also told Joey that he and Matt were damaged. The things they'd seen. The things they'd done. To survive. But there always seemed to be something else. He'd learned not to dwell. That way only took him to deeper pits. And lost focus. They still had to clear up. He turned away and went back to gather up the holdall.

Matt dropped down on his haunches. Staring down at the now calm quarry lake below until Luke came back.

'If you didn't know what was in it,' Matt said, 'you could say it looks quite picturesque, couldn't you?'

'Every picture hides a story?' Luke asked, as he unpacked the guns.

Matt nodded. But was asking himself the question he knew had no answer. Why does it always have to be like this? People in terror of psychos. Who always weaponise the kids. He knew the tactical reason. Because of what had just happened. The good guys always baulked at harming kids. That gave an advantage. A weakness to exploit. And that thought alone, he reflected, proved how screwed up it all was. Calling it a weakness? Caring about kids?

His attention was caught by three splashes as Luke tossed the cut-down shotguns over the edge. Then the Skorpions.

'Shame about the Glock,' Luke commented as he

followed its trajectory to see the splash. But, on top of everything else, they didn't want to get caught with weapons that might be traced back to whatever Leather and his crew had been up to. The bloodied baseball bat and its two companions went next. It would be a long time before anyone ventured into that chemical stew. And even if they did, the odds were that the guns would be traced back and the assumption made that it was all part of some drugs war.

Luke then turned to Matt. 'You OK?'

Matt nodded and stood up. 'You mean can I hold it together?' There was more than a slight edge to the question. But it was controlled.

'Well?' Luke asked again. Adding his own edge. 'Nothing new.'

'Except it's on our own friggin' doorstep?' More edgy.

'Which is why we agreed to do this. Yeah?' Luke spat back. 'That kid . . . Those like him. No matter what we think. Or feel. About where and how they got like they do. You know. They'd still kill us if told to.'

Matt hesitated. He did know. But that didn't make witnessing it any easier. But after a moment he nodded. 'Just . . . I get it when we're away. Foreign. But it shouldn't be . . . Not back home.'

'And I should be happily married now?' Luke asked, the irony weighing heavy.

This brought Matt back. What Luke had been through. Why they were doing this. He finally touched his friend on the shoulder. 'Sorry. Didn't think anything could get to me any more. Perhaps my PTSD is wearing off.'

'Do you want a hug?' Luke asked, adding a grin.

Matt gave a sardonic smile. 'Now who's engaging in displacement therapy?' He bent, picked up the holdall and tossed it into the lake. The moment had come and gone. 'What now? We still on for the other?' he asked.

Luke nodded and held out another wide five. The pact was solid. 'Just need to sort the other two out first.'

Matt took a last look down at the lake. Still once again. It was anyone's guess what's down there, he thought as he turned to follow Luke back into the weighing-in shed.

'Got away did he?' Mr Muscle asked, sneering, as he heard Luke and Matt enter.

Luke went over, checked he was still cable-tied to the pipe, then pulled the hood off. He was still in his balaclava but wanted to see Mr Muscle's eyes. Wide, glaring, hard. Hate. 'Let's just say he's not with us any more. OK?'

Mr Muscle stared back, trying to process this information, until Matt helped him out. Lifted the muzzle of the MP5 and pushed it against his nostrils. He didn't have to phone a friend. He could smell it. And, finally, the eyes narrowed. Fear.

Matt moved across to the driver and repeated the process. 'What about you? Want to follow your leader?'

'No. No. I said . . . Before . . . I said . . . I'll take the deal back. I swear.'

Matt turned to Luke. What do you think?

Luke looked at the two remaining captives. Even Mr Muscle now looked subdued. But Luke kicked him to test his reaction. He didn't get one.

Matt took over. 'C'mon. You go along with it?'

Mr Muscle nodded. But it wasn't enough.

'I'd like to hear it,' Matt prompted, putting the Blackhawk knife against his face.

'OK. I'll take the deal back, too,' he shouted. The eyes back wide and full of hate. 'We won't come over here. But, if I ever see you anywhere near our territory . . .'

'Yeah, yeah,' Matt said as he pulled the hood back over his head. He then went to do the same to the driver. Who immediately tried to pull away.

'I'll . . . I'll do . . . I'll do anything you want. Or say. I will,' he gabbled quickly. Still petrified.

'All right. Chill. We have a deal, don't we? Someone will come and get you.'

The driver flopped backward. Relief. Exhaustion. But found himself being pulled forward as Matt tugged the hood off again.

'One last thing. That kid. After what your mate seemed to have done to him . . . Why? Why'd he . . .' he glanced in the direction of the lake, thinking of the way the young lad had tried to stop Leather from falling. 'Why was he so protective?'

The driver looked away. He didn't want to go there. But Matt yanked his head round. 'What?'

The driver hesitated again. 'What?' Matt asked again. More forceful.

'Pete was his dad.'

Matt almost stumbled backwards. But Luke was already right on his shoulder, thankful that bit of news hadn't come out earlier.

At the swing bridge Hilary was talking to her officers who had responded to a call about an abandoned car blocking the bridge. She was off duty, having stopped on her way back from visiting her parents. She learned that no one seemed to have seen anything. The occupants of the car had just disappeared. Already there was talk of an alien abduction. While Hilary considered they might be alien to Highbridge, she was sure they were of this world. Regional Crime had flagged the car as registered to one of the regional drug lords. And the APNR had it logged as coming in and out of town a few days ago. It was enough for Hilary. Two and two were not only making five. But six, seven and eight.

'It should make you feel better, shouldn't it?' Matt asked, as they tossed their bags into the hire car outside the cottage. 'Knowing you've dug out a parasite. But . . .' He shook his head and went back to contemplating the question with no answer.

Luke set the cottage alarm, locked up and headed for the driver's seat. He was not going to let Matt get them pulled over for speeding. Before he dropped into the car he took a long look at the cottage, then across the roof of the car to Matt. 'It makes me feel better, if that's any help.'

'That'll do, for now. But . . .' he carried on, as he got into the car, 'another one'll pop up. They always do.'

'But it'll buy time. That's what we always do. C'mon, let's get it finished and get gone.'

He had already texted Joey on the pay and throw, which he had then dropped into the bag along with the others, the Motorolas and the drone, which they would leave for Billy Higham under the railway bridge. They were still in their blacks. The balaclavas and body armour were on the back seat. With the MP5s. Within reach.

Having served its purpose, the Transit van had been collected and was now being driven down the track that led down to the old salt quay, long abandoned since canal barges had been displaced by trucks. The only people who went down there now were hard-core dog walkers and the occasional teenage taboo breaker. And the summer kayakers who usually generated a bit of interest in trying to restore the quay as a tourist attraction, reminding everyone that it was the Romans who originally built it. No one took any notice.

Nor was there anyone around to notice the driver get out and go to the engine compartment. Nor would anyone have noticed him remove a spark plug and squirt in a bit of water. They might have noticed the clanking clunk as the engine fired, then seized solid as piston, water and cylinder head all met with the explosive impact of ignited diesel. As water cannot be compressed it was the steel that gave way. The engine was now useless so the van could not be driven away. Soon it would be an easy target for teenage curiosity and spares vultures. A stripped carcass to the passing onlooker, but a cornucopia of mixed DNA to a forensic examiner.

In all this, the only thing anyone might have noticed was the shock of red hair as Bobby McBain's car park manager jogged away into the night, tossing his biodegradable rubber gloves into the canal.

Joey had received the text from Luke and deleted it straight away. It took him a moment or two to gather his thoughts, then his tool kit. With Natasha off fetching Tanya, it was an easy win getting the boys to stay put by saying he had to pop out. In the Jag. If Natasha left them alone while he'd been away, he was sure they'd be OK for half an hour.

Twenty minutes later Joey had pulled the ancient fuse that still controlled the street supply. Everywhere went dark, including the chippy's CCTV system. But not Joey's phone. It vibrated. It was Luke again. On his real phone. TA MEET COTTAGE 20. A few seconds later he heard the jangling crash of the chippy's front door being smashed. He headed off up the street, not looking back. Just as he was told.

Inside the chippy, Fatchops had shown another turn of speed as he came out of the back to see what the commotion was, only to find himself grabbed, spun, slammed into the tiled wall and dazed, as his arms were pulled back and zipped together. He was then shoved through back into the rear. The biggest human shield Luke and Matt had encountered to date.

They passed though the neatly tidied workspace, everything cleaned and stored. Just so. Everything as Fatchops's Mr Sheen POLO. It smelt of disinfectant. Unlike the smell that greeted them when them went through the door to the living space. Tobacco. Alcohol. Cannabis.

The bearded one was there. Sprawled on a settee watching *Newsnight*, with two young girls leaning either side, neither of them appearing too interested in current affairs. One looked asleep, drunk or drugged, while the other was stripped down to her underwear and undergoing a slow breast massage.

It was a moment for the bearded one to realise that Fatchops was walking rather oddly. Like some form of giant, obese penguin. With two smaller penguins following. Too late his vision cleared and the penguins were upon him. He tried to react but even without the weight of the girls he found himself trapped under the falling mass of Fatchops. Luke stayed with them as Matt went on through the house, MP5 raised and ready.

It took him seconds to check the ground floor and go up the stairs two at a time, opting for speed and surprise rather than stealth. Four doors off a small landing. He went into the first. Bathroom. Nothing. Second door. Messy bedroom. But nothing. He crossed the landing. Third room. This was it. On the bed was a man having sex with a girl young enough to be his granddaughter. He was overweight. White. To one side were two others, more like uncles, one black, recording it on his phone while the other, Asian, was stripping off. Obviously next.

The girl was crying and asking for the old guy to stop which, unfortunately, seemed to be what he was after, as he turned and played up to the phone. His gurning face turned to shock as he saw Matt, but the phone-holder didn't, until he was flipped round and felt the full force of a head butt. He fell next to the other one, now trying to dance away with his jeans round his ankles, who then felt his legs kicked sideways, his head hit the floor and then his chest crushed as Grandpa was yanked backwards off the girl and dumped on top of him. As Matt's boot came down on Grandpa's genitals, the girl rolled off the bed and curled up in a corner.

While zipping all their hands, Matt tried to make reassuring noises and gestures to the girl until she calmed down, finally appreciating that he might be a good guy. He then indicated that she should stay put, while he went to check out the remaining room. When he got there, his stomach turned. Curled up on the bed was Joey's girl's mate. The one he had seen being dragged away the other night. Damn.

Downstairs. Luke had other problems. Crunching glass. Someone was in the chippy. Having secured the bearded one Luke knew he wouldn't be going anywhere, especially as he had tethered him to Fatchops. He gestured for the girls to be quiet. They nodded. Too frightened to do otherwise. He then slowly made his way back through the food preparation area and took a quick look from the darkened space into the chippy, lit by the sodium glow from the street lights. It was Hilary Jardine.

11
Resolution

Joey had made a critical mistake. He had let his heart rule his head. Despite being told not to stop, not to look back, for anything, he couldn't walk past the old boy struggling to get his wheelie bin out the front door. In the dark. The darkness he was responsible for. He stopped to help, but then found himself inevitably turning and glancing down the road – to see Hilary Jardine stepping into the chippy. Could he just walk away now? Not look back? Knowing what Luke had told him about fighting his way out?

No matter what. Luke had repeated it. Over and over again. No matter what. You can't get involved. Walk away, Joey told himself. Walk away. But he couldn't. Not when two of his oldest friends were about to confront each other. It would only end badly for one of them. And Joey knew that would be Hilary. No matter what came after, right there on that street, he knew Luke would do anything to get away. And if anything did happen to Hilary, it would be his fault.

Luke was also running through the scenario. She's sussed it. But she was alone. Out of uniform. No blue lights. What's that mean? Trying to prevent something? Old times' sake? Only one way to find out. He took another quick look. She had her back to him, examining the smashed door. He pulled off his balaclava and unclipped the MP5 as he quietly stepped out into the shop, putting the gun just behind the counter, out of her sight.

'What you doing here?'

She spun round to face him. The confirmation clear. 'Should I be asking you the same?'

'Just saying goodbye, actually.'

She started to walk across but he held his hand up, with a quick glance sideways to the MP5. 'Don't.'

'Why?'

'There's something here you shouldn't see.'

'Really?' It was a challenge. He was questioning her authority. She pointed at his body armour. 'And I suppose that is to protect you from the hot oil?'

He held her stare. Knowing this was the point. No going back. Win or lose. But one last try.

'Hilary, please, can you just take my word.' Then he hardened the edge. The language became clipped. Of command. 'You do not . . . Want to get involved in this. Right now.'

'Think I've seen enough already,' she responded. Her own crisp tone now that of the Superintendent, not the old friend. This was her jurisdiction. Her authority.

But he came back. Harder. One of them had to get the upper hand. 'Believe me. If you do get involved you'll have to act. And . . .' He paused. Another of those moments. No going back. 'And I'll have to respond.'

It was unemotional. Calm. Cold. A coldness that Hilary had not been expecting. Just as she had not expected to feel her pulse rate increasing in direct proportion to her anxiety, as the preconception of the hot-headed guy she used to know was forced out of her head. This was now nothing more than a threat standing in front of her. The past friendship might just allow her to back away, but nothing more. She had to let the training come though. Even though she was wearing a Per Una Quilted Stormwear overcoat instead of body armour, and armed with nothing more than her John Lewis Coney across body handbag.

So they stood. The head girl up against the playground vigilante. But a lot of time, water and trauma had flowed by. And, back then, neither of them carried weapons. She was sure that was what he had on the countertop. Just as she knew he was right. If she saw him with a weapon there was no choice. No going back. He was also right about one other thing. She didn't want that. Right now. Which is why she had come alone.

'OK,' she said. 'I'll blink first, if that's what you want.'

She moved to one side, deliberately allowing him to see

that she was obscuring any possible view of what he might have on the countertop. But she also wanted to let him know that she was working it out. She pointed at the single point sling hanging from his shoulder. 'And I don't suppose that is for attaching your ID to?'

'Among other things,' he replied. But he smiled. That moment had been defused.

But not for long. Luke suddenly caught something in his peripheral vision. A head taking a quick glance through the window. He stepped towards the counter – towards his weapon, Hilary thought, as she saw his eyes were now locked on the window. She turned to see a figure, silhouetted against the street lights, slowly making for the door.

'No, stop,' Hilary called, spinning back and forth between Luke and the approaching figure. 'Stop. Stay where you are. Both of you.'

She was relieved to see Luke step back from the counter, but surprised by the reason.

'What? What's going on?' Joey asked from the door.

Back in the house, Matt had corralled the gang-bangers downstairs and had them lined up, on their knees next to Fatchops and the bearded one. A motley multi-ethnic mix. He had the phone they'd been using upstairs, and was going along slowly, recording each of their faces. A bewildered Becky was helping the now dressed but still sobbing girl from upstairs into the room to sit next to the equally bewildered girls on the settee. They had come for a party and had ended up in a horror movie.

'What the hell you want?' Fatchops asked. Defiant. 'No money here.'

The beast within Matt was on him in a moment, back-handing his head. Not enough to put him down, just enough to shut him up.

'What I want, is for you to stop doing what you do out there.' He pointed to the chippy, then turned to the others, held up the phone. 'What I want, is for you lot to leave these kids alone. But you probably can't, can you. So I'll have to stop you, won't I?'

He raised the MP5 and put the red dot on Fatchops's head. Which was when he heard someone fumbling with the back door. Someone was trying to get in.

Out front, Luke and Hilary were still holding their ground, holding their stares, as Joey was babbling about having fancied some fish and chips, then saw the door smashed in, and then seeing them. Hilary knew this was all nonsense. She had seen the look that quickly went between Luke and Joey. She hadn't been able to read it but she knew it was connected to her earlier suspicions about Luke's return.

'Go on, then. What's going on?' Joey asked again. Carrying on the charade. Hoping to find a way out. For them all. But that wasn't likely to happen as the street outside started to strobe blue.

They turned to look in unison. Joey looked alarmed as Luke again moved towards the MP5. Hilary turned back and held out an arm for him to stop.

'It's nothing to do with me. This time, trust me, Luke. Let me check.' Then she turned to Joey. 'Stop him. Whatever he's planning.'

It was the old friend, now crunching across the glass towards the street.

Joey and Luke watched her pulling her warrant card from her handbag as she met the approaching patrol car. Ordinary markings. And ordinary beat bobbies getting out. This was not an armed response team.

'I told you not to—' Luke started to say, but Joey cut across him.

'I know, but what did you expect me to do, seeing her coming in here? But now's your chance. Take it.'

Luke took another look outside. Hilary was in deep conversation and pointing up and down the street. It didn't seem like she was summoning reinforcements. There was still time. He picked up the MP5, causing Joey to step back in surprise.

Luke grinned. 'What did you think we were going to do? Hand out Bibles and hope they found God?'

'Er . . . No . . . But I . . .' He was back to the gibbering schoolboy in front of the military pro.

'We're doing this because we want to, Joe. Remember. Our choice. Just as it's our choice not to be taken. Win or lose.'

'What? You'd really shoot . . . You'd shoot your way out?'

'That's what we do. And what you do, is forget this.' He tapped the MP5. 'And tell her –' he nodded out the window – 'you know nothing.'

'OK,' Joey said, turning to glance at Hilary outside. When he turned back, Luke had gone.

Matt, behind the rear door as it opened, stepped out and hit the new arrival square between the shoulder blades with the MP5. Even with live rounds it was still a very expensive, but effective, club. The new arrival hit the wall opposite and then sideways, his head going one way, his legs the other as Matt executed the well-practised move, letting the target's own body weight do most of the damage. Matt was just bringing in the prone figure to add to the line-up when Luke came through from the front of the shop, carrying his MP5 and saying they had to go, and Becky started screaming.

'Stop . . . Stop . . . You can't . . .'

She flung herself on the new arrival. It was Husani.

Luke pulled her away as Matt forced Husani down on to his knees. Was this more of what he'd witnessed up at the quarry? Victim dependency? But there was something else in her voice.

'Please . . . please . . . He's not one of them. He isn't.'

And then it echoed back. 'I'm not, I'm not,' Husani gabbled, realising the situation he had walked into. He then turned to Fatchops. Anger. Real. And rattled off something in what sounded to Matt like Serbian, but whatever it was the disgust and disdain was clear. As was the blaze of anger in Fatchops's eyes about something of which he'd just been accused.

Matt stepped forward and backhanded Husani across the head. 'English.' They had been in this one before, too.

Becky leapt up. 'Leave him alone. He's done nothing.'

Matt rounded on her. 'And you can understand English. So, sit down and keep quiet.'

She did so, but only after Husani nodded. Then turned to Matt. 'I said he had let me down. I asked him to watch over her.'

'And I did,' Fatchops replied angrily. In English. 'She was safe in another room. Until they came.' He glared at Luke and Matt.

Husani ignored him, still trying to make a connection with Matt. 'I asked him to do this, while I,' he threw another look of disdain at Fatchops. 'Until I went to get money.'

'What for?' Matt asked. Still suspicious.

Husani hesitated. And looked to Becky. She didn't hesitate.

'We're going away. To get married.'

She might as well have thrown a stun grenade.

Outside in the street, Hilary had discovered that the patrol car was just that. And had been asked to check out the chippy in case there was a young girl, Becky Hargreaves, hanging out there. Then they saw the street in darkness. Hilary had explained her presence by saying she had been passing and saw the chippy door broken. She was about to call for backup, but in the meantime they should check with the neighbours who were out trying to discover what had happened to the electricity.

She stood for a moment. Point of decision. Or no return. She looked up and down the street at the growing number of people drawn by the blue lights. Sometimes they attract more trouble than they solve, she thought, as she reached into the car and switched them off.

'That might give Luke some reassurance,' she said to Joey as he stepped out of the chippy, still trying to digest what Luke had just told him.

'He's gone anyway,' Joey said, hoping it would slow her down. It didn't. She pushed past him and went inside, making sure she was out of earshot of the street before calling Luke's name.

Joey decided, this time, to take Luke's advice and stayed outside.

After a moment, Hilary decided to go through to the back, but found her way blocked by Luke. That was the last thing he wanted her to do. Once again he left the MP5 out of her sight.

'They came looking for a young girl,' Hilary immediately offered.

It worked. He relaxed. Slightly. 'She's in the back,' he

told her, but then added quickly, seeing her concerned look, 'She's OK. With her fiancé, apparently.'

She looked a little surprised, but that wasn't her concern right then.

'I can't just let you walk away, Luke.' She glanced outside. 'Not now they are here. They know I've been in here.'

They held each other's eyes again briefly as Luke digested her words. The chain of command. 'OK,' he said. 'This time I'll do the blinking. We'll go out the back.'

'No, that's not what I meant.' Neither head girl nor old friend. Back to win or lose.

Luke considered. Then nodded slowly. 'I understand, but . . .' he paused again, trying to find the words. 'OK. I know you'll have figured out what this is all about. Who and what we've become. Just as you know what this is for.' He flicked the lanyard.

'I have my own weapons team,' she countered.

'You have. But you need to know that we will use ours to get out.'

That was it. The last step. No going back.

'That a threat?'

'Just a fact. And your call.' He stepped back. His voice became clipped again. 'I've always liked you, Hilary. I respect what you have to do. But you must be clear. Right now. Don't follow.' He held her stare, before adding, 'Please.'

With that he stepped away and went through into the back.

She stood for a moment. Should she follow? Would he really harm her – or respect her authority? But the training came through. Don't be a hero. Call for backup. She turned and headed outside for the police radio.

On the pavement Joey was hovering. He followed her to the patrol car.

'What's going on?'

'It's an operational matter now, Joe. Keep out of it.'

'Are you sure you really want to do that?'

'I have no choice.'

'And neither does he. Did he tell you that?'

She rounded on him. What did he really know? 'Tell me what?'

Joey saw the look. The official look. The look that said he had to be very careful. 'What he's told me a thousand times in the past. That, after Janey, he just doesn't care what happens to him.'

She turned away, dismissing that as pub talk. Joey tried again.

'What about suicide by cop, Hilary? Have you thought of that?' Joey was making it up as he went along, trying to make sure he didn't say anything that could be tagged to a conspiracy charge later. Like Hilary, he knew the old relationship would only get him so far. But it got her to hesitate.

'And even if it's not that, are your guys really up to taking on those two psychos?'

'It's what they are trained for, Joe.'

'Are they? Really? I'm guessing here, but they might be good on the practice range or in training drills. Or taking down the odd psycho or schizo with superior numbers and weapons. Perhaps keeping the lid on something until someone like Luke turns up to clear it? But how good will your guys really be under a military-style attack? What's your acceptable body-bag count, Hilary?'

It hit home. Whether she liked it or not, it had elements of truth within it. She knew the firearms teams would do what was asked, but she also knew that part of their ethos was avoiding conflict. Containment was what they were trained for.

'What do you expect me to do, Joe? I can't just turn a blind eye.'

'It's what I don't want you to do, actually, Hilary. Like causing someone to write letters to the families of the guys you will lose. Explaining that they died needlessly. Or, just guessing again, will that come from some later investigation?'

She tried to respond, but couldn't immediately. Her mind was still sorting the cascade of images it was conjuring up from Joey's words and Luke's chilling response. Before she could get things sorted, Joey threw one more at her.

'Do you really want to put your team in harm's way?'

Fatchops now felt in harm's way as Luke had dragged him back into the food preparation area and told him to start the fire.

'I . . . I can not . . . They, they'll come. Worse than you.'

'I doubt that,' Luke replied. 'Get on with it. I want you to burn your own house down.'

'Why? Why you ruin my life?'

'Maybe because you've been doing that to the kids round here.'

'That not me. That just life.'

'And this is a life-changing moment. That's if . . .' Luke suggested, 'you want to keep your life. Your choice.'

It was decision time. For Luke and Matt it was only what they left behind. For Hilary it was everything. The final decision wouldn't be hers. She knew the chain of command as well as Luke. But her duty was to set things in motion. Refer up. If she didn't, her career, at the very least, would be over. If she did . . . well, she had spent enough time reading the post-trauma reports. Could she cope with that? To send in the tactical response team wouldn't be her decision, but she knew, ultimately, that she would shoulder the responsibility if it went as Luke had warned her. No matter. She knew what she had to do. She reached for her phone. At least Luke would have ten minutes. And she guessed he would know that too.

Having used some of those precious minutes on Fatchops, to Luke the smoke that was now billowing out of the chippy seemed to indicate that he had made the right choice. That same smoke now masked the departure of Becky, Husani, and the three young girls, shepherded by Luke and Matt, MP5s at the ready, but pulling off their balaclavas. Matt was carrying the girl from the bed. He put her down at the top of the alley.

'Take her to the health centre for a check,' he said. 'And tell them what happened to her. OK?'

But the girls hesitated, throwing worried looks down the alley at the smoke billowing out of the chippy.

Matt took out the phone he had taken from the Asian granddad. 'This is going to the local paper. So their families, friends, neighbours and assorted bigots and racists will know what they've been up to. I doubt they'll stay around for long. Now go. She needs help.'

They all nodded and walked away. Matt watched them go, still controlling the beast, as he knew this one would survive, before turning to Husani.

'How'd you get in? I could have blown your head off.'

'Borrowed the keys from my cousin. The one with the beard,' he explained.

Matt nodded. 'Sorry about back there. Occupational hazard.' Then added, 'But behave with her, OK?'

Husani didn't know whether this was meant as advice or a threat, or whether to say thanks or tell him to mind his own business. But looking at the guns he decided just to nod.

Luke turned to Becky. 'We're probably sounding like

bossy uncles or something, but phone home and tell your folks you're OK.'

She felt she didn't have to apologise or complain, but knew what she wanted to do: reach out and give him a hug. He held on to her for a moment longer. 'And good luck,' he nodded towards the waiting Husani.

She smiled, thinking he meant with the intended wedding. He didn't explain that he meant when she told her parents.

He turned to Matt. 'Time to get gone?'

Matt nodded and they walked away, stripping off their body armour as they did.

They had left the others face down in the back of the chippy, reasoning that after a while, as the fire got closer, they would risk defying the final order to stay put or be shot. One by one they'd come stumbling out into the alley and into the arriving armed response team.

Up at the cottage, Joey had stumbled into something he hadn't been expecting. With Natasha back home with Tanya, he had told her he needed to pop out. She hadn't asked why.

Outside the cottage was not Luke, but Bobby McBain, leaning against his Range Rover and offering Joey an envelope. Inside was £5,000 in cash.

'What's this?'

'Down payment on the rest of the job?' he said, and indicated the cottage. For once the gravelly voice was sombre as he tossed the cottage keys to Joey. 'Lukey, wants you to finish it. And get it ready to sell.'

'What? What you on about, Bob?'

'Reckons the memories have changed. Time to move on, he said. Also said you'd know what he meant.'

Joey just nodded, understanding the real meaning. And if Bobby was delivering this message, had he been involved all along? 'You been playing me, Bob?'

'How'd you mean?' It was genuine surprise.

'You had Luke sorting out the competition for you?'

But Bobby shook his head. 'No, Joseph. And if we didn't go back a ways, I'd be a bit offended now. I wanted those scumbags out, sure. But I wasn't in that game. Christ, you can make more out of smuggling tobacco than you can for selling your soul to those psychopaths.'

'Then what?' Joey asked.

'I'd like to say I was all public spirited and that but, well, Fatty and his clan were bad for business. Attracting too much attention from our Hilary and her merry men. And you couldn't get boys like Luke and his oppo for five hundred quid now, could you? So, bit of cash to help them out. Why not?' He just shrugged. Good business.

'You were paying?' Joey asked. Shocked.

''Course I was. That's what that envelope is really about. You couldn't have afforded some of the gear they were after. Or had the contacts for all the other stuff. Especially if it escalated.' The gravelly laugh returned. 'Clever bugger, though. Kept us apart until the end. Tradecraft. Need to know. Small cells. All that special ops stuff.'

Joey was struggling to take all this in. He'd thought he was the one helping Luke, but now it seemed he was just a pawn.

'So he played us both?' he finally asked.

'Played us all, mate, played us all. But we're all grown-ups, aren't we? Got what we wanted.'

'Did we?' Joey asked. Unconvinced. Remembering something Luke had said. Wherever they went, a military solution could only nullify the current threat. Buy time. Then it was up to people to find a political solution. 'He might have left us with a bigger problem.'

Bobby gave a nod of agreement. 'Got the same war and peace lecture. He wins the war and we have to win the peace? But that's down to the likes of your Sean, isn't it?'

Joey didn't look too convinced.

'Don't look so depressed, Joe.' The gravel started to rattle in his throat. 'Like the rest of them, he won't be able to create too much trouble. Without you behind him. Lukey might have pulled the trigger, but it was you and yours he was doing it for. Janey was just the excuse. Not the reason. And your Sean won't do much unless the likes of you are behind him. Pushing. Keeping him on track.'

'Do you reckon?'

'I do. But I was up at the old chemical quarry before. Bit of tidying up to do.'

Knowing its usefulness for the likes of Bobby, he didn't

ask for the details. As he'd told Natasha, it was best not to know. He just waited, wondering where Bobby was taking him next.

'Reminded me of you.'

This should be good, Joey thought. It was.

'A catalyst. That's what you are, Joe. Something that makes other things happen.'

'I . . . I didn't do anything.' He waved the envelope. 'Not even this, it seems.'

'But you did, Joe. You stepped up. Crossed the line because you knew no one else would. Takes real bottle, that. To put, as our Lukey might say, yourself in the line of fire. And you're over that line now, mate. No going back. People will look to see what you do in future. People like Gazza down on the bridge.'

Joey tried not to react to any of this, but the predator opposite spotted the telltale eye flicker. And held up his phone.

'Told you, I know everything. And if this knows,' he tapped the phone, 'I also know that you are stuck with it now. You're like the town conscience. We should call you TC, for short.'

'Er . . . That's a bit much to lay on me, Bob?'

'Y'reckon?' he asked. Deliberately mimicking Joey's earlier dismissive response. Then cracked the pebble-dash. 'You were born to it. People don't like cops or politicians. But they'll follow real people. Real leaders.'

'Oh yeah. And what about you in all this? You seem to have it all figured out.'

'Joe, I'm a villain, aren't I? People like the cheap fags, fake designer gear or free parking. But "Vote for Bobby"? Nah. You're stuck with that role, TC. The power behind the throne. Our own *Game of Thrones*. But someone always needs to bankroll 'em. And your Sean will need it too.' He tapped his chest and then Joey's. The meaning clear. It was going to be them. Then he turned away and headed for the Range Rover.

'As you will,' he shouted back. 'And I'll always need a good sparky every now and then.'

With that double-edged sword placed at Joey's feet he sped off, this time without his customary bang on the horn.

Joey turned and looked at the cottage, then at the cash, and wondered where his friend was now.

It was something that rattled round his head as the week rolled on with no word from Luke. Not even when the local paper came out with its best front page to date. A big picture of Craig Harlow, with Sean and Sandra opening Santa's Garden. Out of focus behind their shoulders were, as promised, the Chairs of Planning and Education, but the main headline was: Craig Harlow to be Santa's Helper. Below which ran a second strap: Owner set to run for Council. In the sidebar next to it there were two teasers.

A picture of the burnt-out chippy with the caption: *Chippy Owner Sought In Child Sex Scandal, See page 5*; together with, on page 3, *No Clues In Alien Abduction Theory*.

'Plenty of news this week, then,' Natasha commented, coming up behind Joey and nuzzled his neck as he made his morning Colombian. But she felt the tension.

'What's wrong?' she asked. 'You're in the clear, aren't you?'

'Yeah. No worries,' he replied, trying to sound casual.

'C'mon, what is it? Your neck muscles are like steel.'

'My secret identity out, is it?'

'Joe?' she pulled him round and saw a sadness in his eyes she wasn't expecting. 'What? What's happened?'

'Nah, I'm just being daft. Having a moment,' he said as he tapped the newspaper. 'We might have saved the town. And I might have the town gangster as a future in-law thanks to Tanya's choice of boyfriend, but . . . I may have also lost my oldest friend.'

She put her arms round him and cuddled into his chest. 'He'll be back, Joe. When he needs you again. Just as we need you, and I'm so glad you're back.' Then she smiled. 'Especially for the lie-ins when you do the school run.' She finally felt him relax slightly, as she continued, 'And, anyway, I thought I was your best friend.'

'You are. My best . . . mate,' he said, emphasising the word mate, before adding, 'If you don't suffocate me with your hair.'

'Oh, I can find other ways to do that.' She pushed back

and opened her dressing gown, revealing the pink and black nightdress they had bought on a weekend in Dublin, the first time they had managed to get away alone after Lucy turned five.

'No point in you being back,' she continued with a wicked, grin, 'if we can't take advantage of the kids being at school, eh?'

'No point indeed,' he replied, starting to follow her to the door, just as the doorbell sounded and his phone vibrated. Typical, Joey thought as he went to the door while looking at the phone. A text from Benno. HOW'S LIFE? Joey smiled as he opened the door. A DHL courier offered him a package. Back in the kitchen he opened it to find a slate plaque with the words *Pro Bono Ad Populum* engraved on it. He opened the small card inside to find the translation printed: For the Good of the People. On the other side was: For Old Times' Sake, Conscience and a Better Future.

Joey knew it was from Luke. So he must be safe. Somewhere. As he heard the floorboards above creak, he went to finish the tea while looking at the sender's address on the packaging. Domino's Pizza in Birmingham. His face broke into a satisfied smile as he sent a reply back to Benno. LIFE? INTERESTING.

Acknowledgements

There are two things every producer dreads in television and film: agreeing the billing at the beginning and the credits at the end. In many cases, at the end of a difficult shoot, you sometimes feel that instead of a list of credits, it feels more like a list of who to blame. Fortunately, this particular endeavour has not been like that, but like any creative activity it has required a great number of people to bring it to fruition 'behind the scenes', many of who I simply do not know. But thanks to every one of you. I hope we can meet one day. Also, another wide acknowledgement to all those folk who have given me answers to questions they might not have fully understood at the time, I did it that way to keep them free from blame and protect their reputations. But I am also grateful to them all.

However, all writing is a collaborative activity that requires someone to write and someone to bounce the ideas off. Francesca Pathak at Century has coped brilliantly with being bounced off, while Susan Sandon at Penguin Random House has kept the faith and made sure I got this far.

And, finally, even if it is a bit corny or clichéd, but something learned the hard way about the power of the off switch in television, is that fiction is nothing without its readers and audiences. So, thank you to anyone reading this. At least you showed some interest.